WAR WITHOUT F...

Former British Pr...
Harvey, is now a ...
Brussels and he puts forward a bold new
project for the European Commission: a
merger of the British and Italian motor
industries, both of which are threatened by
workers' revolts. Since the merger must be
completed by the European Summit, Sir
Patrick has only seven days to settle its
terms. Success depends on absolute secrecy.
However, he has not reckoned with a
determined, ruthless terrorist organisation
which has already infiltrated Brussels. They
are unscrupulous, have no qualms about
kidnapping and murder, and will go to any
lengths to secure their aim.

'The story races down its marathon length at
gold-medal pace. The writing is quick-witted,
the research thorough. And the locations,
from official Rome to a hill farm in Wales,
from a terrorist hide-out in the Dordogne to
the Brussels suburbs are gloriously apt and
visual. Here is a piece of intelligent
entertainment it is difficult to fault at any of
its chosen levels'
David Hughes – *Mail on Sunday*

'Very much a tale of our time and compelling
reading just because the scenario is so
familiar'
Sunday Telegraph

'A well-written and marvellously enjoyable
thriller'
Literary Review

'A very exciting and entertaining thriller'
Spectator

**Also by the same authors,
and available in Coronet Books:**

Send Him Victorious
Scotch On The Rocks

About the Authors

Andrew Osmond has been a full-time writer
since 1967. Before that he was, variously, an
officer with the Gurkhas, a diplomat, and one
of the founder-members of *Private Eye*,
London's famous satirical magazine.

Douglas Hurd has collaborated with Andrew
Osmond on three previous occasions to write
similarly stylish political thrillers with an
unerring degree of veracity. These were
SEND HIM VICTORIOUS, THE SMILE ON THE
FACE OF THE TIGER, and SCOTCH ON THE
ROCKS. After thirteen years at the Foreign
Service, and a period as Minister of State
there, in September 1985 he became Home
Secretary. He is Conservative MP for Witney.

WAR WITHOUT FRONTIERS

Andrew Osmond and Douglas Hurd

CORONET BOOKS
Hodder and Stoughton

Copyright © 1982 by Andrew Osmond and
Douglas Hurd

First published in Great Britain 1982
by Hodder & Stoughton Ltd

Coronet edition 1984
Second impression 1986

British Library Cataloguing in Publication Data

Osmond, Andrew
  War without frontiers.
  I. Title   II. Hurd, Douglas
  823'.914[F]   PR6065.S6
  ISBN 0 340 35479 8

Printed and bound in Great Britain for
Hodder and Stoughton Paperbacks, a
division of Hodder and Stoughton Ltd.,
Mill Road, Dunton Green, Sevenoaks,
Kent (Editorial Office: 47 Bedford
Square, London, WC1 3DP) by
Cox & Wyman Ltd., Reading.
Photoset by Rowland Phototypesetting Ltd.,
Bury St Edmunds, Suffolk

For Thomas, Louise and Alexander

AUTHORS' NOTES

In our first three books the work was evenly shared. But while we were still planning this one, a general election changed my way of life. So this time most of the thinking and writing has been Andrew's.

Douglas Hurd

Nevertheless I am grateful to my partner for sticking with this long story through the real-life dramas of government. I should also like to thank my wife, who typed the whole manuscript and made many good suggestions. This book, and this author, owe much to her constant support.

Andrew Osmond

And we both add thanks to Margaret Body whose skilful and patient editing contributed much to this joint enterprise.

AO, DH

Wednesday

1

Rosa Berg woke with a gasp. Her eyes opened wide and her heart thumped about in her chest. Rushing up to consciousness she had started half out of her seat, and she found herself still in that position, her body poised rigid as she cast about for the threat.

None appeared.

Behind her, the door which led out to the deck was swinging gently on its hinges. Beyond it she heard some vague movement, receding. That was all. Except for the first light of day, now whitening the windows, the scene had not altered. In the green leather seats, arranged like an aircraft, people were sleeping. The boat was still throbbing ahead as it had through the night.

And yet it was fear that had woken her. She had a queer feeling that her face had been brushed by a bat. Perhaps it was a dream, she told herself, although she couldn't remember one. Her pulse settled down. She relaxed in her seat and peered at the sea through the salt-smeared window at her side. The Channel was more grey than blue; flat calm. The sky too was grey, without pattern of cloud. It was still very early.

The boat was packed full. People lay curled on the floors and even the stairs. Here in the starboard saloon they sat collapsed together, with their heads at odd angles and their mouths gaping open, like corpses on a battlefield. No longer fearful, Rosa's eyes travelled with cold deliberation from one sleeping form to the next. Although they were pressed close around her, she felt distinct from the mass. She examined them from an inner distance.

This boat was steady as a bus, but even so some of the people had managed to be sick, rushing off with handkerchiefs pressed to their faces. A few hadn't made it, and mixed with the stink of perspiration and cigarette smoke was another smell, faintly sweet, that she put down to vomit in the carpet, or rather the disinfectant used by the stewards to clear it up.

Some of the people had been sick, and some had got drunk. Some had got drunk and then sick. When the bar closed they had stuffed bottles into their pockets and gone off to swill through the night, propped together, until they fell apart in senseless heaps. Most of the drinkers were British. Getting unconscious with alcohol was the British idea of fun. The Germans drank too, but not in the bar. A group of them had set up a base in the other saloon and walled it around with their luggage like a fortified camp. The French dashed about and prattled incessantly, as if in receipt every moment of fresh dramatic news. Prattle was the French idea of fun. The Italians protested, but uselessly, knowing it was useless; for fun. One of them had made a fuss because the purser's office ran out of *lire*. The Scandinavians perched aloof in corners, slim men with very elaborate rucksacks and neatly trimmed beards, women with babies on their backs.

And all of them had trooped through the shop. Oh *merde*, thought Rosa, the shop. All the time until it closed the people had queued for their duty-free cigarettes and Calvados, the potions brewed by avaricious monks and the sickly-sweet perfumes to dab on their bodies. Since leaving Southampton the people on this boat must have spent more money than passes through a slum of Calcutta in a year. And now they were sleeping it off, surrounded by the debris of their own consumption. Cartons, cans, bottles, paper cups and paper plates had filled the whole ship to the edges. Well, she was glad to have seen it. The sight made her angry, and with anger came strength of purpose, of which she was glad on this hot July morning. All Europe was here and it stank.

Scrambling up from her seat, she walked out on deck.

The sky had turned pink in the east. France was just visible ahead: a blur on the southern horizon. Glad to see France, glad to be alone, Rosa stood at the rail and breathed in the warm salty air, watching the bow-wave roll into flatness. Clarity of purpose came easier in solitude.

It was not that she hated the people, she told herself. She just saw too much to be one of them. That was the difference. Not many people had that sort of vision. It set you apart, and to hold to it needed some courage, of the sort shown by Lenin in exile, working on at his books among the drunks of Siberia, taking long walks across the ice to keep himself fit for a day so far off that he couldn't imagine it. That was the spirit. To change things you had to resist the suction of the mass, never ceasing to believe you were right when others thought you mad. I am right, you must say, and keep on saying. I am right. I am not mad, and I must not give up, because what I have seen is the truth. . .

A man had come out on deck behind. He advanced to the rail and stood beside her: English *petit-bourgeois* by the look of him, the sort who talks to strange girls on ships.

"See it, did you?"

"What?"

"The kid on the stretcher." He looked at her covertly, wanting more reaction. "There's a party of children up the front, you know, all cripples. On their way to Lourdes."

"I know."

"Well, one of them just died. The priest brought the body through, quiet as a mouse."

Or a bat, thought Rosa. The brush of a priest, like a bat in the dark, and the sweet smell of death – or was it sanctity? She took hold of the rail.

The man moved closer, delighted to have caused this effect. "French, are you?"

"Yes," she said, "French."

"Oh well then, you'll understand it. But if you want my opinion . . ."

Rosa could think of nothing on earth that she wanted less than this man's opinion. She had a strong desire to throw him in the Channel, that convenient ditch which protected the English from anything resembling a moral idea. But instead she turned away and kept going, ignoring the small yap of protest at her back. She reached the stern and found some iron steps, which she climbed, then more steps, which she climbed at a run, until she was alone at the top of the boat.

She sat there all the time until it docked.

As soon as they had liberated Paris, the Allies turned back to Le Havre. The Germans had walled themselves in there, under orders to hold the Channel port at any cost. The battle went on for ten days. Every day for a week the town was bombed by British aircraft and shelled by naval guns, while the Germans themselves, as defeat became inevitable, smashed the harbour with mighty explosions. No port in Europe suffered worse damage. The mess took so long to clear up that rebuilding proper could not begin till 1946.

That was the year of Rosa Berg's birth, but she knew more about the battle for Le Havre than most French of her age, having heard about it often from the person she was now about to visit. This was the harbour where her aunt had fought at the end. Scuttled German ships across the entrance, Simone said, quays crumbled like landslides, half-sunken submarines, corpses in the water, the sea itself on fire with blazing oil . . . Well, maybe. Often as she'd heard about it, Rosa herself could not imagine the scene. She did not try. It belonged to an uninstructive episode of history and had less power to move her than the band of little pilgrims below, being helped down the gangway and put in their private bus to Lourdes. An ambulance was waiting on the quay for the dead one. The priest in black habit was flapping among them: a bat caught in daylight. But Rosa's interest was no longer in him. Her eyes were on the crippled children. She watched them with sympathy, feeling drawn to them, almost at one with them as they stared from their own inner distance at the mass of other passengers. The physical freak, she thought, is as lonely as the visionary. All men are equal except for the sick.

And then she watched the *flics*.

A couple of gendarmes with submachine-guns were standing on the quay, posted either side of the gangway as the passengers filed off the ship. Was that normal?

Ten minutes later, passing between them, she kept her false papers at the ready. But neither man made a move. She let out her breath and walked on, taking out her genuine passport at the *guichet*. The official flipped through it, glanced up at her face, then back at the photograph. "Next," he said, and gestured her on.

No longer on her guard, Rosa followed the green path through Customs. But there, to her utter surprise, an official stepped forward and asked to see her camera. No effort of control could stop the blood rushing from her face, rushing back again. She felt her colour change, her pores opening. "But I've had it for years," she said in a tight voice. "It was my mother's."

The man nodded casually and handed it back.

Rosa walked out of the passenger terminal, found her car in the parking lot, got in, and sat at the wheel for several minutes, regaining control. Then she drove out of the docks.

The sun was now up but still low, bathing sea and land in the golden glow of an early summer morning. But no warmth of light could soften the lines of Le Havre, where the bleak style of reconstructed Normandy had reached its extreme. Dun blocks of rectilinear concrete stood ranked around a square the size of an airport, off which ran streets wide as runways. Le Havre's resemblance to the new towns of Russia was no special thing to Rosa, but over the years she had grown to like the place, pleased by the functional way it fanned out from its massive new postwar harbour. It was a town built for work. And home, besides, to the person she admired more than any in the world.

Knowing her way, she drove down the Avenue Foch and out to the suburb where her aunt still lived. There was almost no traffic. A few early cyclists in berets and overalls, *bleu de travail*, pedalled along between the double lines of plane trees. A municipal water-truck sprayed and cleaned the cobbles with a rotary brush. But Rosa wanted total solitude. She drove on until she found a street with no life of any sort, where she parked and took her camera from its case. Inside it, held by spring-clips, was a small lightweight pistol of Czech manufacture, her CZ50. She cocked the gun and put it in her bag.

A few minutes later she locked the car and set out on foot. After turning several corners she crossed an empty square and walked towards a block of state-built apartments which over-looked the beach of Le Havre from a height. She could see nothing wrong. She was calm and in control. Going up in the lift she took out the pistol, slipped the safety catch off, and again checked the forged identity card in her bag.

But neither was necessary. Simone Salvador was waiting, as arranged by telephone the night before. Propped on a stick, the old woman pulled her niece into a tremulous embrace. Kissing her, Rosa felt the bones beneath each cheek, frail as a bird's, then followed her aunt into the kitchen, where coffee and fresh heated *croissants* were waiting. The old woman's passage was painfully slow, and either from the effort of movement or habit derived from a life of conspiracy, she did not speak until they were seated. "Well," she said then, "how was England?"

"Barbaric," answered Rosa, at which they both laughed: an old shared joke. "But the news is good."

"Tell me."

Commanded to give her aunt good news, Rosa Berg then described the state of strife at Ash Valley, the factory in the British Midlands from which she had come the day before. The workers there were ready to revolt, she said. And things were even better in Italy. There had been shooting already in the car plants at Naples and Milan. So now, this week, was the time for the interventions planned by the Iskra, both in England and Italy, to make sure that these situations developed in the proper revolutionary manner.

Reporting this, Rosa expected approval. She personally needed it, here above all places, and so was dismayed to see doubt, and then fear, invade her aunt's face, followed by an expression akin to irritation. The sight was so surprising that she stopped in mid-speech. For a moment the little room was silent, except for the trickle of coffee being poured by her aunt into two thick mugs with a shaking, arthritic old hand. Far below, on the beach, an early-morning jogger was pounding down the water-line, intent on some objective of his own.

Simone set the jug down hard on the table. "So," she said, "you've come for the trunk."

"Yes. It is time."

"Well, I cannot prevent you. But I wish to hear, exactly, your purpose."

Rosa explained in more detail the steps to be taken, the objectives in view. And she was eloquent. As the Iskra's founder, its leader and tactician, she could explain the movement's purposes better than any other member.

But Simone, having heard the plan, was unconvinced. "It is too soon," she said. "The masses are not ready, especially in England. Premature action without a social base leads only to martyrdom."

"We're a vanguard party."

"You and your international brigade – yes, very fine. But you are not a party." Simone shook her head and went on to warn of the many times that revolutionary action had failed by being premature; Russia 1905, Berlin 1919. "These are the lessons of history."

Rosa listened with respect. Her aunt had more right than most to quote the doctrine of Marxism, having fought for Republican Spain as well as the French Resistance. Simone had been given a medal in Moscow. She had worked for the Communist Party of France all her life, until they kicked her out for excessive independence of thought. She had cared for her exiled Spanish husband until he blew his brains out, and now she lived alone in this comfortless town, with the Iskra's most dangerous secret in a box below her bed. Even so, a saint could be wrong. And for every revolutionary text, there was another: a game at which Rosa herself was adept.

"History is sometimes too slow, aunt. We must hurry it on."

"At any cost?"

"Personal cost, yes. You should know that."

"By any means?"

"By any means appropriate. The justification is success."

"And you expect success?"

"I hope for it."

"Answer the question."

"*Eh bien*, yes. I expect it."

Simone's eyes were those of a thrifty old pensioner picking out good vegetables from bad at market. "Let us be perfectly clear," she said. "You have reason to expect a political success in this case which will justify the means, and the risk, you have in mind."

Normally Rosa loved her aunt best in this dialectical mood. But this morning she found it exasperating. "Simone, we can't spend the whole of our lives discussing the state of the world late at night. There comes a time to act, and for us it is now. There won't be a better chance. The others agree, by the way – if it makes any difference."

"So it's war."

"No, just a battle. The war will be finished by others."

"After you're dead, you mean."

"Perhaps. I can't tell. But I'm taking the trunk."

15

Rosa was depressed by this interrogation. Her mood had dropped like a stone.

But Simone's face had softened. "Good," she said. "You take it. As to practical effects, I think you may hope for too much. But that is an old woman talking. What matters is that you understand your own action." She paused, reaching over the table to grip her niece's hand. "The only thing I fear is that your life will be wasted by incorrect thought. You have a head, my girl. Use it. That is all." She sat back, then reached for her stick and dragged herself up. "Now I shall fetch the boy who lives above. He will help you to put the box in the car."

"Wait. Let me fetch him."

"No, drink your coffee. And call your friend Yup. He rang here before the birds were awake.

Rosa laughed. "Not Yup," she said. "It's Yope, spelt J-o-o-p. You know that."

Simone shrugged, not amused. "Yup, Yope – how do I know what your dangerous friends are called? The Dutch, they speak like turkeys, gobble, gobble. The number's on a pad by the phone."

The old woman limped away. Rosa sat on in the kitchen, still smiling as she heard the outer door slam. Dear Simone. And dear Joop, to call at this moment, always at hand when needed. Joop Janssen and Simone Salvador – action and thought – were the best of the Iskra. So long as she had them, she wasn't alone. Encouraged, she moved to the parlour, which was in the general style of Le Havre: a purely functional room. Chairs to be sat on, books to be read, a powerful radio set in one corner. No frills or flowers, no mementoes of the dead. Telephone in the right place.

She dialled the prefix for Brussels, then the number on the pad, listening for the faint click and static of extra connections. There were none. Waiting for the hotel operator to answer, she rehearsed the peculiar name, false but also Dutch, under which Joop was travelling that week. His voice, when she was put through to him, was soft and casual. They spoke in French, avoiding mention of their own names or any unnecessary detail.

"Hello," she said to him. "It's me."

"Ah, good morning. How are you?"

"Well."

16

"Good trip?" he asked.

"Yes. Good trip."

"And now you're at auntie's."

A faint note of sarcasm tinged this remark. Rosa ignored it. "That's where I am."

"Got the luggage?"

"Yes," she said. "I'm taking it now."

"To Paris?"

"Yes."

Joop was silent a moment. "All right," he said. "But don't mess about with it, will you? We don't want any accidents."

"Of course not," Rosa said more sharply, taking command of the conversation. "And how are things your end?"

"All set," came the answer from Brussels, spoken in the same low expressionless voice. "Harvey's back in town. He flew in last night. If he keeps to his usual routine, he'll leave his house in thirty minutes."

"Good," Rosa said. "That's good. Will you call me if there's news?"

"As you wish," Joop replied, and rang off without a good-bye. Rosa smiled at the curtly formal phrase. As she wished, Joop Janssen would do. Her reliable Dutchman. She replaced the receiver and sat for a moment in the small warm room, feeling more buoyant all the time. Her spirits rose as swiftly as they fell. Things are beginning to move, she thought. Only Harvey can get in our way now, and he is too late. We are one step ahead and that's how we'll keep it.

Twenty minutes later, left alone in her flat, Simone Salvador was less confident. She wished she had spoken out more strongly for caution. Now it was too late. With the trunk had gone her right to advise, and such purpose as remained in her life. She had existed too long, she felt. The world belonged to strangers, and now even Rosa was gone.

It shamed her that she'd not been more frank. To be honest, she had only kept the trunk for the fun of the risk. She did not have the smallest faith in the poor girl's objective, or even, any longer, in the grand old theory which inspired it – that dream of a world where men would stand equal and dignified, not taking from each other but contributing each what they had for the benefit of all. For one brief period of her own long life that dream had seemed to come true, back in Barcelona 1936. The red and black flags at every window, the churches demolished, the shops and trams claimed for the people . . . The cafés had been taken over too, but a drink came anyway, and another, and another, no one paying, while the revolutionary songs blared from the speakers and the crowds milled about in the streets all day and for most of the night. That was how it was in Barcelona, each day a lifetime, and all a little blurred now, except for that crisp December morning, bright as a postcard, when Anton Salvador came striding down Las Ramblas with his comrades of the party, then broke away to meet her, the new girl from France.

And how had it ended? To remember how it ended had angered and grieved Simone Salvador for many years afterwards. Now she no longer cared. She no longer thought about it. To her, in old age, the outcome of Barcelona 1936 was neither surprising nor even very interesting. To believe in a better world you had to be twenty, that was all Spain proved. When you were old the future was a bore, because you had none left yourself. There was only the past to be picked over, and the present, oh how slowly creeping on, to be endured.

She glanced at the clock on the wall. The hands were coming up to 7.30.

The day ahead seemed intolerably long. She could not think of anything to do, so sat where she was in the kitchen, staring out at the beach, at the flat sea beyond and the promontory over to the right where the British torpedo boats had waited to catch the German submarines at night.

While aware of her aunt's inner fight against cynicism, Rosa would have been shocked to know how thoroughly it had been lost. She thought of Simone as a religious person, hanging grimly on to the forms and language of the church although her faith had burned low with old age. The dialogue just past, while it might have contained some pretence, was a serious test. And it had been passed. Her own resolve was the stronger because of it.

But now she had already ceased to think of her aunt. By 7.30 she was out of Le Havre and crossing the Seine on the main road inland. The wheels of her dusty brown Simca were splayed by the weight of the trunk, but Rosa drove as fast as the car would go, across the Pont de Tancarville and left along the river bank, past the slow barges floating downstream, through the cider orchards and fields of dappled cattle, then away on the wide road to Paris. She felt as alive as a person can feel. Her car was rushing on and her mind leapt ahead of it, on towards Paris and the things she had to do there, on further into the future, everything rushing past so brilliantly fast that she felt she might take off and fly at any moment.

Yes, she thought, yes, Simone is right. This is war.

2

At 7.30 in the morning the residential suburb of Kraainem, on the eastern side of Brussels, was a picture of wealthy seclusion. The comfortable houses of the Belgian bourgeoisie, some of them now leased to senior officials of Europe, stood spaced at wide intervals among the trees and rhododendrons, each house set back from the street in its private enclosure of smooth green lawn and trim shrubberies. The first to arrive here were servants, coming by bus from the city's sleazy immigrant quarters. In term-time the first to move out were the children, most of whom travelled to school in big chauffeured limousines. But now it was late July. School was over for the summer, and the first sign of movement came, as it often did, from the house of the Harveys.

Each house in Kraainem expressed a rich man's fantasy. The Harveys', which was rented from a local banker, was Swiss in inspiration. The big projecting eaves and maroon wooden shutters were those of a mountain chalet, though the walls were of yellowish brick instead of logs. .At the apex of the roof stood a dovecote, itself like a miniature chalet, around which a flock of white pigeons cooed and fluttered in the quiet. A grey one had got in among them, so some of the little pigeons were coming out piebald, which was not going to please the Flemish banker when he saw it. But Lady Harvey was an English-woman. She refused to get rid of the grey plebeian bird. She said it was racialism.

Her touch was apparent in other ways. Flowers not seen before in Brussels had been added to the garden, and half the windows in the house had been open since first light. The garage was shut. But parked in the drive was a big blue official

Mercedes, and beside it a uniformed chauffeur stood chatting to an armed security guard, on loan from the Belgian police. They had arrived five minutes before.

At 7.30 exactly the front door opened and Sir Patrick Harvey, wishing each man good morning in English, as he always did, stepped into the car's back seat. The chauffeur got in behind the wheel. The guard sat beside him, looking more alert. The Mercedes rolled away down the drive and turned left at the gate.

As the car pulled into the street, Harvey watched to see if his wife would wave from the house.

She did not.

He kept on watching until the house was out of sight, and then sat back with a small inner sag of disappointment. In the old days it had been a ritual. Each morning, when he reached the corner of the street on the way to the station, he had always turned, and she had always waved. But that was a long time ago. Now it was almost twenty years since he'd gone to work by train. At Number Ten he had not gone to work at all. The work had come upstairs to him, into the flat with his breakfast and the newspapers. Even so, as Prime Minister of Britain he had spent a very large part of his time being driven about in cars – or so it now seemed, looking back. Up the Mall to the Palace, down to Chequers at weekends; to factories and parade grounds, summer fêtes, constituency surgeries . . . Bill Rivers had been his driver then. Old Bill, who'd always known the way but many times lost it. He could still see the pitmarks on Bill's stubborn neck.

After leaving the suburb of Kraainem the Mercedes accelerated south down the ring road, then turned into Brussels along the Avenue de Tervuren, passing through the royal museums and the Parc du Cinquantenaire. The route to work was changed daily, to foil imagined terrorists, and Harvey always waited with a mild degree of interest to see which way would be chosen. Glancing up from his newspaper as the car purred smoothly through the park, he watched a group of equestrian Belgians, brightly equipped, cantering down the ride between the birches. Traces of mist still hung between the trees, not yet dispersed by the sun. It was going to be another warm day.

There were no pits in the back of Paolo's neck. Paolo Santini was young and very handsome. In Brussels itself he drove

21

slowly, so that everyone could see the beautiful driver of the beautiful car of the former Prime Minister of Britain who was now Vice-President of the European Commission with special responsibility for Industrial Affairs. But out in the countryside a different Italian trait asserted itself. Paolo drove fast and loudly, sweeping simpletons out of his path.

Harvey settled deeper into the car's beige upholstery. At this stately pace he could read *The Times* without feeling sick, and once they were out of the park there was nothing to see. The architecture of Brussels had varied down the ages, but in every street the spirit was the same, solid and grey. Most of the buildings looked like banks. A lot of them were. But that was all right, he had come to think; that was how it should be. When it came to choosing a capital for Europe, only this modest grey burg of the Belgians had been acceptable, and the choice was a sound one. A place of compromise, tawdry at the edges, commercial to the core, sane, rather ordinary – Brussels expressed the age perfectly, and with luck contained the future. But that didn't make it any better to look at. He went back to his paper as Paolo drove into denser traffic.

The Times, for Harvey, was like a favourite piece of furniture: something he carted round the world to give himself the feeling of being at home. After numerous closures and changes of ownership the paper now belonged to a socialist millionaire, a radical brewer from Scotland, who had turned it into a sort of journalists' cooperative, like *Le Monde*. But the product was virtually unchanged. Its opinions were still the most sensible, its letters page the only one worth reading or writing to. It was certainly more fun than *Le Monde*.

Usually he managed to get as far as the rather prissy gossip column by the time that the Berlaymont Building, headquarters of the European Commission, came in sight. But today they were jammed for a minute or two in an underpass. He had started on the business page, when the car swung round the Rond Point Schuman and down the ramp to the sunken entrance of the Berlaymont.

Harvey glanced up at the building as it loomed ahead. At first he had disliked it: thirteen storeys of steel and dull glass, star-shaped, looking out over a mish-mash of uninteresting streets. But now he was fond of it, just as he had grown more fond of his job, fond of Brussels. The Berlaymont was full of maddening people; maddening things occurred in it every day. But after a time you could see the joke, and behind the joke the work that was worthwhile. The European dream had fallen into the hands of ordinary men and a mediocre architect, but so what. The better the times, the less the need for giants.

The Mercedes pulled up. The Belgian policeman jumped out, looked round for Irish marksmen, then tapped on the roof. Paolo held the door open.

"Home for lunch, Excellency?"

"No, Paolo, I'll walk to lunch. Usual time here this evening."

"Usual time, Excellency. *Bene.*"

The handsome young Italian touched his cap in a nonchalant salute, then drove off to polish the car, or whatever he did all day.

Left alone outside the entrance, Harvey stood for a moment to breathe in the gently radiant morning, still unpolluted by petrol fumes. The city, still only half awake, was giving off a vague muted rumble of sound. Almost no people were about. Before him, ranked on tall masts along the front of the building, were the flags of the nation-members of the European Community. With the recent accession of Portugal and Spain the organisation now stretched from the Baltic to Africa, from the Hebrides to Crete, and this, in so far as it had one, was Europe's head office. But the twelve flags hung limp in the windless air, as though tired out by the mere act of getting into line; and that very often seemed true of the nations as well. The idea looked better on a map than it turned out in practice, and here at headquarters was the start of an ordinary working day, too hot and rather lackadaisical, already touched by the mood of the coming August holiday.

But Harvey saw it otherwise. What he had to do this morning would affect the lives of many thousands of people. If successful, it might even alter the powers of the Commission itself, this great official hive which sat at the centre of the continent, so much less powerful than the pioneers of European unity had hoped . . . No, that was probably putting it too high. Still, win or lose, today was important.

Nudged into motion by the thought, he turned on his heel and entered the big glass building, acknowledging the bevy of ushers with a nod as he walked across the lobby. Although now in his middle sixties, he was a sprightly man, quick and light of step. And like the other Commissioners, he reached his office well before most of the junior staff. Only in England was laziness in the morning considered a badge of high rank.

But things could go wrong in the Berlaymont, too.

The lift was out of order again – or so said the card in nine languages hanging from its button.

The other lifts had a good record, but the express lift which carried the European Commissioners direct to their offices on the thirteenth floor was always in trouble. It was said to suffer cruelly from the extra weight of its passengers as they returned each afternoon from the many fine restaurants of Brussels. Not that it mattered much. There were plenty of other lifts. Harvey chose one at random and shared it with a young Spaniard whom he knew slightly as a rising star in Directorate-General One. Spain's admission had unleashed a swarm of eager new officials into the Berlaymont, all trying to make their mark in an office already housing five thousand people.

"Good morning, Sir Patrick," said this one. "I hear you are meeting the chemicals men today."

"That's right."

"I should warn you, they are angry with the Koreans. They will ask for some emergency action."

"So it said in the brief." Harvey smiled to soften the snub. "If they ask for action against the Koreans, I shall refer them to you in DG1. Rows with Asia are your province."

"It may come up at the summit. What if they ask for a cartel?"

"Then that is my province."

The doors opened at the eighth floor. The Spaniard hesitated, wondering whether to ride on up to the thirteenth and snatch a few more sentences with the man of power. Pride prevented. He stepped out.

Left alone, Harvey felt his spirits rise with the last upward surge of the lift, all his inner systems perceptibly quickening – it was almost a sense of release – as he stepped from his troubled private life into the cold, clear air of high office. The quickening of his heart, though, was something to be careful of. A mild case of cardiac arrhythmia had been diagnosed. The doctor had prescribed some pulse-settling pills and warned him to think of retirement. Harvey wasn't ready for that. Retirement would come in due course and would bring its own pleasures – time to read, time to think, the headship of a university college perhaps. But not yet. His term as Commissioner had two years to run and he meant to finish it. His faculties were sharp and he enjoyed using them.

He went to work with pleasure. And his step, too, was quickened by the Spaniard's mention of the summit. There were three such meetings a year, but the most important was the one coming up, in late July, when the heads of government gathered to tie up the business of the year. This year it was going to be held in Rome, starting a week from today. That was not long, Harvey thought. For what he had in mind, seven days was horribly short. But either it would have to be done in that time or not at all. After this summit would be too late.

Feeling suddenly that even minutes counted, he hurried from the lift to his office, crossing the thick green carpet of the thirteenth floor in a series of short, fast strides. Today, unusually, he was not in ahead of his staff. Neither was at this moment in sight, but he saw from their desks that both of his closest assistants were already here. Probably poaching coffee from the French. No matter. He was glad of a few more moments alone.

Sitting at his desk, he took *The Times* from his briefcase and returned to the business page – to the piece he'd been reading in the car, which had to do with the British motor industry. The latest dispute at Ash Valley, it said, could spell death for the city of Coventry. But Harvey knew that without being told. Skipping the predictions of doom, he glanced at the various solutions proposed, then breathed a small sigh of relief.

There was no mention yet of a link with Italy.

3

Two hundred yards away, in a modern hotel which rose level with the curving glass cliff of the Berlaymont, a man was standing at the window of a tenth-floor bedroom.

His name was listed in police files as Emil Johan Janssen, but his friends referred to him only as Joop, pronounced Yope – the Dutch abbreviation for Joseph. A scrawny man, with white hairless skin and several scars on his hard muscled body, Joop Janssen was naked except for a set of bulbous yellow headphones, through which he could hear Sir Patrick Harvey's breathing. He was watching each move the Commissioner made through the telescopic sight of an Armalite rifle.

So this was the man, he thought.

Making a fractional adjustment to the focus, the Dutchman steadied the sight until the cross of its hairline intersection was exactly in the centre of Harvey's head. Then he began to move it slowly up and down, left and right, inspecting each one of the Commissioner's features. Grey hair, cut short and neatly parted . . . eyes still sharp, and between them a frown of concentration . . . pale face, sallow at the edges. A man who spent his life in rooms full of talk, this Harvey, but alert and quick of movement as he took a sheaf of notes from his briefcase and made some corrections with a red ballpoint pen. An old British work-machine, Joop thought to himself, still functioning well; and not to be estimated lightly. Rosa was right.

Lowering the telescopic sight, to which no weapon was attached, he pressed a finger to the headphone on his left ear, hearing the ring of a telephone in Harvey's outer office. At the sound he quickly returned to the apparatus spread on his bed.

Why had Harvey spent the last two days in Britain? How

much did he know about the state of affairs at Ash Valley, Coventry? What was he going to do next?

Those were the three questions Rosa had asked.

Crouched nude on the bed, Joop Janssen waited for the answers. Now that Harvey's secretary was back in her office, he thought, the talk would begin.

Harvey heard the telephone ring in Laura's room and then glanced up as his secretary came through the door, marvellously dressed as she always was on these summer mornings – on any morning. Today it was a cotton dress he hadn't seen before, rust-coloured, soft and loose-fitting. Probably French, he thought, like the coffee in her hand. Laura was an all-round Francophile.

She gestured back towards her own office. "It's Lady Harvey on the line. Shall I put her through?" ˙

The question was neutral, but Harvey sensed a barb in it. He was never sure how much his office staff knew of his relations with his wife, with whom the day had started badly. He had apologised before he left home, but no doubt Margaret had sat brooding out there in Kraainem, alone in that mock-Swiss house she hated, until she found a new angle of attack. Well, she could wait.

"Just a minute," he said with his hand up. "What's on today?"

Laura produced a typed diary card and gave it to him. This was the day on which the seventeen Commissioners traditionally met in full conclave, but this morning the meeting had been scrapped. "You have the European Chemicals Federation at eleven," she said. "The *Die Zeit* interview is at twelve. And the Portuguese Ambassador particularly wants . . ."

"I know what he wants. Put him off, will you? And make my apologies to *Die Zeit*. No press today."

"Not even *El País*? They're due this afternoon."

"No, but be nice to them," Harvey said, still treading carefully with Spain.

Laura's face assumed an expression of deliberate patience as her carefully constructed schedule fell in ruins. "Has something come up?"

"I must see the President. He's in today, isn't he?"

"Yes, he's in Brussels. But he hasn't arrived up here yet."

"I need half an hour with him alone."

"I'll go and see how they're placed. It would help if I could say what it was about."

Harvey nodded in sympathy. "I know it would. But I can't risk any loose chat in Riemeck's office. This one's for him and me alone.'

All right, said Laura's eyes, but you can tell your own staff, can't you?

"Don't forget Lady Harvey's on the line," she said sharply, and left the room.

Harvey turned to the phone on his desk and picked up the receiver, holding it a little way back from his ear. But his wife, as sometimes happened, had swept the quarrel out of her mind. Her fresh cheerful voice sounded twenty years younger than it had an hour earlier.

"Hello there. Busy already?"

"Yes," he said, relief warming instantly into affection, which he never really lost. "A big day today."

"Well, sorry to break in, but John Clabon has just rung from Coventry – that factory of his, what's it called?"

"Ash Valley."

"Oh yes. Funny name. Ash as in cinder, I suppose, not tree."

Harvey smiled. Margaret's capacity to wander from the point was a kind of artistic creation which kept politics in place. Sometimes it was just plain mischief, but this morning he would let it run.

"Talking of trees," she went on, "you never told me you'd been at Cwm Caerwen. I thought you were in London."

Cwm Caerwen was their cottage in Wales, far from all human disturbance. The only sounds to be heard there were the repetitive bleating of sheep, the trickle of invisible streams and the high, thin cry of the buzzards which circled the hill. It was the perfect antidote to Brussels, and Margaret went there often, usually alone.

"It was a sudden thought," Harvey said. "John Clabon wanted somewhere quiet to talk, so we met there yesterday."

"Was there any water?"

At Cwm Caerwen the water came brown from the hill. If the weather turned dry, so did the taps. If the weather was wet, the pipe clogged with particles of peat, and the taps stayed dry. In that case you struggled up the hill and stroked the filter with

28

your hands until the pipe was clear. It had always struck Harvey as a human achievement of particular charm, to make water unattainable in so drenched a land.

"We climbed the hill," he said, "and stroked the filter."

"I'm amazed you remembered how. And did you see May?"

"Yes, I took her the sheets when we left. Why did John Clabon ring?"

"Did you give her extra for the sheets?"

"Yes, and Owen for cutting the nettles. Why did Clabon ring?"

"Oh, it was a message for you, very personal. Now let me get this right. John said to tell you that he's spoken on the quiet to the ministers concerned, and it's all right on the British side. You can go ahead. Does that make sense?"

"It does indeed. Thank you, sweetheart."

Half-turning from his desk as he brought the conversation with his wife to safe harbour, Harvey saw that Laura was back in the room. She had heard his side of the conversation. And so had Erich Kohlman, also now standing in the room. That meant a decision. Were they to be involved in this or not? His mind now working on two levels, he looked across the desk at his two closest aides, assessing them both in a way he had never quite needed to before.

Laura Jenkinson, though mad on the French, and indeed almost Latin in appearance – olive skin, raven hair – was as British as her name. The daughter of army people, said to be an excellent rider, she lived with an aristocratic Belgian family out at Tervuren, whose horses she exercised in the Forêt de Soignes instead of paying rent. She was a bit of an intellectual show-jumper too, which could be a mite irksome. Rather a touchy girl, rather tense and volatile, with modish opinions of a leftward kind. But marvellously competent. She had been with him two years as Personal Secretary.

Erich Kohlman was even more valuable. An efficient young member of the German diplomatic service, seconded from Bonn; immensely quick and helpful. Slim and smartly dressed, with feather-light blond hair, Erich was fond of music and kept a cello at home. An inner romantic perhaps, of the classic German sort. Who could tell.

Both were aged about thirty, both unattached so far as Harvey knew. Their private lives were closed to him. All he saw was their work, and it was good. He had faith in their discretion, but had still not decided how much to tell them as he turned first to Laura. "Have you fixed up a time with the President?"

"He's coming in. They tell me he's set aside the whole day for Lomé Five."

Harvey understood the Eurotalk. Yes, he thought, Riemeck would need to know his brief for the next aid agreement with the Africans and others, especially since the Germans were due to foot most of the bill.

But his own matter couldn't wait either.

"I'm sorry," he said, "but you'll have to try again. I must see him this morning."

Laura hesitated, knowing the weight of argument needed to break the pattern of the President's day.

Harvey saw her predicament. "Look," he added, "tell them that the President would look very foolish if the news I have to tell him broke this week and he knew nothing of it. Hasn't he got a press conference on Friday?"

Laura nodded, her face yielding suddenly to a girlish smile of mischief. Riemeck's last press conference had been a disaster.

As she left the room, Harvey realised he had no choice. If he was to operate at all, then Erich and Laura must know. But he would try to keep it to those two alone, he thought, as he took out a folder from his briefcase and added it to the handwritten notes on his desk. "Well," he said to Kohlman, passing the papers across, "here's the story. You know John Clabon, don't you?"

"Of course. The chairman of BMG."

Kohlman had kept quiet while Harvey and Laura dealt with procedures. He dealt with substance: a distinction he liked to underline. But now he was eager to get going. There was a hint of excitement in his voice. It struck Harvey that he would get to know this self-contained young German much better before the business now beginning was over. But it wouldn't do to rush things. He kept his manner formal as he explained.

"John Clabon rang me from England last week requesting a meeting, no reasons given. So I saw him yesterday, at my wife's cottage in Wales. We talked for eight hours in absolute privacy. In this folder are the papers he gave me, and here are my jottings in the plane last night. Get Laura to type them out, will you? Four numbered copies only."

Harvey paused, then decided to change his manner after all. If Kohlman was going to share the secrets, he might as well learn to share the excitement, the fellowship of work under pressure. It was worth a try, anyway. Risen to in the right spirit, this thing could be as much fun as Downing Street. He scooped up the papers on his desk and handed them over with a smile.

"Here. You'd better take all this stuff off, Erich. Read it through carefully and then we'll have a chat. I want to know what you think."

As Kohlman took the folder a lock of thin hair flopped across his forehead, making him look about eighteen. A faint blush of pleasure appeared on his pale, controlled face.

Then Laura returned. "Twelve forty-five," she said. "The President's going to put his lunch back."

"That's fine," said Harvey, giving her a smile too. "Well done."

Laura's smile was one of grim satisfaction. She liked to have her own way, and she didn't like the staff of Professor Otto Riemeck, who were known among the girls of the thirteenth floor as male internationalist pigs.

In the hotel bedroom, two hundred yards away at a parallel height, Joop Janssen bent down closer to his little receiver, pressing the left headphone tight to his better ear, touching up the volume again as Harvey's two assistants withdrew to the outer office and closed the door behind them. There was a moment's silence. And then the girl, Laura Jenkinson, laughed. "Another fight with Margaret," she commented tartly. "But peace now declared."

Kohlman made a non-committal noise, implying that he had no interest in gossip.

Laura sat down at her desk and started sorting papers. "What is all this, anyway? Why the big rush to see Riemeck?"

"Something to do with cars."

"British cars?"

"Yes," said Kohlman, "British."

"What's the matter with them? I thought they were having a revival."

Kohlman made no answer, obviously still head down in the

papers which Harvey had given him. He had sat down to read them at the desk belonging to the typist. "This is incredible," he murmured after a while.

Laura stopped her sorting. "Ah, a secret. Come on Erich, tell."

"Laura, please," said Kohlman irritably. And then he stood up, his voice growing loud as he came across to her desk. "Here. Type these out, will you?"

"Typing is Lucy's job."

"Not in this case. Look at the classification. He wants four numbered copies. Separate red jackets, distribution by hand. Manuscript into the shredder."

"*Jawohl, Herr Kapitan.*"

A pause, then Kohlman said: "That is not funny."

"It's what they always say in British war films."

Kohlman did not laugh, but the timbre of his voice was altered by a smile. "Oh yes? And what is my line?"

"*Achtung*," said Laura airily. "Just keep saying *achtung* and we'll put you in the picture." She began to hum an old British march, then lost the tune and broke off. "You know, Erich, you're quite attractive when you smile. You should try it more often."

Kohlman was standing over her. "What is the matter with you this morning?"

"I'm bored."

"So why are you making these jokes?"

"To keep awake."

"You look happy to me."

"I am happy."

"Happy and bored also?"

"Erich, *cher collègue*, it is possible to feel two emotions at once. I am bored because I am here. I am happy because I shall soon be lying on a beach in Corfu," said Laura, but absently now, losing interest in the banter as she read her chief's notes. "Golly, I see what you mean. This will give the shredder indigestion. Oh, I do wish the man could *write*. What's that word?"

They put their heads together, coming closer to the microphone as they tried to decipher Harvey's handwriting. The unreadable word, they eventually agreed, was "amalgamation". And then, thanks to Laura, it came right out. "So he wants to join BMG with Mobital," she said. "Well now, that's not so boring, I must say. A merger of the British and Italian car industries, to be fixed in one week flat. No, I would say that was interesting, quite interesting, wouldn't you?"

"Please, not so loud," murmured Kohlman. "I would say it was mad."

"And Riemeck? What's he going to say?"

"The President will not permit it, I think."

"Erich, he'll go out of his tiny bald *skull*. Poor old Uncle Otto. Oh yes, I think this is going to be fun."

Laura began to sing again as she wound paper into her typewriter. Kohlman's steps retreated to his own room, then a door closed behind him. He had gone off to read the dossier Harvey had given him.

So there was the answer. Listening to them from the hotel opposite, Joop Janssen slapped his knees in triumph, and then yelped in pain as a heavy machine-gun started to fire rapid bursts through his skull. He snatched off the headphones with a short Dutch oath – a sound like a man being choked – then turned down the volume and leaned back on the pillows, watching the sound-level needle jump to red each time that Laura's fingers hit her typewriter.

The receiver on the bed between his legs appeared to be an ordinary cassette-recorder, but plugged into its side was an aerial, thin as a thread, which stretched across the carpet to an antenna clamped outside the window. The main alterations, done by himself, were internal. One button was now a fine tuner, and the others had been converted to waveband selectors, for monitoring three microphone-transmitters.

The mikes were in their telephones – Harvey's, Laura's, Kohlman's. All three were working well. But now there was nothing to hear, which gave Joop a chance to call Rosa.

Still watching the needle, he picked up the phone beside the bed and dialled a number in Paris. A man's voice answered, rough as a cement-mixer.

"Yes?"

"This is Joop."

"Hello, Joop." The man's voice dropped. "She's not here yet."

"No, I know that."

33

"So what's new?"

"When she arrives," said Joop, speaking fluent but dissonant French, "just tell her it's on. They're going to do exactly what she thought."

And that was all. Since no more needed to be said, Joop rang off abruptly and lit himself a cigarette, never once taking his eyes off the sound-level indicator. His breakfast tray was pushed to one side. The sheets of the bed were flecked with crumbs from a half-eaten *croissant*. Tobacco ash had settled on the pillows. His clothes were scattered on the floor of the room, sodden towels lay discarded in the shower. Having gone to some trouble to get into it, he felt obliged to show his contempt for the Hotel Europa.

The gesture was automatic, untroubled by the thought of the maid from Portugal who would have to clear up the mess. Thought was not Joop's speciality. He was a technician. That was what Rosa sometimes called him, and it was a term he liked better than 'executioner', a word she only used when excited. His pride was in his skills. The political allegiance to which they were harnessed was simply a habit: something he had fallen into many years ago, and now a way of life, which he sometimes grew tired of but could not get out of, since his name made the lights flash on every police computer in the West.

It helped that they thought he was dead. Even so, he could not make a move without elaborate precautions, and what he grew tired of was the sheer inconvenience of being someone else. His false identities were so many and various he sometimes forgot which one he was using. He didn't like wearing a suit, he was not a travelling salesman in cassette-recorders. He disliked using luxurious hotels. It had annoyed him to cut his hair short. He had considered tinting it with dye, but had stopped short of that, knowing well enough how peculiar his hair looked already. It was tufted and patchy. In parts it did not exist at all, and its overall colour, once fair, was now a dull ashy grey. The skin of his face was mottled by burns; his left ear worked better than his right. He was not an attractive sight and he knew it. Another disadvantage of the life that he led was plain loneliness. Girls turned away in the streets, and those that didn't could not be approached, only stared at in a crowd or through glass.

Still naked, he returned to the window of the bedroom and raised the telescopic sight to his eye again, to watch Laura Jenkinson type. Her fingers were dancing over the keys like a pianist's and her head was held at that odd, upright, sideways angle of the practised secretary. He liked her legs.

The lay-out of this office in the Berlaymont, the functions of each individual employed in it, were familiar to him. There was another girl, an ordinary typist, still to arrive. She did the paperwork and filing, nothing else. Laura, whose clearance was higher, only typed secrets. As Personal Secretary her job was to organise Harvey's public life. Erich Kohlman, the German, was Harvey's *chef de cabinet*. He drafted the Commissioner's letters and speeches. All the important stuff passed through Kohlman. And Harvey seemed to like him. They got along well.

So who had planted the microphones?

That was something Rosa was keeping to herself. She had an ally inside the Berlaymont, but who it was she wouldn't say. That was her right, of course, and a sensible precaution. Joop had no personal objection to it. And yet he was curious to find out the answer if he could, and so had spent some time speculating. Anyone with access to the thirteenth floor could have done it, perhaps on a Sunday or at night, and it had to be someone from another department surely. The risk made no sense for Harvey's own staff, who were privy to his secrets in any case, and could spill them to Rosa with a phone call. Or was that considered too risky? Perhaps the mikes had simply been placed as the safest and most rapid means of communication, in which case it might have been done by one of Harvey's staff.

Joop thought about that for a while, and then shifted the telescope's aim to Erich Kohlman, who was in his own office now, reading the papers that Harvey had given him.

As a terrorist Joop had always found it difficult to get along with Germans, of whom there were many in the people's war. Their word for it, *volkskrieg*, sounded a whole lot too similar to *blitzkrieg*, that rush of grey steel through his village long ago. He could not be friends with a German of any sort, and even now, watching this inoffensive and dapper young official at work, he felt his gut tighten in hostility. The emotion passed. The telescope shifted again, further right, back to Harvey himself, who was still also reading, his grey head propped against one hand as though in prayer.

And here came the proletariat.

Taking the scope from his eye, Joop looked down to the pavement below, where Commission staff were swarming to work now, an army of ants on the move. For a moment he watched them from his high isolation, without fellow-feeling. Then he turned away from the window. The sun, still rising, had obscured the thirteenth floor in a blaze of reflected light.

The time was 8.45.

He put on some clothes and sat on the bed again, thinking things out in his own slow methodical fashion. So Harvey was going for a merger of BMG and Mobital. But how was he going to do it? And did he know what was in store if he failed? Rosa's second question still hung in the air.

Yes, thought Joop, there were several more answers to be had here, and the rest of the day should reveal them. Turning up the volume on the speaker, he put his breakfast tray out in the corridor and settled in for a long vigil. Twenty minutes later he heard Laura put Harvey's notes in the shredder. And then she came back to shred the Portuguese Ambassador, whose invitations had clearly been turned down before. For half an hour hers was the only voice audible as she rapidly cleared Harvey's week of every engagement until the summit in Rome. She put off the local correspondent of *Die Zeit* and cancelled all further press interviews. But then, at 10.03, she herself received a call from *The Times* of London, whose editor came on the line in person to request a word with Sir Patrick. Laura stalled him adroitly. Then she went through to tell Harvey about it.

The Commissioner laughed. "The Workers' Voice," he said. "No, we can do without them for a week."

"It seemed to be a gossip item," Laura said casually. "Apparently you were seen riding about the Welsh hills in a golf cart with John Clabon."

At that Harvey did not laugh. He was silent a moment, and then, in a carefully calm voice, he asked Laura what she had said in reply to this query from *The Times*.

"I told him that Wales was your private retreat, and you hoped it would stay that way."

"You did well," said Harvey after another long pause. "But that was close. Just bear in mind that if the press get one tiny sniff of this, we're finished."

4

In London, because of the time difference, it was only 9.15. The morning was warm but overcast, with a promise of rain. But Jack Kemble was not aware of either the weather or the time. He didn't care whether the sun shone or not.

He was lying in the bedroom of a flat in Hampstead, with a woman asleep beside him. The curtains were drawn. The room was in darkness and smelt of old sex. A fly or a bee was trying to get out of it, buzzing all over the window in search of an aperture. The woman was snoring. Kemble's eyes were fixed on the ceiling, which he felt might collapse at any moment and bury him. There were cracks spreading out from the light fixture.

He had been lying this way for an hour, maybe more, because a problem he had with trying to kick alcohol, one of the problems, was that it made him wake early. And then there were the waking dreams. Something in the process of withdrawal set off a sort of electrical static in his brain, a crazy rush of images of the kind they say happens to a drowning man. If he opened his eyes, he could stop it. But then it started up again, and this morning it was death and destruction, a movie of his tour in Vietnam.

That Marine with his head blown off . . . the chopper full of press, very slowly careening . . . the strong type from Langley who wept in his beer at things he had to do, so upset that he crumpled the can. Yes, here it came again, the usual old war flick of barbecued flesh, blood and litter. All that steel junk, piled high on the beach . . . a sampan splintered to matchwood . . . those child whores scrapping for custom in My Tho, worst place in the world, and that other night the car went over in a monsoon ditch because the stupid Aussie was stoned at the wheel. Funny really, some of it. No, funny anyway, all of it, funny and horrible at the same time, because it is the special mad art of Americans to make death hilarious.

He closed his eyes.

That was another way to stop it.

To open or shut the eyes stopped the show briefly, but to shut them was best, because it got rid of the rotten British ceiling as well.

Most of the memories that came to Kemble's head were American. Although born English, he had been gone to the States seven years, chasing money, chasing women, pursuing his craft in the intervals. And some of it had gone quite well, in the early days at least. So what in the hell am I doing back here, he thought. I have been going down a long time, but here in this pad, in this city, with this woman, is surely the bottom of the pit.

Wanting blackness, he kept his eyes shut, but images of ruin began to quiver at the corners of his mind again. And then they were scattered by the ring of a telephone, loud and very close, coming from the floor on her side of the bed. The woman woke up with a grunt. She reached down to take the call, spoke a few words, then sat up abruptly with her hand cupped over the receiver. "Jack, wake up. It's for you," she said. "Frank Holroyd."

"Holroyd?"

"He's the editor of *The Times*. Come on, get a grip, clear your throat. This could be work."

The call was brief and obscure, but work was what it sounded like – enough to get Kemble out of bed. Half an hour later, after strong black coffee and two diet biscuits, he was seated at a desk in the big bay window of the lady's flat, which looked towards the cemetery where Karl Marx was buried. In London the weather had been so dry that Hampstead Heath was scorched to a pale shade of brown. In a couple of places the bracken was black from brush fires, and scattered in the grassy parts were little heaps of litter and dog turds, unmoved by the present shower. It made him think of a park in downtown Cairo.

He held the heath briefly in view, and then dived again at his elderly portable, hitting out the words as fast as could possibly be done by a man using only the index finger of each hand. His mind worked in short, prefabricated paragraphs. Whole sentences fell out of him, three or four at a time, before he straightened up and stared back at the rain, automatically reaching for the cigarette burning beside him.

He kept at it hard all morning, correcting but never improving what he wrote, except to eliminate adjectives. Second thoughts were for thinkers, fine prose wouldn't pay the alimony. Words were what facts got turned into, and they gave him no pleasure; the plainer the better. What gave him pleasure was the digging up of facts, the hotter the better. But there lay the problem. At the age of forty-three, he was pushed to find stories worth his talent or editors to print them. In America scandal had gone out of fashion after Watergate. He had quarrelled with every decent paper in Washington and one of them, the *Star*, had folded up beneath him. Now the quest for work had brought him back here. His life had come full circle.

He was back to old haunts and a very old flame. Even her flat had that consciously plain, crafted look which went with brown rice and the sixties. The ashtrays had been moulded by a potter with hands full of gravel. The chairs were of rattan or cane, imported from poor parts of Asia. The fabrics were faded William Morris and the carpet a sort of prickly buff hessian, stained here and there with red wine. Set against the walls were jumbo cushions. Old copies of *The Guardian* lay stacked in one corner, concealed behind a rubber plant so tall and straggly that it must have lived since the sixties itself. There were a great many books, too many for the shelves, and the new ones, stacked flat, were the sort with odd titles that turn up in second-hand shops, sold off by reviewers to supplement their fee.

Reviewing bad books was what she did for a living. From a room in the back came the rattle of her own word machine: faster rattles, longer pauses for thought. A refugee from marriage, like himself, she had jumped at the chance to put him up in London. Separate beds at first, now one. But agreed to be a temporary arrangement.

At 12.30 she stopped and came in. "You'll be late," she said.

"No," replied Kemble, "finished." He pulled the last sheet off the roller and went quickly through it, then put it with the others. "Well, there's the bait. Let's hope Holroyd bites."

She looked over his shoulder. "My God, you write fast. What *is* all that?"

"My memoirs, chapter one. Patrick Harvey at Number Ten. Jesus, I spent my whole youth tailing that old sod."

"Yes, I remember."

"And nothing was quite so good afterwards, I must say. Spoiled me really, Harvey did, for Blighty. Hence departure New World."

Bending over him, the woman took the sheets of typescript and clipped them together with a little yellow stapler she kept in a drawer of the desk. "And this is what Holroyd wants?" she asked in a dubious voice.

Kemble stubbed his cigarette, squashing it hard until the filter disintegrated. "Think about Harvey, the man said. Well, there you go. I think best on . . . Goddamn, it's *raining*. Why didn't you tell me?"

She was keen to take care of him. She found him a cab on the phone and made him put a tie on. Better wear a tie for *The Times*, she said, even if it was a bloody bolshevik cooperative.

The rain had stopped before he left Hampstead. The heath was steaming in the sun. Riding down Haverstock Hill, Kemble felt thirst in the gills turn to all-over need, but kept his mind fixed on the peculiarities of the London taxi cab, so strangely like a hearse, and just about as comfortable. He had been away so long that even London itself looked peculiar, too big and yet too small, a never-ending toytown of narrow brick streets crammed with miniature cars and tall scarlet buses. The shower had left no freshness in the air. Garbage lay piled in plastic bags on the sidewalks. Arab women drifted through the shoppers in billowing black garb, and over Regent's Park, burnt brown as the heath, rose the glossy minarets of a mosque. The Cairo of the West.

As the cab turned below the Post Office Tower he had a brief attack of the shakes, but knew the drill to follow, from the clinic in Connecticut, and was back into fragile equilibrium as he stepped out at the restaurant in Charlotte Street. He hurried inside. Holroyd was late. Kemble was glad of it. Seated alone at a central table, he worked quickly through a bottle of mineral water as the place filled up with London's *literati*, assembling for the midday assault on their publishers' expense accounts.

They came through the door like people arriving at a party, looking around to see who else was there, and although he'd been seven years absent, Kemble was not quite forgotten. Unexpected people stopped to talk to him. Some waved and smiled, some merely nodded. A few stared curiously. And some, though expected to stop, swept by with their noses high.

An extra discomfort was that Kemble himself was not sure how well known, or unknown, he was. Since arrival he had made one appearance on television, but not many people seemed to have seen it. Perhaps they all watched the other channel. Perhaps they didn't watch television at all.

When the eating began, it would be better. Heads would go down to the trough. But meanwhile the business of sitting exposed like this in the favourite spaghetti house of literary London was making him very depressed. He had once been big in this town, but return to the scene of past success only sharpened the sense of present failure. He felt worse than low. He felt a fool. And that, in particular, was the trouble with journalism. It was fun to begin with but hard to end well. Like sport, like showbiz, it raised you high quickly and then left you on the skids, pretending you didn't like booze as you waited in line for work, any work, and other people pointed at your face with knowing smiles.

He glanced at his watch, then barked for a packet of cigarettes, taking it out on the waitress. The restaurant was loud with animated chatter now, everyone fully absorbed in food or their own repartee. Kemble began to feel more and more conspicuous, alone at his table for two. He felt the mocking eyes on his back, sensed malicious smirks all around. But salvation was at hand. The cigarettes came swiftly, and soon after them came the editor of *The Times*, which may have knocked a few of the smiles off a few of the faces. Frank Holroyd's entrance was typical. He pushed through the door like a sheriff for the shoot-out, paused as if to draw, then strode directly forward before the head waiter could accost him.

"Jack," he cried. "Long time."

"Hello, Frank."

"Sorry to be late. Taxis not what they were, you know. End of civilisation as we know it."

"Should be worth a couple of paragraphs," Kemble said, rising.

"No, too late. We did the end of the world last week."

They laughed and pumped hands, then sat down.

Holroyd was smart in a grey lightweight suit and pink shirt, all male and proud of it, with hair cut short as a convict's, flecked with grey. First man to be elected editor of *The Times* by a vote of the writing staff, first Australian to hold the post, he was reputed to be a secret Marxist, but wrote his leaders straight down the middle of the road, just like every previous editor of *The Times*. Although now podgy with prosperity, more of a businessman in appearance than a journalist, he had altered very little in the ten years since Kemble had known him. Still smooth and sharp, still sneaking a look at every girl in the room. As good a man to turn to in trouble as Judas Iscariot.

"And what are the Gadarenes eating today?" he said, snatching up the menu as if in a hurry to return where he came from. He chose *ossobuco*, then stared at Kemble's glass. "On the wagon, eh? Good idea, I'll join you."

Kemble took out a cigarette and waggled it ruefully. "One vice at a time, Frank. Got to specialise at our age."

"Too true, old boy. I'm working at mine like a mule." Holroyd smirked in reference to a girl in his features department who was known to be getting more exposure than her talent deserved, then he shook out his napkin with a violent downward flick, inspecting the restaurant to see who was there, friend or foe. "So, you've come home, Jack."

Home, for Jack, was a neat box of clapboard tucked into the woods of Bethesda, just off the Washington Beltway. But there was no point in talking of that. "Yes," he said. "Been back a while. Looking around."

"Going to stay?"

"Might."

"But you were more Yankee than the Yanks. Land of the free, you said, more muck to rake. Something go wrong?"

"No, not really."

"Wife?"

"Still paying for the first one. But number two's a sport."

"So why are you shacked up in Hampstead with our favourite bleeding heart of the books page?"

Kemble saw then it was hopeless. "Okay, Frank. You can tell me."

Holroyd's black eyes had been flicking round the restaurant, small and quick as a snake's, but now he lunged forward, hissing for the kill. "I'm sorry, Jack, but it's all over town. The *Post* kicked you out, and so did your good second lady in Bethesda. And if anyone here was still wondering why, you gave them the answer on Monday night."

Kemble recognised a reference to his TV appearance. "Oh?" he said. "You watched it?"

Holroyd nodded and sat back. "You were smashed, you silly bastard. And it showed."

After that they talked of other things, mainly a fresh dispute between *The Times* and its printing staff, who refused to have anything to do with the writers' cooperative. Holroyd was bitter about it. Did Kemble know that the Russian revolution of 1905 had been started by printers demanding the same pay for punctuation marks as letters?

Kemble did not, but listened with patience, wondering which way this political acrobat would have jumped in Russia 1905. Both ways, probably, and landed on his feet.

Meanwhile the meal continued. They were through the *ossobuco* and into raspberry sorbets before Holroyd raised the subject of Patrick Harvey.

"Now there's a man you still know better than any of us, Jack, even if you have been long gone. Struck me this morning."

The name was enough to make Kemble's spirit sag. Harvey. Square One. Nodding glumly, he pulled out the article he had worked on in Hampstead and tossed it across. "Try that for starters," he said.

But Holroyd, after flipping through quickly, tossed it back with a shake of his head. "Not for us, I think."

"That's good stuff."

"Rather old hat, though."

"Come on, Frank, I need a job. Take me on the paper."

But this appeal to friendship fell flat. The soviet of New Printing House Square was not about to open its ranks, it seemed, to any old buddy of the editor. Holroyd smiled in regret, if such a thing is possible. "Times have changed, Jack, and so has *The Times*. I'm elected to my job, you know, and plenty others want it. Have to watch my step."

Kemble felt hatred and the need for a Scotch rushing up into his gorge with equal sudden violence. You bogus opportunist little creep, he thought. But at that moment Holroyd took out a phial of saccharine tablets, dropped one in his coffee and smiled in a different way. "However," he said, "I do have some *work* for you."

"You do?"

"Nothing regular, just a one-off. That's why I rang."

"Go on."

"Officially I'm asking for a half-page profile of Harvey. Where is he now query, saviour of the nation query. Eight hundred words, pound a word – make it a grand, expenses on top. You'll have to see him, of course. I shall need some quotes, and we ought to have a pic. Greatest Living Englishman, stuck in Belgian suburb – you know the form."

"I know, and can do." Kemble mustered up a posture of gratitude. "Thanks, Frank. That'll be a start. How soon do you want it?"

Holroyd sat back, smiling archly. "Well," he said, "now that we're getting down to detail, I don't want it."

Kemble was dumb.

Holroyd continued to smile. "Officially, a profile is what we will ask you for, and if that's the best you can get, bring it back. We'll print it. You'll get your money."

Kemble was still bemused. "This is starting to sound like a cover," he said. "Don't tell me you're a spook on the side."

"Certainly not. But you're right, it's a cover." Holroyd dropped his voice. "As I told you, I'm only allowed to farm out specialist features. You're a Harvey specialist, fine – I can swing that on the comrades. But if they heard I'd given you a news job, they'd hang me from a rafter of the chapel."

"Okay, Frank, I've been away a long time. So just spell it out for me, nice and slow. If you don't want a profile, what the hell do you want?"

Holroyd leaned closer, dropped his voice lower. "Harvey is up to something. I want you to find out what, and I don't care how you do it. But it won't be easy. You know the man."

"I know him."

"He's got a girl laying down barbed wire. You'll have to go underneath."

"My, my, a commando job. And if I get caught, you'll disown me, right?"

Holroyd smiled uneasily. "You'll have to do this on your

own, Jack. But bring it back exclusive and you can name your price."

"Terrific," said Kemble as the bill arrived. "But I'll tell you my price when I hear what you want. And I'll need the thousand greenies up front, profile or no profile. I don't get off my butt for less than that."

Holroyd took a moment to respond. "Fair enough. Can be done, I think, just. I'll have a private word with the boss."

"Oh, you do *have* one then?"

"Indeed we do," said Holroyd. And now at last, from his repertoire of smiles, out came the honest one. "The company's run by elected committee, oh sure. But he still holds two thirds of the voting shares, the canny old bastard. Nor is he any friend of Harvey's, I'm glad to say. So let's go back to the office and set this thing up. I'll tell you what I know on the way. Just a few straws in the wind, though, I warn you. There's everything to do."

Holroyd paid the bill with a credit card. They walked towards the door, and then suddenly, glancing round the crowd of uproarious lunchers, Jack Kemble was glad to be back. What cranks the English were, he thought: jolly in defeat, stuffy yet corrupt, masters of the fast buck but essentially bored by money, an egalitarian society with more social flavours than a layer-cake. Perhaps they would take him back after all. Perhaps he should never have left.

Already keenly wondering what it was, this secret *The Times* wished to prise out of Harvey, he followed Holroyd into the street, where the air was less sweet than Cairo. Mingled with the kitchen aromas was the all-pervasive stench of warm, decaying garbage. Stacked high outside every restaurant were banks of black plastic bags. But here between them came a taxi with its light on, arriving as if by private and prior arrangement for the famous Australian editor. All he had to do was raise his hand. He was that kind of man. At home or abroad, in peace, in war, when the revolution came, when the world ended, Frank Holroyd would be all right.

5

At 11.45, Belgian time, Erich Kohlman began to dictate a profile of each company. He cleared his throat with a nervous little cough, then proceeded in a flat mechanical voice, without hesitations.

"BMG, the British Motor Group, has now absorbed every motor vehicle manufacturer within the UK, except Ford. The group's success to date has been based on specialist cars and commercial vehicles. It owns a joint research company with Saab and Volvo, for engine development. It also has subsidiaries manufacturing motorcycles, aero engines, pumps and power boats. The total workforce is approximately 120,000. Since the group was first formed, the equity holding of the UK government has been steadily reduced. Control has now passed to the private sector. The chief executive, John Clabon, comes from a background of private industry. His support for the principles of free enterprise is well known. The proposal for a merger with Mobital comes from him. Despite the group's progress to date, he does not believe that BMG can survive in isolation."

Kohlman paused. He was dictating a covering minute for the dossier which would go through to Dr. Otto Riemeck, the President of the Commission, when Sir Patrick Harvey went to see him in one hour's time. Having finished with BMG, he said "paragraph", then waited for Lucy Maclean to catch him up in shorthand.

Lucy Maclean was the typist, a pretty girl from Scotland whose principal interest in life was not the European Community. She habitually arrived late to work, as this morning. Harvey had decided to bring her into the secret, on the grounds that they couldn't get through the week without her. But to Lucy it was neither here nor there.

"Do you want it double-spaced?" she asked.

"Yes," said Kohlman, "space it out. New heading. Are you ready?"

"Ready."

"Automobile Italia, brackets Mobital. Text begins. Mobital is also a semi-private company, partially owned by the Italian state. A quarter of the shares are held by Fiat. But the dominant portion of the equity is in independent private hands. The group was formed by the junction of Lancia with Alfa-Romeo. It employs 130,000 people. It has various subsidiaries, including a research company jointly owned with Macchi Aircraft Corporation, for metallurgical development. The chief executive, Carlo Guidotti, comes from a background of government service. Guidotti's motive for accepting a merger is likely to be political. In Mobital this aspect has now become explosive."

Kohlman hesitated, perhaps wondering how an aspect explodes, then went on in his soft precise voice.

"Text ends. New paragraph, new heading. A Role for the Commission."

"Hold it," said Lucy. "All right, got it. How many copies, by the way?"

"Four will do, no more. Destroy your carbons and attach four photostats of last year's directive on mergers. Here it is. Now, last paragraph," said Kohlman. "Are you ready?"

"Ready."

"Text begins. Full proposals for action by the Commission are attached, but they can be summarised as follows. The merger will not succeed without our assistance and substantial financial support. An attempt should therefore be made to present an outline agreement for approval in principle by heads of member governments at the forthcoming European Council in Rome."

"That's a bit of a mouthful, isn't it?" Lucy said, still scribbling.

"I think Dr. Riemeck will understand," replied Kohlman in the same even voice. "Text ends there. Leave space for a signature, then add the distribution list. That's all."

"Big thing then," said Lucy, standing up. "Hush hush."

Kohlman made no comment. "Just do it as fast as you can."

She went off to type.

The time was twelve noon.

Kohlman returned to his office. He had been waiting for a further discussion of the merger with Harvey, but that had been overtaken by the chemical meeting, which was still going on. Then, at 12.20, the meeting broke up. The delegation left. Immediately Harvey summoned all his staff to his office, including Lucy.

"Now's the time for lunch if you want it," he said. "I expect to be with the President for about half an hour, so please be back here by 1.15. We could have a busy afternoon. I should also warn you that your social lives may suffer in the week ahead."

"So it's battle stations," Laura said, mocking the world of men.

"Let's just say we could be pushed, from now until the summit. Off you go then."

The two girls withdrew. But Kohlman hung back and said: "Can't I come with you? I'm briefed on this now."

"No, Erich, thank you. This is a case for two old men alone. Dr. Riemeck will be nervous enough as it is."

"Yes. I understand."

"But now that we have a moment, let me hear your own snap reaction. Is it possible?"

"Perhaps," said Kohlman cautiously. "There is very little time."

"True."

"It has not been done before."

"Also true."

"We shall have to cite last year's directive. I have attached it to the papers."

"Well done."

"Even so, it will need a lot of money. I do not think the President will be easy to persuade."

"No, nor do I," Harvey said, then rose from his desk and walked away from it. He said nothing more for quite a long moment. When he spoke again, it was in the fatherly tone he had tried once already. "Politics is sometimes called the art of the possible, Erich, by which people usually mean that not very much can be done. But I would say the art, not possessed by all politicians, is to see and make others see the hidden possibilities for action. The chances for that, on a big scale, don't come often. However, I think this is one, and I hope you will help me."

"Of course," replied Kohlman. "I am at your disposal."

"Good. Well, don't forget to eat now – and bring me back a sandwich, will you?"

In the hotel opposite Joop Janssen, too, got ready for a break. Fully dressed now, he dismantled his receiver and put it away in a suitcase. He took a last look at Harvey through the telescopic sight and then, glancing down to the pavement far below, he saw Laura and Lucy come out of the Berlaymont Building, laughing together in the sunshine. Moving quickly back to the suitcase, he locked away the scope, then hurried downstairs to the café where he knew the girls would lunch. He meant to sit beside them, get a closer look, the way he had yesterday.

But then he changed direction.

Stepping out of the hotel, he walked straight across the street to a waiting taxi, having seen a signal in the lobby which meant that he was summoned to an immediate meeting with higher authority.

So Moscow want to know what's going on, he thought in the back of the car, which resembled a Belgian taxi in every respect. Well, I'll have to tell them. Rosa can have her little secrets, but I have mine too. I wonder if she would understand. No, she would not. She would kill me. Oh yes, she would too.

Alone now, Sir Patrick Harvey stood at the window of his office looking out at the city of Brussels spread below: the banks and big hotels, the stock exchange built like a baroque cathedral and the sky-prodding emblems of international companies, ITT, Siemens, Monsanto, Shell. No, he thought, this thing wouldn't be as much fun as Downing Street. That had been a vain expectation. But there was work to be done here; and the scale was big enough. A quarter of a million people, according to the minute just signed, would fall or prosper on the result. And that was just direct employees.

Prompted by Laura's little military sneer, he had a brief picture of the companies as armies in distress, to be joined and boldly led forward across the map. But the image wouldn't hold. Here, at the air-conditioned centre of Europe, all conflict came down to statistics. And just as well too, he thought. Generals should keep their heads out of the smoke.

His own head now clear, he picked up the relevant papers and walked to the opposite end of the thirteenth floor.

Time to visit Caesar in his tent.

Everything in the President's room was big except the President.

Desk, chairs, sofa, the Matisse and the Rouault – all were enormous, and quite out of scale with the small Social Democrat professor who had been picked to head the European Commission at the very last minute. The favoured German candidate, a far more forceful man, had died of a heart attack while speaking in the Bundestag.

Otto Riemeck, like Brussels, was a compromise. And like the Belgians, he sometimes seemed appalled by what he'd taken on. As he listened to Harvey's report he kept clapping one hand on top of his head, smoothing out the hair that was no longer there. Behind his metal-rimmed spectacles his eyes began to dart about the room, as though in search of a bolt-hole, and then he said, almost pleading: "But that is impossible. Impossible, surely."

"Clabon was perfectly clear," insisted Harvey. "As things are, BMG are going under. Unless there is a change he will have to announce a closure within the year."

"Total?"

"So he says."

"I cannot believe it."

"Bits will be sold off, of course. But the break-up will be total. The group as a whole will cease to be viable."

"But their last figures were good, quite good."

Harvey nodded. "Since they took over Lotus and Rolls Royce, they have done very well on the whole. Profits up, production up, steady repayment of government loan – it's all in Clabon's dossier."

"Well then?"

This was going to take time, Harvey thought. The President spoke perfect English, but that was not the point. There had to be translation, not between languages but between ways of thought. And at the end of it he wanted Riemeck to take a brave decision.

He tried a short cut.

"Look, Otto, this is important. Let me take you out to lunch."

But that didn't work.

In the big padded chair behind the big desk, Professor Riemeck stiffened in resistance. His normal demeanour was jolly – Laura said he looked like a bald Santa Claus – but at times he could be stubborn, and when shifted to an angle of suspicion, as now, his glasses reflected the light and turned to blazing discs, which was rather unnerving.

"It is kind of you," he said, "but impossible. Already I am behind time. I have to make myself perfect with the Lomé Convention."

Harvey had never yet been at ease with Riemeck. The trouble was partly one of relative fame. To the world at large it seemed odd that a former Prime Minister should submit to the authority of a former Professor of Jurisprudence. Harvey had done his best to overcome this difficulty, but today it was close to the surface. Begin again, he thought. Take it slow.

"Last year's figures weren't too bad, as you say. But the new ones, for this half year, aren't so good. In fact they're darn awful. You'll find them in there, not published yet." He nodded at the dossier still lying unopened on Riemeck's desk. The printed instructions on the jacket were in red, the colour reserved by the Commission for deepest trouble. "The trouble is simply that BMG have sunk all they've got – previous profits, and some very heavy borrowing – into a new volume car. I'm informed, by those who know, that the basic decision was sound. But the car which actually emerged from it has been a catastrophe. It's called the Pilot."

"Yes, I have seen it," said Riemeck. "An ugly thing."

"The design goes back to the fuel crisis, Clabon told me. They went all out for economy, but apparently others did the same thing better. The group's other cars are successful – the luxury and sports models. But apparently that's not enough to stay in business these days. As you know, the whole European market is under great pressure."

"Yes, of course. But demand is expected to recover in a year."

From harsh experience Harvey distrusted all academic forecasts, especially from economists, but he knew they were Riemeck's life-blood. And that, more than relative fame, was the difference between them.

"The problem is," he pushed on, "that BMG doesn't have the strength to wait for the market to pick up. They'll be dead long before they can introduce a new model which might save their fortunes. In fact they're reducing their private sales forecasts so fast that they haven't dared show them to anyone. You'll find what Clabon said in my notes, and that's far more than he's told the British Government."

"Nevertheless the government will of course rescue them – again." Riemeck didn't bother to conceal his disdain.

"Maybe they would, if they were asked. But they won't be asked. BMG, remember, was created on the clear understanding that it was to pay its own way. And that's a commitment John Clabon takes seriously. He refuses to bail himself out with public money."

Riemeck sniffed dismissively. "That is a bluff."

"I think not. I know him well, Otto. This man's got free enterprise tattooed on his chest."

Riemeck was silent.

"And that is an attitude we're bound to applaud," Harvey added quickly, knowing well that Riemeck, as a German, believed almost more than himself in the postwar philosophy enshrined in the Berlaymont – free trade between nations, undistorted by government restriction or subsidy.

He saw that he'd scored a point. And now he made another. "There is also a political aspect to this that you should know about. BMG are being pulled down by the very tough attitude of the men at Ash Valley, where the Pilot is made. Most of Clabon's troubles arise from that plant, so the first thing he'll do is close it down. But that will rock BMG utterly. Counting in the engine and body divisions, thirty thousand men will be out on the street – if they agree to go."

"If?" said Riemeck. "What do you mean?"

"You won't find it mentioned in any of those papers, but there's a real danger here of another factory seizure by the workforce. Clabon has the evidence. It's frightening."

"I see."

"Industrial failure, political extremism – it's growing, Otto, all round the edges of the market."

"Yes, that is true."

"Time we played a stronger hand, I think. And well within the scope of the Treaty."

Harvey rested his case, although there were other points he might have made. He knew that in Riemeck's mind, as in his own, would be several previous industrial collapses – the dockworkers of Trieste, the coalminers of Marseille, the ship-builders of Dunkirk. The disaster to Coventry of BMG's closure would be worse than any of these. But the President did not need telling. He had accepted the facts now. Leaning back in his chair, he swivelled it gently from side to side, then put his hands together in front of his face and closed his eyes. It looked like prayer, but meant a pause for reflection which was not to be interrupted. After a while he lowered his hands to speak.

"So Clabon would like us to arrange a merger with Mobital."

Harvey was so surprised that his mouth fell slightly open. The project for a merger had not yet been mentioned, so how did Riemeck know? Never mind how. This leap in the argument was a promising sign, and happened to coincide with a shaft of bright sunlight which picked out a Degas on the President's wall: a drawing of jockeys and mounts shifting into the pattern of order from which a race could begin.

"Yes," Harvey said, collecting himself, "a merger. BMG must expand or shrink drastically. So they want to go in with the Italians."

Riemeck nodded, without surprise. "Because of the engineering, I suppose."

"And other factors. Each company is strong where the other is weak."

"But Mobital have no money."

"That's true. The bride would need a dowry."

"From us?"

Harvey nodded, gaining confidence. "Yes, from us. For a merger across national frontiers, it will have to be European money. That's the only kind Clabon will take."

"And Mobital? What do they say?"

"I expect Guidotti to jump at it. But you never can tell with him."

Riemeck unhooked his spectacles and started to polish them with a big white handkerchief, although they were spotless already. "Why does Clabon not go to the banks? If he is, as you say, such a man of free enterprise."

"He'll go to the banks. But we must take the lead."

"A loan or a grant?"

"A loan, secured against assets of both companies. But no share of the equity."

"How much?"

"I suggest a billion."

Riemeck replaced his glasses and looked up – again the flash of discs. He said nothing.

There was a pause while the figure was digested. Although he had not denominated a currency, what Harvey meant by a billion was one thousand million Ecus, or European currency units. This was the unit of account that Europe's officials used between themselves, to keep the books, and it was a symptom of the time that most of the people of Europe had never even heard of it. The Ecu could not be drawn at a bank or kept in a wallet, but in value it was roughly equal to the US dollar.

"A billion is what the project will need," repeated Harvey firmly. "And it could be a good investment. When I met him in Wales, Clabon showed me a very startling piece of research."

But Riemeck did not want to hear any more. He had swivelled right round until only the top of his smooth bald head could be seen above the back of the leather armchair, like a pale pink egg. Then even that disappeared from view as he bent down over the dossier, now held in his lap. A further silence ensued.

Harvey wondered what was coming. Riemeck, though cautious, was not without resolve. He had once defused a small student riot in the University of Württemberg. His six months as Commission President had yielded a few good speeches, a minor showdown with the French, a modest success with the American President. But this was a challenge of a different order, Harvey thought as he waited for the swivel chair to turn. But when it did eventually turn, he could not read any decision in Riemeck's face. Nor did the President's tone yield a clue.

"I recognise the importance of the proposal, Sir Patrick," he said with slow deliberation. "And it would, of course, come within the scope of last year's directive."

"There's a copy attached."

"Thank you. I am familiar with it." Again the flash of glass. "Personally, I am inclined to favour this initiative. But not all our colleagues will take the same view."

There was just enough encouragement here for Harvey to show his whole hand.

"Otto, there's simply no time to consult them. If we try to win round the whole Commission at this stage, the story will be all over Brussels in an hour. So what I suggest is this. I should call a meeting of the companies – just the two chairmen. Perhaps I can get them together this weekend. By Tuesday I shall aim to have a plan agreed in outline, which you can then put direct to the summit in Rome."

"That is a very short timetable."

"I know. But worth a try, surely."

"It is also quite irregular," said Riemeck after another long dubious pause. "According to the Treaty, an initiative of this sort should come from the Commission as a whole, then go to the Council of Ministers – the Industry Ministers, in this case."

"Yes," replied Harvey with a reckless touch of asperity, "but in my view this is a case for short cuts – as I said. To bring this thing off at all, we shall have to go straight to the top."

And then, once again, Otto Riemeck surprised him – this time with a smile. "The French and the Germans will not be putting out flags in the street, I think, when they hear what you plan to do for Britain and Italy."

Harvey saw consent on the way. "They'll be even less pleased if either firm falls to Ford," he said. "Or if the Reds take over Milan. Or if the British break the Treaty with some crazy rescue plan of their own."

Riemeck made no response. He sat for a moment in silence. Then he rose from his chair and went to a high mahogany cabinet set against the wall. Inside was a single green bottle and a few tall glasses. He took out the bottle.

"I do not wish to be involved in the detail," he said as he drew the cork, "but please keep me closely informed of the main developments. I reserve my approval until I see what is agreed."

That was enough for Harvey. He raised his glass for a toast. "To the first real European merger."

Riemeck raised his own glass and smiled again, not quite with the warmth of Santa Claus. "Your good health," he replied.

6

At 1.15, exactly when he had predicted, Sir Patrick Harvey was back in his office. "It's on," he told his staff.

"The President agreed?" said Kohlman in surprise.

"With some provisos, yes. In fact he's been looking in his tea leaves."

"You mean he knew about the merger already?"

"No, I don't think so, not exactly," Harvey said in a pensive voice. "But I must say, he was remarkably quick on the uptake. All right now, let's go to work."

In the hotel opposite, Joop Janssen was back at his post, having spent some minutes in apparently casual conversation with a man drinking beer at the bar of a working men's café in the Boulevard du Midi. That was where the KGB's taxi had taken him. And the site of the rendezvous had been well chosen. The district was crowded with visitors to the *Foire du Midi*, an annual street fair held in that part of Brussels. Balloons, banners, hurdy-gurdies, roundabouts, big wheels, folk dance and jugglers had filled the boulevard from wall to wall. Joop had strolled unnoticed through the noisy festivities until he saw the Cuban at a stall selling fritters. Together, at a signal, they had entered the café and pushed through the throng to the bar, where they stood side by side for as long as it took to drink a glass of Stella Artois. Their talk had been low and brief.

"You should continue to cooperate with this adventurist group called the Iskra," the Cuban had said, "since their action, although theoretically incorrect, will help to expose the growing weakness of capitalist industry in Europe."

Coming from Reinaldo Herrera Valdes, a fat young attaché of

the Cuban Embassy in Paris, this instruction seemed to Joop Janssen to be getting very close to sanctimonious bullshit. However, an order was an order, and this one had certainly not started life in Havana. So he did as he was told. Returning to the Hotel Europa, he set up his audio-surveillance equipment again and listened to proceedings in Harvey's office until 1.30. Then he telephoned Rosa Berg in Paris, the founder and leader of the Iskra. She wanted to know where he had been.

"Out to lunch," replied Joop.

"So what's the situation?"

He told her.

Rosa listened. And then she said: "So they're going for a merger, fine. I expected that. But do they know anything about the . . . countermeasures? You know what I mean?"

Joop smiled at Rosa's efforts to talk cryptically on the telephone, at which she was almost as shaky as arms drill. "I know what you mean," he said. "No, there's been no talk of anything like that."

"That's good. That's very good. Thanks, Joop." There was a halt in Rosa's voice, as though she were winded by exertion, and then she added: "I'll be with you tonight."

"You will?" Surprise hardly altered the tone of the Dutchman's reply.

"Yes," she said, "I'm coming with Mitzi."

"As you wish."

In Paris, having heard the answers she wanted, Rosa Berg put the phone down too hard in excitement, so hard she almost cracked it in two. Correcting this momentary loss of control with a single deep breath, she composed herself and turned back to face the central committee of the Iskra, all of whom were gathered in an upstairs room at the Café Babylone, a dim leftist drinking hole in the Boulevard Raspail, a cobble's throw from the Sorbonne.

"So there you are. Now we know," she said to them, having repeated Joop Janssen's news. "Harvey's going for a merger of the companies. And he's got a fat bribe in his pocket." She translated one billion Ecus into francs.

Someone whistled softly.

But Rosa was confident. "Don't worry," she said, "don't worry. It is nothing like enough to save them. And Harvey will run into trouble at the summit, you know. France will speak for Renault, Germany for Volkswagen. They'll tear the thing to bits, and him with it. As clever old Riemeck is very well aware."

No one present had the knowledge to dispute this analysis. But little Mitzi Hoff, who liked to see action, the more dangerous the better, pulled a face of disappointment. "Surely you're not going to let this Harvey go ahead?" she said, pouting.

Rosa smiled at the question, coming as it did from the mind of a reckless German child. "No," she answered, "that would be too big a risk – even if the odds are against him. This project for a merger has to be stopped before it goes any further, and in my view the best way to stop it is to take some immediate action against both companies, of the kind we have many times discussed. That is to say, we should immobilise the management. At the same time we have to accelerate political action by the workers if we can. Both things must happen at once – one without the other is no good. And the moment is now. We must act within the next two days, no later. You all agree?"

All agreed. Or rather, none argued.

Rosa glanced round at their faces, some young and ardent, some getting older now, touched with doubt. New recruits and veterans, nine people in all, were gathered in the small dark room where the Iskra had begun. As well as the French hard core, whom she knew and understood the best, there was Mitzi Hoff from Berlin. And sitting at the side, chewing gum with a vacant expression, was the shiftless American, Hal Fawcett. Rosa had little faith in him, but knew he would not be the first to resist her authority. Her relationship with each of these nine, her power over each, was slightly different. Together, in a mass, they could be troublesome. But now, when it counted, she had their attention and respect. She took another deep breath.

"Very well then. The moment for action has come. Either we take this risk now, or our lives are a pathetic joke, and our talk has been wasted breath. Will you open the box, Marc?"

She turned to the big Algerian sitting at her side, a man as dark and unkempt as his café, who got to his feet and bent down to open the box she had brought from Le Havre. It was not so much a trunk as a long wooden military crate, with some of the markings on its side painted out. The items inside were covered by a blanket. Marc Bensaîd pulled off the blanket, then stood back for all to peer in.

There was a moment of silence. Somebody whistled again. Then, one by one, they reacted.

"*Look* at that stuff."

"God, Rosa, where did you *get* all this?"

"Joop got it."

"American, is it?"

"Some is. Some not."

"What are we doing? Starting World War Three?"

Reactions were different, some slow, some quick; not all delighted. Rosa watched their faces, caught the flicker of doubt and pushed on before it could catch. "Hal, I want some of this delivered to Italy by tomorrow. You'll have to get going immediately. The rest goes down to the house."

"What house?"

"A base we've prepared in case of trouble. Marc knows where."

Two of them had taken out pistols.

"That's right," Rosa urged. "Help yourselves. If you have the courage, don't get taken alive. And if you are taken, don't talk."

Everyone then took a pistol out of the trunk. Ammunition was distributed.

"Remember the Iskra's tradition of silence," she told them in conclusion. "It has never been more important than now. Harvey is acting in secrecy, and that is what we must do too. Our aim is to kill off this merger in a way that cannot be traced back to us, or even blamed on the Left. The last thing we want is to set off an anti-Red scare in the press. You agree?"

All agreed, although young Lucien Seznec, whose life had not equipped him to understand more than a street fight, was white to the lips. He waited till Mitzi took a gun before he armed himself.

Rosa, looking round at them all with a stern expression of command, was inwardly leaping with exultation. She had not been sure they would follow her, but now the moment of resistance had passed. "Very well then," she said. "To work."

In London, twenty floors above Euston Road, the chairman of the British Motor Group was smoking a short square cigar. His office was panelled, thickly carpeted, hushed. The murmur of traffic hardly reached it.

Hugely built, with close-cropped ginger hair and hands like mechanical grabs, John Clabon was the sort of man in whom leadership took a form close to physical force. He stood at the panoramic plate-glass window with his feet set apart, his swollen grey eyes fixed unblinking on the opposite office blocks. Then he took the cigar from his mouth and smiled: a small private smile of satisfaction, with something voracious about it – a hint of old scores settled. At lunch he had received advance word of a knighthood.

But the smile was quickly gone as he turned and walked back from the window to his desk, on which were spread sheets of statistics. Self-congratulation was premature. Everything so far done at BMG had been a rescue operation, nothing more. Any more figures like the present ones, he thought, and the axe of dismissal would fall on his head before the royal bloody sword.

His gloom was interrupted by a buzz. Absently he pressed down a switch, leaning his head towards the speaker at his side. "Yes?"

"Sir Patrick Harvey on the line, sir, from Brussels."

"Ah, good. Put him on." Clabon snatched up a phone. "Patrick?"

"Hello, John. Glad to find you in." Harvey's voice, diffident always, sounded close and yet strangely far away, as if he were speaking from space. "Where are you going to be late this afternoon?"

"Ash Valley. Leaving now."

A pause, then Harvey said: "Can we use that landing strip – the one by the works?"

"Yes, no problem. Just clear it with traffic control as you go."

"We've hired a small plane, you see. I thought we should keep this thing on the move."

"Good idea. I'll send a car to meet you."

"No, not me. I'm sending a member of my staff. His name is Kohlman – Erich Kohlman."

"Does he know what's up?"

"He does. And you can trust him."

"All right. You're the chief. What time will he land?"

Arrangements for a rendezvous were made. His voice gave little indication of it, but Clabon was pleased by the speed of

Harvey's action. Good, he thought, good. So something gets done in that Eurocratic glasshouse after all. Then, for the second time in minutes, satisfaction gave way to anxiety. He stared again at the latest sales forecast in front of him, which had come handwritten from his Finance Director, Michael Oppenheim. It was even worse than the one he'd shown Harvey in Wales. After studying the figures a moment, he picked up another phone, short-circuiting his secretary.

"Oppie, I've seen it. And now I'm going to destroy it, right?"

"Right. I understand."

"You do the same. I want no record anywhere. You can bring this up at the board next week. Till then, not a whisper."

"Okay, John. Good luck."

Good luck? *Good luck*? Clabon, having put down the telephone, glared back at it suspiciously, wondering if the secret had got through to Oppenheim. He had told none of his directors about the plan for a merger. If it failed, he preferred them not to know of it; if it worked, he would slap it down on the boardroom table as a triumphant, accomplished fact. That was his style with them, and none of them liked it. But only Michael Oppenheim, Finance and Planning, was clever enough to make such tactics difficult.

Still, within the company the secret was probably safe. If Oppenheim had guessed the truth, he would at least keep it to himself. Much the greater danger was that smooth Aussie hack at *The Times*, Frank Holroyd, who had telephoned in mid-morning with some awkward questions. Holroyd had got the idea, from where he wouldn't say, that a merger with Mobital was in the air. He was also the only national editor to have picked up that piece of local gossip from Wales.

"An open-air vehicle apparently, John, without any engine sound. Yellow thing, rather like a golf cart. Scooting up and down a track in the hills, the man said, very fast and very quiet, with our former Prime Minister in the passenger seat. The driver sounded rather like you."

"No, not me, Frank. You're up the wrong tree."

But oh Lord, no, it was the right tree, and keeping off the press was like trying to shoot down a pack of monkeys, thought Clabon. They kept coming back until you ran out of lies.

Shredding as thoroughly as any machine, he tore Oppenheim's figures to pieces, then leaned again towards the speaker at his side. "All right, Mary, we're off. We'll do those letters in the car."

"Yes sir."

"And call the police at Ash Valley. Tell them I'm going in through Gate Five, and I want some protection."

Talking low in the back of the taxi, on the way from the restaurant to his office, Frank Holroyd had told Jack Kemble of the two small straws in the wind that were making his news nose twitch. The first originated with a Welsh schoolmaster, who had come down from a hike in the hills and immediately phoned the local paper in Builth Wells to report a remarkable sight.

But Kemble, having heard what the schoolmaster saw, was slow on the uptake. "So," he said, "what was it?"

"Electric car, Jack." Holroyd, leaning closer, breathed the answer through a cloud of garlic. "There's been a bit of chat around BMG about a new battery engine, developed with Saab and Volvo. And if that thing in Wales was the prototype, it goes like a bomb, I can tell you. Could be revolutionary."

Kemble's interest had risen. "Okay, good story. I'll get it if I can. But why the demonstration for Harvey?"

Holroyd's answer was that European money, and very large amounts of it, would be needed to bring such a toy to production. And Patrick Harvey held the purse strings. Even so, BMG was rather small to tackle such a project alone, or to be in volume cars of any sort. This was well known. They needed a partner. The Swedes wanted no closer link than they had already, and anyway were outside Harvey's spending area. However, there was one other good candidate. Last year, when he came to London for the Motor Show, Carlo Guidotti of Mobital . . .

Kemble had taken the job.

But first he had doubled the fee. Two secrets to crack, so two thousand sterling up front please, cash, expenses on top.

This had strained Holroyd's goodwill to the limit. Muttering darkly about geese and golden eggs, he had gone off to clear it with his boss.

Kemble, while he waited for the answer, had been hidden in the paper's boardroom, well out of sight of the staff. The room was out-of-date modern, with a long oval table and chairs like aircraft seats. On the wall was a portrait of the paper's new proprietor, or rather the impartial chairman of its elected managerial committee, who also just happened to control the company. It was a fairly grim picture. The man who had brought democracy to *The Times* appeared to be going up in smoke.

At one end of the table was a telephone. Kemble stared at it a while, then picked it up. He asked for an outside line, dialled the prefix for America, then the area code for Bethesda, Maryland, then the number of his little clapboard box in the woods. He caught his wife alone in the house. He told her he loved her. He told her he hadn't touched a drop for a week. He told her about the job and the money. She listened in silence.

"Kim, come on," he said. "I'm trying."

"Yes, Jack. I know that."

Her soft southern voice sounded close in his ear. In the background he could hear heavy traffic on Huntingdon Parkway: the usual exodus of minor foreign diplomats, always the last to go to work in Washington.

"Just give me time," he said. "See what I can do. Give me a week."

"Okay," she said eventually, sounding tired enough to sleep on the spot. "But no promises. Good luck, Jack. I wish you the best."

Kemble had hoped for no more. He meant to keep trying. Having cleared up his sins in Hampstead, he caught an afternoon plane to Brussels in purposeful mood and sat at a window with Europe spread below him. The land was flat and domesticated, laid out in delicate rectilinear patterns of fields, roads, canals. He stared at it without affection. He didn't give a damn for this continent's secrets, he told himself, and didn't much care for the English after all. His wife was American and so was his heart. He would make a quick score here, then get the hell out, go home, find work, stay dry, sort things out, make it up to her.

Advancing down the aisle of the aircraft, wheeled by a hostess of Lufthansa, was a trolley with many small bottles on it. The bottles were clinking merrily together amid the clatter of ice cubes being shovelled into plastic beakers. Kemble closed his eyes as the sound drew closer. The best thing would have been to fall asleep, while still in a state of virtue, but since the trolley was only two rows away he tried to hold his mind on the task ahead. The best way to Harvey, he thought, would be through his girl, whose name was Laura. And the way to Laura . . .

"Cocktail, sir?"

On one of the *autoroutes* coiling below, like broad strips of tape on the map, Rosa Berg was also on her way to Brussels.

She had passed through Paris like a whirlwind, scooping up everyone at her command and flinging them out on new errands. From the meeting at the café she had gone to her bookshop in the Latin Quarter, *Berg Livre*, which was more of a democratic commune than *The Times*. All profits went to political purposes. Each worker-comrade was equally paid, with small variations according to need, but only one of them knew of the communications code concealed in the shop's mail-order trade, by which the Iskra kept in touch with its members in other parts of Europe. As she rushed through the place in the early afternoon, delegating jobs, removing papers from files, Rosa had left the impression that she was clearing up for good. But nobody asked any questions. She frequently vanished for fairly long periods, but was quick to check the figures on return. For a Marxist, it was generally agreed, Rosa Berg was a pretty tough businesswoman. And, for a woman, plain tough. Rosa had the strength of a peasant, her friends would say with timid smiles. And she herself knew what they said. She took a pride in it. She had been travelling round Europe for a week already, but seemed to gather strength with motion. After crossing the border into Belgium she handed the wheel of her car to Mitzi Hoff and immediately slumped asleep in the passenger seat. She had the knack of instant slumber, and slept so deep that she needed very little of it. Within twenty minutes, as Brussels approached, she had pulled herself upright in the car and was staring with wide-awake eyes at the grimy industrial scene either side of the road. Then she turned with a sudden, broad, ebullient smile to the German girl who was driving.

"Mitzi, my dear, do you know what Trotsky's word was for a nation which abandons all principle to commerce?"

"No," replied Mitzi to cue. "What was it?"

"Belgianisation!" cried Rosa in delight, and laughed out loud at the eloquent insult. Good old Trotsky had a tongue like a whip, she thought to herself, and used it on friends as well as enemies, which did him no good in the end of course, but made him more fun than most of the Bolsheviks.

Mitzi laughed too, but sourly, and less at Leon Trotsky than the Belgians. "Yes," she said, "they're pigs."

Mitzi Hoff was the youngest of the Iskra, and the latest to be recruited. A tiny girl, dark, and curly-haired, she could have been sixteen. She was in fact twenty-six. Her style in clothes was all her own. Next to her skin she invariably wore some sort of tee-shirt, fitting close to her small shapely torso, and suspended over it by straps from her shoulders a pair of flappy dungarees, either bright green or striped, to the front of which were pinned a number of political badges. Her feet were either bare or in sneakers, depending on the weather. Today the tee-shirt was black, the dungarees green. She had kicked off the sneakers to drive barefoot. She was a pretty girl, especially when she pouted, and gave off a powerful sexual lure of a most disturbing kind, half-knowing, half-innocent, like a child depraved. Most of the men in the Iskra were hot for her, although only Lucien, the waiter at the Babylone, was known to have had success. The rest consoled themselves with exotic rumours that Mitzi did not confine herself to men. She would do either, it was said, she would do anything. To Rosa it was extraordinary, amusing, disgusting, to watch the effect that this slip of a girl from Berlin could have on a pack of hard-boiled Parisian Marxists. In the end she had put a total ban on discussion of Mitzi Hoff's love life.

And yet she herself was strangely fascinated. For a few moments after the laugh about Trotsky she kept her eyes on the pretty young German, who was driving flat out, returning more in temper than haste to the city where she lived in sullen exile. Mitzi's job for the Iskra was in Brussels. She had been there three months, for a purpose known only to Rosa and herself, and would stay as long as required. Her home was Berlin, though, and perhaps that accounted for her fascinating, other-worldly strangeness. She had dropped, as it were, from an alien planet, where the rules of life were not as here. There was no telling what her reasons were, this sad-happy child of the east-west border, most of whose friends were locked up or dead. She could do the most startling things. Several times in her life she had burst into violence. Most of the Iskra, Joop

Janssen especially, distrusted her. Some of them thought she was mad. Only Rosa had faith in her. Only Rosa had seen that underneath Mitzi Hoff's wanton exterior was an unswerving loyalty to friends and a faculty for sticking to orders, once accepted. The latter of these German qualities she had come to rely on especially. Rosa knew without stopping to wonder that Mitzi, although she might argue and pout, would always do what she had said she would, and would do it to the letter – to death.

"You can drop me off at the hotel," she said as the city of the Belgians closed around them. "But I want you back at midnight, ready to take over the listening from Joop."

Mitzi's ball of dark curls bobbed once, in wordless obedience. Her eyes remained on the traffic. "Shall I have a room at the Europa too?" she asked in her simple, toneless French.

"No, you'll have to do it from your car. It won't be comfortable."

"For how long?"

"As long as is necessary," Rosa said. "A few more days. Perhaps a week."

"So where's Joop going?"

"To England."

"Why?"

"That's what I'm coming here to tell him, Mitzi. But I don't think I ought to tell you, do you? We should each know as much as we need to, no more. That's a sound old Leninist tactic."

Mitzi's baby-cheek dimpled. Her smile was at the same time mocking but sweet. "Comrade Lenin, Comrade Trotsky – you talk all the time of dead Russians. But can they help us now, these old men?"

"Oh yes, they can," Rosa started to reply with some vehemence, preparatory to a declaration of faith. Then she stopped herself. It was this sort of speech, exactly, which couldn't be made to a child of the East-West divide. Abashed by her own political naivety – that was what Mitzi made it seem – Rosa fell silent. And then, for reassurance, she started to think of Joop Janssen, her hard and trustworthy Dutchman. At the thought of reunion with him her spirit rose cheerfully and her body began to ache with pleasant yearning.

In Brussels the rush hour had begun. The whole central city was thundering with homeward-bound traffic. But high in the double-glazed calm of the Hotel Europa, Joop Janssen was still at his post, his radio-surveillance equipment still spread on the bed. He had been listening all afternoon to the business of Harvey's office.

At his side was a pad filled with notes, each note carefully indexed to the relevant portion of the relevant cassette, in case Rosa wanted to listen to a replay.

But now there was nothing more to hear from the Berlaymont. Erich Kohlman had left for England two hours before. Lucy, the typist, had skipped away home on the clock. Harvey himself was in another part of the building, conferring with the Director-General of his department, who would handle other business while the effort at a merger was on. Only Laura Jenkinson was left on duty, and whatever she was doing, she was silent.

The light was gradually fading outside, reduced by a rising pall of dust and exhaust fumes. The bedroom was almost in darkness. But Joop switched on no lights. He considered a trip to the window to take another look at Laura, but could not be bothered. He had done enough. He was tired. He swung his feet up on the bed, stretched out and closed his eyes.

And then, minutes later, he was woken by the ring of Laura's telephone, coming loud through the speaker at his side. Immediately he sat up and put on the headphones. The tuning was already set exact. He could hear Laura's voice with perfect clarity, and also that of the caller: a journalist just in from London who wanted to interview Sir Patrick. He was speaking from a phone booth at Zaventem Airport.

"I'm afraid the Commissioner is busy." Laura repeated the formula with weariness. All day she had stalled for Harvey and Erich while the two of them put their clever heads together, and she had had enough of it – today, for ever. "I'm sorry, Mr. Kemble, but there's nothing I can do. Sir Patrick is completely tied up for the next seven days."

"So what about you?"

"Me?"

"Well, what I want to do is a general piece – centred on Sir Patrick, of course, when he's free to see me, but basically Life in the Berlaymont. The New Europeans, you know, hope of the world, all that stuff." The man broke off and laughed. "Oh boy, what crap I do talk. I've been doing this too long."

Laura laughed too. "Foot in door, eh?"

"Foot in door. And I'm getting worse at it. Must be gout."

"Who's the piece for? What paper, I mean."

"Whoever's mug enough to buy it. I'm freelance. Basically I see it as magazine·stuff, maybe ladies' market. Plenty of pictures and personal detail."

Laura laughed again. "How nice for the ladies," she said with an edge. "Well, Mr. Kemble, I'm sorry I can't help. We're awfully serious up here, you know. All work and no play."

She was about to ring off, but then he said: "Wait, Laura, please. Look. I don't know this town, or a damn soul in it. Can't I start with you? Take you out for a meal or something?"

"You know my name?"

"Yes. I got it from Jenny in Washington."

"Jenny?"

"Jenny Hall, at the embassy."

"Oh," said Laura, remembering no Jenny, but assuming the lapse was in her own mind. "So you're new to Brussels, are you? That's a cruel fate. Where are you staying?"

"The Europa."

"Well, Mr. Kemble, it's nice of you to ask me. I already have a date tonight, as it happens. But I could call round for a drink – about eleven? Would that be too late?"

"It would not," he said with simple boyish glee, practically undressing her down the line. "I'll be in the bar."

Yes, she thought, the bar is where you would be – and have been already by the sound of it. "*À bientôt*, then."

"Excuse me?"

"Till later. It's what the natives say here."

"Oh, sure," he said, sounding now just a little too simple to be true. "Till later. I'll see you at eleven."

Laura rang off with a catlike smile. Whatever excuse they began with, American men were quicker to come to the point than the English, which made them more fun to discourage – or yield to. She had no intention of yielding to this one, whose voice made him hard to place in any case. He was either American pretending to be English, or vice versa. This ambiguity did not increase his charms. On the audible evidence he had few charms of any sort. And yet she was happy to hang a small question mark over the end of the very dull diplomatic evening ahead.

7

Descending on Coventry in the chartered jet, Erich Kohlman inspected the country which three of his uncles had died to defeat. It was hard to see why they had bothered. The Midlands looked exactly like the Ruhr. A greater air of dereliction perhaps; more red brick, less new apartment blocks. Spread below the plane in the smoky evening light were the usual mazelike patterns of close-built terrace housing, unique to Britain. But otherwise no difference appeared from the air. Here too among the small fields like patchwork were towns running into each other, distinguished only by their churches, factories everywhere and motorways snaking through the pylons and slagheaps, all below a sulphurous yellow-brown haze. A blot on the landscape; a blot so big it had become the landscape, and certainly not worth dying for, in either direction. The mark of industrial man was everywhere the same.

In the city of Coventry itself he could see the bomb-blackened spire of the old cathedral, preserved as a memorial of war, like the *Gedächtniskirche* of Kaiser Wilhelm in Berlin. Here, as on the Ku-Damm, a new church had been put up beside the ruins of the old. Then the plane banked, and he saw the big BMG assembly plant, its long green hangars passing close below. Ash Valley was a city in itself. The day shift was just coming off, a huge tide of men pouring out of every gate and away in separate streams to their homes.

Excited, almost scared by the sight, Kohlman tightened his seat-belt for landing. Parked beside the runway he could see a green BMG Jaguar, which he guessed must belong to John Clabon. He wondered what the man would be like.

"A very tough nut," Sir Patrick had said, "and bound to make a fuss. But don't let him bully you, Erich. Just tell him the plan and come back."

John Clabon glanced up from the papers on his knee as Kohlman was led towards the Jaguar. So this was Harvey's messenger. A surprisingly young man, given his job. Blond and neat; pale as a ghost. Airsick or scared? Maybe just pale as a ghost.

Even when noting mere physical details, Clabon assessed a man in terms of his own self-interest. How useful, how dangerous would he be? With Kohlman he came to no instant conclusion.

"Welcome," he said, stepping out. "I assume you wouldn't hire a plane to tell me it's off."

Once they were seated together in the back, the young German started to make a reply, but Clabon interrupted him. "Later," he said, thrusting all his papers across to his secretary in the front seat. "We'll talk when we get to my office. But first I'm going to show you something. Just sit tight and watch. Don't speak, and don't get out of the car."

Kohlman sat obediently silent, stiff in his seat as the car pulled away from the airstrip.

Clabon then spoke to the driver. "Be ready to stop when I tell you. But keep the engine running."

The driver nodded. The secretary scrambled to get rid of the papers. The Jaguar was travelling fast through the middle-income suburbs of Coventry: matching pairs of bow-windowed houses, semi-detached, sumac trees and washing-lines, gardens strewn with gaudy plastic toys. Then the BMG factory came in view. Ash Valley loomed over the town like a green tin mountain. Still pouring away from it was a stream of men on bicycles, which thinned to a trickle as the gates of the plant drew nearer. The day shift were almost off the premises. The night shift were already in. But packed around Gate Five, when it came into view, was a crowd of perhaps a hundred people. Most of them were gathered round a brazier of coke, on which a picket of strikers were boiling a kettle for tea. A bus was parked to one side with a pair of police cars. The police were gathered round the brazier too, apparently waiting for tea.

The sight of this fraternisation reminded John Clabon of a story he'd heard, that during the General Strike of 1926 a

71

photograph of English miners playing football against the police had been published by a French communist newspaper under the caption THE BRITISH ARE A CIRCUS NOT A NATION. The story had always made him laugh. Not today. Confronted with the fact, he felt as exasperated as any French dogmatist. Let's either go to work, he thought, or have a flaming revolution. It's this tea on the barricades which will finish us.

Leaning forward to the driver, he made him stop within sight of the crowd, but still at a distance from it. Then he turned to Kohlman.

"The picket are Scotsmen," he explained. "They arrive here every day in that bus. They make our steering-wheels in Glasgow, you see, and they want more money for it. So they go on strike against their own employer. Fine. Democracy in action. But then they come down here and set up that picket, to stop our two other suppliers delivering any steering-wheels. Which is not so fine, I'm sure you agree, and is causing us some bad production problems."

Kohlman then spoke his first words. "But surely," he said, "this is not allowed. You have a law against secondary pickets."

"The 1980 Act, oh yes, sure." Clabon nodded sarcastically. "But these fellows know how to get around that one. They don't actually call themselves a picket at all, you see. When the coppers ask them what they're doing, they say they're not here to stop men or vehicles passing through that gate. But they're there, aren't they? That's enough. I mean, take a look at them." Clabon waved his hand forward, at the same time turning to watch Kohlman's face. "Would *you* like to go through that lot if you knew they didn't want you to?"

Kohlman shook his head.

"This has been going on three weeks," Clabon added, facing forward again. "And if it goes on much longer, a lot of men here in this factory will be out of a job. But as you see, the Scots are not getting any stick from their brothers at Ash Valley. Far from it. The men at BMG accept the action of this picket. Some of them have even joined it. And now they're all having tea together. They could be discussing the New Jerusalem, I suppose, but I've a shrewd idea they're talking football."

Kohlman smiled, a little nervously. But Clabon was not joking.

72

"I am supposed to be running this company, Mister Kohlman. And yet I have no power to stop this situation. Now if that isn't bloody dictatorship by the proletariat, would you mind telling me what you would call it?"

For a moment they stared together in silence at the scene: the cloth caps and bobbies, the factory behind and the sky tinged with smoke, so very little different from an old sepia photograph of 1926. Then Kohlman spoke again.

"I would call it Britain."

Clabon laughed harshly. "You're too damn right," he said, and then told his driver to advance very slowly, at the same time leaning right forward himself to get a better look at the crowd ahead. It had been swelled by some students from Warwick University. No doubt there were some onlookers, there for fun; a few local press perhaps. And the BMG men who had joined the picket itself were grouped below a banner of the Industrial Workers Alliance. The IWA were militant Trotskyites, the best drilled political group at work within Ash Valley. Clabon had expected to see them here. He tightened his tie, then laid a warning hand on the shoulder of his driver. "Right, this will do. Stop here."

He was out of the car before he was recognised. The police, forewarned, ran to put a cordon round him. But Clabon pushed through them, strode forward into the centre of the crowd and roared out a single question.

"Is Stephen Murdoch here?"

The jeers died away. There was a moment of surprised immobility. Then a pale young man, spare and short, with a thick shock of wavy red hair, stepped forward in the silence, emerging from the group of BMG workers. "I'm here," he said, his pinched face taut with ill will. "What of it?"

Clabon turned to face him with the smile of a bear offered meat. "Ah, hello, Murdoch. I thought you'd be around."

"The IWA is here in support. As is our right."

"Got the day off for it?"

"Don't worry, you've had your quota."

"So you do make cars as well. I'm surprised you have time."

"Come on, Clabon, cut the bloody play-acting. What do you want?"

"I want to tell you, Murdoch, that we know about the organisation you work for – I mean the foreign one. But I doubt

73

if your mates do. And I'm damn sure these chaps from Scotland don't." Raising his voice, Clabon looked first at the knot of BMG workers, then turned to the men of the picket itself. "So why don't you ask him, gentlemen? Ask Comrade Murdoch here about the Iskra."

But the word was lost in a chorus of jeers. Clabon tried to say more, but could not make himself heard, so gave up and walked away, ignoring the storm of foul abuse behind him. The police jumped forward to protect him. A brick hit the boot of the Jaguar. There were two arrests.

A few minutes later, standing in the quiet of his office, John Clabon was still a little high on the pleasure this incident had given him. But he made no immediate further mention of it.

"The Commission's plan? I thought it was my plan."

"There have been some changes since you spoke to Sir Patrick in Wales," replied Kohlman, still holding the thin red dossier with SECRET stamped across it in four languages.

"Sit down, sit down," said Clabon, and they moved to some low easy chairs, made of tubular chrome and black leatherette, set square around a glass-topped table. "How about a drink?"

"No thank you."

"Bit early, I suppose. Oh the hell with it, come on. Wet your throat."

"Nothing, thank you. But please, serve yourself."

"Yes. With your permission, I will. Those Trots give me a thirst."

Striding across to a cocktail cabinet, which lit up like magic when he opened it, Clabon poured himself a whisky of fierce proportions. He had once been a factory foreman and was proud of it. He had learnt his business style on Midland golf courses, driving his way to a personal fortune contract by contract, tee to tee and back to the club-house for a quick one. As saviour of the national motor industry he'd had to learn a new style, but part of it was to pretend he was stuck with the old one. A rough diamond, even if fake, could cut a lot of corners.

"One of these, then?" The cigars were short and square, made in Switzerland.

"No thank you."

Clabon gave up the effort at courtesy, feeling baffled, as

often, by the ways of modern Europe. The merger, if it happened, would be a heavy blow to the German motor industry, and yet here was this keen young German, handing him the plan in the name of an institution whose chief, come to think of it, was also a German.

"Are you telling me that Riemeck has already bought the idea?"

Kohlman placed his briefcase at his feet as he sat. "Sir Patrick had a meeting with the President this morning. That paper was drafted after lunch on their joint instructions."

"Have Mobital seen it?"

"I go to Milan tomorrow."

"Well, I'd better take a look then."

Swiss cigar ignited, Scotch drink in fist, Clabon sat down himself and opened the folder from Brussels.

They were on the first floor of an office at the edge of the BMG assembly plant. From the tall green hangars all around came the mountainous rumble of mass production. The windows of the office looked north across a cricket ground, towards a belt of larches which screened the first suburbs of Coventry. But today there would be no cricket. The entire field was covered with cars. They stood in mute rows by the hundred, their unpolished bodies lack-lustre in the dusk. A uniformed guard was walking between them with a dog.

Glancing up, Clabon caught Kohlman's eyes fixed on the sight. "Notice anything?"

"That is the Pilot 1500."

"Anything else?"

Kohlman looked again. "The ones near to us have no steerage wheels."

"Correction, none of them has a bloody steering wheel. So now you see the damage those Scots are causing. Two other firms, one British, one Dutch, are tooled to make interior components for the Pilot, but neither of them dares to deliver through that picket. At least the British one won't. The Dutch haven't tried yet."

"Yet the BMG workers support the picket."

"A few of them."

"A few support, the rest do not oppose," insisted Kohlman, "as you told me yourself. At the gate, just now, it was your own man you treated as the enemy."

Though irritated by the correction, Clabon was beginning to be rather impressed by this handsome young German, who was not quite the wraith that he appeared. Even so, something was absent. Imagination? Humour? Character? A strange lack of *substance*, one felt, in these clever young Europeans – perhaps because they seemed to have no nationality. Anyway, there was no choice. Show the boy the worst.

"Yes, you're right," he said. "The Scots aren't the problem. The enemy is here." He stared at Kohlman a short moment longer, then jumped to his feet and pressed down a switch on his desk. "The P.I. chart, Mary. Would you bring it in please? And the Security List."

A grey-haired woman came in with a sealed buff envelope. Clabon ripped it open and spread the contents on the glass-topped table.

"Know what P.I. means?"

"Not yet."

"Production Interruptions. A simple concept, like life and death. To start with, we were running at seven hundred stoppages a year. Then things got better. Now they're getting worse again. Look here." Clabon's fingers darted over the sheet, then stabbed at it forcefully. "On the basis of that graph, we're back to an annual rate of twelve hundred interruptions. It makes me miserable even to look at it."

But Clabon was not really miserable, being a man who needed problems as a bulldozer needs rocks to push. He stroked the flame of a heavy gold lighter over the end of his cigar, until it glowed red, then pushed the chart away and sat back.

"All right, so the stoppages are up. But there's something very odd about them. Take another look."

Kohlman already had the answer. "Most of them occurred at Ash Valley."

"Damn nearly all of them. So what do you make of that?"

"Bad management?"

Clabon shook his head. "Could be, but no. The management here is as good as at Rover and Jaguar."

"But the car is not."

"The Pilot has its problems, I admit."

"Problems so severe they could close the plant," Kohlman said in a voice of gentle reproof. "And in view of your most recent figures, that risk now extends to the group as a whole."

"Ah, so it's the lemming theory."

"Lemming?"

"Lemming. Kind of rat." Clabon's left hand scampered downwards in grotesque imitation of a suicidal rodent. "Thirty thousand men catch the deathwish, just because they happen to work at Ash Valley. Is that it?"

Kohlman ignored the question. "I suppose you are going to tell me that there is a plot in this factory."

"Too right I am."

"But surely a conspiracy, among so many, does not seem more probable than suicide."

"No, of course not. A few conspire. The mass just follow." Clabon's voice sank in volume but intensified in passion, his whole body leaning into the argument, like a boxer's weight applied to a punchbag. "Look," he said, "I'm telling you, there is a plot. But so few people are actively involved in it that we could fix them with one quick firing squad."

Kohlman's face was shocked. "That is the language of violence."

"All right, too strong. But violence, Mister Kohlman, is what I see coming unless we act quickly. We're up against a group of fanatics here."

"And this group has chosen Ash Valley for special attack?"

"Indeed they have. For attack and sudden death, followed by a full political showdown – the revolutionary choice, as they call it. Want to hear how it works?"

"Please tell me."

"All right, listen well." Clabon poked his cigar at Kohlman's chest, narrowing his eyes in the thickening smoke. "First they stir up so much trouble that we are forced to close down the plant. Then, next step, they persuade the men to take the place over – I mean physically occupy it, until we agree to give them their jobs back. We, of course, refuse. We can do nothing else. So then comes the showdown. Either the men are starved out, or they try to make the Pilot themselves, with the help of the government. A people's car, made by the people for the people, with the people's money – you know the sort of madness. We've seen it here with one or two other things."

"Yes, and in other parts of Europe," said Kohlman. "But never on a scale so big. Would the government help them?"

77

"I doubt it. Not this one."

"Without that I cannot see how they would succeed."

"I find it rather difficult myself," said Clabon with sarcastic mildness. "But that is the plot, I assure you. And the really pathetic thing is that the men themselves don't realise it. Just an inner group. Here, let me show you."

He then spread out on the glass-topped table the second of the documents brought by his secretary. It was a long list of labour disputes, with the names of the men involved. A third column showed their political connections. Clabon's finger stabbed down the list.

"The same names, you see, again and again. And always the Industrial Workers Alliance. IWA, IWA – keeps cropping up. They've packed the factory and recruited hard inside it. And guess who's their founding father?"

"The man you spoke to at the gate?"

"That's right," said Clabon. "Stephen bloody Murdoch. Here, take a look. You see, Murdoch's always at the centre of the punch-up. Here he is. And here. And here again. Separate negotiating structure for toolmakers, a softer brand of paper in the shithouse – you name it, Murdoch is in there. Murdoch, Murdoch." He paused, staring grimly at the name on the page. "Yes, there's the enemy."

"And the Iskra," asked Kohlman. "What is that?"

"Oh yes, the Iskra." Clabon straightened up and drained his whisky at a single gulp, then leaned right back in his chair with a malignant smile. "Well, to be honest with you, that was a bluff. I just said it to shake the bastard up a bit."

"The word is a Russian one, I think."

"Correct. It means 'The Spark'. Name of Lenin's party rag – or so I'm told by Special Branch. The coppers think it's some kind of gang that Murdoch belongs to, probably violent, probably foreign. Apparently he's boasted to his cronies that if things get rough, help will come from abroad."

"So your information comes from the police?"

"It does. But if that gets out, bang, up we go. There'll be no more tea on the barricades."

Clabon quickly scrabbled together all the BMG papers and took them out to his secretary, then came back and stood at the window, staring out morosely at the field of ghost-cars. The day was fading fast.

"Of course," he said after a pause, "if it came to a showdown, the men would lose. We'd leave the poor bastards shut in here to rot. Eventually they'd give up – or some would, and that would be the end of it." He dragged at his cigar but it was out. He took it from his mouth, stared at it irritably, as though it had betrayed him, then forgot it and turned from the window with his hands out, a dark silhouette against the lights of Coventry. "But that's not the way I want to win, Mister Kohlman. It would be a disaster for this town, and for many good men who have worked here all their lives. So now you see what this is about. Together with Mobital, and some European cash in my pocket, I can offer the workers who work some intelligent hope for the future. I can keep this place open and clear the Reds out."

Kohlman hesitated in plain disapproval. "The plan I have brought," he said in a prim voice, "was prepared on a different basis. The European Community is not a strike-breaking institution."

"Good God, sonny, I know *that*!" Clabon flung back his head and laughed in scorn. "Of course we shall all have to wear our best classless hats and pretend that there isn't a war on. But if you're going to handle this, I thought you better know the true position."

"The plan assumes . . ."

"I'll read it this evening. Now what about that drink?"

"No, Mr. Clabon."

"What did you say?"

"You will please read the plan at once. Sir Patrick requires your comments by tonight. In his opinion the merger has no chance at all unless it is agreed in time for the European summit."

"But that's next week."

"It is. Starting Wednesday."

Clabon gaped for several seconds. Then he strode swiftly inward from the window, slapping his thigh like a rodeo rider. "All right, why not, let's do it in a week. So what's the next step?"

"A meeting this weekend," Kohlman told him, "starting Saturday morning. Just yourself and Mr. Guidotti, with Sir Patrick in the chair."

"I agree. Where?"

"Sir Patrick has friends who maintain a small château near Tours, in France."

"Tours," said Clabon, opening the cocktail cabinet. "Yes, I had a funny idea it was in France."

8

In his room at the Hotel Europa, Brussels, Joop Janssen had stowed away his equipment and was stretched out flat on the bed. Outside it was almost dark. He was asleep.

And then he was woken by a knock on the door – a hard, peremptory rap of the knuckles, open up or else. Automatically he reached for the pistol concealed below the mattress, but his hand stopped short of the gun. Recognising the knock, he swung his feet off the bed, walked across to the door and unlocked it.

She patted him casually on the cheek, but said nothing. Her eyes did a slow, contemptuous tour of the luxurious room. She walked to the window with that swift heavy stride of hers, stared briefly at the late-working staff in the Berlaymont, then turned to face him with a small reckless smile which said there is only one thing to do in a place like this, so why not?

Joop started to speak. But Rosa, still smiling, planted a finger on his lips. Then she told him to turn on the lights.

Knowing what she wanted now, Joop pressed every switch until they were standing in the full bright overhead glare of an operating theatre, then he waited by the bed without moving while she took off her clothes. The curtains were undrawn, the Berlaymont loomed in the night like a grandstand, but Rosa undressed without hurry or shame, deliberately exposing her big pale body to the world.

Under her shirt, strapped tight around her ribs, was a sort of canvas corset with deep vertical pockets. Joop assumed that this had started life as a money-belt for gold or currency smugglers, but Rosa had used it for years as a bandolier-cum-holster. Jammed into one of the pockets was her small Czech

81

pistol. She was also carrying a spare magazine, he noticed, some loose clips of ammunition and two fragmentation grenades of the green oval sort, M 26. So Rosa had put her hand into the trunk. Take cover, friends as well as enemies. But he made no comment as she undid the buckles and laid the belt on a chair. It clanked metallically as it came off.

Her shirt was the grey sort they issue in prisons, and her skin very white, the way a prisoner's might be. Her breasts were so big she kept them strapped in a brassiere, otherwise they got in the way of the gun. Released, they seemed to swell as they sagged, huge skins of milk no child had ever tasted. Watching them, Joop felt a stir of excitement.

Then nude in the glare, no longer smiling but concentrating, she walked across and started to undress him in turn, as though she were unwrapping a present. Here was an object she wanted and deserved, her manner declared, something she'd waited for and would now enjoy as she pleased, even if the whole damn world was watching. Joop remained passive. The initiative was Rosa's. She pushed him back on the bed, spread him flat and took her pleasure. She didn't make a sound throughout. Silent, expressionless, she worked at it methodically, breathing harder, moving quicker, until at the climax she expelled a jet of air through her teeth in a long, slow, satisfied hiss.

And Joop enjoyed himself too. The moment he heard her exhale in fulfilment he reversed the roles suddenly, brutally, flinging her over so that he was on top and then pinning her back by her short damp hair as he in turn used her, despoiled and degraded her with all his superior strength. Rosa resisted him, but feebly, and when he exploded inside her with a shout, she shut her eyes tight and went rigid, from top to toe, opening her mouth very wide, even wider, still wider, and wider again, until it emitted a small guttural croak of utter abandon and defeat, like a death rattle.

Afterwards, relieved, they lay with their slack limbs entwined, like sleeping children. Neither spoke. Then Joop got up, switched the lights off and lit a marijuana cigarette. That was the only kind Rosa enjoyed. They smoked it side by side on the bed, the burning tip passing between them like a firefly. And still they did not speak. Words risked sentiment, a weakness that Rosa despised above all others. And Joop was untalkative by nature. Endearments were superfluous, in any case, for a couple who lived in the shadow of doom. They had the camaraderie of war. Like soldiers at the front, they preferred to keep things practical, and so after a while, when he thought she was ready, Joop began a formal recital of the new information he had. He spoke in French, fluent but wierdly accented, while Rosa sucked in the last of the joint, blowing sweet grass smoke into the dark.

"So the companies are getting together," she said. "I told you they would."

"You were right."

"When is this meeting in Tours?"

"Saturday morning."

"And this château, do we know where it is?"

"I have the details," said Joop. "The girl fixed it up on the phone."

"Ah, the little Laura. How is she?"

"She types like a firing squad."

"You like her, don't you?" Rosa said, amused.

"Her knees are agreeable. And she smells like a flower shop," Joop replied in a neutral voice.

"You must have got close."

"There's a café she goes to for lunch, with her friend from Scotland."

"Well, be careful. You shouldn't get too close." Rosa rolled sideways and stubbed out the joint. Then, lying back, she reached for his hand and caressed it. "You are the best of us," she said to him softly. "The strongest, and the best."

Joop was so startled by this unusual gesture that he couldn't think of any response. Puzzled, he lay stiff beside her, suspecting that compliments from Rosa boded no good.

He was right.

"Tell me," she went on after a moment, "could you teach Mitzi how to work your box of tricks?"

"Yes, I suppose so. It's not very difficult – for a rational being."

"You're prejudiced."

"Rosa, she's crazy. I've seen the type. A crazy little German killer."

"Mitzi has never killed anyone."

"You wait," said Joop with a sniff.

"And what are you, my friend? Saint Francis?" Rosa snatched her hand from his in irritation, then took a deep breath and went on again in a low controlled voice, less affectionate now, more commanding. "All right, so none of us understands Mitzi. She makes her own rules. But she isn't a fool, and she isn't going to talk. In any case she'll have to do the listening from now on, because I've got another job for you."

"You have? What is that?"

"Action. More dangerous."

"Go on."

"We have to stop this merger, Joop. If the companies combine, they'll survive. Our work will be wasted. If they don't combine, they will fail, and the workers will take them over. It's as simple as that. All we have to do is keep them apart."

"So you want to break up this meeting in Tours."

"I want to stop it happening at all."

"You'll have to be quick," Joop said. "That bastard Kohlman is getting pretty busy."

"There you go again. Let's keep your racial feelings out of this. Just tell me again, what exactly is the schedule?"

"They're all due to reach the château in France on Friday evening, arriving by different routes – Harvey, Clabon, Guidotti. The talks will start next morning."

Rosa was silent for a moment, thinking. Then she said, by way of a premise: "We should leave things undisturbed in the Berlaymont."

"To protect your friend inside, you mean."

"Yes."

"Whoever that may be."

"Whoever that may be," repeated Rosa with a snap. "And don't expect me to tell you. That's the whole point of this system. Why do you think I brought you up here, to shoot Harvey dead at his desk?"

"I gave it some thought."

"No, Joop. In Brussels we listen. In Italy we can shoot, if we want to, because that is normal in Italy. But in England we must be more subtle. The political context does not permit the same degree of violence."

About to explain what it was that she wanted her Dutchman to do, Rosa paused to pick her words, more embarrassed than in the act of sex. But this time it was Joop who took the initiative, turning his head towards hers on the pillow with a friendly, invisible smile. "So you have found a way to cut Clabon's balls off," he said. "Within the political context, of course."

For reasons not clear to Jack Kemble, the Europa's bar had been done up in Scottish style: antlers and crossed claymores, Cameron walls, Mackenzie carpet. The barman's clan lay along the banks of the Congo, but the whisky was genuine, and after a dram or two even the tartans were blending quite nicely in Kemble's eyes. Having stepped off the wagon on the plane, he felt better, much better, and was now at that agreeable stage, known only to serious tipplers, where his head seemed more clear, more steady than when he had started.

And then he felt hungry. So he crossed to the hotel's coffee shop, where he sat at a table with a view of the lobby, watching out for Laura Jenkinson. He knew from her voice what she would look like: too brainy to bother with sex appeal, vain enough to want her face in the papers. But she was late. It was nearly midnight.

Beginning to feel stood up for the second time that day, he studied the coffee shop's menu, which was printed on a plastic bat. He ordered *croque monsieur* and a brand of beer known in the pubs of Hampstead as Eurofizz, then sat watching the people around him in a mood of increasing, irrational malevolence. The Belgians were a race about whom he had three fixed ideas. One, they ate too much. Two, they tended to panic at the least provocation. Three, they had less ability to handle an automobile than any other branch of *homo sapiens*. The third of these notions had been confirmed in hair-raising manner on his ride into town from the airport. Panic he had not yet observed. But here now in front of him was greed of a quite revolting order.

They had come into the coffee shop close behind him, a man and a woman, slightly furtive, touching hands, Not young, either of them – late thirties, early forties – and not exactly credit-card fraternity. Out of their element, they seemed to be, and rather enjoying it, though they must have had a room in the hotel – the man was carrying a key with ball and chain attached. Perhaps they were on their honeymoon. Perhaps they had just robbed a bank. But whatever they were doing, it had given them an appetite. After one quick look at the menu bat they had ordered cheeseburgers, two each, with two large portions of *frites*, bread rolls, and green salads on the side. Each had drunk a pint of beer. And now they were settling the whole thing down with chocolate milkshakes.

Kemble watched them with appalled fascination. The girl had tits you could drown in. She was a big girl all round, dressed in a long skirt and boots, with her upper equipment swinging about below a rough grey shirt, too thick for the weather – the sort of shirt that gets handed out in prisons. She had a wide, almost Slav sort of face and short brown hair, severely cut. Her fringe was bedraggled and damp with sweat. She looked tough as a peasant and yet at the same time hysterical. Even while she was eating, Kemble had the impression that she might at any moment jump up and yell some appalling obscenity.

The man was all skin and bone, with the desperate eyes of a pub brawler: a hard man, with nothing to lose, and therefore quite ready to cut your throat. While talking to the girl he had an odd way of holding his head, as if his neck were cricked. There was something peculiar about the skin of his face, a sort of stretched look, and his hair appeared to have been cut with garden shears. It was spiky and tufted, in parts holed through to the scalp. Its colour was a dull ash-grey. He was wearing a terrible suit, brand new but crumpled, ill-fitting, which no man who knew or cared a thing about suits could possibly have bought. Perhaps he had just got married in it. Yes, that was what it looked like: a once-only outfit bought for a formal occasion by a rough-living man.

There had been some celebration certainly. Both were pink-eyed. They had been smoking grass, you could smell it, and now they had almost done eating. Muttering together in French, snickering at some private joke in the pauses, they were sucking up their milkshakes through straws striped like barber's poles. Kemble wondered what they'd have next. Coffee and éclairs, probably, with cheesecake on the side, then back upstairs for more of the red-eye. Typical damn Belgians, he thought. Then he noticed a pause in the banquet, as first the man, then the girl, stared up in surprise at the door of the coffee shop. He looked in the same direction himself.

But by that time Laura had turned and left the room. She was walking away across the lobby.

Her sleek black hair and the smartness of her cream satin dress, seen from behind, made Kemble doubt that she was English. Even so he was about to go after her, thinking this must be Harvey's girl, when his eye was distracted by another girl.

Mitzi was coming, Laura was leaving. Their paths intersected in the lobby. Each paused to glance at the other, then walked on.

By this time Kemble's eyes were on Mitzi: a lissom little creature hardly more than five feet tall, dressed in black tee-shirt and flappy green overalls, with badges of protest pinned on her chest. Immediately, hard to say why, his mind turned to lechery. Convinced but amazed that this was Harvey's secretary, he rose from his seat to greet her. But she walked straight by him and sat down with the two marathon eaters.

Kemble then searched for the first girl, but she had now vanished from the lobby. He hurried outside in pursuit of her – too late. Standing on the steps of the hotel, he saw her drive off in a snarling red Porsche.

All this Jack Kemble observed, quite by chance, on his first night in Brussels. But it meant nothing to him. He continued to wait for Laura in the bar, and when she didn't come, began to drink in rage, which was always the cause of his worst excesses. Soon he was blind. The details receded in an angry red fog, turning quickly to the black of sweet oblivion. And the last face to go was Mitzi's.

Thursday

1

The big Volvo truck started out on its journey from Holland a little after dawn.

First Joop Janssen heard it, and then he saw it, rolling out through the factory gate beneath an arch of curly iron lettering which wrote the words *Torenstra Automobiel Werken* against the pale, blank, early sky. The lorry's huge engine sputtered and growled, clearing its throat like a drunk the morning after, as the driver accelerated over the railway lines and into the empty streets of Rotterdam. He had obviously made the trip before. He knew the way and drove too fast for safety. But Joop was ready for him. Slipping Rosa's Simca into gear, he caught the truck up and then settled in behind it at a distance of about sixty yards.

"He is Eurasian," Rosa said. "A man called Piet Bommel."

"From Indonesia?"

"Yes. His mother came from Bali."

"See how he drives," said Joop. "The scab."

"He needs the money. We should not blame him."

They were passing through a dismal district of Rotterdam's dockland. Behind the cheap housing rose cranes and ship's funnels. Seagulls were scavenging in the litter. The few men already cycling to work had swarthier skins than the Dutch. Most of them were Turks.

Rosa watched their faces, stoically blank in the cheerless light.

"The employers will always use immigrants to do the worst jobs. That is not surprising. What depresses me is the way that our own working class exploits another. Europe seems to generate new victims."

91

This was a little too complicated for Joop, who grunted and kept his eyes fixed on the road. He had been driving since two in the morning. Before checking out of the Hotel Europa they had gone back up to the room and done it another way, excited by the prurient staring of that drunken American. Half the fun came from proving the worst suspicions of the bourgeoisie correct. Sex was a political act, at least it was with Rosa. Give her a good Marxist reason and she would do anything.

He glanced at her beside him in the car, lost in some inner dialectic set off by the bicycling Turks. An anti-dresser, usually in boots, she smelled of herself. Her hair hung short round her head, bedraggled like a dog's. Her body was too big, her mouth too small. But he had got used to her. He liked her body and respected her mind, which had more power to plan than his own. He wondered if he'd see her again.

From Brussels they had driven to Antwerp, leaving Mitzi to carry on audio-surveillance of the Berlaymont. Crossing the border into Holland had caused no problems, except that it made Joop feel trapped, as always. A sort of claustrophobic rage, an urge to smash and run, had taken hold of him as they entered the overcrowded flatness which was home, the manicured fields in the moonlight and the neat little brightly lit towns, one after another, just the same, human boxes by the thousand, no mess or surprise. Boxed in was what Joop felt in Holland. Boxed in was what he could not bear to be, not even for a moment.

They had stopped to smoke a joint. That had not helped, so he had taken a walk by himself, below some poplars along a canal, fifteen minutes out and then back to the car in the moonlight. That had helped. Then he had changed out of the fake executive's suit into his own clothes, frayed jeans and matching short jacket of faded blue denim. That had helped more. They had driven on to Rotterdam, Rosa at the wheel while he read the map.

But something had gone wrong in Rotterdam. For reasons still unexplained, neither local member of the Iskra, one of whom worked inside Torenstra factory, was waiting at the rendezvous agreed, an all-night bar in the Afrikaanderplein. So they had pressed on unguided, driving round this dismal slum of Turks until they found the entrance to the works. They had started to worry that the truck might have left.

But there it was ahead now, still using sidelights. All was well. And here are we too, on our way, leaving home, breaking free, Joop thought to himself, seized with a strangely childish delight to be getting out of Holland. He made no effort to explain his mood to Rosa. But her spirits, too, were now high. Driving out of Rotterdam they talked of this and that with bright inconsequence, small things, funny things, since there was nothing else useful to be said about the dangerous business ahead. The sun was almost up, the top of the Euromast was breaking through the mist; and now they were clear of the city on E.36, heading out east towards the Europort. It was going to be a fine Euroday.

The lorry had picked up pace on the wide empty road, so Joop put his foot down as well, to keep at a constant distance, glancing down at the Simca's speedometer as he did so.

"Look," he said, "look at the speed. This Bommel is crazy."

"I am told he is a big man, possibly violent," Rosa said, turning suddenly serious. "Be careful with him, won't you?" She took out a package from the glove compartment. "Here is the money. And here's the map of Ash Valley," she added, digging a crumpled brown envelope out of her bag. "Better study it again before you get there. Steve Murdoch will be waiting with a car the other side, at Gate Seven – there, you see, it's marked. But what happens after that I don't know. I left the arrangements to him."

Joop nodded and stuffed each item into separate pockets of his denim. "I'll ring you tonight."

If I'm still in one piece, he thought.

And perhaps Rosa thought the same thing. "No," she said, "don't ring tonight. I'll be in Rome. Just get back to Paris as soon as you can. We'll meet again there."

"As you wish."

"Good luck, Joop. And thanks for doing this."

"I'm under orders, aren't I?" Joop smiled at his own double meaning.

"Just stay alive," she said, rubbing her hand up and down the nearest thigh of his jeans in a fierce, affectionate massage.

"You too," he answered smiling, and reached out to tap the weapons-belt under her shirt. "Keep the safety catch on, unless you have to draw. And for God's sake get rid of those grenades. You'll blow yourself up."

Rosa smiled back but made no reply. Half an hour later, as the ferryboat pulled out of harbour and sailed for England, she waved goodbye to him, standing alone beside her car at the end of the concrete mole. And then, while Joop watched, astonished, from the rail of the ship, she took the two grenades from under her shirt and lobbed them into the sea.

Joop waved back at her, chuckling, and clenched his hand into a fist. Crazy girl, he thought. Poor old crazy Rosa, she'll kill us all.

For a few minutes longer he remained at the rail while the passengers beside him flung crumbs of bread to the low-flying seagulls. And then he went off to find Piet Bommel, the Dutch-Indonesian driver who had rashly agreed to deliver a cargo of five thousand steering wheels for the BMG Pilot 1500.

2

Erich Kohlman was also up before light, preparing for a second excursion from Brussels. He had returned late and tired the night before from his visit to John Clabon in Coventry, but after only four hours' sleep he rose to the bleeping of a digital alarm clock, did some exercises, took a shower, shaved electrically, dressed, made his bed, and then percolated coffee in the well-equipped kitchen of his bachelor flat. He lived in a diplomatic ghetto of the Belgian capital, an ultra-modern hive of luxurious apartments known as the *Quartier d'Europe*, and his home was neat as a pin. Everything in it was new or very nearly, made by Braun, made by Grundig and other fine firms of West Germany. Everything worked. His life had the perfect drill of loneliness.

At five he caught the news in French on Radio Europe, and then, still seated in the kitchen, he took out a dictaphone and played back the tape he had made the night before to bring Sir Patrick Harvey up to date.

"Mr. Clabon is not telling us the truth," he heard himself say. *"The chairman of BMG assured me that the group as a whole could survive without Ash Valley. A workers' revolt would be ignored, he says, by both himself and the UK government. I do not believe so. The company would cease to exist as a private enterprise, and Clabon would be replaced as chief executive. So for him this merger is vital. The Pilot is bleeding the whole group to death, but amputation of this model is no cure. A transplant is urgently required . . . "*

No, that wouldn't do. Knowing the functiontal style preferred by his master, Kohlman erased the medical metaphor. He played the tape again. Satisfied, he put it in an envelope, drank his coffee, ate a bowl of cereal, washed up, then lay for ten minutes stretched out on a sofa listening to Bach through a pair of headphones, his eyes closed in meditative attitude. He chose Brandenburg Six, for the absence of a flute. He wanted no chirruping today, but the steady sawing rhythm of the gambas, proceeding to their proper conclusion.

At 5.30, as arranged, he was picked up by Paolo Santini and driven to the airport in Harvey's Mercedes. At Zaventem the same chartered jet was waiting. Before take-off Kohlman gave his taped report to Paolo, addressed to Laura Jenkinson for typing. Then he left for Italy.

At first view the Alps were pink in the sunrise, but by the time the plane flew across them the peaks had blazed into dazzling whiteness. Kohlman was stirred by the sight. Nervous, tired as he was, he could not resist a surge of elation at this magnificent daybreak. There was the summit of the continent, and here was he above it, the high-flying herald of a new and better Europe.

Then the plane dipped into Piedmont, and he saw the factories of Fiat round Turin. The old royal city, all its colonnaded squares clearly visible in delicate miniature, appeared to be besieged by a huge industrial army encamped in long sheds of grey tin. The company's flags flew from masts at every gate, its name was painted on the roofs for the benefit of air travellers. Kohlman peered down with special interest. Here was the biggest battalion of capitalism in Italy, whose recent manoeuvres were much to the point. Fiat had allowed its subsidiary Lancia be joined to the ailing state enterprise of Alfa-Romeo. The result was Mobital, partly owned by Fiat itself, partly by the government in Rome. Each hoped to gain full possession in due course, but meanwhile control had passed to the balance of the shareholders, a consortium of banks and private interests whose nominated spokesman was Carlo Guidotti.

It was a very Italian way of doing things. A working stalemate, one might say, and as such well suited to the talents of its chief executive. As a young man Guidotti had fought with Rommel in Africa, but had switched his allegiance to the Allies at the opportune moment. He had joined the Foreign Ministry and risen to the rank of Ambassador, then resigned to go into politics. He had joined the Christian Democrats, then broken away to seek alliance with the Communists. Now he had broken away from politics altogether to take command of Mobital.

"Guidotti likes to be called Ambassador," Sir Patrick had said. "But he's no slouch at business either. Don't let him fox you, Erich. Just pin him down and come home."

Kohlman recalled the warning with a smile, having done more research than Harvey realised. Mobital's chief was a master of diplomacy, he didn't need telling, and the company's geography reflected the fact. To give himself a neutral position between the great car towns of Turin and Naples, Guidotti had set up his general headquarters at a factory near Milan.

The Commission's jet flew on there, descending in a long slow gradient across the Lombard plain, over the big flat alluvial fields beside the Po and the dusty white roads lined with poplars. Brussels was warm, England dry, but here the land was baked to the colour of cement. And then Milan itself came in view, a grey smudge pierced by a spiky cathedral. Again Kohlman peered from the aircraft with interest.

This was where the battle for Italy would be won or lost, it was said, perhaps the battle for Europe. In Milan revolution was almost a fact, yet business continued as usual. Commercial as Zurich, red as Bucharest, the city existed in an uneasy truce. Milan could explode any day.

At the airport, called Malpensa, the air was muggy, although it was still early morning. A car was waiting, and with it a girl from Guidotti's office who could have been a fashion model. She welcomed Kohlman formally in German, then cleared his path in short, sharp barks of Italian. Officials fell before her like slaves to a queen. They were soon on their way. Once seated in the car, the girl reverted to German. Automatic courtesies reeled out of her like the announcements of an air hostess, but Kohlman's attention began to drift. He was tired. He was hungry.

Mobital's factory, when it came in view, appeared to be defended like a military base. A high wire fence ran around it with floodlights and observation towers. At each gate were striped booms, armed men, dogs and guns. But nothing un-usual occurred until the car pulled up at head office, a big cube of tinted glass on the Como Road. There, at the gate, they were stopped by a uniformed guard, who leaned in to give the girl an urgent message. And from that point things began to happen quickly. At her order the chauffeur drove fast along the fence, then entered by another gate, tyres yelping as he braked at the factory itself. As the car came to a stop the girl, who had lost her composure but was struggling to maintain an all-is-well manner, like an air hostess after bad news from the pilot, turned to Kohlman with a rigid face.

"There has been an accident," she said.

It had occurred in the paint shop.

The bodyshell of a Mobital Sparta GT had fallen from the overhead conveyor, smashing in the head of an elderly spray-gunner. A tank had also been split, so the old man's dead body lay doused in a pool of yellow paint, into which the blood from his skull still oozed. Standing in the centre of the mess was Ambassador Carlo Guidotti himself, dressed in overall and gumboots, his silver hair escaping in wisps from underneath a yellow hardhat. Grim but unruffled, he issued orders quietly to the growing crowd of company officials around him, who were joined in due course by a squad of police and four khaki-uniformed *carabinieri* toting submachine-guns. An ambulance arrived, siren howling, and two men in white ran up with a stretcher on wheels. Having certified the death of the victim, they stood to one side as a priest hitched up his soutane and waded to work in the pool of spilt paint.

The girl retreated in horror to the car, but Kohlman stayed to watch, still holding the black official briefcase he never let out of his grasp. It was only his third visit to a factory of any sort. He had expected noise, but now the whole assembly line had come to a halt. The normal whine and rattle of machinery, the explosive hiss of spray-guns had stopped. Half-coloured body-shells hung in the air, still swinging gently on the overhead conveyor, while through the doors of the paint shop came workers gathering from all round the plant, a dark Latin crowd in matching blue company overalls, unusually subdued for a Latin crowd confronted with violent death. Advancing no further than the edge of the scene, they muttered together in the hush.

Watching the men of the paint shop itself, who were standing in a separate group, Kohlman was suddenly reminded of a football team who have brought down an opposing player. While the casualty receives attention they withdraw together, hiding guilt in numbers, looking back nervously for the verdict of the referee. If accused they will all wave their arms together, protesting their innocence, but without much conviction, because they know very well that it wasn't an accident; they know it was deliberate, and they know who did it, but they will never say, and since they can't all be sent off, the game will eventually go on.

First the sporting image came to Kohlman, and then its explanation.

He had been summoned to a murder.

Half an hour later Guidotti confirmed it.

"Yes, he was killed. One of them pulled the release – we shall never know who. That is the third death this week."

The office of Mobital's chief was cool and quiet, superbly more stylish than that of John Clabon. Pale carpet, abstract art, exotic plants – the room was a plate in a glossy magazine, and so was Guidotti himself. On the way from the paint shop he had used an executive changing room and emerged in full customary elegance. His grey suit was perfectly tailored to his thin, stooped frame . His tie was pure silk and his shoes bore the small brass hallmark of Florence's most famous fashion house. With his tan complexion and smooth silver hair he looked the sort of rich Latin sugar daddy that Saxon girls dream of meeting on holiday.

But Kohlman had already seen the other side. "For what reason?" he asked, speaking English – their best common language. "I mean, why was this man killed?"

Guidotti spread his hands in a gesture of helplessness. "We wish to automate the painting here, but the Reds demand more payment for redundancy. All of them refuse our offer, except this old man. He accepts the company's compensation. So they kill him, *pah*, like that."

The action of dropping a Mobital Sparta GT on the head of a scab was mimed economically, then Guidotti waved Kohlman into a chair. Between them, on a low marble table, were two cups of black *espresso* coffee and a plate of Milanese pastries. Kohlman accepted gratefully as Guidotti served them out and went on talking.

"You do not see such things in Germany, but here the Reds are strong. Soon they will take everything. No one can stop them. The government in Rome are cowards. Centre Left, Centre Right, what is the difference? The politicians can do nothing, so they care for themselves. The police do nothing. They also are afraid. I am alone here."

While he was speaking Guidotti took a mouthful of coffee and lit himself a yellow cigarette from a crocodile case. He didn't offer one, but smoked by himself, morose and introverted. Each puff ended in a sigh.

In the ensuing silence Kohlman noticed that across the road two men in overalls had started to scrub a painted slogan off the facing brick wall. WATCH OUT FOR YOUR PRETTY LEGS, CARLO.

Guidotti ignored the sight. He smoked on in silence, and then said, reverting to the victim in the paint shop: "First he was at Lancia, then here. Twenty years of his life that old man was making cars for Italy. But today, *pah*." He repeated the mime with less vigour, shook his head mournfully, and then struck off at a tangent, talking as though to pass the time. "And Sir Patrick? How is he?"

"He is well," replied Kohlman, but added no more, determined not to state his business until asked to do so. Guidotti was manoeuvring already, he thought, with this silly pretence that a messenger from Brussels was of no particular interest to the great chief of Mobital, locked in lonely combat with the Sparta-dropping, cisalpine Reds. Something deeply German in his nature was affronted by the Italian's obliqueness. The purpose of this visit was obviously important; therefore an explanation should be requested, at which point it would be duly given.

But Guidotti smoked in silence, and seemed prepared to do so indefinitely. In the end Kohlman had to give way. Opening his briefcase, he took out a copy of the Commission's plan and handed it across.

"I am instructed to show you this, Ambassador."

Guidotti glanced at the jacket of the folder, then opened it with the weary expression of a man who had better things to do.

"It was drafted yesterday," Kohlman began, intending to explain how the notion of a merger with the British Motor Group had been born. But he got no further. Guidotti stopped him, hand raised in a signal like a Fascist salute, then sprung to his feet with surprising alacrity – the first really energetic movement he'd made.

"Please, Herr Kohlman, say no more of this thing, or we are dead men. Come with me."

3

Ambassador Carlo Guidotti liked to speak of his enemies generically as Reds, but there were many fine shades of that political colour in Italy, as he himself would readily admit when not trying to scare foreign visitors.

The violence in industry was coming from two different factions. In the first place there were the Red Brigades. These were tightly organised, secret cells led by discontented members of the intellectual class. They were inclined to random acts of terrorism, such as kidnaps and shooting factory managers in the legs. The Red Brigades' purpose was to create a general climate of fear in which all authority, political, industrial, judicial, would cease to function.

Then there were the autonomists. Less tightly linked and directed, these were independent revolutionary groups with particular objectives of their own. In the factories their aim was workers' control. And they were especially strong in Mobital. Guidotti's main present anxiety was the autonomist movement, behind which lay a mysterious organisation called the Iskra. Almost nothing was known of that except its name.

The PCI, Italian Communist Party, although its flag was red, could hardly be classed as his enemy. The party was hoping to win an electoral success in the autumn and wanted no blood on its hands. It disowned the other two violent factions of the Left. The Communists urged negotiation rather than shooting through the kneecaps. And Carlo Guidotti was expert at playing on this difference. Better than any other industrial leader in Italy, he knew just how far he could count on the Communists to help him keep control of his company.

Erich Kohlman was not so ignorant of these gradations as the chairman of Mobital supposed.

And nor was Laura Jenkinson.

Left alone in the Berlaymont Building, Brussels, Laura had moved into Kohlman's room during his absence and taken command of the office, a promotion she always enjoyed. But this morning little was happening. A lull had followed yesterday's bustle. Having gone through her in-tray and Erich's – nothing interesting – she wandered off to the Press Department and came back about ten o'clock with a clipping from *La Stampa*, which she sat down to read. She was fluent in Italian as well as French.

At Harvey's request the cuttings girls were now under orders to provide his office with any press reference to Mobital or BMG. This was the first to arrive. Laura studied it with interest. A long piece, spread across the two middle pages of the paper, it discussed the relationship between the two extreme wings of Italian leftist politics. The Red Brigades were strongest in Rome, it said, but the autonomists were gaining ground in Milan. In the factories of Mobital, especially, control was breaking down. A physical seizure of the company by its workers could not be discounted.

Laura laid the cutting aside with a sigh. As usual, she had been left out. What really mattered was happening elsewhere. Sometimes the desire to do more than she did came over her so strongly that she wanted to scream or commit some act of shocking physical violence. Even now she could feel a knot of frustration start to form in her stomach, but after a while it dissolved into numbness and she sat at the window, simply bored, thinking how dreadfully dull Brussels was to look at, even on a bright summer's day. The office blocks reduced to insignificance the shabby old houses around them. Either kind of architecture would have been all right on its own; together they were just a mess. Free enterprise, left to itself, created only ugliness, but really there wasn't much point in getting worked up about it. One might as well dive in the mess and splash around some money.

One mood led swiftly to its opposite. Having glanced at the diary to see what the day held – nothing important – she decided to take a long lunch hour, shopping for bikinis. Perking up at the prospect, she dashed through her work and by midday had assembled a big pile of typing for Lucy Maclean, with whom she was cross.

Lucy had come in late, as usual. She said she had been to the dentist. She did indeed have a somewhat bruised and dopey look about the face, Laura noticed, but not of the kind a girl gets from having her teeth drilled. They spoke in taut monosyllables. Lucy accepted the bundle of paper in a sulk. Then the phone rang. Laura picked it up and heard again the semi-American voice of that persistent pressman, Jack Kemble.

"Hi," he said cheerfully. "So we blew it. Sorry about that. Trouble with blind dates, I suppose."

"Oh, hello," she said, "it's you. Where *were* you?"

"Eating – in the coffee shop."

"You said the bar."

"I know. But meat is required as well as drink, you know, even in my trade."

"I'm sorry, Mr Kemble, I got there rather late. But I did look around for you."

"You did. You wore a cream dress and you drive a red Porsche. I like your legs."

Laura laughed. "Yes, they are rather beautiful, aren't they?"

"Careful what you say now. Hope is beginning to rise in my breast."

"Where are you now?"

"Right here, downstairs. In the hall of mirrors."

"Wait there. I'm coming down."

Laura rang off with a smile, cleared away her papers, locked Erich's office and left the key with Lucy, who looked up to ask where she was going.

"To the dentist," she said. "All right?"

Kemble's alcoholic orgy of the night before was still pulsing lightly round his temples, but his brain was taking messages in clear from the libido. Her front view didn't quite live up to the promise of her back, he thought, watching Laura advance from the Berlaymont's top-floor lift. She was too lean and bony, rather taut round the face. All the same, not bad, not bad. A dark girl, sleek, well dressed, drenched in scent – she must have had a bath in it – and smiling at him boldly as she held out her hand.

Laura was also pleasantly surprised. The man looked arrogant yet about to fall to bits: a not unattractive combination. He was older than she'd thought from his voice, forty at least, and not at all the sort of mug he made himself out to be on the phone. His hair was receding, touched by grey, and his body needed all the concealment it could get from those comfortable American clothes. His face was like a battered room. Good times and bad had roared through it: a wild, unguessable history. She knew straightaway that he had been lying to her, but the consequent sensation of risk was entirely in tune with her mood of the moment. She held out her hand with a smile.

Shaking hands, they stayed light on their feet, like boxers before the fight. Then Laura said: "Well, shall we go?"

Kemble was surprised. He looked at his watch. "What, right now? Don't you work?"

"Only when there is some."

"How nice of Sir Patrick."

"Sir Patrick's away."

"That's a pity," Kemble said, bouncing off the ropes. "I was hoping you'd help me sneak up on him."

"He's unsneakable. I told you."

"Where's he gone?"

"Away."

"Will he be back?"

"Now just a minute," Laura said, counter-punching. "Surely, after all that sweet talk, you're not going to stand there and ask me questions about my boss."

"No, of course not. Sorry." Kemble held back his hands in a peace gesture. "Just checking things out."

They went outside and walked towards her Porsche, which shone like a brilliant red toy amidst the mass of dimmer vehicles. On the way Laura said: "So you've come from Washington?"

"Yes."

"But you're not American. You're English."

"Yes."

"Born somewhere up north, I'd say."

"Middle to north," replied Kemble curtly. "Not quite down the mine, if that's what you're getting at."

"I'm not getting at anything. Just checking things out," she said, mimicking his accent as she bent to unlock the car. "So you want to see how we live here?"

"That's the idea."

105

"All right then. First you can help me choose a swimsuit, then we'll go to the Leopold. Do you know it?"

"No."

"It's a bar. A drink at the Leopold costs about the same as a three-course meal in America. So we'll have a few drinks, and then you can ask me some questions about Sir Patrick, none of which I'm going to answer. How's that?"

"I think that's a very fair deal," said Kemble. "Let's go."

4

In Britain an ex-Prime Minister attracted little attention. One or two heads had turned at the airport, and the driver of the car had gone so far as to say that the country needed him back. But the porter at Nuffield College, Oxford, looked up with an indifferent nod as Harvey tapped on the glass of the lodge.

"Lord Doublett, please. He's expecting me."

"Straight ahead, second staircase on the left." The porter, having come out to point the way, stood peering across the quadrangular goldfish pools and shaven lawns, the sculpture like rusting scrap metal. "There, you can see him at the window. Still having his breakfast, looks like."

So Doublett still had two breakfasts.

This eccentricity had kept the press amused when Doublett had served as head of the Central Policy Review Staff, commonly known as the Think Tank. One breakfast in his house at Chinnor, another to be served at his desk in Whitehall. There was nothing wrong, the Professor had explained, with the breakfast cooked by his wife. It was just that he would rather have a second breakfast than lunch.

Now Harvey, still standing under the arch of the lodge, could see the familiar dark shaggy head. Doublett was sitting at a desk in the window of his first-floor study, partly obscured by a pile of books. He was bent forward, apparently in thought, but then a fork appeared, darting up rapidly into his mouth.

"Probably forgotten you were coming," said the porter.

But Harvey knew better. Arnold Doublett might forget to put a tie on, but would keep an appointment to the second, with every small relevant fact prepared in his head. In government service he had turned out to be a ruthless investigator. His job had been to ferret out wasteful expenditure, and during Harvey's time as Prime Minister it had grown to be something of a hobby between them. Doublett was one of the very few personal friends that he had allowed himself in office.

Laura and Erich had not understood this. It had mystified them why, when time was so precious and the problem was cars, he had chosen to spend half a day in Oxford with a man whose principal work was an acclaimed edition of Thucydides. Harvey had not been able to explain. But he was glad that he had come. He needed someone on his side who had no career to advance, no profits to promote. Above all he needed someone with his own kind of English mind, oblique yet practical, steeped in the past, detached yet wanting to succeed.

"Ah, Patrick! Come in, come in."

Doublett wore a shapeless cardigan and baggy yellow corduroy trousers. He was sixty, and had looked it for twenty years: a big, shambling, untidy man, hirsute as a bear, so rapid of speech that many people couldn't understand him at all. He snatched some papers off a chair and padded round looking for a flat space to put them.

"I was glad to find you in college," Harvey said, sitting. "I thought you might have disappeared by now."

"No, we at Nuffield take no notice of vacations. Our labours are unending, as you see. Ceaseless toil." Doublett waved at the books on the desk, at the plate still spattered with egg.

"But not so intense, I hope, that you can't find time for this."

Harvey took out the merger plan.

Immediately Doublett's manner changed. He took the document and flipped through it quickly. "Twenty-six pages. Then the annex – ten pages. This will take me eighteen minutes to read. Here is the newspaper. Would you like a cup of coffee?"

"No," said Harvey, "I had enough coffee on the plane. I'll take a turn round the quad. I get less air than a convict these days."

Doublett nodded, without reply. He was already reading.

Harvey slipped out of the room and walked slowly round the too-neat enclosure below, enjoying the warmth of the sun and the pleasantly superior feeling – a Cambridge man himself – inspired by the architecture of Nuffield. Built of stone like fudge, half barracks in style, half Cotswold, the college had been founded by a motor tycoon. Lord Nuffield was father of the Morris, but would not have liked this plan for a European merger. One of his regular jokes had been to call Frenchmen "manure" instead of *monsieur*.

Still, old Nuffield had fitted with his own generation all right, founding an industry, a college, a house which was now a museum; a rough man of deeds, not words or thought. Nowadays the British were full of words and thought, but they founded nothing, or so it seemed to Harvey, who observed his countrymen more clearly from Brussels than he ever had as their Prime Minister. They talked all the time about how silent they were, they boasted all the time about their modesty. Yes, he saw them more clearly, but not because he had ceased to be one of them. That was the trouble with being European, you didn't stop being a Frenchman or an Englishman. Or perhaps it was the point.

Ten minutes passed. Time to go back, he thought, and took a short cut across the seared square of grass towards Doublett's staircase. Much would depend on the next half hour. Either the merger could be done or it couldn't. He would soon hear the best opinion he could get. Erich Kohlman's mission in Milan was important, but this trip to Oxford was more so.

The Professor continued to read without stirring as Harvey re-entered the room and sat quietly, letting his eyes wander over the bookshelves. On one side were classical texts, he noticed, not the little red and green Loebs which he himself had at home, with the Latin or Greek text opposite the English translation, but big volumes, many of them edited in German. One entire shelf was devoted to the Greek trireme, and above the fireplace hung Doublett's sensational map of the Battle of Aegospotami, BC 405. But across the room the subject matter changed. The opposite wall was filled with parliamentary debates, blue books, company reports, General Motors, BMG, Peugeot, Daimler-Benz, Mobital, Ford. Few people knew it, but Doublett's hobby was the motor industry, a subject in which he had kept up an interest since his days in government. Although the study of Thucydides was clearly of much greater relevance to the modern world, he liked to say, there was a certain intellectual fascination in the problems of car manufacture.

And now he had finished his reading. At the end of eighteen

minutes exactly he wheeled in his chair and spoke with suppressed excitement, like a connoisseur who has just seen a rare work of art from his period. "What exactly do you want to ask me?"

"First, your snap reaction," said Harvey.

"Bold, magnificent, necessary. But, as it stands, two snags."

"Let's hear them."

"Smaller snag first," rapped Doublett without the slightest pause. "The deal's lop-sided. BMG don't have enough to offer to interest the Italians."

"They have more than appears."

"Sorry, don't follow."

Harvey hesitated. "You'll have to keep a secret, Arnold."

"A secret? But I'm full of them, mostly from you." Doublett snorted in merriment, tilting up his chin with the back of one hand. "So full of secrets can't open my mouth at high table. One more won't hurt, I think."

"All right," conceded Harvey, "I'll tell you, but keep it very strictly to yourself. BMG have developed a battery engine with Volvo and Saab."

"Have they now? Really, really."

"John Clabon showed it to me himself on Tuesday. He met me up in Wales with a funny little buggy under wraps on a trailer."

Doublett's eyes shone with something like greed. "Top speed?"

"Seventy. At least, that's as fast as we went."

"Acceleration?"

"Like a normal car. Nought to fifty in about twelve seconds, but that was in this thing like a plastic golf cart – very light in weight, so rather a cheat. The power-weight ratio is what they're still working on. They either need more power or a very light body."

Doublett nodded. "And the battery itself? How heavy?"

"Pretty heavy. Several hundred pounds."

"How far will it go before recharging?"

"About five hundred miles. That's with normal driving."

"How's it done?"

"Now don't expect me to get too technical," Harvey said. "But there's a rather big flywheel involved, and the battery itself has some kind of element, it looks like a silver tube, which

110

can be taken out and replaced at petrol stations. The operation takes about half a minute."

"Yes, that's new." Doublett's head nodded up and down, with a rapid jiggling motion. "Yes, my word, that evens things up a bit. Guidotti would give a lot for that."

"Clabon is hugging the secret so close to his chest that it's hard to see how we can bring it into play. Still, it may help if we get bogged down. Now, Arnold, tell me, what's your second snag? The bigger one."

"Money."

"Go on."

"Whole thing's going to cost more than you think. A lot more."

"How so?"

"Add it up. Takes a billion dollars to launch a new car, more if it's electric, maybe twice as much," jabbered Doublett in his strange donnish speedtalk. "And you've got to buy out both governments. Can't have either London or Rome messing about with the new joint company. Once it's merged, it has to be free, quite free."

"I agree."

"BMG's about clear of public debt, so far as I recall. Some interest outstanding, few million, nothing to worry about. But you'll have to buy the state out of Mobital."

"Of course. We've provided for that."

"Election year in Italy, so they'll squeeze the orange. Could be dear."

"I still think our figure's enough."

"You're the better judge," Doublett rushed on. "But the workers will cost you more too."

Harvey began to feel like a student defending a faulty essay. "More in what sense?"

"You'll have to go for parity, same rate for same job, in Coventry and Milan. Essential. Got to level up from the start, or each end will leapfrog the other."

Harvey thought about parity, the figures spinning off in his head like the distances of galaxies. "In that case the unions will have to get together, British and Italian. We'll need a joint labour structure."

"It will grow anyway." Doublett's face darkened in sudden disapproval. "Evolutionary process."

"I'd rather provide for it. Did you notice the section on consultation between workers and management?"

"Don't," snapped Doublett. Guzzling cold coffee as he flipped quickly back through the plan in search of the offending paragraph, he made a noise like a dentist's saliva pump. "Pay high, don't consult. It's the wage-packet warms the heart, not service on a joint committee." He found the clause concerned and snorted in contempt. "Consultation, participation – all hooey, take it out. Average working man doesn't want to think, you know, doesn't want responsibility. Rather watch the boss get it wrong."

Harvey had forgotten his friend's views on labour relations, which were almost as crude as Lord Nuffield's. Pay 'em high, drive 'em hard, don't consult, watch the profit – it seemed an unsuitably primitive formula for the age, but what other was there which worked as well? He'd never quite cleared up his mind on the point.

"Back to money then," he said.

"Of course all this should go to consultants," barked Doublett, looking up. "But I would say four."

"Four what?"

"Dollars, billions American – or are you working in Ecus? Yes, of course, Ecus. Well, same figure. Four thousand million."

"Arnold, do please stop talking in telegrams. Explain yourself."

"That's what a merger will cost. You've allowed one billion from Community funds. But it will need four."

"*Four!*"

"Spread over a year or two, mostly at the start."

Not one billion, but four. Harvey considered this estimate for approximately four thousand milliseconds, then closed his briefcase and got to his feet. "That is all very easy for you to say, Arnold. Do you have any conception how difficult it would be?"

"Seen you tackle worse."

"Ah yes, but then I was in charge. Brussels isn't Downing Street, you know. Nor are the streets paved with gold. Otto Riemeck will have a fit."

Doublett's eyes sharpened at the name. "Is he in on this?"

"Of course he is. Why? Do you know him?"

Doublett's head bobbed again, but slower, more reflectively. "Good man, Otto Riemeck. Rescued Jews in the war, you know. Brave thing to do."

Harvey failed to see the relevance of Riemeck's war, fine and unusual though it was. Preparing to leave, he pointed to Doublett's copy of the plan. "I want you to keep that and think about it. Have you a safe?"

"A safe? Of course not."

"Oh well, hide it under one of those then." Harvey gestured at the stacks of paper all round the room.

"You won't stay to lunch?"

"No, I must get back."

Doublett stood up and rubbed his hands. "Well, this is rather fun, isn't it? Quite like old times."

"Yes. Only then we were planning to save money, not spend it."

"The pleasure is the same. It's the problem that interests me, not the philosophy."

Harvey considered this remark on the way back to Belgium. If professors had become the solvers of problems, he thought, where on earth were we to go for philosophy?

However, in this case even the problem remained.

Four billion was impossible.

Disappointed by his trip to Oxford, he wished he had gone to Milan instead. But before he was back at his desk in Brussels he had started to change his mind. And soon, thinking more about the money, he began to consider a very risky tactic.

5

In Milan it was so hot that Kohlman could feel the sun burning through his hair. To keep in the shade while he waited, he strolled up and down the Galleria, the arcade of shops and cafés which led off the Piazza del Duomo. Under the high roof of glass and arched iron, like that of an old railway station, it was cool and the light was dim. The footsteps of pedestrians resounded upwards hollowly, just as they had in the cathedral itself, and the people in the cafés seemed to talk quietly, almost in murmurs, relieved to escape the fierce sunshine outside. In Milan the sun was an inconvenience. The trees were bleached with dust, the pigeons too listless to fly.

Kohlman found it hard to believe that a revolution would happen in this grey and respectable city, so similar to those of northern Europe. The place seemed as dour, as hushed as a bank. As prosperous, too. In the windows of the shops he found the same sort of goods as in Berlin, at the same sort of prices, and then to his pleased surprise the arcade filled to the roof with thin strains of Austrian music. A four-piece orchestra, seated on a platform at the biggest of the cafés, had struck up a waltz by Strauss. Kohlman stood listening for a while to the sweaty and not very skilful quartet, all fiddling away in bankers' suits, and then he walked back to the rendezvous. A few steps behind him was Guidotti's second thug, a swarthy type, from Sicily perhaps, hugely broad in the shoulders and so low of brow that his hairline collided with his eyebrows. He, too, was wearing a suit. In Milan musicians and bodyguards, probably even the Red Brigades, dressed like bankers. That was the oddness of Italy. Blood and elegance.

This midday ramble in the city had been suggested by

Guidotti. Mobital's chief had taken the merger plan off to his home, demanding some time to read it alone. In an hour he would send the car back, he had said, and then they would lunch together. Guidotti had refused to talk at all in his office, alleging no secret was safe there, but once they were driving into town he had found some preliminary comments to make. A merger was an interesting suggestion, he had said, and clearly of very great value to the British. But where was the advantage to Mobital? He would need to be shown some substantial advantage before he could promise to attend any meeting. However, he would read through the plan and think it over. They would discuss it at lunch. Until then the best thing to do was go off and see the sights with Angelo . . .

Or was it Aldo?

Guidotti had two of them. They shadowed him everywhere. But which was which Kohlman couldn't remember. He found it hard to retain facts of any sort from conversation with Carlo Guidotti. Evasions, half-truths, bluffs, pretences – the man was impossibly devious. And why did he need to read the plan by himself? He had been alone at his home now for more than an hour, quite a lot more, and was clearly playing for time. Was he on the line to Rome or to Fiat? To General Motors, perhaps. Kohlman liked none of it. This whole Italian end of things made him feel exposed and outmanoeuvred. He began to perspire with anxiety as well as heat while he waited beside the cathedral for Guidotti's car to come back.

It was late.

He tapped the face of his watch in complaint.

But Angelo, or was it Aldo, merely shrugged and grunted, exposing two rows of crowded yellow teeth in an ape-like smile of amusement.

Kohlman could not see the joke. Standing in the heat of the great open square, a swarm of fat pigeons round his feet, he felt panic coming closer like the birds, beginning to flutter and peck at the edge of his mind. What had he got himself in to? What was the proper thing to do? He had a sudden desire to run away and keep on running until he was lost in this big, hot, sombre, foreign city.

Then the car arrived. It was a long grey Mobital Alfa, accompanied now by two police motorcyclists – an extra precaution arising from the murder at the factory, perhaps. Angelo or Aldo held the door open, and then they were speeding away through the dusty trees and wide cobbled streets, jumping lights, dodging trams, with the white-strapped motorcyclists opening up their sirens at the slightest obstruction. Outside its central showpiece the town was spray-painted with Marxist slogans. Red flags hung from windows and high iron balconies. Two weeks ago the mayor had been shot in broad daylight.

Guidotti's home was a fortress. It was in a modern apartment block built of concrete, the sort with the plank-marks left in, and set well back from a quiet residential street. The garden had been stripped of bushes or any kind of cover. Floodlights were fixed to the walls at high points. All the lower windows were barred. There was a guard on the entrance and another in the basement garage, to whom Guidotti's driver chattered by radio as the car approached. A closed-circuit camera watched them in the lift going up. Another scanned the third-floor landing, swivelling slowly in perpetual motion while they waited outside the door. Then the door of the apartment itself, which was plated with steel round its peephole, was opened on a chain by Guidotti's other guard, a thinner and younger man, with the quick cunning look of a rat. With a muttered exchange Angelo and Aldo showed Kohlman into a sitting room and shut the door sharply behind him.

Feeling a long way from home, he waited for Carlo Guidotti to appear.

The interior of the flat was practically in darkness, the way Italians like to keep their homes in summer. Through the slats of the blinds Kohlman could see that the balcony outside had been caged in with chicken wire, presumably to catch grenades. The air-conditioning hummed softly. The air was chill as winter but smelled agreeably of a hot and saucy Italian lunch, being cooked somewhere out of sight. The room itself was austerely modern, with plain white walls and a floor of grey marble, but everything in it was ornately antique. A magnificent Persian carpet was spread in the centre. Medieval altar carvings hung on the walls and bits of Roman statuary stood in the corners, dismembered as if by a bomb. Guidotti's wife was dead. He lived here alone with his mother, aged ninety, and a housekeeper called Serafina.

Entering, he held the Commission's plan high in the air and

116

then dropped it on a painted consol table. "I will come to this meeting in Tours," he announced. "But I make two conditions."

He filled two small glasses with *Punt e Mes*, the aperitif named to commemorate a price on the stock exchange, and held one out before Kohlman could refuse it.

"The first condition is this," he went on. "There must be no publicity, and no record kept in writing. These talks must be strictly private."

"That is already understood, Ambassador. Sir Patrick insists on secrecy himself. And what is your second point?" Kohlman, who was learning to read the signs, could see that something much bigger was coming.

Guidotti sat down and lit one of his thick yellow cigarettes, then spoke deliberately through the smoke. "I wish to make it clear that Mobital, as the larger and more profitable company, must be the controlling partner."

Kohlman had picked up his drink. Now he put it down again. "But that is a major point of negotiation," he said, his voice cracking upwards like a boy's. "It can't be decided before the talks begin."

"Mobital's supremacy must be accepted in principle. Otherwise I cannot come to Tours."

Insisting on the point, Guidotti shook his head sadly, his face set into an expression of regret at the harsh moral laws which governed both their lives. He shrugged, as though there were no more to add, and then sat smoking in silence, until a small woman in black came in with a mumbled announcement, at which he stood up.

"You like *lasagne*?"

Kohlman replied that he did, though too bemused to recall which type of pasta this was.

"Ah, but you do not know the *lasagne* of my Serafina," said Guidotti with genuine feeling, his whole manner brightening as he led the way into a small, square dining-room adorned with fine old tapestries. "You have never tasted *lasagne* like this, I assure you."

And that was true. In the whole of his life, which included a modest career as a gourmet, Erich Kohlman had come across no dish from Italy remotely as good as the *lasagne verdi al forno* served up by Guidotti's Serafina. It came much drier than is usual, still sizzling in an ovenproof dish. Guidotti cut it like a cake. Each portion was lifted out carefully and placed upright on a plate, so the layers were visible in cross-section. And Kohlman was able to eat it like a cake. He sliced his helping into segments that only disintegrated when his teeth closed upon them, munching the crisp green wafers of pasta into the white cheese sauce and spicy mincemeat.

The wine was also unusual for Italy. It was white, very cold, dry and light, almost colourless as water. No bubbles were visible, but when swallowed it seemed to fizz very slightly on the tongue. Kohlman enquired about its origin.

Guidotti's gaunt face lapsed into a smile of almost lascivious cunning as he lifted the dewy-wet bottle by its neck and rotated it, to demonstrate the absence of a label. "This is a secret I tell to nobody. It is made by friends of mine – a very old family of the nobility, you understand." He picked up his glass and took a taste, then opened his eyes very wide, as though the bubbles had popped in his head. "Magnificent, yes? Tomorrow, in Rome, I shall get some more. If God protects me."

Kohlman decided to risk a joke. "God has some assistance," he said with a nod towards the kitchen, where the body-guards could be heard enjoying a more boisterous lunch with Serafina.

But Guidotti did not smile. "Did I not tell you? Ah, I thought I told you. Tomorrow, in Rome, they will try to kill me."

"Kill you?"

"That is correct."

"Who will try to kill you?"

"Some band of crazy Reds. They are led by a woman."

Kohlman put down his fork and sat still. "How do you know this?"

"She has told me."

"Who?"

"The woman. Three times she has telephoned, each time to a different place. Always she knows where I am, but she speaks bad Italian. I believe she is French."

"What does she say?"

"That I will die if I try to make an accord with the workers. She talks like a Fascist, but that is a pretence. This woman is a Red. It is the Reds, you see, who wish to stop agreement. They want a war of the classes. They believe it will lead to *autonomia* –

118

control of the factories by the workers. But this is very old and foolish nonsense. We have seen it before in 1920. It ends in workers' blood, not control."

"And she will kill you tomorrow?" Kohlman asked in amazement, his food untouched since the topic had arisen. "Did she tell you that?"

"No, of course not. She is not so stupid." Guidotti waved his fork sideways with a small erasing motion. "But tomorrow it must be, if she wishes to stop me, because tomorrow I go to Rome, not only for wine. I am there to make an agreement with the three confederations of labour. And this will be a historic accord, you understand, with many new democratic features. After it the Reds will be finished. The Iskra know that. They must act to prevent me, if they wish to have their foolish nonsense of a war."

"The Iskra? That is their name?" Kohlman's interest grew more intense still.

But Guidotti's was declining. He had finished with the subject. "The Iskra. Yes, I believe so," he said in an offhand way, going back to his food. "There is a band of that name encouraging disturbance in the factories. It is said that their leader is a woman."

"Have you told this to the police?"

"The police – what can they do?" Guidotti chucked up his chin in contempt. "They send men on motorcycles to ride beside my car."

"Have they no information?"

"No information," said Guidotti, munching a mouthful of oozing Lasagne. "I make my own enquiries, I make my own protection. That is how it is to be a businessman in Italy, Herr Kohlman."

Kohlman, returning to his food, reported that John Clabon, too, had heard of a gang called the Iskra.

Guidotti asked for the details, but without much interest or surprise. "They are international, such people. It is usual."

"You are not worried?"

"No, Herr Kohlman, I am not worried. In this country there is violence, yes, of the Left and the Right, but it is done by a few. There is much inefficiency in industry and government, yes, that is true, and for me, for you, it is very annoying. But it is a matter of littlest importance to most of the people, and they

119

know that it will not change. The state does not work, but the state does not fall. In Italy life continues, *malgrado*."

Kohlman suspected this speech was an act. He could not tell. But whether it was feigned or not, Guidotti's nonchalance suddenly vanished. He had spoken in a flat and languid voice, but now he jumped to life again, dark eyes burning as he leaned across the table and prodded the air with several quick thrusts of his fork, held aggressively upright.

"This woman makes threats to me on the telephone, her friends make trouble in the factories. That is easy. But tomorrow, in Rome, we shall see who is strongest. If they wish to stop me, they must take more risk."

6

Long before they sat down to lunch, Jack Kemble had given up any fixed plan for dealing with Laura Jenkinson. He had no plan at all. He didn't know whether to bluster or flirt or come clean or wheedle, and so held himself ready for anything, waiting to see which way she would jump. The problem was she jumped so often, so fast that he couldn't begin to tell where the real girl was situated. All he could do was jump with her, in response, keeping light on his toes. If less had been at stake, and the weather slightly cooler, it might have been fun. As it was, the effort had brought on a terrible thirst.

Was she under some pressure, or several pressures, pushing her in different directions? Kemble didn't know. He couldn't guess. He had spent his whole youth chasing smart English girls of exactly this type, but here was one full of surprises.

And the greatest surprise was he liked her.

For one thing she made a great fuss of his career, which was a quick way into the heart of a man without a job. The big kill in Washington especially impressed her.

"You mean he actually tried to deport you?"

"The FBI did that. But I assumed he was behind it. He held me responsible."

"And so you were."

"No, not really. Others built the coffin. I just drove in a couple of nails."

"Still, what a story."

This exchange occurred in a small boutique called *Ma Petite Folie*, while he sat perspiring on a fragile gilt chair, watched by several suspicious Belgian ladies, and Laura stripped off behind a curtain. Then she had started to step out in different bikinis, displaying her body in a manner both awkward and brazen. And how upper-English that was, Kemble thought, remembering similar disrobements in the boudoirs of Chelsea and Knightsbridge long ago. But why on earth was *this* girl doing it? Did she want him or didn't she? Laura herself gave no sign. Swooping in and out, accepting his verdict by signal, she kept on talking, and not about beachwear.

"So you smashed the most powerful man in the world. What next?"

"You really want to know?"

"Of course I do. How do you follow a thing like that?"

"I'll tell you when we get to this bar."

"No, tell me now," she called, back behind the curtain of the cubicle. "Go on. I can hear you."

Kemble smiled uncomfortably at the watching Belgian women. "Okay," he said, "here's what you do after Watergate. First you divorce your wife and run off to live with a film star in Hollywood. She's so rich you don't have to work at all, but then she turns into a junkie. So you come back to Washington, get married again, and go back to work on the paper. Things get better, then things get worse. So you turn freelance. By this time Nixon's men have got to be millionaires telling their side of the story, but you're just trying to keep yourself alive, picking up the bills for two wives and another man's kids. So you work at it. You write about life in Brussels for tacky magazines who want some grey stuff to go between the pictures. But there are compensations, I will say. You get to see some nice girls in swimsuits. Yes, I like that one."

"Which? The blue one?" She was dressed again, spreading them out on the counter for final selection.

"Yes, the blue."

She took the yellow one.

And then she pounced on a matching yellow beach-hat and bought that too, with an arch, delighted cry of "*Quelle trouvaille!*"

At least she hadn't asked the name of the film star until they were out of the shop. He told her. Again she was impressed, or pretended so. "Lucky you. She's beautiful."

"She's mad."

"Is she really a drug addict?"

"No, not really. Her drug was other chaps."

122

"Oh dear, poor you. Still, she is beautiful."

Then she had wanted to know about his second wife and first, in that order, and he'd told her, though starting to put up some faint, feebly laughing resistance. "Laura, please, do we have to go through this? It really is not my favourite story."

"Sorry," she said to him breezily. "Just checking things out. *Look* at that ridiculous thing."

"Ah, the famous little tiddler."

"This is just a copy. The real one's in a museum, with a nice new suit of gold donated by the British when we joined the Common Market. Don't you think that's sweet?"

They were passing the Mannekin Pis. And then they came into a big open square enclosed on all sides by tall grey buildings of intricate stonework. Kemble's eyes felt shrivelled by the light. He put on a pair of dark glasses as Laura, a person who touched as she talked, laid a hand on his arm and pointed across at a blue and white awning beyond the flower stalls.

"There you are. The Leopold. Prepare to be parted from your francs."

Downstairs it was a medieval pub, dark wood and sawdust, beer from the tap, but Laura had led the way upstairs to an air-conditioned restaurant with carpet on the floor, pink cloths on the tables, potted palms below the beams and a gipsy violinist to take your mind off the prices. They had drunk iced champagne and eaten stuck pig from the grill, followed by a species of waffle unknown to Howard Johnson, thick and fluffy, drenched in liquefied loganberries.

Outside in the medieval square a bunch of jolly young people in medieval costume were doing a medieval dance around a gothic-written banner advising all tourists to visit the *Foire du Midi*. But inside the Leopold, once the gipsy ceased playing, there was only the low hum of money, and it struck Kemble then that somewhere in the last ten years America had lost all claim to be the world headquarters of luxury. The District of Columbia was the bush compared to this. By his own calculation the upcoming check had already reached eighty-three dollars less service, cover charge, tax on value added and any supplementary ideas the Belgians might have had in his absence.

Still, *The Times* was paying. So he let the occasion develop, enjoying it for its own sake. A smart girl, music and champagne; a sunny day in Europe at Holroyd's expense. The view from the pit was improving.

But now the time for business had come, and he still didn't know which way she would jump.

They were discussing her job in the Berlaymont, and she had just told him what it paid her, tax free: a figure to water the mouth of the best rewarded secretaries in Washington.

"So why don't you like it?" he asked her.

"How do you know I don't like it?"

"You don't."

"No," she said, "you're right. I don't."

"Well?"

She twiddled her glass by its stem, back and forth, back and forth on the pink linen cloth. "I suppose you'll think this is ridiculous, but I was once good at riding horses."

Kemble could not see what horses had to do with it. "A perfectly harmless occupation," he said. "Therefore better than most."

"But also perfectly useless, and far too expensive for my parents. So then I went to Oxford to learn economics. And I was good at that too, you know. I knew about things like demand curves and cost-push inflation."

"Plenty of that around here."

Laura didn't smile. Perhaps she didn't hear. She had turned to stare down at the square, but was looking back to Oxford, eyes misted with nostalgia. Then she sat up and waved at the scene around her, a vaguely contemptuous gesture which stretched from the Café Leopold to the Berlaymont. "Well," she said, "you see how it ended. Now I'm nothing much. No good at anything, not even horses. Some of my friends are quite famous, you know."

"You mean the girls?"

"Yes, the girls. On TV, writing novels, doing great things – one of them's even in the government, damn it. Or they're married, of course. Fat with babies." She wrinkled up her nose, then looked at him soulfully. "Think I'd make a mother?"

Kemble laughed and shook his head. "Hang on to your demand curves."

"A film star? A junkie? Come on, man, I want to *break out*. How about a journalist? Now that I could do, surely."

"Grief no, stay clear."

"Why?"

Kemble replied in the words of his first wife, a clever English girl not so different from this one. "It takes a good mind to simplify the facts but a cheap one to make them entertaining."

Laura continued to look at him in a bland, friendly manner. "So you've taken to drink"

"Off and on, yes."

"And freelance means fired, I suppose."

Confronted with such frankness – it was what he liked about her – Kemble could only be frank in return. "Yes," he said, "fired," then raised his glass. "Join the press, see the world, become a lush. Let's have another bottle."

"Half," she said.

"Okay, half."

He ordered it, and while he was doing so Laura talked about the journalists she knew, the gang of political trusties who hung around the Berlaymont in suits and worried frowns, pretending to be statesmen. "Still," she said, "I like them better than diplomats. All *we* ever do is oil the wheels – the grease between nations."

Kemble clapped her. "Baby, you're making nice copy. Grease between nations is good." He took the new bottle directly from the waiter and refilled her glass. "Okay, come on now, it's time. Let's hear about Sir Patrick."

"I don't know him."

"Oh yeah?"

"Really, I don't. He's polite. He's quite kind. Sometimes he makes a joke. But he isn't the tiniest bit interested in my existence, so naturally we don't talk much."

"You mean he's supercilious."

Laura took a sip of the new supply, peering at him cautiously over the rim of the glass. "No, not exactly supercilious. He's too polite for that. He's deep, even wise, I suppose. Experienced, anyway. But the trouble with Harvey is he can only relate with any real ease to people of his own importance. As for me, well, you can imagine. Nice enough girl, but a bit pretentious. He employs me, that's all."

Kemble nodded ruefully. "Yes," he said, "that's Harvey."

"You sound as if you know him."

"Of course I know him. I was still in London when he was

PM. Harvey made the news and I wrote it. We were a travelling roadshow for years."

Laura's bland expression didn't alter. It merely shifted from natural to controlled. "You didn't tell me that."

"You didn't ask me."

"It's him you want to talk to, isn't it?"

"Professionally, yes." Kemble's chips were on frankness.

"And you're just using me to worm your way in."

"I'm enjoying that part of it most. Personally, I'd rather worm with you than talk to him."

"Who exactly are you working for?"

"I told you, I'm freelance."

"But you're not here at your own expense, are you? Somebody's paying for this, and I'd like to know who. American magazines use stringers for this kind of thing. They don't send us reject reporters from the *Washington Post*."

Kemble blew out his cheeks, as though punched in the belly, then nodded and help up one hand for peace. "Okay, so I'm down and out. And my only way up is to prise a good story out of Harvey. If I try to prise it out of you, you'll be in trouble. Want to be prised?"

"Certainly not."

"No, right. So I'll have to try him direct – not so easy when he's put a ban on all press interviews until the summit. Obviously nobody's going to get close while this merger is on."

"I have absolutely no comment to make."

Laura had jumped up to go, but Kemble pulled her back again, sat her down and held her, one arm pinned firmly to the table. "Wait," he said. "Listen. It's not so much to ask. After all, ban or no ban, I could get to him myself – and that's what I'll do if I have to. But drop me in his path and I'll take him nicely, which, as you know, is the best way to take him. Old Harvey will hide as long as he can, but once he's caught fair, he will never leave a working pressman with nothing to print."

Laura made no reply. She was stiff as a plank. Kemble let go of her arm. "So that's all I want," he said. "Now do me a favour. Please."

"Why should I?"

He answered by holding up the bill. One hundred and eighteen dollars, service still to add.

"Not enough," she said. "I cost more than that."

"It's a story the public should hear."

"Rubbish. If it's not kept private at this stage . . ." She tried to swallow the words.

Pretending not to have heard them, Kemble looked up from the bill with the most stupid smile he could manage. "Do it because I'm a nice guy then. Nicer than him."

"Huh! I'm not so sure of *that*."

Again he held up a hand for peace. "Okay, let's keep it strictly business. Lay this thing on and I'll get you a job."

"Oh yes? And how are you going to do that?" Her spite came back with her confidence. "You haven't even got one yourself."

"I can do it. It'll have to be London, though. The Yanks won't give you a permit."

"*Woman's Own*, I suppose."

"No, I was thinking of *The Times*."

"I see," she said. "So that's who sent you. Commissar Holroyd. Well, well. I might have known."

"Don't pry now. Just happen to mention where I can run into Harvey. I'll forget where I heard it and fix you up with a new career. Now that's a good deal, you'll have to admit."

Kemble waited. He had no more chips left.

She looked at him for a long moment. And then, to his great relief, a smile spread slowly across her face. "All right then."

"You'll do it?"

"I will," she said.

"God bless you. I knew you were a white man."

"There's a dinner tonight, at the Portuguese Ambassador's."

"That's fine," said Kemble. "Couldn't be better. But how am I going to get in?"

She narrowed her eyes at him, turning on the twinkle, and then leaned close to pat him on the hand. "I believe I can fix that myself. I happen to know they're one short, you see, and looking for some extra clout from England. Shall I say *The Times*?"

"Yes, if you like. Why not?" Kemble smiled back at her, twinkling in his turn. "Say *The Times*."

7

The boat from Holland landed just before noon. The last commercial vehicle to roll down its ramp was a big Volvo truck belonging to Torenstra N.V. of Rotterdam, manufacturers of automobile components. Customs clearance took thirty minutes. There was a short queue. Inside the Volvo were five thousand steering-wheels designed to fit the BMG Pilot, packed in cartons and secured by nylon tape to shelves either side of the long aluminium container. A few of the boxes were opened for inspection. A dog walked between them, sniffing for drugs. But there were no problems. Within half an hour Piet Bommel, the Dutch Indonesian driver, was on his way into central England, rumbling through Essex and Suffolk on a cross-country road which led to Cambridge.

The little brick villages shuddered at his passing. Old English ladies glared in hostility from their rose gardens. Once they had tried putting nails in the road. Now they were resigned. The statutes of the European Community had no clause on rose gardens. Even so, a continental lorry of this enormous size, the maximum allowed, could not pass unnoticed, and afterwards a number of people were found to confirm that at this stage there was a passenger riding with Bommel in the driver's cabin, a pale and scrawny man with oddly cut hair, dressed in faded blue denim. He had been on the ferry from Holland as well. The two men had talked on the boat – both Dutch, it seemed – but had disembarked separately. Nobody saw them join up again, but they must have, because they travelled on together from Harwich.

And for Joop the ride was a pleasant one. The sun was shining bright, the fens were tall with crops. Kestrels hovered and butterflies jigged above the verges, where poppies grew red in the unmown grass, their blooms dancing wildly in the violent slipstream of the truck. From the Volvo's white cabin he looked out with affection at this country which, tilled to the corners as it was, had always felt more spacious than his own. It rolled more, the fields yielding suddenly to unfenced downs or patches of woodland, and away out of sight but always in mind – that was what made the difference – it spread into mountains and waterfalls, the emptiness of Scotland and Wales, Atlantic surf pounding the cliffs. He had hiked here as a boy. Britain had been his first escape. In a hostel near Wrexham he had known his first girl, and camping illegally north of Loch Ness, chased from glen to glen by angry men with shotguns, he had first tasted life on the run. Perhaps that was how it had started. Perhaps this, today, followed from that.

The idea drifted into his mind, drifted out again. For a while, between Bury St. Edmunds and Newmarket, he relaxed enough to dwell on pleasant memories. But then he went back to watching Piet Bommel. The Eurasian driver was a big swarthy man, his forearms black with hair below his rolled-up shirtsleeves. He was in command of his vehicle and pleased with his job. He wouldn't be easy, whichever way it went.

Not wishing to hurt the man, Joop assessed him carefully, and eventually formed a plan of action. But he made no move until four o'clock.

By that time Bommel had joined the motorway outside Northampton. He drove along it for about eleven miles, then pulled off into a service area, where he parked with the other commercial vehicles.

From here it was a short run to Coventry. But the truck was not due at Ash Valley until five, just after the change of shifts. The timing was important, and so was the point of entry. Bommel's orders were to arrive at Ash Valley on the stroke of five, no sooner, no later, and present himself at Gate Two. What he did then was up to him.

Joop knew all about those orders, but not from Bommel himself. The Eurasian had made no mention of the dangerous circumstances in which his cargo was due to be delivered. Nor did he now. Having pulled off the motorway, he cut the engine with a grunt of accomplishment, checked the tachograph, then leaned back to light a small cigar.

"So," he said, "here I will stop for some English tea. But then we must say goodbye."

Joop made no verbal response. His only luggage for the trip was a khaki webbing satchel, placed on his knees with the flap open. His right hand was resting on the pistol inside. With the other he took out an envelope containing four thousand guilder, which he tossed into Bommel's lap.

Meanwhile, eleven miles north, a fierce reception was being prepared.

Word had reached Ash Valley that the Dutch were going to try a delivery. The information, which was very precise, had come from Stephen Murdoch. Torenstra were sending in five thousand steering-wheels from Rotterdam, he said, and their vehicle was due at five o'clock. He seemed to know what he was talking about.

The Scots believed him, anyway. They had pickets deployed at each of the factory's ten gates. Some of the men had heavy implements hidden in their clothing. Others were singing as they waited. The mood was a strange combination of hilarity, anger and confusion. The Dutch had been expected to withhold delivery until the dispute in Glasgow was settled. So why this sudden attempt? Had they changed their minds, or had they been got at by Clabon? At any rate they would not pass.

The truck was expected at Gate Five. That was the normal delivery point for body components, so the largest picket was there. About forty men were bunched tight either side of the gate, ready to fan out across it. Ready to restrain them was an equal number of police.

Strangely, Stephen Murdoch was absent. Some people were there from his organisation, the Industrial Workers Alliance, but by 4.30 in the afternoon Murdoch himself and two other leading members of the IWA had disappeared from the scene. Nobody noticed. As zero hour came closer the picket and its sympathisers were joined by a television crew, about a dozen press, some union officials and a fairly large number of BMG workers who had come off the day shift. At Gate Five there were now about three hundred people, lurching backwards and forwards in a haze of dust. The police were trying to keep a way clear for traffic. The situation was very nearly out of control.

The other gates were quiet by comparison. A small group from Glasgow stood at each, with a pair of police.

And the smallest picket of all was outside Gate Two, an entrance which was normally kept shut.

Only three Scotsmen were sitting on the pavement there, chatting to the single young constable who was keeping them company. The gate was chained and padlocked. But just before five o'clock the Scots heard the chain come off with a sudden sharp rattle. Startled, they jumped up to see the gate opened from inside, not by the usual company guards but a pair of junior BMG executives. Questions were asked. The BMG men were shifty. The younger of them smiled in an unpleasant way, and that was enough for the Scots, one of whom went running for help. The other two received a lecture from the constable, who turned immediately formal and started to recite a warning from the rulebook.

At that exact moment it appeared, coming up fast from the motorway, an articulated Volvo with TORENSTRA in a big blue lettering on the ribbed aluminium of its side. The two Scots immediately flung themselves down, end to end across the gate. The constable got ready to pull them away. The BMG executives stood clear. The truck roared up to the gate, but then it went straight on past and round the corner out of sight, following the supply road which skirted the factory's perimeter.

Bewildered, the Scots got back on their feet. The constable whistled in relief. But most surprised of all were the two BMG men, who stood with their mouths open, their eyes slowly widening in horror as they followed the Volvo's engine note into the distance and then heard it merge with a noise like a football crowd.

"My God," said one of them, "he's gone to Gate Five."

They were hammering on the windows and the hollow steel panels of the driving cab, mainly with fists but also things heavier, beating at the radiator, trying to spike the tyres, and there went the headlights, first one and then the other, exploding in a shower of glass. And now there were men on each running board, trying to get the doors open, but they couldn't, because the doors were locked, so they just kept on hammering with their fists, yelling and spitting at him through the glass.

Joop took no notice. He knew they couldn't reach him. He was not at all concerned with what was happening on his flanks, but concentrating utterly on the interplay of brake and accelerator, trying to control exactly the slow forward thrust of this mighty vehicle into the crowd of men in front. There was the danger, in front. He was almost up to the gate now, but some of them had started to close it.

Others were trying to link arms across his path, the fools, and now the police had lost control completely, a flailing blue line at the edges of his vision. A solid wall of men had formed across the road, about three or four deep, linked together, some of them actually trying to push the truck back while others pulled the factory gate shut. The fools had made a trap for themselves and it was closing. Those right in front of the truck were being pushed back against the gate, some of them starting to scream in fear now as well as anger. But Joop didn't hesitate. He had to go on. He must not stop. The only thing to do was to keep moving forward at a steady even pace, allowing the mass of men time to yield and reform, yield and reform, their numbers thinning out gradually without falling over as he edged them back towards the gate. He must not stop and he couldn't accelerate, because there were men still in front, pressed so close to the bumper that he couldn't even see them. And now the police were back in the picture. They were fighting to clear him a path, yes, the chain had broken, the gate was swinging open . . .

He slammed his foot down.

The Volvo surged forward, knocking back the heavy iron gate with a clang, and what happened under his wheels Joop could not hear or see. At the moment of break-through all the accumulated tension broke out of him in a single wild yell, and then he was away and up to forty, scattering works traffic as he tore along the internal roads of Ash Valley.

Three men of the picket came with him, still hanging on to the side of the cabin. Then one tumbled off at a corner. Another lost his nerve and jumped clear. But the last man clung to the driver's door, furiously banging on the roof with the flat of his hand and shouting "Scab! Scab! Scab!"

Joop ignored him. He was thinking only of the route, watching intently for the various landmarks which came up before him, just as described in Rosa's map. So far, so good. No other vehicle had followed him. Then he came out on the factory's far side and saw a stream of office staff leaving through Gate Seven, just as predicted. The plan was to step out and join them, walk away quietly, but that wasn't going to be possible now, not with this mad shouting Scot hanging on. Now there was only one way to do it, Joop decided, and in the same instant he did it, keeping up speed as far as the fence and then putting all his weight on the footbrake. The wheels locked and screeched, the truck went into a slide, slammed into the fence, knocked it down and stopped athwart it. He kicked the door open and jumped out.

The Scot had been flung to the ground, as intended. But he was a very tough number. Bleeding from the hairline, cursing horribly, he picked himself up off the flattened mesh fence and came at Joop with his fists raised. The Dutchman let him come. The Scot took a swing, and then was down again, felled by a vicious chopping blow to the neck of the kind which is taught by Russian instructors at Camp Matanzas, Cuba. And this time the Scot did not get up. He flapped like a turtle on its back, then groaned and lay still.

Joop knew that he wouldn't get up. Without pausing to look at the man once he'd hit him, he quickly reached back into the cab for his haversack and then ran through the breach in the fence, off the factory's premises and away towards the car which Murdoch had waiting.

8

John Clabon was at his house in Summerhill when it happened, taking tea with his wife on the patio. A sprinkler was squirting a dry patch on the lawn. Two Labrador dogs were chewing bones on the grass. From the distance came the rumble of traffic on the motorway, a sound as natural to the people of the Midlands as the boom of the sea is to coast-dwellers. It was a golden, drowsy evening.

Summerhill was where the big money of Birmingham liked to live. Close enough to see the factory smoke, far enough away to be clean, it was a carefully landscaped estate of very large houses put up in the twenties and thirties, now hidden in the ornamental foliage like shy millionaires. The Clabons' was largest of all, a black and white Tudor-style mansion with swimming pool, tennis court, emergency generator, two stables, four garages and a billiards room. It was called Fair Lawns. The oil bill in winter was £1000 a month. The family lived more in London now, but in summer they came here as much as they could. Fair Lawns was home, especially to Clabon himself, who liked the place better than his wife did, she being more aware than he of the difficulty of cleaning dark-stained woodwork and several hundred small leaded window-panes, or rather of finding someone else to do it, preferably of white complexion, at the market rate of £2 an hour.

"We shall have to get rid of her."

"Yes," he said, listening for the telephone. The time was 5.05. The Jag was set to go.

"John, you're not listening."

"No. Sorry."

"What's the matter? You seem edgy."

134

Clabon turned to look at her, sitting beside him in a deckchair with her skirt rolled up. Susan had a very good figure for her age, still remarkably free of those foam-rubber dimples which women called cellulite. Once he had burned for her. A glow remained: enough for them both. She took care of his appetites and ran his home like a ship, seeing to every last detail, such as the tea now spread on a trolley beside them, complete with a pyramid of egg-and-cress sandwiches cut into damp white triangles with the crusts off.

Admiring her legs, enjoying the tea, Clabon smiled as he smiled at no one else. "I'm waiting for news. We're trying to bust that picket."

"About time too."

"Torenstra has sent his toughest driver. We're hoping to get the man through the back gate."

"Will there be trouble?"

"Oh yes, the Trots will go mad. Even if we do get the truck in, Murdoch will try to black it."

"Him again."

"Yes."

"He ought to be shot."

Clabon laughed loudly at his wife's remark. "That's what I told Patrick Harvey's young German," he said, chuckling on. "Poor boy wasn't amused at all. Anyway, there'll be no shooting today, just the usual boring old barney. Murdoch will say the Dutch delivery shouldn't be touched until the strike is settled in Glasgow. I shall turn up and say come on, chaps, leave the Scots to sort out their own problems, let's make some cars here, or we'll all be out of a job. The unions will dither. The men will decide, one way or the other, probably tonight. And probably against me. But it's worth a try."

"They're such fools."

"Sometimes."

"Why *must* they be so greedy?"

The question was foolish, not meant to be answered, but today Clabon thought about his wife's opinions seriously as he watched his two chunky-limbed daughters, ginger-haired and freckled like himself, playing energetic tennis on the hard court beyond the roses.

"The workers are greedy because they are normal," he said to her. "They get as much for as little as they can – just like me."

"Oh come on, John. You work jolly hard."

"And enjoy it more than they do. In any case I'd rather have them greedy than foolish, I assure you."

"Is there a difference?"

"Oh yes, a big one. If the men and I were left to fight it out, like perfectly normal greedy human beings, we'd be better off, and so would the country. That's the natural law, you see, eat or be eaten, combine to hunt for food. The trouble only starts when someone mucks about with that in the name of some other law, progress, justice, I don't know what – a better world, I suppose, where people don't eat each other. That's what muddles the poor bastards up. Give me greedy men, without any fool ideas in their heads, and I'll make you some motor cars."

Even as his creed came out, Clabon realised it was more of a wish for things past than a hope for the future. In either case it had got a little too abstract for his wife, whose face was raised blank to the sun. He took another sandwich and swallowed it whole. Then the telephone rang in the house.

He walked quickly in from the patio to answer it. For about half a minute the only sound at Fair Lawns was the steady bop-bop of girls' tennis. Then the phone was slammed down with a four-letter bark. Susan Clabon rose from her deckchair to see what the trouble was, but when she reached the hall, her husband had gone. The front door was open. The Jaguar was racing away down the pea-grit.

The time was 5.15.

At 5.35, half way to Ash Valley, John Clabon changed his mind.

All he knew was the Dutch truck had gone through Gate Five, not Two, and there had been casualties. Surprise, annoyance, bewilderment, anxiety passed through him in rapid succession as the car sped at eighty down the elevated motorway. Then he began to think about tactics and told the driver to take him to the Royal Midland Hospital.

It was his second mistake.

Each of the emergency operating theatres was in action. He peered officiously through the observation windows, without really looking, then pushed through a second set of doors and stood on the edge of a room where casualties were prepared for surgery. It was a battlefield. Yellow faces lolling, spattered sheets, overhanging drips, dials twitching, tubes pumping, the urgent squeak of plimsolls on lino – was there any sight on earth so frightening as a nurse on the run? Clabon felt suddenly faint. He was not good at hospitals. He wished he hadn't come.

"How many here?"

"I've really no idea," said the sister who had followed him, protesting, all the way from the hospital's entrance. "I think it might be better if we got out the way, Mr Clabon."

A surgeon came up, green-overalled, flexing his fingers into a pair of transparent gloves, like an extra skin. His eyes, above his mask, were cold with recognition. "Well, Mr Clabon, this is quite a little skirmish you've won here today. I hope the profits are worth it."

Clabon stood dumbfounded by the sneer, only then beginning to see the true trouble he was in.

But a worse shock immediately followed. When he paused to say a word with the relatives, they either stared glassily or turned their backs. None of them would speak except one, a stout woman of about fifty, who spat in his face.

"That's what I think of you, Mr Clabon."

By the time he got back to the hospital's lobby, where the press were waiting to question him, John Clabon was not thinking straight.

"Much as we deplore this type of illegal picket," he told them, "we would never consider the use of force."

But that should have gone without saying. None of the three reporters present had thought of accusing the BMG management. Astonished, they stared at him a second, then scribbled frantic shorthand on their pads.

"Where were you when it happened?" asked the quickest of them.

"At home. I came straight here."

"So you knew there would be casualties?"

"No, of course not. Nothing like this."

"But something like. You knew, in advance."

"Now watch it. I was told that some men had been hurt, so I came here immediately. That's all."

"But the general feeling is, Mr Clabon, that this was a deliberate act. The driver of the lorry went through the picket without even stopping, and then he got away in a car which was waiting for him. So it looks as if the whole thing was organised, doesn't it, by people with views against secondary pickets rather similar to your own?"

Clabon realised then that he should have stayed in Summerhill until he knew more. He should not have come to the hospital first, and he should not be talking to the press at this point. Three mistakes already. He stared at the questioner balefully, then pushed him aside. "You print any allegations like that, sonny, and I'll sue your bloody arse off."

But they followed him out in a rush, the other two straining to catch every word while the clever one kept firing questions.

"The unions say they had no prior notice that a delivery was being made from Holland today."

"Were they entitled to it?"

"Mr Clabon, did you yourself know that Torenstra were sending a truck to Ash Valley?"

"No further comment."

"Some of the management knew, didn't they?"

"No comment."

"The men who opened Gate Two knew, isn't that right? They were ready to let the driver through, but he went the wrong way. What do you have to say to that, Mr Clabon?"

"Get out of my way."

But of course they would not. They stuck with him out to his car, two cameramen running up to join them. The clever one came right up to the window and yelled his last question through the glass.

"Who opened Gate Two, Clabon? That's what you'll have to answer."

Clabon began to raise two fingers, but quickly turned the gesture to a wave as a flashbulb popped in his face. He sank back into the Jaguar with relief. Three mistakes was enough. The way this was going, two fingers could finish it.

138

9

He left the hospital with seconds to spare. As he drove away from it he saw the Scotsmen's bus, bringing members of the picket to visit their injured mates. Stopped at a traffic light, the Scots were yelling their rage at bewildered passers-by, who might have mistaken them for football fans, except for an improvised placard being vigorously waved from one window. BMG OUT, it said. This slogan was no surprise to Clabon. When he reached Ash Valley, he found that the picket had transferred its main strength to gates used by BMG employees, who were now being urged to strike in sympathy.

That was the first thing to stop, he thought. BMG itself must not be involved. This week of all weeks the group must keep working, even if it was stocking half-finished cars on old aerodromes. The illusion of prosperous motion had to be maintained until Guidotti's pen touched paper.

With this aspect top of his mind, Clabon entered the factory at speed, passed through a lane of police and proceeded direct-ly to his office, where a bunch of frightened management were waiting to bring him up to date. He told them to wait. Pushing straight into his room with Mary Williams, his secretary, he poured himself a very large drink while she tracked down the Scotsmen's employer in Glasgow.

She held the receiver out. He snatched it from her.

"Joe? You've heard what's happened? All right, so I want you to settle it. Now, tonight. Give them everything they want. Put the buggers back in their bus and take them home. Never mind what it costs. You can pass the cost on to us . . . I know it's not what I said last week. It's what I'm saying now. Oh, just do it, that's all. Goodnight."

Clabon slammed the phone down in disgust. Damn Jocks. Resent even blood money. Still, they make this stuff.

He took another swallow of the whisky, then turned to his secretary, fire in the belly.

"Quick as you can, then. What went wrong?"

Mary Williams was ready. She recited the facts as known at that point, ticking them off on a pad as she spoke in a voice of exaggerated calmness. Clabon listened carefully, watching her, not interrupting. Mary had been with him for years, in bad times and good. She lived for nothing else. She had no husband, no children, no hobbies, no affairs that he knew of. She read romantic novels, three a week, and kept a large family of indoor plants. Every year she took two weeks' holiday in Minorca. Prematurely grey, dressed for neatness rather than attraction, she was more good to the company than she was to herself. In two minutes flat she had laid out the whole situation.

Even so Clabon could hardly take it in.

Something extraordinary had happened here, something more dangerous than he'd realised. There were some very big questions still to be answered. Thinking them over, he stood at the window in the soft evening light and carefully inspected the scene below him. Beyond the factory's boundary fence he could see the field full of unfinished Pilots, the watchman still patrolling between them, as he had the day before. Further away, to the right, the fence had been flattened. Across it stood the truck from Torenstra of Rotterdam, now ringed by intensely bright floodlamps. Police were swarming all over it. A bunch of BMG men stood guard, to make sure the load of steering-wheels stayed put, and even from here the Scots could be heard baying mad at every gate. But the plant was still running. That was something.

And there, beside the truck, was Piet Bommel, the original driver from Holland. A swarthy type in shirt-sleeves, half Indonesian according to Mary, he was smoking a cheroot, half-hidden in shadow as he waited to reclaim his vehicle.

Clabon watched him with a hostile glare. "Just tell me again, Mary. What exactly does he say, this man Bommel?"

"He says he drove as far as Watford Gap – that's the last service stop on the motorway. After that the other man, the one who made contact on the boat, took over as arranged."

"*Arranged*? Arranged by whom?"

"I don't know," said Mary Williams with a shake of her tightly permed head, then she took off her pink-framed spectacles and let them hang from a gold-beaded chain round her neck. "Apparently that's the only statement Bommel would make until you got here."

"Me?"

"Yes," she said, looking at him in a worried way, rather like a mother who wants to help her son, but can't until he owns up. "You."

"What have I got to do with it?"

"You can explain, he says. The police should either talk to you or his own head office in Rotterdam."

At that point Clabon began to see an all-round answer which chased the warmth of Scotch from his veins. This whole gory mish-mash, he thought, bore the elephantine mark of Niki Torenstra, who was one of those types you can meet in Dutch business, a man so far out to the political right as to be very nearly invisible from any normal standpoint. Give Niki Torenstra a nudge about bypassing pickets, and this was what you got – a half-witted darky for the run-up, then a homicidal madman for the crunch. Well, if that was it, Torenstra would have to answer. There was some very urgent washing of hands to be done here.

"Right, Mary, listen. I want you to get Bommel up here as fast as you can, on his own, no police."

"He doesn't speak much English."

"He speaks enough to drop me in the shit."

"The police are trying to find an interpreter."

"Never mind. Bring him up here on his own. And then get me Niki Torenstra in Rotterdam. He'll be home by now. Just find him, wherever he is, and put him straight through."

"Right, sir. I'll try," said Mary Williams, lifting pad and spectacles like a soldier standing to. She called him "sir" because she liked to. She made a point of it.

Clabon, as often, was glad to have her with him. "You can let them all in now," he added to her back, referring to the flock of scared BMG executives waiting beyond the door. "We might as well make a full meeting of it."

But he was not as well briefed as he thought. While he had shut himself up with Mary Williams – mistake number four – the situation had taken two turns for the worse. Both of these

141

new developments were known to the men outside his office. But neither new problem emerged in the very brief meeting that followed, and that too was largely John Clabon's own fault, since one of his techniques for putting the wind up incompetent managers – error five – was to fire questions at them and then change the subject before they could answer.

"So Gate Two was opened?"

"Yes, sir."

"And you did it yourselves."

"Yes."

"Was that clever? No, it was not. Never mind. Too late now. Do the men know?"

"It's getting around, sir. There's no way to stop it."

"Any action yet?"

"The stewards are meeting at the moment."

"Are they? Right, hold everything. I'll get across there and talk to them myself."

The faces round the room expressed dismay. There were several half-uttered warnings. But Clabon was already on his feet, on the move, not listening. "We've got to stop this spreading," he said as he left. "So keep the gate business fuzzy if you can. We knew the truck was coming, yes, but we didn't expect or intend to bring it in through any direct opposition, especially from the main picket. In any case we don't, repeat don't, regard this as a BMG dispute. Our plan is simply to keep the place running, turning out cars for people with no hands, while the Jocks fight it out with the Dutch. Right?"

There was a half-hearted titter of assent. The younger ones had risen to their feet as he withdrew, but the old ones stayed put. Some of them had an odd look on their faces, which Clabon later realised was embarrassment; a wish to be dissociated from him. Others stared dully, too weary to argue. Beaten men.

He turned back to face them at the door. "Come on now, start drafting a statement for the press. But don't make a move until I get back. Don't talk to anyone and don't let this throw you. The drinks are in there."

They're a tired lot, he thought as he left. And walking from the managers' meeting to the workers' one, he himself felt some weariness of spirit. Ash Valley was a hard place to run. The men he was leaving had the responsibility, the ones he was going to had the power. The two sides met only to argue, and the wrangles between them left little time for cars. In today's case the workers would be represented by the CSSC, Combined Shop Stewards Committee, a body of eighteen men each one of whom represented a different craft union. The members of this committee spent a lot of time fighting each other, but together, in a bunch, they were hard to say no to, since they spoke for nearly thirty thousand men. They met in a room off the body-in-white shop, Assembly Building 14.

Clabon went straight there, walking alone through the build-lines and finish-lines of the BMG Tiger 1800, a sports car in strong demand abroad. The car's unpainted body was being put together by an old-fashioned process, the moulded steel panels of it coming in by overhead conveyor while the smaller parts were lifted from pallets along the assembly track. Each piece came to hand at the right place and time, then was punched to the car's main frame by spot-welders, experienced men who moved with the effort-saving ease of long practice as they wielded their bulky apparatus, like weightless machine-guns, each jig suspended from the ceiling by pulleys.

Some of them nodded as he passed. None smiled. Most expressions were blank, a few hostile. One spat on the floor. Others mouthed unaudible insults. But none took their eyes off their task for more than an instant, and that was enough for John Clabon, who did not expect to be loved. He liked to see cars being made, that was all, deriving an almost aesthetic pleasure from the way that low silver body of the Tiger took shape. Walking on down the assembly track, he watched the car shells move from jig to jig, passing through the fusion-welders, bent down behind heavy masks to apply their points of blue fire, and then on to the finishers, who pounced on each small imperfection with a screech of their fast-rotating files. Whine and hiss, thump and rattle – even the sounds of mass production had the power to lift his spirit, as another man's might be by music. Whatever the problem, once into the factory proper he was always filled by a sense of human achievement, especially in the less automated plants such as this, where the integration of man and machine was more impressive.

Beyond the Tiger's track was another, then another. The bodies of three different BMG models were assembled in this one building, which covered three acres and was too big to see across. The ceiling was obscured by a maze of conveyors along

143

which the various body-parts, suspended like limbs in a slaughterhouse, travelled through the air towards their proper destinations. And the floor was busy, too. Fork-lifts and pallet-transporters, also made by BMG, were speeding up and down the lanes between the jigs, keeping to the left and sounding their horns as they would in the streets of a city.

At each intersection Clabon paused to let them pass, looking both ways. These silent, electric-powered vehicles could kill. Each year there were a number of accidents, and even today, despite his care, a fork-lift brushed past awfully close, whooshing swiftly by on its soft rubber wheels. But he crossed the floor without further incident. For a moment he stood beside the escalator, where the bodies of all three models converged for their onward journey to the paint shop, and then he felt his stomach muscles tighten, half in dread, half in anger, as he passed through a door with the number fourteen on it.

Plant 14 was a tall airy hangar, glass-roofed, purpose-built, in which the entire low-drag body of the BMG Pilot 1500 was assembled in four minutes flat by computer, all of its light-alloy pieces arriving at speed to be slammed automatically together, in great explosions of sparks, by a series of robot multi-spot welders. This was what the tourists came to see at Ash Valley, and even today, in the midst of crisis, a group of them stood by the wall exclaiming and gaping at the fireworks with a man from the PR department.

But all that John Clabon saw was the biggest mistake of his life. Here was the wonder car that nobody wanted, even when it did have a steering-wheel. Planned to roll out at a thousand a day, the Pilot was selling at a thousand a week. To set up this model had cost £500 million, a miscalculation which would kill BMG unless it could somehow be turned to account in a deal with Mobital. Now even that last hope was under threat from the eighteen shop stewards who were talking up some fatuous gesture of protest in the room half-way down to the left.

There were causes enough here to constrict any chief executive's stomach, but as he turned left down the side of the plant what Clabon was actually braced for, half in anger, half in dread, was the sight of Stephen Murdoch.

By union decree this automated body shop still employed a number of redundant men, among whom, predictably, was Murdoch the Mole. The founder of the Industrial Workers

144

Alliance was drawing £200 a week to service man-operated jigs on a floor where nothing was done by man. The thought of this, let alone the sight of it, was sufficient to drive John Clabon to the edge of violence. Indeed it was reckoned by Michael Oppenheim, the Finance Director, that over the years of his employment in BMG, through the many disputes he had started and led, Stephen Murdoch had single-handed cost the group £50 million, a fact which made it difficult not to punch the little weasel in the middle of his Trotskyite face.

But today he was absent from his post. The toolmakers' workshop, where Murdoch sat plotting the company's doom on company time, was empty. He was nowhere to be seen on the floor.

Clabon unclenched in relief and walked on, past a group of men who were watching the wonders of the Pilot with their mouths open, just like the tourists. So Murdoch's clocked out, he thought. He might of course be whipping up the Scots at the gate, the way he was yesterday. But at least he isn't here to provoke me. And nor is he whipping up the CSSC.

That was Murdoch's only slip in six years. He had lost his position on the stewards' committee, having been expelled by his union for unconstitutional behaviour. But they wouldn't allow him to be sacked from the factory. Nobody, unions or management, dared to let Murdoch be flung on the street, because of the very large number of men that would follow him. So here he still was, being paid to watch robots. Murdoch was unofficial leader of the toolmakers, he was plotting a workers' occupation if Ash Valley closed. He was ready to take over the company and would no doubt sort out the country in time, abolish parliament, lock up the sovereign, declare a republic and join the Warsaw Pact. But meanwhile he was not on the Ash Valley CSSC. And for that small temporary victory John Clabon was joyously grateful. Among the committee's eighteen members were a couple of wild ones, he knew, listed by Special Branch as Reds. But the rest were open to reason. He expected to persuade them.

Working up the speech he would make to them, he was heading towards the closed door of the rest lounge, thirty yards further on, when he saw an old man in brown overalls, sweeping up some filings that had fallen to the floor. He walked across to him.

145

Later Clabon counted the minute thus lost as his sixth mistake, but a pause to talk to Jim Hunnicut seemed wise at the time. They had worked together all their lives. At Clabon Engineering in Darlaston, Jim Hunnicut had spoken for all the men employed. Now the old man was retired, but he came here twice a week to top up his pension. There was no better barometer of the mood within the works.

"Hello, Jim. What's the weather?"

The old man neither replied nor looked up. He kept sweeping.

Clabon repeated the question. "So what have we got here, a shower or a thunderstorm? Or is it going to be a bloody earthquake?"

Still Jim Hunnicut continued to sweep, not raising his head.

Clabon dropped the weather-talk, a code which they used for reasons of tact. "Will they go or will they stay? Come on, Jim, how should I tackle this?"

Hunnicut looked up then, with no trace of deference or even goodwill in his eyes. "They'll walk. And I'll walk with them," he shouted, then went on sweeping as he added a further remark, inaudible except for the single word "killer".

Clabon stood staring in shock, wondering if he could have heard right. The Pilot's assembly process, while more modern, was a great deal more noisy than the Tiger's, so the air here was full of the crash and clash of metal, huge weights colliding under pressure – quite frightening for a person not used to it, and difficult for conversation. Perhaps the old fellow hadn't understood the question.

Disturbed, but still in haste, Clabon started to walk on, then heard his name called through the din. He turned to see one of the computer operators, standing at the door of the control room. The man beckoned him, miming a phone call. Clabon walked back. The door was closed behind him. Inside the double-glazed room there was no noise at all except for the faint click and chatter of an electronic brain, making cars that nobody wanted. He picked up the telephone. It was his secretary, Mary Williams.

"Oh," she said, "thank goodness, I've caught you."

"What's up?"

"Bad news, sir. I thought you should know before you went in."

"All right, let's have it."

"There's been a death at the hospital, just after you left there." She paused to let him take it in. "And another man's had both legs removed – not a member of the picket, but a BMG employee."

Clabon was silent. "God help us," he breathed eventually.

"I'm afraid that's not all," said Mary Williams as gently as she could. "There's something else, sir."

"Go on."

"Apparently everyone knew this in the managers' meeting here just now. They thought you knew too."

"Knew what?"

"The police have taken a statement from Bommel – that's the original driver."

"Yes, I'm aware who he is. So what does he say?"

"He says he was paid four thousand guilder, that's about a thousand pounds, by a man who was carrying a letter of authority from you and Mr Torenstra, signed by you both, on BMG paper. The letter instructed Bommel to hand his lorry over and pick it up here later on in the day."

Clabon suppressed all emotional reaction. "Does he still have it – the letter?"

"Apparently not. The other man kept it."

"Yes, he would."

"But Bommel has the money, sir – four thousand guilder, just as he says."

"What does Torenstra say? Have you found him?"

"Not yet. He's left the works in Rotterdam, but his home doesn't answer."

"Keep trying. And connect me as soon as you catch him. You realise what's happened here, don't you?"

"No, I don't, sir. Please tell me," said Mary with feeling.

"I made some quiet arrangements to outflank that picket. But Torenstra arranged to ram it, the fool. And he's made sure I'm implicated."

"Can I tell the managers that? They're pretty depressed."

"Certainly. But don't let it go any further for the moment. I assume the police are keeping Bommel's statement to themselves."

"No, sir, that's the trouble. It was made in front of several BMG people, and one of them ran straight off to tell the CSSC."

147

"I see. All right, Mary, thank you. Hang up, hold the fort. I'll be back."

Clabon put the phone down. The clock above his head said 6.55.

His own plan to outwit the picket, he saw now, could not be hidden from the stewards' committee. He would have to admit the tactic at Gate Two in order to clear himself of murder at Gate Five. But would they accept the distinction?

And then, turning round, he saw he was too late. On a panel above the computer's main console a series of small red lights were coming on, first one at a time, and then several rapidly at once. The computer men were busy throwing switches. Ash Valley had started to shut down.

Immediately he rushed from the room, ran to the left and burst into the rest lounge. But it was empty. Nothing remained of the shop stewards' meeting but smoke, cigarette ash, crumpled paper cups and red plastic chairs arranged in a circle. The CSSC had decided and gone.

Clabon thought of going after them, but knew in an instant that it was no good. They had taken a public position now and could not be seen to back off it. There would be a stoppage, and it would have to run its course. So better to stay here and let the place clear.

Turning back to the door, he closed it behind him, then lit a cigar and sat down in the room. The machinery outside was already silent. Lights were going off. Groups of men passed by, unaware of his presence, laughing and chattering as they walked out. The lounge was almost in darkness, illuminated only by the bulbs of a fruit machine. Round the walls were pictures of vintage British cars. Clabon sat smoking alone there for about twenty minutes, thinking of the many mistakes he had made and the ways, not so easy, by which they might be rectified.

But then he made one more.

At 7.15 he set off for his office the way he had come, returning through the paralysed robots below their glass roof, and then down the Tiger's assembly track, which was also now stopped and almost in darkness.

Did they see him by chance or were they waiting? He never knew. It was never even proved who they were. Their faces were invisible, but there were three of them, possibly more, and they jumped him unseen among the static machinery. Two of them grabbed him from behind while another hit him from in front, several times, about the body and face. Clabon fought like a bull. Eventually he threw them off by sheer might and rage. They ran away into the dark. He himself stumbled a few steps further, then fell. Nothing seemed broken, but he couldn't get up. Coming and going, on the edge of consciousness, he made himself wait until his strength returned. No one came to his aid. He was too faint to shout for it. The last lights went off, doors slammed shut. Again he tried to get to his feet, but could not. Above his head the weld-guns hung from the ceiling, still swinging gently on their pulleys, like vines in a forest at nightfall.

10

In Brussels the time was 8.20, ten minutes to go before dinner. The guests of the Portuguese Ambassador were still dispersed in groups about the garden of his residence near Tervuren, drinking champagne below the paper lanterns strung between the trees. It was a warm, balmy evening. The sun, almost down, was casting long shadows on the lawn. Two peacocks were strutting about, like gentry entertaining the tenants, and in a small arbour by the lily pond a band was playing Portuguese folk music.

It was an elegant scene, thought Jack Kemble, very similar to diplomatic Washington, and almost as dull.

He himself was as elegant as he could manage. The Brussels correspondent of Associated Press, last seen at Tet with a fragment of mortar shell lodged in his backside, had lent him a white tuxedo. The tux was so tight that Kemble couldn't button it, but would serve. Clipped to it like a fountain pen was a microphone wired to a small flat recorder in his pocket.

His plan was to soften Harvey up with some chat about the old days, then tap him on the merger after dinner. But Harvey hadn't arrived yet.

There were two American generals, a rather impressive Belgian baron with a monocle, and a visiting African statesman, whose teeth gleamed even whiter than his robes. There were ambassadors to the European Community, ambassadors to NATO and ambassadors to Belgium itself, all resident in Brussels and most of them speaking in French. Kemble had never seen so many excellencies collected on one lawn, even in diplomatic Washington. European Commissioners also counted as ambassadors, he was told by the girl who was taking him round, and there were two of those here as well. But not the Commissioner for Industry, he noticed. Harvey was nowhere in sight.

Then dinner was served at a long table set out of doors, overhung with baskets of flowers and lit by flaming torches. The guests first clapped this display, then sat at it, warily inspecting the *placement* for errors – at which point Kemble saw the numbers were complete. Harvey wasn't here, and Harvey wasn't coming.

Seated next to his host's social secretary, the Portuguese girl who had introduced him round, Kemble asked her casually what had become of the former British Prime Minister, whom *The Times* had been hoping to come across tonight. She replied to him in rapid, hoarse English.

"Harvey? He cancel, he always cancel. His wife don't like parties."

"When was this?"

"Laura telephone me yesterday. Harvey cannot come, she says. Then she call me back this afternoon, say you come instead. And for that I am happy. Laura is my friend."

But not mine, Kemble thought as he bent towards a glass of Portuguese prawns. Oh dear no, not a friend of mine. Laura is a treacherous English bitch, and before I get inside her tight little drawers I am going to apply a little pain.

The Portuguese, as latest recruits to the European Community, were still being made to feel at home. It wasn't done to refuse their parties. But Patrick Harvey had backed out of this one to be with his grandson, David, who had come to stay in Brussels while his father and mother took a holiday in Kenya. The boy had arrived that morning. And this was the cause of the quarrel still crackling on between his grandparents. Harvey had clean forgotten that David was coming, and so had let the week fill with other engagements, to the very great annoyance of his wife. Now the weekend had been taken too, reserved for the merger talks in France. Only this one evening, Thursday, had been cleared for fun and games with David.

But it was disappearing fast.

Still in the Berlaymont at 8.35, Harvey watched the light fade with dismayed frustration, ruling out one by one the things he might have done with the boy. They could have gone boating in the park perhaps, or played French cricket in the garden. But the way this was going, he would get home too late. David would be in bed, and Margaret would be grim with annoyance, banging things about in the kitchen as she warmed up a left-over portion of supper.

No, she would not be annoyed, she'd be furious. Neglect of a grandchild was the surest way to bring her temper up to the boil from the depths in which it usually simmered, contained by thirty years of married life. And he knew, word for word, how the row would go. She would say he had put his work first again, not from pressure of events – that was just an excuse – but because he enjoyed it more than family life. That was what she always said. And sometimes she was right. But tonight she would be wrong, Harvey thought, aggrieved already by the argument to come. It was all very well for Margaret to accuse. She should come here herself and tell Otto Riemeck it was time he stopped talking because out there in Kraainem a nine-year-old English boy was waiting to play French cricket . . .

And of course, she would. Yes, that is exactly what my dear wife would burst in and say, thought Harvey to himself, trying to conceal his impatience as the President came to the end of the point he was making.

"So that is an aspect you have not considered, Patrick. Your proposal may be in contravention of Article 85."

Oh dear, this really was the lawyer talking. Yesterday Riemeck had seemed quite enthused by the plan, or at least willing to let it be tried. So what had gone wrong in the interval? Had somebody got at him? Or was this the academic mind taking over, seeking quibbles as trained? Harvey was once again struck by how little he knew of this German professor from Württemberg.

"Otto," he said, "do we really need to worry about the fine print? This thing will start life, if ever, at a summit."

"Yes, yes, I know. But are we not creating a cartel, in breach of the competition policy? We shall perhaps be in trouble with the European Court."

Harvey glanced across at Kohlman, sitting beside him in the President's office. The problem raised by Riemeck was irrelevant, but there was a perfectly good technical answer to it, of the sort which any alert *chef de cabinet* ought to provide at this point. Was Erich off guard or evading exposure? In either case he obviously wasn't going to speak. Irritated, Harvey took care of the point himself.

"I can't see that this will be a problem, Otto. Even if the companies do get together, they won't be the biggest of the car groups in Europe, not by a long way. And their share of their own home markets will still be well under half."

Riemeck nodded in acknowledgement, pleased by the technical answer. He said no more about Article 85. There was a pause, and then he picked up the dossier left with him the previous day. "A billion, you say. Will that be enough?"

"Oh yes, I think so."

It was a lie. One billion Ecus would not be enough, Harvey knew, having thought about it more in the course of the day. The BMG Pilot alone had cost that; the effort to rescue American Chrysler had cost three times as much. To put it in American terms, a thousand million dollars, for the purpose of modern mass car manufacture, was an opening stake. To stay in the game required more. In this case there were two firms, not one, to be saved; two governments to be bought out, two model ranges to be integrated. Funds would be needed to pay for a unified wage scale, development and launch of new products. Chuck in immediate cash problems, and according to Arnold Doublett, who ought to know if anyone did, the whole thing was going to cost four times as much.

Not one billion, but four.

Harvey's first reaction to that had been annoyance. A typical piece of donnish unrealism, not worth the journey to hear. But after more thought he had changed his mind. Doublett was right, he'd decided. Four billion was what it would take. Converted, he had spent the afternoon in his office doing sums. A billion from this year's budget, and the same again next year, drawing on Social Fund, Regional Fund and Contingency Reserve . . . a soft loan from the European Investment Bank . . . a raid on the new Mediterranean Fund, because of the Italian connection . . . a special guarantee, perhaps, to persuade commercial banks to make up any shortfall.

Yes, there were ways that it just might be done. Consulting no one, using only his own very basic arithmetic, Harvey had scribbled himself four billion. Of course he ought to have consulted his colleague, the Budget Commissioner, but that would have led to all sorts of trouble. This thing would have to be agreed at the top, at a stroke, or not at all. Even so, it wasn't going to be easy. One billion might be too little; four was a tall order indeed. The figure to go for lay somewhere between, perhaps. And eventually Riemeck would have to be persuaded of it. But to mention a higher sum now might scare him off the project altogether. It would certainly keep him talking past sundown.

And so it was that Harvey, thinking partly of his grandson, told one of the riskiest fibs of his life. He stuck to one billion and explained how the sum would be raised.

"If, of course, we ever get that far."

Riemeck nodded, seeming satisfied. "You think you can do this thing, Patrick?"

"We'll soon know. The test will be in Tours."

"They have both agreed to come?"

"Yes."

Kohlman turned to his master in surprise, knowing that this was not the case. Only Clabon had agreed to attend the talks; Guidotti was still hanging back. But already Harvey had risen to his feet, obscuring this second and smaller untruth with some hasty scooping up of papers. The President saw them out and closed the door behind them, apparently still not finished for the day. They walked away towards their own office. Then Kohlman made his first remark for ten minutes.

"Congratulations."

But Harvey found the comment unsuitable. He felt out on his own now, responsibility settled on his shoulders like a mountaineer's pack at the start of a climb. "Congratulations come later," he said in a curt voice, stepping out at a brisker pace.

In the harsher light of the corridor it was clear how tired Kohlman was. The skin of the young German's face, drawn tight across his skull, had been broiled to a light shade of pink by the Italian sun. There were swellings like bruises below his pale eyes. His suit was crumpled from two days' plane travel.

It was time to send him home, Harvey thought, himself now filled with that longing for things familiar – his chair and his books, even the anger of his wife – which tiredness and too much travel brought on. But where was home for Erich? Was there a girl waiting somewhere in Brussels? An angry girl perhaps, about to warm up supper? A lonely girl, giving up hope in Lübeck or Bonn? Maybe there were lots of girls. Or maybe there were no girls at all.

He had given up guessing at his staff's private lives, but in this was like an ex-smoker who couldn't resist the odd puff. What a mystifying blank the boy was, he thought, as they walked together in silence to the opposite end of the thirteenth floor. Then he stopped wondering about his assistant and turned his mind back to the merger, about which he felt a sudden surge of confidence at the close of this second day.

Clabon and Guidotti were two exceptionally difficult men. But there was just enough to bring them together, and the skill required to do it was his own, a politician's. Once he had them at his side in a nice house in France, with luck, and some good meals between, he could conjure up agreement.

"Clabon's all set then."

"He will come," said Kohlman. "Or so he said yesterday. You read my report?"

"I did, and I agree with it. John Clabon has no choice, as you say. If he shuts down Ash Valley, the group will fall apart. Did you meet Oppenheim?"

"No."

"He's the dauphin. A very different man. What did you make of him, by the way? I mean Clabon."

Kohlman's smooth brow was creased by a frown; his head shook slightly in puzzlement. "He treats his workers like fools. And yet he has great affection for them. It is a strange thing to see. An English thing, perhaps."

"Yes, I'm afraid so."

"He believes that a group of extremists are trying to destroy him."

"He would."

"But so does Guidotti. He spoke to me of the same group."

"Reds under the bed."

"Excuse me?"

"We invent the enemies we need," Harvey explained, sitting down at the desk in his own office. He opened his briefcase, looked up from it and smiled, unconcerned, as he took out a technical magazine that Doublett had given him to read on the plane. He spread it open on his desk and began flipping through it, page by page, as he talked. "Now, Erich, time to go home. The problem is this condition of Guidotti's. You say he

155

won't come to Tours unless we promise to give him control?"

"Yes."

"That's out of the question."

"So I warned him."

"Do you know where he'll be in the morning?"

"He is going to Rome for a meeting with the labour unions."

"Right then, here's what you do. Track him down early and try to make him come. If he still refuses, you can tell him to get hold of this magazine and read the article on page forty-three. Tell him the suggestion comes from me." Harvey held the magazine up and then pushed it across, open at a double-page spread, on the latest developments in electric power for automobiles.

"That will be enough?" asked Kohlman in surprise.

"Oh yes, that will bring him, I assure you. He'll be waiting on the doorstep with his tongue out."

11

Arriving in Italy, Rosa Berg showed her passport with exactly the same weary air as the other people coming off the last flight from Paris. Then hitched up her shoulder-bag and walked straight on, skipped the queue for luggage and passed through Customs without a sideways glance. Once again she was carrying her camera, with the pistol concealed inside it. But there was nothing nervous in her manner. Her tread was firm and her gaze direct. She had nothing to declare but death to the state.

Waiting for her in the airport's arrivals hall was a plump man of typically Latin appearance, about the same age as herself, with a monkish bald patch in his hair and a fluffy black beard all over his face. He wore tinted spectacles, heavy-framed, and a soft rumpled suit of white linen. His manner was nervous as Rosa's was not. When she came through the barrier he jumped up to greet her, hesitated, pumped her hand, started to chatter, then ran out of words and hurried along beside her as she kept on walking with long, heavy strides across the hall and out to his car.

It was not the car of a poor man. Rosa expected a Fiat, but the bearded man led her to a brand new Mobital Sparta 1500, bright yellow, with a black racing flash down each side. All right, she thought, we can all have one of these when they're made for the people. Not yet.

The night was hot and close. Thunder was rumbling like gunfire in the hills. A damp aroma of salt was coming off the sea, somewhere close to the west, and as the man ushered her into his car Rosa caught the smell of his fear, which was like bad breath.

157

In the car were two younger men, sharply dressed. She was introduced to them. And then she turned back to the bearded one. "So what's the news? Did Hal deliver?"

"Yes," the man replied in a gloomy tone. "We have the equipment."

"And Guidotti?"

"He'll be here. He's coming from Milan in the morning."

"That's good."

"Where's Joop?" asked one of the youths in the back. The question had a cocky male sneer to it.

"He's busy," said Rosa without turning round. "Can you manage without him?"

"No problem. We've used one before."

"Are you ready to show me?"

"We're ready."

And twenty minutes later they showed her, far out on the marshes of Ostia, beyond the fenced boundary of the ancient port. The noise was covered by a crackle of thunder, the flash just another in the flickering night.

Rosa was satisfied.

"Good," she said. "Let's go."

And then they all ran for the car as the rain gushed down, falling so fast that it formed instant ponds on the road to Rome.

Friday

1

Waking early in Rome, when the storm was over, Rosa Berg lay in bed and thought of Trotsky. The first light of day, just starting to show through the shutters, brought a picture to her mind of that other fine morning in Mexico, 1940, when the old man had made the last entry in his diary.

I shall die a proletarian revolutionary, a Marxist, a dialectical materialist, and consequently an irreconcilable atheist. My faith in the communist future of mankind is no less ardent, indeed it is firmer today, than it was in the days of my youth . . .

She knew the passage by heart. She quoted it often to her friends and this morning in Rome she said it to herself, moving her lips but making no sound as she watched the light grow beyond the shutters. The elegant bedroom in which she was lying had less familiarity for her, less reality even than the room she had conjured into her head, that small ground-floor study of the house in a suburb of Mexico City, as it was more than forty years ago. From photographs in books and frequent imagining she knew every detail of it, down to each article of furniture. And clear enough to touch she could see Leon Trotsky at his desk, the straggly grey hair and sharp jaunty beard, the eyes still bright behind the pebble-lensed spectacles as he lifted his head and turned to the window, smiled at what he saw there, continued to reflect a moment, then picked up his pen and bent to the page again.

Natasha has just come up to the window from the courtyard and opened it wider so that air may enter more freely into my room. I can see the bright green strip of grass at the foot of the wall, and the clear blue sky above the wall, and sunlight everywhere. Life is beautiful . . .

Repeating them, Rosa felt warmed by these words, which for her, as for many of the faith, were a metaphor. Whether he meant to say so or not, it was a fact that from his own point in time Leon Trotsky could not see the world he had worked for, still obscured by the wall of human repression and ignorance. All he could see was fragmentary glimpses: the grass below the wall and the clear sky above it. But that was enough. He believed in the unseen fields beyond, where men would walk as equals, in dignity, on a day which surely could not be far off.

I shall die with unshaken faith in the communist future. This faith in man and his future gives me, even now, such a power of resistance as cannot be given by any religion.

Those were the diary's last words. Having written them, bent over double like an old Jewish watch-maker, Trotsky straightened up and examined the page, his head on one side, his pen still poised. Rosa stayed long enough to watch him add his signature, then left him still seated at the plain wooden desk where Stalin's assassin smashed his skull.

The light had hardly changed behind the shutters.

She peered at the watch on her wrist. It was just five o'clock. Here in Rome there was nothing to do yet but wait and think calmly, keeping dread at bay with that strength beyond religion, for which, if nothing else, she would follow Leon Trotsky to the grave.

Religion, for her, was not strength of any kind, but weakness. Like a disease it had scarred her in childhood and left its mark still. Even now, to this day, she could not set foot in a church without feeling sick. All that mumbled self-abasement and grovelling for mercy, glorified despair and suffering enshrined, the hopeless view of man and his future – so ignoble! So plain damn stupid! At the sight of good people on their knees she wanted to barge in and yank them to their feet, shout and slap their faces to wake them up. But it was more than that. Underneath this rational anger was a deep instinctive horror at the ritual, primitive as voodoo, which had ruled the first eighteen years of her life. It turned her stomach even to think about the sibilant, secret-sucking priests behind their wire grills, so close you could smell what they'd eaten for lunch; the sweet stink of incense; the clicking of beads, the drinking of blood; the corpses in effigy and scraps of the saints, the rota of martyrdoms which had punctuated childhood, the rush to light candles when baby brother caught mumps – no good: he died anyway – and the years, endless years of kneeling to a bell in that dark, ornate chapel of the convent school in Nantes. Darkness was what these memories brought back to her: fear and guilt in the dark, and shame so heavy it could crush you to nothing, make you wish you were nothing, annihilated. With the greatest of ease she could not only see that dark chapel, lit by a ghoulish yellow glow from the disembodied heart in the window, but remember how it felt to be herself at that age, eyes shut tight in intense concentration on her own utter worthlessness before the flaming eye of a harsh and dissatisfied creator. And always at hand, poised to slap down the first sign of pride or even childish joy, were God's own bullies, those grim faced ex-women in billowing grey habit and starched white linen, getting their own back on life. The sheer damn *cruelty* of nuns, forcing small girls to scrub lavatories for laughter in mass! And oh, the blind stupidity of the parents, obediently bobbing up and down to the tinkle of the bell while they worried about the fees, but wasn't it worth it, yes, look at Rosa, so sweet in her little white dress . . .

Merde! Even now it made her sick to remember; and yes, afraid, as though if she peered too long into that clammy darkness it would reach out and snatch her back.

Reminded of these early years of her life, knowing very well that hence came the strange cast of mind that made her repeat Trotsky's words like a prayer, Rosa had stiffened in the bed. Her breathing had quickened and her hands were clenched. So strong, so black was her hatred of this pious childhood that it had destroyed every trace of affection for the strict Breton mother who had forced it upon her. Nor could she ever forgive the mild, half-Jewish, half-socialist father who had not had the nerve to oppose it. Even Nantes, the ordinary town in which she had grown up, was shadowed by this dark cloud in the memory. Its castle and brewery, steelworks and flour mills, the solid bourgeois suburb where her mother still lived, the alleys

163

leading down to the rivermouth port – every feature, every image of Nantes was repulsive to her. She thought of it only as a place where she had endured a long and painful illness.

Yet the strange thing was that she had no memory of the cure. No person, no event attached in her mind to the moment of escape from the Christian religion. What had happened to release her? Who had talked her out of it? Now, almost twenty years later, she could not remember. One day, aged eighteen, she had just gone to Paris and left all that sick provincial humbug behind.

Yes, she thought, Paris was where my life began.

Her first years at the Sorbonne were a vague glow of happiness in the memory; pure pleasure and freedom; escape from Nantes. But then came a clear and specific event. Unlike the day she'd lost God, the day she found Marx was distinct: the place and the weather, the man who was talking, and especially her own extraordinary feeling as she first saw the world and its history, entire, in this way.

Most of the Marxists she knew had a similar memory. Some of them likened it to first hearing Bach, others to the gift of second sight. But she had always thought of it as stepping through a door which led off a maze of old streets, quite an ordinary door, often noticed, never tried, which one day flew back to her touch and was found to open into a great modern building made of steel and glass, clean of line and flooded with daylight, aesthetically satisfying whichever way you looked. What she liked especially was the symmetry, the soaring mathematics of it. And right from the start she had felt quite at ease within that stern architecture. She had found a home and never left it.

Or rather found myself, she now thought. Because faith is identity, and at that stage in Paris I had none to speak of – no faith, no identity. I didn't really exist as a conscious individual until that long rainy afternoon at the Café Babylone when Blaise Chabelard sat making a tower of sugar-lumps between the pools of rain on the table-top, carefully piling them higher and higher as he built up the theory of Marxism. So that was the true beginning of my life.

Remembering how the sugar-lumps fell but the theory did not, Rosa smiled in pleasure, and then frowned to herself in remorse at the ludicrous botch she had made of this fine new existence. Having opened her eyes, Blaise Chabelard had opened her legs; and that she should never have allowed. Extraordinary really, after so long, how much it still hurt to remember that sunny little attic Blaise kept in St. Germain, and the tap which kept dripping, drip, drip all day long as he lay with his eyes shut, dreaming of another girl, or maybe just bored, while she stroked him in exploratory wonder, amazed to be alone with, let alone in bed with the celebrated leader of *Jeunesse Communiste Révolutionnaire*.

Poor little Rosa from Nantes, love unrequited had very nearly left her stone-dead as her saints.

But when it was over, there was Joop Janssen, offering plain Dutch comradeship. And there, too, at the moment required, was Simone Salvador, the communist aunt in Le Havre whom her parents refused to mention, unseen since childhood, but now stepping firmly into the centre of her life with the sharp reminder that a theory of history should not be confused with sex or even love. Marxism wasn't a gift, said Simone, but a task, unrelated to personal feeling. Rosa could still hear that stern advice, uttered on a long corrective walk down the beach at Le Havre. With hindsight she suspected her aunt of touting Karl Marx as a cure for the heart, but in any case that was when she'd read up the theory for herself and started to work at it, organising, demonstrating, starting to lead even, flexing her strong new identity through the autumn and winter of 1967. Did she sense what was coming? Did anyone? No, not really. But surely I must have sensed something, Rosa thought, to have hung on in Paris through that extra year, sweating out the pain of lost love and enrolling for a doctorate I never did want.

And now again she smiled to remember, for a Doctor of Political Science she was not. She had barely read a book when the Sorbonne blew up, Paris blew up, all France, oh the bliss of it, began to blow up in that wondrously rapid chain reaction of May 1968.

Drunk with incredulous joy, she had marched and fought and shouted with the best, hacked trees and rolled over cars, dug up the streets for *pavé* to fling. *Tout est possible*! had been the cry at the time; and so, for a while, it had seemed. Things thought impossible, things never dreamed of had kept coming true, day after wonderful day. Paris had swarmed end to end with marching columns and the Sorbonne had roared with unshackled humanity, just like Petrograd 1917. The students had led, the workers had followed. Ten million had come out on strike in three days. And this had been her highest own moment: the closest she'd come to changing the world. Trusted as a leader by the Trotskyist cadres, she had been sent down to Nantes to address the aircraft workers whose action began the great shutdown of France. Ah, the sweet revenge of it, to have raised the flag of godless revolution in that miserable town, yes, waved it in the faces of those stiff-wimpled bullies at the convent! A moment not forgotten, still a joy to remember . . . But brief. And also futile, as her aunt was the first to foresee. Simone had come especially to Paris for the fun and had laughed to see the marching and the flags, black for anarchy, red for equality, the slogans splashed on walls, the emergency canteens and the action committees who talked so much they never could act. So like Barcelona 1936, she had said. Just the same, except for one thing.

"Spain was serious. This, my dear, is not. You want to know what this is? Publicity, that's all. Copy for newspapers, film for television. Your young friends, they understand publicity, yes, and they understand it better than the government. But that is the only thing they understand. When the summer comes, they will go off to lie by the sea. The government will still be the government, the papers will write of something else. The workers will accept a few extra francs, and France will continue as before. You will see."

What a terrible shock it had been to hear Simone say that, and to sense straightaway that she was right, even though the battle was still at its height. They had been walking by the Seine at the time, from bridge to bridge along the towpath, the river running silently by while the gas bombs exploded inside the Latin Quarter. But Simone was quite unimpressed. Staring over the water at the smoke already rising, as evening gave way to another night of furious street battle, she had smiled with wordly-wise sadness.

"Enjoy it," she had said, "so long as it lasts. But please, don't count on it, will you, *ma chère*? Revolutions are like love affairs, too good to last. To make them endure you need stamina, as for a marriage. It is not so much fun. You will see."

Stamina, yes, thought Rosa now, you needed that all right. But you also needed hope. In the long haul both were required, hope and strength, faith and discipline, the undimmed vision of Trotsky and the undeceived eye of Simone Salvador. It was a question of balance. To believe in the future yet act in the present, that was the balance which had to be held.

In 1968 the future had seemed very close; the hard thing had been to gauge present reality. The students had let their hopes run far ahead of the facts, yes of course. After that moment of truth by the river, even while marching at their side, arm in arm, she herself had seen the whole thing going wrong, exactly as Aunt Simone had predicted. And when the workers, commanded by their unions, gave up possession of the factories and accepted a straightforward wage deal – that was the turning point, May 28th – she had called together the best of her friends, the few who had shown they would last, and led them on a different path.

How clear it was still, that original meeting of the Iskra, upstairs at the Café Babylone on the night the workers of France backed down. Looking back to it, as she did often, Rosa could still see the thick swirling smoke of *caporal* cigarettes under a single dim light-bulb, the bottles of cheap red wine and the crusty loaves of bread, half-eaten. She could not remember what she had said to them, only the reaction of each as they listened; the objections, the suggestions, the doubts diminishing, the growing acceptance, the mood of bitter disillusion transformed through the night into hard new resolve; then the moment of decision, the ring of young faces set solemn as each took the pledge. She remembered the lapse into laughter after it was done, the intense sensation of comradeship, and then the tired dispersal at dawn through streets still strewn with flung cobblestones – the start of the journey which had led to today. And her choice of followers had been sound. Since that first meeting, in May 1968, only three had fallen by the wayside. One had died mad, one was in jail. And one – the great traitor, Blaise Chabelard himself – had changed his mind, abandoning his pledge to the future for contemptible present success. But all had kept their promise of silence. The Iskra lived still undiscovered. Of the twelve originals, nine were still in action, not counting new recruits and casual supporters. It was enough.

And for that, Rosa thought, the credit is mine. I thought of it, I started it. It was I brought them into that room, it is I who have held them together ever since. Her chest swelled with pride at the thought. Aware that today, in Rome, could be the end of the journey, still half-addressing Trotsky, she offered up the Iskra for approval: her own contribution to history.

To begin with, in the backwash of 1968, as the tide of protest receded, they had scattered to their various lives about Europe, bound by nothing more definite than a pledge to break the system, and keeping in touch through a postal code she had devised – a system of messages concealed in books. Some of the members had gone underground and some had joined orthodox socialist parties. Some, like Steve Murdoch, had set their hands to agitation in industry. Others, by contrast, had risen high to posts in government and business, deliberately breaking all overt connection with the Left. Joop had gone to fight for the Arabs. New recruits had been found. The organisation had survived but not achieved much; and for her that wasn't enough. She had seen that it needed more precise objectives. So in 1972 they had met to talk tactics, and since then had held four reunions, each time more resolute in purpose, their aims more defined than the time before.

The big change had been to go for seizure of individual factories by the workers – revolution by degrees and by example, as Mario called it – rather than the grand old Russian scenario of a unified and instant uprising of the mass, the whole people led by party élite. Trotsky would not have liked this innovation. Simone was doubtful of it, too. It went against every traditional doctrine of revolutionary tactics. To achieve change piecemeal, in isolated pockets, each worker-run factory linking up with the next as their numbers gradually grew, was not the normal method of Marxism-Leninism. But given the present conditions in Western Europe, it seemed to be the best, the only hope of change. Mario believed so. Rosa was persuaded. In the end all had agreed. The promotion of workers' control, by any means short of violence, had become official policy of the Iskra. That had been in 1975. Then, four years ago, after some small successes in other parts of Europe, it was realised that something much bigger was needed to push history on, so the organisation had narrowed its targets exclusively to BMG and Mobital. Now each of those citadels was poised to fall in a pair of linked, simultaneous victories which would make the workers' movement unstoppable in Europe. Conversely, failure could not be allowed. This, right now, was

168

the make-or-break moment, and in its harsh undeniable light the Iskra had finally brought itself to a state of war. Two days ago, at the meeting in Paris, the rule against violence had been dropped. That too had been a very good session, Rosa thought, recalling their shock at the opening of the trunk from Le Havre, then the way that each of them had rallied in turn, taking out pistols one by one, gathering courage together as they had on that night back in 1968, although of course nothing in all the time since had equalled the marvellous electricity of that first youthful pledge in the smoke-filled room above the Bab.

That was where it started, and this was where it led – to a comfortable bedroom in Rome. Uncomfortably comfortable. We must be getting old, Rosa thought. Never mind. Our purpose is clear, our will is still strong. This morning the Iskra will fire its first shot.

2

Steadied by reflection on the long chain of political incident which had led to this day – it put the coming action in a wider, less personal perspective – Rosa fell asleep. When she woke, the sunlight had grown and the shadows had moved, but only by a fraction. Surprised at how little time had passed, she looked at her watch again, checked the hour and the minute, then followed the thinner hand, travelling round in twitches, one per second.

Almost 5.30.

How quiet it was now, after the storm.

According to the two young men of the Red Brigade, it was the worst storm to hit Rome for years. Coming back here from the airport, full of their success with the bazooka out at Ostia, they had pranced at the windows and jabbered excitedly as lightning flashed over the rooftops and rain crashed down on the terrace. To Rosa they seemed a pair of ludicrous fops, even if they did know how to shoot a rocket. Disgusted, she had left them and gone to bed with the thunder still slamming and crackling directly overhead; and it had rumbled on for most of the night. But now it had stopped. The rain had stopped too. The city seemed stunned into silence. She had a brief impression of it spread at her feet like an unconscious man, just beginning to stir, still vulnerable. Individual sounds reached her ears: a trickle in the gutter, the snarl of a scooter in the street below. Spread out in the wide double bed, she lay on her back and let the time pass slowly, exploring the room with her eyes.

The light was making stripes on the walls now, gathering brightness.

How handsome it was, this apartment of Mario Salandra's,

plain white all over with touches of brown and a floor of glossy patterned tiles. Mario had good Italian taste. Mario had too much damn money. This was the nest he shared with his child-bride, now sent to visit her parents in Rimini. His first wife had run off and left him, which had taken the fire out of Mario, and then he had married this beautiful child, who was no incentive to change the world either. Mario had a nice home, a nice car, and also a nice post at Rome University, where he lectured on the works of Antonio Gramsci. Known to be a man of the Left but approved for that reason, to balance the faculty, he had done the job for years.

Job, wives and money had all done their bit to jellify Mario Salandra, who was not the man he'd been in Paris '68. Oh yes, he still believed in the future all right – Mario was a true scholar of the world to come, the Iskra's chief ideologist – but his will to act in the present had weakened. Following her orders he had spied on Guidotti and secretly guided the workers of Mobital towards a seizure of the company, all very well. But then, without orders, he had brought in two of his students from the faculty's Red Brigade to deal with this morning's rough stuff. Mario couldn't face theory turned to blood, that was the truth of it. And now he was in an utter funk.

Reviewing her team for the job, Rosa felt a stab of fear herself. Two cocky juveniles and one scared political philosopher, she thought, were not much to pit against Carlo Guidotti, who had a pair of armed bodyguards and might well have called in extra police, expecting some trouble today. Thinking ahead to what had to be done, she wished very much that Joop Janssen was with her, as originally planned. This was Joop's job. He ought to be here. Missing her Dutchman badly, her fear now extending to include him too, Rosa wondered if the ruse at Ash Valley had succeeded. There were so many things that might have gone wrong. She wished now she'd never even had the idea. But only Joop could do it, there had been no choice. And he had agreed to make the attempt of course, without any question or argument, like the perfect soldier he was; no hesitations and no bravado, just straight into action, whatever was required. Dear Joop, what a plain man he was. Dull really, simple in the head, and strangely . . . empty. Was that it? Yes. An empty man. Yet hard. Effective, too. Not like these foppish Italians, posturing always for effect. A third of the nation votes communist, Rosa thought, and still they haven't changed a damn thing. Italians were nothing but gesture.

It was hard to believe that pair could kill.

And yet they had killed twice already, according to Mario. These two young *brigatisti* from Rome University belonged to a team who had shot the chief magistrate of Padua and then fired a burst through the guests at his funeral, one of whom had later died. And now they were acting for the Iskra. For years, Rosa thought with misgiving, we have waited to take this supremely serious action, and now it is going to be done by a pair of pretty boys who clap thunderstorms. But I should stop worrying about this. Who pulls the trigger is not so important. What matters is the political effect, and if I have judged that correctly, it will justify the action and all concerned. In death even Carlo Guidotti will make a contribution to history.

"Rosa, you are awake?"

"Mario?"

"Yes, it is me."

"Come in," she said, pulling up the sheet.

Mario Salandra opened the door and stood at it, hesitant, dressed already in the rumpled suit of knobbly white linen he had worn at the airport the night before. His dark hair was tousled round the monkish bald patch, and he hadn't yet put on his tinted spectacles, so the whole of his sad inner state was revealed in his deep brown lap-doggish eyes. Poor Mario. How old he looked, she thought, how scared. He smiled at her bashfully through his black fluffy beard, in which a few wisps of grey had appeared in the last half-year. "You slept well?" he asked in his sonorous French, not so rapid but more correct than Joop's.

"Yes, very well."

"You would like some coffee?"

"Please," she said, "yes. And bring in that radio. Let's try to get London."

He shuffled away in loose-fitting Moorish slippers with up-turned, pointed toes. Rosa put on a shirt and got up. Standing at the bedroom's window she peered through the horizontal slats, then wound the shutter up a few inches. The day outside was brilliant, already hot, but the tiles of the floor were cool beneath her feet, cooling her all the way up. She breathed deep and stretched, then went back to the bed and sat on it, cross-legged, smiling, wide-eyed. She felt good.

172

A few minutes later Mario came back with a big pot of milky white coffee and two thick slices of bread with jam, which he knew was the sort of food she liked. He laid the tray beside her on the bed and then sat fiddling with the knobs of a radio. The many different voices of Europe came out of it in snatches, but London was not yet transmitting.

"It's too early," he said. "The first news is not until six, British time."

"Just leave it tuned then. And calm yourself."

"I am afraid, Rosa."

"That is very obvious."

"Please, I ask you. Is this wise, what we're doing today?"

"Who knows what's wise," she said, starting to eat. "It is logical, that's all. So far as we can judge, the time has come to take this action. The advantage outweighs the risk, so we must do it. The choice is not ours to make, Mario. However, if we find the risk is greater than we think, we shall withdraw."

"I beg you to consider that."

"I shall consider it. Where are your two little soldiers?"

"Not here yet."

"Do you trust them?"

"Oh yes," nodded Mario, mumbling into his beard, head lowered to stare at the counterpane. "They're both good boys."

"But they don't know the target yet, do they?"

"No, I haven't told them."

"And how will they react, do you think, when they know it's Guidotti?"

"I don't expect it will worry them."

"You mean they'll kill anyone," Rosa said, trying to sneer with her mouth full.

At that Mario turned on her, quietly indignant. "I mean youth is brave, Rosa. The bodyguards won't worry them, the man's power and name will not frighten them."

She smiled and patted his hand. "Yes, youth is brave," she said, remembering how Mario himself, the fierce young Italian graduate from *Science Po*, had stood on an overturned car in Paris 1968, lobbing bottles of petrol at the oncoming wall of CRS riot shields. "I can still see you clout that big gorilla when they came at us over the barricade. Oh, what a marvel. He went down like a tree. And you didn't even have a beard."

"No, no beard."

173

He tried to smile back at her, but even the glories of May '68 could not brighten Mario today. Rosa took his hand and held it gently between her own. "Poor Mario, you shouldn't have married her. It just makes things harder."

"Yes," he said, dropping his eyes. "Harder."

"How much does she know?"

At that he looked up in real alarm. "Francesca? She knows nothing, nothing. I have told her nothing, Rosa. She must be kept out of it, please. On that I insist."

"But of course, *caro*, that is understood. Calm yourself . . . Ah, turn it up."

The British time signal was coming from the radio, like a faint distress call from space. Mario adjusted the tuning until the bleeps were louder. Then they heard a cool British voice, announcing the BBC World Service.

"Here is the news."

A pause, and then the first headline.

"Two men were killed and five injured when a Dutch lorry forced its way through a picket line of strikers at the BMG assembly plant near Coventry yesterday afternoon. One of the injured is still in a critical condition. The identity of the driver is unknown. After ramming the picket he escaped from the factory and was driven away in a car. A full police search is continuing . . ."

The announcer moved on to other headlines.

For a second Rosa stared at the radio, catching up with the English in her head. Then she grabbed the second hunk of bread from the tray and started to smear it with jam. "So, first blood to the Iskra."

Mario's head had dropped at the news, and now hung forward from his shoulders, as if his neck were broken. "Yes," he said. "Workers' blood."

3

"Today all production has stopped throughout the British Motor Group in protest at what has been described by one union leader as a deliberate act of aggression by the Dutch supplier in connivance with BMG management. The charge has been vigorously denied by John Clabon, the group's chairman, who has been assisting police with their enquiries. Mr Clabon himself was physically assaulted by members of the Ash Valley workforce yesterday evening, but is said to have suffered no serious injury . . ."

The hot chocolate had splashed on the plastic tablecloth, Sir Patrick Harvey noticed in annoyance as he refilled his grandson's mug to the top. Bad news had not always made his hand shake.

"Meanwhile a watch has been mounted at all ports and airports for the driver of the lorry, who did not take over its wheel until just before arrival at the factory. Police have described this man as . . ."

Seated stiffly in the all-wooden mock-rustic kitchen of his house at Kraainem, Belgium, Harvey listened to the news from England with mounting dismay. Whatever had happened here, bad luck or plot, it would make a discreet excursion to Tours very difficult for Clabon.

"When are you coming back from France, grandfather?"

"Not until Monday. Quiet a moment, David. I must hear the rest of this."

Now a union leader was on the air.

"As general secretary, I am convinced that these deaths of my members were the direct result of strike-breaking by right-wing extremists. It remains to be seen how closely the BMG management were involved . . ."

Worse and worse. Harvey listened for half a minute longer,

until the subject changed, then switched off the radio and sat deep in thought. In the sudden silence the pigeons could be heard on the roof of the kitchen, their feet like the scratching of rats. The clock on the wall showed 7.10. In London it would be an hour earlier, but Clabon would certainly be up, he thought, already pacing around some room in a state of high agitation. Perhaps he should be steadied with a phone call.

"Would you like me to cook another crossing for you, grandfather?"

Harvey came back to the boy with a smile. It had been his own idea that David should get breakfast, to give them a little more time together. But now that, too, had been spoilt.

"I won't have another one," he said, "but warm it up for yourself, why don't you? And finish off that jam. It's called a *croissant*, by the way. *Croissant*. The French have spent years thinking up these difficult words, you know, so we mustn't turn them into ordinary English ones."

No, he would not ring John Clabon. He would act as if things were on course, which might help to keep them so.

Anxious to be on his way before this tactic could be spoiled, Harvey sat waiting for the sound of his car. Then he thought of the dead at Ash Valley, of breakfasts in other kitchens, each with an empty chair, ordinary fathers and husbands snatched away by the wild talk of dreamers. Blood and rhetoric, the compulsion to see political argument as heroic drama, the urge to resolve it with violence – how many men had died in Europe for such foolishness? There must be a better way to run the place. Yes, there was a better way, of course there was. It meant committees and dull institutions, heavy papers, hours of talk, grey men like himself half-asleep round long tables, interpreters droning on in glass boxes, weekends spoiled, angry wives and disappointed grandchildren, all contributing their unnoticed fraction towards a safer, more reasonable society.

Was it worth it?

Not according to Margaret, who stood in the doorway now, still too annoyed to smile or say good morning. She turned aside into the hall and put down his suitcase, which she had packed because she always did, sweeping the bedroom of his personal things as though clearing junk. Then she came back to the kitchen, advanced to the sink, and filled a kettle with water.

176

Harvey looked into his wallet and gave David a thousand Belgian francs. "For holiday spending. Enjoy yourself."

The boy said nothing.

Margaret Harvey turned off the tap and spoke without a glance at the table. "Thank your grandfather."

"Thank you, grandfather."

Then the bell rang. Harvey went out to the door, and there was Laura Jenkinson, all dressed up for her weekend in France and looking so smart in the bright morning sunshine that she was almost beautiful. The sight annoyed him. He told her to get in the car, then picked up the suitcase and turned to kiss his wife, who had made no effort to improve her appearance since getting out of bed. But she had already gone back to the kitchen.

"Goodbye," he called. "Goodbye, David."

They shouted back together, and to Harvey it seemed that they were laughing. He was glad of it. Hoping they would have some fun without him, knowing they would not have more if he stayed, he shut the door and walked out to the car, wishing Paolo Santini good morning. The handsome young Italian, looking hardly less glamorous than Laura in his smartly tailored chauffeur's uniform, took the case from his hand and stowed it in the boot of the shining Mercedes. There were briefs laid out on the seat for him to read. Harvey picked them up and set them on his knee, not bothering to look at the house as the car pulled away into Kraainem. He was back in the world where he did well.

A few miles away, at his flat in the diplomatic quarter of Brussels, Erich Kohlman had also heard the BBC news. After it he waited fifteen minutes, in case Harvey rang with fresh instructions. But the telephone stayed silent. Kohlman was not surprised. In Sir Patrick's hands non-communication could be an evasion, a snub, a tactic, a riposte, a command, a whole speech. The English Commissioner had as many different silences as an Italian had gestures. And in this case the message was: "No change, Erich. I've heard it too, but I'm going to Tours. So carry on as planned."

Kohlman got the message, but thought it optimistic, in view of the news from BMG. As soon as he reached his office he started to hunt down John Clabon on the telephone.

The BMG offices in Coventry and London were unmanned at

that hour. The Clabon home in Summerhill, Birmingham, didn't answer. But Susan Clabon was at the family flat in London. Unsurprised by an early call from Brussels, she said that her husband had spent the night at his club, to escape the press.

"He'll be in the pool, Mr Kohlman. Do ring him before he has a coronary."

Swimming up and down in the basement of the Royal Automobile Club, Clabon had already passed the limit suggested by his doctor. But it was a good cure for other things. Gradually the all-over, top-to-toe ache brought on by this form of exercise had diffused the pains left by his beating up at Ash Valley. Rage, disappointment, perplexity had given way to plain fatigue. After twenty-two lengths there was only one problem left in the world. Could he do twenty-three?

That would be a personal best. Determined to try it, he turned and toiled back one more time with slow splashing strokes, so tired that the water felt sticky. But what better training could there be for the British motor industry than a brisk swim in treacle? To see where you wanted to go, to be in a hurry to get there yet unable to go any faster, your limbs moving more and more slowly, as in a bad dream . . .

He made it.

Red-eyed with chlorine, he hauled himself out and lay gasping on the tiles like a beached white whale. Gradually the problems of the moment came back to his mind. But none of them seemed as hard as twenty-three lengths.

He had been framed, that was now clear. And the Dutch had nothing to do with it. Torenstra's driver had been replaced by another one, put in by some unidentified party to breach the picket. This could have been done by rightist fanatics, but Clabon was convinced of the opposite. It was a ruthless intrigue of the Left, he felt sure, designed to rouse the men of BMG against him.

The main, immediate problem was how to make anyone believe it. The police were unconvinced. The unions were due to hear his case at eleven, the board at two o'clock. Frank Holroyd was coming in person to take a full statement for *The Times*.

Yes, it would be a long day, Clabon thought, and it could end in jail instead of France. He stood up and towelled himself vigorously as the club's porter backed towards him with a telephone, paying out a lead from the wall. He took it and snatched the receiver.

"John Clabon."

"Erich Kohlman here, from Brussels."

"Yes, what is it?"

"The Commissioner has heard of your difficulties."

"That's a pretty word for them."

"You are injured?"

"Nothing much."

"Sir Patrick conveys his sympathies. However, he intends to go ahead with the plan."

"Let me speak to him."

"He has left."

"Already?"

"The Commissioner expects to meet you in France at the time and place agreed. There will be no other opportunity."

Clabon could detect no hint of a personal attitude in the young German's flat, neutral voice. "I'll be there," he said.

"You can guarantee that? From the news it seemed that you were in some kind of legal trouble."

"My friend, I am always in trouble, not all of it legal. That's business. So you just stay in that glasshouse and leave the real world to me. I'll see you tonight."

Clabon rang off, then smiled as he handed the telephone back to the porter, an elderly man in serge uniform with a rainbow strip of medal ribbons stitched to his chest.

"Arthur, how did we win the war?"

"Don't know, sir. Must have been the Americans."

Kohlman replaced the receiver, then stared at it, thinking. He did not believe what he had heard. John Clabon's troubles were worse than John Clabon would admit. His presence in Tours must be doubtful. Despite Harvey's confidence, the talks were in danger, and the time had come to say so.

The thirteenth floor of the Berlaymont had the quietness of all high places, faintly sinister to Kemble's mind. Having sneaked his way up from the Press Department, he was standing alone in a carpeted lobby surrounding the lift shafts. The Commis-

sioners' offices fanned outwards down very long curving corri-
dors, but there was no way of telling which way to strike. At the
heart of bloody Europe you needed a compass.

As he paused in uncertainty, a uniformed usher came up to
him. Kemble prepared to bluff it out in one language or
another, but luckily the man was English, a dignified type with
the manner of a high-class butler, or maybe a middle-class
dropout. It was hard to tell these days, especially with the
English.

"Sir Patrick hasn't moved, has he?"

"No, sir. Half way down on the left."

"Thanks."

Oh the poor English, so easy to bluff, thought Kemble,
proceeding on his way. Each Commissioner's door had a label
on it, so Harvey's was not hard to find. He opened it softly and
found himself in a secretaries' room, with two desks and two
typewriters. The room was empty. He caught Laura's scent on
the air. Harvey's own office was empty too, but through the
open door of another came the voice of a man talking German.
Kemble poked his head round to look, then crept back to a chair
and sat down to eavesdrop. But his presence had been de-
tected. The German voice stopped abruptly, and then the
speaker appeared: pale and fair, very neat in a lightweight suit.
Just a boy really, or rather so creaseless that he looked a bit
unreal, aged anywhere from twenty to thirty.

"Who are you?"

"Oh, hello. My name's Jack Kemble. I'm here to interview Sir
Patrick."

"My name is Kohlman. I am in charge of Sir Patrick's office. I
do not think you have an appointment."

"Is that necessary?"

"Certainly it is. How did you get up here?"

"Same way as you did, I expect. In the elevator."

"You have a pass?"

"Sure."

"Let me see it, please."

Kemble handed over a green slip of paper. The German
examined it briefly, then looked up with even less warmth.
"This is a pass for the Press Department."

"Oh really? Doesn't run to the top, you mean."

"It does not. The correct procedure . . ."

180

"I know the procedure, Mr. Kohlman. But you'll find that Sir Patrick and I can get along without it. So I'll just wait here until he arrives."

"You will have a long wait."

"How long?"

"Until Monday."

"That's too late. Can you tell me where to find him?"

"I cannot."

"You mean you won't."

Kohlman had stepped out into the corridor to beckon an usher. "I mean I have no authority to do so," he said, turning back. "And you have no authority to be on this floor, Mr. Kemble. You will please return to the Press Department and apply for an interview in the ordinary way."

"This is ridiculous. Where's Laura?"

"Not here. As you see." Kohlman's face changed to a look of curiosity. "Miss Jenkinson knows you?"

"Oh yes, we're old buddies."

"I shall tell her you called."

"Please do that," said Kemble. "I'll go downstairs now and give the computer my fingerprints, then I'll wait at the Hotel Europa. Tell your boss I'm here to do a profile for *The Times*. And tell Laura she has until noon to shape up. After that I play dirty."

Left alone again, Kohlman returned to his room, where he made his second phone call of the day, to Mobital's office in Rome.

"You may have heard, Ambassador. There has been some difficulty in England."

"I have heard," said Guidotti.

"However, the plan is unchanged. The Commissioner wishes you to know that he has left for the rendezvous."

"And what about . . . the other party?"

"I have spoken to him. He says he will be there."

"And myself? What am I to do?"

"Yourself, Ambassador?"

"Herr Kohlman, I made a condition when we met in Milan. Do not tell me that you have forgotten it."

"Of course not. I reported it with care. And Sir Patrick believes a solution can be found."

"At the rendezvous?"

"At the rendezvous, yes. You must come to hear the answer."

There was a long, hostile silence.

Kohlman sat it out. On his desk was the magazine that Harvey had left with him, a technical monthly called *New Science*. The article it was open at described a sensational break-through in the effort to develop a battery-driven car, but omitted to mention which company had made it. Kohlman had read the piece carefully during the night and could see what it might mean to Mobital. But the bait was unnecessary. Guidotti gave in with a small, soft laugh.

"You know, Kohlman, we Italians are always treated like this. We are very subtle in negotiation, we agree to nothing without conditions. The difficulty is that no one believes us."

"You will be there?"

"I shall be there. But tell the Commissioner I have not changed my mind. It is just that I wish to present the point directly."

"I will tell him." Kohlman closed the magazine. "And you yourself, Ambassador, you have had no trouble this morning?"

"Trouble?"

"You were expecting some attack."

"Ah *si*, the woman. So far they hide their faces. But do not fear. We are ready."

4

"So Guidotti wants to do a deal with the labour unions, and it has to be something big, sufficient to put an immediate stop to the movement for workers' control. That is why he's here today."

Standing on the terrace with the sun at her back, Rosa paused to let Mario translate. The two young men of the Red Brigade – *brigatisti*, as they were called – professed to speak French, but she was unwilling to take a chance on their wits. As they listened to her lecture they were lolling in deckchairs, limbs akimbo, dressed to kill.

The bazooka was spread on the terrace beside them. Its khaki tube glinted in the sunshine, dismantled into sections, with the shoulder-rest and sight-attachment laid to one side. It still bore the markings of the US Army, stencilled in yellow on the tube, though some of the numbers had been scratched away. The rockets were still in their box. To Rosa the whole apparatus looked so dangerous and complicated that she was relieved, after all, to have the help of these seasoned young assassins. Still, they should understand why they were doing it.

"So Guidotti is in Rome," she went on. "At this exact moment he is in his office on the Via del Corso, where the unions will come to meet him this morning, and he will go to them this afternoon, at the communist union headquarters. On both these occasions he will be well protected, by police as well as his own men. However between the two meetings he has a very private engagement, which he thinks we don't know about. For this he will leave the Mobital office by a back entrance, with only his bodyguards, no police escort. He will tell his associates he is going to lunch with his friend Count di Rufolo. But that will be a lie. Guidotti will go to di Rufolo's flat, as he often does when he's in Rome, but this morning the Count will be conveniently absent. The person Guidotti will meet there is Fernando Vico.''

Vico – at the mention of the name both students sat up in surprise, but Rosa turned away from them, stopping again to let Mario translate. The sun was already hot and the sky very blue, without a smudge of cloud. The day had that brilliant sharp clarity which follows a storm. Pink geraniums, freshened by the rain, cascaded from terracotta pots along the railing of the terrace, and beyond them all Rome was spread to view, its many domes and cupolas jutting up like buoys in a sea of orange pantile that undulated out to the ring of Sabine hills. To Rosa's eye the city appeared less beautiful than decadent, its ochre walls rotten as cheese. Too many churches, she thought. And over there, sharp against the skyline, the dome of St. Peter's itself. Down with it.

As Mario finished she turned back to the terrace, just in time to catch a filthy digital gesture from one of the two *brigatisti*. She felt the blood drain from her face in annoyance. ''What's the matter with you?''

''Me? Nothing,'' the youth replied to her in French, then turned to titter at his friend.

''So why did you do that?''

''What?''

''That.'' She made the gesture herself.

''Oh, that.'' He smirked at her. ''That was for Vico.''

''Vico is a dirty reformist,'' said the other one in support.

Feeling her blood rush back, Rosa put up her hands and worked them over her face, as if to wash it. ''A reformist, yes, you are right,'' she went on. ''That's the word for him. As you know, Fernando Vico is a Communist deputy in the Assembly, and his voting record is a disgrace. He'll side with any party that furthers his interest. However, what matters to us is this. Guidotti has picked this man to represent the unions on the Mobital board. Shall I go on, Mario?''

''Yes, I can recap. But Rosa, I wonder whether this is necessary? Both these boys understand . . .''

''Just shut up and listen. The Iskra doesn't blow people up without a proper analysis.''

Mario's head dropped in submission. Turning from him, Rosa continued to the other two in French: "Do you follow me?"

They nodded at her, each in turn, no longer smiling. She went on.

"Vico is a pure opportunist, without a revolutionary thought in his head. With him as its first representative, the movement for workers' power will be dead. We can see that clearly, can we not? And so can Carlo Guidotti. Vico's appointment as a company director is so much in Mobital's interest that Guidotti is meeting him in secret, between the formal talks, in order to arrange it. That is what they mean to do. And we are going to kill them while they're at it."

"Both of them?"

"Yes, both."

"That's good," said the older student. "I have wanted to do away with Vico for years."

Mario shuffled his feet uneasily. "Could we not achieve the same effect by revealing what we know? A word to the press, and these two men are finished. The collaboration between them, at least, will come to nothing."

But this suggestion was promptly cut down by the other two in a burst of hot Italian. The argument went on for some time, and when she saw that youth had prevailed, Rosa was able to sum up in French, unopposed.

"The collaboration of Vico and Guidotti will be clear from their corpses," she said. "And after it is done we shall make no public statement, so the Left will blame the Right, and vice versa. The result will be an intensification of the struggle for power in Mobital. With Vico dead, the workers will push for full control. And as to Guidotti, the fascists will never find another old fox like him. Ambassador Carlo is the only man alive who is clever enough to save this company for capitalism."

While Mario translated this for the younger student, whose French was not so good, Rosa walked across to the bazooka and squatted down to stroke its steel tube, now hot in the sun. More properly called a 3.5 rocket-launcher, it had been stolen from a NATO base near Heidelberg, then purchased by Joop from the remnants of the Baader gang. Best thing there was, he said, to make sure of more than one man with a single shot fired from a distance, especially if the target was in a closed space. The

185

rocket went off in a ball of white heat, exploding outwards with a shower of fragments . . .

Mario had finished. She returned to his side and sent him back into the flat with a muttered command. He nodded in reluctant obedience. As he went off his face was a strange shade of grey behind his beard, like putty.

"Very well, so much for objectives," she said to the students. "Now let's discuss the method. We still have plenty of time."

Out of their chairs now, the two *brigatisti* had started to unpack the rockets, transferring each of them carefully into a canvas grip padded with blankets. Rosa stood propped against the railing. All her blood racing now, too fast, too fast, she gripped the iron bar very tight as Mario came back to the terrace and spread a map of Rome at her feet.

5

"Right, lad, watch out. Here comes a googly."

"Americans can't bowl *googlies*."

"Oh no?"

"They don't even *play* cricket."

"Okay, that does it. Cut the talk, smartass. Stand by your crease."

Kemble stood in the centre of the lawn, rubbing one side of the ball on his trousers to work up a shine. The boy stood ready to bat. He was plump and freckled, with the pudding-basin haircut pioneered by Henry V, still favoured by English prep schools. About nine years old. But ready to tell the world the rules.

Kemble began to trot towards him, then broke into a lumbering run. "Here she comes now, your special . . . unbeatable . . . all-American . . ."

"No ball!"

"*What*?"

"No ball. You're too close."

Kemble came all the way up to him, then leaned down slowly into his face. "Oh yeah? Who says I'm too close?"

The boy's eyes widened behind his magnifying lenses. His voice faltered. "You're supposed to bowl from that stick."

Kemble smiled at him, then straightened up and stared at the house behind, which looked like a very large cuckoo clock, taken over by pigeons. No movement came from inside. "What we need here is an umpire," he said. "Where's your grandpa?"

"I don't know. Gone to France."

"France? What's he doing in *France*, for Pete's sake?"

187

"I don't know," said the boy with a shrug, getting ready to bat again. "He's busy."

"When's he coming back?"

"Monday, I think. I don't *know*. Can we play now?"

"We can, my friend. But no more of these Belgian rules, if you please." Kemble retreated to his bowler's spot and turned to recommence his run, scraping the grass with one foot like a bull before the charge. He rubbed up the shine of the ball again and spat in his palms. "Ready? Okay, stand by. Here it is now, the Kentucky fried googly." He started to run, speeded up, checked at the twig, delivered the ball over-arm, then ducked as the boy whacked it back past his head, straight over the lawn and into a shrubbery. "Oh, terrific shot. Six runs. Two more if you can find it. Is your granny in?"

She was, Kemble knew. He had watched from a place of concealment as Lady Harvey hobbled back into the house, struck on the knee by a singing off-drive. He was surprised she had walked off at all. Although made of rubber, the ball was a hard one. And Margaret Harvey must be almost into her seventies, he thought, although not much changed in ten years. An angular woman with an outdoor complexion, slightly taller than her husband. Better born, too. The power was Harvey's, the class was his wife's. She had never liked politics, but here she still was, playing the game out in Kraainem, Belgium. Her hair had turned white.

And now she was at an upstairs window, about to pop out of the cuckoo clock. Pretending not to notice her, Kemble watched the boy dive into the shrubbery, then turned to raise his arms in an umpire's signal for six. "Oh, Lady Harvey – hello."

"Jack Kemble, isn't it?"

At this his surprise was real. "That's right. You remember?"

"Of course I remember." She smiled at him inscrutably. "Wait there, I'll come down."

Kemble stood tense on the lawn. He had a good line as seeker after truth, and another as breezy cynic, but neither would kid Margaret Harvey. At Downing Street she'd chopped down the press like weeds in her garden. Play it straight, he thought, and hope for the best. No other way.

She came towards him limping from the bruise on her knee, untidily dressed, and now he could see she had aged. Her face had an arthritic's lines of endurance: aches and pains ignored, life got on with despite, buck up and make do. He had always rather liked her.

"Jack Kemble. Well, this is a surprise. I thought you went off to America."

He smiled and shook her hand. "Went off, came back. Still scratching around."

"I suppose you want to see Patrick."

"Hoping to, yes."

"I'm afraid he's away for the weekend."

"Duty calls?"

"Oh no, Mr. Kemble; pleasure calls. We're the duty." She nodded at the boy, still thrashing about in the shrubbery. For a moment her lined face was grim with anger, then she led the way over to a circle of white wooden chairs set out in the sun. "So who are you working for now?"

Kemble dropped the name of *The Times* and then talked of other things, working his way back carefully to Harvey. "Can you tell me where to find him?"

Margaret Harvey was silent for almost half a minute, then smiled as her grandson broke cover with the ball. "You'll have to convince me it's important," she said, still watching the boy.

"It's important."

"And urgent?"

"Yes, of course, urgent. What isn't?"

And this line of Kemble's worked well. "You're right," she said with sudden feeling, turning her smile from her grandson to him. "It's always urgent, isn't it? Always. If there wasn't a crisis, they'd make one up. They do so love it, you see." As she spoke, the amusement vanished from her face. Her eyes turned cold and her wrinkles set grim again. "Do you believe in revenge?"

Kemble was too surprised to answer.

"Acts of revenge," she went on, "they purge the temper, don't they? Help to clear the air. Only small ones, of course."

"I once had a wife who agreed with you."

At that her smile returned, a shade more malicious. "All right, I'll give you a number to ring in France. But don't say you got it from me."

She got to her feet. The boy ran up. Kemble sat absolutely still, as he'd learnt to do when luck came. He must say or do nothing to scare it away. She went into the house, then came back to the garden with a sheet torn from a small memo pad.

"Here it is. He'll be there tonight," she snapped, grimmer than ever. "And don't bother lying. Say you got it from me."

"Thank you," said Kemble, reaching out as he rose.

"One condition." She pulled the sheet back from his grasp.

"What's that?"

"You bowl at least four more overs to this wretched boy. Good idea, David?"

"Yes! Good idea!" yelled Harvey Minimus. "Come on, smartass!"

A Mr Kemble was calling from Brussels, said the girl on the switchboard of *The Times*.

"Yes, put him through. Hello? Mr Kemble?"

"Hi. Who are you?"

"I'm Mr Holroyd's secretary. Judy. Judy Keith."

"Hello, Judy. Let me speak to him, will you?"

"He's out at the moment. In fact he's just left for BMG, to talk to Mr.Clabon."

"Okay, never mind. Pencil out, Judy. Take this down. 47,56,00,52. That's a telephone number in France. What I want, double-quick, is the name and address of the subscriber. Can the co-op deliver?"

"I should think so, Mr Kemble. I'll call our Paris office."

"Tell them I'll be here in Brussels, at the Hotel Europa. They can page me in the bar."

"In the bar. Yes."

"Partaking of a little light liquid refreshment, prior to commencement of the chase."

"Naturally."

"Comrade Judy."

"Yes, Mr Kemble."

"If a poor American boy tried to join the shop in which you are closed, could you swing the votes of the typing pool?"

"I have some influence."

"Wield it."

"I will wield."

"You're a white man. So Frank's gone to see John Clabon. Can you get hold of him before they start talking?"

"I might, if I'm quick."

"Okay, message is that cards are on the table. Harvey's girl practically told me so. And she's with him in France all this weekend, at the mystery address."

"Sounds nice."

"Don't eat your heart out, baby. It's not that kind of merger."

Preparing himself for *The Times*, John Clabon spent a few minutes alone in his office high above Euston Road. The room contained several souvenirs of his career. There were silver models of cars, some golfing trophies, an aerial photograph of Clabon Engineering in Darlaston and one of the Spitfire plant in Castle Bromwich, taken the morning after a German bombing raid. As he strolled among them Clabon drew some extra resource from this small collection of personal objects. The battle was not lost yet, he told himself with cheerful defiance. Nonetheless, it had been a heavy morning. The unions, refusing to accept his denial of violence against the picket, had told him they would keep BMG shut down, all thirty factories, unless he resigned. Their cigarette smoke and heated words still hung in the air of the room. But now that long meeting was over. The unions had gone and he was unmoved. Nothing unforeseen had occurred; nothing was worse than it had been before. The real test would be the board, he thought, due to meet at two this afternoon. And they would listen better.

Meanwhile there was Frank Holroyd.

"Send him in, Mary."

"He's taking a call from his office, sir."

"As soon as he's ready then. And no interruptions, please. If the cops come, park them in the boardroom. I'm damned if I'll be charged with manslaughter in front of *The Times*."

"Surely it won't come to that, sir."

"Maybe not. Holroyd goes in half an hour, anyway. Lunch here for you and me alone, meat and two veg. Something for the scaffold."

A sympathetic cry came out of the intercom. Clabon flicked it off with a smile and got behind his desk, settling into the chair like a man digging into a defensive position. One eye was swollen, half closed by a bruise. A tooth was loose. His ribs were strapped. His balls still ached, and also his kidney. His cigar had gone out, its end wet and frayed with nervous chewing.

191

But he had a plan. He was smiling as Holroyd came into the room.

The editor of *The Times*, surprisingly camp for a hefty Australian of middling years, immediately threw up his hands in dismay. "Jesus, John, *look* at you! Can we have a mug shot?"

Clabon grinned through his wounds with boyish pride. "Be my guest."

"I'll send a camera round. That shiner is front-page stuff."

"Happy to oblige, Frank. But no obits, please."

They talked for about fifteen minutes. Holroyd sat and scribbled with a slim gold pencil, acting up the role of humble reporter, while Clabon told his side of the story. And the mood was more relaxed than it had been with the union leaders. Clabon readily admitted a degree of collusion between himself and the Dutch firm, Torenstra of Rotterdam. The plan had been to sneak through a side gate, he said, not smash the picket. There had never been any talk of money or a substitute driver. That had been someone else's idea.

"All right, John. Whose?" Holroyd laid down his pencil and spoke very quietly, as a barrister does when the witness is about to make a really stupid statement.

"You could ask the Industrial Workers' Alliance."

"The Trots? Oh, come on, this is hardly their style."

"Not normally, no, I agree. But this time they're in it with friends. Have you heard of the Iskra?"

"No, John. I haven't."

Clabon told what he knew of this organisation, which was really nothing. "There are some very wild men at Ash Valley, Frank, and they want me out, so they can take over. This thing is a frame, can't you see that?"

Holroyd shifted in his seat and looked away, through the window. He had stopped writing.

"At the time that picket was bust," Clabon went on, his finger rising like a soapbox orator's, "the leader of the IWA was nowhere to be seen. And he hasn't surfaced since it happened, which is pretty damn odd, don't you think, considering that this is his moment."

"You mean Stephen Murdoch?"

"Yes, I mean Murdoch. He's not at home, and he's not leading the walk-out. No one knows where he is. Total shutdown, Frank, and our chief rebel takes a holiday."

But Holroyd's mind seemed to have wandered, like his small black eyes. "It's not enough, John. We'll look into it, of course. But meanwhile I'd like to discuss something else."

"What's that?"

"Why did you meet Patrick Harvey in Wales and take him for a spin in your battery-driven prototype? There's a perfectly reliable witness, you know. He's the local schoolteacher. A hill-walking type. Not likely to hallucinate."

Clabon didn't move, dug deep behind his desk, but his hands slowly clenched into fists. His face had turned white around the mouth. "Do you want this interview exclusive or don't you?"

"Of course."

"Let's stick to the goddamn subject then. And now I want to go off the record. Can you promise me no attribution?"

Holroyd shifted uncomfortably. "Tell me what it is. Then I'll tell you how we'd put it."

Clabon stood up, still dizzy with anger. Without saying more he walked across to a wall-safe and took out the document he had shown to Erich Kohlman, the list of factory incidents and the politics of the men responsible. Laying it down on his desk, he went through a moment of nervous hesitation. The act of trusting Frank Holroyd was akin to that of placing the head in a noose while standing on a very fragile platform.

"Take a look at this," he said, "then forget you ever saw it. We put it together with Special Branch."

It was Holroyd's turn to go still in his seat. "The police?" he said in a voice of careful, quiet detachment. "They've helped you to check on your own men's politics? You realise what this could do, I suppose, if it ever got out."

"I realise." Clabon nodded, still white around the lips. "But I want you to see this. I want you to know why I'm saying there's a plot."

Ten minutes later Holroyd stood up. "All right," he said, "a Trotskyist plot. I accept the possibility. We'll run that theory on Monday."

"What's wrong with tomorrow?"

"There are things to check, John."

Clabon's hands thumped his desk in frustration. "You mean you don't believe me. You think I bust the bloody picket myself."

"It's your friends, the police, who don't believe you." Holroyd smiled at him silkily. "Where can I find you this weekend?"

"I'll be at home. Sunday night I will, anyway."

"And from now until Sunday, where will you be?"

"Who knows, Frank, who knows. I could be anywhere with this on."

"Well, don't run too far." Holroyd walked away to the door, then turned back, as casual as an actress on camera. "By the way, are you in touch with Carlo Guidotti?"

"No. Why should I be?"

"We've been trying to catch him for a comment, since he's had a few similar troubles himself. But his secretary says he's away until Sunday."

"Oh," said Clabon. "Really."

"Is Mobital in some kind of flap?"

"Italy is permanent flap, Frank. They just make good cars."

"Does that mean . . ."

"It means what I say. They make good cars. Now off you go, while I get out my prayer mat."

Holroyd nodded, but continued to stand by the door a moment, glancing once quickly round the room, as though in a last check for clues. Clabon stared back at him woodenly, feeling that one careless word, or even the minutest change of facial expression would bring the merger into print. Go on, he thought, get out of here, you awful fellow-travelling Aussie creep.

6

Waiting for Carlo Guidotti to come into her trap, Rosa sat half way up the Spanish Steps. Behind her, at the top, rose the elegant belfries of Trinità dei Monti, the church built in Rome by the kings of France. On the flat space below her, between one flight of stairs and the next, sprawled a crowd of hippies, lackadaisically watched by a pair of khaki-clad *carabinieri*. At the foot of the steps were the booths of the flower sellers, then the sunlit expanse of the Piazza di Spagna. The whole near side of the square was jammed with green and black taxis, squat purpose-built cars from Fiat and Mobital, lined up hugger-mugger for fares in the space between the steps and the fountain designed by Bernini in the form of a waterlogged barge.

Most of the people in sight were tourists. Among them was a party of Englishwomen, searching for the place where John Keats died. Pointing the way to the poet's last digs, posing for snapshots and generally adding to the charm of the scene were two ceremonial guards in dark blue uniform, with swords and white straps, red cockades in their sideways-worn Napoleonic hats. Their black boots creaked and their silver scabbards clanked softly on the steps as they mounted the staircase very slowly, side by side, towards the point where Rosa sat. She wondered what they'd do when it happened. Draw swords, perhaps, and wait for the cameras to click.

Across the square, half right, at its junction with Via della Croce, was the flat belonging to Count di Rufolo. It was on the fourth floor of a tall stone building and so level with her post on the steps. Once the guards had passed her, Rosa scanned its tall windows with field glasses. All of them were shuttered except one, and that revealed nothing. The flat was in darkness. There was no movement inside it.

She lowered the binoculars and looked for Mario, easy to spot in his white linen suit as he stood at the entrance to the building. He signalled to her negatively. No one had arrived yet.

It was 1.25 by her watch.

Five minutes to go, if both parties were punctual. Vico might be late, she thought, but Carlo Guidotti would turn up on time. She waited for him, calm, but already drenched with sweat inside her loose cotton dress. The sun was hot on her neck. The glare of it beat back into her eyes from the pale porous stone of the steps. Down in the square the traffic had gradually piled up until every driver in Rome, it seemed, was blowing his horn, the noise spreading right across the city like an orchestra tuning up. The tourists held their hands to their ears and laughed in astonishment. Rosa smiled too. Noise without motion, she thought, is the problem of Italy. But we shall take care of it.

Raising the glasses, she went back to watching the square's far side. There, not so easy to see because in deep shadow, was the thoroughfare that ran left to right across the front of the old Spanish Embassy. Because of the traffic system, this was the only way Guidotti could come.

And two minutes later he appeared, exactly on schedule. As foreseen, he was not in his usual car, but a smaller one, taken from the pool at head office. Like all the company's vehicles it had a tall radio aerial, as used by the police. The windows were tinted, so the occupants could not be seen. Noticeably lower on its wheels than most Mobital Alfas, because of the armour plate, it was inching slowly forward through the pile-up, occasionally mounting the kerb with a lurch.

Rosa raised her hand in a signal to Mario, who jumped to the alert and waved in acknowledgement. She saw him tread out a cigarette and take up position. Good, she thought, Mario is steady. Then she looked back to the car. It had stopped. As she watched through the field glasses, Guidotti's two bodyguards scrambled quickly out of it and hurried ahead on foot. Ignoring Mario, they inspected the entrance to the building, then stood either side of it, scanning the square and its overlooking windows. Satisfied, they signalled back to the car, which moved quickly forward and deposited Guidotti – a flash of pale suit and silver hair, quickly gone. The car then turned left, round the corner of the building, and vanished down Via della Croce.

Mario remained at the entrance, on the look-out for Fernando Vico.

Rosa raised her glasses to the flat, four floors up, and saw the shutters opened by the bodyguards, who stood at each window in turn, looking out. One of them checked the windows commanding the square, while the other took care of the two overlooking Via della Croce, just out of her sight. As the flat's corner-room filled with light from both sides, Guidotti could be seen in the centre of it, taking off his jacket. And someone was with him. It was Vico. Yes, Vico was already there. He must have been waiting inside, perhaps on the stairs. A short man, bullet-headed, paunchy. He, too, had taken off his jacket and was pulling up chairs to a table. Guidotti poured drinks. They sat down, spreading papers between them. Rosa waited until they had settled. Then she lowered the binoculars and got to her feet, beckoning Mario towards her.

They met at the bottom of the steps, behind a flower booth. Mario didn't look so steady close up. Despite its manly beard his face was a picture of fear, off-white like his suit, glistening with sweat, eyes staring wide behind his thick tinted glasses.

"Vico's there already," she said. "Sitting pretty."

"Rosa, please. I cannot do this."

"Shut up. Let's get on with it."

"I cannot see the value of this insane risk."

"That is the reasoning of fear. It's a good risk. Now go and get your brave little kneecappers, or I'll do it for you."

Intending more discussion, he took out a cigarette and tried to light it. She knocked it from his hand.

"Go, Mario. *Go!*"

Still his feet didn't move. But he stared at her differently, first in surprise and then with dull hate. At that point she knew he would do it. She gripped his arm in encouragement. He shook her off, turned away and walked across the square, between the parked taxis, into a narrow street which lay out of sight behind the terminal lodgings of Keats.

Rosa climbed back up the steps. Just as she resumed her position, she saw a small white van cross the square and disappear right, into Via del Babuino. Now it would be pulling up to park in the first available space. The driver, a friend of theirs, would stay at the wheel, all set to drive them away when it was done, but by now the two *brigatisti*, both wearing overalls, would have got out the back and gone to work, one of them carrying a TV aerial, the other a heavy brown toolbag. Already they ought to be riding up in the lift of an unguarded building, with a duplicate key to a door at the top which opened onto the roof.

This Rosa could not see, so had to imagine, timing each step in her head. All she could see for the moment was Mario, resuming his original post, from which he would act as a link in the signal chain. He raised his hand to tell her the van was in position. Rosa immediately lifted her binoculars to the roofs on the far side of Via della Croce, directly across from and level with the windows of Count di Rufolo's flat. And there, a moment later, the two *brigatisti* appeared, conspicuous in their green overalls. Still carrying the television aerial as well as their bag, they manoeuvred awkwardly among the chimneys, then disappeared from view in a valley behind the first slope of orange pantiles.

It was not until then that Rosa panned back to the flat and saw that both guards were standing at a window on the square, staring straight at her with great concentration. She felt her heart leap. How long had they been there? Had they seen her talk to Mario and watch the roofs opposite? She dropped the binoculars into her lap. Neither man moved. Perhaps it wasn't her they were looking at. Then she knew that it was, as both men ducked back into the flat and dashed to the windows on Via della Croce.

But here, just in time, came the two brave boys of the Red Brigade, rising from the tiles of the opposite roof with bazooka assembled. One of them was resting the tube on his shoulder, eye to sight, hand on trigger, while the other crouched behind and slipped the first rocket in. Though still connecting the rocket electrically, he raised a hand to tell Rosa they were ready. Rosa could see Guidotti's guards drawing pistols, crouching to shoot, but she raised her hand to Mario, who signalled in turn to the driver of the van, preparing him to go. There was no signal for stop, but it didn't matter now, because there went the *flash-whoosh-bang* of the rocket, hitting home with a short, sharp explosion like a door slammed. Rosa saw a puff of pale dust and flying masonry, a brown cloud blossoming upwards from Via della Croce. The rocket had struck. Smoke was pouring out of the flat. It filled the windows and hid the interior, but had not quite obscured the roof opposite, so there she could see what had happened. The rocket had struck, but so had the pistols of Guidotti's guards. The bazooka slithered down the tiles as she watched, immediately followed by one of the students, who fell into the street like a sky-diver, limbs spread wide in green overalls. Perhaps he was already dead. And the other, the loader, had been caught in the back-blast. His body was suspended in the chimney pots, blackened and smouldering. Bits of debris were still falling out of the sky, clattering down all round the square, on the roofs of the cars and the heads of the people.

Then smoke hid the whole of the scene at that end.

All this had happened in seconds. Watching it, Rosa had jumped to her feet and was now standing rooted to the spot, hardly aware of the utter pandemonium in the square or the people rushing past her on the steps, staggering, screaming, climbing frantically to escape they knew not what. Her eyes were only on Mario, who could not see her signals and was scampering about at the entrance of the Via della Croce, trying to make out what had happened. Eventually he seemed to work it out. With relief Rosa saw him wave the van on its way and start to run towards her, picking his way through the chaos of stalled cars and terrified people.

Then she saw that he was being chased.

One of Guidotti's bodyguards, the smaller one, had staggered out into the square with drawn pistol. Obviously dazed, perhaps hurt, he stood lurching on his feet, then spotted his quarry and started in pursuit, shouting for people to help him.

Rosa watched the chase calmly, assessing the speed of hound and hare, then hitched her bag over her shoulder and trotted up the last flight of steps, until she was close to the top. There she turned to wait. Mario was past the first landing, where the hippies had sat, before he realised he was being pursued. But by that time he was too short of wind to climb faster. He was screeching for air when he reached her.

"Don't talk," she said without looking at him. "Keep going. Get in the car."

He went on up. Rosa backed after him, two or three more steps, then stood with one hand in her bag.

For a moment she thought it was going to be all right. Guidotti's man was nearly on his knees, climbing slower all the time as his strength gave out. Like the victim in a cartoon film, he was blackened and frayed by the explosion of the rocket. His face was running with blood, eyes rolling, mouth gaping wide as he waved his pistol and croaked unintelligibly. So far he hadn't been able to get in a shot, because of the crowd still milling about on the steps, but some of them were starting to come to his aid now. He passed her, still going upwards. Rosa turned to follow him, keeping close behind. She was still hoping that he would collapse, but near the top of the steps the crowd parted for him, he got a clear field of fire, planted his feet and aimed at Mario's back. So she shot him point-blank through the head.

7

Jack Kemble was glad to be leaving Brussels, if only to escape the girl he had left his first wife for. Her latest film was showing at half a dozen cinemas in the city. Everywhere he looked he saw her sharp white teeth and perfect little breasts, blown up to wall size. Such was the special, well deserved and altogether ludicrous torment reserved for those who lost their manhood to movie stars.

He was also escaping another girl.

Mitzi Hoff had given up surveillance of the Berlaymont and was following him out to Zaventem Airport in her old-fashioned, snub-nosed Volkswagen. There was no caution in her pursuit. At the airport she pulled up behind his taxi and walked straight into the departures hall, where she stuck close enough to see him catch a flight to Paris, with onward connection to Tours.

And Kemble became aware of her.

Turning to leave the check-in desk, he noticed her standing right behind him in the queue but could not immediately recall where he'd seen her before. He smiled at her. Mitzi smiled sweetly, boldly back. A small girl, with dark curly hair and dimples in her cheeks, wearing striped dungarees. Pretty in a milkmaidish way, with eyes that knew more than a milk-maid.

Still wondering where he had seen her before, Kemble walked away, through passport control and luggage search. Then he remembered. This was the girl who had crossed with Laura in the hotel lobby, who had sat with the two big eaters in the coffee shop. He looked back. She had gone. Waiting for the flight to be called, envisaging a little mild flirtation on the plane, he kept an eye out for her. She did not appear. She was not on the plane. For the second time Mitzi Hoff dropped from his consciousness.

The job was now top of his mind in any case, spiced up by the pleasure of the chase and a keen desire to maul Laura Jenkinson. Even his thirst had dropped to second place.

For *The Times*, it seemed, the main attraction was a chance to maul Harvey. Some old grudge was at work in the mind of the paper's new Scottish proprietor, reflected with every fine nuance in the voice of its Australian editor. On the telephone, reading out the name and address that went with the number supplied by Lady Harvey, Frank Holroyd had sounded quite vicious with excitement. His accent returned down-under in spite.

"Well done, Jack. That's the home of Harvey's oldest friend in France. But I don't think he's gone there for fun."

"No, nor do I."

"Get after him then. Blank chit for expenses, and don't be too fussy how you do it. I want to print on Monday."

A long way from Brussels now, the Mercedes was overtaking everything in sight. A year ago such speeds had terrified Harvey, but now he relaxed and left Paolo to it, pleased to pip the French on home ground.

He glanced across at Laura, curled up at his side with her mouth open. Asleep she was really quite pretty, he thought, with her dark hair falling loose and that tense little frown of ambition erased from her face. They had not had a very happy morning. Annoyed by the day's bad start, he had pushed her harder than necessary, dictating replies to every one of the papers she had brought. But now he was feeling more benign, a mood which expanded to keen expectant pleasure as he watched the spires of Chartres rise ahead.

Laura had hoped to stop in Paris. A long sulk had given way eventually to slumber. But Chartres would make her happy, Harvey thought, as it once had his wife. They had stopped here for two days and nights on their honeymoon. That had been Margaret's first visit, not his. He had come to this place in childhood, again as an undergraduate, and as often as he could in the busy years since. Even in the back of a high-speed

Mercedes he felt like a medieval pilgrim, returning to fall on his knees at the home of the Virgin on earth.

Either side of the road was a flat expanse of wheat almost ready for harvest and as the two spires reared above it, so familiar, so oddly mismatched, Harvey's mind filled with a picture of the great collective effort which had gone into rearing this mountain of stone in the plain, all the people of the town heaving carts from the quarries in a strict devotional silence, princes and paupers side by side in harness, merchants and labourers, landlords and peasants all tugging at the traces without a single sound until, at a signal, they would lift up their voices in psalms when the half-finished church came in sight. By day the dust of those stone-bearing convoys had darkened the sun, it was said. At night the plain had twinkled with their camp fires. Devout books described the building of Chartres as a miracle, but to Harvey it had more romance as a human achievement. What stirred him was the plain good organisation of these men still emerging from an age of darkness, the confidence and energy with which they had laboured to realise the fantastic vision of an unknown architect. And it pleased his down-to-earth English mind, drawn to the commonplace in mysteries, that they had a sound commercial motive as well. A good church was good business, then as now. All right, never mind. Blessed are the entrepreneurs, for they shall enrich us all.

A few minutes later they were there. Paolo had taken the car away and Laura was brushing out the creases in her suit. Uncertain where this girl stood on higher matters, Harvey kept the tone worldly as they mounted the steps to the great western entrance.

"Of course," he said, "the Church was the great power of Europe in those days. It bought the best talents and it had no frontiers. The masons just travelled round from country to country, like the priests."

"Or like us – the servants of the great Church of Berlaymont," she said in a sour voice. "That's what you're thinking, isn't it?"

"It crossed my mind."

"Do you think that's a valid comparison?"

"No, just a thought," Harvey said with an inner sag as he started to walk left to right along the carved portals. Pointing

203

out his favourite details, he led her along the famous statuary, the strange kings and queens in their elongated drapery, the shepherds herding sheep next to Aristotle bent at his writing desk. A couple of tourists tuned in to his commentary, glad to have found a free expert. But Laura trailed behind looking tired. And the sun was very hot, he noticed suddenly.

"Shall we go inside?"

She smiled as a teenager smiles at a boring old parent. "I've seen it before, you know."

"Yes, so have I."

"Why don't I go and find the restaurant? I'll meet you back here."

"That's a good idea."

Glad to be rid of her, Harvey walked into the nave and stood by himself among the huge shafts of stone splaying into the vault. He lifted his head in a sort of upward greeting, but did not expect too much in reply, his friendship with his maker having always been marked by a certain mutual diffidence. Sincerely half-hearted, content with a vague mix of symbols and literal truth, he had made a conscious effort to keep his faith alive across the years, mainly because, like his party, it sustained him with a sense of continuity. He was a conservative, he was a churchman. Doubt was a personal indulgence.

Even so, Chartres always came as a welcome refreshment. If ever he caught sight of more, it was here, in this hollow stone mountain of the French. Today, still hoping for something, he wandered about in the shadowy silence, eyes lifted to stained-glass pictures of the heavenly city kaleidoscoped with proletarian life, the butcher and the baker still at work in the windows donated by their unions. In the distance great shafts of misty sunlight slanted down between the pillars, as they might through gaps in a clouded sky, and from each far, dusky recess of the walls came a glimmer of votive candles. Human voices, human feet were reduced to a rustle on the air.

But it was no good. This morning, for Harvey, Chartres had lost its spell. His irritating secretary and his irritated wife kept plucking at his mind. Eventually he gave up and walked back to Laura at the door, feeling mildly depressed. He didn't want to have lunch with her.

At first, however, lunch went better than expected. The restaurant, in Rue de la Poissonerie, had not changed a jot in thirty years. There were the same stained beams, the same red and white chequered tablecloths. Only the waitress had altered since he'd sat here with Margaret on their honeymoon. The prices had altered too of course, but so had his salary, and today the Commission was paying expenses. Deciding, unusually, to profit from the fact, Harvey ordered vintage champagne and let Laura loose on the menu at 75 francs, one down from the best. The wine came, the food came. She brightened up.

They talked about the pleasures of France: food, wine, sun, clothes, scandal, straight roads. Laura admitted that for her the heavenly city was Paris. This in turn led to a longish discussion of the reasons why seriously, money apart, she had taken the job in Brussels. She declared a wish to do something more important with her life, still unsatisfied.

"And you," she asked then. "Why politics?"

"At the start, you mean?"

"Yes, at the start."

Harvey looked up at the ceiling, looking back in time. "I suppose it just seemed the thing to do – a thing I might be good at. I'd been a bit involved at Cambridge before the war. And after the war, of course, one felt a certain sort of missionary pull to put the world to rights. That's why I so enjoy the Berlaymont – all those cross words instead of bullets. And even the words get blunted, don't they? It's difficult to draw much blood by simultaneous interpreter."

Laura had the look of a woman with more to say, but she held it until the main course, poached turbot, and the third course, wild strawberries, had gone. They were sitting with coffee. Harvey, who only smoked on high days, had lit a small cigar, when she suddenly returned to the subject. "But don't you feel a bit disappointed in it?"

"In what?"

"United Europe."

"You mean the institutions?"

"I mean those dreary chemists on Wednesday, whining on about Korean phosphate. Cartels, quotas, subsidies, tariffs – we never seem to stop talking money."

"Ours is the money department."

"Yes, but the *level* seems so trivial. Common Market – that's a good name for it."

"Peace will always be too dull for some people," Harvey said in a colder tone. "Excitement in politics is a thing I distrust."

At that she lunged, like a fencer. "But *boredom* in politics can be dangerous too, don't you think? We've got no beliefs, that's the trouble with Europe. We live in a sort of luxurious vacuum, so people get carried away by the first breeze that blows."

Harvey half-drew on his cigar, half-puffing out again quickly, as rare smokers do. "Surely we're not so fragile as that," he said, half-frowning, half-smiling in a facial expression wholly maddening to women, as he himself half-knew.

Laura drew back, the better to lunge again. "All right," she said, "I know, some good things do get done in Brussels, and there are a few beliefs at work there. But oh, the opportunities *missed*! Every day I see them."

Harvey controlled himself, curious to see how much further she would go. "What exactly are you thinking of?"

"Well, this car thing."

"Yes?"

"It's just a plain business deal, nothing more. All we're providing is the cash."

"If those two companies fall, it will rock the whole system."

"So, let it rock. It might come out better."

Harvey's annoyance overcame his curiosity. "That is wild talk for a member of the staff," he said, "and a great deal too easy for someone whose livelihood isn't at stake. Now let's get the bill."

"I'm just *telling* you my *own* opinions. Can't I have any?"

"Of course you can, Laura. And I can disagree with them, especially when they start to sound callous. Have you ever been unemployed? No, you haven't. So let's stop this now and get on. I suggest you put a call through to Erich while I settle up."

She went off then, upset. And what was upsetting her most, Harvey saw, was that she hadn't finished saying her say. He made no point of her being a woman or even a subordinate, but disliked being lectured by a person half his age, especially after a nice French lunch. Oh, the indiscriminate seriousness of youth, he thought. They've got a view cooking on everything, and out it has to come, however half-baked. There's the generation gap.

Had he and Margaret been like that? Yes, very probably. But not with each other. Their early life together had been very largely a matter of secret shared jokes. As he paid the bill he had a sudden sharp image of her sitting across from him, not at this table but the one over there, laughing as she plucked the plastic flowers from the vase and put in some wild ones she'd gathered on the road from Rambouillet.

He squashed his cigar out in shame and annoyance. To have come here at all had been a betrayal of his wife. He should have known better.

A few minutes later he was waiting for Laura in the narrow street outside, now in shadow. But she was nowhere to be seen. Paolo turned up, still smart in his uniform, then went off to get the car. Harvey, while he waited, stood spinning a display rack of postcards. Suddenly one caught his eye. He picked it out, paid for it and put it in his pocket with a small wintry smile.

Then Laura arrived, her smart patent shoes clacking over the cobbles, and straightaway it was clear from her face, from her step, that she had had some kind of shock. She had made the call to Brussels from the Post Office, she said. "I thought it might be quicker."

"Well, what's the news?"

"Someone has just tried to kill Guidotti."

Harvey stood still in dismay. "Oh no," he said softly.

"He's hurt – Erich's not sure how badly."

"What about Clabon?"

"He's all right. He's coming."

The Mercedes appeared at the end of the street. Stepping back into it, Harvey was still wondering what to do. More information was needed. But then it turned out that Paolo Santini had the facts, having listened to Italian radio in the car during his long idle break. Yes, he said, Ambassador Guidotti had been attacked in Rome by communist assassins, who had fired on a restaurant in the Spanish Place with an anti-tank weapon supplied by the Soviet Union. Many had been injured, many killed. The Ambassador himself had survived, however. And such was the courage of this man, one of Italy's best, that despite painful injuries he had made an immediate statement to the press, requesting calm. Two of the assassins had been killed. But two others, a man and a woman, had escaped in a car. After further shooting they had fled up the Staircase of Spain and driven off into the gardens of the Villa Borghese. But now they were trapped within the city, surrounded by a very strong cordon of armed police and units of the *Squadra Anti-Commando*. There was no way they could escape . . .

"Thank you, Paolo. Let's drive on now."

For the second time Harvey refused to be stopped by news of violence. As with the picket trouble at BMG, he thought this attempt best ignored. If Guidotti could talk to the radio, he must be all right, and if he was even half-way all right, he would come to the meeting at Tours. Even so, these incidents were worrying. They showed what the companies were up against, and made a solution seem even more urgent. It was strangely bad luck they should happen today, just as both men took a step towards a merger.

As his car hurtled southwards Harvey sat thinking for some time in silence, then put the whole matter from his mind and took from his pocket the postcard he had bought. It was a quotation from the writings of Bernard of Chartres, Chancellor of the Cathedral in 1114.

> *If we can see further than the ancients, it is not because of our own strength of vision, but because we are borne up by them and carried to a great height. We are dwarfs mounted on the shoulders of giants.*

The card had been on sale in four different languages. He had almost bought the German one for Riemeck, but thought better of it, remembering that the President was in fact rather on the dwarfish side, physically speaking. Now he sat reading the English text again. Then he held it out to Laura with a smile.

"You say our society has no beliefs, Laura. Well, there is mine, more or less. So what's yours?"

"Mine?"

"Yes, yours – the new crusade. What's it going to be?"

But the telephone call to Erich had driven the subject from her mind. "I don't know," she replied with a blank, surprised stare. "I really don't know. I just see the lack, that's all." She took the postcard and read it, without any facial reaction, then handed it back at arm's length, simultaneously turning away to the window. For a while she watched the fields rush past, half-harvested, some tall with crops and some down to stubble piled with bales. Her interest appeared to be in the sunlit French countryside, but then she spoke again in a dull, tired voice.

"Perhaps the lack's in me, not the world. In any case as soon as this is over, I'm going to resign. I'm sorry, but I have to. I feel as if I hardly exist."

Harvey could think of no reply.

They drove on in silence to Tours.

8

At 2.45 John Clabon stood at the window of his office, watching cloud-shadows chase over London.

Something in the style of the room, the walls of smooth veneer or the pale recessed lighting, suggested an ocean liner. Others had said so. To him it was not a point of interest. But now he remembered the comment, since he felt like the captain of a very large ship with its engines stopped, standing alone on the bridge while thousands of tons of dead weight drifted slowly under his feet, unresponsive to any command. All hands had mutinied below. And now, God save BMG, there was trouble with the officers.

Having heard his case on the broken picket, the board had been in session without him for the last twenty minutes. This blush-saving procedure had been suggested by Michael Oppenheim, who had spoken up strongly on his behalf. But now it was over. A decision had been taken. Hearing the door of the boardroom open, Clabon turned back from the window as his Finance Director came in.

"Well, Oppie?"

Oppenheim's visage was grave. A morose man by nature, soft of speech, swift of mind, he had come from a top merchant bank. Clabon had learned to rely on his pessimism. Each of them exaggerated his nature to balance the other's, a game that had served the company well. But today there was no pretence at all in Oppenheim's doleful expression.

"No good, John, I'm afraid. I did what I could."

"You mean I'm out?"

"I'm afraid so."

Clabon began to blow up, then contained himself. After a

moment he sank carefully into the chair behind his desk. "The fools," he said quietly. "The bloody ridiculous, chicken-hearted fools. And who's taking over? Donahue, I suppose."

"No, John. I am."

"You, Oppie?"

"Yes."

Clabon absorbed this extra news slowly, staring at his colleague in silence. Then he nodded. "Well, that's something, I suppose. No, really – that's good."

Oppenheim looked down at the carpet. "They'd like you to come back in now and hear a vote of thanks."

"Oh, that's touching."

"Then they want to settle on a line for the press."

"Yes, of course. Good thinking. Well, you go ahead. I'll join you in a minute."

"I'm sorry about this, John. It's a sad day for me, as well as this company."

"That's all right. Go on now."

Clabon sat on, immobile at his desk. He felt nothing. His mind was empty. The emotion he was nearest to was laughter. He wondered if this was how a stroke felt.

Mary Williams, his secretary, was in the room now. She advanced a few paces from the door, then stood with her mouth open. Clabon saw the problem. If she spoke, she would cry. Already her cheeks were damp below her pink-winged spectacles.

"Cheer up, Mary. Worse things happen."

She tried to indicate that worse already had, then blurted it out. "The police are here."

"For me?"

She nodded at him, dumb with fright.

Immediately Clabon stood up and began to give orders, speaking with the sudden calm resolve of a man with no more to lose.

"Right, now here's what you do. Ask them to wait downstairs while we whistle up the lawyers. Get Michael Oppenheim back in here quick, then put a call through to Kohlman in Brussels and tell him what's happened. Then get my wife. I'll speak to her myself."

By early evening, some three hours after this event, no word of it had reached the château of La Maréchale, near Tours. At the local airport a car was still awaiting John Clabon, who was expected to arrive there by the next commercial flight from Paris. Meanwhile, at the château itself, Sir Patrick Harvey and Laura Jenkinson were already entertaining Ambassador Carlo Guidotti of Mobital. The three of them were seated outside on a terrace, enjoying the wine of the house, and in the absence of more dramatic news the talk was of murder in Rome.

"A great inconvenience" was all that Guidotti had to say about it, putting up one finger to touch the narrow strip of sticking plaster on his cheek. "The glass of the window fell inwards and struck me."

Mobital's chief was so busy playing the tight-lipped hero that it took some time for Harvey and Laura to extract from him any exact information about what had happened. But eventually the details came out, and they added up to a narrow escape indeed. Guidotti's bodyguards had saved him by a fraction of a second. Having spotted the students on the opposite roof, they had shot the one holding the tube of the launcher. As this youth died he squeezed the trigger, so his friend, who had fixed the electrical connections but not yet stepped to one side, was blown away by the back-blast. The rocket itself, its aim slightly lowered, went through the wall of the flat below, which was empty. Guidotti and his men were hit by flying glass, and bits of the floor came up all around them, along with a lot of heat and smoke. But they lived.

"Then one of your men was killed?" asked Harvey. "How did that happen?"

"Yes, in the *piazza*. Aldo pursued and was shot on the steps. The killers escaped, a man and a woman. Angelo can tell the details."

Guidotti's surviving guard stood a few yards off, at the edge of the terrace, a hulk of a man with a very small head. A dressing had been applied to his skull, in a clearing cut out of his negroid hair, and unlike his master he had come straight from the battle without a change of clothes. The front of his shirt was stained pink and his suit appeared to have been peppered with shot. In parts the cloth was ripped into many small holes and in other parts, mainly round the trou-

212

ser legs, scorched brown with heat. He seemed a little wounded in spirit as well. Reporting on the death of his partner in Rome, he crossed himself, then stood beside the table with a tragic expression while his master translated into English.

"In addition to Aldo and the students with the rocket, one person was killed in the square – an old woman. Some stones fell down on her head. Many others were injured in the same way." Guidotti paused for effect, putting up his hand again to the wound on his cheek, around which were many smaller scratches. "The consequence is that I was delayed for this charming evening."

As he said this he dipped his head to Laura, who was dressed up for dinner, but still very stiff and on duty. Harvey would not have been surprised to see a notebook in her lap. What an odd girl she was, he thought. Smooth on the surface, jagged inside. Broken glass in silk. He expected her to stay in the job after all, but was not going to knock himself out to persuade her. Inconvenience apart, the prospect of life without Laura had a certain attraction.

"And you were alone when it happened?" she asked. "Apart from your guards, I mean."

"Yes. My friend, the Count di Rufolo, escaped without harm."

"The radio said he was in Venice."

"In Venice, yes." Guidotti sat back in his chair and breathed a perfect ring of cigarette smoke into the still evening air. "A fortunate misunderstanding in the circumstances."

"So presumably the rocket was meant for you," Laura said, still pushing for the facts like a news reporter.

But Guidotti didn't mind. "In Italy today," he replied to her gravely, "any person of distinction is a target. We have lived with that fact for several years. It does not deflect us from our duties . . . or our pleasures." He refilled her glass and his from the slim-necked decanter, then pulled his chair closer and started to tell her how it was to be a person of distinction in Italy.

Harvey's attention wandered. The sun had dipped below the trees of the garden but its light still suffused the sky. At the foot of the unkempt lawn, cut for wild flowers not croquet, stood an avenue of huge mature chestnuts, dark against the luminous west. The trees had been planted by Louis XV's Marshal at the time he built this château for his mistress. As châteaux went, it was a small one, and Harvey had always supposed that the lady must have been past her best. The gift of such a house at modest cost, a long way from Versailles, would have been the Marshal's goodbye.

To his own mind La Maréchale was close to perfection, the loveliest human habitation that he knew or could imagine, and sitting outside it now on the raised gravel terrace which ran along the front he felt far from all human ugliness or folly, charmed almost out of the world. In such a place how could two men disagree about the manufacture of motor cars?

Still hoping that Clabon would make it for dinner, they had moved out of doors to sample the previous year's vintage, a beautiful cloudy yellow brew, the colour of fully ripened grapes on the vine and still tasting of them. The chairs they were perched on were of grey rusted iron, not painted for years. The balustrade of the terrace was cracked here and there, as though by a minor earthquake, and the whole façade of the house was in need of renovation. In English hands, money permitting, it would have got the works. But the French knew better when to leave things alone, Harvey thought, pleased to find so little changed since the last time he'd been here. The sand-coloured paint on the many-paned windows had blistered and faded even further. The magnificent wistaria which grew up the front, thick-limbed as a tree, had climbed all the way to the steep slate roof, nudging shutters and gutters out of line. Its pendulous mauve blooms still scented the air, though most of them had dropped to the gravel. Built of the pale flaking stone of the district, La Maréchale was not a small house by any modern standard, but nonetheless delicate, stylish in decay, with something intrinsically feminine in its tall, slender lines. An appropriate monument to a love affair.

Now it belonged to a Parisian businessman, who certainly had enough money to spoil it, but would not, Harvey knew. Louis Royand was good taste incarnate. And also discretion personified. He had agreed to lend the house and all its staff without asking why, enjoying the whiff of conspiracy no doubt, but also delighted to help a friend he had given up expecting to ask him for anything.

Harvey had met him in the war. For two exhausting years

they had manned the liaison line between the Free French and Churchill, who had called them into his study once and given them each a bottle of champagne, saying as he signed the label that it would have to do as a medal. Royand still kept his, undrunk. After the war he had gone into business, making money with the frightening speed that some Frenchmen achieve. But Harvey had not looked too close. Never mind how it was bought, La Maréchale had always been a happy place. He had brought his sons to stay here on two, or was it three, summer holidays. They had learned to play *boules* with the Royand boys on this same terrace. At La Maréchale they had learned to eat cheese before pudding and shake hands each morning with everyone, however long it took. They had even learned to speak a little French. Margaret had loved it all too, the picnics in the woods, the long sets of very bad tennis, the endless stream of guests, the witty quick-moving conversation and in particular evenings like this, when the bright talk faded with the day and it was enough to sit looking over the lawn to that wonderful double line of trees, the new wine glowing inside you.

Harvey felt gladdened and supported by these memories, but immediately behind them came a doubt. Perhaps he should have left La Maréchale undisturbed and set the talks in some plush new hotel. Clabon would certainly have preferred it. Guidotti too, perhaps. Pretentious menus describing dull food, elaborate cocktails, a bright blue pool beside a polluted sea – that was modern Europe, and a setting more suited to this "plain business deal", as Laura called it. His own inclination was to see the thing historically and try to bring it some grace, but maybe that was simply absurd, like dressing up dull food with a pretentious menu. He wasn't sure what to think. Increasingly, as old age approached, he felt out of touch with the charmless world fashioned from his own recent past.

And Guidotti seemed to sense this line of thought. Abruptly breaking off his conversation with Laura, before the advantage of early arrival slipped away, he said it was time for business.

Harvey smiled warily. "But this is an evening of pleasure," he said. "We can't do business until Clabon gets here."

"It is often the preliminaries to business which are the most pleasant, Sir Patrick. Also the most important." Guidotti put out his cigarette and uncrossed his knees, looking suddenly very tough indeed. "And we are still in the preliminaries, I remind you, because they have not been settled to my satisfaction. When I met your assistant in Milan, I asked for an assurance that Mobital should take the lead. I repeat that. We must be the senior partner. The name of the amalgamated group, in addition to its structure and financing, must admit our priority. Without this I cannot talk at all."

"But why should John agree to that?"

"Why should I agree to anything else?" Guidotti said in a harsh voice, dropping all deference to the social occasion. "I know the BMG figures, and I know mine. The good models, the good engineers, the good sales – they are all mine. It is not I who am the *demandeur* in this case."

"There are other things, which can't be measured in figures," said Harvey after a pause, noticing that Laura did in fact now have a notebook out on her lap. He signalled her brusquely to put it away. She did so, but missed the small extra flick of his head which meant she should leave. Still wondering how to turn the subject, he looked back to Guidotti and held his eye. "May I call you Carlo?"

"Of course. It will be easier."

"Then why are you here, Carlo? If all goes so well with you, why did you accept my invitation? For you it means risks of many kinds."

"Yes indeed." The Italian smiled ruefully and reached up to touch the plaster on his face for a third time, more theatrically still. "Let us say it was an exciting proposition. As you know, we Italians like to lead an exciting life."

"I'm sorry, but that's not enough. We shall have to try and speak more frankly."

Harvey had been as curt as he dare, but could think of no softening remark to follow. Guidotti had to be drawn off this. But how?

They sat in silence for one full minute. The sun had gone down a little further. The chestnut avenue in front of them ended in a tall iron gate wrought with the Marshal's arms. Beyond that a country road lined with poplars stretched straight and flat into the distance, towards the town of Tours. A

216

car had come into view, still about two miles away. Perhaps it was Clabon.

Guidotti must have had the same thought. As soon as he saw the car, he answered the question. "Very good, I will be honest with you. I am here because Mobital needs more money than I can raise in Italy. The funds that we require for development must come from Brussels. But European finance will be easier to arrange for a two-nation project, I understand that. And so I must consider an alliance with the British, to please you."

Harvey nodded in encouragement. "That is frank."

"But of course there is more than that. To succeed, I must also be political. I have to watch my country."

Waiting to hear what came next, Harvey saw that the car had passed a crossroads. Instead of taking the turn to the village, it had come straight on.

"As you know," Guidotti said, making a see saw motion with his forearm, "the political battle in Italy is now very bad. It could go this way, that way. I do not know who will succeed, Left or Right. But for Mobital there is a danger in either case. If the Left win, they will make us a state corporation. If the Right win, the Reds will smash the factories. Perhaps there is no escape from this. But we have a better chance, I think, if Mobital becomes an international company, with some of its branches outside Italy. That is the way to make Italians respect us and leave us alone."

Guidotti had said his piece. Harvey nodded again in thanks for his honesty, and then both of them, Laura too, watched the car advance down the avenue. It was Harvey's own Mercedes, which had been waiting at the airport. All of them thought it would be Clabon, but when Paolo hopped out and opened the door, the passenger revealed was Erich Kohlman.

The German was quickly beside them on the terrace. He nodded at Laura, shook hands with Guidotti, then hesitated, looking intently at Harvey.

"You have heard?"

"Heard what, Erich?"

"The news from BMG."

"What news?"

"Mr. Clabon is no longer chairman. He has been dismissed by his board."

They sat appalled.

"He has also been arrested," Kohlman added, glancing at each face in turn, as if their surprise might be a practical joke.

Harvey was the first to collect himself. "How do you know this?"

"His secretary called me."

"When was that?"

"Just before I left Brussels. You have heard nothing here?"

"No."

"Mr. Clabon's replacement will be here to negotiate, she told me. A man called Oppenheim."

Guidotti groaned.

But Harvey had an old habit, already exercised twice that day, of refusing to accept bad news at face value. If you checked, you often found something retrievable.

"Right," he said calmly. "We have three personal numbers for Clabon. Try them all, Erich, now, before we have dinner. The telephone is in the study, to the left of the door as you go in. If you find him, fetch me."

Kohlman went into the house, Paolo following with a suitcase. Laura disappeared to arrange things. Harvey continued to sit on the terrace with Guidotti. It was cooler now. A breeze had begun to stir the chestnuts as the long summer day slowly faded. Guidotti was the first to speak.

"Oppenheim is not good news."

"We shall see," Harvey said.

"He is a banker, not a businessman."

"Is there much difference?"

"Patrick, you know there is. I may call you that?"

"Please do."

"Oppenheim will not have the courage for this project. He will not even desire it. He supported the British attempt to leave Europe."

"Yes, he did. I remember."

"He does not even believe in free trade, this man who is coming. Last year I myself have heard him speak in favour of a state-supported motor industry, with controls on imports if necessary."

"We'll have to change his spots then," Harvey said, still thinking only of Clabon: the achievements thrown away, the knighthood that would now never be. A boss who liked his workers more than most, but also felt free to despise them, because he had risen from their ranks. A characteristic fall, therefore. But sad. A great loss. And terribly timed. What next? Oppenheim. Bad news indeed.

Guidotti lit another cigarette. "Poor John. He had courage, but no wisdom. For a bull the odds in the ring are not good."

"He's not dead."

"No, not dead – except in business."

"And I wouldn't count on that either. He'll be back," Harvey said, starting up expectantly as Kohlman returned to the terrace. "Any luck?"

But none of the numbers had answered.

"What, none of them?"

Kohlman shook his head. "They ring, but don't answer."

"That's odd."

"Perhaps he is dead after all," Guidotti said.

Harvey felt a sudden sharp need to be alone. Asking Guidotti to show Kohlman round the house, he sent them both off while he took a last stroll on the terrace. Disappointment had brought tiredness. I am a long way past my best, he thought. Getting old, beyond refreshment.

On the roof of the stables a familiar clock chimed seven. His feet fell in step with the repeated tinny note. Turning at the end, he looked back down the long stretch of gravel and saw four small boys, two English, two French, arguing over a game of *boules*.

Then the telephone rang in the house.

Hope rising instantly, he hurried inside and reached the open door of the study in time to see Laura take the call. As agreed, she spoke in French. All incoming calls were first to be taken by her or the housekeeper.

"*Allo? Allo?*"

She repeated the word several times, then seemed to get an answer. She stiffened all over. For a short moment longer she continued to listen, then turned to face him with a shrug.

"No one there," she said, starting to put the receiver back.

"Wait. Let me." Harvey took it. "Hello," he said, English fashion. "Hello?"

There was no reply, and yet the line was definitely live. The silence on it had a sinister quality of breath held. Harvey kept listening, until he heard a click, followed by deeper silence. He turned in puzzlement to Laura.

Two spots of colour had appeared in her cheeks. Her eyes were wide.

9

Both of them.

Beautiful.

Kemble rang off with a twitch of vengeful pleasure, somewhere low down and not unlike sex. Still undecided how to take the castle, he had kept his mouth shut except for a quick French *allo*, to hold her on the line. Had she recognised his voice? Yes, she might have, but couldn't have heard enough to be sure. Hoping to have spoiled her sleep, no more, he withdrew his head from the plastic bubble of the phone booth and returned to the strange companion he had picked up in Tours.

Waiting on the bar were two glasses of Pernod. He splashed water into his own and stooped to watch the chemical change.

"Hal, my friend, this is a very mean potion. What's it made of?"

"Lizard's balls, man."

"That why it turns white?"

"You got it. A seminal reaction."

"Up yours then."

They clinked their glasses and drained them.

Kemble slammed his on the counter with a tortured grimace. "That is a *mother* of a drink," he said, then swivelled on his stool to gaze in dumb shock at the Café Univers.

The coincidence was that he had been here before, a very long time ago, hiking south to the sun with an early girlfriend. They had dawdled in Tours for several days, he remembered, detained by nothing more than the pleasure of sitting in this very place. In those days the Univers had been the heart of the town, a typical wooden-floored old barrack of a café, murky with smoke and packed to the walls with citizens talking their

221

throats dry, for or against French Algeria. In sunshine its tables had spread across the pavement under the trees, waiters in white shirts and tight black waistcoats weaving between them with tin trays held high, and at night the best place to be was a big room behind where old men in berets played pocketless billiards, cannoning on round the worn green felt in incredible breaks.

Now it was a branch of Las Vegas, with fruit machines and rodeo decor, wall-to-wall carpet and thumping music. The billiards had gone, and the customers too. Apart from a man with red hair, drinking beer by himself in a corner, there was only a bunch of local *jeunesse* sucking milk shakes in the din. The waitresses were wearing stetsons.

That was the French for you, Kemble thought. Either they left things alone or they vandalised them totally, whereas the British liked to tinker with everything, just enough to spoil. Hard to say which was worse.

He felt suddenly homesick. Mock America, America mocked, made him miss the real thing. Nothing was easy here, nothing was simple, quick or cheap. *Le snack* in this bar was *un rip-off*.

"Hal," he said, "the Universe has changed. Let's go find another."

"Right on, man. Take your poison and away we shall go."

"Where to?"

"There's a place across the river. French tail, cheapee, cheapee."

Reminded now of Saigon, Kemble turned round to find two more Pernods. This time they were doubles. And in the same moment, glancing up, he caught a quick exchange of sly smiles between his free-spending, high-talking companion at the bar and the solitary man drinking beer in the corner.

This annoyed him. He left his glass where it was. "Enough liquorice for me," he said. "Drink it yourself."

Hal Fawcett did so without a blink. First one glass, then the other was tipped down his throat without the aid of water.

Kemble watched him with new dislike. Now that he knew this American fool was trying to get him drunk, he was not so amused by him. What was going on here? Who were these two?

The man in the corner had wavy red hair and a thin freckled face with an unloved, unloving expression. He had kept his distance, but Kemble had the definite impression that he was English. His beer was, certainly.

As to the dispenser of Pernods, he was the sort of American that made you glad to be in Europe. A lanky Californian in his late thirties, built for football but playing Bohemian, Hal Fawcett had long yellow hair to his shoulders and a straggling yellow moustache that curled on down to his chin. Suspended round his neck were bits of African and Indian gear, strings of dried beans and a ju-ju of lion pelt, leather thongs, Cherokee beadwork. More things were hanging from his wide leather belt. Keys, chains, timepiece, cigarette lighter and coke-sniffing spoon clinked and rattled round his waist when he moved. In this hot weather he was wearing a very old combat jacket, US Army, but sewn to its sleeves were circular patches with the fork of Mars reversed, the anti-nuclear symbol.

To Kemble there was something false, something studied in this heavily dated style. Sensing a guilty secret behind the fast talk and weak doped eyes, he was next to certain that this American-in-France was a Vietnam deserter, still on the lam for some reason or other. But if that was so, Hal Fawcett was not short of funds. He had thousand-franc notes to burn, and his car, when they walked out to find it, turned out to be a big Peugeot station-wagon of the largest and latest type, maroon in colour, not clean but nearly new. Its interior had that new-car smell. On the other hand it had been driven hard and far, this car, in its brief life since leaving the showroom. Six thousand kilometres were already on the clock, Kemble noticed as he was driven off to another bar some distance out of town, across the River Loire.

Having no desire for more French drink, and even less for French tail, he went along from plain curiosity. Who were these fellows who had picked him up in Tours? What was their game?

The questions hung in his mind unanswered.

Perhaps they were some rival outfit of the press – the underground press, from the look of them – who made a habit of dogging professional newsmen to see what turned up.

Then he noticed something else. In the back of Hal Fawcett's car was a trunk, or rather, on closer inspection, a big wooden box, more long than broad, with strong rope handles either end. It had been painted black in a slapdash fashion, but glimpses of stencilled yellow lettering showed through, and patches of dull olive-green. Kemble immediately recognised a small-arms crate of the US Army.

So the guy was a gun-runner.

No, wrong. Fool he might be, but even Fawcett wouldn't use a box as obvious as that. He was just keeping his shirts in it. There was a kind of freak who liked to boast that before becoming converted to peace he had been in a real, killing war. Like the born-again Christian, the reformed alcoholic, he held up his previous sins for display. Of course, yes, that was Fawcett.

Or, perhaps a gun-runner.

10

The proletariat has no fatherland, it had to be admitted, was bunk. Pure theory, at least. The fact was the opposite. Nothing worked the people up like nationalism, Rosa thought, and it made silly monkeys of most intellectuals too. Look at me. All I want now is to get out of this hateful country and back to my own. And look at the master of theory out there, the famous priest of universal brotherhood. All the fool can do is weep in his beard because he is leaving home soil.

Poor old Mario, he was in a bad state. He had hardly said a word all the way. Even on the mad drive away from the steps, with the *carabinieri* loosing off shots behind, he'd done nothing but whimper half-audible exclamations and call out the name of his wife – *"Che fare, oh Dio, Francesca"* – the same words over and over, just whimpering in panic and driving too fast in his stupid sporty car with the stripes down the side, going no-where, tyres screeching, up hill and down dale through the Borghese Gardens, until she herself had thought what to do and yelled at him to head for the nearest known address of a Red Brigade.

And that had been a good idea. Not everyone here was a fop and a bungler. In fact it was astonishing to see how tough the Italian Reds were, how well organised and practised in subterfuge, like a wartime resistance movement. No needless questions had been asked. Every decision required had been taken in minutes and put into action by fast-moving, matter-of-fact people. She had never even caught their names, but one of them had taken off the car to dump it on a road leading out to the airport while another drove them straight to the railway station, telling her exactly what to do in rapid calm French since Mario was speechless with shock.

"Get on a train," he had told her. "Now, immediately. Any train; going anywhere, doesn't matter where. Just get out of Rome. Then ring us at this number when you're clear. If you're travelling in the wrong direction, get off at the first main stop and we'll work out a route from there."

She had taken the advice without hesitation. It had always been Joop's advice, too. "If you ever have to run," he had said, "use a train or a boat. It's the roads and the airports they watch."

So trains it had been all the long afternoon, first north to Viterbo, then back to the main western line at Civitavecchia, change, again north to Grosseto, where another Red was waiting with money and instructions, then away on this overnight express from Naples to Paris, a long silver beauty of a continental train travelling fast up the Mediterranean coast in the pearly evening, through the crowded resorts of Viareggio, La Spezia, Sestri, Rapallo, about to stop at Genoa any minute now, then on to the border with France.

Mario stood in the corridor watching his homeland flash by, the beaches planted with coloured umbrellas and the brown sandy people packing up for the day, the pollarded palms along the tessellated promenades and the flat sea beyond with the sun dropping into it. His white suit was rumpled, stained with sweat below the armpits, and something in his motionless posture, the sag of head and shoulders, suggested such abject despair that Rosa was frightened it might be noticed. She glanced round the four other passengers on the seats of the cheap-class compartment, but all were asleep or otherwise occupied. None had shown any curiosity. The danger would come from now on, she thought, when people would have seen an evening paper or the television news. In Genoa some luck would be needed. So far their luck had been good, but they had not relied on it. At each stop since Rome, however small, they had put their heads out of the window and watched for boarding police. Between stops, just to be sure, they had taken turns to stand in the corridor, so as not to get surprised by a search on the train. Mario had been on guard since Pisa, but was showing no wish to sit down. She would leave him to brood a while longer.

Poor man, he had cause. By now the police would be tearing up that clean white flat of his and grilling his pretty child-wife, to whom he could not go back. Two of his students, assassins though they were, were dead because of him. In effect Mario's life, too, was over. It was impossible not to feel sorry for him. Even so, Rosa thought, he had better buck up when the train got to Genoa.

Her own mood surprised her: this clear-sighted calmness which action had brought. It had started from the moment the rocket went off and had lasted intact through the day, except for sudden collapses into sleep. An uncontrollable drooping of the eyelids, a forward drop of the head into senselessness – that had happened three or four times in the afternoon of train travel. But each time she woke to the same fact, cold and clear. She had killed a man, and she had done it in front of so many people that now it could only be a question of time, a day, perhaps hours, before she was hunted by name. Therefore her old life was over. Her flat in St. Germain, the bookshop, her unpolitical friends, all the pleasures of ordinary existence in Paris – there was no going back to any of that. From now on, like Joop, perhaps with him, she would have to live on the run, and at the end there was nothing to look for but a prison cell or a police bullet, at best a long exile like Trotsky's, years cooped up with other western renegades in some dismally boring foreign state.

All this she saw, at first with no feeling at all. But now, on this faster train, her spirit was lifting as Mario's declined. It was odd. She couldn't help it. She felt carried forward by the force of events, and simplified. The explosions of the morning had stripped her life clean of every complication. Childish fears, intellectual doubts, self-serving calculations, unnecessary ties – all blown away with a bang. Now there was only the Iskra, for which she could burn like a beam of concentrated light. Her mood was one of hopeless joy. Despair and elation, she felt them both equally, without contradiction, as the fast electric train rocked beneath her, rushing on to France with a power that nothing could impede. She was damned, she was blessed, she was unstoppable. She had squeezed her finger and down he had gone, bang, just like that, so easy, the blood splashing out of his head on the steps as she held off the people and backed towards the car parked under the church.

Yes, there would be, wouldn't there? Always and every-where, a church looking down. And inside it, no doubt, the same sepulchral gloom: cold marble, polished pine, the starchy crackle of a nun bending close. Lower your head, Rosa. Close your eyes . . .

Again she dropped into deep black slumber. But almost immediately her head jerked upright at a change in the rhythm of the train. It was slowing. Tall blocks of flats had appeared either side of the line, ships' funnels, dockside cranes etched sharp against the sunset. Genoa. She blinked and stood up, hitched her bag over her shoulder, then walked out to join Mario in the corridor, feeling for her gun and spare passport. She had a better chance than he did. Mario had no false papers to show, only his normal ID card. By this time his name and description must have been broadcast. He had turned up his collar to hide his beard and had put his mauve glasses in his pocket, but this was hardly a disguise. Genoa, for Mario, was going to be dangerous. And what a typically cruel joke of fate it was to place the test here, in the town where his father's father, an early believer in workers' cooperatives, had been thumped to death by a Fascist patrol. Was Mario thinking of that? No, probably not. She put her arm round his waist and squeezed it.

"All right?"

"Yes," he said.

"Genoa."

"Yes."

"From here they start checking for the border. So now we get off."

"Yes."

"Your friends will be under the clock in the station con-course. Will you recognise them?"

He shrugged apathetically. "Perhaps, perhaps not. It de-pends who comes."

"Well, try to be steady now. We should be all right."

"Rosa, I have something to tell you."

"Yes, I can see that. Not now, though. Let's get out of here first."

The red sky of evening slowly disappeared as the train rolled into a cavernous station. They moved down the corridor to a door of the carriage, and then, leaning out, Rosa saw straight-away that they were in trouble. The border officials, about to get on for a passport check, were wearing flak jackets. And bunched at either end of the platform, ready to work through the train to its middle, were soldiers with submachine-guns. That meant another armed party at the platform's ticket-barrier, perhaps a full document check for passengers getting off at Genoa. But better to try the barrier, Rosa thought; better to keep moving and mingle with the crowd, hope that tickets only would be required. Her mind was made up by the time the train stopped. She stepped down to the platform. Mario followed, unaware of the danger. Together they joined the throng walking down towards the ticket-barrier, at which more uniforms were instantly visible. But before they had gone much distance they were stopped by a girl coming up the other way, towards them, against the tide of people. A small girl, quite young, well dressed, very calm. *Brigatista*.

"Wait," she said, speaking Italian. "Pretend you've forgotten something. Go back. I'll follow you. Don't rush."

They got back on the train.

The girl followed them into the coach. Immediately she crossed to its other side, slid down the window of a door and put her head out very carefully, inch by inch, until she could look up and down the railway track itself, in the narrow gap between their train and the next. She turned back inside and spoke to them softly.

"Four men watching. One at either end, and two in the middle, about twenty metres away. Move when I do. Don't stop for anything."

She opened the door a few inches, then held it, ready to push it fully open and jump. Rosa and Mario stood close behind her. As she waited to go, the girl peered back across her shoulder towards the platform they had left, from which the next instant came a very loud bang, reverberating right through the station.

Rosa had not been expecting it. She jumped nearly out of her skin. Mario actually yelped. On the platform people screamed and scurried in panic, fell flat with their hands round their heads. But the girl already had her head out the other way, peeping up and down the gap between the trains to see if the four men watching had been distracted. "Don't worry, just a firework," she muttered, still glancing up and down, her head further out, and then she was gone. She had pushed the door open and dropped to the black oily gravel of the track. They jumped out after her. The girl took the time to reach up and close the door behind her, then she crouched down double and led the way under the wheels of the neighbouring train, to the platform beyond it. As they climbed out the other side, people reached down to help them, asking what had happened.

"Terrorists!" the girl cried. "Quick, they've got a bomb!"

Carried almost bodily from the station by the consequent stampede, Rosa laughed aloud for sheer happiness. And a few minutes later, riding fast out of Genoa in a car full of jubilant friends, even Mario managed to smile.

Then the girl, who was driving, took out an evening paper and passed it across. On the front page was a picture of Carlo Guidotti, addressing the press after treatment for cuts.

Rosa stared at it and nodded, without surprise. "His men shot first," she said in a flat voice, "so the rocket's aim was spoiled. It went too low, I think."

"Still, that was close," said the girl.

"Yes, close."

Rosa's chest heaved and fell in a single deep breath, in and out, as if for a doctor's stethoscope. She passed the newspaper to Mario. She had spoken in French, and it was in French that the girl of the Red Brigade now spoke back, one hand on the wheel, the other clenched into a fist, her teeth flashing into a fierce, vivid smile.

"Leave Carlo Guidotti to us," she said. "We shall get him another day. And now, Comrade Berg, I shall take you to France. We are going to meet your friend Yoppo."

Two hours later, not long before midnight, the Iskra's flight from Italy was almost accomplished. Rosa Berg and Mario Salandra were alone again, finishing their journey on foot by the light of a clear and nearly full moon. The path they were on led up a steep hillside above the Mediterranean coast, between Ventimiglia and Menton. Down to their left was the sea, up to their right were higher hills. The border with France lay half a mile ahead.

The bold girl from Genoa had brought them as far as she could, then turned her car round and driven away with a short staccato fanfare of her horn, like a bugle call. They had watched her lights zig-zag downwards, and then she was gone, a spark drawn back into the bright stream of traffic on the coastal *autoroute*. She had left them to finish the journey on their own, but all her instructions were good. For twenty minutes afterwards they had climbed the rocky slope in silence, keeping without any difficulty to the path she had marked on the map. Now, however, Rosa wished she could call the girl back. Although she had been expecting it for the most of the day, the crisis between herself and Mario had come so late, so suddenly that it had caught her unawares. She could not think what to do or say.

"Mario, please."

"No, I cannot. Leave me here. You go on."

"But you can't just take to the hills."

"No, of course not. I shall go back. This is my country, Rosa. My friends are here, also my family."

"And what about your enemies?"

"Them too. For me the fight is in Italy, nowhere else."

"That is stupid nonsense. The fight is also in Britain and France, it is all over Europe. I have heard you say so yourself many times."

"But my own task is here."

"No, it is not." Rosa's voice thickened as she grew more angry, its note turning hoarse and guttural like a man's. "The Iskra has decided collectively to take this action. None of us has the individual right to put it at risk. In Italy now your face is on TV, in the papers. If you stay, you will be caught – within a few days, perhaps hours. And then you will be questioned. I cannot allow that."

The night was shrill with crickets. The ground still radiated heat, although they were quite high up now, and had reached the limit of cultivation. Around them grew a few stunted olives and vines, where the earth had been hacked into shallow, ragged terraces. Immediately below and behind them was the last of the farmhouses, two of its windows still lit. A dog had started to bark there. In front there was only scrub, rising steeply to a ridge of bare rock. The path twisted up it, white in the moonlight, its dust scuffed with mule tracks.

And Mario had stopped like a mule. In front when it happened, Rosa had now come back to where he stood. Eye to eye, they argued in tense subdued voices, so as not to excite the dog, which was leaping about on a chain at the farmhouse. She took his arm. He pulled himself loose.

"My friends will protect me," he said, turning downwards. "I shall walk back until I find a telephone, then call them to fetch me."

"No, you will not."

"So, you will prevent me, Rosa, will you? And how will you do that?" Mario's voice rose on the question, setting off the dog again, and then he stepped back up towards her in a sudden little rush, gesticulating wildly, almost shouting. "You will shoot me, is that it? Oh yes, I think that would be very easy for you, just like this morning. And for me, perhaps best. Go ahead then. Shoot, shoot!"

He held his arms wide, then spun away from her and sat on a rock, head bowed for execution.

Rosa had not thought of killing him till then . . . or had her hand gone to her bag before he spoke? She wasn't sure. In either case it was there now, angrily clamped round the butt of her CZ50. But the pistol remained in her bag. She withdrew her hand, embarrassed, then sat down at Mario's side on the rock and waited for the dog to settle, noticing suddenly how fine the view was.

Inland rose the foothills of the Maritime Alps, dark against a sky full of stars. Spread along the coast far below were the lights of Ventimiglia and Menton, the *autoroute*, the railway, a train travelling fast into France with all its windows glowing like a miniature electrical toy. Beyond and below that again was the sea, shining silver in the moonlight. The border itself, she thought, must run along the line of the ridge ahead, beyond which Joop would be waiting. There was so little further to go. Italy and all its bloody nightmares were almost behind her. Now this.

When the dog quietened down at a shout from the farmer, she took Mario's hand in her own. "That is a mad way to talk," she said to him softly. Then she laughed. "And not very kind, I must say. After all, the only reason I shot a man this morning was to stop him shooting you."

He nodded in acknowledgement, but without any gratitude. The reaction so annoyed her that it instantly threw up an image of his head jerking forward with the force of a bullet, blood spouting. Shocked that such a thing should come into her mind, Rosa suppressed it in fright and kept talking.

"It is their job to kill us," she said with a wave back to Italy and all the many forces of pursuit. "Ours is to survive, and finish this thing if we can. Our lives have no other purpose. Can you think of one? Can you tell me why else we have existed in the world?"

"I have a wife, Rosa."

This she had expected, all the way from Rome. Her answer came prepared. "Yes, there is Francesca. But how will it help her if you return? If she conceals you, she will get caught, and then she will go to prison for months, perhaps even years. Is that what you want?"

He shook his head miserably, still slumped in the same position on the rock. Urging him back into motion, Rosa squeezed his hand, smoothed it and patted it.

"In France you will not be so easy to catch, *caro*. We have a place prepared, you will see. Stay with us until this is over. It can make things no worse for you, can it? And when the job is done, we shall find a safe refuge. Then, if you wish, you can ask your wife to join you."

"I want no more blood."

"I agree. We must find another way."

Immediately Rosa regretted this promise. To blur it, she stepped quickly back into the path and stood waiting.

Mario raised his head at last, and then, in a gesture of exasperation which had come all the way from Rome, he stuck his chin up in the air and waved his right hand in a series of quick, jerky stabs at the rocky hills around. "But we are lost," he blurted out, setting off the dog one more time. "Lost! Lost! Lost! How can we go on?"

Rosa knew then that he would come.

"No, we're not lost," she said. "Just a little more climbing to do."

11

Harvey woke suddenly and stared at the canopy over his bed. A yellowish light was playing across the silk draperies. It swooped round the walls of the room, then went out.

A torch, at this hour?

He lay still and listened, his heart beating faster than it should. Perhaps it was Guidotti's thug, he thought, on a night patrol of the grounds. But no voice or movement came from outside. Only the chestnuts in the avenue were stirring: a sound like the sea below cliffs. Much closer, like very soft blows of a hammer, the old stable clock ticked on towards midnight.

There seemed to be no cause for fear, and yet he was filled with a vague sense of menace, which any small thing could now stir to life. In the back of his mind, discussed with no one, a sinister pattern had begun to take shape. An attempt to kill Guidotti, on this day of all days? John Clabon toppled by a violent labour quarrel, on this day of all days? The timing was either pure coincidence or very alarming indeed. He wondered if anyone else had spotted it.

He sat up abruptly as the light came back, playing full on the windows, brilliant yellow. But with it now came the noise of tyres on gravel, the powerful throb of a turbo-charged motor. The car pulled up with its engine running. A door was opened, then shut with a bang.

Harvey swung his feet to the floor and moved to the window. A man was striding through the beam of the headlights towards the terrace steps. It was John Clabon.

"John?"

"Ah, Patrick, there you are. My God, you tuck yourself away, don't you? I've been looking for this place for hours."

"Hold on. I'll let you in."

As he put on a dressing-gown and hurried downstairs, Harvey wondered whether to ask for explanations. It was often better not to. On the other hand he had to know on what basis Clabon was here.

"We heard you had some trouble," he said, pouring brandy.

Clabon sat heavily, the fragile glass clamped in one ginger-haired fist. His face was discoloured and swollen, like a boxer's after the fight. "Trouble? Oh boy," he said. "Got to Paris all right, late flight, but missed the last connection to Tours, so had to borrow that thing outside from our agent. Damn it, the man drives a Peugeot. I should have fired him on the spot."

"I meant trouble with your board."

"Oh, that. Yes, well, it held me up a while. But that's all finished." He wrenched down his tie and loosened his shirt. "Where do I sleep?"

"Finished in what sense?"

"What's that to you?"

"Nothing at all," replied Harvey evenly. "Unless, of course, it affects your power to negotiate."

At that Clabon dropped the attempt at breezy normality. He said nothing for a while. His eyes were staring grimly at some remembered scene in his head. He had not even noticed the magnificent *salon* in which they were sitting, a tall panelled room, milky grey and gilt, with several fine impressionist paintings on the walls and Winston Churchill's bottle of Pol Roger set in an alcove.

Harvey walked across to the door and closed it, hearing movement upstairs. "Come on, John, I need to know. Did your board dismiss you or not?"

Clabon nodded wearily, one hand still holding his drink, the other clenched in a tight ball against his forehead. "Yes," he said, "they did, the treacherous bastards. Can you imagine? All of them, even old Oppenheim, were in that boardroom, just sitting there waiting for me to tell them how to put it to the press." He leaned back with a sigh, eyes closed. Then the fist unclenched from his forehead and dropped to the arm of the chair. He opened his eyes and smiled. "That was how we were when the law arrived."

235

"The police?"

"Yes, bless them."

"We heard you'd been arrested."

"No, false alarm. They'd put it together by that time. That picket was bust by the Reds, as I'd said all along." Clabon sat up again, his free hand held out. "Imagine that, Patrick. Running down your own side with a forty-ton Volvo, just to put the boss in a bind."

"Yes, I've been thinking about it."

"Well, there you are. It was done by the Trotskyites to frame me. They're hoping to bring the whole house down, you see, so they can take over the ruins. And they don't mind losing a few of their own kind to do it. But it was too much for one of them, I'm glad to say. He turned himself in to the cops and squealed."

Clabon sat back again, his face set into an expression of numbed recollection: the soldier back from the front. He looked ready for bed. But Harvey now pulled up a chair and sat down himself.

"Who were they then, these people?"

"That's not so clear. So far the only name we have is a man called Murdoch, our leading resident Trot. He organised the getaway with two of his comrades, IWA men from London. But one of them grassed on him, so now Murdoch's done a bunk himself. The law found his car at Luton Airport. They think he belongs to some terrorist outfit in Europe."

"The Iskra?"

"Yes, that's right." Clabon looked at Harvey in surprise. "So you know about it?"

Harvey shook his head. "Only what you told Erich Kohlman at Ash Valley. The odd thing is that Guidotti thinks he was attacked in Rome by an organisation of that name."

"Really? They're probably Italian then. Typical. How is Carlo, anyway?"

"All right. Just a scratch or two."

"And making the most of it, I bet."

Harvey's nod, and the smile that went with it, were almost too small to be seen. "He was telling us about it at dinner. An international gang, he says, led by a Frenchwoman."

"A woman," Clabon said with more interest. "Yes, that's what Special Branch think. I hadn't heard she was French."

"That's Carlo's own theory. He believes the gang is run from France but aimed specifically at Mobital."

"They're certainly aimed at BMG."

"So it would seem," said Harvey slowly, frowning at the hunting scene woven in the carpet. "A violent international Marxist gang, then, aimed at both your companies. I think you two had better put your heads together."

Clabon nodded, but wearily, unable to grasp another problem that day, or maybe unwilling to share one with Guidotti. "They could be after the whole motor industry, I suppose. Soft underbelly of the system and so on. They must have had someone in Rotterdam, for a start, to have known that lorry was coming."

"What worries me is they may know about these talks."

Harvey dropped this suggestion in a quiet voice, undramatic, yet charged with the utmost seriousness. There was a pause. Then Clabon looked up at him, reacting slowly.

"Do you have any evidence for that?"

"No, not really. Just the timing. I mean here you both are with your heads broken, walking wounded before we even start."

Another pause; then Clabon waved his hand dismissively. "Business is war, Patrick. Happens all the time. Especially in Italy, and increasingly, alas, *chez nous*."

"But both of you? Attacked by the same bunch of people, just as you try to get together?"

"Coincidence."

"A rum one."

A third and longer pause, while Clabon frowned in thought. Then he shook his head. "No, Patrick, this is just bad dreams. Come on, I'll tuck you up with a pill." He drank the rest of his brandy and got to his feet.

"You're probably right." Harvey stood up himself. "It's just that almost anything seems possible these days. I'm getting rather old for the times, I'm afraid."

"You'll do," Clabon said with a cheerful grin, picking up his suitcase and starting to the door. Then he stopped, the grin wiped away by doubt. "How many people have you told about this?"

"Just my own staff, and Riemeck of course." Harvey made no mention of Doublett. "What about you?"

"My secretary knows. And Oppenheim may have smelled a rat. Talking of rats, *The Times* have been nibbling round too."

"Yes, I know," Harvey said with a rueful nod. "Frank Holroyd tried to catch me for a comment in Brussels this morning. I'm afraid my girl may have been rather rude to him."

"Oh, deary-me. Poor Frank." Clabon's battered face broke into a school bully's grin, then to Harvey's surprise he reached out and whacked his former Prime Minister on the shoulder. "Well, old chap, you've got us here."

"Yes. Just."

"So what's the programme?"

"Jaw, jaw." Harvey's smile was a schoolmaster's. "No more black eyes, I hope."

"There's a lot to cover."

"There is indeed. So we'll start at eight."

"Do you think it can be done?"

"We're here because it can. But only so long as you keep your temper, John."

"The group's survival is at stake, you realise. Not to mention my own."

"I do realise. But there's something that you must understand too."

"What's that?"

"I'm not here as an Englishman."

Clabon nodded. "No favours, you mean."

"No favours. My allegiance is to European money and European jobs."

"Money and jobs. Well, I'll drink to that. But first sleep."

"Yes, sleep. I agree. Follow me then."

Harvey switched off the light. He had in fact decided to do one more thing before going back to his bed, but first he wanted Clabon out of the way.

They groped into the hall. Somewhere upstairs they heard feet retreating, then a door shut.

"The housekeeper," Harvey said softly. "Better make it up to her in the morning or we'll get slung out."

He tried to find another switch, but couldn't, so led the way up the central staircase by moonlight.

"Holy Moses," shouted Clabon, half-way up. "Where *did* you get this place?"

"*Shh*," replied Harvey, one finger to his lips. "*Des amis français — très riches, très discrets.*"

Clabon stared into the château's upper darkness. "Lead on then," he said in a barely lower voice. "And for God's sake try to speak English, even if you aren't. No wonder we keep seeing bogies."

Saturday

1

Soon after midnight Rosa had the feeling that she was in France.

There was no fence, but she reckoned the frontier must run along the ridge, which dropped sharply leftward into the sea. The *autoroute* and railway passed underneath it in tunnels.

At the top of the ridge they paused to rest, but she kept on her feet, showing off more to herself than to Mario. She had strength in reserve, but was not sure how much she would need in the days ahead. Had they done enough to stop the merger, she wondered, or to delay it at least? In Italy, surely, they had caused enough shock and confusion to keep Guidotti tied down. But what about John Clabon? What had happened in England? Soon she would know. Eager for news, relieved to be in France, she hurried on over the top of the ridge.

Ventimiglia disappeared behind, the lights of Menton emerged below, and after that everything was easier. A breeze had come up from the west: the piney, herby breath of Provence. Rosa felt it play on the dampness of her face as she slithered down over the ridge's bare rock and then on down further, through the spiky *maquis* of the lower slopes. Mario came behind gasping. The breeze diminished as they came off the heights, the scrub grew thicker, and then they were out of it, scrambling quickly down a dry white streambed in the moonlight. Eventually they reached a dirt track. They walked along the track leftwards until it joined a tarmac road, and there, at the intersection, stood a blue-lettered sign of shiny enamel embedded in a squat concrete arrow. Now they were certainly in France.

Rosa led the way down the road, Mario shuffled behind. Her

own feet, flapping on the tarmac in sandals, were almost too sore to put down. They walked along in slow, tired tandem under the bright, white glare of the moon. Crickets were bleeping all round them, but otherwise the night was still. They seemed to be quite alone. But then they came round a bend and there was the car, parked on the road, a short way ahead of them.

Joop Janssen flashed the lights, once, twice, then got out to greet them. Rosa walked up to him, lengthening her stride but not rushing. She put her arms round him and held him very tight, her face pressed into his chest. Joop raised his hands to her shoulders with a slight answering pressure, not moving or speaking till she did. Mario stood patiently by. Then Rosa lifted her head and smiled at each of them in turn, the smiles broke into soft laughter, a few quiet words. Mario shook hands with Joop. They got in the car and drove down to Menton.

Mario, slumped in the back, was instantly asleep. Rosa sat in front, her legs aching painfully. Having told her story, she made Joop tell his, in detail and from the beginning, all that had happened since their parting on the quayside in Holland. He reported the facts in his fluent toneless French, without any comment, but she caught a note of resentment when he told how the picket attacked the truck at Ash Valley. Nothing in the Iskra's instructions, he said, had prepared him for such fierce resistance, so the moment of crisis had left him no choice.

"I could only go forward, through the men. I could not stop."

"Of course," she said. "It was not your fault."

"You intended such injuries?"

"No, we intended an effect. And that you achieved. We heard on the radio that Clabon is getting the blame. It will take him a week to extract himself, at least – don't you think so?"

"Perhaps," said Joop. "We shall see."

He went on with his story. The resistance of the picket was the first surprise, he said. Then came a second. When he ran from the factory, he found a car waiting, just as arranged, but Stephen Murdoch wasn't in it. Waiting instead were two total strangers, who turned out later to be members of the Industrial Workers' Alliance, brought up from London for the purpose. For the dash from Ash Valley they used a stolen car, which they dumped in a quiet street of Coventry. They joined up with

Murdoch on the edge of town, then the four of them had driven off together, down the motorway to London, using Murdoch's own car. That was when the trouble began. Murdoch's car had a radio. Soon news came through of the casualties to the picket, then a death was reported from the hospital. The IWA men got upset. They accused the Iskra of murder. But most of their fury fell on Murdoch. They said he had tricked them. The IWA had not been created to kill the working class, they said, swearing and shouting at him from the back seat. Murdoch kept flinching and turning his head, expecting a blow from behind, and violence was close at that point. As more news came through from the hospital, an amputation, a second death, the IWA men became inarticulate. One of them was crying. The other screamed abuse. But there was no hitting. After a while they conferred in agitated whispers, and then came up with a statement. They wished to dissociate themselves from what had occurred, they said in a formal way, and the organisation would take no responsibility either. Murdoch must quit the IWA, immediately and for ever, or they would see that his action was exposed. Meanwhile they wished to be taken to the nearest rail station.

"So we dropped them in Bedford. They took a train from there."

"That was kind of you," Rosa said sharply.

Joop paused to stare at her. "What would you prefer? These people had helped us. For me, at the factory, they took more risk than Murdoch. So I am to shoot them?"

Rosa left the question unanswered. "The English are pathetic," she snapped, one hand flying up in dismissive, exasperated scorn. "They fail at capitalism, they fail at revolution – and for the same reason. They can't accept the results of their actions. Well, go on."

Joop continued in the same cool voice. After that things went better, he said. He and Murdoch drove on to Luton Airport, where no extra checks had been mounted. He himself flew off to Paris without any problem, leaving Murdoch to stir things up in Coventry.

"That was the idea, anyway."

Rosa sat up in surprise. "What do you mean?"

"I mean he never went."

"What?"

"Except to get his passport. He might have gone for that."

But probably not, Joop went on. More likely Murdoch had his passport with him all the time. In any case he caught a flight later that night, from Luton to Madrid. And then he came on to Paris. At noon the next morning there he was, sitting in the Café Babylone with the others when Joop himself turned up. In fact they were all at the café – Steve, Hal, Lucien, Marc, three others. The whole Paris section of the Iskra had come to the Babylone and were gathered round a radio upstairs, tuned alternately to Britain and Italy. The mood was high. The news was good. BMG had shut down from end to end, because of the picket affair, and Guidotti had turned up in Rome for talks with the labour unions.

"We reckoned you would hit him at lunch time. We practically had the champagne out."

"Oh *là*," said Rosa sarcastically, annoyed by this detail of the story. "Champagne."

But Joop took no notice of her comments. "That was how we were," he said, "all at the café and waiting for news, when we got a call from Brussels."

"From Mitzi?"

"Yes."

"So Mitzi kept listening to Harvey's office."

"Yes, she did."

Rosa nodded in pleased satisfaction. "I told you she would. And what did she have to report?"

"Quite a lot. Some good, some bad."

"Let's hear the bad first."

The bad news was, Joop said, that the Iskra's existence had been discovered. The chiefs of both car companies had heard of the organisation. Each had told Kohlman about it, and Kohlman, in turn, had told Harvey. But Harvey, to judge from his voice, was not much concerned.

"Know what he calls us?"

"Tell me."

"Reds under the bed."

"Ha! He better watch out for his sleep," grunted Rosa, unamused. She peered at her watch in the dark of the car's interior and saw that the luminous hands, faintly green, had formed a single vertical line. It was half past midnight. "So they know about us, do they? Well, that's not too bad."

"There's more."

"Go on."

Joop was driving fast as he talked, sweeping down the hairpins of the steep mountain road in stomach-heaving, ear-singing loops. He lit a cigarette and went on. The middling news from Brussels, he said, was that a journalist had started to sniff out the merger. The man was so keen to question Harvey that he'd bust right into the thirteenth floor of the Berlaymont, unauthorised. An American, working for *The Times* of London. And the strange thing was that this was the same fellow who had sat sodden with drink in the Europa's coffee shop on Wednesday night. So, at least, Mitzi reported. She was speaking from a telephone in the hotel, where she'd gone to see what this pressman did next.

Rosa listened to this without much interest. To stop the merger was the main thing; to stop it before it leaked out to the press was desirable, but not of the first importance.

"So," she said, "what was the good news?"

The good news from Brussels, Joop replied, was that Erich Kohlman thought the merger was off, because of the problems at BMG. Mitzi had heard him say so.

"Oh? Really? Who did he say it to?"

"Don't ask me, Rosa. Ask your *Fräulein*."

"Yes, I will." Rosa sank into thoughtful silence. "So that was all?"

Joop nodded. From Mitzi Hoff, yes, that was all. She rang off. Attention in Paris turned back to the radio. This was late yesterday morning, about 1.30. At that point the mood at the Babylone was tense. Marc went down to run the café, Lucien brought up sandwiches and wine. Murdoch insisted on beer. Hal clowned around a bit, but nobody laughed. To pass the time, they cleaned the weapons in the trunk, de-greasing them one by one. The radio played music from Italy. At two o'clock they turned up the volume for the news. Nothing was mentioned until the end, when the woman announcer came back with a late item. There had been an explosion in the Piazza di Spagna. That sounded good enough. There was immediate jubilation at the Bab. Cheers, clapping, shouts for champagne – cut short. The phone rang again. It was the Red Brigade, calling from Rome.

"Their discipline is good."

"Yes," Rosa sighed, losing interest. "It is."

"They gave us a map reference, to say where you'd cross the border. So I flew to Nice and hired this thing." Joop patted the dashboard of the car, then leaned down to look at its clock. "So, here we are," he said, concluding in methodical fashion. "It's 12.45. And this, if you're interested, is Menton."

He held a hand out to the windscreen. Rosa peered forward as they swept on down between white moonlit villas spiked with dark cypresses, then into the brighter-lit streets of the town. The car was a Citroën, one of the big kind, very comfortable. Its instruments glowed like a plane's. And Joop, of course, had them off pat. Without slackening speed he pulled out the lighter knob and held it to a second cigarette, then slapped it back into the dash with the flat of his hand, swift and sure, a man at his ease with all sorts of machinery. Watching him, Rosa felt better than at any time in Italy. She reached across and massaged his leg with a strong, kneading motion of her fingers. "I'm glad to see you."

"It's mutual." He patted her knee. "What now?"

"We'd better find a phone."

He nodded and drove on down to the sea, where they turned along the palm-lined *corniche*, cruising past a number of cafés. Two or three were still doing business. Joop stopped at the biggest. Rosa went in.

She was gone for half an hour. Joop sat and smoked in the car for a while, then stepped out for air, wishing that Rosa Berg would stop her war long enough to take a bath. Mario Salandra slept on, curled up in the back seat like a dead man.

Despite the hour, Menton was lively. Tanned boys and girls drifted past arm in arm, calling out to others below the awnings of the cafés. Watching them, Joop felt immeasurably old. Somewhere a disco was thumping. The sea hardly stirred.

At 1.15 Rosa came back to the car, carrying sandwiches. She got in, slammed the door and sat without speaking. Joop let her sit. Then she turned to him, laying one hand on the dashboard.

"How fast is this thing, Joop?"

"It's fast."

"Do you need to sleep?"

"No, I've had some."

"Then let's go." She put down the sandwiches and opened the glove compartment. "You drive, I'll work out a route."

Joop started the car and turned off the seafront, heading back up through the town. "So where are we going?"

The question seemed basic, but it annoyed Rosa. "To Tours," she snapped. "Where else?"

She took out the folding paper road-map of France supplied with the car and opened it, concertina-wise, having shut the glove compartment with unnecessary force. Joop left her to it. After climbing through Menton until he reached the *autoroute*, he took the westward lane and picked up speed. The road, cut into the cliffs, snaked along at some height above the rich and thickly populated coast. At his side Rosa wrestled with the map as if it were a living and contrary-willed thing, pulled it open, bent it back, punched it and slapped it, until it lay quiet on her knee. Joop, to assist her, reached across and pulled out the reading light, poising its snake-like articulated neck above the map. She didn't thank him. There was silence in the car as they flew high and fast along the French Riviera, into tunnels, out again. Monaco passed below to the left, its casino and palace, a harbour full of glittering white yachts. For a long time Rosa remained hunched over the map, perhaps in an effort to control herself. Then she looked up.

"It's a thousand kilometres, mostly *autoroute*."

Joop worked it out, distance into time. "We should keep to the speed limits, if you don't mind. Can't risk a chat with the *flics*."

"I agree."

"Ten hours then, near enough. Say we'll be there by noon."

"Good. Noon will do."

Folding it, she punched the map in the face one more time, just to show who was boss, then put it away. Joop made her use the seat-belt. They passed the big illuminated sprawl of Nice, then the seaside airport where the car had been hired. After that the road cut inland, looping round behind Cannes.

Rosa glared sullenly ahead.

"They're all in Tours," she said at last, "the whole filthy bunch of them."

"Clabon too?"

"Yes, Clabon too. Murdoch's friends saw to that. Oh, the *English!*" Her voice was throttled.

Joop let a moment of silence go by. "So what did you expect?" he asked her.

"I don't know." Rosa shook her head, momentarily calmer. "I thought we might have held it up – enough to make them miss the summit."

"When's that?"

"Wednesday."

"So?" said Joop. "Today's Saturday."

"Yes."

"They'll be in Tours tonight, and most of tomorrow."

"That's Harvey's plan."

"In an unguarded house."

"Yes," said Rosa, nodding, her eyes and voice still far away. "Guidotti's got his thug, the one we missed. That's all."

How did she know all this, Joop wondered. Who had she telephoned from the café in Menton? He left the question unasked. "Well then," he said. "You still have time to do it."

And that set her off again. "Do *what*, Joop?" she snapped at him, twisting in her seat. "What do you suggest?"

He shrugged. "It's your war."

She strained towards him, held back by the belt. He thought she might yell, but she twisted round further, to look at Mario sleeping, then sank back into her seat. "I promised him no more blood."

"Did you mean it?"

"I hoped it. We've killed enough people already."

"The wrong people."

Then, at last, she yelled. "Don't you talk to me about right and wrong, Joop Janssen! What in God's name do *you* know about it?"

God just slipped out: always a bad sign with Rosa. By way of correction she started to swear at random, words of such creatively brutal filth that even Joop, an old hand at *argot*, lost track. He held his hand up for peace. She stopped and flung away from him, rigid in her seat, panting like a sprinter after the race. He ignored her and drove on, going faster as the road veered away from the coast, towards Fréjus and Aix. Rosa's breathing slowed. She said nothing more for a while, then reached across and touched his inner leg, rubbing the denim of his jeans.

Joop laid his hand on hers. "Take it easy," he said. "You did well."

"In Rome, you mean? Well, it just happened. There wasn't

much choice.'' She withdrew her hand and sniffed. ''The baptism of fire.''

''Welcome to the faith.''

She laughed, then fell silent. When she spoke again, it was in her most serious, deliberate voice. ''We shall kill if we have to. But it must make sense, Joop. We're not a bunch of anarchists.''

''Perhaps we should go to Paris first then,'' Joop said, thinking of certain items that might be needed.

Rosa guessed his calculations. ''To pick up the trunk, you mean? No, there's no need for that. Hal Fawcett's got it with him. He's in Tours now, with Murdoch.''

Joop's chin lifted in contempt. ''The Marx Brothers.''

''And Mitzi's on her way from Brussels. She'll meet us there.''

''Mitzi too. Oh well then, we can't go wrong.''

''You don't trust anyone, do you?''

''I don't trust those three, especially not your *Fräulein*.''

''Just because she's German,'' Rosa said. ''You really do hate them, don't you?''

''Well, you know why.''

''That was another war. Irrelevant now.''

''They killed my father,'' Joop said. ''To me that's relevant.''

Again silence fell between them as the big car hummed on, speeding deeper into Provence along valleys flooded with moonlight, then up into steeper hills topped with stone villages. The country grew wilder, the night more aromatic. Pine and cork-oak gave way to gorse and heather, and at one point the car was filled by the strong smell of lavender. Mario slept on. After a while it was Joop who spoke again, his voice lowered.

''I think it's time you told me the truth, Rosa.''

''The truth? About what?''

''About Brussels. About Mitzi Hoff. What's she doing there?''

''She's listening. As you know.''

''Come on,'' Joop said with a touch of impatience. ''She's been there three months. As you know.''

''Who planted the microphones, that's what you want me to tell you, Joop, isn't it?''

''And whatever else. I have a right to know.''

Then at last, swivelling in her seat with dangerous slowness, Rosa turned to look at him. ''A right?'' she said softly. ''A *right*?

What you mean is you want me to tell you, so you can tell your Cuban friend, who will then tell the Russians, who will tell you what to do next."

Joop's head spun in surprise. He could see that she was smiling at him, her face half-lit by the moon as she went on in the same friendly-dangerous voice.

"Oh yes, don't worry, I've known for some time. So just keep driving, Joop, and give a little thought to whose side you're on. We'll talk about it later. I'm going to sleep now."

He started to reply, but she let down the back of her seat and curled up away from him. Joop turned back to the road and drove on. Soon he was the only one awake. He smoked a cigarette, then another. His mind worked slowly, dulled by fatigue.

That she should have guessed at some past connection with the Russians was not a complete surprise. But the present connection, through the Cuban in Paris, was his most closely guarded secret, and it shook him to the core that she knew of it. How had she sniffed out that? Did she really know or was she guessing? Should he admit the truth to her? And if so, what then? What would she do? And what should he do himself? Whose side, in the end, was he on?

No decisions came. But his feelings, now that the issue was out in the open, settled down to one of relief. He shook his head, then chuckled once, briefly, to himself. There was no stopping Rosa.

2

She slept for a hundred kilometres, then straightened up the angle of her seat, wide awake. Joop braced himself for an interrogation. But her mind was back on the business of the moment, still scheming. "There is one other factor," she said, as much to herself as to him.

"What's that?"

"This journalist. Kemble."

"Oh, him. You mean the man in Brussels."

"He's not in Brussels now. He's in Tours," she said in an offhand voice, thinking the situation through by herself. "Steve and Hal are keeping an eye on him. I wonder what he knows. I wonder what he'll do – that's the thing."

"Does it make any difference?"

"Oh yes, it might. In Harvey's view premature exposure would wreck the merger."

Joop spread a hand, palm upwards. "Well, there you are. Your bloodless solution."

Rosa considered it, then shook her head. "That's Harvey's view, not mine. He's thinking of the opposition that would get stirred up once the plan was known. But there'd be some support as well, quite a lot perhaps."

Joop had the car at high speed, but his mind was slowing up, left behind by her reasoning. He said nothing.

"For us this isn't a reliable solution," Rosa said in the end, then turned to look at Mario, still snoring behind. "However, I know it would appeal to our Roman professor here. Tipping off the press is his favourite idea."

"Well, you don't get arrested for it."

"No, you don't."

"So?"

"So nothing, Joop. I'm thinking, that's all. What's the time?"

The Dutchman's eyes flicked to the lights of the instrument panel, faintly glowing through the one-spoke steering wheel. "Half past three," he said. "It'll soon be light."

"Are you tired?"

"A little. Aren't you?"

"Yes," she said, "I'm tired. Can't sleep, though. Where are we?"

"That's Aix."

"Ah yes, Aix." For a minute Rosa watched the town pass, to the right of the road and above it: a fortress-like bulk against the stars. "Fine city," she added in a lighter voice. "This is where the Romans beat the Germans, you know. A really grand slaughter. I expect you wish you'd been there."

Joop smiled in the dark, but made no retort, still wondering when she'd get back to the dangerous subject. But her mind was on something else. Again she glanced over her shoulder at Mario. Then she turned to the front and sat hunched in her seat, eyes fixed dully on the yellow-lit road as it curved slowly northward up the delta of the Rhone. When she spoke again, her voice was hushed.

"I nearly killed him back there, do you know that?"

"Mario? Why?"

"On the frontier – he wanted to go back. And I could have done it, Joop. I could. That's the truth."

"Yes, it gets easier," Joop said. "After the first time."

"When was the first time for you?"

He hesitated. "I don't remember."

"Come on."

"I don't."

"You're a liar, Joop. You want my secrets but you won't tell your own. Well, please yourself."

And with that she reached for her bag, a voluminous affair of canvas and leather which she carried with her everywhere, suspended from her shoulder by a strap. Now it was on the car's floor. She heaved it to her knees, rummaged inside it, then placed it at her feet again. She had taken out her CZ50. Glancing sideways, Joop saw her press the pistol's release catch, so the magazine slid from its housing in the butt and fell into her lap. She pulled back the slide until the top cartridge was ejected; inspected the chamber; let the slide go with a metallic snap. For a moment she stared down dully at the gun, as though it had just fallen into her hands, and then she turned and pointed it at him, very slowly extending her arm until the mouth of the barrel touched his temple.

"Mind instructs finger," she said in a husky voice. "Squeeze or don't squeeze. But it's quite hard not to, isn't it? Like vertigo. The finger just wants to . . ."

She squeezed; the gun clicked; she lowered it with a snuffle of laughter, then drew in her breath with a sudden sharp hiss, perhaps remembering Rome.

Throughout this Joop hadn't stirred or made a sound. He kept driving, eyes forward to the road. "You did it right then?" he said to her coolly. "Close in to the head?"

"Very close, yes. The way you taught me."

"You did well."

"I'll tell you a funny thing." She was pressing the loose cartridge back into the magazine, biting her lips as she forced down the spring. "I told someone once how you'd taught me to shoot, and you know what they said?"

"What did they say?"

"That's the KGB style, they said. In close to the head – straight arm, one hand, several shots."

"It's the style for girls who can't hit a tree at five paces."

Rosa ignored the jibe. She reloaded the gun and then held it two-handed, muzzle down between her legs, pointed into the folds of her skirt. "All those years you were gone," she went on quietly, "weren't spent with the Arabs, I know. For some of that time you were in Russia – after you were hit by the Israeli bomb. The Russians patched you up and they still pay you money. You're never short, are you, Joop?" She turned to look at him, laying the loaded gun on her knee.

Joop had run out of cigarettes, but was otherwise prepared. "They have helped me, it is true. But I give them no more than I want to. They don't control me."

"And what do you give the Russians for their money, Joop? Information, I suppose – is that it?"

"Sometimes, yes. If I feel it won't hurt."

"About what?"

"Oh, the whole scene." He waved a hand vaguely at the surrounding night. "Palestine, the underground movements in Europe – the way things are going, you know."

"About us? About the Iskra?" Rosa's voice had gone tight and very small, as if her throat were constricted. Now it was down to a hoarse, strangled whisper. "Information about *me*?"

"No, of course not."

"I hope not," she said, still watching him. "I hope not."

Joop turned to her, taking one hand from the wheel in protest. "Come on, girl, what do you take me for?"

"A good party man." She smiled at him, softening a little. "Like your father."

He looked back to the road, less worried now, still craving a smoke, driving on. "Rosa, these people aren't our enemies. They can help us."

"They can also destroy us," she retorted. "You know Moscow's line as well as I do. So long as we contribute our bit to the problems of the West, they'll support us from a very long distance, at second or third hand, with gloves on. But if we try to mount an alternative strategy of the Left, in deviation from official party tactics – and that is exactly what the Iskra is about, Joop – then Moscow will see to it we're crushed. Remember Paris '68."

"The situation has changed."

"In some ways, yes. The Russians have not. In any case, I want you to make me a promise."

"What's that?"

"If it comes to a choice, between them and me, you will tell me."

"So you can shoot me first?"

"So we can discuss it, Joop. And meanwhile I'll keep a few secrets to myself." She sat half-turned, still watching him. "Well, is it a contract?"

"A contract. Understood."

"Until this is over. And then you are released from the Iskra, if you wish." She paused. "And from me, if you wish."

Joop glanced sideways as the pistol came up again. But now she was holding it out to him reversed, by the barrel.

"Here," she said. "You take it."

He pushed it away and leaned across her, to tap the glove

compartment. "In there, please. Cocked, with the catch on."

"It is cocked."

"No, it is not, Rosa. Take another look."

"Oh, you're right," she said in surprise. She pulled back the slide again to cock, then turned the gun over on its side, bending down to look for the small red dot which showed when the safety catch was off. "Red is dead, right?"

It was a cautionary rhyme he had taught her, but Joop was appalled that she still had to look. "Yes, red is dead," he said. "And so will you be if you play silly games with that thing. Now put it away. If the *flics* stop us, we'll form a committee and decide democratically who pulls the trigger."

She laughed as she shut the gun away, catch applied. "Dutch Stalinist swine," she said, then lowered the angle of her seat again and turned away from him to sleep. "Wake me up if you can't remember the meaning of history."

Joop breathed out in relief and drove on. There were contracts and contracts, he thought to himself, and some had been made under less duress than this one. For a time he held balanced in his mind, weighing each against the other, his allegiance to the forthright French girl at his side, who commanded such personal feelings as he had, and his fealty to an obscure Russian general of State Security, Department Five, last seen at lunch in Odessa – the central authority of his life, and one which went back further than Rosa. He wondered again what, in fact, he would do if it came to a choice. But again the question dropped behind him unresolved, swept into the darkness like the road. He believed in taking things as they came, when they came, not before. A soldier's habit.

It was the blackest hour of the night. The moon had gone, the dawn had not appeared. In front of his eyes there was only the never-ending ribbon of yellow-lit concrete, rushing up to meet the shark-nosed Citroën. The tar-swollen joints thrummed on below the tyres, on and on, like a heartbeat, mesmerically regular, but he was now wider awake than at any time since leaving Menton. Conversation with Rosa, armed, was a very fine stimulant.

And now she herself could not sleep. After ten minutes she gave up the effort, half-raised her seat and sat with her head back, eating a sandwich. She said she was thinking about

257

the situation in Tours, but she watched each move that he made as they filled up with petrol. As he got back into the car, she tapped the fuel gauge, then prodded the wallet in his jeans.

"Better watch out, comrade. That's going to show in the KGB's budget."

He grinned at her but made no reply. They drove on. Joop lit a *caporal* from a new packet, Mario continued to sleep. Rosa's teeth tore at the crusty sandwich, then she lowered it and watched the lights of Avignon pass to the left, home of French Popes. That set her off again.

"I was brought up to love an idea, you know – to believe in another world, better than this one. Blaise once told me that's why I'm a Marxist. Rosa loves the people, he said. She just can't bear people."

Joop stiffened in automatic hostility at this reference to Blaise Chabelard, the flashy French leader of the Trotskyist students in 1968, who had been Rosa's lover before himself. "Very neat," he said sourly. "The traitor's excuse."

"He knew me."

"At the time. Not for long."

"I am trying to say something, Joop – to you."

"Go on."

"I am saying that personal love, for me, isn't easy. But . . . a contract, is that all we have?" She went on quickly before he could answer, her voice turning harsh in denial of sentiment. "Yes, I suppose so. Perhaps it's all we ever had – a working arrangement. Perhaps that's the best I can do."

"It's lasted."

"Yes, it has." She had gone very serious. "And I'm frightened of it ending, especially since I can't go home now, back to Paris or any of that. So you see, it's pure selfishness talking – nothing very fine. This time I want to stay with you, wherever you go, because for me there's nothing else."

"I would like that."

"But would you? Would you really?" She turned to him passionately, all pretence at hard-heartedness gone. "You'll be a lot easier to catch with me on your back."

"That's not the position you'll be in."

At that she laughed aloud and sat up. Immediately reverting to her crude and boisterous self in things physical, she leaned across and kissed him, took his ear into her mouth and chewed it, still holding the sandwich in one hand, the other going straight to his crutch. She massaged his jeans until she felt some result. "Fair exchange?"

"I'll take payment later," Joop said, pushing her back with a smile. "Go to sleep."

She released him and sunk her teeth into the sandwich, eating like a hungry peasant. "Cuba – is that where we'll go?"

"Or east, or south. Depends who'll have us."

"I think I'd like Cuba."

"What would you do?"

"Grow tobacco, have babies. Try not to think too much."

"Roll cigars for John Clabon?" said a soft voice behind.

Rosa spun round. "Mario! How long have you been there?"

"Long enough to be embarrassed."

"Spy!" She took hold of his beard and waggled it. "Here, have a sandwich."

Mario accepted one and spoke with his mouth full. "Tell me, are my wife and I to be included in this Caribbean paradise?"

"But of course, we'll start a commune. Now you come in front and talk to the chauffeur here, who needs a little basic theoretical instruction. I'm going to have the back seat."

Joop pulled in. They got out to stretch their legs, all suddenly noticing the sky had turned pale, all suddenly freezing as a police car slowed to inspect them. Joop waved to indicate no engine trouble. The police moved on. As their car pulled out of earshot, Rosa jeered in defiance. But now she was exhausted. Within a few minutes she was deeply asleep, spread out in the back.

The other two had little to talk about. For most of the time they sat in silence, each to his thoughts, while the Citroën sped northwards up the valley of the Rhone and the sky slowly lit to the east. They passed Montelimar and Valence. By 6.30 they were skirting Lyon, slowed up by industrial traffic, and then they were on the last section of *autoroute*, prior to the westward, cross-country run which would lead to Orléans, Blois, and then Tours. As Joop drove on over these great distances his eyes began to grow heavy with fatigue and his mind wandered idly ahead, to the château of La Maréchale and what they would find there.

So Mitzi is coming from Brussels, he thought, and she's bringing the listening kit. That means we have a friend in the castle.

3

"It's so quiet here."

"Yes," said Kohlman. "A beautiful place."

But Laura turned the conversation round on him, the way she so often did. "Except for that damn clock," she said, "ticking on all the night like a death sentence."

What a very strange turn of expression, Harvey thought. And what a jumpy pair they were, how competitive. But both of them looked good as new after sleep. The young seemed younger at seven in the morning.

"We have been in Brussels too long," he said to them. "A country weekend will do us all good."

They turned towards him, startled by his entrance. As they bickered they had stood face to face in the window of the dining room, their heads touched by the early sunlight, striking down through the trees outside. Each was smartly dressed, each holding a clipboard, ready to go. From where they stood came a mingled aroma of expensive soaps and lotions.

The room was laid out for the talks. Chairs were set in position round one end of the table, along with pads, pencils, blotters, glasses placed upside-down and a bottle of Perrier water in each place – all the quite useless little touches required for such an occasion, at least in the minds of these two young professionals, trained in the council halls of Europe. Neither had yet caught the style of the occasion, Harvey thought. Neither understood the casual, relaxed mood required to generate an impulsive act of trust between these hard men of business, and nor did they have the faintest inkling what a raw, bitter fight for money and power would break out beneath this pretty moulded ceiling if the mood went wrong.

Well, at least they hadn't put out nameplates, or miniature flags. And more to the purpose than the blotting paper was a three-directional microphone, placed at the centre of the table, its lead coiling off to a tape-recorder laid on the floor below one chair.

That would be Laura's place.

And Kohlman's was the one where the papers were already spread out for work.

Set square on each of the other three positions was a folder of documents prepared in the Berlaymont, expanding particular points of the merger plan. But in none of these papers was there yet any mention of money. The sum to be offered in support was still hovering in Harvey's head. One billion, as cleared with Riemeck? More? How much more? He had slept on it. He still wasn't sure.

Walking once slowly round the table he examined the name on each folder, to see where each principal was placed, and then came back to the window, where the other two stood waiting for his comments.

"Ashtrays?" asked Laura.

Harvey thought before replying. Clabon smoked cigars, Guidotti fat yellow cigarettes. If he tried to stop them, it might speed things up, and would certainly make things more pleasant for himself. But the strain on temper would be too great.

"Yes," he said, "ashtrays. If you can find some."

She already had. Scooping them off the sill behind her, Laura dealt heavy glass ashtrays like cards on the table, one here, one there, bang bang. Harvey watched her, beginning to feel more awake now himself. He was wearing a red silk dressing-gown, not new.

"No," he said. "It's wrong."

She turned on him. "What's wrong?"

"The two of them should sit side by side, facing the window. Move the chair with arms to the head of the table – that's for me. And you two sit together on my left."

Yes, that was better. The world could be run without blotting paper, but the placing of bottoms was important, here as in Downing Street. The power of the British Prime Minister depended very largely on the fact that in cabinet he alone sat in a chair with arms.

Laura consulted a list on her clipboard, announcing facts from her own small field of decision. "We start at eight."

"Yes."

"Lunch will be at 1.30."

"A late lunch. Yes, good."

"But you can stop for drinks before that," she said. "I've set them up in the *salon*. Scotch for Clabon, vermouth for Guidotti. Sparkling water for the workers from Brussels."

"Fine."

"And we'll need a break," she said. "I will, anyway."

"Yes," agreed Harvey after a pause. Guidotti would start the day with a swallow of *espresso*, Clabon would be missing his bacon and eggs; both would be hungry by the middle of the morning. "Coffee with biscuits, ready at ten. But not to be brought in until I give a signal."

A meeting going well could be ruined by coffee. A meeting going wrong could be saved by it.

"No coffee till green flag," said Laura, making a note. "So the kitchen will just have to keep it percolating, won't they, until it tastes like Bovril."

"That's right. They will."

It was hard to tell where her sense of humour began. She looked at him, pert but unsmiling. "And how long will we go on? I have to let the staff know."

"All afternoon. Perhaps this evening too. You should plan for dinner."

"Yes, I plan sheepmeat. What about tomorrow?"

"I can't say yet. Ask again at lunch."

Harvey was suddenly irritated by the details. This was a moment in the history of Europe, yet here was this girl, simultaneously officious and flippant, fussing on about coffee and *placement*. And Kohlman was not much better, conscientious but too literal-minded, sitting already at the table to study some trivial annex to the brief. This taking things too literally, too strictly in sequence, was Erich's professional weakness – a German one perhaps. Or was that just an Englishman's verdict? Harvey distrusted racial generalisations, especially since living in Brussels. The British gift for improvisation, for instance, could as well be described as a talent for muddle.

"Listen, you two."

263

They both turned to look at him, blank-faced, as he switched to a friendlier tone.

"You will have to be quick today, because we're tracking two beasts of the jungle here, suspicious creatures, both of them, on the look-out for traps. They could go for each other any moment, or they could turn and go for us. We shall need all our instincts to get them in the same cage by nightfall."

"Instincts?" Kohlman rose from the table.

Perhaps he had not understood the word. Erich's English was so nearly perfect that it was easy to forget he wasn't born with it.

"Yes, hunting instincts. There will be no agenda, no time-table. I will move from point to point, apparently at random, sometimes trying to frighten them, sometimes reassure. And the odds, I should warn you, are against success." Harvey stopped, annoyed with himself now. He had been showing off. "Well, I must go and get dressed."

Kohlman stood silent. In Brussels he was on his own ground, self-assured and effective, but here Laura had the advantage, bossing the staff around in a moving cloud of perfume, flirting with Guidotti by candlelight. Now she stood waiting to go, the woman with better things to do, unmoved by talk of big-game hunts.

Harvey, glancing crossly from one to the other, gave up the effort to alter the mood. "There's one extra thing," he said to them, his voice sharpening back to its official tone. "I've decided that we're too exposed here, so I made a few phone calls in the night. Commission Security are sending down two guards, and we're also getting six local gendarmes. All eight men will be armed, and they'll be posted at various points in the grounds so long as the talks are in progress."

The reaction to this, from both Laura and Erich, was identical. They stared at him, open-mouthed, as if surprised that he could be so effective. Harvey walked away to dress. At the door, on an afterthought, he turned back and added one extra instruction.

"Let me know when they get here, will you? And I want the gates closed and locked, with someone on duty at each. Erich, will you see to that?"

"Of course."

"Straightaway, please. You understand the reasons."

"I understand."

Six miles to the south of these preparations, at the same early hour of the morning, Jack Kemble woke to a view of the central square in Tours, which was actually a circle, called the Place Jean Jaurès. The hotel he was in smelled of putrefying plaster and bad drains, plus some kind of wax linoleum polish. The bed was flat and hard, with rough starchy sheets and a bolster which had cricked his neck. His eyeballs hurt if he moved them left or right.

Outside in the square it was horribly bright. A few early cars were screeching round the cobbles, and then the city fountains came on, all squirting up together between the trim flower beds. From where he was lying, head propped by the bolster, Kemble could see the upper arc of their jets, so brilliant in the sunshine that they made him think of Hollywood – the pool of her house in Bel Air, the splash as she dived in each morning.

The memory filled his head: the way that he used to watch her swim up and down, the muck of the world simply rolling off her back as she splashed about in the light and he lay in shadow, selected from millions to sleep in her bed because he had bought her a meal or two when she was Juliet in the park, her voice hoarse from shouting at Romeo over the whoop of police sirens.

Jesus, what a terrible mistake.

But hard to walk away from when she would come back still slippery wet and pull him down on that shaggy white carpet, lithe as an eel, fantastically, frantically inventive, dragging him all round the room until he was cast aside, limp. Her breakfast.

And down the hill, under the smog, her lunch and her supper were waiting.

Kemble shut his eyes. He lay a moment, frowning, the smells of the cheap French hotel in his nose. Then he rose from the mattress and struck the bedside cupboard with a violent outward swing of his fist, so hard that it toppled over on the linoleum and broke into several separate pieces.

After that he got up.

For breakfast he returned to the Café Univers and sat at a table on the pavement. Outside, by day, the place had changed less. A spruce young waiter in a waistcoat brought strong black coffee in a very thick cup. The *croissants* were warm from the bakery and the sun shone down through the leaves of the plane trees with the dappled effect of a Renoir. It was a perfect summer's morning in France. But to Kemble it brought no joy. Nor did it really bring pain. Now that his brief waking rage was over, his mood was more detached than depressed: a sort of numb resilience. Thinking of the lives he had thrown away – London, Washington, Hollywood – he felt like a multiple refugee, cast up in a new land once again with nothing but his wits and the moment, this place and this chance, here, today. His past was irrelevant, the future a blank. And this, he thought suddenly, is probably the last of my lives. Well, so what. I am nothing but a skill I am tired of.

It was 7.45.

He sat on drinking coffee, making plans. He was waiting for the shops to open. There were things to be bought and a car to be rented.

Across the street a newsvendor added an airmail edition of *The Times* to his rack.

Kemble bought the paper, then returned to his table, and immediately was staring in surprise. BMG CHAIRMAN CLEARED OF PICKET DEATHS, said the headline. Below it was a picture of John Clabon, and beside that another: an indistinct photograph of Stephen Murdoch, a Trotskyist agitator wanted by police. Kemble looked at this second picture hard. The details were not quite sharp enough to be sure, but the man in it closely resembled the red-headed stranger who had sat drinking beer in this café, in Tours, last night – the non-speaking friend of gun-running Hal.

Immediately Kemble's mood changed to one of eager interest. He read the story quickly, then checked the café, outside and in. Neither man had made an appearance this morning, and yet they were not far away, he was sure. Having paid the bill, he inspected the street, and then started to walk slowly down it, in the shade of the plane trees, waiting to see what else moved.

Any rapid motion by Hal Fawcett was unlikely. He had quickly drunk himself stupid. All the same, he had kept the secret in his black box. Just as he seemed about to open up or collapse, the long-haired American had vanished, taking off alone in his car from the bar they were in at the time. Perhaps he had been frightened off by a question. Kemble's memory of the conversation was blurred, but it had been a dull one, unrelieved by a glimpse of French tail. Hal Fawcett had indeed run from Vietnam, on his own admission, and seemed likely to run from guns of any sort. It was hard to believe that his secrets amounted to much.

However, if his red-haired friend was really Stephen Murdoch, the runaway rebel from BMG . . .

Again Kemble stared at the newspaper. He could not be sure from the photograph, a fuzzy enlargement of a single shouting face, taken no doubt from some turbulent scene of industrial protest, that the man he had seen was the same one. Even so, the possibility was worrying. And firmly lodged in his mind now, impossible to explain yet impossible to dismiss, was the idea that he might have been followed to France by people with a sinister interest in the car business.

In that case they must be spotted and shaken off, or this day was going to get messier than it already promised to be.

So calculating, still trying to draw his unseen suspects into the open, Kemble continued to wander slowly down the Avenue Grammont, until he spotted a Europcar rental office, just opening for business. As he crossed the street towards it he watched the traffic nervously for a red Peugeot, then searched the faces on the opposite pavement for a shock of red hair. He felt exposed, yet no longer depressed. At the first hint of danger to his person he had given up any idea of retiring from the planet.

4

Clabon had already shifted his place down the table, away from Guidotti. But there they sat, side by side, and that in itself was something. Harvey felt confident as he led the talks off.

"You see the recorder beside Miss Jenkinson. It will run all the time unless either one of you asks her to stop it. But no use will be made of the tapes without your agreement. You have my word for that. In addition, Miss Jenkinson will make a note of the points on which we agree. These will be presented for initialling at the end. Is that convenient?"

Clabon grunted in assent. He looked terrible. In addition to the wounds inflicted by his workers, he had cut himself shaving.

Guidotti had turned up on time, dapper in a pale grey suit with a tiny pink rose pinned into the buttonhole, but his manner was reluctant, as if he would rather be elsewhere. For a moment he stared at Laura's gadget, then his eyes turned balefully on Kohlman.

"I have said before. I want no record."

In the end it was agreed that the tape-recorder should sit in the centre of the table, within sight of all. Each completed cassette would be sealed in an envelope, numbered, indexed, then left on the table until the close of proceedings, at which point the need for a verbatim record would be considered again.

"And what's our friend here going to do?" asked Clabon.

"Herr Kohlman is here to help me," replied Harvey sharply, annoyed by the question. He moved straight on. "Well, so much for procedures – except for the matter of security, which has two aspects. First there is the security of the meeting, which

268

must be absolute. I must therefore insist on no phone calls, in or out, except for my own communications with Brussels." He saw them bridle, but did not pause. "And then there is your personal security. Within the grounds of the château we accept responsibility for this, and have taken precautions, as I told you. Outside the gates we can guarantee nothing."

Clabon changed from grunt to growl. "So we're asked to consider ourselves your prisoners."

"Guests." Harvey hardened his voice. "And you can leave now if you wish. What you cannot do is leave and return."

There was silence, except for the murmur of two Italian voices. Guidotti's guard Angelo was outside the window, keeping as close to his master as he could get. They could see him propped against the terrace's balustrade, flipping through a picture magazine. Paolo, the chauffeur, was with him. Eight armed men were deployed at other points. Harvey had ceased to worry on that score.

"Now we can get down to substance," he said. "But first I have a preliminary word. I don't need to tell you that this could be a crucial day for Europe. An agreement between the Commission and your two companies, approved at next Wednesday's summit, would be the biggest step yet towards industrial integration. The Community has been faltering lately, but I take it you share my own hope that the early impetus of this great postwar idea can be restored."

Harvey's taste for rhetoric, always sparing, had diminished still further with age. Still, he thought, hard men could sometimes be moved by a platitude, and this one had given them time to relax. It was also, incidentally, true.

Then Clabon surprised him by replying to it. "There are no flags on my factories," he said. "No political donations, nothing for charity – we don't even sponsor sport any more. And the same applies here. For us Europe's not an ideal, it's a market. BMG is a business, I am here to talk business. Nothing more."

Harvey let him finish, then left a little silence. "To judge from the latest figures, BMG is hardly a business," he said in a cold voice. "It's a national emergency."

Even Guidotti was surprised.

Laura's head flicked up.

Kohlman sat rigid, as he had from the start.

269

Clabon gaped the widest, then banged the table with the flat of his hand. "That is a lie – and a bloody insulting one too," he blustered, pushing back his chair and surging to his feet. "I won't be spoken to like that, even if you were once Prime Minister."

He loomed above them angrily; but having stood, faltered, still too bewildered to leave. Harvey waved him back into his chair.

"Sit down, John. And simmer down. Everyone round this table knows what you've done for the British motor industry. You saved it, you built it back up. It wouldn't exist today without you. We know that, and we know very well what a fight it has been. To remind ourselves of that, we have only to look at you."

Saying this, Harvey smiled in sympathy, and his hand, still extended, made a gesture at Clabon's battered face. It was just enough. Like a slowly falling tree, the chairman of BMG sat.

"However, facts are facts," continued Harvey quietly, "and mistakes are mistakes. The Pilot was a big one. There have been others. The full cost has still to show, but the figures you showed me last Tuesday, projected to the end of the year, will lead to a loss of at least six hundred million." He turned towards the others, addressing the table as a whole. "That's in pounds sterling, by the way."

Guidotti's eyebrows were raised. He was clearly surprised by the true size of BMG's loss, but it seemed to give him no pleasure. His immediate sympathy was with his fellow businessman. Harvey was glad to see it.

But Clabon was really upset now, staring at the table with his fists bunched. "You got those figures in confidence," he said in a grim voice. "You've no right to spread them around."

"Nonsense. We're here to spread confidences. We might as well pack up this minute if we're going to tell lies all day."

The challenge was calculated, but to Harvey's dismay it didn't work. Clabon stood up again, as if to go. Then a hand restrained him.

"Take it easy, John." Guidotti's voice was calm. "Sir Patrick is trying to show who is boss here. Now, please, sit down and listen to me. I have something to say."

Clabon sat down again. Harvey, relieved, turned to look at Guidotti and waited. He knew that the chief of Mobital, having shown how grieved he was for the victim, would now put the knife in. And so it was. In the pause that followed this rumpus the Italian lit his first cigarette of the day, then drew a slip of paper from his pocket.

"It is no glory to me," he said, "that Mobital's position is the stronger. The correct decisions were taken long ago, before my appointment. However, the difference exists, and it would be foolish to ignore it any longer. I have here a plan of my own which reflects the relative strength of each company."

"Sixty-forty, I suppose." Harvey refused to take the flimsy sheet of typescript.

"It is not expressed so crudely."

"But about that?"

"Approximately, yes. The ratio of Mobital's control has been computed on sales and profit."

"Put it away, Carlo. You are in no position to make demands here."

"No? From your own analysis of the British problem, that seems to be exactly my position."

"Not at all. John is weak. That doesn't make you strong."

Guidotti leaned back in a cloud of smoke. "Please make yourself clear," he said in a soft, contained voice.

Clabon himself said nothing, although he had started to recover. He smiled in open contempt at Guidotti's bid for control of the merger, then waited in ostentatious silence for Harvey to answer it.

Harvey kept his eyes on the Italian, trying to assess how far he would go for the point. "Your weakness is political," he said, "as you yourself admitted last night. If the Left come to power in Rome, you are doomed as a private enterprise. If the Right prevails, your workers will seize the factories. Your only hope is to take yourself out of the national arena. That's why you're here today – aside from shortage of cash for a new small car to beat Fiat."

Guidotti's reaction was slow. His face didn't change, but his head tilted gradually backwards, until he was looking at the room's moulded ceiling. Then he blew out a long jet of smoke. "So, Sir Patrick, you have betrayed both our confidences. At least you are impartial. But do not expect us to kiss you on the cheeks. Right, John?"

"Right," said Clabon with feeling. "Never trust a politician."

Guidotti turned to him with a smile. "Spoken like a true Italian."

"I'm learning, I'm learning." Clabon reached into his pocket and slapped a leather cigar-case on the table. "Well, this is fun, isn't it? I'm glad I came."

Harvey let them run on. There was something to be said for a really bad start, especially when it turned against the chair. Deciding at that moment to go for the central issue straight-away, since neither man was going to quit yet, he picked up the line of his remarks to Guidotti.

"To be wholly European, Carlo, you'll have to be half British. Nothing less will take you out of the firing line. And as for you, John, if you want control, you're a fool."

Clabon's head moved in the negative: a minimal response, but unqualified. Harvey pushed on.

"The truth is you need each other equally. Neither of you can survive alone. You can't raise the money to develop new models, and your scale of production isn't big enough to bring down the cost of components – that's the main thing. You're a pair of small boys, fighting giants. If you fight each other as well, you'll end up smaller still, or get eaten up by the Americans, who make a third of Europe's cars as it is. Quite enough."

"So that's it," Clabon said. "The view from Brussels."

"That's part of it."

Again the BMG chairman shook his head, but this time with a small smile, both rueful and honest. "The Americans have problems of their own," he said. "They won't want to take on mine."

"Of course," said Harvey to both, "either of you could become a state corporation, tucked up to sleep behind a wall of quotas. That's a possibility. Or you could simply die. That's another. But we shan't lose a quarter of a million jobs, in the present state of Britain and Italy, without some very bad political trouble."

Clabon nodded gravely, beginning to cooperate. "That's true."

Exploiting the slight improvement of mood, though Guidotti was still not actually contributing, Harvey dropped his hector-ing tone. "Enough of the horrors," he said. "We're all well aware of them. The point is simply that you're in the same bind. And your size, near enough, is the same. You should therefore, in our view, come together as equals. The Commission's proposal is a 50-50 union. In the folders in front of you are further details, but the structure we're suggesting is this. BMG and Mobital stay separate companies, but so closely linked that you work as one. The directors of each firm serve on the board of the other. At the top, between and above the two boards, we create a ruling committee of three men, which takes all the main decisions." Harvey made a pyramid with his hands, then lowered them flat, palms down on the table. "And that's really it. All the rest is fine print."

"The Unilever solution," said Clabon. He was fully attentive now.

Harvey judged that the man had two storms a day in him. One had already burst; the second would take some time to build up. "Yes," he said, "it's not a new idea, and not perfect either. However, it has some advantages. The main one is that it's simple. No share transactions, no problems with national law or taxation. All that's required is a simple commitment to subordinate each company, just as it is, to the three-man committee. In practice that means that each national board will have to delegate its powers to the ruling triumvirate." Harvey paused, then opened the folder in front of him. "Let's take a breather while you think about it."

The pause was a long one. Clabon opened his folder and made a half-hearted show of reading. Guidotti didn't move. Laura doodled. Erich sat with his head down, apparently unnerved by the silence. Outside on the terrace the two Italians were still chattering softly. Harvey sat watching and waiting, quite pleased with the way things were going. The thin fleecy cloud of early morning had cleared. It was going to be another hot day. The meeting was twenty minutes old. It seemed longer.

Clabon was the first to react. He sat back and puffed out his cheeks. "This isn't going to be easy, Patrick. In effect you're asking our boards to vote themselves out of existence. Damn it, mine will throw me out again – or they'll get thrown out themselves, by the shareholders."

"I very much doubt if the shareholders, in either country, will have much objection to what we are doing here this weekend."

"But what about the British bloody government? They'll

want some say, so long as they've still got money in us. Won't they? Eh?"

"Both governments will be bought out. We're coming to that."

Clabon brightened like a beacon at the news. Harvey smiled. "My treat for the day," he added.

Then Guidotti stirred at last: with impatience, not interest. "I do not see the need for these arrangements at all," he said in a bored, weary voice. "If you cannot agree to a structure which admits the supremacy of Mobital, then let us simply agree to cooperate in certain areas – engine development, overseas marketing, whatever else interests you."

Harvey shook his head. "I'm sorry, Carlo, but that's not enough. If you want some European cash, you'll have to do it by the European rules. Each firm will have to be bound in law to the three-man committee, which in turn must answer to the Commission. That contract, between you and us, will be enforced by the European Court, and the terms of it will follow the European company statute – the draft we put out last year, with the new directive on mergers. All right, that's a model which no one's yet followed – I know, I know. But Otto Riemeck will insist on this, I assure you. He wants a bit of history for his money."

Neither executive was much pleased at this. There was an anti-European silence. And then Guidotti said, casually enquiring: "This top committee that you are suggesting, the one of three men. Who will be on it?"

"Yourself, obviously. John for BMG. And a chairman, who will have the casting vote," replied Harvey. "So he ought not to come from either company."

"And how are we to choose him, this chairman?"

"That's my job."

"Yours?"

"As Commissioner for Industry," Harvey said, "I shall be responsible. So long as you're using the Community's money, I, or my successor, will nominate the chairman of the new joint company."

Guidotti's head had turned sharply at this, but now it retracted back into his shoulders, like that of a tortoise. "So," he said, speaking more slowly all the time, "the chief executive of Mobital is to sit on this so-called neutral committee with an

274

Englishman and a chairman nominated by another English-man."

"Now it is you who are putting things crudely, Carlo."

"You insist on this solution?"

"It's the only one possible. And in practice . . ."

But Harvey did not have the chance to say why, in practice, he thought this solution would work. His voice tailed away. With the others at the table he watched in stunned silence as Carlo Guidotti pushed his chair back, then walked straight out of the room.

5

"Cars, cars. Where *are* they all going?"

"To the sun," said Mario with a logical shrug.

Rosa nodded and smiled. "The Highway of the Sun. In a thousand years they'll find it in the jungle and wonder what it was."

They were eating breakfast in a futuristic café which straddled the road in a bridge of bright red girders and tubular glass, *style Pompidou*. Above their heads, suspended from the ceiling, was a perspex cut-out of the European continent with the *autoroute du soleil* marked across it in broad blue plastic, like a river which ran from the Channel to Sicily. No cities were shown, but the site of the café was marked by a light, as though it were the centre of the civilised world. That ought to keep the archaeologists guessing, Rosa had commented as they measured their route by the scale provided. Since Menton they had travelled eight hundred kilometres.

And Joop had been at the wheel all night. Now he was too tired to speak or eat. Rosa had finished his eggs as well as her own, then picked up her coffee and turned to gaze at the double stream of traffic below. This she was doing still, in pursuit of some thought of her own.

"How many cars in Europe, would you say?"

"A hundred million," answered Mario from knowledge. "Ten million new ones a year."

Rosa shook her head, as though at the news of some great, scarcely credible calamity. "A hundred million. Just think of it."

"Is this a good thing for us to think about?" asked Mario in a sharper, almost teasing tone of voice. "Since the Iskra, too, is committed to industrial production?"

Rosa turned on him, stung. "Production for use," she snapped, "not profit."

"And you think that will lead to less waste?"

"Of course it will."

Mario's smile was knowing but sad, as if he were sorry to disappoint a child. "You really believe that the people, given the choice, will elect to have less cars?"

"I believe I have heard enough doubt for today," Rosa said, jumping up from the table with a dismissive, half-amused snort. She drunk the rest of her coffee and hitched her bag over her shoulder. "Come on, Professor, switch your brain off. It's your turn to drive."

Not long after this, by nine o'clock, they had turned off the *autoroute* altogether and were striking south-west towards Orléans. Joop now slept in the back. Mario took the wheel. Rosa read the map, but distractedly, thinking more about what she was going to do next. There was little cause for cheer, and yet she was cheerful. Even Mario had picked up some impetus from constant motion. It was also a lovely morning, bright and airy, of the sort which encourages irrational hope. On one straight stretch of the road they overtook a column of racing cyclists who seemed to catch the spirit of the day, heads down, caps backward, legs pumping in furious effort to reduce the time between two points of their own selection. In the fields huge jets of water were spraying the vegetable crops. The stucco and pantiles of Provence had given way to stone and slate. Since daybreak the soil had darkened from red to brown, and now there were no more rocky hills spiked with cypresses. The land here was soft and fertile, arable, wooded, gently rolling, so different from that of the Mediterranean coast that they felt they were in another country. Mario made a comment on this. All Europe's landscapes converged in France, he said. It was really the heart of the continent, just as the French said, although no one else much liked to admit it. And Rosa agreed, with a raw national pride which she tried to convert into tactical logic. "It's the ground I know best," she said. "I am glad to have the battle here."

"What will you do?"

"I'm not sure. Perhaps nothing."

"Nothing at all?"

"There's a chance that Harvey will fail without our help. We shall listen and wait."

Mario didn't believe it. "But if he succeeds?"

"We shan't wait for that," Rosa said with a sniff.

"You have a plan?"

"I have several." She smiled at him. "Wait and see."

Mario drove on a short way, brooding in silence, then glanced at her through his mauve spectacles. "No more blood?"

"I shall try to avoid it."

He nodded, with a touch of sarcasm. "Yes of course, you will try."

"You must trust me, Mario. Come on now, speed up. You're dawdling."

"I shall try to trust you, Rosa. But I cannot, on my oath, drive faster than this."

"All right, let me."

They changed places. By ten o'clock they were in Orléans, stuck in dense traffic, but once through the town they found another *autoroute* and dashed along the fifty kilometres to Blois. Making up time, Rosa drove like the wind. The big Citroën hummed and quivered in her hands. Her eyes were a little dilated. Mario watched for the police. The Loire appeared to the left, greeny-brown in the sunshine, flowing wide and shallow between its many islands and spits of sand, its banks fringed by poplars and bushy blue-green willows. A file of boy canoeists in crash helmets paddled energetically midstream, between the fishermen in hip-high wading boots, who raised their long rods to let them pass. Along the banks were many camp sites, bright blue and orange, and wherever the land was flat it was striped into neat weedless vineyards, the ripening fruit already just visible beneath the vivid foliage. Above the working homesteads rose cliffs of white rock holed with wine cellars. Outside them were signs saying *Dégustation Gratuite*, and erupting from the heart of each small town that passed were big bulbous châteaux built of the same whitish stone, their towers topped with conical roofs of slate like witches' hats. Far across the river, peeping through a dense mat of trees to the south, they could see the fantastic cupolas and chimneys of Chambord, like a miniature town in the forest.

"How about that for waste?" Rosa said, pointing.

"Production for show," was Mario's answer. "Still goes on, you know – east and west."

"Not for the kings of France it doesn't."

After Blois the road looped away from the river, and then they saw the towers of Tours. At 11.15 they entered the town along the Rue Nationale. Destroyed by the Germans in 1940, the whole street was modern, rebuilt in the same brown concrete as Normandy. Rosa told Mario to look for the Place Jean Jaurès.

"Silly old revisionist," she added with a grimace of scorn.

"He died for peace, Rosa."

"And got his name on a few squares. An example not to follow."

They parked within sight of the town's central fountains. At 11.30, ten hours exactly since leaving Menton, they were walking towards the Café Univers. Seated at a table under the trees were Hal Fawcett, Stephen Murdoch and Mitzi Hoff.

Joop, sharp-eyed again after his sleep, was first to catch sight of them. "Well, there's your army," he said to Rosa. "What next, *ma générale*?"

"A hotel," she replied, and then cackled with laughter to see the look of dismayed surprise which this produced on the Dutchman's face. "No, Joop, not for that. I want a bath, and Professor Salandra here is going to shave off his beard. Then we'll buy some changes of clothing. And then, *petit soldat*, I shall tell you the plan."

The other three, turning round as they heard her voice approach, jumped up from their table under the trees. Rosa strode towards them. fist raised in salute. Mitzi raised hers in return. Hal stumbled over a chair. Steve Murdoch looked ready to run.

The moment that Guidotti left the room, Harvey had jumped up and started to follow him, issuing instructions as he went.

"I'll try to talk him back. Leave us alone for about ten minutes, then you bust in and make a fuss, John. Accuse me of dealing with him behind your back. Erich, work out some variations on the three-man formula. Laura, switch off that tape and remove yourself. Two English people are enough here."

And with that he was gone. They heard his feet hurry across the hall, then a murmur of voices, shut off by the door of the study. The dining room was left in silence. Clabon stood up and began to stroll round the table with the condescending air, half-amused, half-bored, of an adult awaiting his turn in a children's charade. Kohlman bent to his papers. Laura withdrew to the kitchen, where she drank another coffee with the staff. Then she went out to join Paolo on the terrace. He asked her what was going on.

"A matter of face," she told him in Italian. "No women allowed."

The young chauffeur nodded, finding nothing absurd in such a situation. His own *figura* had been much enhanced, in his own eyes at least, by the disclosure that he kept a private pistol concealed inside the Mercedes. This was quite irregular, but in view of the unusual dangers of the moment he had been allowed to keep the gun until return to Brussels. Now he was cleaning it with a rag. As Laura stood watching he snapped the parts together in a practised fashion, then placed the pistol on the round iron table and pulled out a chair for her. His jacket was off and his white shirt unbuttoned, revealing a small gold crucifix suspended in the hairs of his chest.

He really was amazing to look at, she thought. A true Valentino. But there was a hard peasant shrewdness in Paolo, along with a serious formality, quiet and respectful, that she very much liked. They had worked together for two years, in all of which time he had never once tried to narrow the distance between them. Perhaps he didn't like her. Laura didn't mind. Feeling more at ease with Paolo Santini than she did with most men, she sat beside him in silence as he loaded the pistol's magazines from a carton of close-packed, glinting brass cartridges. She was sure he would shoot as well as he drove.

At either end of the terrace, she saw, were the two security guards from Brussels. One of the six French gendarmes was posted at the bottom of the lawn, where the avenue of chestnuts began. The others were deployed further out in the grounds, round the back of the house and at its gates. Angelo, following his master's voice, had shifted down the gravel to stand outside the study. His reading matter lay discarded on a chair, the latest issue of a company magazine called *Mobital Illustrato*. Laura picked it up and flipped through the pictures of company football teams, company housing schemes, company schools and company hospitals, company beauty contests.

Miss Mobital Milan sat bulging in a swimsuit at the wheel of her prize, a Mobital Sport 2000. Laura's lip curled in scorn. She tossed the magazine away and sat with her eyes closed, face raised to the sun. The air was heavy with the scent of dewy wistaria. The silence was intense. They were too far from a road to hear traffic. She no longer noticed the slow hammer-beat of the stable clock. Her ears were tuned only to the soft drone of Harvey's voice in the study, a little along to her right, as he tried to coax Guidotti back to the dining room.

In the end he succeeded. By 9.30 the talks were under way again, all parties having accepted a structural formula for the new joint company. And Harvey had won this first issue outright, Laura learned on return to the table. The chairman of Mobital-BMG would be picked by the European Commissioner for Industry. However, this appointment would have to be ratified by the Commission's President, and if either one of them, Commissioner or President, was British or Italian – as in the present case – they would bring in a colleague of the other nationality, to assist in the process of selection. The balance of the merger's three-man junta would therefore be ensured by a similarly balanced committee of Commissioners, and if either company felt that this balance had been disturbed, it would be able to appeal to the European Court of Justice, whose ruling in the matter would be final.

Laura got it down in shorthand, amazed, as she often was, that matters so important could be so boring. This small master-piece of Eurocratic compromise, she didn't need telling, had come from the mind of Erich Kohlman, who had been left behind in the study to draft an exact form of words. And how very happy he'd be at it, she thought, how pleased with himself as he smoothed away each point of friction with a sub-clause. The grease between nations . . . Suddenly, then, she felt ner-vous, as her pet phrase for diplomats brought with it a picture of the journalist Jack Kemble, sardonically applauding at the Leopold in Brussels. Had that been Kemble's voice on the phone last night? Surely not. Surely, please not. It was hard to see how he could possibly have tracked down the site of the talks. But if he really was here, what next? And oh dear, what after *that*? A number of disastrous scenarios flicked through Laura's head, like clips of lurid film. But now she had no time to dwell on them. Listening to the progress of the talks, watching the reels of tape turn in the cassette-machine at her side, she added fresh points of agreement to her pad.

The first one, *Administrative Structure*, had taken an hour and a half, but now the decisions came every few minutes, a number of smallish things settled on the nod.

2. *Subordinate Boards*
3. *Reciprocal Directorships*
4. *Joint Management Committees*
5. *Accounting Procedures*

Under each heading Laura recorded the substance of agreement in a few lines of shorthand, feeling pleasantly as though she were in charge. These powerful men could talk all they liked. Until her pencil moved, they'd done nothing.

6. *Community Audit*
7. *Reports to Commission*
8. *Products Excluded*

When the clock on the stable struck ten she began to think of coffee, but Harvey pushed on without a pause, darting off into each aspect of the working relationship between the Commission and the new merged company.

9. *Adjudication of Disputes*
10. *Role of European Court*

These were small things, all of them, in some cases hardly worth bothering with, and both executives had started to fidget. Clabon kept trying to move on to cars, Guidotti was itching to talk about money. But Harvey, with unusual pedantry, insisted on his list. And then Laura saw the purpose. He was trying to create a feeling of progress before the next row, and to judge from the way he was doing it – the haste, the piling up of many small points agreed in the same restricted area – the row was close. Something explosive remained from the period of adjournment.

11. *Existing Shareholders*
12. *National Law and Taxation*
13. *Independence from Governments*

282

The points kept coming. They had filled half her pad. She would soon need another. She took out the second tape cassette, inserted a third, pressed the button to record. Discussion droned on, the clock chimed the quarters. 10.15, 10.30. Where was Erich, she wondered, then forgot him. She was concentrating only on her task, but then, as they got into how the merger would shake free of national governments, the talk slowed up. Still following it by ear, but able to relax a little, Laura raised her head and watched Harvey at work. How accomplished he was at this sort of thing, she thought, how impressive. But that was all there was of him. Outside the world of high politics he hardly seemed to exist as a person at all. He was too busy doing to feel much or think very deep, too occupied with public matters to be bothered with private ones. And that was his secret, really. A sort of deliberate shallowness. What made him effective, and so damn irritating, was that he never had a doubt. Or rather he never admitted to one, especially doubt of himself. Politicians called that resolve. But really it was just an act, which fooled a few people for some of the time. And for this man, surely, the play was almost over. Watching him, Laura had the sudden impression that the moment Harvey ceased to perform in the role of public man he would fall over flat, like a cardboard cut-out, and then there'd be nothing left at all, just air. Well, she thought, bending to write again, I won't be there to see it. When he dies the papers will write long columns of praise and there'll be a service in some big church full of people as famous as himself. But no one will really care. Not me, not even his wife. Fancy that. All the world knows him but nobody cares . . .

"Laura."

"Sorry, yes. Not listening."

"Go and find Erich, will you? Let's hear what he's done."

But there was no need. Erich Kohlman came in through the door at that moment and laid his verion of the three-man formula on the table. He had made several carbons on Laura's typewriter, which was sitting on the desk in the study. Each person present was given a copy. Harvey read the document aloud, clause by clause, and then looked up at each business-man in turn.

"Any objections, gentlemen? If not, I propose we initial this, by way of a start."

There was a silence.

Clabon had turned to Guidotti. A look passed between them. They had obviously had private words, and now, when the Italian spoke, he was speaking for them both. "So," he said, "neither of us can reject your choice of chairman."

"On your own, no. For reasons explained."

"Then who is this man to be, please? Tell us now."

"I haven't thought about it," Harvey said irritably. "We can get around to finding a man in the summer."

"No. I cannot accept that."

"Carlo, you have already accepted it."

"I have agreed to your right to choose future chairmen, so long as we borrow your money. But the first one remains within my veto."

"What's that supposed to mean?"

"It means, Sir Patrick, that Mobital will not come into this at all until we know who the chairman is to be. Until that is settled, I sign nothing. I agree to nothing."

"What about you, John?"

"I'd like to know too," said Clabon more sheepishly. "Make it easier with the board."

"You realise what this means," said Harvey, staring coldly at both. "You're asking me to find a man by next Wednesday. Because we can't go to Rome half-committed, I assure you. By the time this thing goes to the summit it must have your full, unconditional agreement."

Guidotti nodded, unrepentant. "Let us hear some names. You have some ideas, of course."

But Harvey ignored the suggestion. He was staring now intently at Laura, as if there were some profound secret in all of this that only he and she understood. Laura nodded, jumped up, and went to press a bell on the wall. The secret, she had realised after a fractional delay, was coffee and biscuits.

284

"Let's take a break now. Coffee's on the way."

The two or three minutes that followed this announcement of Harvey's were comically awkward, though the funny side didn't occur to him till later. First there was a loaded pause. No one spoke. No one moved from the table. He himself sat where he was, saying nothing. The businessmen's refusal to let him appoint the new chairman had left him too annoyed to make any small talk. This, however, left the initiative to Guidotti and Clabon, who were not in the mood to change the subject. Exchanging a quick glance of mutual defiance, they began to drop the names of potential neutral chairmen into the silence, waiting after each to see his reaction.

"Come on, Patrick, tell us. It is time to pull the hare from the hat."

Clabon began to correct this remark of Guidotti's, but Laura, returning to the table, cut in on him. "Oh," she said, "please, let's not split rabbits."

Only Erich Kohlman, who was paid a large salary to deflect conversations such as this, was silent.

Harvey ignored them, so then the two businessmen turned to each other, swapping names of potential chairmen loudly enough for him to hear. At that point he thought of going to the lavatory. But he was too interested. He wanted to hear their ideas. So he stayed in his seat and kept his eyes fixed on the dark varnished picture which filled the whole opposite end of the room.

It must have been there since the house was built. As a painting it was not very good, but there was a lot in it to look at.

In the sunlit foreground the Marshal's lady was picnicking with two female friends, picture hats spread on the grass. Beside them an overdressed boy, presumably the Marshal's bastard, sat bored on a swing. In the dim background a man on a prancing white horse, presumably the Marshal himself, was leading a column of infantry up a hill, from which emerged puffs of white smoke. The battle of Fontenoy, Harvey thought. Or perhaps Minden. In any case La Maréchale had had quite enough of it. The look on her face reminded him of Margaret, waiting for the men to finish the fooleries and get back to tending their women.

Still listening to the car men, still pretending not to, he glanced at Erich Kohlman, seated speechless on his right. What was the matter with him? Since the talks had started, Erich had seemed more rigid than usual. And Laura even more volatile. As she kept the record, her expression had veered from amused to bored to contemptuous: shifts of mood unrelated to the state of proceedings. Now she had rushed from the room.

Silence returned. Clabon and Guidotti had run out of names. The clock on the stable struck 10.45. Then Laura appeared again, holding back the door from the kitchen, through which, at last, arrived coffee.

And Harvey had to smile. The girl who brought it in was so wonderfully pretty that she must have been the prize of the district; but never before, perhaps, had so many men in one room been so pleased to see her. As she put the tray down with unnecessary help from all sides, she blushed from the roots of her hair to the neck of her dress, then stood back and put her hands up to her cheeks with a sweet little laugh.

Everyone laughed with her. She fled. Laura poured. Eyes met. Guidotti raised his cup in salute. "Patrick, you're a master."

Clabon shook his head, staring after the girl. "I'm not sure that she's in the rules."

Harvey smiled at them both, feeling suddenly very old indeed, but quite cheerful. "We only bring that one out in emergencies," he said. "Next time you see her, you'll know you're in trouble."

He took a cup from Laura, intending to talk about the painting at the bottom of the room, since now, if ever, was the moment to get away from cars. But again he missed his chance.

Before he could open his mouth a new point was raised by John Clabon.

"So where do you want to put the head office? Or can we choose that for ourselves?"

"Will you need one?"

"I think so. This top committee will have to have a staff. And Chairman X can't live in a jet, now, can he?"

Harvey had hoped to take the point later. "In that case London," he said.

"I agree," said Guidotti immediately.

"Right, headquarters in London." Harvey nodded at Laura to take it down, concealing his surprise.

But Clabon's eyes narrowed in half-amused suspicion. "What's going on here? I won that too easily."

Guidotti smiled at him blandly. "London is better for finance," he said, "and also for security. I wish to retire without holes in my knees." He took a long swallow of coffee, then carefully put down the cup, as if to have both hands free. "However, there is a condition."

"Oh-oh. Let's have it."

"The company's name will be Mobital."

Clabon, too, put down his cup. And then, to Harvey's real amazement, the chairman and saviour of the British Motor Group replied with a nod. "All right, I agree. On one condition."

"What is that?"

"On every car made within the UK, the letters GB must be added to the logo – like this."

All parties watched in silence as Clabon snatched Laura's pad and pencil, drew a rectangle, then wrote within it.

> *Mobital Pilot 1500/GB*

"There," he added, standing back. "In chrome, please, bolted on tight. So if any frigging foreigner tries to take it off, there are holes in the frigging bodywork."

Guidotti laughed aloud. "Condition agreed," he said. "That will look very nice in a museum."

Harvey took this to be a crack about the future of the Pilot, rather than GB, but he wasn't going to lose the initiative again.

"Working languages," he said on the instant, like a gambler dealing a fresh hand quick, before his luck turns.

Guidotti reacted first. "We shall have to use both."

"Nonsense," snapped Clabon, defensive again. "English is the language of engineers and money men."

"Not my engineers."

Harvey jumped in. "I agree with Carlo. There should be parity."

Clabon stared at him aggressively, then yielded with a nod. "All right, so we go bilingual at a technical level. But let's use English at the top. What do you say to that, Ambassador?"

Guidotti lifted his shoulders and spread his hands wide. "*Non capisco. Ma sono d'accordo.*"

Laura's laughter was like glass breaking.

Even Erich smiled.

But Harvey had gambled enough. "Let's stretch our legs now. Straight on at eleven."

Everyone then left the room except himself. Years of such meetings had left him with a bladder of iron, or so Margaret used to say, in the days when she still made jokes about politics.

He was glad of a moment alone in any case. The problem, as perhaps for the Marshal in the painting, was which way to lead the troops next.

The girl in the kitchen should be given a medal, he thought. Jokes from Guidotti was very good, and at last the Italian was saying more what he meant. Clabon, on the other hand, was showing more subtlety. Also good. Both men were now trying hard.

And before Laura sniggered too much, she should hear what had happened in the interval, while she sat out on the terrace. Guidotti really had meant to leave. All that had held him was a massive adjustment to the deal, still too hot to record. In order to even up the size of the companies, four big subsidiaries of Mobital were to be hived off – motorboats, pumps, hotels and computers. Guidotti's idea was to sell them to Fiat, thus getting the larger firm out of his hair, but he would have to do it before a breath of the merger got out, so it hadn't yet appeared on Laura's pad.

To Harvey's mind this was a really inspired contribution. And hardly less fine was Clabon's decision to leave BMG's aerospace division included in the deal, although it was disqualified from European aid by its present healthy profit. That, too, had taken some hard private talk, in which he had seen Clabon suffer like a man on the rack.

Yes, it was going all right, he thought, and the way they had ganged up against him on this business of a chairman was in one sense a good sign – their first act of collaboration. It was a clever bit of bargaining, and Guidotti's concern on the point was understandable, since any announcement of the merger before a neutral chief was appointed would certainly open him up to the charge of handing over Italy's finest cars to English control. Even so, this bid for a veto had to be stopped. Harvey wondered how to do it. No answer came to mind. Momentarily blank, he couldn't think how to proceed from the break, which was due to end in three minutes.

The pretty girl came back to clear the coffee cups. He smiled and thanked her, for more than she knew. She took the tray out.

Erich Kohlman then came in and sat down, immediately burying his head in a deep pile of paper.

Still wondering what to do next, Harvey strolled about the room, then stood beneath the painting and took a closer look at the battle in the background. While his horse reared beneath him, upset by the puffs of white smoke, the Marshal was pointing bravely one way and looking rather anxiously the other, as if to tell the troops that he had the rear exit in view, but meanwhile it was forward that they must, without delay, go.

"Erich."

"Yes."

"Come over here a moment, will you? I've had an idea."

Two minutes later the businessmen were seated, looking to the chair for a lead. And Harvey led off the way they expected. "I suggest we now leave the question of company structure," he began, "and move on to other things."

But immediately Kohlman interrupted. "There is one aspect you have not considered."

Harvey turned to him, frowning. "What is that?"

"Industrial relations."

"We'll come to that later. It's not a structural point."

"Except in one respect."

Harvey's frown deepened. "And what is that, Erich?"

"Consultation between management and workers," said

Kohlman coolly. He took out a paper and held it up to show the number, so the businessmen could find it in their own dossiers. "We have drafted a code of conduct to be included in the main merger contract. The text is based on the labour clauses of the draft European company statute."

"What does it say?"

The question came from Clabon, who was staring at Kohlman as if he were a creature from outer space, completely unintelligible, possibly dangerous, perhaps just a joke.

But Kohlman was not put off. His answer came from memory. "These clauses make consultation with the workforce compulsory," he said without a glance at the text in his hands. "The employees will be given representation on the board of each national company, plus a right of appeal to the ruling three-man committee."

There was a long appalled silence, which Harvey did nothing to break. Seated immobile on his white horse, he watched his young Prussian lieutenant ride into the guns.

Clabon fired first. "How much representation?"

"Two places in five."

"You mean to tell me that two in every five directors of BMG must be chosen by the workers – is that it?"

"That is correct, Mr. Clabon. And two will speak for the shareholders. If you keep to a senior board of five, that gives you, as chairman, the casting vote."

"Oh thanks very much, I'm sure. That's nice of you. Jesus Christ. Will you let me know which way to part my hair?" Clabon pushed all his papers away in disgust and sat back, staring up at the ceiling to control himself.

Then Guidotti went into the attack. "When we met in Milan, Herr Kohlman, I informed you that decision-sharing with the labour force was a subject I could not discuss at this meeting, because it is a matter of very great political danger in Italy. You informed Sir Patrick?"

"Yes."

Guidotti then turned to Harvey. "So," he said in a voice cold with anger, "it is you who insist on these provisions."

But Kohlman continued to draw the tycoons' fire. "The Commission, as a whole, will insist," he said. "These ideas have already been approved in the new model statute. As the first real European company, you cannot be seen to do less."

Guidotti turned away, throwing up both hands. "This is madness."

Then Clabon spoke again, leaning forward in one last effort to explain the industrial facts of life to this ignorant bureaucratic youth. "These democratic notions may look nice on paper, but no one has ever run a business that way, laddie. No one ever could."

"The Germans do," Kohlman shot back.

Clabon could find no argument to this, so turned in appeal to Harvey. "Drop it, Patrick. Put it away in a drawer until the last trump, when we're all changed into bloody angels."

"Truly, it is not for this world," agreed Guidotti.

At which point Laura made her second intervention of the morning. Her head shot up from her pad and she said in a tart voice, addressing herself to Guidotti: "I really can't see why *you* should object. According to *La Stampa* a couple of directorships would make your communists happy. And once you've got them on the board, they will help you to squash the autonomists, who want full control of the company. So this ought to suit you pretty well."

Guidotti, unnerved, looked round for assistance, but no one else spoke. She had struck them all dumb with astonishment. Harvey especially was appalled. Since their quarrel in Chartres Laura's manner had been ever more peculiar. Now she had lost all sense of her place, it seemed. And Erich, too, had gone far enough with this fire-drawing manoeuvre. It was time for the Marshal to take command.

"I understand your objections, gentlemen, and I have some sympathy for them. Speaking for myself, I am not at all sure that a fixed proportion of workers' directors is the answer. However, I do think we have to try something. Here we are almost at the end of the century, still quarrelling in the terms of the last – labour versus capital, class war, all the rest of it. Surely it's time we moved on. And if ever there was a good case for experiment, it's here, in the merger of your two companies. Indeed, as far as relations with your workers are concerned, I would say that your situation is that of the terminally ill. Any cure is worth a try, because the alternative is worse."

Guidotti and Clabon didn't like this. They hated it. Each man looked ready to leave again. They glanced at each other for

291

support, then glared at Harvey together as he laid a hand on the table, palm downwards.

"Now just hear me out. Whatever you think of that diagnosis, I assure you it's the one now current in Brussels. Your labour troubles are now regarded as the two worst cases of a sickness that threatens the continent. And it's that, to be honest, which makes you prime candidates for assistance from the whole Community. However, there are some strings attached. You are a political problem. Europe's new answer to that problem is a system of workers' directors, two in five, and you will have to accept it if you want Europe's money."

Having made his point, Harvey withdrew his hand from the table and sat back, reverting from stern to sympathetic. "I'm sorry, but Erich is right," he concluded. "You must swallow the medicine."

Clabon shook his head, more in sorrow than anger. "It's the cure, not the sickness, that will kill us."

Guidotti was more angry than sorry. He stared straight ahead, saying nothing.

"Well, we shall leave this now," Harvey said, "but let me be absolutely clear. I am not going into that summit unless you are both committed to the structure, by which I mean workers on your boards and a chairman chosen in Brussels. As to the latter, I shall try to produce a man by Wednesday. But if I can't, you must sign nonetheless – or the deal is off."

Neither man stirred.

Then Guidotti spoke sulkily, not even turning his head. "What deal? You've offered us nothing."

"I'll come to that later."

"Let's come to it now."

"No, Carlo, money comes last. First I want to hear how you'll spend it."

In fact Harvey had not decided yet how much to offer. But he knew they would sit there until they heard a figure. So now we will come to the heart of the matter, he thought, which is where the blood really will run.

"Let's talk about cars," he said aloud.

7

"Together you will make 1.5 million vehicles a year. That doesn't top the giants, but it does make you big enough to fight. You'll be able to bring costs down. And once you have integrated, you will offer the public a better range of models. Your bad cars will be dropped, your good ones stepped up."

Harvey had meant to make this speech at the start, but now it was coming out flat. Each executive was waiting for the catch. And there was one.

"We reckon that this integration will take you about four years. Obviously a lot of very technical decisions will go into it, and also some painful choices, which I dare say you'd rather not discuss today. All right, we can leave the technical details. But not the hard choices. To be specific, I want you to decide here and now, this weekend, which products are going to be phased out."

"That's impossible," said Clabon immediately. "We can't."

"You can try. Just the main, strategic decisions."

"We can try. We won't succeed."

"In that case you won't get your money," Harvey said flatly. "Unless they can see a joint plant of production, the Commission won't put this to the summit. The merger shouldn't start life with any big rows still hovering between you. So the really hard choices must be taken. However, I propose to start with some easy ones."

He moved straight on before they could object, and within ten minutes they had merged dealer networks: a decision in which the mutual advantage was clear. BMG was strong in the old British empire, Mobital better spread in Europe. Each had a third of its own home market.

Laura's pencil started to flick again, leaving symbols like Arabic on her pad. Harvey was glad to see her head down. He kept it there by pushing through the junction of BMG's aerospace division to Mobital's sideline in light civil airframes. This was music to Guidotti, and Clabon stuck firmly to what he had promised: his precious aircraft engines to be swept into the deal. So far, so good.

Continuing to take the easy things first, Harvey then came to commercial vehicles. Vans, lorries, tractors, buses and jeeps – production plans for each were settled in minutes, since in each case one firm was obviously dominant. The only real sacrifice came from Guidotti, who abandoned his tractor plant in Brindisi, striking out twelve thousand jobs with ominous ease. Wondering which British town would die in return, Harvey thought briefly of the hot dusty port from which he had once sailed to Greece. Men with nothing to do had stood about in the streets, so bitter that they spat at the tourists.

And the point brought Laura's head up again. "So," she said, "goodbye to Brindisi."

Harvey was so very angered by this that he felt momentarily suffocated. "Just keep the record, Laura. If we want your comments, we'll ask for them," he said to her, speaking as harshly as he ever did. He paused to catch his breath and then turned to the businessmen. "Right, gentlemen. Now we come to cars."

Taking out the relevant paper from the brief, Harvey noticed that it was headed *Redisposition of Model Ranges.* But long words by Erich wouldn't help, he thought. Here was where the trouble would come. To delay it as long as he could, he began with luxury and sports cars, drawing their attention to a list in which the roughly comparable models of each firm were set out side by side.

> *BMG Jaguar/Mobital Alfa*
> *BMG Rover/Mobital Lancia*
> *BMG Tiger/Mobital Sport*

Six different models in this department, he told them, was too many. In the long run they ought to come down to three – two saloons, and a single sports car.

Guidotti shook his head. "The sports cars cannot be compared. The Tiger is a toy for the young. Ours is for those who like quality, and also has a roof."

"All right," said Harvey, jumping in before Clabon could, "so the sports cars don't really compete. I know that. And to some extent the same is true of the luxury saloons. Each has its steady clientele – Lancia people, Rover people. So you won't want to change the badges in a hurry. Your aim will be to standardise more and more components, until they become in effect the same car. Am I right?"

"You are right," said Clabon. "But it takes a long time."

"Even so, I should like you to knock out a brief written plan for three cars instead of six – just the main objectives, as precise as you can. It'll help me to sell you in Rome."

"Paper, paper," groaned Clabon. "You live in a world where it counts more than action."

"That's not quite right, John. I work in a world where action is sometimes paper. And luckily I understand it better than you do. So please put your heads together and draft me some prose on specialist cars."

"Now?"

"No, later. Because now I am coming to volume cars. And here, as you know, the problem is more difficult."

Harvey paused, watching Clabon, then addressed them both.

"To survive among the giants, you must hit the world market with a popular, medium-sized car. Otherwise this merger will fail. And this is not a case for gradual tinkering. What's needed here is a single strong model from the start, produced in each country at an overall rate of ten thousand a week. Am I right?"

"Ideally, yes," muttered Clabon. "You are right."

"Very well," said Harvey quickly, "so let us consider the models you're both making now. At 1500 cc there's the BMG Pilot, made in Coventry. And then there's the Mobital Sparta, made in Milan. Both are cheap family saloons, designed for mass sale but not yet achieving it." He paused again, still watching Clabon. "Well, there's the choice. One or the other of those cars has to go."

On an impulse he stopped at that point. He was ready to make his own suggestion, but something in Clabon's demeanour made him wait. Guidotti, too, had the tact to keep silent, taking a sudden close interest in the state of his finger-nails. Even Laura sat with her head down. Erich was waiting for a signal, ready once again to present the hard facts. But Harvey had finished with that tactic. He let the silence continue, the pressure slowly mounting within it, as if they were sinking to the bottom of the ocean in a bathysphere.

Then John Clabon broke it with a very small sigh.

"All right," he said, "we'll kill the Pilot."

There was a general stir of relief. Still no one else spoke.

"But I've got a few conditions, and they're going to be expensive. Want to hear them?"

For Harvey the pressure continued to mount, constricting his breath and making his ears sing. "Go ahead," he said tightly. "All right with you, Carlo?"

Guidotti nodded. "Go on, John."

Clabon himself was quite unemotional. He closed a freckled paw round his bottle of Perrier, forced off the half-opened cap with his thumb, poured and drank. His manner, when he spoke, was matter-of-fact.

"The Pilot, as you say, was an error. It's cheap to run but costs too much to buy. And we got a little over-excited in the wind tunnel. I have to admit it's a pig to look at, and yes, all right, the damn thing is selling at the moment like bacon in Israel. I've got bloody thousands in stock."

"How many?"

The question came from Kohlman. Harvey, annoyed, turned to silence him. But Clabon swept on.

"I'll tell you that when I've had a drink, sonny, and I don't mean this stuff." He emptied the Perrier and thumped the bottle down. "So the Pilot gets the chop. The question is how to do it neatly. My own plan is this. First I cut the price, move it out at a loss, then I'll scrap the saloon and close down our robot assembly. But I'll keep the estate version on, butched up with heavy-duty tyres and military paint, to sell to the hunting-shooting set. We'll make it on a manual line and phase it out over a longer period."

"And the Sparta?" said Guidotti. "You will sell it instead?"

"Oh yes, you bet. Fine car, Carlo. Just ship it over. We'll have one in every showroom the day you sign. Then we'll start to improve it."

"Improve it?"

"We've got one knocked down at Ash Valley already. I reckon that we could be building the Sparta there inside a year, putting in our F series engine and some of our best bits and pieces. Meanwhile I'll get rid of twelve thousand men, to match you in Brindisi. But the rest must stay, every one of them, until we get back in full production. That means some very long lay-offs. And when it comes to making the Sparta, the robots will have to be taught some new tricks, which is going to set you back a few Eurobob. If you don't know how much it costs to tinker with those things, Patrick, then you're going to need a drink too."

"One moment, John. Please. One moment." Guidotti had at last got a word in. "Are you saying that BMG will only sell the Sparta if it becomes a British car?"

"About half and half will be enough."

"And you expect me to use your components in Milan?"

"Some I do, certainly – the best of them. Not the rubbish."

"This needs discussion."

"Indeed it does," Harvey said, suddenly standing. "So work it out between you and have the bill ready in about half an hour. Erich, will you take the chair?"

Clabon stared up at him in surprise, disappointed not to be praised for his heroic compromise. "Where are you going?"

"To check the defences," Harvey said.

"Is that really necessary?"

No, it was not. But Harvey couldn't answer. He hurried from the room.

Staggering slightly, he crossed the hall and mounted the stairs to his bedroom, where he swallowed some pills and lay down. Within ten minutes his heart was pumping evenly, the trip in its beat smoothed out by the drug. Recovering, he lay on his back and breathed slowly in and out, as prescribed. The air, stirring in from the open window, was fresh. He felt better, though damnably tired.

The drill when this happened was to stay very calm, but that wasn't easy when things were going so well. After less than four hours, he thought, the job was almost done. There was nothing left now which would lead to a serious quarrel, though already it was clear that one billion Ecus wouldn't be enough. He would have to offer more and take a chance on talking Riemeck round. After Riemeck would come the French and the

Germans, who wouldn't much like it, but none of the smaller nations . . .

To stop himself, he stared at the canopy over the bed, thinking only of the pattern in the sun-faded silk and the way that it fell in dusty folds from a central knot. Then he managed to think about nothing at all. He shut his eyes and instantly fell into a short, shallow sleep.

As soon as he woke, he felt refreshed. He raised himself off the bed carefully, waiting for the dizziness to clear. It did. He moved to the window and stood looking out.

And that was when he saw the movement in the park.

About half a mile away, beyond the chestnut avenue, the boundary wall of the château was intermittently screened by thick clumps of shrubs and smaller trees. A human figure was moving along it, appearing to bend between each gap in the cover, as if trying not to be seen.

Harvey assumed it was one of the gendarmes. He looked down to the terrace, which was right below the window.

"Paolo."

"Excellency?"

"Meet me inside, will you? I'm coming down."

Startled to hear Italian, Guidotti's guard had jumped up off the terrace's balustrade and started to reach in his jacket.

Harvey turned back to smooth the bed. The pills were lying where his hand had released them. He picked up the phial and put it with the other two: an old man's luggage, but not yet required at all times in the pocket. Of such small distinctions consists an old man's pride.

He went downstairs, found Paolo Santini in the hall and took him through into the kitchen, which was now full of steam and appetising smells. The pretty girl was dicing carrots on a chopper board. Watching her do it was the cook, a typical old French crosspatch whose bibulous habits were as famous as her soufflés. Annoyed at the interruption, she glared at Harvey with bloodshot eyes. He smiled at her and held out both hands, slightly bending his knees as if for a very heavy load.

"The key, if you please, madame."

This was an old joke. The door to the cellars of La Maréchale was a huge slab of barred and bolted wood which could only be opened by a key not much smaller than a tennis racquet. The cook, unamused, led them down a white corridor and showed them where it hung. Harvey took the key off the wall. Paolo lit a paraffin lamp and held it high as they passed through the dungeon-like door and then down a long flight of worn, smooth steps. The air below smelled equally of putrefied stone and fermented grape, with a dash of dead rat. The bottles stretched away into shadow, their labels obscured by white dust.

"Help yourself, my friend," Louis Royand had said. "You know where the best is."

And that was true. From many previous visits Harvey knew his way around this store of ancient liquid treasure. But the best must wait until the end, he thought. For lunch he had already settled on a favourite Muscadet. Stooping under the vaults, he walked straight to it, but Paolo wouldn't let him touch the dusty bottles, so he stood back and watched as the keen young chauffeur slid them out of the rack, blew on them, wiped them, then placed them carefully in the basket provided.

"Four will do."

Paolo nodded gravely, his face lit in chiaroscuro by the lamp, like a boy in a Caravaggio painting. "This is very old," he said, "very fine. The French understand these things."

"Try some yourself. Take a bottle out to the kitchen when you've served it."

"Thank you, Excellency. I will do so." The chauffeur picked up the lamp from the floor. "It goes well, this conference?"

"It goes well," replied Harvey, noticing the angular bulge of the pistol in Paolo's pocket. "And thank you for your help, Paolo. I appreciate it."

Suddenly they were in absolute darkness. The lamp had gone out. Harvey stood still, his heart bouncing out of its rhythm again as something scuttled past close. But Paolo was calm. He put down the bottles and relit the lamp, turning up the wick for a stronger flame. Then he led the way back to the steps. Harvey followed him, feeling like a child.

A few minutes later he returned to the dining room, where the car men were arguing still about components for the jointly manufactured Sparta 1500. Laura had made out a list for him.

Power unit	Suspension
Radiators	Brakes
Carburettors	Steering columns

Petrol tanks　　　　*Ventilation*
Exhaust systems　　*Instruments*
Trim

Beside each item she had written the country it would be made in, though some still carried a question mark, and alongside steering columns was the tart comment *Anywhere but Holland*. Harvey wondered if the quip was her own. No, he thought, that's Clabon speaking. He sat down and let the two men run on a bit while he thought what to talk about next.

The room was swirling with smoke. Each man had filled an ashtray. And Clabon had taken off his coat, which was not a good sign, Harvey thought, having long ago noticed one cultural division in Europe. Northerners shed clothes at the first touch of heat, southerners buttoned up tight. And in this case the temperature was rising on the subject of windscreen wipers, British or Italian.

Half following the argument, he lifted the cover of his brief and studied the private agenda he was keeping underneath it, a handwritten checklist of points to be covered, not necessarily in order. Then he took the list out and put it in his pocket.

"Gentlemen, it's getting rather stuffy in here. What would you say to a walk in the garden?"

Both men agreed with this idea.

"You can come back to these nuts and bolts later. There are better things to talk about now, and perhaps some rather easier ones too. We can take them as we go."

The agreement to that was even stronger. The meeting broke up. Harvey led the two men outside, then away across the lawn towards the shade below the avenue of chestnuts. He expected no trouble.

8

The day was now hot. Crossing the lawn, John Clabon took his tie off and rolled up his shirtsleeves. Guidotti, too, had removed his jacket and was walking with it over his arm. Harvey kept his on, feeling shivery.

Behind them was Angelo, Guidotti's private ape. When they came up to the French gendarme posted under the trees, Harvey asked him to walk in front. The two Commission guards were out on the flanks, right and left, one of them leading an Alsatian dog.

"Good grief, just look at all this," said Clabon in a loud voice. "Where have you put the artillery, Patrick?"

Harvey's smile was bashful. "Well, now they're here . . ."

"I don't much like the look of the rearguard." Clabon made a show of watching his back. "Where did you get hold of that one, Carlo?"

"Angelo comes from Sicily," said Guidotti, "where his family is very well known. So you must be nice to him."

It was all a bit deliberate: an effort to lighten the atmosphere. And Harvey, grateful for it, was struck by how much he had come to like and respect these two utterly different men.

John Clabon made you aware of the sheer, almost physical force required to prevail against the sloth of British industry. Apparently he liked to set his top managers impossible targets, in which there was no bluff at all – if they failed, they were out – but then he would make sure they didn't fail, inspiring them somehow to match his own terrible pace. So went the legend, and today it looked true. Clabon was virtually in the lead now, pushing and pulling the talks on forward with alternate demands and concessions of great boldness.

And Guidotti was the opposite of the hot, demonstrative Latin. Strolling along with his tame *mafioso*, he made you aware that to be an industrialist of any sort in Italy was an act of personal courage.

Harvey liked both of them. They also appeared to like each other, which was more to the point. Most big mergers, Arnold Doublett had warned, were done on a whim. They stood or fell straightaway on the personal compatibility of the top men. Harvey had no doubt at all that this was true, as in politics, and it pleased him that after four hours of argument the three of them could still be at ease together, even if the jokes weren't good. He was also pleased, at that moment, that he'd left behind Erich and Laura. A walk for three was what the moment required, especially since he was about to raise the most confidential point of the day.

They were under the left line of chestnuts now, keeping to the shade beneath the great trees, whose foliage whispered high overhead, stirred by a breeze not felt at ground level. The leaves were already curling brown at the edges. The grass underfoot was littered with sprigs. Half way down the avenue was a small medieval dovecote, still about sixty yards ahead. The doves had been bred in different shades of grey, Harvey noticed, almost black to almost white, or perhaps they had managed this effect on their own, like the pigeons on his own house in Kraainem. These birds of Royand's were in commotion now, wheeling up suddenly against the blue sky, each circle narrower as they closed back in on the old *colombier*. Something must have disturbed them.

"Of course," he said casually, "a joint car at 1500 will only half-solve your problems. You'll also need to make a small one, won't you?"

"That's where the real volume is," Clabon said. "And also the profit, provided you get the car right."

Harvey, encouraged, went on, still watching the doves. "It's whispered that you both have small cars coming off the drawing board. Is that right?"

Both executives nodded, but warily, waiting to hear what followed. So he came straight to it.

"The question is, can they be combined? Because you ought to produce a small car together, from scratch. I'm sure you agree."

Neither man answered. They were walking with their heads down, watching their feet.

"All right," said Harvey, "I realise that we're on dangerous ground here, since this is an area of commercial secrets. However, it is also the area where your development costs will be highest. A joint small car, if you do it, will use a lot of European money, so I don't think we can leave it aside."

Neither executive responding, they emerged from the trees and walked towards the dovecote. The château's long drive passed round it in a circle before continuing straight, between a second stretch of chestnuts, to the rusty iron gates. All round the wide gravel circle stood a thick wall of ancient rhododendrons. Harvey's intention was to take a turn round the dovecote and then walk back to the house in shade, down the opposite side of the avenue, but as they came into the open circle Guidotti paused automatically, waiting for Angelo to catch him up. He stood on the edge of the drive, looking back towards the château, which was seen at its best from this angle, its elegant façade framed neatly by the trees. Then he answered the point.

"What you say is true, Patrick. For Mobital the chief attraction of this merger is extra finance for research and development. We do not have sufficient money to build a new car alone. And the same is true for John, I expect, especially if he plans to go electric."

Clabon jumped as if stung. "Who told you that?"

"Nobody told me," Guidotti said coolly. "I read about it in a magazine."

Harvey, appalled, began to protest. "Carlo, just a minute."

"In the American magazine called *New Science*," Guidotti said regardless, "there is a description of a new battery engine. The performance, if true, is remarkable. The chemical formula is omitted, also the name of the manufacturer. But this work has been done by BMG, I believe, in association with Saab and Volvo."

For the second time Harvey felt breathless with anger. "Damn it, Carlo, will you shut up? I told you to leave this subject to me."

"*You* told him!" Clabon barked, jumping again. "*What* did you tell him?"

"Only to read the magazine," said Harvey, seeing already that he should have kept silent. "That's all."

"That's *all*? Holy shit, Patrick, that's *enough*!"

"But you told me nothing," Guidotti said to Harvey, clearly bewildered. "I study this magazine for myself, all the time. I do not understand what is happening here."

Harvey then realised the measure of his blunder. He turned to stare uselessly at the blond German head on the terrace of the house, now nearly half a mile away. "Erich Kohlman told you on my behalf," he said, "to take a look at that article but keep it to yourself."

Guidotti swept his hands sideways in total, vigorous denial. "Herr Kohlman told me nothing, nothing. We did not even speak of it. I study the technical press for myself." Then he spread his arms high and wide, in a papal appeal for reconciliation. "But is this not excellent news? If BMG have developed a battery engine, then let us discuss it. I believe that Mobital may have something of value to add, and these trees, these birds will keep our secret."

This poetic suggestion seeming good sense to Harvey, he turned to persuade Clabon into it. But the damage was done. Clabon was already walking away to the dovecote, his neck pink with anger. Desperately Harvey started after him.

"Wait here, Carlo, will you?"

All parties then changed position. Guidotti withdrew to the shade of the trees, Angelo edging up closer beside him, while the Englishmen sorted out their quarrel in the centre of the weed-grown circle. As they argued in low angry voices they stood face to face in the lee of the dovecote, which was built of stone, a round tower in miniature, full of little square holes for the birds. The doves cooed and rustled inside, holding a conference of their own. The French gendarme stood watching them, his submachine-gun slung from his shoulder. He was smoking a cigarette. The two Commission guards, a pair of young Belgians in suits, strolled round the circle with their dog, chatting quietly. The dog watched the birds.

A few minutes passed.

Then Guidotti was called across to hear the verdict. He emerged from the shadows, and the three of them stood together in sunlight, by the dovecote, while Harvey explained.

"John will agree, in principle, to collaborate on a new small car."

"That is all?"

"For the moment, yes. What about you?"

"I agree, naturally." Guidotti smiled, the only one in good humour. "This will make Fiat jumping mad."

Harvey continued stiffly, like a man who has been insulted. "The formula John suggests is this. The Community's funds may be used for development of new products, but neither company is obliged to reveal the details of its current research until the merger is a legal fact."

Guidotti's smile vanished. He looked at Clabon. "You insist on this, John?"

"I do, my friend."

"Can we not trust each other?"

"I'm sure we can. But let's wait until the politics are over. Then we shall know where we are."

Clabon would say no more. He looked ready to quit again. Harvey opened his mouth to speak, perhaps in apology, but right at that moment the dog began to bark – and immediately panic struck the doves. There must have been a hundred of them, scrambling out through the holes of their fortress one after another, as quick as they could, and then all clattering upwards together, darkening the sky as they swooped round and round overhead with a whoosh of many wings. The Alsatian went on barking, hoarsely, furiously, leaping and straining on its short chain leash.

Both executives and Harvey jumped in fright at the sudden commotion, but the two guards from Belgium were unworried. They held the dog tightly, then eventually calmed it. "*Il a peur des oiseaux*," one of them called across, laughing.

Only Clabon refused to smile; or perhaps he had not understood. "Let's go and find a drink," he grunted, starting back the way they had come.

"We'll walk back this way," Harvey said, leading off towards the other side of the avenue.

Clabon made a show of hesitation, to indicate that any suggestion now made by the chair, however small, was grounds for suspicion, but eventually he followed in surly silence. They passed through a gap in the rhododendrons and reached the shade of the opposite chestnuts. The four-man escort deployed as before. The return to the house began, no one speaking. Harvey was depressed. The mood was broken, the fault was his own. Slow thinking, hasty speech. An old man's lapse, he thought. Damn.

And then he saw Kohlman, running towards them from the house.

The bodyguards, taken by surprise, rushed in close, drawing weapons. But Harvey waved them back and stood waiting calmly under the trees. He was thankful for a distraction, whatever it turned out to be.

"What is it, Erich?"

Kohlman stood before them, flushed and panting from his run. "There are people in the grounds," he blurted out, his voice as shrill as a frightened boy's.

"What people? Where?"

"The staff have seen a man round the back, and we have just seen one up there." Kohlman, still gasping for breath, pointed back towards the rhododendrons. "When the dog barked, he came out and ran away into those trees, over there, beside the wall."

"Who saw him?"

"Laura and I, from the terrace."

"Where is Laura now?"

"Laura? I . . . don't know." Kohlman turned back to look. "She has gone in the house perhaps."

"Right," said Harvey quickly, "we'd better get inside too. Erich, take the gendarme up to those bushes and show him exactly what you saw. Better take one of our own men, too – the chap with the dog. We'll keep the other one with us until we're back in the house. Get going now, quickly."

But that was all.

Nothing else happened, and no intruders were found, despite a careful search of the grounds.

Harvey considered a search of the house itself, but rejected it as unnecessary. Instead he brought four of his sentries in close, to cover the approaches, and sent Paolo off on a tour of the other four with instructions that they should keep a sharp watch on the perimeter. That, he thought, would do for precautions. The alarm had probably been a false one. But whatever the cause, it was wonderfully timed, for it had brought back the mood of embattled togetherness. The quarrel below the dove-

306

cote was forgotten; John Clabon had regained his humour. And that was what mattered the most. Exploiting the moment for all it was worth, Harvey let the two businessmen loose on the drinks and then, to amused groans of protest, led them back to the dining room.

"Industrial relations, gentlemen, non-structural aspects of."

Following Doublett's advice, he told them they would have to go for parity of wages, same pay for same job, in both Britain and Italy, adjusted to the highest going rate.

They agreed.

From this it followed, he told them, that the unions would have to combine across frontiers, so this might as well be encouraged by a clause about unified negotiating structure, which Erich would draft after lunch.

They agreed.

As to productivity, he told them, the aim must be to raise output-per-man from five cars a year to eight, the level now current in Germany.

"More milk from the cattle," muttered Laura, apparently to herself, in a voice which, though soft, was perfectly audible to all round the table.

And for Harvey this was too much. He had no idea what was the matter with her – nothing like this had occurred in two years – but the reasons could be gone into later.

"Erich, take over the record, will you? Laura, please go and tell the cook we're nearly ready, then wait for me in the study. I'd like a private word before lunch."

There was a silence as she left.

Then the businessmen glanced at each other, close to laughter. Clabon was the first to speak.

"Not all our redundancies will be quite so easy as that," he said with a broad, roguish smile. "Eight cars per man means a hefty drop in the workforce."

"Yes," snapped Harvey. "It does."

"I thought we were here to save jobs."

"Yes, we are here to save jobs," Harvey said more calmly, pleased to see them ganging up again. "But that can't be done without some tightening, as you both know perfectly well. I am thinking of a four-year programme of gradually phased reductions in each country, agreed with the unions and properly compensated."

"Compensation," said Clabon, "on the scale you envisage, is going to cost a bit."

"It is."

"Will you help?"

"Of course," said Harvey, nodding. "This will be a fair call on Community funds."

"Patrick, do you have any idea of the bill you're running up?"

"Some idea, yes."

"Tell us then."

"Not yet. Money after lunch. You agree to these labour provisions?"

They agreed.

They were now so hungry and tired, Harvey saw, that if he suggested it, they would probably agree to give up making cars altogether and go into sweets or dry cleaning. But he was tired, too. It was time for a break.

"Make a note of those points, Erich, then clear all this stuff off the table for lunch. We're going back to the drinks."

And so the merger talks were adjourned. The three older men left the dining room. Waiting for them in the hall was La Maréchale's housekeeper, a blonde French widow with the face of a bank teller. Her news was that Lady Harvey had telephoned from Brussels but refused to leave a message, seeming somewhat annoyed that she wasn't allowed to speak to her husband in person. Harvey nodded in exhaustion. Clabon made some crack about a programme of phased redundancy. Guidotti said, rather sadly, that a cross wife was better than no wife at all. They returned to the *salon* for fortification. Harvey poured himself a small shot of whisky, drank it, then went to find Laura in the study.

She was speaking in French on the telephone when he came in, but the moment she heard him enter she slammed the receiver down and turned to face him, white about the lips, shiny-eyed.

"I said no calls, Laura, so long as the talks go on. That applies to you as well."

"But you've just kicked me *out* of the talks," she said in a brittle voice. "So the rules don't apply to me."

"Calm down."

"I am calm."

Harvey gestured at the telephone. "Who were you speaking to?"

"I don't have to tell you that."

"I think you'd better."

"All right. Friends in Paris. They're offering me a bed. Sir Patrick, I'm off." She picked up the lid of her typewriter. "This is mine. I'll leave you the paper and pencils."

Harvey held up a hand. "Now wait, just a minute. This is silly. What on earth is the matter with you?"

"Nothing's the matter. You and I don't fit, that's all. I'm going."

"Suddenly? We've been together two years."

Seeming momentarily shamed by this, she groped for some polite form of words. But the truth came out naked. "Yes," she said, rolling her eyes to the ceiling, "two years. And I can't stand another *day*. I'm sorry, but I really can't."

Harvey dropped his hand with a sigh. "Well, if you must go, you must. But you've picked a bad time for it."

To that she was going to make some sharp retort, but she stifled it, buttoning her lips between her teeth.

Harvey, suppressing his own annoyance, attempted a last appeal. "I sent you out just now because of your extraordinary remarks, which were not well judged for the occasion, along with some other things you've said this morning. But I want you to come back and act with your normal tact, Laura. Your part in these proceedings is important."

"Important, is it? Oh thanks," she sneered, clipping the lid on the typewriter. "You'll get by, I think."

"Yes, we will – if we have to."

"Well then."

Harvey was used to not understanding women, but this was more than peculiar. It was unreal. Either Laura was mad or she was pretending, but he had no way to talk to her except his own, and so he went on a little longer, seeking normal male reasons for abnormal female behaviour. "Perhaps you're in the wrong job, I can see that. But surely this is no way to end it."

"I agree, it's messy. But I'm going." She shrugged, then lowered her head, still standing by the desk.

He could see that she wasn't going to cry, but took the lowering of the head to be a wavering of purpose. "You're presenting this as some sort of difficulty between yourself and me," he said to her quietly, "but is that it? Is this really a personal thing?"

"Oh, I don't know. It's final, that's all." She looked up. "Anyway, what do you mean?"

"I was wondering if it was political. You've been unhappy about this whole business from the start – that was clear on the journey down here. And now you seem to be more unhappy. In fact, if you'll permit me to say so, you've been talking like some kind of wild leftist bigot. Has someone been getting at you?"

And that, he saw immediately, had torn it.

"Bigot," she repeated with a cold, bitter smile. "That's just your word for a person you don't agree with. If you liked my opinions, you'd call me strong-principled, wouldn't you? Except that you can't believe a woman has opinions of her own at all. She must have been 'got at', presumably by a man. Oh, you make me sick, the whole lot of you. Goodbye."

Taking hold of the typewriter by its handle, she swung it off the desk and started for the door.

But Harvey stepped in front of her, no longer bothering to hide his anger. "Very well," he said, cold-voiced, cold-eyed. "Go you better. But there are a few formalities. Would you give Erich your pass, please? And hand over all your papers, so that he can check them off. When you're ready to leave, the security men will take a look through your luggage, and I'd also remind you to be very careful what you say when you've gone. If a word of this meeting gets out before Wednesday, I'll know where it's come from."

And that, at last, took her aback. "My God," she cried, "what do you take me for?"

Harvey shook his head at her ruefully. "Laura, I have no idea what to take you for. I don't understand this at all. But I don't have time to go into it and there's too much at stake to make allowance for your feelings. So that's how we'll do it, or you won't leave at all."

Harvey thought then she might strike him. She had put down the typewriter and was standing close in front of him, trembling with several emotions at once – shock, annoyance, injured pride. Then her face composed itself into the closed, grim expression of the woman wronged, unable to retaliate immediately, sworn to long-term revenge.

"Can Paolo take me to the station?"

"No, you can phone for a taxi."

At that she became calmer still. Taking the typewriter off the desk for a second time, she turned back and stared at him, eye to eye, and then, as she finally broke with the whole convention that had governed their two-year relationship, she laughed. "You're a bastard, do you know that?"

"Goodbye, Laura. Thank you for your help."

9

Taking with him a boy from the stables, Paolo Santini made his tour of the four gendarmes guarding the château's perimeter. Two were far out in the grounds, east and west, and had to be found on foot. But the two at the gates, front and back, could be visited by car. Paolo had a packet of sandwiches for each of them, prepared in the kitchen, and a bottle of beer. The stable boy was carrying a shotgun. His job was to pass on Harvey's general alert in French, but he was more interested in the Mercedes. Eyes alight with wonder, murmuring appreciatively, he kept stroking it, inside and out, as if it were a thoroughbred horse.

The front gate, at which they called first, had been closed all morning. Nothing had been seen there. The old *flic* on duty was half asleep. Unimpressed by the talk of intruders, he muttered that the beer was too warm and sent them off.

The back gate was closely surrounded by woods. Here, at the rear of the property, the trees grew thick to the château's boundary wall and continued beyond it. And this forest was good for game, the stable boy tried to tell Paolo in French, screwing up his eyes and squeezing an imaginary trigger to make his meaning clear. "*Pam-pam!*" he cried, blasting off with both barrels, then flopped over sideways in the passenger seat with a moribund porcine grunt. But Paolo wasn't interested. His eyes were on the back gate as he drove towards it down a long, straight drive of loose gravel. Like the one at the front it was made of wrought iron, tall and rusty, chained and padlocked at the centre, where its two halves joined. And beyond it a car was drawn up, apparently trying to enter from the road which ran along outside the boundary wall. Leaning down into this car, already in discussion with its driver, was the gendarme on duty here, a younger man than the others, in *képi* and shirtsleeves, with only a pistol on his belt. He straightened up in surprise as Sir Patrick's Mercedes pulled up on the drive, just inside the gate.

Paolo tapped the horn and stepped out, in a hurry to return to the house, since he was due to serve the wine at lunch, a task of more importance than this one. The stable boy got out too, still carrying his shotgun, and together they walked quickly up to the gate, beckoning the gendarme to talk to them through the bars.

Outside and directly opposite the gate, concealed in the trees which grew thick on the road's other side, Rosa Berg watched to see what would happen, then turned to whisper at Mitzi Hoff, who was slithering up beside her in the undergrowth.

"Look who's trying to get into the castle," she breathed, shifting her pistol into her right hand. "See? Over there – the man in the car. He's been talking to the *flic*."

Mitzi looked and nodded. "That's him," she said, "our favourite journalist. Is he going to get in?"

"No, I don't think so. Let's see. Harvey's chauffeur's just arrived."

"Where's Joop?"

"Still up at the house."

In fact Joop was nearer than that. Though still in the grounds of the château, he was only just over the boundary wall, crawling up on its inner side for a last, closer look at this back gate. In an effort to blend with the scene he was wearing country workman's clothes, bought in Tours, and had armed himself with a pump gun, which could be mistaken for a thing to shoot birds with. Inching forward on his belly through the trees, he held the barrel of the weapon carefully clear of the ground, to keep the muzzle clean. He had been right up to the house, close in and all round it, then had circled back through the park, counting sentries. He made the total eight. As soon as he had checked this last position, he meant to hop over the wall, back to Rosa. He was in no hurry.

But then he heard voices, so speeded up his approach, running forward in a low crouch. At the edge of the trees he lifted his head with great care from the bracken to get a clear view of the drive, and then stood perfectly still to watch. Standing on the drive, in discussion with the gendarme through the bars of the gate, was Harvey's Italian chauffeur. At the chauffeur's side was a youth with a shotgun. And then a fourth man joined the group, advancing to the gate from the car drawn up on the road outside. It was Kemble, the drunken pressman first seen in Brussels, and he seemed to be delivering a letter.

Joop stiffened in extra interest, his mind immediately quickening. This could present a chance, he thought.

Three hundred yards away, in the forest which spread beyond the château's perimeter, Hal Fawcett's car was tucked out of sight. The Iskra's other two cars had been left in Ambillou, a village nearby, since neither was suitable for this reconnaissance. But Hal's muddy Peugeot estate, parked straddling the ruts of a track in the thick outer woods, had just the right landowning look for the district.

In the back of it Mario Salandra was smoking a cigarette, his face made weak by the absence of a beard. Hal himself sat at the wheel. Beside him, in the front passenger seat, was Stephen Murdoch. All three were leaning inwards, heads down in concentration as they listened to Joop Janssen's short-wave radio receiver, brought from Brussels to do more service here.

They heard Laura Jenkinson telephone the railway station in Tours. She asked for the times of trains to Paris and was told that the first express, going straight through without any stops, was at 4.05. "Thanks," she said in French, "that will do fine." Next she phoned a local taxi service and asked to be collected from the château at 3.30 prompt. Then she rang off and spoke in English. "Oh, hello. What do you want?"

"I have heard the news," Erich Kohlman said, standing stiffly in the doorway of the study. "I'm sorry."

Laura sighed, one hand still resting on the telephone's receiver. "Yes," she said in a voice flat with weariness. "Well, there you are. It's been coming a while."

"You are really leaving?"

"Yes."

"What happened?"

314

"The Commissioner was rude, I was ruder. Usual thing, you know, but worse." Her shoulders twitched in a tired, careless shrug. "So away I go."

"He told us it was personal."

"Well, he would, wouldn't he? Actually he thinks I'm a secret Marxist."

"That is ridiculous," Kohlman said.

"Is it?" Laura laughed and moved towards the door. "I was thinking he might be right. By the way, I'm leaving you the typewriter. I'll pick it up some other day."

Kohlman's voice rose in urgency. "Please, this is foolish. Don't go. You must apologise to him."

"No."

"Is this your menstrual period?"

"Oh Erich, for heaven's sake. Do please pull yourself together and get out of the way. You can bring me some food upstairs while I pack – and bring my pad. I'll do the record for you in longhand. And then, if you're good, you can search my person."

From the dining room came the sound of male laughter. Harvey and the two tycoons were already at lunch, getting down to chopped carrots and radishes, a fine assortment of *crudités* taken from the château's own garden and set out in a many-sectioned salad dish. The pretty girl who worked in the kitchen was standing by the sideboard, waiting to serve from a plate on which lay a huge grilled fish, still steaming, already cut into cross-sections. Kohlman came in from the study and spoke a few words to her. Then he went over to the papers heaped in one corner, found Laura's pad and went out with it. Two minutes later he came back to the room and sat down at table with the three other men. The pretty girl served the fish, then put a piece on Laura's plate, added some vegetables, and took the plate out. The meal got under way. Several minutes passed before Harvey glanced across at the bottles of Muscadet, still unopened on the sideboard.

"Where's Paolo?"

The chauffeur, it was learned, had still not returned from his tour of the outlying gendarmes. Kohlman, having got up to find this out, went across to the sideboard to deal with the wine.

"No, Erich, you sit and eat. I'll do it."

Harvey then got up to do the job himself, continuing to talk in a relaxed, cheerful manner – he was telling them about the huge key to the cellar – while he drew the cork on the first two bottles. Then he paused at the sound of his car braking sharply below the terrace: the unmistakable tick of the Mercedes' engine, revved up and switched off. A single pair of feet dashed across the gravel, up the steps, into the house and over the flagstones of the hall, suddenly slowing to a walk as they approached the door of the dining room. The door opened. Paolo Santini came in, slightly breathless and straightening his uniform. Harvey smiled at him indulgently and held out the bottle, ready to pour. But the chauffeur, still flummoxed, advanced with an envelope – a personal message for His Excellency.

"For me? Who from?" asked Harvey in Italian.

"A man at the gate," said Paolo. "He gave no name. I believe he was American."

"Is he waiting?"

"No, he has gone. He said it was a matter of urgency."

"Very well. Let me see it. You take this."

Handing over the bottle, Harvey took the envelope to the window and opened it. For about thirty seconds he was perfectly still. Then he put the message in his pocket and came back to the table.

"Friends of Louis Royand," he said casually. "They seem to think I'm here to play bridge."

The meal resumed.

Only Guidotti wasn't fooled. He stared at Harvey's helping of fish, cleared away half-eaten, then at Harvey himself, whose jests, like his face, had become a little wan. A quick look of mutual comprehension passed between them. No questions please, said Harvey's eyes. The Ambassador obeyed.

After lunch there was coffee, then both the businessmen retired to their rooms. It was agreed to resume the talks at 3.15.

Erich Kohlman was sent upstairs to clear Laura for departure, check her luggage and sign for receipt of her confidential documents. His face was set cold as he went to do it, obedience prevailing over friendship. Or perhaps there had never been any real friendship between those two, thought Harvey, once again struck by how very little he knew of his closest subordinates. He himself kept out of the way. Shut up alone in the study, he took out the letter that Paolo had brought him from the gate. As he studied it again he held it out at arm's length, by the tips of his fingers, as though to avoid contamination. His face was that of a man confronted by a disgusting object but determined to give it some serious analysis.

Dear Sir Patrick,

I enclose a snap which has come into my hands. If you want to discuss it, please raise the portcullis. Otherwise I print what I guess, upcoming merger and a joint electric car, to be built with Euro funds. Sorry to be crude. Hard times, foreign ways.   *As ever,*
                                                              Jack Kemble

P.S. Shall wait here till 4.

The note was written on the paper of L'Auberge de la Chasse, a restaurant of some repute in the nearby village of Ambillou. In the envelope with it was a polaroid photograph, black and white, very clear. The picture was of Harvey himself in deep conversation with Clabon and Guidotti. The three of them were standing beside the stone tower of the medieval dovecote, at the centre of the wide weedy circle of gravel, half way down the front drive of La Maréchale. All four bodyguards were looking in various wrong directions. Only the Alsatian dog was alert. Held on a short chain leash by one of the young men from Belgium, it was staring straight across from the circle's far side, ears pricked, mouth open to bark, eyes fixed on the camera lens hidden in the bushes. The whole scene was framed by the dark undersides of rhododendron leaves.

Harvey laid the print on the desk, beside the letter. For a moment he stood looking down at them both, his feelings still held in check. Then he opened an interior door and let his anger loose. Like a big mad bird it swooped right out of him and round the room with a silent rush of wings, about to break something. Then it was gone. He was calm again.

His mind now totally engaged with this new threat, he sat down to read the note for a third time, then held it out to Erich Kohlman as he came through the door. First the letter, then the photograph were studied by Kohlman in silence. Surprise, dismay passed briefly over his face, but he made no unnecessary comment, proceeding directly to the extra facts required.

"This man was chasing you in Brussels. He came to the office without a pass. I sent him away."

"So how the devil did he find us in France?" Harvey pointed to the photograph. "He took that himself of course, though you notice he's careful not to say so."

"He knows Laura, this man."

"What! You think she told him we were here?"

"No," said Kohlman after a pause, "that is not possible. When he came to the office, he was looking for her as well as you. He was obviously annoyed with her."

"Well, we better ask her. Go and fetch her, Erich, will you? No, wait." Harvey held up his hand. "Is there anyone else who could have told him?"

There was, and Harvey knew it. Kohlman knew it too, but did not feel able to say. He stood looking out of the window with a thoughtful frown, remaining fixed in that posture until his master noticed the pretence.

"All right, Erich, thank you. Let's get her on the phone."

A call was then made to Lady Harvey.

As Kohlman picked up the receiver, the mouthpiece came loose. He screwed it back on, then dialled the number for Kraainem, Belgium, while Harvey talked on, for some reason choosing this moment to offer a glimpse of his domestic life.

"The worst thing a man can do to a woman, Erich, is ignore her. My wife sometimes uses the press to remind me of that, only this time she doesn't quite know what she's started. And the fault is my own, I'm afraid. I told her a little, but not quite enough. If she'd known how important it was to keep this quiet, I really don't think she would have . . . What? No answer? All right then, leave it. It doesn't matter, anyway, how this man found us. The question is what to do now that he has. You say you met Kemble in Brussels?"

Kohlman put down the receiver with a nod. "He claimed to be a friend of yours."

"A friend. Yes, he always did have the most infernal cheek."

"You know him?"

Harvey nodded, his face once again set into an expression of fastidious, controlled disgust. "Yes, I know Kemble. I thought we'd exported him. Who's he working for?"

"*The Times*, he said."

"Surely not."

"That's what he said."

Harvey shook his head in dismay at the world, then bent to study Kemble's note for a fourth time, the single sheet of scrawled longhand still set face upward on the desk like a bacteriological exhibit. "Well, someone's paying," he said after a moment, one finger-nail tapping the printed letterhead. "This inn he's waiting at has two rosettes in Michelin." And with that Harvey finished his analysis. Moving with sudden brisk decision, he put both the note and the photograph back into the envelope they had arrived in, then handed the envelope to Kohlman. "Keep this safe, Erich. We may be able to use it later. Now, listen carefully. Here's what we're going to do. First off I want you to ring the special exchange in London. You know the drill. Say you have a call from me, immediate and personal for Chieftain, on an insecure line."

"I know."

"Get cracking then. I'll tell you the rest while you do it."

They went to work like a well drilled team. Kohlman picked up the phone, Harvey began to explain his plan. But before they had got much further there came a knock on the door of the study, a short double rap, sharp yet nervous. It was Laura, ready to go in her smartest grey suit. She was carrying her suitcase. She advanced a step and put it down. Her manner was stilted and her face very pale, as pale as if she were ill. She said she had come to say goodbye. Harvey called her in, shut the door behind her, made her sit down. Then he asked her point-blank if she knew Jack Kemble. The question clearly unsettled her. Her eyes flicked at Kohlman. Yes, she replied, she had met Jack Kemble at a party in Brussels. He had tried to wangle an interview but she had told him it couldn't be done; that was all. Admitting this, Laura's voice pitched a little higher than usual, the words tumbling out in a rapid, tense monotone. But Harvey believed her. He had a sound instinct that Kemble's information had come from his wife.

In some perverse way, however, this made him even more hostile towards his errant secretary. As Laura gave her answer he examined her with cold, deliberate suspicion. He meant to interrogate her further, but before he could ask another question he was called to the telephone by Kohlman. The British Prime Minister was on the line . . . no, not quite yet, but walking in now from the garden at Chequers.

Harvey nodded and took the receiver. As he did so he had the peculiar sensation of being in two different places at once. The English house at that end, its terraced lawns and rosebeds, was more familiar than the French one at this. Then he thought of *The Times*. His face slowly tightened in anger as he waited.

10

It cost a hundred francs, *rien compris*, but lunch at L'Auberge de la Chasse was almost worth crossing the ocean for. After it Jack Kemble sat by himself with cognac, coffee and cigar. The time was three o'clock. Most of the tables had been cleared, but at one of them a bunch of French businessmen, radiant with profit, were talking to the chef, who took off his uniform and sat down to join them, immediately looking like a millionaire himself.

The room was low and beamed, stuffed with antlers, boars' heads, huge curly bugles and other obscure bits of hunting equipment. It all looked quite fake, except that somewhere close by was a kennel of hounds. For a while the pack would settle, taking it in turns to let out a low woof of hunger, then away they would all bay together, not itty-bitty fox-chasers, to judge from the sound, but a terrible brood of stag-eating monsters. Perhaps it was a tape, made to go with the decor.

Kemble had had enough of dogs. Though frozen with fright, he had gone to the end of the film, clicking steadily on inside the rhododendron bushes while two of Harvey's guards restrained their German Shepherd. And that had been an act of magnificent professional courage, he thought to himself, looking back on it now from the comfort of the restaurant with pride and no little astonishment. This cigar, this brandy, were deserved.

He spread the prints out on the cloth again, trying to decide which was best. In all of them Harvey looked anxious and old. He was greyer and thinner, more frail than the man of ten years ago, and yet there was something tough about him: still sharp of eye, still light on his feet as he picked his way through the grounds of the château in his dark suit and shiny town shoes.

Looking at the old fellow now, caught and shot for *The Times* in polaroid, Kemble felt the sudden affection of a hunter for his prey. The feeling didn't last. He put the prints away and paid the bill. Fair game. Hacks must eat.

At 3.15 he moved to the lounge and sat scribbling notes for the story he would shortly ring through to *The Times* in London, with quotes from Harvey or without. Saturday being the day of rest, for daily newsmen as well as the Hebrews, he only expected to talk to a copy-taker, so it came as a double surprise when a few minutes later, just before 3.30, he himself got a call from the paper's editor. Kemble had not even told *The Times* where he was. It was a call from the château down the road he was waiting for, and as he stepped into the restaurant's phone booth, still clutching a glass of brandy, he was braced for an angry conversation with Harvey. The adjustment to a different voice on the line took him several seconds to achieve, a sideways skip of the mind not assisted by previous intake of hunter's reward.

"Frank?" he gaped. "Frank Holroyd?"

"Yes, Jack, it's me, your temporary employer. Don't sound so bloody surprised."

Kemble pulled himself together, recognising the sharp Aussie twang, more pronounced on the phone than in the flesh. "Of course I'm surprised," he said. "How in the hell did you know I was here?"

"I've just had a call from Harvey. He told me where to find you."

"Oh no."

"Oh yes, Jack."

"How come?"

"The electric car – you shouldn't have mentioned it in your note to him. I've been asking about that too, so he guessed that we must have briefed you."

"So now you're in trouble."

"We are. Quite a lot. I told you to stick to the rules if you used our name."

"Okay, so it's not your fault if I jump over walls. Don't worry, Frank, I'll tell him that."

"I've already told him," Holroyd said, an edge coming into the twang. "But he won't believe it. He's threatening to do us for trespass, invasion of privacy, undue duress, you name

322

it – complaints to Press Council pending. He's even got the bloody Prime Minister on our backs. Gross breach of national interest, we are told, if we print a word about the merger. The PM's asking us to hold it till the summit. No, demanding."

"And you've agreed to that?"

"We have agreed."

"Chicken."

"Great national paper, Jack. Can't rock the boat."

"Yeah, I'm saluting," Kemble said. "So now what?"

"He's going to give you an interview."

"He is? You mean Harvey?"

"Yes, I mean Harvey. He's coming to see you in that pub you're in now. His German flunkey is just about to ring you. Now listen to me, Jack."

"I'm listening."

"He's made us a very fair deal, so don't muck it up. Just behave. If you still want a job, that is. I assume that you do?"

"You assume correct," said Kemble. "So what's the deal?"

"Harvey will give you the stuff for a profile. Ring it in quick and we'll do it on Monday, as from Brussels. He will also give you an exclusive on the merger, but only if we hold it till Wednesday and don't use your pictures. What do you say?"

"I say yes."

"Clever boy. And by the way, off the record, well done. The boss is tickled pink."

"I thought he was always that colour."

"Shut your big American mouth, Jack. Out with pad, down on knees. And hand back those naughty snaps. You got us the story. Just don't push your luck."

Back at work in the dining room with the two car executives, Harvey plodded on through some last minor points. He was keeping the record himself now with quick, nervous scribbles of a pencil. In Laura's machine the tapes were still turning, forgotten.

The curtains were half-drawn to keep out the sun. The windows were open but no breeze came through. Outside on the terrace the two guards sent by Commission Security paced up and down through the sultry afternoon, their Alsatian dog still padding between them. Harvey was conscious of their steps on the gravel, up and down, up and down. Each time he glimpsed it through a gap in the curtains, the dog's head was hung a little lower with heat and fatigue.

For his own sake he'd finally asked the tycoons not to smoke, and they had agreed with good grace. Clabon had been dulled, Guidotti enlivened by the wine at lunch. Their mood was pliant, but now they were bored. There was only one big thing left to discuss, and that was the money.

They wanted to hear how much. They were waiting only for that. But Harvey stalled on, refusing to come to it, while the backstage crisis grew ever more obvious. From the study came repeated pings of the telephone as Kohlman made call after call, piling up the pressure on *The Times*. Laura was in there with him, assisting perhaps, or just waiting to go. She had not changed her mind.

This continued till 3.25.

Then the telephoning stopped and Kohlman came back to the dining room. Walking in from the door he made a quick affirmative signal, unnoticed by either executive. Harvey nodded in thanks and went on with the minor business. A few minutes after that Laura's taxi arrived. He saw her shake hands with Paolo on the terrace. She seemed about to kiss him, but did not. Paolo took her suitcase. Head high, Laura walked down the steps, disappeared from view and was driven away. For Harvey she had already ceased to exist. Turning in from the window, he brought the minor business to a stop.

"Gentlemen, these are just details. I think we can leave them. The four main points which remain to be settled are these. Would you like to write them down?"

Obedient as schoolboys, the chiefs of BMG and Mobital reached for their pads. Their heads went down as he gave them dictation.

"One, your acceptance of the Commission's right to choose the new chairman. Two, your agreement to workers' directors on each national board. Three, your plans to co-produce the Sparta. Four, your commitment to a joint small car."

At the last item Clabon's face turned to a scowl, but Harvey ignored him, winding up quickly.

"On all these points I need something firm, so see what you can do within the next hour or so. Erich will stay to do the drafting and answer your queries. And he'll take over the chair now. I'm going to take another breather."

Both businessmen raised their heads, surprised by this sudden change of plan. Clabon especially was suspicious, Harvey noticed. All the credit in their friendship had been used up. And in any case John Clabon was the sort of man who regarded a rest, when taken by anyone except himself, as downright slacking.

"You're going to leave us for an *hour*?" he barked crossly.

"Or so," repeated Harvey. "In fact let's make it two. I'll rejoin you here at 5.30."

"That's a long breather. Are you all right?"

Harvey left the question unanswered. "An old man's privilege," he said to both of them blandly, tidying up his end of the table. He wondered which one would be the first to take the cue.

Guidotti, as usual, was quickest. He held up his hand. "One moment, Sir Patrick. If you are to leave us, you must also leave your money on the table. We have waited long enough."

"Ah yes, the money." Harvey nodded, as though he were glad to be reminded of it, then signalled to Kohlman to take down his answer word for word. "Given your agreement on the four points outstanding," he went on carefully, "the Commission will recommend a mix of grants and loans, to be disbursed over the next four years. Some of these funds will go to pay off your governments. The rest will be applied to the purposes discussed this morning, in proportions we will work on tomorrow."

Both of them were listening intently as he paused, then Clabon's face erupted in amusement. "Patrick, you're getting awfully formal. Is this a good sign or not?"

"I am trying to say what I mean," Harvey answered unsmiling, and added in a more severe voice still: "Since you seem to doubt the word of politicians."

"I hope you're going to mention a figure."

"I am. But you must understand that it isn't a hard cash promise. The Community's funds are not within my gift. There are several hoops still to go through, and at the end, if the money approved at the summit falls short, we might have to make up the balance with some form of bank guarantee. However, the sum I shall mention is what I think you need. It is also what I think I can get, provided you give me your full cooperation. And by cooperation I mean an effort to work out a joint production programme, all secrets shared, starting now."

Clabon nodded impatiently. "All right, all right. We'll try. So how much?"

"Four billion."

The figure was received in silence.

Clabon's eyes bulged, then slowly lit up.

Guidotti was still as a waxwork. His face went rigid with the effort not to show any pleasure.

Kohlman's mouth fell open in shock. The last he'd heard, it was one billion.

Harvey looked from one to the other. "That is four thousand million," he said precisely for the record, "European currency units, roughly equal to dollars American. To be paid in four equal tranches, beginning at the start of the next calendar year. Until then you'll have to meet your needs from the banks."

He squared off his papers, then stood to go.

"Well, there's the offer, gentlemen. Now it's up to you."

That was the last thing he said to them, and with it he was gone, before any one of them could find their voice. From the dining room he went upstairs and lay on his bed for the second time that day, eyes closed, body relaxed, working up the strength to deal with Jack Kemble. Their meeting was fixed for 4.30.

This time he took no pills, feeling more winded in spirit than body. The offer he'd left on the table was a gigantic gamble – exactly the sum recommended by Doublett in Oxford, four times the sum agreed with Riemeck in Brussels. To turn it into cash would take all his energy and skill. But that didn't worry him. The challenge would somehow produce the strength required. What turned like a worm in the soul was this business with Kemble, the grubbiness of it, the need to respond at the same grubby level. Press relations were always the thing he'd found hardest to cope with at Downing Street, where the actions of journalists, especially the British ones, had often seemed no better than vandalism. And Kemble, he remembered, was one of the worst. A devious and insolent drunk, whose skills got their edge from deep social spite.

Old rages stirred in Harvey's breast, like wounds playing up. It upset him that negotiations of such importance, affecting the livelihood of hundreds of thousands, could be threatened by one worthless scavenger. It upset him even more that his wife had probably been involved. Along with an utter lack of principle there was in Jack Kemble, he remembered, a sort of raffish charm which worked well with women. But that Margaret, of all women, should fall for it – that was a sad and shaming thing. Each time he thought about it, Harvey felt more depressed.

However, revenge had been arranged. In the terms agreed with *The Times* was the strict condition that Kemble was not to be accepted on the staff of the paper. As soon as the merger was out, he was finished, but until then he had to be lulled with the promise of a job, in case he tried to sell the story somewhere else. Harvey had no doubt at all that this deception would work, being well within the scope of Frank Holroyd, a man who had the low self-preservative cunning of a creature from the outback, not found so often in editors of *The Times*. It was sad to see the paper in such hands.

Three kilometres away to the west, Jack Kemble was making his own preparations in the village of Ambillou. As the clocks were striking four he entered the Post Office. In his hand was an envelope, addressed to himself in London. He had it stamped, then dropped it in the box. Inside was the best of the photographs he'd taken at the château.

Then, coming out, he stopped in surprise.

From where he was standing he could see the whole village, which was huddled around a wide irregular square. Its buildings of pale stone and blue-grey slate were overshadowed by the forest which pressed in close on all sides. At the top end was a church, and beside it an edifice with small barred windows, like a jail, in which the staghounds were shut. The square's southern side was formed by L'Auberge de la Chasse. Half-timbered and smothered in creeper, the inn's walls carried numerous enamel plaques testifying to gastronomic excellence. In the centre of the square was the usual gravel patch, bright in the sun, with a low fence around it and a sign saying *Union Boulliste Ambillou*. Trimmed trees, neat as mops, encircled this central playground, and several cars were parked there, noses inwards to the kerb.

The scene had the peace of a clearing in the woods, but what stopped Kemble in surprise was the sudden arrival of a vehicle he knew. Appearing from the right, a dusty red Peugeot station wagon dashed into the village and made a rapid circuit of the square, depositing passengers at two other cars. One of the cars was a big white Citroen, the other an old snub-nosed Volkswagen. Immediately all three vehicles went off together, in convoy, at speed, tyres squealing as they took the narrow road to château La Maréchale. And that was all. The hounds in the kennel woofed restlessly, then settled back down as the deep rustic silence closed in.

Kemble stood still a moment, not certain whether to believe what he'd seen. He had not only recognised Hal Fawcett's car, but four of Hal Fawcett's five passengers. Thinking about it, he walked from the Post Office back to the inn. Half-way across the square he accelerated into a trot. By the time he reached the inn he was running.

At 4.15 Harvey reluctantly stirred into action. A little refreshed by his lie-down, not much, he crept across the landing and down the back stairs to the kitchen, where Paolo was waiting.

"Ready, Paolo?"

"Ready, Excellency."

"Lead on then. As quiet as you can."

Following his chauffeur down the back corridor, where the big key to the wine cellar hung, Harvey continued to walk on the balls of his feet. He did not want his departure to be heard from the dining room, where the businessmen were still at work with Kohlman. And this subterfuge was aided by the ring of the telephone, which started at that exact moment, conveniently covering all lesser noises. From the hall came a clatter of footsteps as the housekeeper hurried to answer it, but the bell was still ringing when Harvey left the house. Gently he closed the back door, then stepped into his car. A few seconds later Paolo had the Mercedes started up and in gear, rolling out of the courtyard and down the back drive with hardly a sound. They were on their way to meet Kemble in Ambillou.

In the dining room only the telephone was heard, then the murmur of the housekeeper's voice as she took the call in the study. But neither executive took any notice, since they knew that no interruption would get past the stone-faced, stone-walling Frenchwoman. She had blocked every incoming call so far and she would no doubt block this one, whether it came from President or Pope. In any case their attention was back on the job. Enticed by more Ecus than the world's population, they were putting together a co-produced version of the Sparta 1500, piece by piece. It was a three-box car, and Clabon was trying to make the boot bigger, to capture the British fleet market – police, taxicabs, commercial travellers and so forth.

"Don't ask me why, but the cops like big boots."

Guidotti wouldn't have it. The bodyshell could not be altered, he said, but he would agree to a change in the suspension, which could be softened for the better roads in Britain. The motorways in Italy were falling to bits, along with the political system, so the Sparta's springs were as tough as a jeep's.

Next they moved on to fuel consumption. Each man knew by the pricking of his thumb what each had paid analysts hugely to predict, that the price of petrol would rise even further, so they quickly decided to build an economy model using BMG's F series engine, which could do sixty miles to the gallon.

"What about an electric version, John?"

"Forget it, Carlo. Battery won't pull at this weight."

Guidotti kept prodding at the great British secret. Clabon still refused to release any details. It was clear that this would eventually lead to a row, but Kohlman made no effort to prevent it. At first he had copied Harvey's style in the chair, deflecting quarrels, hustling agreement. But now he sat quiet and kept the record, his tired gaze wandering out to the terrace each time the talk digressed into technical detail . . . and then they were all three up on their feet at the sound of two shots – very loud and very close. Turning in fright to the gap in the curtains, they saw Guidotti's man Angelo tumble to the gravel of the terrace, his pistol already out. The Commission's dog barked so hard it was almost a scream.

At the moment when his car passed through the château's back gate Harvey noticed that the gendarme on duty there, while saluting, turned his head sharply back up towards the house, as though he had heard something. Then he was closing the gate behind them.

The Mercedes, once out of the grounds, turned left towards the village of Ambillou, down the narrow road which led through the forest. Now they were going along it. But Paolo kept the pace down, since the road was pot-holed, and in parts hardly wider than the wheelbase of the car. The trees pressed so close that they met overhead, forming a long green tunnel. The sun pierced this canopy of leaves in shafts of hot light which dappled the road's gravelly surface.

Harvey felt soothed by the beauty of the scene. As usual on this obscure byway, there was no other traffic to be seen, but then they came round a bend and found an accident. A big white Citroen had collided with a Volkswagen. The German car had skidded half into the trees, the Citroen was slewed across the road. A girl was lying on the verge, two people bent over her, while a local man in beret and working country clothes, a farmhand perhaps or a gamekeeper, stood watching unhelpfully with a shotgun over his shoulder.

"Better stop, Paolo. Somebody's hurt."

Paolo pulled up, got out, walked over to the group on the verge and bent to examine the victim. Harvey also stepped out, but hung back, impractical and squeamish, aware of his uselessness in such situations. Then to his great astonishment he saw the injured girl jump from the grass, the two people over her also quickly straightening, all three of them reaching up with their hands to grab Paolo, who jerked back free of them and started to dash towards the Mercedes, simultaneously pulling out his pistol. As he ran he was signalling and shouting a warning, which may have held him up for a fraction of time. In any case he wasn't quick enough. Harvey watched helpless as the bystanding man with the shotgun unshouldered his weapon and fired from the hip, straight into the young chauffeur's midriff. The force of the shot picked Paolo off his feet and flung him to the opposite verge, where he fell with a cry, still struggling.

Harvey instinctively started to duck back into the car, then a fury stronger than fear pulled him up, made him turn and shout in protest. The killer looked casually towards him, then pumped the gun to reload it and fired again into Paolo's body.

When he heard the second shot from the forest, the stable boy pointed frantically towards it. "You see," he cried, "it happens very often here! This is a region well known for the hunt, well known, it happens all the time – *pam-pam*!"

He was utterly bewildered by the furious reaction to his own two shots, especially that of Angelo, who had charged across the lawn from the terrace and struck the gun from his hands. Now, as others of the château's security force closed in on him, the boy scurried off into longer grass and picked up the hare he had killed. "*C'est la chasse, la chasse!*" he repeated in desperate appeal, holding the dead beast aloft as though to explain his whole existence to these crazy strangers who had filled his master's house.

But his troubles were over. The first man to laugh was the pink-faced gendarme advancing from the chestnuts, quickly followed by the two Commission guards, who had finally calmed their Alsatian. The businessmen chuckled from the terrace, exchanging heartfelt looks of relief. Even Angelo was no longer angry. In fact Guidotti's bodyguard had lost all interest in the trigger-happy youth and was staring pensively at the distant woods, where the other two shots had come from.

Kohlman's smile was forced. His face, always pale, had been turned greenish-yellow by the incident. For a moment he seemed unable to move or speak, and then he made an effort to take control of proceedings, suggesting in a stilted manner that they better return to work, since Sir Patrick expected some progress in his absence. Following him into the house, the executives smirked behind his back, becoming more than ever like a pair of naughty boys.

This silly mood was further encouraged by the sudden appearance of the stern-faced housekeeper, who took Kohlman off to the study for a private word. Left alone together in the dining room, the businessmen chortled in amusement. Carlo Guidotti took out his yellow cigarettes for an illicit smoke. He opened the case with a mock-furtive glance, left and right, and held it out. They both lit up and inhaled. There was a pause. Then Clabon, still bouncy, but getting back to business, walked over to the table and switched off the tape-recorder.

"All right, Carlo, just listen to me while I tell you what I dare. We call it the BMG-BDV III. But between you and me it can be the BDV. That's short for Battery Driven Vehicle . . ."

Shut into the phone booth at L'Auberge de la Chasse, Jack Kemble had heard no shots. He had also got nowhere at all with the hard-voiced woman who answered at the château. She either could not or would not converse in the English language.

So far as she could be understood at all, she seemed to be saying that she had no knowledge of a person called Patrick Harvey. Kemble's garbled attempt to convey both urgency and some degree of possible danger had made no dent in her comprehension, but the moment he said the word *"presse"* she'd hung up on him. He had not tried again. His alarm was probably unjustified. It was certainly vague, and its causes were small. Yet he could not dismiss it from his mind. It hovered there uneasily, coming and going, flaring up and falling like a flame in a draught while he stood in the porch and waited for Harvey.

By this time Kemble had taken a room at the inn for the night. He had brought in his case from the car, unpacked, changed his shirt and freshened up. The fumes on his breath had been sweetened by a mouthwash. The forbidden photographs, all but one, were in his pocket. Now he was ready to face the beak.

But Harvey, most unusually, was late.

It was 4.30.

The shadows had started to lengthen in the square, but nothing else was moving in Ambillou. No people were about and no sound broke the silence of the all-surrounding woods, not even a woof from the hounds in their kennel. Perhaps they were eating.

11

At La Maréchale the end, when it came, was quick and painful.

Puzzled by Harvey's long absence, assuming he must be asleep in his bedroom, the businessmen sent Kohlman upstairs to fetch him. A few minutes passed. Then Kohlman returned to say that Sir Patrick had left the house, apparently to visit French friends in the district. It was the best excuse he could think of.

"Well, blow me. The sneaky old rascal," Clabon huffed. "Ring him up, lad. Tell him to come back here at once."

That wasn't possible, Kohlman explained. He himself didn't know who the French friends were, so could not get hold of Sir Patrick for the present.

At that both men became exasperated. Guidotti silently threw up his hands, Clabon swore in open disgust. They got up and walked out together, back to the drinks in the *salon*.

Immediately Kohlman shut himself into the study and put a call through to the inn at Ambillou. The call was answered by the inn's receptionist. She put it straight through to Jack Kemble, who was now in a furious state, having twice more tangled with La Maréchale's housekeeper. His telephone messages had been ignored; an attempt to call at the château in person had been turned back at the gates. Kemble had plenty to say, and a wide range of Anglo-American vocabulary to say it in, but became so carried away by the saying that he forgot to answer the question of the moment. Kohlman had to ask it a second time.

"Please, Mr. Kemble, listen. Are you telling me Sir Patrick did not arrive to talk to you?"

"You're damn right he didn't. He didn't come, and he still isn't here. And that's not the only thing." Released at last,

Kemble's news poured out in a loud, fast spate slurred with alcohol. He told what he'd seen in the village, and how it related to previous incidents. "Pretty damn peculiar, don't you think?"

"Yes, this is worrying." Kohlman was silent for several seconds. "So something has happened? Is that what you say?"

"Don't ask me, chum. But if you haven't heard from him either, I suggest you start thinking foul play."

Again Kohlman lapsed into anxious silence. Then he brought the conversation to an end. Not waiting to hear what sorts of foul play Jack Kemble had in mind, he thanked the journalist curtly for his help, told him to stay where he was until further contact, and rang off. For a while he sat wondering what to do. Then he summoned the two Commission guards and asked them to search the district, calling first at the inn at Ambillou. A few minutes later they drove away quietly in their car with two of the local French gendarmes as guides. The time was now 6.45. The tycoons were wetting their throats in the *salon*, but Kohlman was reluctant to join them, having nothing he yet felt ready to say, so he stayed in the study and started to type out the points agreed in the course of the afternoon. With no idea what to do next, he did his job.

And then the whole matter of the merger was lifted from his hands. At seven o'clock he received a call from Dr. Otto Riemeck, the President of the Commission, who phoned in from Brussels to check on the progress of the talks. They spoke in German. Riemeck was not much worried by Harvey's unexplained absence; he seemed to regard it as in some way typical. But his voice immediately turned to a bark of appalled surprise at another piece of news conveyed by Kohlman.

"*Four*, did you say? He offered them *four*?"

"Yes, four."

"That's in Ecus?"

"Four billion Ecus," repeated Kohlman with certainty, "spread over four years. I was rather surprised myself."

About two minutes after this Erich Kohlman appeared in the *salon* of the château and asked both executives to go to the study, where the Commission's President was still on the line and wished to speak to them in person. Announcing this, Kohlman could not conceal his embarrassment, which came out on his face as plain fright.

334

"It seems . . . there has been a misunderstanding," he said, his voice fading even as he started to speak. "I regret . . ."

The two men strode from the room, already grim. Kohlman made to pour himself a drink but got no further than picking up a glass, which he held in distracted fashion. He heard the businessmen talk on the phone, first one and then the other, their voices rising in disbelief. Then they rang off and spoke to each other more quietly, still conferring in the study. After a time they came back in silence. Guidotti stood in the centre of the room, looking down at the carpet as he lit the last cigarette in his case. Clabon drank a large shot of whisky, then spoke for them both. His voice was level and quiet, very tired; past anger.

"Well, that's it," he said. "We're off."

"But surely you will wait till Sir Patrick returns?"

"No, Mr. Kohlman, I don't think we will. This sort of thing is hard to forgive, you know. But if you don't mind, we'll leave you to tell him so."

And by 7.30 they were ready to go.

But first, at Guidotti's insistence, a cremation occurred in the stables. Both men stood watching while Kohlman fed every typed paper, every handwritten note, every doodle, every carbon and tape cassette through the door of a huge, old-fashioned boiler. Within a few seconds all record of the merger of BMG and Mobital had turned to ashes on the white-hot coke.

No epitaphs were said. In gloomy silence they walked from the boiler room to John Clabon's car. Angelo was already sitting in the back. Guidotti climbed into the front. John Clabon was last to go. He shook Kohlman's hand and patted his shoulder, then turned away without a word. But about to get in behind the wheel he paused and turned back, as though feeling that he must, after all, find something to say. "Are you sure Sir Patrick's *all right*?"

"You mean in health?"

"I mean in the head."

"I have noticed nothing unusual," Kohlman said.

"Isn't *this* unusual? I mean, where is he, for God's sake?" Clabon's hand flew vaguely round the scene, then dropped to his side. He shook his head and sighed. "And anyway, what ever got into him, telling us a fib like that?"

"Fib? What is that?"

"A lie."

335

"I believe it was an error, Mr. Clabon."

"Erich, no man in remote command of his faculties makes an error of three thousand million."

This was the first time since they had met that Clabon had used Kohlman's Christian name. Having done so, he got quickly into the car, as if to cover a lapse, and wound down the window for a parting shot.

"He must have gone ga-ga – it's the only explanation. It's certainly the only damn excuse. Still, rather sad, when you think about it. Surprising, too. Seemed all right, didn't he? Well, I don't know . . . When he deigns to turn up, you tell him from me that it's time he packed it in. Goodbye to you, my friend. And thanks for trying "

The car's wheels span angrily on the gravel. It scorched away, and for a full minute afterwards the noise of its motor receded in the distance as it sped down the long chestnut avenue, round the *colombier*, through the front gates and down the road to Tours, until it was out of sight and out of earshot, only the dust of its passage still floating up slowly in the warm, still air of early evening.

After that Kohlman sat alone in the *salon*. The house was so quiet that all he could hear was a moth beating round in a parchment-shaded lamp. Fatigue and strain had made his head ache.

He wondered if he should have told the businessmen of Kemble's worries about Harvey's welfare. That might have kept them at the château. On the other hand Harvey's own strict parting orders were that Kemble's presence in the district should be concealed. In any case it made little difference. Riemeck had scotched the whole project, so now there was nothing left to do here – except, of course, to clear up the mystery. What had happened?

Soon after that the mystery deepened further, when the search party came back from Ambillou. Sir Patrick's Mercedes had been seen to pass at speed through the village, they reported. It had not come back.

At which point Kohlman decided to act. So far he had sheltered under existing orders, which was his own natural instinct when confused. But now it was clear that fresh orders were required, and the only man left to give them was himself. With a nervous effort of the will he went about it. By 8.15 he had the whole of the château's defence force assembled in the kitchen, the two young Belgians and the six French gendarmes. He questioned them closely, each in turn, while the pretty girl gave them something to eat and the old cook muttered in the background, forced to cast her culinary pearls before swine. Each man spoke up in turn, and although nothing definite emerged, a number of fragmentary observations, if put together in a certain way, began to suggest a rather frightening possibility. All the men saw it at once. Panic spread through them like a gust of wind, turning every head in Kohlman's direction. But he had already gone. Returning to the phone in the study, his feet were heard to cross the hall at a run.

His first action was to call Lady Harvey, who ought to be informed, and might just possibly have some explanation for her husband's peculiar absence. But the house in Kraainem, Belgium, didn't answer. This was surprising, since she rarely went out, and never alone. Kohlman tried the number a second time. No reply. He rang off, picked up the receiver again. For a number of seconds, finger hesitating, he thought of going straight to the French police, but then changed his mind and dialled Brussels a third time. A few minutes later he had Dr. Riemeck back on the line, having dragged him from a banquet at NATO headquarters. The President, irritated, tried to dismiss the matter, but Kohlman insisted, his normally respectful manner disintegrating into an agitated shout.

"Please, sir, don't you understand? Something's gone wrong here, and it's looking very serious. I need some help."

Back at the start there had been some shouting and banging about, more angry than frightened. Most of it seemed to be distress for his chauffeur, but perhaps there was some panic too, Rosa thought, since the space was so small and dark. In any case she'd had to stop it. There was a risk he would be heard, especially in stationary traffic, so a short distance out of Tours she had pulled off into more woods, where they bound and gagged him. To assure him he could breathe, she had fired a hole through the lid of the boot, then held the silenced pistol to his head.

"You speak French?"

He had nodded, lying trussed in a bundle.

"Well listen to me, Harvey. If you want to live, keep still and shut up. Any more noise and we'll shoot you. We can do it any time, you know, by firing through the back of the seat with this. Understand?"

After a pause he had nodded again, but not in fear of death. Now that the first shock was over, his eyes had a flat, steady look, resigned yet determined.

She had shut him back in and driven on, determined to have the hired Citroën off the roads by the time the alarm went up. Mario Salandra read the map while Stephen Murdoch sat behind, half-asleep, crammed over to one side of the seat by the trunk full of weapons. The car hummed on until nightfall, and Harvey had done as he was told. For the last three hours there had been no sound from the back.

But now, quite suddenly, this frantic commotion. His feet were kicking the inner rear wing and his head was beating up against the back of the seat. They could hear muffled grunts, increasingly desperate, and this was more than any of them had the heart to ignore.

"Let him out, Rosa, please! This is too much, I cannot support this! *Veramente*! *Ti prego . . .*" Mario went off into Italian, imploring her to stop the car, and Murdoch agreed, not as ruthless as he'd like to be. "Sounds as if the old bugger's choking," he shouted in English, a little more coherent, though cracking up fast. "Better take a look, Rosa, don't you think? Shit! What is it? What's the matter with him?"

But Rosa, claustrophobic herself, needed no urging. She was already searching for a place to stop. "Shut up! Shut up! Shut your stupid pig mouths and look for a turning!" she yelled at them in French, and then broke off into furious incomprehensible oaths as she tried to find a way off the crowded main road. They were out in the country but going along in heavy traffic, unable to park on the verge unobserved. Then an opening appeared to the right. Rosa yanked the wheel and turned off the highway down a grassy track, which ended in a desolate quarry. Tall cliffs of chalk rose around them in the dusk as the car came into a flat open space heaped with rubbish. They jumped out and opened the boot.

When they took off the gag, he was sick. And that had been the cause of the problem. He had been choking in his own vomit. He had also, while struggling, gashed his head on some metal projection. Blood was running down his face and had spattered his shirt. When they lifted him out of the car, he fell to the ground, wracked with cramp. His breathing was agonised, like that of a man saved from drowning. He was drenched all over with sweat. Eventually, when they raised him to his feet, he stood bleeding and shivering, near swooning, his suit smeared with chalk dust, his grey hair dishevelled. Then his legs gave way and he sagged against the car again, helplessly, sliding downwards.

Mario and Murdoch rushed in to support him. But Rosa turned away and took a few steps, dismayed by a wave of moral doubt.

"Put him in the back," she said harshly over her shoulder. "Flat along the floor, Steve, under your feet. We're nearly there now."

Still waiting for news at the inn in Ambillou, Jack Kemble picked at a two-rosette dinner. He toyed with each course as it came and kept to a bottle of Vichy Water, his desire for wine, his appetite for food destroyed by the increasing whiff of sensation. He was now nine-tenths certain that he had bumped into a story far bigger than the one he'd set out for, possibly the biggest of his life. Twice he had telephoned Kohlman at the château. Each time the answers became more evasive. "Please stay where you are," the German had said, "until further notice."

"Let me come up to the house."

"No, you will be visited. The police are here now."

"Ah! So there is something wrong."

"You will be informed, Mr. Kemble. There has been a delay, that is all."

And further delay there had been, ever since, in passage of information from château to inn. But Kemble was no longer puzzled by this. He had guessed that it was a trap to catch him out, presumably set by the French police, who must suspect him of being involved in whatever it was that had happened. The moment of realisation had come when the phone was cut off at his third attempt to call *The Times*. Just as the paper's exchange came through, the line was disconnected. This had happened three times in a row, and then he had noticed that a pair of dour-faced young Frenchmen contrived after some short delay to turn up in each public room of the inn that he himself wandered into. Clearly not habitual gourmets, they had followed him into the restaurant and given themselves a hearty meal, but had drunk very little, and received no bill. Never once did they raise their voices or laugh. Nothing that moved in the room escaped their eyes. The poor little sweets, they might just as well have worn boots.

After dinner he went upstairs to his room. He knew they would come to get him there eventually. He was so sure of it that he was wide awake, cold sober, and still in his clothes when he heard several cars pull up in the square towards midnight. Stretched out on his bed, he listened with a smile of pure enjoyment to a furtive commotion of soft-talking, heavy-footed men. The crept up from the inn's porch to the corridor outside his room. And a few seconds later they crashed straight in, weapons drawn. Without a word they frisked him and searched the bed, his clothes, his luggage, every drawer, every cupboard. Then they took him downstairs to see their chief.

He was waiting alone at the bar, a hugely overweight man with heavy-lidded eyes and a drooping black moustache, about fifty years of age. He introduced himself as Serge Daladier. His comfortable, fleshy appearance and dark grey suit suggested a man of business, perhaps on the banking side. There was nothing especially police-like about him, and he made no mention of his post or rank. But Kemble knew power when he saw it. Lack of formality was a sure sign of clout, especially among the French. And on that test Serge Daladier had plenty. Not stirring from his stool, very quiet and relaxed, yet watchful, he pushed a bottle of whisky and an empty glass down the surface of the bar.

Kemble, still on guard, held up the hand of temperance. "No thanks, I won't."

"*Vous parlez français, j'espère.*"

"Not enough for this, I don't. Sorry."

"*Eh bien*, you must tolerate my English." Daladier filled his own glass and took out a gnarled black pipe, of the type used by all true detectives. "I have some questions to pose, Monsieur Kemble, concerning your presence in this place."

"You've lost him, haven't you?"

"Sir Patrick is absent, it is true. We do not know where. That is all. His wife is also missing."

"Is she now? Really," Kemble said, turning down his mouth and raising his eyebrows in a grimace of surprise.

"Can you explain this thing?"

"No, I can't. But I know who might."

Kemble then gave descriptions of the people, three men and two women, who had crossed his path in various combinations since Wednesday: first at the hotel in Brussels, later in the café at Tours, and today in the village of Ambillou.

"Thank you," said Daladier. "This is valuable."

"I'll have that drink now."

"Please. *Servez-vous.*"

Kemble helped himself to ice, to Scotch, then swilled them round together, staring into the glass. "So what do you think?" he asked, beginning to assume himself a friend of this soft-spoken, pipe-smoking, mild-mannered sleuth. "Is it kidnap?"

"Kidnap. Yes, perhaps," said Daladier, nodding slowly, his eyes still watchful. "You heard the shots?"

"No, I did not hear the shots." Kemble forgot the drink in his hand. "This is pretty hot stuff," he added quietly, putting the glass down untouched. "Can I tell my paper?"

The Frenchman raised one finger and wagged it. "Not yet, if you please. No publicity."

"Why not?"

"Because I do not wish it."

"Can you stop me?"

At the moment this question was put to him Daladier had disappeared in pipe smoke. But when the smoke cleared, he was seen to be wearing a patient and kindly expression. "*Cher ami,*" he replied in the same even tone, "this is a serious investigation. If you do not cooperate, I shall lock you into prison."

Kemble could not quite believe it. At no point since leaving Bethesda, Maryland, had he felt so far from home. "Well," he said, "that's nice, isn't it? Very nice." He swallowed the drink entire. "So now what?"

"Please pack your baggage," replied the Frenchman casually, sliding his bulk off the barstool. "We are going to Paris."

Sunday

1

From the moment the French police picked him up in the early hours of this Sunday morning, Jack Kemble started to note each small thing that happened around him, feeling suddenly blessed with that specially heightened perception which people outside the trade of journalism achieve by eating tropical mushrooms or thinking very hard about atomic particles. So far he had been chasing a story; now he was in it, and it was improving. Kidnap beat mergers on anybody's breakfast table.

At first it looked like murder. Half way between the village of Ambillou and the château of La Maréchale, on a narrow road deep in the woods, a team of detectives were examining the verge under floodlamps. Tyre-tracks had been found in the grass, also a pool of blood. But analysis soon showed that the blood wasn't Harvey's. Scraps of blasted uniform revealed that the victim was his chauffeur, and dead he must certainly be, this Paolo Santini, since no human frame could survive two short-range shots from a Viking pump gun loaded with nine-ball ammunition. The ejected cartridges were nowhere to be found, but the whole scene was peppered with bloody spheres of lead, and the French had no doubt about the weapon used, since they used it themselves in close combat.

Standing by the car which had brought him from the inn, Kemble watched the scene with ravenous interest, the road-blocks like tank-traps, the glare of the floodlights and crackle of radios, the woods looming black all around. While no one was looking he tried a couple of snaps, though the film in his camera was not of the right type for night work. Nor was his French up to pump guns. For an explanation of what was going on he had to rely on occasional asides from Commissaire Daladier, the hugely built chief of detectives who had come to collect him at the inn.

A few facts about this sombre, taciturn man had been volunteered by one of his subordinates. Commissaire Serge Daladier was one of the top policemen of France. Well known in the press for his coups against terrorism, he was chief of the BRVP, the crack section of the criminal police which dealt with political violence. His staff called him Groucho, because of his drooping black moustache. He had flown from Paris to take on the case. Before arrival at the inn he had spent some time at the château, and now, having taken a look around the scene of the crime, he returned to the car and sat in silence, filling it with smoke from his barbarous pipe. The car, at his orders, remained where it was. Kemble asked what was going on.

"J'analyse, mon ami. J'analyse."

Kemble thought this was a joke. It was not, he realised, swallowing a humorous retort of his own just in time. And then they were plunged into darkness. The floodlamps had been switched off. The gendarmes were hurriedly dismantling the roadblocks, the detectives stowing their equipment into vans. Daladier had ordered the site to be cleared. But he did not wait to see it done. With another curt command he told his driver to proceed to the château. The car started up and rolled forward. As it purred on slowly through the trees, picking out a startled deer in its headlights, Kemble sat still and held his tongue, content to watch and listen until he was spoken to. Then the Commissaire tapped him on the knee.

"The camera, if you please, monsieur."

Kemble handed it over.

Daladier, switching on the car's interior light, casually took out the film and put it in his pocket. He didn't appear to be angry. As the car turned in through the gates of the château, he conveyed the fruits of his analysis in calm, slow English.

There was no evidence, he said, that Harvey himself had been harmed, so this was presumably a kidnap. But if so, a very unusual one. The Mercedes and its driver had been removed; no threats or demands had been received. The conclusion must be that these Leninist bandits, whose name was believed to be the Iskra, had tried to remove Sir Patrick without a trace.

". . . and we must allow them to think that this deception has succeeded. If they believe we know nothing, they will make a mistake."

"So, no cameras," said Kemble drily. "Is that it?"

"*C'est ça*. No pictures, if you please, and no talking to your paper. We must keep a bottom profile." Daladier handed the camera back and stared at Kemble reflectively, still watchful, if no longer suspicious, before he switched out the light. "It is important that we understand ourselves," he added after more pipe-puffing in the dark. "Tonight you are working for the French police. It will be a long business. You are tired?"

"No, I'm not tired."

"Then turn your brain to this, Monsieur Kemble. These people, the Iskra – how does it happen that they know so much?"

The car had come up to the back of a big country house, tall white stone and steep slate roofs, very elegant from what Kemble could see of it. Circling round to the front, they pulled up beside some cracked steps, an ivy-grown balustrade. Parked on the drive was a silverish grey Rolls-Royce. On the lawn, fifty yards away, stood a helicopter.

Winding down the window to tap out his pipe, Daladier sat in the car and continued to ruminate. He had a Frenchman's habit of bringing up the contents of his mind in a beautiful verbal display, like a peacock's fan. Noting this, Kemble resolved to play American dimwit.

"What do you mean?"

"*Eh bien*, listen to me. I will tell you what I mean."

This merger of automobiles, the Commissaire went on, content to spread his logical feathers, was supposed to be a secret, was it not? Yet in each of their three interventions the Iskra had shown themselves very well informed. In England, in Italy, the gang had known when and where to strike. So also here, in France. They knew that the talks were being held in this house, they knew when Sir Patrick would leave it. The question to which the mind should now be addressed is how did they know all these things.

Timidly breaking the silence which followed this elegant exposition, Kemble ventured an answer. "You think they've got an inside man, then."

"A man, perhaps, yes. Or a woman."

An inside woman. At this suggestion of the Commissaire's,

dropped as it was with a casual shrug, Kemble's slow-witted surprise was genuine. "What? Laura Jenkinson? No, come on, you must be joking. She's just a horsy little egghead."

"She is intellectual, you mean, this English girl?"

"I mean she has brains but they're scrambled. She fools around with lefty ideas because they make her feel interesting."

"Ah – a lefty egghead of the upper class. In France we say *bolchevique de salon*."

"Well, whatever, she'd never get into a thing like this."

"We shall see," said Daladier, nodding slowly in receipt, not acceptance, of this opinion. He sat a moment longer in thought, then opened the door on his side. "We shall go in now. But you will say nothing, if you please. Be content to listen and observe."

Kemble bowed in his seat. "I am at your command."

The Frenchman's nod changed to one of full agreement. "That is true," he said gravely, stepping from the car, which perceptibly rose on its springs as he transferred his weight to the gravel. They trotted side by side up the steps to the terrace of the house. Coming into the light from the windows, Kemble glanced at his watch. The time was 1.30. Harvey had been gone nine hours.

They were inside the château for thirty minutes. Commissaire Daladier was busy for all of them, but Kemble, as instructed, stood and watched, allowing the paragraphs to collect in his head.

Opening off a stone-flagged entrance hall were delicate rooms of milky grey panelling edged in gilt, where the style was more luxurious: hunting tapestries, impressionist pictures, chairs too pretty to sit on, carpets too fine for the feet. The Rolls outside belonged to the owner, Louis Royand, who resembled an English country gentleman, until you noticed the cut of his tweeds, so much better than anything the English would wear. He seemed as much distressed by the invasion of his house as the loss of his statesman friend. And who was this person, he wanted to know, pointing in annoyance at Kemble. Daladier calmed him down.

Also there was Erich Kohlman, the German who worked for Harvey in Brussels. The man was still smart as a tailor's dummy, though ruffled in manner now, white with exhaus-

348

tion. Kemble, remembering their encounter in the Berlaymont, could not feel sorry for him.

The gendarmerie were out searching the grounds. They could be seen from the windows, advancing in line like beaters, the beams of their torches probing under the trees. The house itself was swarming with detectives. One of them was taking apart the telephones, another was sweeping the walls with a metal-detector, moving it carefully over the apples and onions of a small Cézanne. In charge here was Inspector Jacques Biffaud, a short man of military neatness, with thin steel spectacles and hair cut *en brosse*. He was Daladier's deputy in Paris.

The lofty, fat, dark-suited Commissaire dominated all, moving from problem to problem with lugubrious calm. Kemble noted each thing that he did.

At 1.45 he made a phone call to Dr. Otto Riemeck in Brussels, President of the European Commission. This took place in the study, behind closed doors, so nobody heard what was said. Emerging, Daladier ordered Kohlman to tell him the names of the people who were privy to the merger of BMG and Mobital. Kohlman did so, in the hearing of all. Daladier wrote down the names, studied the list a moment, then put it in his pocket. Speaking in French now, he asked where the company chiefs, John Clabon and Carlo Guidotti, had gone.

To that Kohlman had the answer. Both men had flown off from Tours in Guidotti's private plane, he said. They were spending the night at Clabon's home in London. They had telephoned in at about ten o'clock, hoping to talk to Sir Patrick.

"And Miss Jenkinson, where is she?"

Kohlman's reply was surprising. He told how Laura had fled from the château – to stay with friends in Paris, so she said. She had left no number or address.

Daladier's questioning sharpened. "At what time was this?"

3.35, replied Kohlman with precision. A taxi had come to collect her. "She was going to catch a train from Tours."

"Was it known at that time that Sir Patrick would leave this house to meet Mr. Kemble?"

"It was known."

"Did she know it?"

Yes, replied the German with no discernible emotion, Laura

knew of the appointment in Ambillou. She had been with him in the study when he made the arrangements.

"Thank you, Monsieur Kohlman," said the Commissaire, who sounded most dangerous when polite. "I shall now pursue this matter in Paris. You yourself, if you please, will remain in this house. If there is any communication from Sir Patrick or his assailants, you will be instructed what to say by my deputy, Inspector Biffaud, who will also remain here. If Miss Jenkinson herself should get in touch, we wish to know where she is. Meanwhile I have another task for you."

Kohlman, blank as a soldier on parade, awaited his orders.

"I understand that no record exists of the business discussions which occurred here," Daladier said to him. "It was destroyed, for reasons of security, at the order of Monsieur Guidotti."

"That is correct."

"In that case I wish you to reconstruct it. In French, if you please, from memory – each point agreed, each point of difference. No detail must be omitted."

For the first time Kohlman hesitated, his pale grey eyes slightly widening in anxiety. "For that I shall need some authority."

Daladier was getting more polite all the time. "Herr Kohlman, this is a homicide enquiry in the territory of France. My own authority is sufficient. You will make one copy for Dr. Riemeck, and another for me. That is all. You understand?"

"Of course. I will do it at once."

Saying this, Kohlman nodded submissively. Under the smooth diplomatic shell there seemed to be a soft and rather likeable person, with that serious, child-like gentleness as often found in Germans as severity.

Even so, he had taken a damn long time to react. Four hours, no less, had elapsed between Harvey's departure from the château and Erich Kohlman's calling in the French police. Rather long, surely. Too long.

This suspicious thought flitted through Kemble's head as he followed Daladier out of the house, down the steps across the lawn to the helicopter. And then, running in beneath the rotor blades, he was thinking of Lady Harvey.

She, too, was missing, and had been so for nearly six hours.

Kohlman had first tried to call her at 8.15. The time was now two in the morning.

Inside the helicopter Daladier kept working. Wearing a bulbous white helmet with built-in earphones and mouthpiece, he distributed orders throughout the flight, talking by radio to parties unknown. The noise inside the machine was tremendous. Kemble, strapped into a hard canvas seat, made notes on his pad in a mixture of words and shorthand symbols intelligible only to himself. His purpose, at that moment, was less to keep a record of events than forget he was riding in a helicopter, a method of transport still haunted by memories of Vietnam. Instinctively, uncontrollably he braced himself for the clatter of bullets on the hull, the sudden white death of a missile . . .

But soon they were over Paris, a great lake of light with the Seine winding blackly through it, and over there Sacré Coeur, shiny-white on its hill like a Disneyland castle. Descending, they turned at the Eiffel Tower, and then they were following the bends of the river, toward the twin stumps of Notre-Dame. French police headquarters, rebuilt the year before, was a massive cube of glass on the Île de la Cité, close alongside the cathedral itself. The helicopter, noisily hovering, planted its wheels on the building's roof. Daladier was out before the rotors stopped. Kemble jumped after him, and then, riding down in an aluminium elevator, was hit by a trembling so strong that he couldn't conceal it. He smiled in apology. But immediately, to his surprise, the Frenchman understood. "You were in *Indochine*?"

"Yes, that's right."

"I also, in the previous pig's mess. It has left a suspicion of parachutes."

Saying this, Daladier covered his privates and stared at the floor, pop-eyed, as though the lift were dropping to hell. The gesture was comic in a man so grave. Kemble, laughing, forgot to shake. He had come across this twice before, the only real bond of feeling between the French and Americans; and in the present case was specially glad of it. He hoped to stay close to the hunt for Harvey, but soon, once his evidence was given, there would be no excuse for his presence. A favour was required of this Frenchman.

Meanwhile there was plenty to record.

The huge smoked-glass building they were in was known as the Quai des Orfèvres, Quay of the Goldsmiths. Headquarters of France's criminal detection force, the famous *Police Judiciaire*, it was as modern inside as out. Here as elsewhere, the French had gone whole-hog for the future. Waiting for Daladier to take command of it was a large operations room, so well equipped it resembled the mission control of a moonshot with its rows of desks and many telephones, chattering Telex machines, clocks showing times around the world, electronic display panels, consoles, computer terminals and banks of small, palely flickering monitor screens. In the centre was a tabular map of French territory, made of glass, lit from below, over which women were pushing plastic markers, like croupiers in a casino, or rather, to Kemble, like the girls at Fighter Command in the Blitz. Every post in the room was taken up, either by detectives in shirts of many colours or uniformed police in shirts of pale blue: about forty men in total. All were already at work.

Over the exits, and at other high points, red lights were blinking. This was a signal for secrecy, Kemble learned. Until the red lights went off, no one involved in the search for Harvey was allowed to mention the fact outside this room.

And so long as that search continued, Daladier would have a priority call on all the other units of law enforcement in France, of which there were far too many for foreigners to understand, with names too long to remember. The Commissaire's own unit, the BRVP, came out in full as *Brigade de Répression de Violence Politique*; and closely allied with it was the DST, *Direction de la Surveillance du Territoire*. The difference of function was small but precise. The DST kept a watch on subversives in France; the BRVP broke their necks if they tried anything. So today, assuming kidnap, the BRVP were in charge, and it was Daladier who took up command in the office set aside for the chief of operations.

This was a carpeted room with a plate-glass wall overlooking the rest of the show. Branching off it were two other rooms, in one of which sat the Commissaire's own staff, drafted in from the BRVP. In the other was a telephone exchange, operated by a pair of women whose expertise consisted in calling up anyone in the world, high or low, at a moment's notice. And they were soon busy. All the time until dawn Daladier was almost continuously on the telephone, sometimes with an interpreter at his side. At various points of the night Kemble noted calls to Rome, London, Amsterdam, Brussels, Bonn and Washington, besides those inside France itself, one of which went to Interpol at St. Cloud, and another, behind closed doors, to the Minister of the Interior.

At the same time, while he was talking, Daladier kept making notes on the list of names that Kohlman had provided. The British Prime Minister had been crossed out, Kemble noted with relief, but everyone else who knew about the merger of BMG and Mobital was being investigated.

Kohlman's own name was on the list, a circle drawn around it. And Laura Jenkinson was underlined. Though assumed to be in Paris, she couldn't be found.

Nor, more alarmingly, could Lady Harvey. Towards morning Kemble overheard Daladier suggest to the Belgian police it was time they broke into the Harveys' home in Kraainem.

Meanwhile a bigger search was being conducted for the kidnappers, and Kemble soon learned to judge its progress from the scene in the well of the ops room. The red plastic markers being pushed about the luminous map were watching posts of the police, not roadblocks but pursuit cars, all set to follow and report if the gang were sighted, at which point Daladier himself would take command by radio. The markers formed a pattern of concentric circles around the town of Tours, and fresh circles kept being added by the croupier-like ladies, the search widening steadily outwards as more time passed. So far there had been no contact. And the wider the circles spread, the lower fell the hope of success. The trouble was the general alert had not begun until 9.15, which had given the gang almost five hours' start. They could have been tucked into hiding before the search began, or they might be out of France altogether.

Daladier's natural gloom deepened. He abandoned his pipe and smoked his secretary's cigarettes. Each time he made a phone call, a queue of his staff built up. They closed round his desk the moment he hung up, then split away quickly one by one as they got fresh instructions. Some of them were starting to show signs of strain, patches of sweat below the armpits, faces drawn tight under stubble, and Kemble himself was tiring, kept busy all night in an effort to identify the members of the Iskra.

This went better than the search on the ground. And strangely enough it was this, more than anything else he had seen, which made him think of Europe as a single country. Interpol could only deal with criminal cases, he learned, so the member states of the Brussels Community had a separate and secret agreement to exchange information on political undesirables. It was done on a network of linked computers.

Stephen Murdoch was first to be put through the programme. At the push of a button his whole life's story came through from British Special Branch. First his face appeared on a television screen: a pinched white visage in close-up, several shots in quick succession. Kemble, peering close, confirmed that this was the man he had seen. The French computer operator, nodding in silent acknowledgement, tapped on the keyboard of his terminal, whereupon another screen lit up with green lines of data from London. Paris pressed for print-out. Immediately a nearby typewriter, untouched by hand, started to rattle at incredible speed.

Transferred to paper, Murdoch's political record was two yards long. His first rebellious act had been to break up the canteen at Birmingham Poly in protest against the cost of lunch. He had come to Paris for the rumpus in May 1968 and ever since that time had stirred up the Trotskyist cause on the floor of British industry. He had been at BMG eight years. WMG, Workers' Motor Group, was what he was going to call the company when justice and reason swept him out of the toolmakers' ranks and into the chairman's seat.

Kemble studied this furious life with some fellow-feeling, himself the son of a steelworker from the British Midlands. I escaped, he thought; I got my revenge with a typewriter. Murdoch did not. This was his. And now let's see how they do it in Italy.

The print-out on Mario Salandra was even longer, though slower to come. He, too, had been in Paris in 1968. But the notable thing about this Roman academic was how his career followed that of his grandfather, a pioneer of workers' cooperatives killed by the Fascists in 1920. Italy had come full circle, it seemed, arriving right back at the bloody political feuds which had brought Mussolini to power. A depressing thing to contemplate, if you were Italian. But if you were American, merely foreign. Americans didn't die for ideas, Kemble thought; they fought for a patch on the prairie. And this was borne out by the third of the Iskra, who seemed to be merely an outlaw, though the data on him, rattling through from Military Intelligence, Fort Holabird, Maryland, could have filled a book.

Early in 1968 Hal Fawcett had sought asylum in France, following desertion from the US Marines. Later he had visited Hanoi with other protestors. Later still he had changed his tune and returned to the States, making apologetic speeches to the press. After a spell in Camp Pendleton, California, he had been released in a postwar amnesty, but immediately his car had been shot up by angry veterans. He had fled back to Paris and had lived here since. He worked in a shop called *Berg Livre*.

Thinking of the dumb young Marines he had seen go to death for reasons that no one believed in, Kemble felt a special distaste for this man. And Daladier, ex-*Indochine*, shared the feeling. "We should have sent him back," he said, shaking his head at the ease with which Fawcett had found political shelter in France. "For this I am ashamed. But now, to oblige you, we shall put him into prison."

The Commissaire spent a long time on Fawcett's print-out. "Here is the one who will make a mistake," he muttered with confidence as picture after picture flashed up on the screen from Washington. And Kemble, confronted again by those lank blond tresses and weak doped eyes, could not disagree. Prison, indeed, was where Hal Fawcett seemed eager to go. By giving away his name on the bar crawl in Tours he had greatly lessened his chances of escape. The number of his car had been traced, his flat in Paris and his place of work were being watched, his phone had been tapped, his friends were being checked. Even his regular drinking spot, the Café Babylone in the Boulevard Raspail, was now under close surveillance.

Fawcett had not turned up, however. Neither in Paris nor in any part of France had the Iskra moved a muscle.

This was the situation at 5 a.m. – three names known, but no other progress – when the Commissaire, seeking fresh air, took Kemble back up to the roof of police headquarters. Together they strolled across the helicopter landing pad and stood facing east towards Notre-Dame. Behind the cathedral's twin towers the sky lit slowly, like a black and white film dissolving into colour. Paris came up grey and blue, tall streets of stone and steep roofs of lead, its familiar tangle of attic rooms and chimney pots stretching away to slabs of new housing on the hazy horizon. Seen from this distance, the latter looked a little like the gantries of rockets, set around the city for its future defence. The Seine flowed past close below, either side of the island, a domesticated river, its two streams joining and winding off westwards between the walled quays and many bridges. A string of narrow barges, sitting heavy in the water, passed slowly by against the current. Kemble could just hear the putter of an engine.

The air was warm and still, retaining the city's stale breath. And Daladier, after a few deep sniffs, had had enough of it. He lit up his pipe.

"You have been writing notes, I observe."

"Yes," Kemble said. "Do you mind?"

"No, I do not mind. But please be discreet about the origins. Not all the world understands that we talk on computers to Washington."

"So when can I call my paper?"

"Not yet." The Frenchman commenced a slow, circular walk of the roof. "We have prepared our traps," he went on, smoke following his head like a cloud of flies, "and now we must wait, like a hunter, very quiet, to see what comes out of the trees."

To control his impatience, Kemble lit up a cigarette, doing his bit towards the ruin of the morning. "Okay," he said, exhaling like a steam-valve, "we wait. You're the boss. But for me, you realise, this is the best thing to happen in a long time."

"Of course, you are a reporter. This is news."

"It is. Very big news. So I hope, when you do release it, you'll give me a start on the competition – a few hours, at least. What do you say?"

Daladier pursed his lips: a grimace not impeded by the stem of his pipe. "I say you ask a very big favour."

"In return for services rendered – yes?"

"We shall see."

"And I'd like . . ."

"There is more?"

"One more thing, yes."

"Continue."

"Well," Kemble floundered, "this hunt for Harvey . . . it

356

ought to be covered in detail, don't you think, from an English point of view? Considering who he is. And also in a way which brings out the problems, from the point of view of the French. So I'd like . . . I've been hoping you'll let me stay with it – with you, that is – through to the end."

Daladier's eyebrows had risen at this request. Now they contracted in a frown. "We shall see," he said for the second time. Then, after a silence: "The end may not be pretty."

"I'll see you come out of it well," Kemble threw in on impulse, immediately trying to obscure this dangerous remark with a smile. "Make you famous."

"Monsieur, I am famous already." Neither amused nor offended, Daladier paused to stare down at the chain of barges, now passing under the Pont St. Michel. He took the pipe from his mouth and smacked it sharply against the rail which ran round the roof, so that bits of hot tobacco were emptied on the heads of any who dared to walk the Quai des Orfèvres. "Please give me a cigarette."

"Help yourself." Kemble snatched out the packet as if his life hung on it.

Daladier lit one, then started to walk again. "You may remain here so long as you help my enquiries. No other reason is possible."

"I understand."

"Your information has been useful."

"I'm glad."

"And you have, shall we say, an English brain. It jumps about the scene, nilly-willy."

"Oh? It does?"

"For the French, this also is useful. We do not think side-ways."

Keeping his own face straight, to be on the safe side, Kemble searched under the Frenchman's moustache for a smile, and thought he saw a small upturn of the lips. "So what's the problem?" he asked. "Can I help?"

Daladier drew in his breath, as if wondering which problem to pick. "We have three names. It is not enough," he said eventually. "Fawcett, Murdoch, Salandra . . . They were all in Paris, did you notice, for the famous amusements of 1968?"

"Yes, I noticed."

Speaking in slow constructed English, the Commissaire

ratiocinated on. Of course, he said, May '68 had drawn foreign crazies to Paris by the thousand. However a check with *Renseignements Généraux*, Central Archives, had revealed that these three men had a habit of returning to French territory on identical dates. Furthermore all of them, not only Fawcett, were known to frequent the Café Babylone.

"So you think they're here now?"

"It would be rational. To hide in a city is easier."

"On the other hand," Kemble said, trying to be lateral, "they must know you'd turn up the Paris connection."

"That is true. So?"

"So perhaps they're not here at all. The best clue, it seems to me, would be Harvey's own car – the Mercedes. Wherever that's found, they'll have gone the other way."

Daladier stopped in his tracks. "Excellent, my friend! You think like a crimnal."

"Oh really? Is that English too?"

The Commissaire smiled, his face lighting up in the first rays of sunshine. "For the English I cannot respond. But Americans are all a little crook, *n'est-ce pas*? And now let us go back to work."

As they left the roof, a bell was chiming from Notre-Dame. The lift doors shut off the sound. Descending, Daladier carried on thinking aloud. The most urgent task, he said, was to find the names of the three other kidnappers, two of whom were women. The big girl, believed to be the leader, especially if she was French, as Guidotti believed, was sure to be identified soon. The central computer, linked to every security agency in France, was searching its memory for a tall, pale female of Marxist persuasion with short brown hair and a bulky *poitrine*. The little girl might be more difficult. She had come from Brussels, it seemed, and she drove a Volkswagen, but some other clue would be needed to trace her.

"So now we shall apply our concentration to the Dutchman – the one who attacked the picket in England. It is he who is the professional."

2

The big blue Mercedes, glinting dully in the early light, flinched on its springs as the magnet hit its roof. The roof bent inwards, with a crackle like paper, but the lid of the boot stayed shut. Joop was glad to see that. He'd been worried the boot would spring open, revealing the body inside. But now the car was under way. Its wheels swept upwards as the chain jerked taut, and then the whole piece of beautiful shining German manufacture was lifted bodily over the cinders, to be dropped with a thump in the crusher. The magnet, released, swung away. A heavier motor went into action. Immediately the heavy steel plates of the crusher pressed downwards and inwards, squeezing the car to a small cube of metal, glass, plastic, flesh. It was done in half a minute. The plates of the crusher drew back. The heavy motor stopped. The crane swung in again; the magnet descended and plucked up the cube, lifting it high against the pale morning sky. Oil and petrol were dribbling from it, also the blood of Paolo Santini, but the two Algerian operators, one on the crane, the other on the crusher, took no notice. The cube was dropped on a huge heap of scrap. It tumbled a little way down from the peak, then came to rest among the relics of a thousand other cars, among which was Hal Fawcett's Peugeot, already undetectable. The magnet swung away. The crane was switched off. The Algerians stepped down and came to get their money. Joop wondered what it would cost. He had given Marc two thousand dollars, plus an equivalent sum in French francs. Thinking that this was best settled in his absence, he turned away and entered the hut at the edge of the yard.

Inside was a desk, a telephone, a pencilled accounts ledger, a

demure girlie calendar in Arabic. Things were scattered about.
A chair had been smashed. Joop tidied up. Bending down, he
lifted one of Hal Fawcett's eyelids, then shook the fool's head
where it lay on the planks, leaning closer to listen to the bones
of his neck.

Why had Rosa trusted this American? Normally her judgement of people was good. Mitzi Hoff, for instance, had turned
out well. She had played her part in the ambush of Harvey
without a blink, then driven to Dijon and dumped her precious
Volks as instructed. A plucky girl; obedient, thorough. But
Fawcett had always been a fool, even in 1968. Rosa's judgement
didn't extend to Americans, that was the truth. She had never
been there. She didn't understand that all of them, good or bad,
only really cared about America. To Hal this war of hers had
always been a joke. Well, he was out of it now, Joop thought,
straightening up and moving to the window.

Outside in the yard Marc Bensaïd was talking to his fellow-
Algerians. It seemed to be going all right. A packet of notes
changed hands. There were no smiles, but no protests either.
Marc pointed back towards the hut, explaining about Hal
Fawcett. The two men nodded. So, thought Joop, they'll do it.
That's good. Relaxing, he turned from the window and picked
up the telephone.

"It's me," he said before she could speak. "I'll talk for half a
minute. Listen carefully. Say no more than you have to. How
are things your end?"

"All right."

"Car out of sight?"

"Yes."

"Okay here too," Joop said. "All disposed of. And how's
your guest?"

"He's here."

"Alive and well?"

"Alive," Rosa said. "But not very well. His heart is bad."

"To hell with his heart. You're not a nurse. Remember, don't
go out for anything. Don't move, and don't call the café. That
number's not safe."

"What do I do if he . . ."

"You conduct the usual ceremonies," Joop said irritably.
"Dig a hole now, then it won't take so long. Are you listening?"

"Yes," she said.

"We've had one problem this end."

"What's that?"

"Our friend from America went drinking in Tours with that pressman. Took him for a ride, let him see the trunk. Even gave his name."

Rosa took the news in silence.

"Don't worry," Joop said, "it's been taken care of. Now do what I say. Keep indoors, no shopping for heart pills. Put one of your friends in a place where he can watch the road. If there's any sign of trouble, get out. You know where to meet me."

"Yes," she said.

"I'm going to take care of our travel arrangements. I'll be with you tomorrow. That's all."

Joop rang off, disturbed by her voice. It was stuck at a higher pitch than usual. For the first time since he had known her, she seemed to have no plan of action. And for Rosa that was bad. Without a plan she couldn't operate. Was it perhaps that she couldn't speak freely, because either Murdoch or Salandra were listening? No, it was not. She was slipping.

A pity that Harvey could not have been canned with his car, Joop thought as he left the hut. That would have been much simpler, though not perhaps approved of by higher authority, who still had to hear of these events.

The Algerians had backed up a van, preparing to take away Fawcett. They each shook Joop's hand as he emerged. He thanked them and drove away with Marc Bensaïd.

Spread around the cemetery of cars was the dismal Algerian quarter of Paris, a *bidonville* of improvised dwellings flung together from corrugated tin and old doors, petrol cans beaten out flat, breeze blocks and bits of old plywood. Every solid wall was splashed with Arabic graffiti. A child stood pissing in the dust. Skinny dogs nuzzled the rubbish. Merchants were laying out their junk on carpets, and from somewhere close by came the howl of an imam, amplified through loudspeakers. Except for the blocks of flats jutting up behind, a lavish new housing scheme on the French scale, this could have been the Middle East.

And Joop felt at home in it. Years of his life had been spent in such places, plotting the death of Zionist agents, awaiting the vengeance of Israeli jets, eating in silence in refugee huts while

the women tried to crouch out of sight. He thought of the
suburbs of Damascus, the Palestinian camps spreading into the
desert. And then he thought again of Rosa; the way she had
raged for those Turks in Rotterdam docks. The men of BMG and
Mobital, even if fired, would not starve, but here in this grim
Parisian *souk* or in the railway stations of Germany, where the
swarms of *Gastarbeiter* lined up for sale, it was easier to summon
up belief in Rosa's war. She must not doubt now, Joop thought.
It's too late for that. The sooner I get to her, the better. And then
away. But first a little talk with higher authority, whether she
likes or not.

Bensaïd drove through the *bidonville* in silence. His thoughts
could only be guessed at. An Algerian himself, he had fought a
savage war for the freedom of his country, but since the middle
sixties had lived and worked in Paris. A dour and cautious man,
he had lasted out two days of interrogation by the French
Foreign Legion. Shabbily dressed, on this Sunday morning as
always, the *patron* of the Café Babylone had the stubbled
appearance, never clean shaven, never fully bearded, of the
Palestinian leader Yasser Arafat. Joop trusted him more than
any other member of the Iskra.

"That was a service you cannot have bargained for," he said
to him eventually. "Rather dangerous, I'm afraid."

Marc shrugged, without expression. "Money persuades," he
said in his thick, hoarse voice. "You spoke to Rosa?"

"Yes."

"No problems?"

"So far, no. All the cars are off the road. Does the house have
food?"

"Frozen and canned," Marc said. "Enough for three days."

"Good. You thought of everything."

"This I did not think of."

"Nor I," said Joop. "It was improvised. He came out, we
snatched him. Rosa took him off. There was no time to
argue."

"What will you do?"

"Do you really want to know?"

Marc shook his head. "No, I do not."

Out of the slums now, they were passing through the housing scheme; rows of identical apartment blocks set in a wide
terrain, and among them, also planted in rows, hundreds of

flimsy young trees strapped to stakes. Joop was reminded of Moscow. The Russians would not have bothered with trees, though, perhaps because they had so many: those endless miles of silent, dripping forest in which they had trained him to hunt, track, shoot, survive. And what about Rosa? Would she survive in that great Asian hinterland? No, she would die of *ennui*. She liked to think of Lenin taking walks on the ice, doing press-ups in Siberia, but she had no more idea of the place than America. Well, she had better prepare herself. Because those who kill can't be choosers, Joop thought. Once that line is crossed, the only home left is political.

And then, as they skirted Nanterre, he was thinking back to May 1968. Here was the bleak modern campus where the great student uprising had begun. It was here, in fact, he'd first met her, the fierce lady Trotskyist from the Sorbonne, whipping them up with a fresh speech each night. They had met, they had fallen into bed. Even that had seemed easy at the time; a natural extension of political instruction. Poor Rosa, she had thought she was moulding him. She had thought she was filling the empty head from Amsterdam with hard revolutionary theory. But that was not quite how it was, Joop recalled. Even then he had been under orders.

No, the empty head was Fawcett's, in 1968 as now. "Fun city", Joop remembered, was Hal's word for the occupied Sorbonne. The idiot had spent several days dressed up as a medieval halberdier, wandering drunkenly about in a costume pillaged from the Odeon Theatre. And Murdoch was scarcely much better. He had rushed over from his college in Birmingham with a fine reputation for ripping up the faculty's carpets, but had not stood his ground on the barricades of Paris. Confronted by the black ranks of CRS, advancing with mesh shields and riot sticks, he had run, as he had this week at Ash Valley.

No, the brave one in those days was Mario Salandra; and also by far the most serious. A man who knew and practised his Marx, but also a very fine street fighter, dashing about among the gas bombs and water jets with a bright red scarf at his neck, *style* Garibaldi. It was Mario and Rosa, both from the timid school of *Science Politique*, who had shown the most physical courage. And for physical energy, Rosa alone took the prize. Even now she had the most stamina, Joop thought. But in May

1968 she was something else. For a month she had hardly slept. Each day she had marched and orated, each night she had taken all his body could give, burning off the last of her strength with fierce shouts of pleasure. And then the other way round. Sex by day, street warfare by night. *Tout est possible*, he remembered, had been a slogan of the time, often quoted by Rosa in those hectic weeks. And she believed it still. Anything is possible, she liked to say, to those who judge the moment correctly and have the will to act.

He lit two cigarettes, passing one across to Marc Bensaïd. The Algerian took it with a short nod of thanks, then spoke again. "I suppose you won't come back to Paris, whatever you do."

"No, I don't think so."

"And Rosa?"

"Impossible."

"For the Iskra, then, this is the end."

"Probably, yes," Joop agreed. "But if this succeeds, it will have ended well. She has made her contribution to history, as she says."

Marc nodded glumly at the wheel, driving at speed through the empty streets. "Care for her well."

"Of course I will," Joop said, made uneasy by a loyalty to Rosa greater than his own.

"Where will you go?"

"I don't know."

"Please find a way to tell me where you are. And tell her too, from me, that I'm proud to have helped in this enterprise."

After this unusually formal statement the Algerian fell silent. He drove on, smoking reflectively. When he spoke again he was back to his normal manner: a sort of growling, deadpan, cynical humour in which no bitterness appeared, and hardly ever a smile.

"You remember how it was at the start, that May?"

"I remember," said Joop. "I was thinking of it."

"Revolution without change, eh? That is the French contribution to history."

Joop agreed with that. Coming from permissive Holland, where change occurred easily, without much excitement, he had been amazed by the Frenchness of it all: the incredible drama, the lack of result. Even so, he thought, Rosa had been very fine. A true *enragée*, as they said. And it made no real difference that in this fine rage of hers – in their affair, even – there had been an element of personal revenge. Politically, sexually, Rosa had wanted her own back on Blaise Chabelard, the leader of the Trotskyist movement in the Sorbonne. And she had got it. Politically she had shown herself superior to Chabelard and the other leaders, all those overnight celebrities of fun city, May 1968.

It had come down, in the end, to the workers at Renault. That was the real test; and Rosa had been the first to see it, perhaps with the help of her aunt. The Sorbonne didn't matter a damn, she announced about the middle of the month. What really counted was happening over the river at Billancourt, where four thousand men had shut themselves into the car plant. It was her idea to march to the factory in sympathy, though Chabelard took the credit – and also the jibes, poor fellow, when the workers refused to let the students in. Rosa was disappointed, too. But at that stage she kept her head down. For the second two weeks of the month she went back to cleaning the lavatories at *Science Po*, a task of peculiar importance to her. "None of you has scrubbed shit for nuns," she used to boast, "that's what's the matter with you." In any case, whether from foresight or not, she detached herself from the whole sad, disintegrating mess. She must have been hatching her plan even then, Joop thought. But she didn't tell me. She didn't tell anyone. Rosa did not speak up until the black night of Tuesday, May 28th. For the revolutionaries that was the end. The government were offering a wage deal, the unions were urging acceptance, the workers were drifting back to work. Even the hard men at Renault, still shut in their factory, were starting to waver. Chabelard, speaking at the Charlety Stadium, made a last frantic appeal to them. Ignore the unions' treachery, he urged them, make Billancourt a fortress of workers' power. But it was too late. Or rather, historically, too early. The appeal fell flat, and Chabelard with it. By midnight he and Helmut Hoff, the whole revolutionary high command, were sitting dispirited in the Babylone. Upstairs at the café, later still, Marc Bensaïd was pouring free drink in consolation, when Rosa, to everyone's surprise, took the floor. So the task would take longer, she said. Perhaps it would take all their lives. But they should remember the slogan of the Iskra, the paper that Lenin had smuggled into Russia when all seemed lost. From this spark shall come the flame, and the flame will light a fire, and that fire will . . .

"Do you have a gun?"

Marc's question was urgent, sharp.

"Yes," said Joop, instantly reaching for, cocking the Makarov pistol under his jacket, not yet understanding the reason.

"Have it ready then," Marc said. "I'll drive straight past. Act normally. Keep your eyes open but don't turn your head."

They were travelling down the wide cobbled vista of Boulevard Raspail, still almost empty of traffic. The café was in sight a short way ahead. Its blue awning, sticking out under the trees, had the fringe detached at one corner – a traditional danger signal. Immediately opposite, across the road, a team of workmen were digging up the pavement, drilling on down for some emergency repair. Beside the hole stood a fibre-glass hut.

"*Flics*," said Marc.

"The roadmen?"

"Also the flower stall. And him, selling papers on the corner. Quite a party."

They drove straight past, sitting well back, neither turning his head. Joop kept his eyes swivelled right, trained on the smaller streets branching off the boulevard. "There's the back-up," he said an instant later. "See them?"

"No. How many?"

"Two vans, about a dozen men. PJ and gendarmes, plenty of hardware."

"*Merde*," said Marc. "They'll be round the back as well. This is going to be difficult."

Continuing to drive at Parisian speed, he turned left on Boulevard St. Michel, then immediately right, into the Latin Quarter. As soon as he was sure there was nothing behind, he pulled up in a quiet street, close to the Sorbonne itself.

They sat in the car and thought it out.

At some stage a check on the Bab had been foreseen. But this was much quicker, more thorough than expected. Not a raid, but a fully armed trap.

"They must be looking for Harvey," said Joop. "I'm sorry, I had not expected this."

Marc's face darkened in anxiety. "In that case it's the BRVP. And those guys are serious, I tell you. They shoot."

366

"I know it."

"Daladier's the chief. Best *flic* in the country."

Joop nodded, not needing to be told. Like all serious outlaws in France, he had studied the character and professional habits of the two or three Commissaires pitted against him. "So what will you do?"

"I shall go back," Marc replied without a pause. "You're forgetting, we've got Mitzi in there."

"I hadn't forgotten."

Mitzi Hoff, having dumped her car in Dijon, had come back to Paris by train, presumably following some secret plan agreed between herself and Rosa.

"There's a place inside we can hide her," Marc said after some thought. "But that'll be no good at all if they really turn us over. When it's dark, we might get her out."

"Make sure she doesn't start shooting."

The Algerian nodded, without a flicker of a smile. "Bad for trade, shooting, especially on Sundays. What's she doing here, anyway?"

"God knows." Joop shook his head. "I suppose she's keeping tabs on her friend – whoever it was we had helping us in Brussels."

"So you never found out who it was?"

"No, I never did."

"It has to be that German of Harvey's," Marc said. "Or maybe the English girl."

"Yes, I suppose so. One or the other."

"Well, which?"

"Don't ask me," Joop said with a sniffing laugh. "Ask Rosa, damn it. She thinks I'm spying for the Russians."

At this Marc's head turned, still without a smile. "Russia," he said. "Is that where you'll take her?"

Joop didn't answer.

The Algerian nodded, withdrawing the question. "Okay," he said. "Now I shall go. Kiss Rosa for me. Tell her that I shall always be here, at the Babylone in Paris. That is her home, whatever happens."

"I'll tell her."

"Goodbye, Joop. Good luck."

They shook hands, embraced. Joop got out. Marc drove away. Joop watched him go, then walked slowly north towards the Seine, through the dark streets of the Latin Quarter, the putrescent stone and torn posters. He could have found his way with his eyes shut. Since the autumn of 1967, when he first came from Holland, he had spent a large part of his life here, coming and going under various identities, sometimes gone for years, but always returning to this quarter of Paris. Walking through it, he felt secure as a mole in his hole. He knew every turning and tunnel, which doors would fly open at a push, which alleys ended in a wall that could be jumped. If it came to a chase, no one would catch him here. Two blocks away was the small rented room where he kept a few things. He avoided it. Hal lived close by; also Rosa. Joop kept away from both flats. But there was one reconnaissance worth making, he thought; not very dangerous and possibly informative. Following an odd zig-zag route, like a tourist in search of recommended sights, he walked on down to St. Séverin.

On the way he worried about Bensaïd. It was inevitable that Marc would go back to the café. The Bab was his livelihood – his life, indeed. If he ran, that life was over. But if he stayed put and did his job, parrying questions as usual, he had a small chance. His role within the Iskra had always been a passive one. He provided a meeting place, took and passed messages, kept the club's secrets. But now, overnight, he was in the most exposed position of all. In the house he had rented was a kidnapped statesman, in the car he'd got rid of was a corpse.

At least he understood the risk. No member of the Iskra could match Marc's experience of the French police. Even so, tough as he was, loyal as he was, too much now rested on Marc Bensaïd. Rosa in particular, and the others in the house, depended entirely on his silence.

In which case, Joop thought, the house was not a place to hurry to.

This self-preserving shift of mind was confirmed when he entered the square of St. Séverin. In the shadow of the church he bought a newspaper and opened it, flipping through the pages as though in search of an item of news that had to be read on the spot. Close by was a Lebanese foodstall, a chunk of lamb rotating on its vertical spit. The smell made him hungry. As he studied the paper his head was angled downwards, but his eyes were aimed over the top of the page at a shop across the square. *Berg Livre*, closed on Sundays, was deserted. A man was peering in through the window, hands cupped against the glass for better vision. He seemed to be interested in the Thoughts of Mao, going cheap in a big pile of red. But then he withdrew and got into a car, which did not drive off. Joop had seen enough. He folded up the paper and walked quickly out of the square, towards the Seine.

When he reached the embankment he leaned against the wall above the river, pausing to look across the short stretch of fast-flowing water towards Notre-Dame. No one came after him. After two minutes he turned left, walked past the green bookstalls, then up a slight slope to the Place St. Michel. He crossed the square and entered a café on its western side, overlooking the bridge and cathedral. Having ordered a full American breakfast, he bought a *jeton* at the bar, then shut himself into the phone booth.

"Hello, this is Josef," he said softly into the receiver. "Is Miguel there?"

"No, he's not here," said the Cuban, speaking French with a staccato accent. "What number are you speaking from?"

Joop gave a six-digit code, indicating place and method of contact, meeting requested in 45 minutes.

"I'll get him to call you when he comes in," the Cuban replied, loud with fright. "But if you're in a hurry, you could try 89-10-45."

The number meant Luxembourg Gardens, maximum caution, meeting agreed in 45 minutes.

"Okay, I'll do that," said Joop, to indicate acceptance.

The bloody pathetic little diplomatic puffball, he thought to himself, annoyed as always by contact with this shifty go-between. It was regrettable, in view of the present emergency, that no higher contact was allowed to him in Europe. He wondered how much to tell the man; what to ask for; how much time to allow him for reference to higher authority. He couldn't decide. He would think about it on the way to the rendezvous.

Meanwhile there was a certain pleasure to be had from eating bacon and eggs in full view of Commissaire Serge Daladier, head of the BRVP. Deliberately choosing a table outdoors in the sun, Joop stared across at the shining glass block on the Quai des Orfèvres, smiled, then spoke just loud enough for himself to hear.

"Too late, *flic*. You won't catch me now."

369

3

Standing at a south-facing window of the ops room, drinking black coffee from a paper cup, Jack Kemble watched Paris stir to life. Traffic was increasing across the Pont St. Michel. More people were walking about the square on the opposite bank, a few already sitting at the tables of the cafés. He envied them. He was starting to feel acutely hungry. And the weather looked nice, even when seen through glass darkly. He had a private theory – a line of bar talk, anyway – which held that the architectural fashion for tinted glass was a source of much modern neurosis, turning the eyes and mind inwards to problems which might look easier in sunlight. Certainly the French police were getting depressed. In all this hardware the only thing working as well as it should was the coffee machine.

The time was now past eight o'clock, but still there was no clue to Harvey's whereabouts, and no message either from his captors, which was a bad sign in kidnaps. A dead man cannot be ransomed.

At 6.15 there had been a small break. News came through that a big white Citroën of the sort used in the kidnap had been rented at the airport in Nice, Friday night, by a man who sounded like the Dutchman. Its number had been issued to all police units. But none of the cars, even Harvey's, had yet been seen, despite the many road-watching posts. The girls with their long-handled scoops were sitting inactive beside their illuminated map, now covered from border to border in red plastic markers. Next move was the Iskra's, but they weren't playing. The game had stopped.

A bigger break had happened in Italy. At 6.45 the *Ispettorato Anti-Terrorismo*, still in pursuit of the girl who had tried to kill

Guidotti, had telephoned to say that a person of the right description had flown in to Rome on Thursday night, arriving on the last plane from Paris. This had set off a rush of activity in the Quai des Orfèvres. Daladier demanded a passenger list from Air France. It arrived within minutes by Telex. The Commissaire, looking through it avidly with two of his team, was first to spot a name which tallied with *Berg Livre*, the bookshop employing Hal Fawcett. BERG, R. A rush to the computer ensued. But the name, tapped into the terminal, produced a woman aged 72. Simone Salvador, *née* Berg, once active on the French Left, was now living quietly in Le Havre. No other Berg could be found in French records, computerised since 1975. So a call had been made to *Renseignements Généraux*, who had hunted through their old paper files. And there, buried deep, was the leader of the Iskra: a girl whose record had been clean since 1968. The file which came over by *pneumatique*, rolled up in a tube, was yellow with age. But Kemble had recognised the photograph instantly: the close-cropped hair, the wide Slav-like face. This was the girl he had seen in Brussels, again in the village of Ambillou. Taking out his pad, he had noted down the details of her life, some taken from her own file, some culled from the record of her aunt.

BERG, *Rosamunde Bernadine, known as Rosa. Age 36. Born Nantes, educ. Convent Sacred Heart. Father, Henri Berg, half-Jewish origin, survived war concealed as farm labourer in Brittany; was accused by his sister, Simone, of collaboration. Case unproven. After war Henri settled in Nantes, opened jewellery store, Berg Bijou. Rosa born 1946, only child. Conventional childhood, conventional freak-out. Mother, still living, old Breton stock, has not seen daughter in 14 years. Cause of rift, May '68. Rosa, at Sorbonne, turned left; scandalised Nantes with speech urging factory occupation by aircraft workers. Disowned by parents in local press interview. But father, on death, forgave and left her money. Rosa buys bookshop in Paris, Berg Livre, 1970, still in business. No further political activity. Lives Rue St. Séverin, top-floor apartment, not cheap. Boy's hair, heavy chest. Not a beauty, doesn't care. Plain dresser.*

Race, religion, family feuds – the girl was so loaded with personal motives that Kemble trusted none of them. A cover so carefully maintained implied strength of mind. Maybe Rosa Berg believed in what she did.

He had left a page blank for extra details, but nothing had yet come to light. Her shop and her flat were being watched. Her car had been found at Orly Airport, presumably left there when she flew to Rome. All her associates were being chased up. This girl too was a regular client of the Babylone. But she hadn't shown her face there yet. Only the café's proprietor, Marc Bensaïd, had arrived on the premises, turning up by car from some early-morning errand. A thick-skinned Algerian, Bensaïd lived on the border of the law but rarely stepped over it. He was unlikely to be involved in this, the police thought.

And now, at 8.15, there was a lull. The ops room was at half strength. A detective came in with a carton full of doughnuts, handing them round. Kemble didn't get one. Feeling hungrier still, he punched the machine for more coffee, then returned to Daladier's office. The Commissaire was back on the phone to the Belgian police, who refused to break into the Harveys' house in Kraainem.

Margaret Harvey was still untraced. So was Laura. And so was the pretty little girl on the kidnapping team. But the thing that had really depressed the French police was their failure to track down the Iskra's Dutchman. To general surprise and dismay, this man had defied the computers.

But now Daladier was ready to begin a second effort. Having finished with the Belgians, he asked what it was that had made the Dutchman so easy to recognise.

"His face," replied Kemble. "Are we really going to go through this again?"

"We are. Describe it, if you please."

"That's difficult."

The Commissaire's eyes rolled upwards, his courtesy discarded under pressure, along with his jacket and tie. "Your vision is good," he snapped, "your *métier* is words. Please tell me again, very carefully, about this man's face."

Kemble poked his own out of shape. "It's twisted, like this. His skin is rather smooth, wrinkled in the wrong places. Makes his age hard to tell. Perhaps he's had a face-lift."

And then suddenly, triggered by this speculation, a picture of the Dutchman eating burgers with his girl in the Brussels hotel came back much sharper to Kemble, emerging from the

372

alcoholic fog in which he'd first seen it. "Goddamn," he cried, "that's it! The man's had a skin graft – maybe plastic surgery."

Daladier leaned forward in excitement. "He has been burned, perhaps?"

"Burns, yes, could be. Car crash, accident – it sure as hell wasn't a cosmetic job."

"This is new. Let us see what the Dutch say." Daladier signalled through the glass to the computer man, who started pressing his switches.

Kemble held up his hand. "Wait, I've remembered something else. When he's talking he holds his head at an angle, like this. Let's see, he was sitting on her left . . . Yes, I'd lay money on it, this guy is deaf in one ear. The right."

"*Il est sourd! Il est mutilé!*" cried the Commissaire, slipping out of English in excitement. "*Bon*, now we catch him. Come with me."

They hurried across to the computer. The operator of the French terminal, plugged in to criminal records in Amsterdam, tapped on his keyboard. The screen of the visual display unit, set alongside, promptly lit up with a list of different services offered – the menu, as programmers call it. Paris pressed for *IDENTIFICATION PHYSIQUE*. The new details were tapped in: a grey-haired terrorist whose face had been altered by surgery, hard of hearing in the right ear.

"That's all?" asked the blank-faced operator, who seemed impervious to feeling or fatigue, as much of a robot as his machine.

"That's all," said Daladier. "Now ask for names."

A tap on the keyboard. The screen went blank. They waited in silence for several seconds, and then two words appeared from Holland, flickering green as though in fright.

IDENTIFICATION NÉGATIVE

Daladier stared at the screen in disbelief. He seemed about to go up with a bang, but after a moment the steam came out of him in a jet of low, incomprehensible oaths.

"Try Wiesbaden," he said to the operator.

Kemble, not daring to speak, remained at the operator's side while the Dutchman's details were fed to the BKA, German

373

federal police, whose computerised records were the best in the world – indeed just a little too thorough for some people's taste.

The Commissaire himself returned to his office, then passed through a grey steel door behind his desk. Beyond this door, Kemble knew, was an interview room. What happened there he did not see, but he heard about it later from the whispers, half-amused, half-nervous, which travelled round the staff of the ops room. At this point, about 8.30, two people had been brought to the Quai des Orfèvres for questioning.

The first was Simone Salvador from Le Havre: former French Communist, old Resistance heroine, widow of an exiled Spanish Republican. Frontier records showed that her niece, Rosa Berg, had landed in Le Havre on Wednesday, arriving by the early boat from England. Had the girl visited her aunt? If so, the old woman had nothing to say about it. Daladier grilled her for almost ten minutes, at first with some control, eventually bellowing into her face. But Madame Salvador, aged 72, opened her mouth only to spit. Daladier, giving up, ordered her taken to the cells in the basement. "Let the old bolshevik rot!" he was said to have yelled as the lift went down.

Next was a man called Blaise Chabelard.

The name meant nothing to Kemble, but he noticed that it sent an immediate *frisson* of excitement through the building.

Chabelard, he learned, was front man for a weekly show on TV, a highbrow programme concerned with the arts which went out on Sunday evening. As such he was a shining star, in a way that no academic, however handsome or pushy, could ever be in England or America. Adored by millions of culture-hungry French, his private life endlessly photographed by silly magazines, Blaise Chabelard lived in a luxury pad by the Bois de Boulogne, which he shared with a famous model. He owned a private plane, in which he commuted round the European lecture circuit. He held the chair of *Arts Modernes* at Grenoble. He was said to earn a million francs a year.

The risk of annoying such a *personnage* had the ops room agog. But Daladier was so little worried by it he later made a transcript available to Kemble, to show how the big break came. The relevant portion, translated into English, ran as follows.

Daladier:	*Answer my question, or you will be in trouble.*
Chabelard:	*Yes, I was a Trotskyist in 1968. Yes, I was a leader of the students.*
Daladier:	*Come, monsieur, you are too modest. It was you who addressed the workers of Renault. You told them not to give up control of their factory at Billancourt. You called for revolution in France.*
Chabelard:	*Yes, yes, all right, the whole world knows this. I was young.*
Daladier:	*And now? Still a Marxist?*
Chabelard:	*No, of course not. We cannot apply the ideas of the nineteenth century to the technocratic society of the twentieth. I have said this on television.*
Daladier:	*I must try to watch more often. But since I do not, please tell me your views. Today, if they asked you, what advice would you give to the workers at Renault?*
Chabelard:	*Some degree of participation is desirable, but the modern decision-making process is much too complex to be widely diffused. We do not live in ancient Athens.*
Daladier:	*Thank you. I believe you may be right. But what do the Iskra say, when you talk like this?*
Chabelard:	*The Iskra?*
Daladier:	*The secret society to which you belong. An organisation to promote the use of democratic methods in industry, as I understand it.*
Chabelard:	*You have made a mistake.*
Daladier:	*Try to be truthful. And then we can all go home to watch television, among other pleasures.*
Chabelard:	*I don't understand this. Please, if I knew what you wanted . . .*
Daladier:	*Well, for a start, you could talk about Rosa.*
Chabelard:	*Rosa – Rosa Berg?*
Daladier:	*That's the one.*
Chabelard:	*She was a friend.*
Daladier:	*You mean she was your mistress.*
Chabelard:	*We were together, for a time, it is true. Not long. This business – it's Rosa, isn't it? What has she done?*
Daladier:	*So you do still know her?*

Chabelard: *No. But she was always extremist. Love or hate, God or Marx — for Rosa there was nothing between.*

Daladier: *Yes, I see you do know her well. And I take it you must have advised against violence by the Iskra. After so long, I mean.*

Chabelard: *What is this Iskra? I thought she ran a bookshop.*

Daladier: *Please, monsieur, be careful. You are starting to bore me.*

Chabelard: *All I can tell you is who her friends were in '68. Will that help?*

Daladier: *Let us begin with that.*

Chabelard: *Well, there was Hoff. And a Dutchman called Janssen. But they're both dead.*

MORT, the Dutch computer agreed, when given the name a minute later. Janssen, Johan Ivor, familiar name Joop, had been killed in Syria five years ago.

"Let's have a look at him," said Daladier, back at Kemble's side, still panting from his dash across the ops room.

The operator tapped for visual transmission, and they turned to the bigger photographic screen, on which a milky-faced boy appeared, staring straight to camera, his cheeks half-concealed by a mane of lank golden-brown hair, so long that it fell to his chest. The eyes were the right shade of blue, but untroubled. The small frown between them was hard to be sure of, since it was puckered by a horizontal headband.

Kemble asked for side shots and got them: police photos taken in Amsterdam, 1962.

He still wasn't sure.

At French request the pictures kept coming.

Joop Janssen, aged 29, at a congress of anti-war movements in Brussels; Joop Janssen in Paris, May 1968. By that time his hair was cut shorter, already flecked with grey. He was frowning. Later pictures followed, some taken in Europe, some in desert lands. In each of them the frown was etched deeper. The hair grew greyer, the face more thin. The eyes became watchful and guarded. The last picture, taken from a distance by Israeli Intelligence, showed Joop Janssen aged 39, talking to a Palestinian leader in the garden of a house in Damascus. His hair was now short, almost shaved, and very grey. The face itself was

376

tanned, but skull-like, frowning at his feet as he dragged on a cigarette.

"That's him," said Kemble.

Daladier clapped in satisfaction. "You are sure?"

"Pretty sure, yes. But now he looks worse."

"Let us try a second opinion."

Daladier signalled to a uniformed man in his office, who disappeared through the steel door, then came back with Blaise Chabelard.

It was a cruel thing to do. The entire operations room fell silent with breathless glee as the great star of Sunday TV, presenter of *Le Feu Sacré*, advanced down the steps and walked round the map of France. His wrists were handcuffed for all to see, attached by a chain to the guard. And the poor bastard hadn't had time to dress, Kemble noticed. His loose cream shirt was not a shirt at all, but a silk pyjama top. His hair was quite long, dark and curly, very clean, cut for that carefully wind-blown appearance which comes out so well under studio lights.

Chabelard himself was too scared to be embarrassed. His eyes were a picture of miserable fright as he stared at the face of Joop Janssen, then nodded to Daladier.

"*C'est lui.*"

"*Vous êtes sûr?*"

"*Aucun doute. Plus âgé, plus dur. Mais c'est Iaupe.*"

"*Iaupe?*"

"It is what Rosa called him," said Chabelard, continuing in French. "Spelled J-o-o-p. In English, Joe. We all called him that."

"So you knew him yourself?"

"Of course. He was one of our band. Not a person of importance, and later on stupidly violent. But Rosa was attached to him."

"You mean he was screwing her?"

"How delicate you are, Monsieur *flic*. Can I go now?"

"No, you cannot," snapped Daladier. "So where did he get the scars?"

"What scars?"

"The ones he has now."

"I told you, he's dead," replied Chabelard coolly.

"What makes you think that?"

"It was in the press. Famous terrorist killed, bravo for Israel. I

377

telephoned Rosa to offer condolence. She was very upset. She could not answer. Though you, of course, would not understand how a woman of Marxist beliefs might have any feelings.''

"Shut your mouth," Daladier said casually, then turned to the guard. "Take him down to the cells."

"No! Wait!" shouted Chabelard in protest. "You can't do that! What's the charge?"

Daladier shrugged, not bothering to look at him. "Murder or kidnap. It remains to be seen."

"Murder! Kidnap!"

"Both serious crimes, as your lawyer will tell you. Of course, if your memory improves, we might come to some arrangement. Otherwise for you, monsieur, the good life is over. This man here is from the English press. At some time today I shall give him the pleasure of telling the world about your secret games. Off you go now, and try not to get too emotional. You will find our basement quite comfortable."

Chabelard could not believe it. Speechless with shock, close to tears, the chic ex-radical was taken away. As he passed through them the staff of the ops room stirred back to their tasks, embarrassed to watch.

Daladier stayed at the computer, waiting for a print-out on the Dutchman. A copy came in French, then another in English for Kemble, in reward for services rendered. The Commissaire, reading his own copy, wandered off to other business. Kemble found a seat and took out his pad.

JANSSEN, Johan Ivor; called Joop, pronounce Yope. Born 1938 at Ede, near Arnhem. Father, a railway worker, lifelong communist, was shot by Gestapo, 1943. Widow, Margaretha Janssen, still lives Ede. Joop, aged 18, was delinquent. After military service became drifter in Amsterdam, was arrested for pushing narcotics, 1962. Two years jail. On release goes to USA, then Mexico; stays 18 months. Believed to have spent time in Cuba, poss. also Soviet Union. Reappears Europe, aged 28, leads anti-Vietnam movement in Holland. Arrives in Paris for Events of May. From 1969, aged 31, joins Palestinian terrorist groups. Seen training PFLP commandos, north Lebanon. From 1972, believed living France, is hunted by Israeli hit teams for murder Jewish agents in Cyprus and Madrid. Last seen Syria, 1977. Reported killed by Israeli bombing raid,

Hamouriya Camp, nr. Damascus. Body flown out to Moscow. Despite this unusual procedure, J. Janssen classified as dead. File closed.

But he lives, thought Kemble, looking up from these notes. Joop Janssen walks and he kills, a patch-faced ghoul put together by some Russian Frankenstein. Aged 44 now, this Dutchman would be, still flitting round Europe with his multiple identities, still lurking somewhere in France, perhaps at this moment staring into the face of his eminent captive . . .

The image turned into sensational prose: a journalist's automatic internal print-out, suddenly stopped by pity for Harvey. Poor old man. The poor, high-minded, well-organised old bastard, what on earth would he make of these continental crazies who had snatched him from the world of paper, talk and compromise? One minute he must have been thinking how to shut up *The Times*, the next looking into the barrel of a gun.

With pity came guilt; then a wave of fatigue drowning all. Blinking, red-eyed, Kemble stood up and lit himself a cigarette. The time was nine o'clock.

But Daladier was now cockahoop. "Five names out of six," he said with friendly warmth, coming back from a telephone. "Congratulations, my friend. You will soon be a member of the Légion d'Honneur."

"I'll take it in cash."

"You are tired?"

"I'm still awake."

"Please remain so. After breakfast we shall make a new effort to find number six, the pretty little lady from Brussels. But unless we have luck, it will be a long job. These games of computer need patience."

For Kemble the most important word in this statement was "breakfast". Somewhere in the building was a staff canteen, alleged to be open round the clock. In his mind its delights now equalled Maxim's.

They were standing beside the big tabular map, still covered in red plastic markers. Now the girls were pushing two yellow ones into the area of Paris.

Kemble pointed at them. "Press? Chinese Army?"

The Commissaire's moustache remained at the slope, undisturbed by any jokes except his own. "Yellow means a sighting," he explained. "Green is for contact and surveillance."

"So who's been seen?"

"The Dutchman."

Instantly the sleepiness was cleared from Kemble's head. "What! He's here? In Paris? You didn't tell me that."

Daladier, back to his normal heavy nonchalance, stuck his pipe into his mouth and moved across to a vertical glass panel, on which a map of Paris itself was back-projected. "At an early hour this morning a man whose appearance corresponds to Janssen's was seen in a Mercedes saloon, colour blue. The car was observed by members of the public, first here, and then here – in the district of Nanterre, going west." He dropped his hand. "So, my friend, what do you think?"

"Car empty?"

"It appears so."

"I think it's a blind," Kemble said. "They've gone south."

"Perhaps," said Daladier pensively. "But let us not dive to conclusions."

He went on staring at the street-plan of the suburbs, then called out in French to a member of his staff: "Take a look in the *bidonville*. But gently, you hear? Plain cars, no uniforms."

The man ran off to a telephone.

Daladier turned back to Kemble, lifting his copy of the print-out on Janssen. "Now let us study the mind of this Dutchman. They all have habits, you understand, even the clever ones. Places they return to, methods they repeat. It is what betrays them."

"He has to be working for the Russians."

"Very plainly. But abroad, to control him, they would use the agents of some other sovietic country. That is their way."

"Cuba?"

"Perhaps."

"He was trained there."

"So it appears. I have spoken to the Service."

Kemble understood the reference. *Service de Documentation Extérieure et de Contre-Espionnage*, SDECE for short, was what the French called their spooks. The fact had been entered in his notebook with a smile. To call the act of spying "exterior documentation" was surely the purest breath of France.

"The Service are watching an attaché of Cuba at this moment," the Commissaire added, walking off towards one of the red-blinking exits. "He is sitting in the Gardens of Luxembourg, where he has arranged to meet a man called Josef."

Kemble was listening without much interest, his mind having turned again to breakfast. But then came another delay.

One of the girls on the special exchange emerged from her glass box and called out "*Bruxelles!*"

The Commissaire broke away and hurried to his office; picked up the telephone; listened; answered briefly; then wrote on a scratch pad, tore off the top sheet and held it out.

"The Belgians found a message in the house. Lady Harvey has gone to this place."

Kemble looked down at the sheet.

Cwm Caerwen.

Daladier was muttering that this was a fine time to visit the Balkans, Kemble was on the point of saying "Wales", when the guard from the cells came back with Blaise Chabelard. Broken with fright, eyes pitifully pleading, the TV celebrity admitted that he'd been an early member of the Iskra. He would tell all the names he could remember, he said, in return for protection of his own. Daladier was just about to answer this, when again they were interrupted, this time by a yell of excitement in the ops room. A detective came dashing up the steps and burst headlong into the Commissaire's office.

"It's Janssen! He's come into the garden!"

4

It was a widely known fact in Paris that Reinaldo Herrera Valdes, Cultural Attaché at the Embassy of Cuba, was a spy. Among those who followed such matters more closely he was listed as third officer in Europe of the DGI, *Dirección General de Inteligencia*. The DGI, headquarters Havana, had been set up and trained for Castro by the Russians. It was practically a branch of the KGB, and Valdes, like all its other officers, was often employed on errands for Moscow. This, too, was very well known. Everyone knew, and no one much cared, about Reinaldo Valdes. Among his own kind he was a joke. His cover was thin, his technique inept. It suited the French very well to have him where he was. They tapped his phone as a matter of form, and when he received cryptic messages, as he had this morning, they followed him. Sometimes, as this morning, Valdes would take evasive action. The French would let him do so, until he was sure he had shaken them off, and then they would pick him up at the rendezvous, waiting to see who turned up. Usually it was some silly student being nursed into the Soviet camp.

Nothing more than that was expected this Sunday. Valdes, whose duties in Paris were mainly administrative, was rarely trusted with anything hot, by either the DGI or the KGB, and his regular contacts were of so little threat to the secrets of France that the two men who followed him into the Luxembourg Gardens at 8.55, a pair of old hands from the surveillance branch of the SDECE, were not of the highest calibre. Nor were they in a state of high tension, despite the all-stations alert which had reached them by radio from SDECE headquarters in

Boulevard Mortier, out by the Porte des Lilas. Listening in their car to the broadcast description of a wanted Dutch terrorist, they had speculated which of their colleagues would land this big fish. It annoyed them to be stuck with small fry like Valdes.

Not pleased to be working at all on this fine summer morning, they followed him wearily along the gravel paths and watched him sit down on a bench below the plane trees, close to the Medici Fountain, the way that he often did. They saw him open a newspaper and knew without getting any closer that what he was reading was the racing form – *comment elles ont couru*. They knew that at two o'clock this afternoon, as on many Sundays, Ramiro Valdes would go to the hippodrome at Longchamp and try for the triple at *guichet* number six. Sometimes he would meet a Russian in the queue. Always he lost his bet. Valdes was very predictable. But today, they noticed, he was being more cautious than usual. Valdes was clearly nervous. Because of this, the two SDECE men took up their own positions with care, at a distance, out of sight. Even so, they did not expect their skills to be tested. The professional incompetence of Reinaldo Valdes was a bore to them.

Joop Janssen's feelings on the matter were different. It worried him greatly to be making this contact in such an emergency. Walking to the gardens from the river, along the wide pavement of the Boulevard St. Michel, he gave careful thought to his method of approach, the checks he would go through before breaking cover, the facts he would keep to himself in discussion.

He had known Valdes since Cuba, 1964. Fresh out of jail in Amsterdam, determined to follow the political path of his father, Joop had come to that island as a priest to ordination. And Valdes, too, had been a force to reckon with in those days: an ambitious peasant boy, lean and angry, full of fire for his saviour Fidel. They had shared a hut at Camp Matanzas and trained together in the mountains. Weapons handling, map-reading, forgery, disguise, cryptography, evasion of surveillance – together they had learned their craft under General Viktor Shuvalov. Together they had graduated to the second leg in Russia. But at that point their paths had started to diverge. Joop had gone down to Baku for the hard stuff from KGB Section Five, assassination by poison and bullets, topped up with two weeks of military training, mainly sabotage of pipelines, from GRU III at Simferopol. Valdes had stayed at Skhodnya, near Moscow, where the best of the students at Lumumba were brought to learn world revolution. Returning to the West, they had gone separate ways. Joop, after two years spent stirring up the students of Europe, was sent to join the Arabs' armed struggle. Valdes had stayed under diplomatic cover.

Five years later they had met again at Finsterwald, the camp on the Oder, East Germany, where the Arabs came to rest and regroup. Valdes turned up there one day to say what help Cuba could offer. Five years later again, in 1975, his presence in Paris had been useful. Without it escape from the city might not have been possible, Joop had to admit. And that operation had led to the present arrangement. Since his own secret return to Europe, following facial surgery in Prague, Valdes had been his only contact with higher authority. This link, though not of Joop's choosing, had worked well enough so far. Even five days ago he had been content to meet Valdes in Brussels. However, to meet the man now in Paris, with his own face known again and the *flics* on the hunt, was dangerous in the extreme. No errors of technique could be allowed today.

For safety's sake he got to the rendezvous early and watched the Cuban sit below the plane trees. Nothing stirred in the gardens behind. At this hour they were still almost empty. The wide gravel paths were bright in the sun and the grass still brilliantly green, kept lush by sprinklers through the long dry summer. The big elms had gone, destroyed by disease. The small chestnuts planted in their place already had an autumn look, leaves slightly rusted at the edge.

Valdes himself did not inspire confidence. He was wearing white shoes and a blazer with shiny brass buttons, pulling tight across his middle. Life in the West had doubled his weight. But after ten minutes he did the right thing. He walked away out of sight and came back to the same position, so that Joop could watch his back, as practised long ago in the squares and parks of Havana. Nothing happened. Emboldened, Joop himself then emerged from hiding, walked up to the fountain and away through the geometric gardens, round the goldfish pond and the marionette theatre, past the monuments to Verlaine and Chopin, through the neat flower beds and many bad statues, then back along the front of the Luxembourg Palace. Valdes remained in the same position, still reading his paper. That meant the field was clear.

Joop walked up to the bench and sat beside him, still carefully inspecting the scene. They spoke quickly and softly in French, which over the years had become their common language. When he heard the news, Valdes yelped in alarm.

"What!"

"They've kidnapped him."

"Hop, this is crazy."

"It's logical. Without him the merger will fail."

Valdes let out a small groan of distress. He pretended to give the matter some thought, but in his eyes there was only panic. "Where have they taken him?"

"To a place they have."

"You know where?"

"Yes, I know where." Joop added no more, although the question was clearly unconsidered.

"There has been no news of this."

"There will be."

"Harvey is a diplomat," Valdes said after another pause. "Our orders forbid interference with the normal process . . ."

"I know it," Joop cut in impatiently. "But I am not in charge of these people, Reinaldo. I cannot direct their actions."

"The girl, Rosa Berg, will do what you say."

"Perhaps. I wouldn't bet on it. Now here's what I want to know." Placing his message to Moscow, Joop spoke clearly and carefully. "Do I go back to the place where they're holding him? And if so, what shall I do when I get there? The second thing is this. I shall have to come out now, the sooner the better, and I want to bring the girl with me. So how, when and where?"

"You mean you'll take Rosa?"

"That is what I mean."

"Comrade, what is this? You are in love?"

"Mind your own business, Reinaldo. Do I go back, what do I do, how do we come out? Answers by tomorrow, please, early afternoon. I'll ring you at two on the safest number."

"Okay, Hop. Leave it to me."

"And don't muck about with the *rezidentura* in Paris. Go to Uncle Viktor."

Valdes nodded anxiously. "This is a very big business. It could make us trouble."

"Right," said Joop. "So get me some orders from the top. Then we'll be all right. Walk away now and take care. I'll call you at two tomorrow, on the minute. We do still have a safe number?"

"Yes, the same one," replied Valdes. "Until tomorrow, then."

Joop sat where he was until the Cuban disappeared, then stood up and walked towards the gate of the gardens. At the gate he suddenly turned and walked back, as though he had dropped something. Bending down to look for it under the bench, he scanned the gravel paths of the garden and immediately saw the two Frenchmen following. Two minutes later he walked down the steps to the Luxembourg métro station, then immediately up again and back down the boulevard, the way he had come. On Rue Soufflot he turned right towards the Pantheon, changed his mind, struck left again past the Sorbonne. Twice he stopped to look in shop windows. At one point he entered a café and made a brief phone call. Shut in the lavatory, he took out his heavy Russian Makarov pistol, checked it, wiped his hands dry, eased the shoulder strap below his jacket. His shirt was stuck to his ribs with sweat.

Emerging from the café, he walked on slowly down the Rue St. Jacques until he reached its junction with Boulevard St. Germain. On the corner was a shop selling Chinese kites. *La Compagnie Française de Pekin*, said some curly golden lettering on the window, *redonne à l'artisanat ses lettres de noblesse et à la beauté un pourquoi-faire*. Joop went inside. Vivid paper butterflies hung from the ceiling, stirring in the gasps of the tourists. Gong music came from the shadows. Bamboo mobiles spun and tinkled softly as Joop brushed through them to the back of the shop. Unnoticed by the sales assistant, he hurried down a corridor and into an office behind. It was empty. He opened a door and went down some steps to a basement, at the far end of which, he knew, was a fire exit into the street behind, Rue du Sommerand. The basement was stacked high with boxes from China. A girl was tying price labels onto the kites. She stood up in fright as he entered. Joop took out his pistol and held it in her face. They stood like that, immobile, not speaking, for several seconds, until he heard two short blasts on a horn in the street above. The time was exactly 10.15.

"Sit down," he said to the girl. "Put your hands on the desk and do nothing. I am now going to leave very quickly."

5

In Wales it was 9.15, an hour behind Paris. In the small valley town of Builth Wells the chapels were still giving out a blast of song, but the main episcopal church was emptying its small congregation into the rain after holy communion. The vicar saw them off from the porch. He was pleased to see Lady Harvey there, over from the continent again for one of her breaks. All his sheep were equal, in his own sight as God's, but the presence of the wife of a former Prime Minister did lend a certain tone to the flock at Builth Wells. He shook her hand eagerly and made a rather elegant crack about escaping the world of "telegrams and anger", to quote E. M. Forster. It went down well. That was indeed the point of the exercise, Lady Harvey replied, and the rain didn't matter a bit. Her grandson, David, smiled up in agreement. Then together they ran across the square towards a big limousine, very wide and pale blue, American in style.

It had been hired at London Airport the previous day. The car, the petrol, two seats on the shuttle flight from Brussels – the whole spur-of-the-moment decision to switch David's holiday to Wales had cost a large amount of money. But that was no worry to Margaret Harvey. The only advantage to her of her husband's present job was that for once, for the first time ever in their lives indeed, money was in plentiful supply. It was no substitute for the things that she wanted. But sometimes, as now, it helped. Planes could be jumped on, cars whistled up. Decisions, once reckoned to the penny, could be taken on a whim. And for that one ought to be thankful, she thought to herself, still touched by the mood of the church service. Trying to look on the bright side, shamed by the poverty of Wales, she deliberately counted money into her blessings as she drove through the suburbs of the little granite town, then into the bare hills around, along the twisting switchback of a road which led to Cwm Caerwen.

It seemed to take a long time. There were always more miles of Wales than appeared on the map, more bends, more crests than you remembered. But to Margaret Harvey, even in rain, the journey was a pleasant one. How humbly beautiful this country was, she thought, how beautifully remote from the glitter and racket of Europe – from telegrams and anger indeed. Although they were not very high, there was something peculiarly massive about these Welsh hills, more impressive to her than the glassy peaks of Switzerland. Sounding her horn at each sharp corner, she drove on slowly in the unfamiliar car, too wide for the single-lane road. Sheep scattered off the tarmac in front of her, leaping away into bracken and mist. And then, as though in reward for the long trek to worship, there came a sudden break in the weather. The rain thinned, then lifted. The mist rolled back to the crags.

She was glad to see it, for David's sake. There would be no sun here today, but what did small boys care about that? They liked to get muddy and wet, dreaming up adventures in a way which could not be managed in the manicured parks of Brussels, or even on the field of Waterloo.

"Glad we came?"

"Yes, Granny."

"What will you do today?"

He shrugged at the adult's question. "Play around a bit."

"I shall need some more logs," she said, feeling as always that fun at Cwm Caerwen should be paid for with some sort of task, in tribute to the long-forgotten farmers who had toiled to raise its stones.

David nodded, well acquainted with this foible of his grandmother's. "Can I take you for a ride in the lorry?"

"Of course you can. Logs first, then the lorry."

And where shall we go today, she wondered happily. The lorry had rusted for decades in the nettles at the side of the cottage, abandoned by the Forestry Commission in who knows what fit of despair. Boys of two generations – her sons, her grandsons – had sat at that steering wheel, driving for hours across desert and jungle.

Ten minutes later they came over the last of the crests. As they did so, David was stretched against his seat-belt, leaning forward to the windscreen expectantly.

"There's the funny tree!" he shouted.

It was an oak twisted back from the road, pointing a long skinny finger across the valley. A penny always went to the child who spotted it first. Half a mile further on was the opening of the track which led to Cwm Caerwen, to ultimate quiet. A moment later it came into view.

A white police car was drawn across it.

Margaret Harvey knew trouble of state when she saw it. This had happened once before, years ago, in a bomb scare during the Scottish crisis. She turned off into the track and pulled up. A pair of young constables got out of the waiting car. One of them hung back while the other came up to her window, pink-faced under his chequered cap.

She knew him. A recent recruit to the police, not popular at the Old Inn because of his zeal about the licensing hours. Son of the grocer at Builth Wells.

He greeted her politely, then came out with his news in the perfectly grammatical, soft sing-song speech of the district. "I am sorry to be bothering to you, but we've had a call from Cardiff, very urgent. It seems that your husband is missing."

"Missing? He's always missing." She had thought it was death. With relief came annoyance. Then she saw the shock on the young policemen's faces. This was not how a good wife should react – a Prime Minister's wife. "My husband's job takes him all over Europe," she explained to them lamely. "I often have no idea where he is."

"The trouble is, Lady Harvey, that he doesn't seem to be where he's supposed to be. Not that anything's happened to him. At least, not that we know."

The other patrolman cut in. He was English. She had not seen him before.

"Special Branch in Cardiff would like to speak to you, madam. On our radio. They'll tell you what they know."

But Cardiff did not know much. They confirmed that Sir Patrick had been missing in France since the previous evening, that was all. Meanwhile they had a list of questions from the Paris police. Seated inside the patrol car, speaking slowly and loudly on its radio microphone, Margaret Harvey answered them as well as she could.

"Yes, she knew of the meeting in Tours, not what it was about. Yes, her husband had been in good health when he left home in Brussels. "A bit crotchety, that's all." No, she didn't mean anything particular by that – it was just his way. Yes, he was always in good health. Yes, it was true he took pills for his heart, but that was nothing serious. No, no brainstorms, no record of amnesia. No, she couldn't think of any reason why he should *want* to disappear. No, she had no suggestions to make.

As she listened to the hard official voice which was reading off these very strange questions over the radio, Margaret Harvey began to suspect it was holding something back: like a doctor who knows the truth already but is going through the full diagnosis, just to be sure.

Then she thought of a question of her own.

"What about his secretary? Is she missing too?"

"Yes," replied Cardiff. "We understand so."

At that point she very nearly laughed. Patrick and Laura, both lost in France. Well, it wasn't that.

There was a pause, filled by crackling interference.

"That's as far as we can take it at the moment, Lady Harvey." The voice softened. "I expect this will sort itself out. But obviously we need to keep in touch. Where will you be for the rest of today?"

"At my cottage."

"Which has no telephone."

In this there was a note of reproof, to which she retorted: "No, it does not. That's the point."

"In that case will you please keep our car with you? We'll call you back as soon as we can."

Oh well, they could help saw the logs and deal with the water. And David would probably enjoy it.

"All right," she said. "We'll be at the house. It's higher than this, so you might hear me better."

Cardiff said thanks and switched off.

Back in her own car, Margaret Harvey led the way up the rocky track, past the Old Inn and the last three farms, then on, still higher, through plantations of pine and arable fields abandoned to sheep. Still more puzzled than alarmed, she kept her mind on the act of driving. And David had plenty to do. There were three gates to open and close, and at one point, where a stream flowed across the track, she made him put down a line of stones, so their wheels wouldn't stick in the mud.

"You need to take the last bit in a rush," she warned the two constables. "Bottom gear and foot hard down."

She showed them how in the flashy hired car, plunging through the stream and up the opposite slope, over the slippery part under the alders, then out on a wide patch of turf at the top, just in front of the cottage gate. The policemen followed, then stepped out to stare at Cwm Caerwen: the small stone house tucked into the hill, its squat chimney braced against the wind. The English one looked as if he'd landed in Africa. He said he would stay in the car, to keep in touch with Cardiff. The Welsh one asked if there was anything he could do. She suggested he saw some logs, then keep her grandson amused.

She herself wanted a moment alone, discomposed by a vague mounting fear. Stooping, she picked up the big iron key from under its stone, where it lay among wriggling woodlice, then went through the gate and into the house. Seated on the hard rectangular sofa by the big black fireplace, she tried to think sensibly.

She knew so little. But that was her own fault. She never listened when he tried to tell her what important things he was doing. Feeling guilty now as well as afraid, she found a pad in the kitchen, then came back to the living room and made a note of the people who would know more about Patrick's movements than she did. There had been more mystery than usual about the trip to Tours. Even so, she thought, Riemeck must know about it. And John Clabon – he was involved. Louis Royand, perhaps – he had lent his house. And, oh dear, that journalist from *The Times*. Jack Kemble.

She put the pad aside, feeling guiltier still. The house was quiet except for the ticking of the wall-clock, sold off from some abandoned railway station. Outside, the rhythm of a handsaw, the bleating of sheep and trickle of water; the silence of Wales, so far away from everything. Too far. Her anxiety increased.

Yet Patrick wasn't dead, she was almost sure of that. They had lived with the fear of violence so long that it hardly existed any more. Even in his early days as Prime Minister they had agreed to escape from security measures, those special ugly curtains on the windows, special glass in the car, and everywhere special protectors – stout, friendly, maddening – who could probably not prevent your death but certainly made life intolerable. If the bomb or the bullet came, it came. That had been their philosophy. It had never come then, at the time of greatest danger. She couldn't believe that it had come now.

But here at Cwm Caerwen were the special protectors: a rule never broken before. Anxious as she was, she could not help resenting the intrusion. Wondering if they would have to stay the night, she went up to check the spare bedroom. It was musty with damp. She opened the window, then sat on the bed in an aimless daze. Beside the bed, put out for guests, was a copy of *Wild Wales* by George Borrow, an old school prize of hers, the label still gummed inside. She picked the book up, put it back. What a sententious ass Borrow was.

Then she heard the rain coming.

A swarm of darker clouds, massed around the mountaintop, broke on Cwm Caerwen in a sudden, fierce downpour. It was over in minutes, but immediately the taps, now that she'd decided to make a pot of tea for herself and the police, stopped yielding water. It was a familiar Welsh riddle: rain equals drought. And she did, at least, know the answer to this. Glad of something to do, she put on her gumboots and scrambled up the hill to the tank. Having freed the filter of particles of peat, until the pipe gurgled, she started back down to the house.

In a bend of the stream, just below her, a dam of stones was being defended by David and his plastic soldiers, called Action Men. Hidden behind a bush, his log-sawing done, the Welsh policeman was lobbing small pebbles against this fortification, shouting "boom" each time he scored a hit. Descending carefully, digging her heels in so as not to slip, Margaret Harvey paused to watch the battle. Over to the east, a first patch of blue had appeared in the sky, and a bird hovered over the pines of the Forestry Commission. Too small for a buzzard, she thought. Kestrel? Sparrowhawk? Once she would have known.

For a moment, standing on the hillside, she forgot the situation. Then came a different shout. The English constable, out of his car again, was waving his arms at her. Fear rushed in again. She hurried on down, the fronds of bracken shedding drops into her boots.

393

Two minutes later she was back on the radio. She expected the same stilted voice from Cardiff, but instead it was another one, less distinct still, quite different.

"Lady Harvey?"

"Yes?"

"This is Jack Kemble."

"Who?" She had heard, but could not believe it.

"Jack Kemble," he repeated, "from *The Times*. You remember. We met on Friday."

"Oh, yes. You. What on earth is all this about?"

"I'm speaking from police headquarters in Paris. Can you hear me?"

"Yes, I can hear," she shouted back. "Just about. I gather Patrick's missing."

"I'm sorry, it's more serious than that. The French police have asked me to tell you what's happened. Then I'll put on the officer in charge."

Coming faintly by radio, from so far away, the story seemed quite unreal. She knew that it was real, of course, but could not at first summon up the right emotional response to it, so very strange were the circumstances in which the truth was delivered. And in one way this was a good thing. It helped her to answer calmly when Kemble said, concluding: "So you see, there has been some progress. The police have got the names of the gang now, all six. And one man's been seen in Paris."

"But now they've lost him – this man? Is that what you said?"

"Yes, I'm afraid so."

"So haven't they any idea where Patrick might be?" she called out, finding that she wanted the answer to this above all. Not being able to picture his predicament, she couldn't even try to be with him in spirit: a desperate sensation, growing worse as she talked.

"Well, naturally, they think he might be in Paris. But there's still no real evidence of that," replied Kemble. "Lady Harvey . . . there's one thing I want to add. If it hadn't been for me, Sir Patrick would not have left the house – I am very aware of that."

"We are both responsible."

"Oh no, that's wrong. You shouldn't blame yourself."

"But I do," she said shortly, not in the mood to spend time on this journalist's conscience. "Now may I speak to this French policeman?"

"Yes, of course. Here he is now. His name is Commissaire Daladier."

A pause, then the Frenchman came on, expressing his sympathy in slow, calm English. Even at a distance he sounded reassuring; a man who knew his business. She must immediately come back to Brussels, he told her, in case the kidnappers tried to get in touch. If they did, they would probably telephone the house in Kraainem. That was the usual way with these things. An attempt would be made to frighten the person most closely related to the hostage. She must prepare herself for that. At the moment the Belgian police were in the house, waiting to take any calls until she got there. Her return would be arranged by the British RAF. As soon as she arrived in Brussels, he would speak to her again, to keep her *au courant*. Meanwhile he had some extra questions.

But again, to her own frustration, Margaret Harvey could not help. Each one of her replies was negative.

No, the names of the kidnappers meant nothing to her. No, she had seen no one watching the house. No, she did not know where Laura Jenkinson might be.

Damn Laura, damn her. What did *she* have to do with it?

But Daladier pushed on unruffled. The important thing was not to raise the alarm at this point, he said. She should travel to Brussels in secret and make no statement to the press. This was part of his strategy. He hoped, by keeping silent, to lure the kidnappers into a mistake.

"We must be cautious, you understand? Madame? You can hear me?"

"I understand."

"We shall do all that is possible. And remember, we have no reason yet to believe that your husband has suffered any harm."

No reason yet. Returning to the house, Margaret Harvey felt more chill than comfort in the phrase. Actual physical coldness came over her. She sat on the sofa. Neither constable spoke until she was ready. After a fudged explanation David was sent upstairs to pack, her bag as well as his own, while she told the police where to take him. Ten minutes later the fire was out, the windows shut. They were waiting for the RAF, with only the

house left to lock. David, upset now, suspicious, began to ask
questions. She could not answer. Tea, once again, seemed the
thing. She went to fill a kettle in the kitchen. The taps gushed
well but she hardly noticed. Then she saw through the window
that the English constable had set a carton cylinder on the grass,
from which was coming crimson smoke. Horrified, she
watched the red contagion spread across the valley, belching
through the alders, scattering sheep. At the same time all the
little sounds of Wales, water-trickle, leaf-rustle, wind and bird-
song, were flattened by the clatter of an incoming helicopter.

6

Eighty miles to the east, the scene was more peaceful. Seated side by side in the BMG-BDV III, a small yellow vehicle open to the air, John Clabon and Carlo Guidotti sped round the test track at Ash Valley, Coventry. The hiss of the tyres, the whoosh of the slipstream – there was no other sound in their ears. Guidotti's hair was flapping round his face, but his eyes were fixed hard on the speedometer. It was now reading eighty miles an hour.

"Bravo," he muttered. "This is very good, John."

Clabon kept his eyes on the track, occasionally flicking them sideways to the suburbs of Coventry, in search of a snooper from Ford. "Normally we bring it out at night. But what the hell, too late to hide now. Had to show you."

The needle had risen to ninety. "*Bravissimo*," Guidotti said, astonished.

Clabon boasted on as he drove. "We tried all the fuels, you know, from booze to beetroot. LPG, methanol – none of them were really any good. A battery it had to be." He glanced at his passenger and smiled. "And now you're going to ask me how it works."

"Zinc-chloride?"

"No."

"Sodium-sulphur?"

"Too hot and too big."

"Zinc-nickel oxide?"

"Rubbish. Come on, Carlo, you read the piece in that magazine."

"They left out the formula."

"And for that I thank God on this fine Sunday morning."

397

Clabon raised his face to the sky with true devotion. "But there were some horrible hints. Come on now, try harder. You're not even close."

"And when I am close," Guidotti said slyly, "will you tell me?"

Clabon, slowing down, roared with laughter. "No, I bloody won't! You've seen enough. Performance now proven, I trust. Battery life three years, recharges as it goes. New chemical element inserted at service stations, good for three hundred miles of average driving. More I shall not say."

"And you want a body?"

Clabon nodded, pulling up. "A body's what we want. Very light in weight, with minimum drag."

Guidotti combed his hair into place. "Mobital has a new alloy," he said with an answering smile, "strong enough for the frame. We also have a low-drag design, already advanced. Fibre-glass panels, plastic windows. More I shall not say."

"So we're on."

"We are on, if you wish."

"Ambassador, old friend, this calls for a drink."

"At this hour?"

"No, I suppose not. Another breakfast then. Come on, let's go back to Summerhill."

But they could not sustain the mood. Each had worries of his own; both were appalled by the news about Harvey. The merger, however hard they tried to revive it, was probably dead without him, and without Harvey's money they were each in desperate trouble, despite their present plan to collaborate technically. As the battery-driven prototype was put under wraps, like a racehorse brought back to the paddock, they drove away together in Clabon's green Jaguar, depressed again, not speaking, each to his thoughts.

Ash Valley was a city deserted. The great sheds were silent, litter drifting between them. All thirty factories of the British Motor Group had been closed since Thursday, on union orders, and would stay so until the men killed in the picket, now canonised as the "Ash Valley Three", were buried in Glasgow tomorrow.

Meanwhile this morning, Sunday, the whole of the BMG workforce was gathered at a nearby football ground, first to commemmorate the dead, then to debate the trespasses of their chairman. Would they forgive him or not? No one was sure. Although cleared of violence, Clabon had admitted an attempt to break the picket. He had also been thoroughly betrayed by *The Times*, who had gone ahead and published the fact that BMG management were in collusion with Police Special Branch. This was resented by all the workers, moderates included. On the other hand the company's rebels had been so disgraced by the tactics of their leader, Stephen Murdoch, that few of them had dared to turn up at this morning's mass meeting. It could, therefore, go either way. On balance John Clabon was tipped to win the day.

Even so he was nervous. As he drove along he stayed tuned to the local radio station, who had a reporter at the scene. And a few minutes later he was able to show the chairman of Mobital what it meant to be chairman of the British Motor Group. Pulling off into the emergency lane of the elevated motorway, he pointed down to a small tin football stadium, its terraces packed to the top with his workers. They could see the speakers' platform in the centre of the pitch, the surplice of a priest, the cigarettes glowing like fireflies in the back of stands, the placards being waved and the hands shooting up in agreement, while over the Jaguar's radio came the speech of a union leader, and then a reply by the management, both of them having to shout against the heckling of the crowd, who seemed to be swinging to and fro, first for a strike and then against, behind the reporter's excited commentary.

Guidotti's humour returned.

"The English are a sporting nation," he said. "Always you make two sides – in industry, in parliament. And nobody breaks the rules. The game is more important than the result, yes? It is very charming."

"It's bloody ridiculous," Clabon growled. "And the rules aren't what they were either – as in football."

Guidotti nodded, immediately sombre. "In Italy, when the bosses score, they are shot through the legs. At least you do not have that."

"No, we do not."

"For which, my friend, another thank you should be said." The Italian pointed to the sky.

"Okay, amen," Clabon said grimly, turning down the radio as music returned. He pulled back into the traffic and drove on, through the rolling suburbs of red brick and slate, the factories abandoned, the pylons and grime of the Midlands. "Of course," he added, "once this kidnap gets out, I shan't have any bother with them, that's the crazy thing. They'll all turn conservative patriots overnight. The Trots will be finished. And my God, if they kill him . . ."

His voice tailed off at the prospect.

"For my own men I cannot be so sure," Guidotti said. "To many of them this will seem a normal act of war."

Every few miles, between snatches of pop song, Clabon turned up the volume of the radio, keeping abreast of events at the football ground. But he made no comment upon them. And Guidotti kept his thoughts to himself. Though drawn together by their mutual problems, they frequently relapsed into silence, still learning to relate without the mediation of Harvey, like schoolboys deprived of a master. Clabon, the emotional Briton, was truly close to despair. As with many tycoons, his drive, disengaged, went into reverse, turning quickly to self-pity and defeatism. He could not exist in neutral. Guidotti, the cynical Latin, was steadier. Under his bored, weary manner lay a strength which was ever more apparent. Ambassador Carlo Guidotti had so little hope of the world that it could do nothing to daunt or disappoint him.

After a time he said in a quiet voice: "The Reds killed my wife, you know."

"What? I didn't know that."

"Her car went over a cliff in the mountains. It seemed, from the marks, that another car had tried to block her path. Nothing was proved, of course."

Clabon shook his head, appalled and confused by this revelation; finding no place for it among his other worries. "I had no idea, Carlo. I'm surprised you carry on."

"I carry on because there is no choice, John. We must play the game, as you English say. And we cannot tomfool with the rules. That is the trouble with Patrick's suggestion."

"Participation, you mean."

"Two directors for the workers, yes. It is either too much or not enough. They will use it to sweep us away. Either we must rule, strong arm, or a whole new system must be created. There is no position between."

"I thought you were tinkering in Italy."

"That is a pretence. I shall keep my power."

"Well, I don't know," Clabon said, "I really don't know. Perhaps he was right, we ought to try something new. But there's no point in wondering now. We can't do a thing until he's found, alive or dead. Nothing else matters for the moment."

"Of course, that is true. I agree."

With that they went back to talking of the progress of the search, the French police tactic of silence. Since the early hours they had been intermittently in touch with Commissaire Daladier in Paris, who had told them to stay where they were and carry on as though in ignorance of the kidnap. This was not easy to do. Embarrassed by their own inaction, ashamed at their hasty departure from Tours, they had tried to salvage something from the work that was done there. They would give the world a new electric car, they thought, even if it did run on guilt. They had rushed up from London on the impulse, to test-drive the prototype, and now they were on the way to Fair Lawns, the Clabon's home at Summerhill near Birmingham, where Susan, Clabon's wife, would meet them for lunch.

At 10.55, just before they got there, Clabon heard good news from the football ground. BMG had voted to return to work on Tuesday.

And then he had one of the worst shocks of his life.

Arriving at his fine Tudor mansion, tucked back from the road in its palisade of trees, he found two police cars drawn up on the drive. His wife, up from London twenty minutes earlier, was weeping hysterically; and the cause could be seen at a glance. The place had been wrecked in the night. Burned into the lawns with acid were unrepeatable words. The tennis court had been skewered up. The half-timbered, black-and-white house was daubed with red paint. Inside was worse. The furniture was overturned and ripped, precious objects had been smashed, pictures slit down the middle, the walls smeared with graffiti and excrement. On all the mirrors in the bathrooms foul messages were written in toothpaste, "fascist" the word most repeated. The beds had been pissed on. Bottles lay around, and many cigarette ends, trodden into the carpets. The desk in the study had been ransacked.

Clabon wandered through it without a word. The police asked him not to touch anything. He nodded in assent.

Guidotti, his guest, stayed with him out of kindness, then left him, out of kindness, and stood outside smoking a cigarette. Susan Clabon grew calmer. She would never come back, she said. For her this house was finished. She had never much liked it in the first place. Guidotti murmured sympathetically. A few minutes later Clabon himself emerged into sunlight and cleared his lungs. He spoke to the police, then returned to the Jaguar.

"Let's go."

They left in silence, without a backward glance, turning south on the motorway to London. After a few miles Susan Clabon, speaking from the back in a loud shrill voice, began to vent her views on the British Working Man. Her husband asked her to be quiet. She wept again, covering her face with her hands, as if to blot out what she had seen. Cries of disgust still came from her. "Oh, my bed! And did you *see* the carpets? Horrible!"

"Susan, I want you to do something. Are you listening to me?"

"Horrible!"

"Shut up!" barked Clabon. "Just do as you're told and keep your mouth *shut*, do you hear? I don't want to listen to this."

She sniffed and whimpered, then was quiet.

Guidotti, in the passenger seat, had been quiet all along. He held out his cigarette case to the driver. Clabon helped himself and smoked absently, racing southward at ferocious speed. Then he pulled a face and chuckled, taking the yellow cigarette from his mouth. "Damn it, Carlo, these things are worse than my cigars."

"I am sorry, John, that this should happen. Truly, it is too much."

"Spot of bother with the natives," Clabon said, shrugging. "They'll settle."

"Horrible!"

To this third screech from the back Clabon replied in a patient voice, flat with weariness. "Susan, please try to remember you have two other homes. No one has been hurt. This has been done by a few angry men who have seen their friends killed. They believe I'm to blame, which I partly am. So think about that, will you? And then think of somewhere to stop for lunch. Carlo and I are going to call Paris."

In the car was a radio-telephone, placed between the front

402

seats, with second receiver for a passenger's use. Guidotti picked it up and sat listening while Clabon spoke into his own. As previously instructed, they were calling back Commissaire Daladier at noon, British time. Soon they were through to a girl at police headquarters, Quai des Orfèvres. Then the Commissaire himself came on. "*Messieurs.* All is well with you?"

"Hunky-dory," Clabon said. "What about you?"

"Some progress, some annoyances." The connection was good enough to carry the Commissaire's sigh. "We have lost the Dutchman."

"That's a pity."

"Yes, *dommage*. We were not well prepared. He was picked up in a van. But later, when we followed, he was not inside it."

Clabon had pulled up in the forecourt of a service station. To express his opinion of foreign police methods, he grimaced at Guidotti. Then he switched off his engine, the better to concentrate. "So you still don't know where Sir Patrick is?"

"Unhappily, no," said the Frenchman. "We do not have a clue, as my friend of the press would say."

"Is he there again?"

"I'm here," said an English voice the other end.

This journalist, alleged to be assisting enquiries in Paris though apparently the prime cause of Harvey's predicament, was Clabon's chief suspect. "Bloody *Times*!" he shouted. "Still eavesdropping?"

"Helping, actually," came the quick retort.

"Oh yeah?"

"Yeah."

"What's your name, fellow?"

"Kemble. As I told you."

"Make a note of that, Carlo."

"First name Jack," the voice added, rising. "Want me to spell it?"

"Watch your lip," replied Clabon. "You and your paper have a lot to answer for. Commissaire, can't we get rid of this joker?"

"*Messieurs*, please," Daladier cut in. "Let us try to be tranquil. I have some small good news to report – another name."

"A kidnapper?"

"*C'est ça*, number six. A girl."

"Go ahead then," Clabon said curtly. "We're listening."

"She is German, from Berlin. Her name is Hoff." The Commissaire repeated the surname, then added two Christian names. "Mitzi Ulrike Hoff."

A pause, then Clabon said: "No, I'm sorry. Never heard of her."

"And Monsieur Guidotti, please. He is there with you?"

"He's here."

Guidotti spoke up for himself. "*Je ne connais pas cette fille*," he said. "*Elle a quel âge?*"

"*Vingt-six.*"

"*Plus jeune que les autres, alors.*"

"*Et plus jolie*," replied the Commissaire, then switched back to English. "The car of this girl has been found in Dijon, in the parking of the SNCF. We believe that she is at this moment in Paris. But we do not know where."

At that point the Frenchman paused, rather oddly, as if he were fishing for some response. But they had none to give him. After a silence of about five seconds he spoke again.

"It is time that you also came to Paris, *messieurs*. I need your help."

And to that he got an immediate response. Clabon and Guidotti, delighted to be mobilised at last, spoke at once, and as one. Of course, they would be there as soon as they could, they said. They would carry on to London and fly across in Guidotti's plane, now parked at Gatwick.

Daladier listened to this plan. He said it would do very well. After a moment he told them to use a side runway at Le Bourget, approach number six. A car of the French police would be waiting to meet them. From the airport they should go directly to the Ritz Hotel, where rooms had been booked. At the hotel they would find Erich Kohlman, who had come up from Tours with a record of the talks, reconstructed from memory. Also at the Ritz would be Dr. Riemeck, who was flying in from Brussels with copies of the merger plan, that is to say the original papers, as prepared by Sir Patrick before the meeting.

Again Daladier seemed to be listening. Having explained these arrangements, he stopped; then went on to add another. Waiting to join them at Gatwick, he said, would be a professor of Oxford University. His name was Lord Doublett.

"Doublett!" cried Clabon in surprise. "What's he got to do with it?"

"Ask him and you will find out. Ambassador, you know this man?"

"No," Guidotti said. "I do not know him."

At which Daladier seemed to be satisfied, at last, on some obscure point. He spoke more freely. "Then please will you ask this professor, *messieurs*, how it happened that Sir Patrick suggested to you a figure of money so far in excess of the one he agreed with Dr. Riemeck. The difference, as I understand, was three *milliards*."

"It was, and we will," said Clabon, glancing across at Guidotti in excitement. "Mister Commissaire, what are you up to?"

Daladier's voice faded on the air, like that of a ghost who has said his piece and retreats into darkness off-stage. "I intend to make a little experiment," they heard him reply from a distance. "In which I hope you will help me."

"Help you? Of course we will," Clabon said. "Go on, tell us more."

They waited inside the parked Jaguar, heads down to the dashboard, each pressing his receiver hard to one ear. Then the voice of the Frenchman came back again, clear but soft.

"Some person who is close to this affair does not want your companies joined, *messieurs*. So I want you to try it again. When you arrive at the hotel in Paris, please demand a new discussion of your merger. And then we shall see what happens, yes?"

7

Jack Kemble, sitting across from the Commissaire at his desk, hung up with a smile.

Daladier stayed listening a short while longer, as though to judge the quality of the disconnection. Then, for the first time, he laughed: a sudden, soundless puffing of the cheeks, which shook all his fat. The ends of his moustache fluttered outwards in the breeze.

"These men of business, they think they are very hard cookies. They are not. They are boys."

"In America they're not so funny."

"In France, also, the type is more serious."

"Perhaps that's the trouble with England," Kemble said. "The real shits aren't running the factories."

The Commissaire shrugged, losing interest. "But that is not our problem."

"So you think these two are innocent?"

"In this affair, yes. They would not betray their own interest."

"Who's the insider then? You're sure there must be one?"

"*Ah oui*, I am sure. And perhaps more than one. We shall think on this matter at lunch." Daladier started to select from the papers on his desk, making a bundle to take out. "You are hungry?"

Kemble supposed that he was, though his belly had ceased to complain. Too empty for hunger, too tired for sleep, he would run now until he collapsed.

There had been no breakfast: a disappointment quickly forgotten in the frantic excitement of the chase for the Dutchman. Success had seemed close at that moment. The ops room had been in an uproar, people running, shouted commands, every telephone and radio manned, red markers closing around the Latin Quarter as the green one, meaning contact and surveillance, moved out of the Luxembourg Gardens. Hope had risen so high that the Dutchman's escape a short while later had been a very bad blow: the worst moment yet in the Quai des Orfèvres. Daladier, losing all semblance of calm, had exploded in a bellow of frustration. A period of silent despair had followed, too deep for further thought of breakfast.

The BRVP blamed the SDECE, whose men had made the fatal slip. Having tailed the Dutchman as far as the Chinese kite shop, they had posted themselves in front, since there seemed to be no rear exit. By the time they learned better, from the girl in the basement, Janssen was gone. Enquiries soon revealed he had been picked up from the street behind in a small grey *deux-chevaux* Citroën van. The van, though its number had not been seen, was assumed to have come from the Café Babylone. The team who were watching the café had seen one of the waiters, a tough young character of the *quartier* called Lucien Seznac, drive off in a vehicle of the same type. He returned a short while later, but stepped out alone. The van by that time was empty.

Recriminations for this failure were still going off, like sporadic gunfire, but to Kemble it seemed that the truth was quite simple, if inadmissible to the French. The Dutchman had been too clever for them. And, of course, there had been too little time. Janssen had been identified, spotted, tailed and lost in bewilderingly rapid succession, before reinforcements could be called up. And now he had vanished without a trace, though presumed to be still in Paris.

One thing seemed gloomily certain. He would not get in touch with the Cuban again, except by the safest of methods. A big operation had been mounted to keep track of Reinaldo Valdes, but this was outside the scope of the Quai des Orfèvres. And Kemble, despite constant ear-flapping, could find out little about it. When the subject came up, doors were closed.

There had been no progress in the last three hours, but plenty of movement. Lady Harvey was on her way to Brussels, flown by RAF transport with an escort of the Diplomatic Protection Group, a unit of the British police specially trained to guard against terrorist attack. Also in the plane was a three-man team from the Special Air Service. Already famous for similar operations, the SAS were offering to help rescue Harvey if it came to a shoot-out. The French had agreed to this, as a diplomatic courtesy, but had no tiny intention of using them.

Waiting to meet this party at a NATO airfield in Belgium was the chief of the European Commission. This Riemeck, though technically Harvey's boss, was an unknown quantity. Kemble was not sure how to rate him. Nor were the French. But Riemeck, too, was on his way to Paris with a large team of staff, including the Director-General of Harvey's department, and also Lucy Maclean, Harvey's typist, both of whom were privy to the merger.

It was Lucy Maclean, in fact, who had brought to light the mysterious Professor Lord Doublett of Nuffield College, Oxford. Sir Patrick, she said, had gone to England on Thursday to meet this man, returning with new calculations.

To Kemble it seemed very odd that Harvey's *chef de cabinet*, Erich Kohlman, hadn't known of this – or, if he did know, hadn't mentioned it. The Commissaire thought it peculiar too. So when Kohlman came up to Paris in mid-morning, bringing a record of the merger talks, Daladier had asked him why he left the English professor off the list.

The German's reply was cool, accompanied by a small frown and a snap of the fingers.

"*Ach*, yes – Lord Doublett. I am sorry, I forgot him."

To Kemble this sounded so thin that it must be true. But the Commissaire made no comment. He had sent Kohlman off to the Ritz Hotel, where he was at this moment, still under a close police watch. Riemeck would be staying there too, along with the businessmen and Doublett. A meeting was scheduled inside the hotel for four o'clock, to be attended by all parties privy to the merger. At it Daladier would present the results of his enquiries. Then the businessmen would spring their surprise. They would press for renewed negotiations, and wait to see who jumped.

To Kemble the Ritz seemed an oddly luxurious mole-trap. He wondered how far the hotel were cooperating – whether, indeed, they had the faintest notion of what was going on beneath their roof. And one thing still puzzled him. This effort to flush out the Iskra's collaborator seemed deficient without Laura Jenkinson, who was surely a suspect, however unlikely.

Her name had not been mentioned all morning. The Commissaire appeared to have lost his early interest in her. Yet among the papers scooped off his desk, now tucked under his arm, was a file on Laura, delivered an hour before by the UK Embassy in Paris. Kemble tapped it with his finger as they walked out to lunch.

"You don't rule her out then?"

Daladier glanced down at the file, then shuffled it into the others, out of sight. "Not yet. It depends what she does."

Kemble blinked in the bright light of day, which was painful to the eyes after so many hours in the brown-glass building. "It's strange you haven't found her."

"We have found her."

"What! You have? You didn't tell me that."

"Monsieur Kemble, *cher ami*, I do not have to tell you everything."

"Where is she then?"

"She is using the apartment of some friends in the sixteenth *arrondissement*, close to the Place du Trocadero. And that is a very *chic* address – not exactly the bolshevik quarter."

"How did you find her?"

"The typewriter, Lucy Maclean. She knows where her friend Laura stays in Paris."

"So you've found her," Kemble said, catching up. "Well, well. Is she on her own?"

"It appears so. The owners of the house are away. French people, very correct. We can find nothing of suspicion in the place."

"You've searched it?"

"*Évidemment.*"

"You mean she's not there at the moment?"

"She is not," replied Daladier patiently. "She has gone to the races of horse at Longchamp. She has had lunch there, alone, at the hippodrome. Now we are waiting to see what she does."

Daladier offered no more. Kemble, beginning to weary of playing the Watson to this Gallic Holmes, gave up and walked beside him in silence. The day was a warm one, even in the shade. The streets were dusty from lack of rain. The square they were crossing behind the Palace of Justice was a small enclosure of ancient and dilapidated houses, strangely quiet, like a country village in the heart of the metropolis, cut off by the river both sides.

Daladier walked along quickly, almost trotting, his feet scuffing over the cobbles in short irregular steps, as if there were not enough time to take a proper stride. Suddenly he ducked to the left and entered a small cheap restaurant, half-empty, with paper cloths and fixed menu. He walked straight through it and into a private room at the back, an all-purpose living room filled with the sort of ugly furniture, neither new nor antique, which the poor take care of until it comes back into fashion. In the centre a table was already laid for two. An old woman dressed in black, muttering a casual greeting, immediately slapped down a carafe of wine. Food followed quickly, plain but good, two plates of grilled veal and vegetables. Kemble's appetite revived in full force. He tucked in. The Commissaire spread out his papers on the table and studied them one by one as he ate. Kemble had not been allowed to see these documents, but looking at them upside-down, he could tell who was left on the list of suspected insiders. Laura was there, and Kohlman. But there were other names too.

At one point Daladier stiffened in his chair and grunted with interest.

"This man Riemeck – he saved Jews in the war, did you know that?"

"No, I didn't know. Is that a bad mark?"

"It was work in which he was associated with communists," Daladier muttered, but made no more of it. He continued to read and eat in silence, until his plate was empty, then mopped his moustache with a napkin and looked up. "You have made some notes on the German girl, Mitzi?"

"Yes."

"Please open them."

Kemble took out his pad and turned to his entry on the sixth of the kidnappers. The sudden identification of this sad little orphan from Berlin had been the only break since mid-morning. The French TV star, Blaise Chabelard, had named her father, Helmut Hoff, as a founding member of the Iskra. Hoff was now dead, but investigation of his past had led to a print-out on his daughter, Mitzi.

The Commissaire was staring at it now: a long reel of data

from the BKA, Wiesbaden. He smoothed it out flat on the table, then tapped it with the stem of his pipe.

"The answer is in the life of this girl."

But no answer was found. Their conversation shifted to plans for the afternoon. Kemble had gained the impression that he himself was to play some part in the effort to winkle out the Iskra's insider; and this turned out to be the case. His task emerged on the short walk back to headquarters. Having heard what was required of him, he nervously agreed to give it a try. In return he was granted a call to *The Times*, which he made from Daladier's office, the Commissaire listening in. They smiled at the furious editorial scream from London.

"Jack! For Christ's sake! Where are you?"

"Sorry, Frank. Can't say."

"What in the hell is going on here? Do I get this thing or not?"

"Forget the profile. Something better coming up."

"Okay, let's hear it. Stop faffing about, man. We're setting up already."

"That's why I called, Frank. I want you to hold the front lead, four columns, and an inside follow-up, wall to wall. Work up some filler on Harvey and both the companies, quick as you can. And keep some people there. Be ready for a scramble."

"Oh yes? What's so big?" Holroyd's voice calmed as he grew more curious. "Has something else happened?"

Daladier's finger was raised in warning, his hand poised ready to cut off the call.

"Jack?" Holroyd's tone was wheedling now, greedy for news. "Jack, are you there?"

"I'm here," said Kemble, stalling.

"Speak up, man. What is this? What's happened?"

"I'll call you back, Frank. That's all for now."

"You can say something, damn it. Come on, what's the problem?"

"No, you'll have to wait."

At that Holroyd started to scream again. "What kind of amateur are you? This is *The Times*, Jack. We can't hang around for an unemployed piss-head like you. Now tell me what you've got or forget the whole deal."

"Foolish words, Frank. I advise more faith. Bye-bye now."

This call, which gave Kemble a great deal of pleasure, was completed at 2.52, just after the second race at Longchamp.

A few minutes later the horses were assembled for the third race. One after another, some nervous, some calm, the six marvellous dainty-legged animals were led round the short sandy track of the paddock by their stable lads. On the oval of grass between stood their jockeys, in last conversation with trainers and owners. No one appeared to be having much fun. The owners, especially, had the gloomy expression of very rich, very cautious men about to do something which might not pay off. Perhaps they had been forced into it by their wives. The wives were wearing silk like the jockeys, and some of them looked very beautiful, if not, on the whole, as well bred as the horses.

And beyond this magic circle of wealth on the grass, packed tight against the rail of the paddock, stood the punters of Paris. Here the faces were jollier, though some wore the tense expression of people about to risk all that they had. Among them was Laura Jenkinson, who was wearing a soft silk dress, just as smart as any owner's wife. Her face, half-shadowed by a wide straw hat, was both perfectly serious and perfectly happy as she watched each horse pass in turn, judging form.

Then she was lost behind a stir of activity. The horses wheeled into the centre of the paddock, puffing and prancing as their blankets came off. The jockeys, now helmeted and goggled, leapt up and rode out, their legs tucked double beneath them. The grass cleared quickly of millionaires and stable hands, punters broke away from the rail to place their bets. The hand-held camera of French police surveillance wobbled in the rush, then steadied on the place where Laura had been. She had gone. But immediately another camera picked her up in a betting queue, zooming up close with a telescopic lens.

For some reason, not understood by Jack Kemble, this was a moment of particular interest to the men in the ops room at the Quai des Orfèvres. So many heads closed around the small monitor screen that he himself had to step back and watch other screens, each of which was now transmitting a different view of the track. Some of them showed the scene from high points, and on one he could see the horses cantering off for the start,

412

beyond them the Bois de Boulogne, a grey smudge of trees in the distance, spiked by the Eiffel Tower.

The bright summer's day, the arena of grass, the trees and white rails, the silks of the jockeys and the pretty girls watching through field glasses – Longchamp on Sunday looked a nice place to be, even when shot in black and white by the cameras of the French police.

The race was over by 3.22. Immediately a team of workers swarmed out on the track, repairing the damage to the grass. The horses filed off the course through a gap in the rails, beside which Laura was standing.

The winner was a fine big bay from America, to the utter disgust of an elderly woman in the crowd, who flung her handbag at its flanks. The jockey leaned down and raised one finger in her face. This produced guffaws of laughter in the Quai des Orfèvres. But Laura, who was standing quite close, ignored the incident. Four cameras watched her glance down at her betting ticket. She put it away in her bag. Ten minutes later she left the course. One camera followed her into a bus, then went blank like the rest. Each of the eight small screens depicting the sunny scene at Longchamp had turned to blizzards of snow.

"*Alors,* monsieur, you are ready?"

Kemble had almost forgotten where he was. Turning, he started in surprise to see that Commissaire Daladier was offering him a pistol, suspended in a tangle of shoulder straps.

"Surely I don't need that."

"Perhaps you will not," Daladier agreed. "But I do not wish it to be said by *The Times* that you were exposed to unnecessary danger."

"*The Times* will dance on my grave," retorted Kemble with a laugh. He took the gun and examined it dubiously, still swinging untouched in its straps. "But really, it's no good giving me this. As someone once kindly said, the only thing I can kill is bottles."

"You have no experience of pistols?"

"Certainly not."

"In Vietnam?"

"Never."

"Very well, you must practise," Daladier said sharply, turning to summon a member of his staff. "Biffaud will take you

413

down to the *salle de tir* while we see what the lady does next."

Kemble glanced nervously back at the monitor screens, expecting Laura to appear again. "Is this really a good idea? I'm not the type to make a good cop, you know."

"You are trained to ask questions," said Daladier nonchalantly, turning to watch the screens himself. "You are also a very great expert on English girls of this type."

"Did I say that?"

"You did, monsieur. So now we shall put it to the proof. *Allez, au sous-sol.* And shoot well."

8

For the next half hour, as instructed, Jack Kemble tried shooting a pistol in the basement of the Quai des Orfèvres. The range was a long low room adjoining the cells, dimly lit. His ears were shielded by cup-shaped mufflers, attached by a spring across the top of his head. The pistol was American, a Colt .45, so big that it jumped in his hands. The target was an Arab made of cardboard, who kept popping up in different positions. Kemble hit this dervish twice, in the ear and left elbow, despite using three magazines. Twenty-two shots went wide. He could hardly believe his own incompetence. The French police were surprised at it, too. To show him what could be done, the officer escorting him took out his own gun and, holding it cupped in both hands, arms straight out, legs bent in a crouch, placed all eight shots between the Arab's eyes.

"Okay, you can kill," Kemble said to him sourly. "So what else is new?"

The man glared back at him, understanding the sentiment if not the words. They went back up to the ops room in silence.

The name of this marksman was Inspector Jacques Biffaud. Having dealt with a number of terrorists in the manner just demonstrated, Biffaud was almost as famous as his chief. But a different kind of Frenchman. The fussy kind, neat and precise in all he did; pernickety even in the act of killing. He had none of Daladier's easy charm, and physically the two men were opposites. Biffaud was small and trim, clean shaven, with grey hair cut short as a toothbrush. He wore steel-framed glasses and a bombproof watch. He looked the sort of man who runs in the early morning, eats low-fat meals and has fun with his wife at regular times of the clock. He did not smoke and he did not laugh. What Biffaud enjoyed was shooting foreign persons through the eyes. Kemble disliked him from the start.

They had met the night before, at the château of La Maréchale, where Biffaud had been left in charge. This morning he had turned up in Paris with Kohlman. Now, this afternoon, he had been detached to investigate Laura, a task in which Kemble was to help.

Neither of them liked this idea, but both were under orders, so they did their best to cooperate. Talking in signs and monosyllables, they left headquarters at 4.15 and travelled across the city's smartest quarter in the hot afternoon. The car hummed swiftly through the wide cobbled streets, along the arcade of the Rue de Rivoli and into the open spaces of the Place de la Concorde. Paris was quiet on Sunday. Only in the Champs Elysées was traffic of normal density, and glancing up to the arch at the top, Kemble thought it made a good image for the age – the gateway to heaven clogged with motor cars.

The famous vista was gone in an instant as they carried on down the right bank of the river, through avenues of chest-nuts and monumental buildings roofed in green copper. The Tricolour fluttered from every brown lamp-post, in honour of what Kemble could not tell, and there were a great many statues, huge women in stone, bronze horses charging the sky.

"Fine city," he said to Biffaud, though feeling in fact that Paris was just a little too fine. All these virtues in togas went ill with the task ahead, which was back-alley stuff. When Americans wanted to do something nasty they cloaked it in senti-ment, but the art of the French was blatant contradiction. In the land of Liberty, Equality, Fraternity, if anywhere on earth, what made things tick were Discipline, Authority, Malice. It was rather refreshing. A change, at least, from jocular humbug, which was surely the art of the Anglo-Saxons.

But compliments were wasted on Biffaud. When told that his capital city was fine, the bristle-haired Inspector made no response, by word or gesture or movement of the lips. He stared at Kemble coldly through his steel-rimmed spectacles, then turned away to peer at the building where Laura was staying. They drove past the door and circled round the block. On Biffaud's face, as he raised his eyes to inspect the upper floors, was the same intense, meticulous expression he had worn in the shooting range.

Kemble, feeling ever more doubtful about the operation to come, was glad that he had, after all, refused a gun. The idea of shooting Laura Jenkinson, whatever she might do next, made him laugh.

The French, on the other hand, were ready to do just that. Armed men had taken up positions all round the building, on the roof above it and at windows opposite, across the street. They had bugged every room in the flat and tapped her phone. They had also bugged Kemble himself, who was wearing a microphone underneath his shirt, a small thing suspended like a locket round his neck, but powerful enough to transmit the coming conversation to the Quai des Orfévres, and even to Daladier himself, if he chose to listen in.

The Commissaire was now at the Ritz, about to conduct his experiment. All parties privy to the merger were gathered inside the hotel, where the two chief executives would shortly attempt to revive the project.

In charge of the simultaneous operation here, at 27 Place du Trocadero, was Biffaud. The time was 4.30.

Laura had just come in from Longchamp. Listening from a car in the street below, they heard her kick off her shoes, undress, take a shower – then a creak of springs as she lay on a bed. After that there was silence. She spoke to no one and made no phone calls.

They waited a few minutes more, then Biffaud made a signal to Kemble. They left the car together and walked without speaking down Avenue Kléber, as far as its junction with the Place du Trocadero. Number 27, in the square itself, was grand as a bank. The lobby was marble, brass and iron. They strode straight across it and into the lift, which was being held open by a BRVP man. The lift was one of the old French kind, an ornate wooden cabinet, double-doored and panelled in glass. It rose through the well of the building with grinding slowness.

Biffaud got out at the seventh floor, where two more police were installed. Kemble rode on to the top by himself, creak and rattle, like a man being hauled to the scaffold. Tense, and yet close to wild laughter, he was suddenly swept from skull to shoes by desire for a drink. He steadied himself and stepped out of the lift, advanced to a heavy oak door, and pressed the bell beside it, an ivory button in a plate of polished brass. In the door was a peep-hole, for inspection of visitors. He kept to one side, well out of its range. She took a while to come. He was about to press the bell a second time, when he heard her feet approaching. A latch snapped back, and the door was opened an inch or two, held by a strong iron chain. In the gap appeared one big eye, wide in surprise, dark and shiny.

"Hi," he said breezily.

"You!"

"Yes, me."

To that she said nothing, but kept the door open. He carried on talking.

"Jack Kemble. Bought you a cheap snack in Brussels, prior to very useful dinner with Portuguese Ambassador. Remember?"

"What are you doing here?"

"Social call."

"Oh yes, I'm sure. A social call. That's nice."

Kemble smiled out the sarcasm, to remind her how amiably stupid he was. "Well," he said, "aren't you going to let me in?"

The eye flicked downwards. "I'm naked."

"Is that an impediment?"

"Funny guy."

He shrugged and smiled on. "All right then, get dressed. Let's take it from there."

The eye continued to stare at him, unblinking. After a moment she lifted off the chain and stuck out her head to scan the landing. "Wait there," she said, withdrawing, then slammed the door shut.

Two minutes later she opened it wide and let him in. She was still barefoot, but wearing a man's silk dressing gown, bright blue, with glimpses of underwear beneath, white bra and pants. Her skin was the way he remembered it, an even brown all over. Her hair fell loose to her shoulders, black and glossy, still a little wet from the shower, but only round her ears and the nape of her neck. The nails of her toes were painted bright red, Kemble noticed, to match the nails on her fingers. She had splashed on some scent while the door was shut.

"Hey, this is nice," he said, entering.

He meant the flat, which was done up in various shades of white – white carpet, white sofas, white curtains, white walls. The style was neo-thirties, glass and chrome, curves and mirrors, with pale abstract paintings and gruesome witch-masks from Africa. The only splash of colour was Laura herself, who stood in the centre of the room in a manner which declared there would be no sitting until her questions were answered.

"How did you find me?"

"Saw you at the races."

That gave her pause, but only for an instant. "And followed me here?"

"That's right," he said. "Sorry. Just wanted to make sure I wasn't butting in on something. You are alone, I hope?"

Already feeling like an actor in a very bad play, Kemble glanced round the room. The doors leading off it were closed, but no movement came from behind them. The rest of the flat was silent. Outside it, below and beyond, the city seemed ominously hushed. Individual cars could be heard as they passed, a snatch of opera in another apartment. From the street came children's laughter, a dog's bark.

Laura, too, was silent. Still watching him, she stood on the fluffy white carpet, her red-tipped toes almost lost in the pile.

"Yes, I'm alone. As you see."

"Whose is this place?"

"Mind your own business."

"I will try to do that. Nice though, isn't it?"

Avoiding her gaze, Kemble meandered round the sumptuous penthouse. The windows on its southern side were filled by a grand panorama of exhibition Paris. Between the museums and statues a vista of geometric gardens sloped down to the Seine and stretched away on the opposite bank, for a mile or even more, through the broad brown legs of the Eiffel Tower.

Laura had still not moved from her spot. "So how did you do?" she asked, cocking her head at him. "At the races, I mean."

"Oh," he said, recovering. "Won on the third – that's all."

"Name of horse?"

"Fooling Around, from the US of A."

"Sounds like a friend of yours." She sniffed, but didn't smile, still watching him, head at the same sharp, quizzical angle. "And what happened when they came in?"

"A woman threw her bag at him."

"No, you fool, she threw it at the favourite, who pulled the race. And I know how she felt. Still, you were there all right. Now, sit down – over here."

Still standing, her bare legs a little apart, she pointed to one of the long white sofas. Kemble sat on it. She was not a beauty and she knew it, but her legs were more fun than the Eiffel Tower's, and she knew that too. Again he was struck by that odd combination of manner, simultaneously brassy and shy, coquettish and resistant. *Go on then, take me, no, wait a minute, perhaps, let me think about it, and meanwhile keep watching, yes, just like that* – it was all so pathetically easy to read. This girl wasn't a sophisticate of any sort, despite the French clothes and trilingual chatter. And surely, Kemble thought, not a Red. The madness of Marxists consists in fixation. Laura's was too much motion.

"So," she said, "you were at Longchamp. But not by accident – don't give me that. Somehow, I don't really care, you've tracked me down here. The question is what do you want?"

"A chat."

"Purely social, I suppose."

"No, not purely."

"You know I can't talk about my job."

"But you've quit your job."

She stared at him, rigid from top to toe. "Who told you that?"

"Erich Kohlman."

"That was unusually gabby of him."

"Is it true?"

"Yes, it's true."

"So, well done. You walked out," Kemble said. "Why was that? Was there something in the merger got up your nose?"

"Don't be a pain, Jack. I've left my job but I still can't talk about it, as you understand very well. If you're here to trick me, you can leave, right now."

To trick her was why he was there. But it wasn't going to be easy. As at their first encounter, she was one jump ahead all the time.

Inquisitive now, or pretending to be, she sat beside him on the sofa in one swift motion, closing and covering her legs. "So Erich told you I'd left my job, did he? How did that happen?"

"Oh, it came up," Kemble said to her casually. "As you know, I arranged through him to meet Harvey. Later on I had more words with Kohlman on that subject. But by then you'd gone."

"Yes, thank goodness. I must say you do your job well, if that's the way it's supposed –"

420

"Wait. Stop there. So you did know about that interview –
before you left the château?"

Her body was perched on the sofa with the absolute stillness
of a bird about to fly. "Yes," she said. "I knew. What of it?"

"Was that the cause of your leaving?"

"On the contrary, it almost changed my mind. Erich was
trying to persuade me to stay, right up until we said goodbye. I
suppose he thought your treatment of Harvey might melt my
heart."

"Which it didn't."

"No – in the end. It made me laugh. You two are well
matched."

"So you left."

"I left."

"With the merger unsettled."

"Merger? What merger?"

She turned and smiled at him: a vindictive little crinkling of
the eyes and lips, like a politician's smirk when he outsmarts an
interviewer. Kemble, exasperated, reached into his pocket for
the photographs taken at the dovecote of La Maréchale, chose
one at random and slapped it down hard on the knobbly white
sofa.

"In the middle of a working weekend," he said to her
deliberately, keeping his eyes on her face, "agenda unspeci-
fied, but big enough to bring John Clabon and Carlo Guidotti to
a private house in France, Sir Patrick Harvey gets dumped by
his secretary. Now why should that be?"

"Dumped?" she cried, uncoiling like a spring. "Ho! I like that!
He dumped me."

"Did he, Laura? Did he? Or did you force him to? Now,
please tell me, exactly. What happened?"

"Nothing much." She stared at the photograph, then at
her knees. Sliding her hands between her thighs, she rocked
slightly forward and pressed her legs tight together, as though
she were cold. "It was personal."

"Can't you tell me?"

"I could, but I won't." She looked up then, defiant, her voice
shooting straight to a screech of anger, as though she had just
decided that angry was what she ought to be. "And now you
tell me something. What the hell is going on here? What's this
all about?"

Kemble patted the air, palms towards her. "Just a gentle probe."

"Into *me*?"

"Into the state of knowledge between us." He skipped in fright round the *double entendre*, but couldn't think where to hop next. "I am trying to find out, Laura, whether you know as much as I know."

"Oh yes?"

"Yes."

"I see," she said, cooling, but guarded; still watching him. "Well, you've heard what I know. But the rest I can guess."

"You can? he said, surprised. "Okay then. Guess."

"My guess is that you didn't get that interview after all."

Kemble made no reply. He tried to keep his face dead-pan.

"Sir Patrick found some way to stall you," she went on slowly, eyes narrowed now, lips beginning to quiver in a smile of cunning. "Maybe he didn't turn up even."

"Go on."

"It sounds to me as though Erich came to see you instead. In any case, between them, they shut you up – right? So here you are again, sniffing round me. Poor old Jack. You seem to be hoping that just because I had a quarrel with my boss, I might spill his secrets to *The Times*."

Serious now, but more relaxed, she went on before he could answer.

"Well no, Jack, I'm sorry to disappoint you, but I'm not that sort of person. I wouldn't mind working for the paper, you know that – I shall need another job soon. But meanwhile I will not betray my previous employer, even if I didn't much like him. What happened between me and Harvey is private. And nor, I might as well add, am I going to rat on the poor old Commission and all its dull works. I do think we live in a dismal society, yes, and I do think it has to be changed. But it has to stay international. And anything new must start from what we've got."

Kemble listened in bewildered silence. If this was a lie, it was in the gold-medal class.

And now, quite suddenly, she dropped her defences. Drawing in breath, she blew out her cheeks, as though to dismiss her own speech, then turned and smiled straight into his eyes with a softer, rather sad expression, in which at last the real girl seemed to appear, lonely and tired.

"There," she said. "Sorry to be boring, Jack, but I wanted to get that out of the way. The funny thing is, you see, I'm actually quite pleased to see you."

"You are?"

"Yes, I am. Because when you've finished this absurd inquisition of yours, we might get on rather well. Don't you think?"

"We might indeed," replied Kemble. "As I have been saying from the start."

"Well, have you finished?"

"No, not quite."

"Let's have the rest then. I can't stop my job until you stop yours." She lowered her eyes to the white knobbly surface of the sofa, at which she started to pick with one slim-fingered, red-nailed hand. A small puzzled frown had puckered her forehead. "Why are we going back over this anyway? Are you in some kind of trouble?"

"Me?" said Kemble, surprised yet again.

"Am I then?"

She asked this question very softly, in a voice like a child's, then raised her fine dark eyes to his, still with the same quite open, defenceless expression.

Kemble stared back at her. His mouth opened, then shut. He jumped to his feet and took a few paces across the white carpet. "Look – can we have tea or something?"

"Tea?"

"Yes, tea."

Laura's eyes were on him, showing only bewilderment. And then he saw, stealing into them, fright. "Yes," she said, also standing. "Yes, I suppose so. All right, tea. Or a drink perhaps?"

"No, damn it, tea!"

She didn't move.

Kemble made a scrubbing gesture, erasing his last remark. "Sorry, sorry. Tea will do nicely. *Une tasse de thé, s'il vous plaît, mademoiselle.* How's that?"

"Something's happened," she said.

"What?"

"Something else has happened, hasn't it? Something you haven't yet mentioned."

"What makes you say that?"

She came up close and laid a hand on his arm, smiling at him now with a sisterly expression, but still with a trace of fright. "Jack," she said, "for a pressman you really are a very bad liar."

Sighing in defeat, Kemble lowered his head, and then shook it convulsively, as though to make sure it was fastened to his spinal cord. After a moment, still looking at his feet, he laughed. "I used to be better."

Still holding his arm, Laura gave it a tug towards the sofa. "Come on now. Sit down, tell me. What is this?"

"Harvey's been kidnapped."

In order to take her by surprise he said it very quickly, in an offhand voice, simultaneously lifting his head and turning to face her, just as they started to sit.

And surprise he got.

Her dark eyes widened and her mouth fell open.

If this was an act, it was brilliant. But Kemble believed it an honest reaction. The instinct had grown on him that Laura was innocent. Now, with relief, he was sure of it.

So he sat down and told her the truth.

9

As he later admitted to the French, Jack Kemble's decision to trust Laura Jenkinson was less than perfectly objective. Her thin brown limbs shifting quickly about beneath a man's silk dressing-gown, which slid across her skin with a silky sound, had given him a powerful urge to take off that big, ill-fitting garment. He kept imagining how it would go – the dressing-gown falling from her shoulders, and after. Her inhibitions would fall away quick, he thought. With this slim, jittery, refined girl from England he would tumble on this fluffy white carpet, in this chic white room full of mirrors, and do the outrageous things he had once done in Hollywood with a tanned young million-dollar junkie. The picture, once into his head, would not go. He had quite forgotten his wife in Bethesda, to whom he had promised to return in good order. Here, right now, in mid-crisis, he wanted Laura.

Worse still, he liked her. He had liked her the first time, but now he liked her more. Her quirkiness, even her spite, made him laugh. She had spark, and oh, she was a change from Washington, a city whose girls weren't famous for their sense of humour. Even when she was serious there was a bright darting quality about her, erratic and inconsequential. She was not so much a person as a number of roles, which she switched between in rapid succession, sometimes playing for laughs, sometimes in earnest, until she forgot which was which. And in these perverse complications there was something especially English, Kemble thought. As they circled around each other, mutually guarded, she made him remember how it felt to be a poor boy from an English steel town about to make a conquest in the English upper class. And he liked her for that.

He wanted her, he liked her; even worse for his judgment, he pitied her, seeing that in her sudden shifts lay a search for self-respect. Having lost his own – between jobs, between women – Kemble knew the feeling. And this would do, he thought, to explain her behaviour with Harvey.

So he told her the truth.

As he did so he was aware of the consternation his action would cause among the French police, who were listening in to every word. Only Commissaire Daladier, he thought, if still tuned in at the Ritz, might understand the turn that this talk had taken.

Because it was now a long way from the script. The agreed, rehearsed line had been to pretend that the kidnap was still undiscovered; and that he, Jack Kemble, was the only person in France who had started to guess what had happened. These suspicions he would mention to Laura, who would then, if guilty, try to silence him.

But Kemble now thought this ruse absurd. She was far too clever to be told such a lie, and anyway there was no need for it. Instead of being put under pressure to prove her own guilt, she should be given a chance to show her innocence. So he started to tell her the facts. And Laura, at first, did nothing to disturb his confidence. She sat in stunned silence as she heard Harvey's fate.

But then her manner changed. Before he had gone very far, she turned and looked at him sharply, coldly; back on her guard. Then she jumped up and went to the kitchen, to make the promised tea. Standing behind her, still talking, Kemble noticed the tension. As she waited for the kettle to boil she stood drumming her fingers on the counter, and then, before it boiled, she left the kitchen and started to wander at random round the flat, peering out through the windows with unconvincing nonchalance.

She had, of course, guessed the trouble she was in. The Iskra, it was already clear from the story, must have had an informer in the château. And she must be suspect. Laura being Laura, this was enough to enrage her; and it might well have scared her a little. Even if she was innocent, she still had to prove it, and perhaps could think of no way to do so.

Even so, Kemble was disconcerted. Her behaviour was so peculiar it made him think she might be guilty, after all, in which case he had made a bad, perhaps dangerous mistake.

Immediately he changed his tactics. Now that he had started he could not break off in the middle. But he cut the story as short as he could, and also, as he did so, left out one very important fact.

He hoped that Daladier, if listening, would notice this.

By the time he finished speaking Laura had gone into one of the bedrooms – a room which looked across Avenue Kléber, straight into the eyes of the watching police. He heard her draw the curtains, first one and then another, with brisk angry movements. He heard the dressing-gown drop to the floor. "Well?" she called out to him shrilly through the open door. "Go on, go on."

"That's about it," he said. "All I know."

"So where are the rest of them now?"

"The Ritz."

"The Ritz. Yes, of course, they would be."

"Why of course?"

"Because, Jack, I'm used to boring discussions in very luxurious places. So, please tell me, who's there?"

Talking through the open door, he gave her the list. "Riemeck's in charge," he said. "He came from Brussels an hour ago. Kohlman's there, and Clabon, Guidotti – they arrived from England with a fellow called Doublett. Some professor of Harvey's."

"Oh yes. Him."

"Anyway it's business as usual. They're going on."

There was a moment of stillness in the bedroom. Then her face appeared round the door, once again struck with astonishment. "What did you say?"

"I said they're going on. The merger – they're clinching it anyway, kidnap or not. So I'm told."

"I don't believe it."

Kemble watched her face. "Guidotti's idea, I think. Or maybe it was Clabon's. Anyway, they both insist. They say it's now or never."

"Yes, I do believe it. My God, the shits," she said, no longer trying to deny the merger's existence. Her head shook once in disgust, then vanished. "Get that, will you? Help yourself."

The kettle had started to whistle: an urgent, rising shriek which made Kemble jump in fright. He hurried to the kitchen and switched it off. Standing there, he started to shake and sweat, without warning. For a moment he gripped the counter, then swift as a thief in the night he started opening cupboards, one after another, until he found some brandy for cooking. He snatched out the cork and took two gulps, paused to feel them go down, then tipped back the bottle and swallowed a third time, deeply. Feeling steadier already, he replaced the cork and put the bottle away. Carefully he closed each cupboard, leaving the kitchen as it was: a purely white room like the rest, antiseptic as an operating theatre. "Better," he murmured to himself. "Much, much better. *Merci, messieurs.* And now, let us see what we have here."

Completely steady now, firm of hand and eye, he started to search for some tea.

Or, of course, tea-bags. Yes, he thought, bags will do nicely, if there are any. What is the French position on tea-bags? They might rather like them. Or, then again, they might not. Convenience versus flavour. Hard to tell with the French . . . Ah, good. *Trouvé.* One for her, one for me.

"Jack? Are you there?"

Her voice made him think of breaking glass. Something was wrong here, something amiss. Steady, he told himself. Proceed with caution, boy, or you'll start forgetting your own bloody lies.

"Yes," he called. "Coming."

Carrying two mugs he returned to the sitting room, in which she had now reappeared, very prettily dressed in sandals and a cream cotton dress with small wild flowers embroidered on the front. To Kemble she had never looked better. The girlish simplicity of the dress made her look younger, less severe. He sat on the sofa. She sat down beside him, sipping her tea, which he'd placed on a glass-topped table between them. Suddenly, smiling in a dangerous way, she put down her mug and brought her face close up to his. For an amazed split-second, Kemble thought she was going to kiss him. But she sniffed at his mouth, then drew back.

"Yes, well you did help yourself."

"As invited."

"Hm," she said, still smiling. Then she turned to a forward position, parallel to his, not looking at him. Abruptly ceasing to smile, she cupped her hands round her knees with a clatter of

428

thin gold bangles and began to ask him questions in a quiet but sharp, glassy voice. "So our friends are in the Ritz, talking money and cars, while the French police are out looking for Harvey – in secret, right?"

"Right."

"And you are here talking to me."

"Yes," he said.

"Who sent you, Jack?"

"No one."

"The *flics*?"

"No, the police don't know. I came on my own."

"So you weren't at the races."

"No, I'm sorry, I made that up when I saw your pro-gramme." Kemble waved a hand at a crumpled white card on the table, headed *Courses au Bois de Boulogne*. "Actually," he told her, "I saw them on TV."

"At the Ritz, I suppose."

"Correct."

"So how did you find me?"

"Got a tip from Lucy."

"Lucy Maclean?"

"That's right," said Kemble. "Nice girl." Not having yet laid eyes on Miss Maclean from Scotland, he went on as fast as he could. "She's at the hotel with the others – standing in for you, I suppose. She gave me this number on the sly. I got the address and came straight round."

Laura paused, examining her knees; then pulled them up a little, rocking back on the sofa, so her feet left the floor. "So here you are," she said, balancing carefully in that position, going on in the same glassy voice.

"Yes."

"Sniffing around."

"Gentle probe."

"And you think I'm a spy for this gang." At this she rocked forward, so her feet slapped down on the carpet in their sandals. Still holding her knees, she twisted to face him. "What's their name?"

"The Iskra," said Kemble. "No, I don't think you had any-thing to do with it – of course not. But I came to warn you the French police might. They're looking for an inside person. You can understand why."

"An inside person." She stared at him, thinking out her next remark. When it came, her eyes blazed aggressively. "Well, I'm not the only one of those now, am I? What about Erich?"

"Kohlman's been checked. Apparently he's clean."

"Clean," she said, chucking up her chin with a sniff. "Clean. Oh yes, that's Erich."

At that she turned away again, forward. There was another long silence while she thought. She seemed to be calm, but the many gold bangles on her wrist, Kemble noticed, had started to clatter and clink with a tremor, just visible, which was running down her thin bare arm. Then her pose disintegrated suddenly. She threw up her hands and brought them down hard on the sofa, fists bunched, at the same time twisting back to face him.

"This is ridiculous. And bloody insulting! God damn it, aren't I clean too?"

"Yes. Well . . ." Kemble shrank back.

"All right," she rushed on, "so I left my job at an awkward moment. *All right*. Is there anything else? Well, is there?"

"There is . . . one thing."

"What then? What is there? Come on, tell me."

Kemble collected himself to speak, still glad of the brandy glowing in his gullet. Here it was, then, the test. Proceed with caution.

"On my first night in Brussels we had a date," he said to her, taking out a packet of cigarettes. "We were due to meet at the bar of the Hotel Europa. Remember?"

"And you weren't there."

"In the bar, no. I was eating in the coffee shop. And a few yards away from me, at another table, were two of the gang – Joop Janssen and Rosa Berg. The leaders."

Kemble paused, glancing up to catch her reaction. So far he had talked of the kidnappers vaguely, as people he had seen around Brussels. This was the first she had heard of where and when. But Laura showed no surprise. She made no comment.

"Go on," she said, calm but hostile.

Kemble continued to watch her. "You came into that coffee shop just before midnight. And then, a second later, you walked straight out again. Why was that, Laura?"

She hesitated, lowering her eyes.

"You must have seen me," Kemble said, coaxing. "Okay,

you didn't know what I looked like, but there wasn't a crowd to choose from, was there? The place was practically empty."

"Yes, all right, I did see you." She sighed and shrugged, as people do when about to dispense with a lie no longer worth telling. "I saw you and I changed my mind. I came because I said I would. But I was tired, I wanted to go home. So I left before you noticed me. All right?"

"All right," said Kemble. "So you walked away. And that was when I saw you – walking away. Now, think carefully. In the lobby you passed another girl. She was small, middle twenties, curly hair, cute to look at. The way I remember it she was dressed like a factory hand – tee-shirt and overalls. She had a lot of badges pinned on her chest."

As her memory was jogged with this latest fact Laura's eyes suddenly sharpened, and quite a new look came into them – alert, excited even; but guarded; still hostile. "Yes," she said. "So?"

"You seemed to recognise her."

"Did I?"

"You looked at her and smiled. You nearly stopped, in fact. I got the impression you were going to speak to her."

"Is this important?"

"It's important."

"Why?"

"Laura, that girl was one of the kidnappers."

Kemble had still not taken out a cigarette. Keeping his eyes on her face, he noted that it showed no surprise. Laura knew already, or had guessed from his questions, that Mitzi was a kidnapper. Nor had she anything to say about it. Her lips were pressed tight. They seemed about to break into a laugh, of the sort which is never far away in panic or shock. But her face stayed immobile, pale and taut. Seeing that no response was coming, Kemble went on.

"After you'd gone that girl came into the coffee shop and sat with the other two. Next day she followed me out to the airport in Brussels. And yesterday I saw her again, just before Harvey was snatched. So she's one of them, no doubt of that. But who is she, Laura? That's the question. As I said, they've all been identified except for this curly-haired cutie in dungarees. She's reduced every computer in Europe to tears."

Kemble was pleased as could be with this latest lie, which had come to him quite spontaneously, flowering straight to the lips with all the mendacious vigour of his youth. That Mitzi Hoff had also been traced was the fact he'd omitted from the story, feeling that it might be made into some kind of test for Laura. Now it had. She was caught. He waited, attempting to extract a cigarette out of the pack by feel as he kept his eyes on her face.

"Well, who is she?" he said again. "Can you help?"

Kemble wondered what the answer would be with the same sort of passive but intense curiosity as a gambler, awaiting the fall of the cards. He had no idea what she'd say.

But once again Laura surprised him. She refused to answer the question at all. In her eyes, staring back at him, dark and lustrous, he saw the same bewildering mixture of expressions – alert, excited, guarded, hostile – but now her face had taken on a firmer look. She had, it seemed, decided what to do. And when he struck a match, she suddenly reacted, as though that had broken some hypnotic trance. Her hand, bangles rattling, flashed out towards his face. Kemble recoiled. But all she wanted was the cigarette. She snatched it from his mouth and put it in her own. He lit it for her.

"Have you told the police this?" she asked in a casual voice, puffing out smoke before she'd sucked it in. "That I knew this girl, I mean."

"No," he replied. "No, I haven't. Not yet."

"Oh really? Why not? I thought you were helping them."

"I wanted to check with you first. As you probably noticed, I was half cut that night. I might have been wrong."

"So you came here in fairness to me. Oh, how sweet," she said with a sarcastic smile, already stubbing out the cigarette. "However, now you've checked, you're regretting it. You think I'm a spy after all."

"I didn't say that."

"It's what you think."

"It is not." Kemble lit a second cigarette for himself. "But it's what the police will think, unless you explain. They're convinced that this girl had a contact in the Berlaymont. Okay, so you knew her, that's established. You don't have to say any more. However, if you don't, I shall have to tell what I saw, or I'm going to get done for withholding evidence. Right? So let's just sit here and smoke. Drink your tea. Have a think."

"What I think is, Jack, you'd better get out."

"You want me to leave?"

"Yes," she said, standing up.

"Right now?"

"Now, please. Yes."

Again her hand flashed towards him. She took the cigarette from his mouth and punched it into an ashtray. Kemble jumped up in fright. "Now just a minute," he said to her, one hand raised in a halt signal. "Please, Laura, think. Is this wise? I came here to help you clear yourself, and now you're kicking me out."

"Yes."

"That doesn't look good."

"Maybe not."

"Then why?"

She took a deep breath before answering, then dragged up a smile of absolute falsity, as though worn out by her own pretences. "Because I am going to do some checking of my own, Jack. And I'd like some privacy."

Kemble assumed she meant a phone call. "I'll wait in there," he said, pointing to the bedroom.

But Laura's finger was aimed at the main door. "No, I said go. That's an order."

"All right, take it easy. I'm going."

"But don't go too far," she said unexpectedly, pulling out one more surprise from her store. "In fact I want you to sit on that bench, down there." She had moved to the south-facing window, and was now pointing into the street. "See? Down there, where I can watch you. Don't move, and don't talk to strangers. I'll join you when I'm ready."

Kemble nodded in obedience. "Okay, I'll wait. And then what?"

"Then we are going for a walk, my fine fibbing friend." She led him to the door and held it open, her face pale with anger or fear, perhaps both. "I have a surprise for you."

433

10

As he went down in the antique lift, creaking, rattling, slow as before, Kemble saw the bristle-topped face of Inspector Biffaud, glaring at him from the seventh floor. But they could not communicate. Laura had not yet left the landing above and was peering down the shaft, straight into the lift itself, which had no top. Kemble grimaced at Biffaud helplessly, rolling up his eyes in warning, and was carried on down to the marbled lobby. Posted there were two other men of the BRVP. Kemble had no time for words with them. He walked out into the square, and a few moments later was standing by the bench which Laura had pointed to. Her face appeared at the window, eight floors up. He waved. She did not wave back. She continued to watch him for a minute or more, then drew back out of sight.

Kemble wondered what she was up to. At this stage he still thought her innocent, despite every sign to the contrary. He simply could not believe that this horse-riding girl from the deepest interior of the British bourgeoisie, however addled in the head, was a member of a continental terrorist gang. So he did as she said. Legs stretched out towards the gutter, he sat himself comfortably on the bench she had chosen, between two trees, on the south side of Avenue du President Wilson, and waited to see what would happen.

Set into the paving beside him was a ventilation grille of the métro, through which came blasts of hot air and deep rumbles. And the air above ground was itself very warm, even in the shade of the trees. To his left the Place du Trocadero was still in full sunshine, though the light had mellowed. Another dry day was coming to an end. In France, as in England, it had not rained for weeks. Paris was cleaner than London, but scraps of litter had drifted into the gutter and yellowish dust rose in eddies from the cobbles each time a car sped past. Even on Sunday the cars were in a hurry, tyres squealing as they came round the studs of the square. Kemble watched them numbly, worn out by the session with Laura. The brandy had taken soporific effect; the tea had failed to liven him up. His eyes were sore and his head was aching. He had not slept for thirty-six hours.

Assuming she was now on the telephone, he wondered who she'd call; if innocent, if guilty. In the latter case he was in an exposed position, but plenty of cops were around. Sitting there in the pleasant warmth of evening, he couldn't believe he was in any danger. It was, however, necessary not to nod off. Soon he would be on the line to *The Times*, dictating the story of Harvey's kidnap. And any moment now, if things went to plan, the Iskra's mole would break surface, which would be a good story in itself.

So who?

Conversation with Laura had left the question open. Without glancing up to her window, avoiding any furtiveness of manner, Kemble took out his pad and laid it on his knee, then flipped to the last of that morning's entries.

The answer, as Daladier had said, must lie in the life of the sixth of the kidnappers. And she was a German. Therefore this riddle was a German one. Its solution must be concealed in some dark little cranny of the recent German past, or perhaps further back, in the past all Germans preferred to forget. Certain of this if nothing else, Kemble searched again through his cramped, pencilled notes.

HOFF, Mitzi Ulrike. Age 26. Born W. Berlin, only child of Elsa and Helmut Hoff. Elsa was refugee from Leipzig, E. Germany. Helmut, famous rebel leader, brought SDS contingent to Paris, May 1968. Next year couple broke up. Elsa moved to Hamburg, taking Mitzi. Helmut, abandoned in Berlin, became violent anarchist. Arrested 1973, was moved to prison clinic, Heidelberg, but jumped to death from window. By this time Elsa is qualified doctor, living respectably in Hamburg with Mitzi. But press catch up. Publicity following Helmut's suicide smears his widow. Accused as terrorist accomplice, Elsa gives up, returns East, taking hospital post in home town Leipzig.

An important moment, this, for Mitzi. Her father is dead, her mother has fled. She is nineteen years old, alone in Hamburg, exposed to the nastiest press in the world. So what does she do?

Mitzi remains in West. Next year, aged 20, goes University Frankfurt; and turns left. Accuses police of murdering her father, declares allegiance to student terrorists. Arrested for anti-consumerist arson, Frankfurt department store.

So she followed her father. But now for this girl there came another turning point, in the last days of 1977. Germany is poised for a fresh wave of terrorism, and Mitzi, by her own declaration, is set to join the carnage. But what does she do?

Acquitted of arson, Mitzi sobers up. Returns Berlin. Has lived there since, in Kreuzberg, poor district near Wall. Allegiance is now to non-violent Marxist group forming network of worker-cooperatives. No criminal record.

She was not on the wanted list, no, which was why she had been so hard to find. All through the night the ops room had flickered with photographs of missing German girls, some of them wanted for terrible crimes. Mitzi had not been among them. But the moment she was traced, in mid-morning, a new fact about her had been thrown up by the German computer. Mitzi Hoff was missing from her home in Kreuzberg, Berlin, and had been so for almost three months. So where was she?

Border records show Mitzi Hoff entered Belgium early May. Has not returned Germany since. Presumed resident Brussels. Drives blue VW, early model, now found Dijon. Alleged by French DTS to be sleeping with Lucien Seznec, waiter at Café Babylone.

That last little fact, if true, was interesting, Kemble thought as he closed the pad. It explained why Mitzi might now be in Paris. It also ruled out, or made less likely, a sexual connection in Brussels.

So who?

Expecting Laura any moment, he looked across the avenue. She hadn't yet appeared. There were few people about, except for loitering detectives. And less cars too, it seemed suddenly.

The lull made him nervous. Somewhere close by a bell was being rung, a sharp tinny clang of a papist nature, not the solid melodious boom of an empty British church. He went on trying to think.

So who?

Suspicion had hardened round Laura and Kohlman. A connection with one or the other would be found in Mitzi Hoff's record, Daladier had been convinced. But no such connection had turned up at lunch. And Kemble still couldn't see one.

There were, it was true, geographical coincidences. Erich had been a student in Hamburg when Mitzi was living in that city with her mother. Laura had acted as secretary to a long-running conference in Berlin. But that was all. Nothing in all three life-stories suggested a point of contact. In any case, what would bring them together? What connection could there be between the child of a crazed German anarchist and an English colonel's daughter, employed on diplomatic business? It was hard to imagine. And harder still in the case of Erich Kohlman. As a German official entrusted with secrets, Erich came under the all-seeing eye of the *Verfassungschutz*, office of state security in Cologne. The V-men, as they were called, had monitored the poor fellow's life so thoroughly that every small thing he had done, from childhood to the present day, had come reeling out of the federal computers. If Erich had stopped to say hello to Mitzi on the street, he would have been finished as a public employee.

Besides, they came from different worlds. Mitzi was a child of Berlin, born in, drawn back to the brittle society of borderland. Erich belonged to the bourgeoisie of the Hanseatic ports. His home town was Lübeck on the Baltic, where the family owned a shipping firm. His mother was an aristocrat from Pomerania, his father a hero of the Russian front, twice wounded, Iron Cross, nothing nasty on the record. And Erich himself had grown up so straight that his file had little to tell. He did well at school, he took a degree in economics. For two years he worked in the Bremerbank. Then he quit banking and joined the diplomatic service. After tours of duty in Washington and Bonn he had been detached to the Brussels Commission, becoming *chef de cabinet* to Harvey in 1981. And that was all. A nice, clean straight German boy.

Too clean, Laura seemed to think.

Could he just possibly be *queer*?

Perhaps, Kemble thought. It was an idea. The trouble was it didn't begin to explain, or make in the smallest bit more likely, an association with Mitzi Hoff.

Think again.

But each time he thought really hard about Mitzi, Kemble's mind was tugged back to one hard, uncomfortable fact. Among the people privy to the merger, assembled now in Paris, there was only one whose path this girl had crossed.

And that was Otto Riemeck.

It had happened in November 1977. In the early days of that month Mitzi Hoff had led a delegation of students from Frankfurt to visit the famous professor of German law. They came to protest at the death of the terrorists in Stammheim prison, who they said had been killed by police, as also had Mitzi's own father, Helmut Hoff, pushed from a window of the clinic in Heidelberg two years earlier. The law alleged suicide. The students screamed murder.

Riemeck at that time was the Rector of Württemberg University, but a popular man with the students because of his unconcealed dislike of the new anti-terrorist measures. As a constitutional lawyer, he had opposed the sweeping new powers awarded the police. He had charged the judiciary with bias and warned the Bundestag against hysteria. As a citizen of Baden-Württemberg, he was also none too keen on the hyper-secure new jail at Stammheim, in the northern suburbs of Stuttgart, a building which had cost Baden-Württemberg six million dollars. Hundreds of armed police were employed there to guard less than two dozen captives, and yet, raged Riemeck in several press interviews, they still couldn't keep their charges alive. The death of the prisoners had made him very angry. He did not believe that they had been murdered, but suicide was quite bad enough. He demanded an instant enquiry, and to demonstrate his feelings received several student delegations, including Mitzi and her friends.

And from that point onwards, as her record made clear, Mitzi Hoff had quietened down. After her visit to Riemeck, who gave her an hour of his time alone, she broke with her violent friends and went home to live in Berlin.

To Kemble this hardly incriminated Riemeck. But it had the French police excited. And the German police, who were clearly delighted to put the boot into this pinkish professor from Stuttgart, had disgorged every detail of his life.

A very distinguished life it was too. Born in 1919, the son of a Lutheran pastor in Ulm, Otto Riemeck had spent his whole career resisting abuse of power by the German state. He was, from the start, a Social Democrat. In the thirties he had joined the SPD, though the party was already banned by the Nazis. In the war he had worked as a teacher in Stuttgart, soon becoming a leader of the very small political resistance to Hitler. Acting in secret, he began to help the Jews. Soon he was running an escape route to Switzerland. By 1943 he himself was on the run, hidden with a communist group in Munich. Hoping to reach friends in Amsterdam, he had fled to the north but never made it. Riemeck was found by the Allies in Cologne, alone, in rags, half-starved and half-blind.

After the war his politics continued pinkish. He was opposed to West German rearmament, especially atomic. He resisted suppression of the Communist Party. He supported a reconciliation with the East. He fought the Nazi revival in Stuttgart. In 1972 he resigned from a government post in protest at the Radicals' Decree, the law by which all state employees were obliged to submit to a loyalty test – that very process of screening through which Erich Kohlman had just emerged cleaner than clean.

From government Riemeck returned to his university. In 1976 he was made its Rector. In the following years he assisted in drafting new German laws for workers' participation in management. He also became a famous expert on the law of the European Community. In 1979 he published a much-acclaimed book on the subject, defending the powers of the central bodies, Commission and Parliament, against those of the member states. Law against nationalism: it was his life's story. It won him a Nobel Prize.

In 1981 he retired. But six months ago, to general surprise, he had been made President of the European Commission. In accepting the post he had made a speech, from which one passage was frequently quoted. "For us Germans, you understand, this is more than an economic arrangement. It is a break with the past. In Europe we find a new identity."

These various facts about Riemeck passed through Kemble's mind as he sat on the bench and waited for Laura, but not in an orderly consecutive manner. Coalescing, they filled his head for about a minute, adding up to the general impression that here was an admirable man, and a very unlikely suspect. Nobel prize-winners do not, as a rule, lean to kidnap.

There was, of course, the ugly little fact that Riemeck was the only person outside the château of La Maréchale who knew that Harvey was leaving it at 4.15. He knew because Kohlman had told him so, by telephone, shortly after lunch that afternoon.

Even so, *Riemeck*?

No, it was impossible. Not Riemeck.

Laura then?

Surely, instinctively not.

Kohlman then.

Yes, the best bet was Kohlman, still, by a very small margin.

Or was that just prejudice? It was certainly instinct, Kemble thought. Instinct lets off the girl with good legs and comes down against the foreign bureaucrat.

In any case the answer would shortly emerge. And whoever the Iskra's collaborator might be, the problem was not to catch him or her, but to force him or her into some sort of move – a run, a phone call – which would lead to the rest of the gang, and so to Harvey's whereabouts. That was the task that Daladier had set himself in this last hour of the kidnap's conceal-ment, having already arranged for a full press conference at seven o'clock.

But time was running out. Laura had still not appeared. What was she doing, Kemble wondered, again looking up to the penthouse window. Her face was not there. And then he saw Biffaud and two of the BRVP men come out of the building. They walked quickly off to a car, which drove round the square and pulled up on its far side.

Half a minute later Laura herself came out.

"Sorry to be long," she said to him brightly, trotting off the street in her pretty cream dress. "Are you tired?"

"I'm fine," said Kemble, stamping one leg back to life.

She stared at him a moment, a cloud of perfume hovering round her. "You look done in."

"No, really, I'm fine." He stuffed his pad back in his pocket. "What time is it?"

"Six."

"Exactly?"

"Three minutes after."

She came up close and peered at his watch, brushing against him unnecessarily, so he felt the tips of her breasts. "All right," she said, pulling back quickly, still very bright. "Let's walk. We'll go through the gardens and cross the bridge."

"Where are we going?"

"You'll see, Jack. You'll see."

11

Leading him away from the bench, Laura put on a huge pair of sunglasses, which covered up her eyes and much of her face. But Kemble had already seen her expression, simultaneously tense and bright. The glitter in her eye was reckless, and playing round the corners of her lips was a half-suppressed smile, as though at some rather grim pleasure to come, still secret.

He recognised the signals of a woman's revenge.

His instinct was to run, far and fast. But Daladier had told him to do what she said. So he followed her through the central terrace of the Palais de Chaillot, the crescent-shaped exhibition buildings, somewhat Hitlerish in style, that commanded the slope to the river. And immediately, before and below them, the same grand spectacle opened up: gardens leading down to the Seine, the Eiffel Tower and the vista beyond, all bathed in the soft light of evening.

Laura paused at the sight. "There," she said, "isn't that fine? Paris – the heart and head of the world." She dropped her hand and turned to look at him, drawing up her lips from her teeth in a bold, provocative, humourless smile. "As Friedrich Engels said."

"Ah, him." Kemble nodded. "Rode to hounds, keen on Paris. It figures."

He was rather pleased with this, but it drew no response. They walked on down towards the river. On the curving tarmac paths of the gardens some children were roller-skating, children no different from others except that they were obviously rich, their vapid little faces unmarked by any trace of struggle or care. This was Paris 16. Laura, too, looked a woman of the *quartier* in her cream cotton dress and open sandals, brown-skinned, red-toed, clinking softly with gold accoutrements as she swung down the hill in long, graceful strides. Slung from her shoulder was a bag made by Gucci, identified to all who cared by its red and green flash. Her black hair was lustrous in the sun.

Coming up behind, Kemble noticed, were a pair of *flics* from Biffaud's team. As they entered the gardens, they took a different path and caught up, to the left, descending parallel. The Inspector himself stood watching from the terrace, short and angry, his legs braced apart in the shooting position. His steel glasses flashed as he turned away.

Did these men know what Laura was up to, where she was going? Would they intervene, or just follow?

Kemble was distracted. The presence of so many armed shadows, previously comforting, had made him more nervous than assured. But now he had to put them from his mind, because she had started to talk again, still with the same unnatural brightness, and still about Paris. She was comparing it to Brussels, a town that, as usual, drew nothing but scorn.

"The capital of Europe indeed! *This* is the capital of Europe. Don't you agree?"

Kemble shrugged. "Napoleon thought so."

At that a smile of limited and strictly provisional amusement appeared below her glasses. "Hm," she said. "Yes, you're right, he did. And that's the trouble, I suppose. No one forgets it. God knows, he left enough reminders." She pointed to the bridge below them, lined with triumphal eagles, and then at the dome of Les Invalides, shining gold across the river, half-left. "Paris, Rome, Berlin," she added, waving grandly round the points of the compass, as though the three cities were in sight, "they've all had a go at grabbing the continent, haven't they? So poor little Brussels it has to be – a common town for a common market. Oh, I shall be glad not to live there."

Kemble, having heard no good word about it, had started to feel rather partial to the capital of the Belgians. "So where would you be glad to live?" he asked her, purely for something to say. "London?"

"London?" Her head turned towards him sharply, as though she had just seen a chance to make a point. "I always feel London's a bit off the map, don't you? A bit provincial. And

Rome's just a glamorous ruin. No," she added casually, striding on, "the only town I've ever liked, even half as much as this, was Berlin."

She left him to follow this. Kemble obliged. "You've worked there?"

"Yes, for six months, at the end of the seventies. I loved it."

"What's so special?"

Again she turned to look at him. "You want me to tell you about Berlin?"

"Might as well. Unless, of course, you'd like to explain where we're going."

"No," she said, immediately grim. "You'll see."

"Okay then, Berlin."

"Ever been there?"

"Once, for a day. Before the Wall."

"You've not seen the Wall? Oh, well," she said with excitement, instantly shedding all falseness of manner, "that's the first thing you notice, especially flying in – a funny, irregular line running right across the city. Like a tidemark."

"High tide?"

"Yes, let's hope." She nodded, but absently, more interested in the picture in her memory. "As you come down to Tempelhof you can see the line clearly, and the difference either side – all those big ugly squares in the east, like empty parade grounds, and the razzle-dazzle our side. Lots of parks. No proper river, of course, like this" – a gesture at the Seine – "only little trickles, half-smothered in bridges. The Spree is rather a mess, I must say. That's a point against. But the city itself, Berlin, is stupendous. It's so *big*. I expect you remember."

"No, I didn't notice."

"You didn't? But it's really *huge* – much bigger than Paris. It must be twenty miles across. In fact it's not a city at all really, more of a separate country. An island. And all the way round it the communist ocean, stretching off to God knows where – Vladivostok, I suppose. That's the frightening thing about Berlin. You're conscious of it all the time, even when you're driving around in a car. This is far enough, you think, better turn round and go back, because right over there, at the bottom of that street, starts Soviet Asia."

Kemble listened with close attention, convinced that this talk of Berlin, like her walk through Paris, was leading to something. As she spoke of the great divided city of the Germans, her mood had altered. She was totally absorbed in the memory of it. Passing under the shade of some trees, she took off her glasses and put them in her bag. Then they crossed the embankment towards the bridge, dodging traffic. Once over the street, she started up again.

"*Insulaner* – islanders – that's what they call themselves, you know. And it's true, the Berliners aren't like anyone else. They've got this rather nice, wisecracking fatalism. We're doomed, so damn it, let's celebrate. You feel it on the Ku-Damm. The whole street's disgustingly flashy of course, quite frantically so – skyscrapers, discos, neon, porn, the usual tat – and yet at the same time it's all rather harmless and *jolly*. As if they were only really mimicking the West, just to cock a snook at the East. Hooray, they're saying, we're free, look what we can do, isn't it disgusting. Yes, I loved the place, I have to confess. It was one of the happiest times of my life."

They were now on the Pont d'Iéna. Above them loomed Napoleon's eagles on pillars. The river flowed green below. A long *bateau mouche*, glass-roofed, shot the bridge and throbbed westward. Laura paused to watch the boat recede.

"In the Ku-Damm you see one side of the Berliners' character – a sort of crazy bravado. But out by the Wall it becomes something else, rather fine and touching, more serious. Something tougher."

Still leaning over the parapet of the bridge, she stared at the waters of the Seine, but her mind was in Germany, and to Kemble she seemed to be searching for something – an answer, an explanation. Was it herself, or someone else, that she wished him to understand? He couldn't guess; and was getting more uneasy by the minute. In her walk she seemed to be dawdling, as though she were waiting for something to happen. Biffaud's two *flics* overtook them and sauntered on ahead. Laura took no notice. Eyes blank, she walked on slowly, still thinking of Berlin's borderland.

"It takes some guts to live in those districts by the Wall, and most of the people who choose to settle there are young, which is maybe what makes me think of them, rather romantically, as front-line troops. And the area itself, of course, is just that – a front line. Kreuzberg, Moabit, Wedding. Horrid places really, quite bleak, half-wrecked. All concrete and weeds."

445

Kemble's ears pricked up at the mention of these suburbs. Moabit was where Mitzi Hoff had been born; Kreuzberg was where she lived now. We're getting closer, he thought. But he made no comment and asked no questions, since Laura talked on without prompting.

"That's where you start to get frightened and want to turn back. Almost every street you turn down, there's the Wall, saying here Europe stops. A lot of the houses are boarded up – planks and breeze blocks, cement splashed in. The place seems half-empty, abandoned in panic. And too *quiet*. You get a feeling of imminent calamity. Dreadful things happened here not long ago, you think, and might again. That's your first impression. But then you take a look at the people who live in these districts, and what do you find? Misery? Fear? No, not at all. Berlin is quite jolly here as well. The buildings are desolate and drab, but camped among them, tucked into the nooks, there are all sorts of jolly little groups. Most of them are using shared houses – multiple family units and what-not, cooperatives and communes, workshops, artists, small factories even. There are lots of cheap cafés, special prices for comrades, food for free if you're broke, street markets full of quaint stuff. And barter – plenty of that. You've got what I need, and vice versa, so let's swap. Most of the politics is leftish, naturally, but not really violent these days, and quite unconventional. There are just these experimental groups, each with a different idea of sharing – sort of do-it-yourself utopias, made up on the spot. A lot of them have run away from something. Some from the East, of course, and some from the West – mostly to get out of military service. And here they are all together, huddled in the shadow of the Wall, arranging things in their own style. It's amazing. You ought to go and see."

"I shall," Kemble said. "After this."

"It would make a good story, wouldn't it?"

"Well, there's your debut. Go on, write it."

But she hadn't finished. As they reached the southern bank of the Seine, overtaking the two police, who were loitering at the end of the bridge, Laura added another brush-stroke to her picture of life by the Wall.

"Of course, because it's cheap, there are thousands of foreigners living there too – Turks, Greeks, Yugoslavs, Portuguese, Spanish, Italians. The *Gastarbeiter*, as they're called –

446

guest workers – though that's not a very good word for them. They're not exactly guests, I mean, are they? And a lot of them don't have any work."

Pausing to dodge more traffic, she crossed the road towards the Eiffel Tower.

"There are crowds of these people round every town in Germany, but when they fetch up in Berlin it's interesting to see how the others – the young Germans, I mean – really do treat them as guests. They are helped in all sorts of ways – canteens, free beds, advice and so forth."

"Guilt?"

"Guilt? For the past, you mean?"

"The past, the present."

Laura thought about it. "No, they don't feel much guilt. Why should they? They help the *gastarbeiter* out of compassion – no, it's a bit more than that even. They *identify* with them, you see. We who live in Berlin are victims too, they are saying, just like these drifters from Turkey and Greece."

"Do they convince themselves?"

"They certainly believe they're the victims of affluence. Wealth, they'd say, degrades as much as poverty. In fact what they're really against is materialism, of West or East. There's a lot of that feeling in Germany now. Mostly it's rather vague and negative, but in Berlin it takes a more positive form – in places like Kreuzberg, where you find these odd little pockets of self-sufficiency, organised to share on a basis of need. Here, you feel, something new is happening. This is the way that Europe could go."

They were now in the gardens below the Eiffel Tower. As they set out on the long gravel path that led through its legs, Laura had started to walk a little faster. Kemble, glancing back to the street they had crossed, saw Biffaud standing beside his car. The two police following on foot had been replaced by two others, a man and a woman. The car drove off. Laura kept her eyes to the front. Seeming more resolute all the time, chin raised, cheeks pale, she strode quickly over the gravel.

Kemble, still hoping she was innocent, was now in a state of deepest confusion. Where was this leading – the walk, the talk? Was she serious? Was she teasing? Did she really believe this preposterous guff, or was she just putting it out to make a point – a point about someone else? In either case he'd heard enough.

"So it's back to the loom, is it? Knit your own socks."

"Don't be crass, Jack. Don't mock what you don't understand and haven't even seen."

"Sorry, okay. So the future's in Kreuzberg. And the way you keep bringing it up, I assume that's where you met her."

Laura walked on, head down to her feet, not replying.

"It's where you'd seen her before, Laura, isn't it?"

After a moment she nodded. "Yes," she said, but added no more.

Kemble, fed up with her games, pushed harder. "The girl in the hotel lobby, I mean. The one we both saw in Brussels."

"Yes. Her."

"You met her in Berlin?"

"Yes," said Laura curtly, not slackening her stride. "In Kreuzberg."

"Well, go on."

"It was winter. Snow on the ground, a terrible wind. Some miserable street by the Wall. I was driving around by myself, which I quite often did, when I saw her on the pavement, making hot dogs for the Turks."

Kemble took a moment to understand the picture. "Ah, free food for the guests."

"Yes, but not really hot dogs. She was giving them buns, with some kind of flat sliced sausage in, cooked up on a neat little barbecue. The men were in a queue – it was probably some labour office. Mitzi was alone. She was wrapped up so tight I hardly recognised her, but her face is the sort that never changes. The moment she smiled I knew her – those chubby dimpled cheeks, shiny-pink in the cold. And she had a smile for every customer. Each time she gave away a bun, she took out a pamphlet from under her coat, like a child revealing a secret. That was the deal, her smile said. Eat my bun, read my message. And the men were happy with it. I expect you noticed, she has the sort of smile which can cheer up an unemployed Turk in the snow."

"Yes, I saw. She's a doll," said Kemble. "And her name is Mitzi?"

"Mitzi Hoff. Her father, Helmut Hoff, was a terrorist – one of the originals. But you know all about that."

"I do?"

"Yes, Jack, you do."

"Oh? Really?"

"The police have already got this girl's name, I think, as well as the other five. And they sent you to catch me out. I expect they're following us now. So do, please, stop acting the goof."

Kemble could only laugh, giving up on every point without a fight. "How the hell did you work all that out?"

"Mostly by watching your ridiculous face," she said without amusement. "It wasn't very difficult."

"Okay, I'm sorry. I did as I was told. So where are we going?"

"You'll see."

"You're not going to do something stupid, Laura, are you?"

"Just keep walking along, Jack. And don't bother telling me any more lies. You're about to get the answer."

Suddenly, struck by a new thought, she stopped in her tracks.

"You're not carrying a weapon, I hope."

"No, of course not."

"Good. I don't want any violence."

She walked on.

They were passing beneath the Eiffel Tower. Its four huge legs converged above their heads in a lattice-work of brown steel girders which went on up for a thousand feet into the softly coloured, cloudless evening. The air enclosed by its base seemed to echo with very small sounds. Birds were flying in and out of it. A lift was descending at an angle down one of the legs. Laura, still walking along at the same brisk clip, raised her head to look up its innards. The sight made her laugh. Seeming glad to change the subject, she suggested that when every rival had been considered, you had to admit that this thing in Paris was the greatest act of vandalism the world had ever seen. However, she then announced, she liked it. It was so monstrous it was beautiful. Only the French would have dared.

This struck Kemble as a typical remark – the first completely predictable thing that Laura Jenkinson had said. She seemed about to make some other comment, on the vista of formal patterned gardens which was opening out ahead. But he wanted her back in Berlin.

"So you knew this girl already then? I mean when you saw her feeding Turks in Kreuzberg. You recognised her."

449

Laura nodded, serious again, showing no wish to evade the question. "She had been in the press a few months before, sticking up for her father. In fact a photographer was pestering her right there, as she stood in the snow with her barbecue. A horrid-looking flashy type, long-haired. He seemed to be trying to provoke her. But Mitzi behaved as if he were made of air. She smiled for her Turks, and them only. It struck me as a brave thing to do. You have no idea how horrible the German press can be, Jack, especially to a girl like that."

"What? Worse than me?"

"Yes, and a great deal better at deceit."

Laura laughed gaily at this: a joke she really did enjoy. And then, once again, she asked the time. Kemble told her. 6.28. Her pace immediately quickened. She seemed to be trying to speed up the walk but slow down the talk, because she did then expound on the scene in front. These gardens were called the Champ de Mars, she said, and that up ahead was the Military School, built by Madame de Pompadour. But Kemble wanted no tourism.

"So Mitzi Hoff had been in the press. But you must have known her before that – some time before. Her face had hardly changed at all, you said."

Laura, walking fast, was slow to answer. "Yes, that's right. I had met her before."

"Where?"

"Here, in Paris."

"When?"

"Oh, about ten years earlier. Yes, it was ten years exactly."

"So what year was that?"

"1968."

Kemble felt no surprise. His puzzlement had been replaced by a mood of grim foreboding. "May, I suppose."

Laura's nod was irritated. "Yes, of course, May. The Events of. During."

"Mitzi was here in Paris? In 1968?"

"Yes, Jack she was, along with all the others. You didn't know that?"

"It's not in her record."

"Well, she was young. Just a child."

"Twelve," said Kemble after a moment, recalling the date of Mitzi's birth. "She must have been twelve."

450

Laura agreed. "Yes, twelve. She looked about that, even though she was tiny. Her father brought her from Berlin. To start with, she was right in the thick of it, a sort of rebel mascot. And then one day she disappeared. I think her mother must have come to take her home."

"Now just a minute, Laura." Kemble stopped on the path and took hold of her arm, so that Laura was forced to stop too, though she would have gone on if she could. "Just a minute," he said again, facing her. "Are you telling me that you were here too?"

Her eyes met his, hard and bold. The question was inane, but she answered it seriously. "Yes, I was here."

"In Paris, May '68?"

"Yes," she said, back to her least pleasant, vengeful smile. "You didn't know *that* now, did you, Mister Ruthless Investigator?"

Kemble dropped his hand. "No," he said. "I didn't."

"And the *flics* don't know either, I expect."

"No, they don't."

"It's not on my file at all, then."

"No, there's no mention of it."

She nodded, without surprise. "A wise little cover-up by my father. But yes, I was here, Jack. Come on, let's walk this way."

12

From that point onward Kemble should have been afraid, but instead he felt only dismay, for Laura had been fine to watch as she talked of the great, lost capital of Germany. What spoiled her looks, and her person, was dissatisfaction. Enthusiasm made her beautiful. Lit up by something she loved, she was lovable . . . No, too strong. Love was a habit that Kemble had kicked. But he was now falling hard for this lady, there was no getting away from it, and the thought that she might be guilty appalled him. He resisted that thought. He refused to accept it, even as the evidence piled up. He couldn't believe he had got her so wrong.

For some time they walked along in silence.

Leaving the Champ de Mars, she led him down Avenue de Tourville, past the burial place of Napoleon Bonaparte. The conqueror of Europe had been interred below a golden dome, which seemed a bit unfair, considering the fate of Adolf Hitler. But such trivialities were not discussed. There was no more tourism. Laura was now in a state of intense concentration. At one point, shortly after she was back on solid pavement, she stopped to flick a handkerchief over her brown leather sandals, which were white with dust from the long gravel path. The tips of her toes shone red again. She tightened a small brass buckle, straightened up, glanced behind at the following police, and then walked on with her quick neat steps, neither pausing nor rushing, but checking the street-names as she went. She was following a definite route. She wished to be in a certain place by a certain time, it seemed, neither sooner nor later.

Kemble had given up any attempt to work out her purpose. He merely followed her, to see what would happen, and as he did so was vaguely aware of a number of dire possibilities. Joop Janssen was somewhere in this city. So, it was thought, was Mitzi Hoff. The others, even Harvey himself, could be here too. They could be anywhere. Anything could happen. Wait and see, he thought. Keep walking, keep cool. And be ready to dive. When Inspector Jacques Biffaud draws his shooter, the place to be is the floor, especially for persons of Levantine appearance. But even if not, down quick.

Biffaud's behaviour was as puzzling as Laura's. Since they had left the Field of Mars he had passed them twice in the same unmarked car, a Peugeot saloon. At other intersections, a short way ahead, Kemble glimpsed passing blue flashes, and from several quarters close by came the urgent hee-haw of sirens. The forces of order were clearly in a state of agitation. It was difficult not to share it.

But Laura was calm. Walking quickly along, she started to tell how she'd come to be in Paris in the spring of 1968.

She had been seventeen at the time, at a private school in Ascot, England. She had come to Paris to improve her French. Under the terms of the language exchange programme, she would spend six weeks with a Parisian family, attending a *lycée* with the daughter of the house. The *lycée* was in Boulevard Raspail. The daughter of the house was called Jeanne. And when the revolution broke, they were quickly drawn into it.

"Everyone was. Of course, Jeanne and I were especially well placed for it, living so close to the Babylone. We didn't have a revolutionary thought in our heads, but we used to sneak down there to watch the fun."

"What went on there?"

"The Bab? It was rebel headquarters, Jack. You could see the stars there any night – Blaise Chabelard and Helmut Hoff, all the famous leaders, plotting away while the press queued for interviews. That was where I first saw Mitzi – a tiny little thing, like a curly-topped doll. Helmut carried her about on his shoulders. He used to stand her on a table and make her lead the battle-chants while the rest of them stamped and clapped."

"Did she mind?"

"Mitzi? You're joking. She loved it. She was a star among stars, until her energy ran out, and then she'd just curl up and sleep in a corner. But I've run on a bit. My memory of it starts towards the end of April. Up until then it was just a student rag, but early in May it got more serious – I can't remember how – and suddenly we realised that the centre of the whole amazing thing was our rather ordinary little café, the dear old Bab. At least Jeanne and I realised, long before her parents, who were wonderfully slow on the uptake. They never thought of stopping us. We dashed off our homework and went there every night."

She stopped to glance at a street-name, taking her bearings, while Kemble was trying to remember how much he had told her. The Iskra went back to '68, he had said, according to the evidence of one of its original members, the TV celebrity Blaise Chabelard. Yes, that had come out. But about the café, nothing.

There was no time to work it out. She was on the move again, picking up the story.

"And suddenly things did start to move very fast, day to day. One evening we came back from a film on the métro and as we got out of the train, we smelt it, even underground. The gas, I mean. A funny sweetish stink that made your eyes hurt. And when we got up to the street, bang, we were in the middle of a riot. Gas bombs were going off all round us, people running about and screaming. Most of them were trying to get out the way, though the students were starting to fight already, ripping up the cobbles, tearing grilles off the trees. As for the *flics*, they were laying into anything that moved. So we ran. We got away. But after that, obviously, we were involved."

A vision of Saigon in flames passed across Kemble's mind. The peace talks had started in Paris that same May of 1968, too late and too slow to save lives without number.

"It's amazing that no one was killed through the whole thing," said Laura. "But the following week was fierce. The *flics* started using a sort of grenade, shot from the hip with a short-barrelled gun. The explosions were terrific – not really dangerous, though, just flash and noise. And they came up with a new kind of gas, which burned your face if you used a wet handkerchief, which we all did, because it worked with the old kind. Jeanne was quite badly affected. She had to be taken to hospital. And I nearly got myself arrested. We were helping to defend the Bab, which got completely smashed up. Someone dragged a car across the street and set light to it. There was blazing petrol all over the place."

"Nasty."

"Yes, it was. And after that, of course, Jeanne's parents were furious – quite wild with terror, as much for me as for her. We were confined to the house. My father started ringing up every hour, ready to cross the Channel with a British Expeditionary Force. It was agreed that I should go home. Well, you can imagine, Jeanne and I thought that was a rotten plan. So you know what we did?"

"What did you do?"

"We ran away."

Recalling this, Laura looked so much the teenage girl on an illicit spree that Kemble, again, was tempted to trust her.

"We didn't go far," she said, "only to the digs of some students we knew. But that was far enough. With things as they were, we were impossible to find."

"So you joined the rebels."

"We joined a march anyway, up the Champs Elysées, and sang the Internationale at the Arc de Triomphe – or tried to. We weren't too sure of the words, or even the tune. The march that day wasn't big, compared to what followed, but to us it seemed *enormous* – an army on the move. And there was Mitzi again. I can see her now, right up the front on her father's shoulders, fist in the air. She was punching in time to the chants. But that was the end of it for her. I only saw her once more, at the café, being fought over by her parents. They were shouting their heads off, with poor little Mitzi scared stiff between. Helmut had hold of her, and so did her mother – Elsa, was it?"

"Yes," said Kemble, "Elsa."

"Well, mama was the winner. That was the last we saw of Mitzi in Paris. And just as well for her. Because the really big battle was still to come. The *flics* had sealed off the Latin Quarter, so the students decided to take it. The Bab was rather out of things now, because of its position. But our little hidey-hole was bang in the middle, so Jeanne and I saw the whole thing – we were *in* it. This was what they called the Night of the Barricades, and it really was extremely violent. The CRS had come into it by this time. My goodness, they were fierce. And the students were pretty tough, too. They kept track of the battle by radio, so they knew how the others were doing – where the line had held, where not. And the *speed* those barriers went up! In our street they took up the cobblestones with a pneumatic drill. Goodness knows where they got it. Paving stones, traffic signs, furniture, dustbins, everything was grabbed for the pile, even trees – they just hacked them down with axes. And cars of course, turned over on their sides. Some of the piles were turned into bonfires. But the *flics* had these huge, very powerful water-hoses. In fact that's how they got me in the end."

"With a hose?"

"Yes, I'm afraid so. It was rather humiliating. My feet got caught in the jet and *whoomph*, down I went on my head, out cold. I woke up in hospital with a man either side of the bed. One was the British Vice-Consul, and the other was my father – a considerably more frightening sight than the CRS."

"So then you were out of it," Kemble said.

"Yes, that was it for me and Jeanne. Her father locked her up. Mine took me back to England. And that was really the end for the students too, although it didn't seem so at first – far from it. In the week after I'd gone millions of workers came out in their support. But that really did scare the ordinary French – as the government knew very well it would. So they let the thing run a bit, then put it to the vote. When the election came in June, the communists lost half their seats. The Sorbonne surrendered and the factories went back to work. End of shallow analysis."

"Shallow?" said Kemble. "It sounds as if you followed the thing pretty closely."

"Well, yes, I did – of course. I followed it like a player taken off at half-time. And that's the way the match went. But the question is what to make of it now. Was it just a bit of mass excitement, whipped up by the press, or was it something quite important?"

"Which would you say?"

"At Oxford I used to talk about it seriously, mainly to boast that I'd been there. Later, when I went for a job with the Foreign Office, I didn't even mention that I'd been there. That was daddy's idea."

"And what's your line now?"

"Now?" She thought about it, striding on. "Now I would say that what happened in 1968 was a sign of collapse in the West."

"Wow-ow," said Kemble, rolling his eyes. "That's *big*. We could make a movie out of that."

"Shut up and listen. People say 1968 was caused by boredom, meaning the French were fed up with de Gaulle. I agree it was

456

boredom, but deeper. What came out then was real dissatisfaction with the trivial, plush life we lead, and the terrible muck-heap beneath it – the wasted resources and wasted human lives. I mean the moral vacuum in Europe that Harvey thinks there's no need to fuss about, just because it isn't as bad as the war. Moral ideas are just a source of trouble, he seems to think. Well, I disagree with him. Vacuums can suck in trouble, too. Peace needs inspiration. But men like Harvey just don't understand that. They can't see the danger of their own bloody dullness."

"That's a pretty ruthless thing to say."

And pretty culpable too, Kemble thought with sinking heart. But her face showed no flicker of penitence.

"1968 was the start of something, that's all I'm saying. There'll be more of it."

"Consumer revolts, you mean?"

"Yes."

To Kemble this seemed unlikely. "Hm," he said, copying her own expression of doubt. "I seem to remember that while you people were burning cars in Paris, the Czechs were fighting for more of them."

"Their problem is repression. Ours is waste."

Having seen off the Czechs with this ready answer, she came round a corner and entered a minor *étoile*, where five streets met. Around it stood old-fashioned métro signs of sinuous iron. The traffic was so slight that Laura, to take a short cut, walked straight across the central circle. Half-way over she waved a hand round the peaceful, dusty scene.

"I didn't see it, thanks to my father, but people say Paris has never been so lovely as it was in the second half of May '68. There was no petrol, you see. No cars, so no accidents. There have never been less people killed in this city than there were in that month."

"Aha," said Kemble, "so it's not just back to the loom, it's back to the goddamn farm. Solar energy and horse travel, grow your own beansprouts."

Ignoring this, she walked down a boulevard, very long and straight, lined with trees. Kemble glanced behind, but could see no followers, which gave him a turn. He had come to rely on the French armed presence at his back. Then he noticed that Laura's pace had slowed a little. She was calculating distance.

457

Next moment she said in a cold, deliberate voice: "You're a clever fellow, Jack. But like all cynics, you're a fool. And not at all convincing. What do you answer when people ask you what you believe?"

"I tell them that, like Dr. Johnson, I believe all schemes for political improvement are a laughable thing."

"Yes, you would. That's a journalist's attitude."

"Is it?"

"You lot are always jealous of the people whose doings you have to report, so you make out their doings are absurd."

On another occasion, relaxed in his friendly neighbourhood bar, Kemble might have conceded this. Today it was not the point. "And you, Laura, what do you say when serious people, not fools like me, ask you what you believe?"

Walking slower, she answered with a tight, grim smile. "I suppose I would say that I believe in schemes for political improvement."

"Is that why you walked out on Harvey?"

"Partly, yes."

"You said it was personal."

"No, it was more. I felt disgusted at what they were doing." Her voice warmed up and her eyes began to glow again, as fine in anger as enthusiasm. "It seemed a crime to me – a disgrace, let's say, that those three men could sit there, so pleased with themselves, and about to eat a marvellous lunch, having ruined the lives of twenty-four thousand other men with one little scribble on my pad. Twelve thousand to be axed from each company, that was the deal. It took about a couple of minutes."

She had stopped below the awning of a café. She was standing in its shade. Her face had gone pale and her breath was coming fast in indignation – or was it fright? Yes, it was fear she was pale with. On impulse Kemble reached into the pocket of his jacket and disconnected the transmitter wired up to the microphone under his shirt, so the French police could hear no more.

"So you *are* against this merger?"

"I'm against the system it bolsters." Her voice was tired now. "There are men in those factories who want to try another system. They want to take charge of their lives."

"And you're on their side."

"I sympathise."

458

Kemble could hardly speak. He had not believed it till now. "My God," he said, "you *are* in this thing."

"What do you think, Jack?"

"Well, you've been spinning it out, but it's pretty damn clear. You met them in 1968. You were snatched away before they could hook you. At Oxford you started turning left, but then you forgot all about it – until you met Mitzi in Berlin."

"Walk ahead, Jack."

"What?"

"Let's go in here and have a drink. Then I'll tell you." She waved at the café behind him. "Go ahead, lead on."

"Whatever you say." Kemble turned and walked inside, muttering desperately over his shoulder: "It's no good, you know. The *flics* are all set to shoot you on the spot."

"So we have been followed?"

"Yes, we have. They're right behind."

"As I thought. Let's sit there, in the corner by the window. What will you have?"

"Scotch. A large one."

Kemble sat down at the table she had chosen. Laura remained on her feet. A young waiter, slim and dark, came over to her, smiling in wary recognition. Laura greeted him with a handshake, gave him the order, then sat down herself.

"That's Lucien. Fancy, he's been here ever since I was a schoolgirl, bringing drinks to people in this room."

Kemble's innards contracted in surprise. He felt a fool as well as frightened. The answer was obvious, but the question came out of him.

"Laura, where are we?"

"Oh," she said, "sorry, didn't you realise? This is the Babylone."

13

For a short while Kemble did not speak. Recovering quickly from surprise, he passed straight into a state of hyper-observant calm. Within a few seconds his senses had absorbed the Café Babylone. He took it in all of a piece, the whole scene at once, but his brain wasn't working so well. He couldn't think what to do if this or that happened – or that, or that, or that. There were too many possibilities to calculate. With intense but resigned curiosity he waited to see how the end would come, like a passenger trapped in a car that has gone into a skid.

The café itself was one of the old French sort, with no more comforts than a railway waiting-room. Brutally lit by white fluorescent tubes in the ceiling, it was almost full, and very noisy. When Laura first entered a hush had fallen, but now the din had resumed: shouted conversations and wooden chairs scraping on tiles, còins being flung into saucers, cups and glasses clattering on cheap tin trays as they travelled from zinc bar to marble-topped tables. A TV set was on loud in one corner, but no one was listening, because everyone was talking, a wall-to-wall hubbub suspended only for multiple hand-shakes. The air was clouded with cigarette smoke and the walls were exactly the colour of skin stained by nicotine. A dark brown dado of painted wood ran round the room at head height. Above it were mirrors donated by aperitif companies, St. Raphael and Cinzano, and between the mirrors hung por-traits of the saints. Marx, Lenin, Trotsky and Mao gazed down on the company; Guevara stared into the distance. In every space left by this rudimentary decor, pinned to the dado and the walls above it, were hundreds of photographs, some new, some faded and curling with age, some signed and scribbled with messages, as in a place frequented by actors or sports-men – only here the fraternity were rebels.

Laura had chosen a table in the front left corner, just inside the window. She herself sat with her back to the wall, which gave her a view of the café's interior, and also the street. All the tables outside were taken. A dense crowd of shaggy, revolu-tionary persons thronged the green iron furniture spread on the pavement, in the shade of a blue fringed awning. Beyond them a bunch of Daladier's police, disguised in overalls, were digging up the Boulevard Raspail. Beside the shallow pit they had dug stood a fibre-glass hut with a gauze-covered aperture facing the café. Another man from the BRVP was selling papers even closer, on the pavement beside the café's tables. Across the street a couple, man and woman, had set up a flower stall. They were from the *Brigade de Surveillance*, as probably were most of the people who kept drifting up to the stall, lingering to chat, drifting on. No one was buying any flowers.

Then Kemble saw that Daladier himself was on the scene. The Commissaire was sitting in the back of a car across the street, about thirty yards from the flower-stall. So the action is here, Kemble thought, it is not at the Ritz.

Because of the position he was sitting in, facing the corner, Kemble had to twist in his chair, first inwards, then outwards, to take in the scene. And Laura watched each movement of his head, each shift of his eyes. Her glances followed his. She noted what he noted. When he turned back to her, she smiled in malignant triumph, but only for a moment. Her face was taut with tension now, white around the lips and grimly deter-mined. She had something still to do, Kemble thought. What-ever she was up to, she hadn't finished yet.

"So this is the Bab," he said. "Where it all began."

"Yes," she said, "this is the Bab. It's hardly changed at all. Jeanne and I used to sit there." She pointed across the room; then down it, towards the bar. "And that table there at the back, in the corner, was rebel headquarters. Chabelard used to hold court there with Hoff. They were the two big leaders, and their followers sat either side, the French JCR over there, and on that side the German *Studentenbund* – the SDS. You could see them here any night, the whole Berlin crew, with Mitzi curled up on that bench."

"And what about the others?"

"The others?"

"The Iskra," Kemble said in a low voice. "Rosa Berg and her friends – Joop, Hal, Mario, Steve. Where did they sit?"

"Did they come here too?"

"Laura, you know they did. This was their hangout in '68. They've been coming back ever since, and so have you. You found your way here by heart."

She stared at him, calculating. "I'm not ready to discuss it," she replied with a snap, then turned to look out of the window, at the street-digging *flics*. "However, yes," she added in a calmer tone. "I have come back here a few times."

"I suppose you know the whole place is surrounded."

She nodded, still watching the street. "Yes, I thought it might be."

"So what in the hell are we doing here?"

"We are waiting, Jack."

"Waiting? For what?"

"You'll see."

Kemble gave up and lit a cigarette. Laura, turning quickly from the window, took hold of his wrist and twisted it round to see the time. 6.45. Then the waiter arrived with their drinks.

Kemble inspected him with interest. This was Lucien Seznec, a junior member of the Iskra, believed to be Mitzi's lover in Paris. Lucien had worked in this café all his life, between spells in prison. Aged thirty, he could have been twenty; a slim fellow, black-eyed, olive-skinned, with short black curly hair. Even in his waiter's gear, white shirt and black waistcoat, he was somehow deadly in appearance – the gipsy matador. A knife scar, like a white vein, ran across his left cheek from ear to throat. With quick, deft movements he put down a whisky, ice on the side, a bottle of mineral water – prising off the cap with one hand – and then a pink drink for Laura, possibly Cassis. She smiled at him in thanks. He nodded at her warily, tucked the cash slip under a saucer, then withdrew to the bar at the back, where he stood talking to Marc Bensaïd, the café's Algerian proprietor. Bensaïd was a heavy, dark, shaggy man, unshaven and streaked with grey, roughly dressed, much fatter than in the police pictures. His paunch was compressed by the bar as he leaned across it to speak in Lucien's ear. The waiter nodded, then disappeared out the back, through a doorway screened by hanging strips of plastic. A woman came out to take over, perhaps Bensaïd's wife. The Algerian himself went back to work, half-hidden behind an express coffee machine, watching Kemble and Laura all the time as he pulled the levers in a cloud of hissing steam.

At that point Laura stood up.

"Sorry, I won't be a moment," she said, and then, leaving Kemble alone, her drink untouched, she too went out through the door at the back. The coloured plastic strips swung behind her, then settled. Above the door were signs saying *Toilettes* and *Téléphone*.

Kemble was ready to bolt. But then, turning back to his drink, he saw that the *flics* were in the room. Inspector Jacques Biffaud, champion sharpshooter, was sitting at a table five yards away. With him were two other men, presumably BRVP. Kemble watched for a signal, and immediately got one. Biffaud, who was sitting with both hands cupped around a short glass, slowly extended one finger in an order to stay put.

Kemble prepared to dive. His pulse speeded up. He snatched up his own glass and swallowed half the whisky, without any ice or fizzy water. It went down well. He felt calmer. But then, seconds later, he twitched in fright as the café was swept by an uproar. A few people started it, but soon many others joined in, shouting abuse at the television screen in the corner. The face which had appeared on it was that of Blaise Chabelard, the handsome purveyor of Sunday-night culture, in this place regarded as a turncoat. No trace remained from that morning's interrogation. His dark hair shone nicely in the lights. Speaking fluently to camera, the betrayer of the Iskra said his piece and then vanished. It must have been a trailer for the programme to come, Kemble thought, relaxing as the uproar subsided.

He waited for one more minute.

It seemed a good idea not to drink the other half of his whisky, since this was a moment for strict self-control.

He drank it.

The waiter, Lucien Seznec, had not reappeared.

Then Laura came back through the plastic strips. Passing the bar without a sideways glance at the *patron*, Marc Bensaïd, she advanced through the tables. And then, half-way across the room, she stopped and changed direction towards the café's door, opening her mouth to greet a new arrival.

Just in off the street, standing stiff in the doorway, was Erich Kohlman.

Kemble, unsurprised, watched them talk. Then they came towards him.

So, he thought, they're in it together. Well, that had always been possible.

14

Before they joined him Kemble had it worked out. While alone in her flat, Laura must have phoned Kohlman at the Ritz. She had told him to come to the Babylone, where friends would be waiting to help them get away. Commissaire Daladier, listening in, had decided to let this happen, being well enough prepared on the ground to play the game any way he liked. He had come here from the hotel to take charge. And Laura had timed the whole thing to the minute. Walking here from Trocadero, she had carefully avoided a full confession. Now, as the truth emerged, she was ready to flee.

And presumably somewhere in the café were guns – a force strong enough to break through the police cordon. If so, this was going to be a very hot spot. Biffaud, five yards away, had unbuttoned his jacket and placed his right hand beside his glass.

But something else had to happen first. Laura intended to sit before she ran. Bringing Kohlman to the table, she placed him beside her, so they both had their backs to the wall. She was the one in charge, Kemble noticed. Kohlman seemed strangely confused. He was moving like a sleep-walker, without volition. His eyes were glazed, and his face was even paler than usual, set stiff, as if in wax. And yet he was going out in style. For this last appointment of his life within the law, Erich Kohlman had gone to his wardrobe and drawn out a fresh combination from what seemed to be an indefinite supply of grey suits, cream shirts and plain silk ties.

Laura offered him a drink. He shook his head. Speak for yourself, Kemble thought, picking up his own empty glass and staring at it in surprise, as though he had only just noticed the state it was in. But Laura was not taking hints. She sipped her own pink concoction, then put it down and started on her final statement.

"The theory is, Erich, I suppose you know, that Sir Patrick was betrayed by a member of his staff. That's what the French police think, anyway. So they sent this buffoon round to question me, in the hope I'd be lured into self-incrimination by his masculine charms. Correct, Jack?"

"Near enough, yes."

She nodded and went straight on, addressing Kohlman, but not to his face. She was staring at the surface of the table as she spoke.

"I might say there's no proof at all. They suspect me because I ran away from Tours. And now they're in a worse flap, because it's come out that I was in Paris during May '68, when this gang called the Iskra got together. Where were you?"

Kohlman was slow to take in the question. "Me?" he said, turning to look at her with a quick little twitch of his head. "In 1968 I was at school."

"In Lübeck, I suppose."

"In Lübeck, yes. That is my home."

"How very handy for you," Laura said in a suddenly nasty turn of voice. "Well, so should I have been – at school, at home. But I wasn't, as it happened. I was here in this bar, watching Blaise Chabelard and Helmut Hoff plot the end of the world. Helmut Hoff, from Berlin, friend of Baader and Meinhof – remember him?"

Kohlman grew more resolute. Sitting erect, he replied in a firm, quiet voice: "Hoff, yes, of course. Every German knows the name. He killed himself."

"How about his daughter?"

"His daughter?"

"Mitzi."

Kohlman said nothing to this. His face was blank. Laura turned on him, her dark eyes alight with the same vengeful glare she had used against Kemble. Then she stood up.

"Mitzi Hoff was here too, with her father, in Paris. May '68. Here, let me show you."

Stepping away from the wall, she turned back to face it, then moved a little along to the right, towards Biffaud. And now Kemble saw why she'd chosen to sit in this corner. Over her

466

head, on the wall above the dado, was a large blown-up photograph on laminated board, about three feet across. It showed the rebels of 1968 marching up the Champs Elysées to the Arc de Triomphe. An enormous column of advancing people filled the street from side to side and stretched back down to the Place de la Concorde, half a mile below and behind. The uniforms and weapons were improvised, motorcyle helmets to protect the head, goggles and scarves against gas, plimsolls for running in, dustbin lids as shields, hand-painted banners, instant placards, red flags. And the mood was triumphant. Fists were raised, mouths open in chant or song. The first rank carried a horizontal pole, to keep the dressing straight, and walking either side were marshals in armbands. Among these leaders, some in the front rank and some among the marshals, were all the members of the Iskra that Kemble had yet seen pictures of. Rosa Berg was there. She had her Dutchman, Joop Janssen, on one arm and her old lover, Blaise Chabelard, on the other. Mario Salandra, the Italian, much thinner than today, made a dashing figure in his red headband. Hal Fawcett, having seen the photographer, was pulling a face and holding up a beer can. Stephen Murdoch was one row back, his mouth wide open in a shout. At the centre of the picture, out in front of the pole, marched Helmut Hoff. A dark man, heavily built, tousle haired and wild eyed, he was laughing, his rimless spectacles knocked askew by the little girl riding on his shoulders. Mitzi, aged twelve, was shrieking in delight, her curly head tossed back to the sky, both arms spread wide in a victory salute.

It made a very fine news picture, Kemble thought, already judging its usefulness for present purposes as his eyes followed the vivid red nail of Laura's right forefinger.

"There's Chabelard," she said. "This man in front is Hoff. And here, you see, that's Mitzi on his shoulders. Recognise her?"

The question was to Kohlman, who had half-stood and half-turned, leaning away from the wall, peering up. He shook his head.

Laura dropped her hand. "All right then, let's see who Jack knows. Tell us who you know in this picture, Jack."

Kemble stood up and put a name to each member of the Iskra, conscious as he did so that the café had gone rather quiet. Laura stood beside him, watching carefully as his finger moved from face to face.

"And these are the people who've kidnapped Sir Patrick?"

"Yes."

"What about you, Erich? Know them, do you? Any of them?"

Again Kohlman shook his head, as much in confusion as denial: a response that drove Laura straight to fury.

"Well, I'm bloody sure I don't! I've never met them in my life," she said in a loud shrill voice, her whole body quivering with the vehemence of a woman wronged. "Chabelard and Hoff I knew by sight, and that's all. Except, of course, for Mitzi. She's a longer story. Come on, let's sit down."

Starting from the tables immediately around them, a ripple of silence had spread through the café. Many eyes were turned towards them; curious, hostile. The hush deepened further. Laura, unwilling to perform for an audience, sat with her head lowered, nervously pecking at her pink fizzy drink. Kohlman was upright but inert. His eyes stared sightlessly forward with the same dazed expression. Kemble, rigid with fright, caught a movement behind the plastic strips at the back of the room. They stirred as someone shifted behind them. A finger came through them, pulled them slightly apart, let them fall back again. Nothing else happened. Marc Bensaïd, still at the bar, had been struck by the general paralysis. Hunched over his till, the owner of the Bab was staring at Laura with a gloomy, resigned expression. And then, like a ripple which had hit the outer walls, the silence shrunk inwards towards them. Heads turned away; people stirred; talk resumed. Noise closed over them like water. Laura raised her head and went on.

"Jack's been wondering why I came to this café when he never mentioned the place. The answer is I knew about that picture. I thought they'd be in it as soon as he told me their names had come from Chabelard. And I knew for certain that I could show you Mitzi."

She was still addressing Kohlman, but face to face now, with the calm of a woman victorious.

"You see, Erich, I am suspect for a third reason. Four days ago I was seen to recognise Mitzi Hoff in a Brussels hotel. And it's true, I did. I've never spoken to her once in my life, but I've seen her three times before – first here in Paris, then in Berlin ten years later. The third time was only a month ago, in

Brussels. She was in a park with you."

Kohlman didn't move a muscle. Laura went on, speaking quietly.

"It was a Sunday, remember? I was on a horse and you were in a boat, on that lake in the Forêt de Soignes. You had a girl with you. I waved. But you weren't too pleased to see me, were you? You rowed out of sight, round the back of that island, and got rid of her. When you brought the boat in, she wasn't in it. I pulled your leg about it, but you weren't amused. And no wonder. That girl was Mitzi Hoff. I suppose you thought the park was a safe place to meet."

Kohlman stirred to life, as though released from a spell. His eyes came into focus. "You are mistaken."

"Rubbish," Laura snapped. "I'm not blind."

Despite the force of her accusation, Kemble saw that Laura was bluffing. She wasn't quite sure that the girl on the lake had been Mitzi. She was trying to shake Kohlman into admitting it. But Kohlman stood his ground.

"I have no knowledge of this girl," he said, gaining resolve all the time.

"Don't lie, Erich. Let's get this over in a dignified fashion."

"You accuse me to save yourself."

"My God, you've got a nerve!" Laura's voice rose to a screech. "I accuse you because you're ruddy well guilty."

Kohlman was still unperturbed. "You have no proof at all," he said calmly. "You are being very stupid."

Laura controlled herself. "All right, tell us this," she said grimly, tapping the table with one finger. "What was Mitzi Hoff doing in Brussels at all? Because she was there all right. Jack saw her too, in the Europa's lobby, last Wednesday night."

"I have no idea."

"Come on, Erich, think a little harder. You'll never get away with this. Someone must have tipped this gang off – either you or me. And it damn well wasn't me." As she said this, Laura's tone had shifted towards a plea. But still she made no impression. Giving up, she turned to Kemble. "This is going to get rather rough. Come on, let's find the police."

"They're here already," Kemble said, "at the table behind us. So sit still and listen to me, please, both of you."

Kemble had worked out a plan now. To leave the café at this

point, the three of them together, would be premature. What this conversation required, to suit the tactics of the French police, was an extra shove towards snapping point.

"You're right," he said first to Laura. "The Iskra's link in Brussels was Mitzi. She's been in Belgium for the last three months. Naturally, you two were both suspected. Your records were checked, but neither of you seemed to have any connection with the girl, so the German federal snoop-machine came up with another idea. They sent through a print-out on Riemeck."

At this both Laura and Kohlman looked equally surprised.

Laura was the first to protest. "But that's just silly," she said in impatience. "You're not going to tell us that Uncle Otto . . ."

"No, I'm not."

"Come on then. What *are* you saying?"

"I'm saying what you say, that it has to be one of you two." Kemble paused. "The thing is, you see, the Belgians have had a hard look at the telephones in Harvey's office. And someone's been mucking about with them."

Having said this, he left another short pause, then turned to Kohlman, who was staring straight at him like a man before a firing squad: still bold, still defiant, but without any glimmer of hope remaining in his pale grey eyes. So there was the answer. Kemble's voice dropped, in a sort of embarrassment.

"Shall I go on, Erich?"

No reply came, no movement of the head or facial muscles. But at that moment Kohlman's whole person seemed to sag very slightly, as much in relief as despair; a sudden release from some long effort of the will. The light went out of his eyes altogether.

Kemble turned back to Laura. "Yes," he said, "you're right. Mitzi and Erich are friends, but they had to make sure it was never known in Germany. And in Brussels they had to be more careful still. So after you'd seen them, they kept in touch another way. With the Iskra's help Erich bugged his own office, to pass information without any contact."

In this allegation there was an element of guesswork, but Kemble presented it as proven fact, still hoping to cause a reaction. On the evidence collected so far, he said, it was clear that the Iskra's Dutchman, Joop Janssen, had set up a listening post in the Hotel Europa. And the transmitting microphones had been hidden in three telephones, one in each room of Harvey's offices.

"Erich may be wondering how this got pinned on him, since he was careful to leave no finger-prints." Still getting no reaction, Kemble had turned back to watch Kohlman's face. "Well, old chap, sorry, but you can thank me for that. Remember that day I bust in? I caught you right at it, didn't I? I stuck my head into your office, and there you were all by yourself, talking German. But you weren't on the phone and you weren't dictating. You were chatting to Mitzi on the air." Kemble was not at all sure of this, but it passed unchallenged. So he pressed the charge. "That's how you did it in Brussels. And you used the same trick at the château. The Iskra knew exactly when Harvey was coming down that road, and they didn't need anyone to tell them. All they had to do was tune in to your little gadget. Am I right?"

Kohlman lowered his eyes. His head dropped downwards, perhaps in admission; his shoulders sagged a little further. He said nothing.

Kemble answered the question himself. "Yes, I'm right. And there's really no point in trying to deny it. As Laura says, the best thing to do now is come with us and tell the *flics*. Will you do that?"

Kohlman still didn't speak or stir, but his eyes flicked sideways in a glance at Marc Bensaïd, still at the bar. And then, with a start of surprise, he stared at the doorway which led out the back. The plastic strips had moved again. They must have been opened wider, perhaps for a signal. Kemble was too slow to see. By the time he himself looked towards them, they were falling back together from some sudden vigorous disturbance. He turned to Laura.

"Get ready to leave."

"What? Leave? Why should I? He'll just run away."

Kemble slapped the table in annoyance. "Just shut up and listen to me. Do exactly what I say, this second, or somebody's going to get killed."

Laura's eyes opened wide, so the white showed clear around the tawny irises. Kemble directed them towards the window.

"Go straight across the street to that fat fellow with a moustache. There, see him? Sitting in that car, beyond the flowers. His name is Commissaire Daladier. Tell him Kohlman's confessed and we're coming out in three minutes' time." Kemble glanced at his watch. "Okay, go."

Laura went without protest. Hurrying from the café, she stepped through the tables on the pavement and out across the wide cobbled street, towards the men of the roadworks, who were now in a state of obvious alert. The boulevard was half in shadow, half-lit by the warm glow of evening. When Laura was across it, Kohlman also started to rise from his seat. Kemble grabbed his arm and pulled him down.

"Not so fast, buddy. She goes, you stay. Don't move and don't talk. Just sit there until I say different."

Kohlman sat heavily. His movements were jerky now, touched with little twitches and tremors. His face had taken on a yellowish hue.

Kemble, still pinning him down with one hand, made an ostentatious gesture to Biffaud with the other, a sign which said: "This is the man. Get ready to nab him."

Biffaud was taken aback. Uncertain what to do, he sat rigid in his seat five yards away, his eyes darting this way and that behind their steel spectacles.

Then Mitzi Höff stepped through the plastic strips.

Drawn from cover by the obviously imminent arrest of Erich Kohlman – that, at least, was Kemble's intention – she advanced past the bar and into the café. Marc Bensaïd, taken by surprise, was too slow to stop her. She moved quickly forward, quite calm, not running, with one hand tucked horizontally into the front panel of her green overalls, just above the waist. Below the swellings of her small unstrapped breasts, the outline of a gun was clearly visible. She was wearing red sneakers and a plain white tee-shirt under the overalls. Pinned to her front was the same assortment of badges as in Brussels, peace symbols, victory signs, red power, green earth, no nukes – the general message could be seen at a glance – and her face wore exactly the same provocative expression: the fearless gaze of a wanton child. No mark of strain had been left by the last four days. She had hardly changed in years, come to that. The dimpled chubby features were exactly those of the little girl riding on her father's shoulders at the head of the marchers in 1968. Mitzi Hoff was ageless as a doll. And even now, as she strode towards him, about to pull a gun, Kemble was struck by her total attractiveness. Having winkled her out of hiding, he watched her approach with paralysed fascination.

Biffaud, too, was transfixed. He muttered a warning to the two men with him.

Biffaud watched Mitzi, and Mitzi watched Biffaud, daring him to draw before she did. The Inspector, under orders no doubt, stayed put. But she kept her eyes on him all the time, one hand resting on the gun in her clothing. Her entry went unnoticed in the café. The hubbub of talk never slackened as she came right up to the table. Ignoring Kemble, she pulled out a chair with her left hand, swivelled it round to face Biffaud, then sat beside Kohlman. For perhaps twenty seconds they talked together in rapid, soft German. It seemed like an argument. Kohlman was protesting, Mitzi was insisting. Kemble understood none of it. He glanced out the window. Daladier's car, now preceded by an armoured police van, had started to cross the street. Two of the BRVP men were advancing from the roadworks. Then they jumped back in surprise as a small boxy Renault, bright yellow in colour, its bodywork dented and scratched by hard city driving, came screeching down the boulevard. Heeling over on its springs, the car leapt the kerb, mounted the pavement, and screeched to a halt beside the tables of the café, engine racing. At the wheel was the Babylone's waiter, Lucien Seznec. He held back the police with a pistol, waving it through the window, and shouted to Mitzi to join him. But she was already on her way. Pulling out a slim machine-pistol, with long magazine and folded wire stock, she jumped up and fired a burst through the ceiling. A collective shriek of alarm swept the café, followed by a whimpering silence. Kemble, with others, was already on the floor. Mitzi had reached the open door, moving backwards, never once taking her eyes off Biffaud. "*Bougez pas!!*" she screamed, waving her weapon above the cowering heads. Then she called to Kohlman to follow her. But Kohlman wouldn't budge. Having risen to his feet, he stood frozen to the spot, whether in fear for himself or for her was hard to tell. For a few seconds more the two of them argued in loud, desperate German. He seemed to be telling her that it was no good, she shouldn't try to rescue him, or even try to run, because she wouldn't make it.

And Biffaud was ready to shoot. Half-out of his seat, hand poised, he waited for Mitzi to turn her back.

A split-second later she did so.

With a last despairing call to Kohlman, she dived out the door and dashed towards the car. Biffaud dashed forward and dropped to one knee, gun extended. But didn't shoot. He could have killed her easily, but instead merely kept her covered. Aimed at her back as she zig-zagged away through the tables on the pavement, the barrel of his pistol swayed from side to side, rose and fell, like the gun of a tank locked on target.

Kemble understood the plan. The police intended to let this flight occur, so that it could be followed. He stood up to watch how it went, made bold by curiosity.

It didn't go at all as expected.

Mitzi, having reached the car, pulled up short and stood on the pavement, looking back towards the door of the café. Lucien, revving up the motor, was begging her to get in quick. She refused. Shouting at her French lover to save himself, she stayed to be with her doomed German friend. Lucien needed no encouragement. The Renault shot forward through the trees, off the pavement, away down the boulevard. Two police cars set out in pursuit.

Police on foot closed in around Mitzi. She stared at them defiantly, raising her gun. They stopped, spread around her in a circle. Then she flung her weapon to the pavement. The impact caused another shot to go off, but no one was hit. Biffaud, advancing from the café, yelled at her to raise her hands. She would not. The Inspector shouted again, the back of his neck turning pink below the bristles. His gun was still trained on her, held at arm's length. But Mitzi was quite unimpressed. She laughed in contempt, tossing back her curly head, then flung her arms wide in the air, both fists clenched – the very image of 1968.

Two minutes later she was sitting in the back of the police van. Erich Kohlman was beside her. The two of them were manacled together, attached by a chain to the side of the vehicle. Wondering what inner bond held them, Kemble stood watching this strange German pair as the rest of the Iskra, plus suspects, were loaded on board – four people in all. Kohlman seemed utterly broken. His head hung down. But forgetful of her own predicament, Mitzi was giving out all she had left to support him. Her cheek pressed close against his, she was murmuring soft urgent words of encouragement.

That was how they were when the doors clanged shut. As the

van drove away the only face visible was that of Marc Bensaïd, staring morosely from the small barred window in the back. The time was seven o'clock.

15

Arriving back at police headquarters, Kemble saw a large crowd of colleagues assembled. The portals and lobby of the Quai des Orfèvres were thronged with press. Television vans were parked in a line along the river, their cables snaking up the steps to the building. The announcement of Harvey's kidnap had been postponed to 7.30.

Kemble's plan was to put Laura into the coming press conference on his own behalf. She would make a note of what was said while he himself phoned *The Times* on the minute of 7.30. Laura had agreed to this with excitement: her first assignment as a journalist.

Whisked up from the entrance in an elevator, before they could talk to anyone, they were now standing side by side in the BRVP operations room. Laura, who had seen none of this before, listened wide-eyed as Kemble explained the complex scene before her – screens, maps, radios, telephones, computers. Standing a few yards off, Daladier was conferring in mutters with Biffaud. Both men's eyes were fixed on a vertical panel of perspex, through which shone a street plan of Paris. Two girls in headphones were moving coloured markers about the surface, several red ones clumped around a single green. This depicted the tracking of Lucien Seznec, the fugitive waiter from the Babylone, who was still on the move in his car. But the chase was leading nowhere. After a moment Daladier moved away to a bank of small television screens on which could be seen the interior of each detention cell in the basement. Laura and Kemble followed him. Displayed on the screens, like fish caught in tanks, were the captured members of the Iskra, plus a number of suspected collaborators. Some had been locked up alone, some in pairs. Each cell was also monitored for sound.

The Commissaire's interest was centred on Mitzi Hoff and Erich Kohlman, who were sharing a cell. The two young Germans were sitting close together, hands locked, heads bowed, as they had in the van. "Like a pair of lost children," murmured Laura, touched by the sight, as Kemble had been. But Daladier was shedding no tears. He stared at the German couple coldly, reflectively, for about half a minute, then barked out a question in French.

"Have they spoken?"

The answer was no, they had not. At least they had said nothing useful. Mitzi had guessed the cell was bugged. She kept urging Kohlman to silence.

"Take her out," Daladier said. "Go to work on her hard, starting now, nothing physical. Leave Kohlman alone until I say."

Having given this order, Daladier shouted something else to a man across the room, who left with a nod. Kemble failed to catch what he said. He turned to Laura for translation. The press were being told to wait, she told him. The news release had been put back another hour.

Kemble was dismayed. Turning back to Daladier, he started to protest. But the mountainous Frenchman took no notice. Distributing a few final orders to his men, he led Kemble and Laura to his office, closed the door and waved them into chairs. They waited in silence while he made two phone calls. With perilously little time to go until the deadline of *The Times*, Kemble sat scribbling print-ready paragraphs into his pad. Laura was bent over reading a long sheet of telegram the Commissaire had tossed across his desk. She was still reading, Kemble still scribbling, when Daladier put down the phone and addressed them in English.

An hour's delay was worthwhile, he told them, if it led to further information. There was one more thing to try before he broke the news.

"And for this I shall ask your assistance."

As he said this the Commissaire vanished in a cloud of pipe-smoke. When it cleared, he was staring at Laura. He waved at the reel of paper in her hand, which stretched to the floor.

"So," he went on, "you have read the mother's story?"

477

Laura's nod was nervous. "Yes," she said, "almost."

"You understand it?"

"Yes."

"And what do you think? Is it true?"

"Oh yes, I'm sure it is." Laura handed back the telegram. "It explains the whole thing."

Daladier left the document untouched. Removing his pipe with one hand, he smoothed down his bushy black moustache with the flat of the other. His eyes, fixed on Laura, were narrowed in assessment. "You have worked for two years with this man, Erich Kohlman. Did you never suspect him?"

"No, I never did."

"Relations between you were good?"

"We were friends."

"Friends – that is all? Nothing more?"

The question was surgically objective, but Laura recoiled as if insulted. "No, nothing more," she said, "certainly not. In fact I hardly even knew him. We just did our jobs."

"*Eh bien*, come with me." Daladier stood up, so abruptly that Kemble was taken by surprise.

Laura's face had paled in dread. "Do I have to?"

"You do, *mademoiselle*. There is a question that this man must answer. *Allez*, let us go."

Laura rose to her feet, for the first time clearly and completely disconcerted. Kemble could not help enjoying the sight. And Commissaire Daladier was making no allowances. He took her arm and led her from the office, through the grey steel door behind his desk.

The attitude of the French police to Laura Jenkinson exactly resembled that of huntsmen confronted with the hare who had mucked up their chase of the fox. The *flics* had hoped to scare Kohlman into a separate run from the Ritz, a run which might have led to the kidnappers' hideout. Instead of that Laura, to prove her own point, had staged the scene at the café. By asking Kohlman to join her there, without explaining why, she had taken the French by surprise. Daladier, forced to make an instant decision, had told the German to do as she asked. But that had turned out to be a mistake. Now the whole Paris branch of the Iskra was locked up and silent. The only quarry left to follow was a frightened young waiter, still driving in circles round the city.

Considered in the round, Kemble thought, the present situation was of the sort known to fox-hunting men, and others of similar parlance, as a first-class bugger's muddle.

Smiling to himself, he picked up and scanned the telegram that Laura had read, and immediately was serious with interest. He recognised from the first lines that this was a statement by Mitzi Hoff's mother. Dr. Elsa Hoff had been questioned at a military hospital in Leipzig, East Germany. Her statement had been taken at three o'clock that afternoon. Forty minutes later it had been transmitted *en clair* to Paris, but not until 5.23 had it travelled, by hand, to the French police. And in the interval someone had censored it. The teleprinted text, which was typed on detachable strips of white sticky tape, had in parts been removed completely, leaving strange black bars in the script.

Stranger still, the language used was English.

All traces of origin had been removed, but from one of the date stamps Kemble could see it had passed through American hands. The significance of the deletions in the text didn't strike him till later. His interest was held by what was left in. Because somewhere in this expurgated message from the East lay the story of Mitzi Hoff and Erich Kohlman.

It took him a while to find it, since the reel of teletype was five feet long: a sad, strangely garrulous, yet stilted document, revealing more of Dr. Elsa Hoff's concern to show herself ideologically uncontaminated than any anxiety for her wayward daughter.

The story began to get interesting after her rescue of Mitzi from Paris in May 1968. That had been the final rift between the Hoffs. As her husband turned to terrorism, Elsa retreated from Berlin to Hamburg to finish her medical studies, taking her daughter with her. But Helmut's spectacular, violent career had made him an object of distant fascination for the adolescent Mitzi, who started to turn against her mother's attempt at respectability. The crisis between them, mother and daughter, came during a holiday in Plön, a quiet resort in the district of lakes which runs up the Baltic coast from Lübeck. Elsa, made miserable by Helmut's notoriety, had taken to concealing her identity. She registered at the hotel in her maiden name. Mitzi, now aged seventeen, went along with the subterfuge, but sulkily. She worked at odd jobs in the hotel and spent long hours by the lake on which it stood, swimming or sunning, reading books or watching birds. She refused all advances from the boys in the town.

Then the Kohlmans arrived.

Each summer this rich shipping family came up from Lübeck to spend a month in Plön. They knew many people in the hotel, and Elsa was inevitably drawn into their company. At the memory of them her English livened up.

"The Kohlmans were real mucky shit. The wife was angry with Chancellor Brandt for giving away her land, German land, to the Poles. She could speak of nothing else. Yak and yak, all the time, hell to the Poles. Her husband was crazy mad on discipline. Many of the guests admired him. There is the old sort of German, they said. But for me he was a horrible bully to his son. Erich was crushed completely by these people. Both parents were fifty, maybe older. Erich was twenty-one. So pale he was always, so quiet. He does not speak much. He does not argue. But in many things this boy is sensitive and cultured. I liked him. So as well did Mitzi, this to my own surprise. In a few days she and Erich are friends. Maybe it was loneliness which pulls them together, yes, I believe it was that. Okay, so never worry the reason. They started to spend their time together. They go on the lake. They have their own rowboat filled up with food and books, many books. They read to themselves on private islands. And all the time they talk, very quiet, like they are people telling some secrets. That is what I think to myself when I watch them. And yes, my God, I am right. One day I see it. Mitzi has broken our secret. She has told this boy from Lübeck who we are. Erich Kohlman knows that this is the daughter of Helmut Hoff, the famous terrorist, and I am the wife. But he tells it to nobody. And now I understand what is Erich's own secret. This boy hates his parents. It pleases him to be the friend of a terrorist's daughter. This is for Erich a big rebellion, the true self he has not dared to express in his life. But Mitzi is not so good at secrets. In private she attacks me already for hiding my name, and one day she says this in front of the others. She shouts to all the people in the hotel that our real name is Hoff. Okay, you can guess how it was after that. The Kohlmans went crazy mad, like their son had been touched by disease. The others in the hotel are too afraid to help us, so that was the end for Mitzi and me in Plön. Next day we went back to Hamburg. Of course I was very annoyed with her. For many weeks we did not speak. After this happened my daughter was never again my real friend. We did not see the Kohlmans again or hear any words of them, but in the fall of that year Erich came as a student to Hamburg. And soon it was known by me that Mitzi was meeting him. For her this was a matter of amusement perhaps, also of pride. For Erich, I believe, it was more. Only in his friendship with this girl was his true self able to be expressed. But in this I am making a guess, because I never, not even one time, saw these kids together. They were meeting like spies, with many precautions. The reason for this, you understand, was the very great danger to Erich. He did not wish to lose his career or the admiration of his parents. So for him it was necessary to have two lives. And Mitzi understood this. To assist the double life of her friend, she was careful beyond her nature.''

This remark was followed by a long deletion. Whole chunks of the text were barred out in black. Before he read on Kemble lit himself a cigarette, beginning to feel faintly sorry for Elsa Hoff. Having studied her photograph, he could imagine her seated in an office at the hospital in Leipzig, a handsome woman with black hair swept back in a bun, though perhaps there would now be a few wisps of grey above her ears. Her face had none of the ebullience of her daughter's, for reasons which weren't hard to guess. She had lost her husband and her daughter to the incomprehensible frenzies of the West. Defeated in her effort to live there, she had come back to the East with her head down. Disgusted by one world, disgraced in the other, she survived in Leipzig because she was useful; a qualified doctor of medicine. She was safe so long as, and only so long as, she stuck to her job. In which case how frightened she must have been by this sudden request for a detailed confession of her past.

But now she had almost finished.

Since her return to the East, she said, she had seen her daughter only once. But she knew that the secret friendship with Erich Kohlman had continued. And the other great influence in Mitzi's life was a woman called Rosa Berg, a friend of Helmut's from 1968. It was Rosa who had stopped Mitzi running wild in Frankfurt and steered her to more constructive work in Berlin. And when Erich got his job in Brussels, the friendship became three-cornered. Mitzi had introduced him to Rosa.

Kemble's eye stopped again at this point.

So, he thought, Kohlman was a new recruit. He had not been approached by the Iskra until he became *chef de cabinet* to Harvey. That was an interesting fact. But from Elsa Hoff, the last.

"There is no more I can tell you. I know nothing else. And now I would like, please, an insurance in writing that my help in this matter will not affect (*long passage deleted*). You wish me to read this out? Very well, I will do so, and then I will sign it. I am making this statement for the use of the western security services. It is made by my own free will. If my daughter has been engaged in violence against a member of the diplomatic community, of whatever nation, I do not support it. Such methods cannot be approved by the government or people of the German Democratic Republic. Signed by my hand, in the presence of (*names deleted*) at the Fourth District Army Hospital, Leipzig. Elsa Elisabeth Hoff."

Only then did Kemble understand. The self-excusing language, the pattern of details censored – it suddenly came to him. Mitzi's mother was a communist. An official one, too. She had probably been in the party before she met Helmut and all through her years in the West, in which case she must have worked for East German Intelligence.

And of course it was not the Americans who had taken her statement. Perhaps they'd been present while she made it. They must have been involved at some point, since this document had certainly passed through the US Embassy in Paris. But the original transmission, teleprinted on this peculiar sheet of detachable strips, must have been to another embassy. That was where the text had been clipped, by hand and on the spot, before release. Kemble had never seen anything like it, but had no doubt that the censoring hand here belonged to the KGB.

So the French were getting help from the Russians.

Realising this, Kemble felt only a mild passing interest. It had not yet struck him how the search for Harvey, in another direction, would be altered by help from Moscow. He was still involved in the German drama. And now he left Daladier's office to watch its last act.

The Commissaire himself was back in the ops room. Wearing headphones, he stood before the bank of screens which showed the prisoners in the basement. Kemble joined him. Together they listened and watched as Erich Kohlman, deprived now of Mitzi's support, stared back at his questioner with dull, guarded eyes. They saw Laura pull up her stool a little closer and lean towards him. Then she tried again.

"But why, Erich. Why?"

How German he is in defeat, Laura thought. Dignified, but utterly doomstruck. He is brave, but he makes no effort to put a bright face on things, the way a brave Englishman might. He acts up his tragedy as if he enjoyed it; just sitting there, staring at me hopelessly. If he can't have his dream, he will have his despair.

She waited for a reply. And at last it came out in a low, reluctant murmur.

"You would not understand."

"Are you sure?"

"You do not know what it means to be German."

He lowered his eyes to the floor, and then, as she thought he might, started to tell her what it meant to be German. As in a teenager, the desire to explain was as strong as the need to be misunderstood.

"To have no past, no history which can be talked about – that is the difference. The Germans of today are like orphans. We have to make a new national identity. But this we have not been permitted to do. Our land is divided by old ideas. A colony of Russia, a colony of the United States – that is what Germany is today. Okay, in the West we are rich. But what does this mean? It is nothing, Laura. Really, to me it means nothing. Germany should give something new to the world. We have to unite in a new identity. I do not expect you to understand, but that is my true opinion. This primitive yankee capitalism must be destroyed, to create a new synthesis between East and West. That is the proper task for Germany."

"And this is why you joined the Iskra?"

"I did not join them. I helped them."

483

An interesting distinction, Laura thought, and pathetically typical. She held it in reserve.

"In this movement for control of the factories," he explained, gaining confidence, "I see the future. Democracy at work must come, Laura, as it has in the state. The people's intelligence demands it. We have seen this idea crushed in Poland. Now they are trying to crush it here. But I think it will come, in the East and the West. It will be the new synthesis in Europe."

A silence followed, broken only by the low hum of ventilation in the warm, sealed underground cell. For a moment they sat and simply watched each other, competing intellectually, as they had so often in the offices of Brussels. And already Laura felt worsted. She couldn't think what to say next. The amazing thing was that Erich appeared to have forgotten where he was. Just as usual, he was coolly dominant. When he spoke again, before she could, it was with a superior smile.

"I'm surprised that you don't agree. Do you have no sympathy with these ideas?"

"Maybe I do," she said sharply. "But I wouldn't kidnap and kill for them. I'm not in jail, Erich. You are."

And that broke his shell. He blinked, then slumped again, speechless as before.

Laura, in that moment, glimpsed raw schizophrenia. Here was the split personality which had enabled him to work for a project he was helping to destroy. Erich had done his true best for the merger, though secretly committed to its failure. He had faithfully carried out his functions for the Iskra, but was he perhaps appalled by their actions? Appalled was what he looked now. Having boasted about the grand plan, he seemed to be upset by its consequences.

And that, she saw suddenly, was the way to crack him: by chipping at the contradiction.

"Did you know what they were going to do, Erich?"

"No," he said softly. "It was never discussed."

"So you didn't expect Sir Patrick to be kidnapped?"

"No," he said, softer still, and lowered his eyes.

"Are you pleased?"

He didn't answer. His head had gone down, so she couldn't see his face.

"Erich, be honest now. You know I don't like the man, but really, you must admit, this is too much."

His head hung abject. Still he said nothing. Laura waited, then pushed again gently, at the same weak spot.

"After all, he might be killed. Do you want that?"

"No."

"Well then, let's do what we can," she said quickly, as though she were equally to blame. "Where have they taken him? That's the first thing."

This was Daladier's big question. She tried to make it casual, but it hung in the silence of the cell, unanswered.

"Please, Erich, try to help. Do you know where Sir Patrick's been taken?"

"Not exactly."

"But you have some idea."

"They have a house," he said after a moment. "A place to hide in, if there was trouble."

"A house? Whereabouts?"

"It is somewhere in France – I have that impression. In the country. A farmhouse, Mitzi said."

"But you don't know where."

"No."

"Does Mitzi know?"

"No, I don't think so. This was a secret Rosa kept to herself." Head up now, he frowned as he thought about it, doing his best to solve the problem. The conscientious public official had taken over fully from the secret rebel dreamer. And then his face cleared. "There is one other person who knows about the house, Mitzi said. If we were in danger, we should go to him."

"Who's that?"

"The man who owns the café."

"You mean Bensaïd? The Algerian?"

"Is that his name? Yes, he is Algerian."

As he said this, Erich seemed quite unaware of its import. The act of betrayal came with pitiable ease. And Laura had taken as much as she could. Knowing already that this was the most she would get, she relaxed a little, and immediately started to tremble with various unstopped emotions. She wanted, above all, to breathe the open air. She controlled herself and asked a few further questions, as instructed. None yielded more information, though Erich did his best to answer each one. Again, she could see, he'd forgotten his circumstances. But the moment she stood up to go, he remembered.

He made to leave with her, then stopped, looking suddenly bewildered as a child. For a moment she thought he might cry, which had the odd effect of making it certain that she herself would not. Tears in a man always turned her cold. She put out her hand.

"Goodbye, Erich."

"Goodbye. I am glad you could come."

The mask was on again. His face was blank. He shook her hand firmly, then took a step back as the door was opened from outside. She left him standing calm and erect in the centre of the small, clean, white-tiled room. Then the door was shut and she walked down the corridor, back to the lift. Poor Erich, she thought. Poor Germany.

16

Shortly before eight o'clock, while Laura was still in the cells with Kohlman, a greater excitement swept through police headquarters. Lights flashed, men cheered in the ops room as another of the kidnappers was caught and brought in.

Hal Fawcett had been in the *bidonville*. A team of detectives, chasing rumours through Paris's kasbah, had found him locked up in the home of two Algerian brothers who ran a scrap-metal yard. On arrival at the Quai des Orfèvres he was taken to the basement and questioned with urgency, since more was wanted for the imminent press release. But Fawcett was too dazed or scared to speak. So at 8.15 an old drinking chum was sent in to help him.

"Use your head, brother. Or you're going to do a long stretch."

Kemble could not be bothered with the gentle touch.

And his shock approach had quick effect. Half a minute later Hal Fawcett was talking. He told how his own car and then the Mercedes, with Harvey's chauffeur inside it, had been crushed to scrap. He described himself as a helpless, unwilling participant in the kidnap: a crime into which he'd been forced by Rosa Berg and her crazy Dutchman, Joop Janssen. To prove it, Fawcett pulled back the collar of his shirt and pointed to a long yellow-purplish bruise along the base of his neck.

"Son of a bitch nearly killed me."

Kemble leaned forward to peer at the damage. "Say, that's nasty. Why'd he do that?"

"I'd been drinking some. Joop didn't like that. And he was annoyed because I talked to you in Tours. I was supposed to follow you, that's all."

"So he knocked you cold in the scrap yard, then got the Arabs to lock you up. Didn't want you to talk to anyone else, I suppose."

"Yeah, I guess so. Crazy bastard." Wincing in pain as he buttoned his shirt, Fawcett mentioned a very unnatural act between the Dutchman and his mother, then spread his abuse to the Iskra as a whole. "They're all fucking crazy. This whole thing is crazy. You gotta believe me, man, I never expected them to do a thing like this."

"You didn't?"

"Hell, no, the Iskra was Rosa's little game – like a secret society or something. She had these friends from '68, and some she picked up later. They all had a mail account at her shop. For a code, when we sent out the books, we marked the letters with a pin, and the message always started on page 68. So it was a game, see? Just a kid's silly game. There was nothing ever like this."

"Marking the books was your job?"

"Right, man. I did the pinwork."

"So you could give us the names."

"Sure I could."

"Better go to it then," Kemble said, passing his pad across. "Might do you some good."

Fawcett jumped at the chance for treachery. He snatched the pad and began to write, his blond hair flapping round his face as he made up the full, final list of the Iskra. He was dressed as before, in a bleached combat jacket, but the French had stripped him of all his beads and amulets. Even his belt had been removed, presumably as a precaution against self-strangulation.

"Comrade Fawcett."

"Hold it, man. Let me finish this."

"No, that can wait. You listen to me. Two more questions."

Fawcett looked up from his list, then immediately started to weep. "You gotta get me out of this, man. Please, will you do that? There's got to be some kind of deal I can make here."

"Tell us some more then. What was that box in your car?"

Fawcett was jolted by the question. His eyes showed first fear, then cunning. "Oh, that, yeah. I don't know. It was Rosa's."

"She's got it now?"

"Right, man, Rosa's got the box. She took it away in the Citroen."

"What's inside?"

"How should I know?"

"You should know," Kemble said with patience, "because that was a small arms crate of the US Army."

Fawcett said nothing, though his mouth was open.

"Make a list of the weapons she's got," Kemble snapped. "And now you better tell us where she's gone."

"Shit," Fawcett groaned, "oh shit." He lowered his head and shook it. "I knew you'd ask that."

"That's the only deal you can make," Kemble said. "Save Harvey's life and you might get a break. Nothing else will make much difference."

"I know it, I know."

"So? Where's she taken him?"

Fawcett's voice broke as he answered. He started to whimper and sniff again. "God help me, I'd tell you if I could. Like I said, there's this house Rosa talked about. But I've never been there."

Kemble believed him. "After the kidnap, then. Which direction did she go?"

Fawcett's head shook again. He looked up desperately. "I didn't see. Jesus, man, how am I going to . . . Oh Jesus Christ, this is terrible. Listen, can you get me a lawyer?"

"No, I can't. Have a cigarette. They're cheaper."

Fawcett took a cigarette, but could not put it to his lips. Holding it between his knees, he shook with wet sobs. "Thanks, man. I'm sorry. Just give me a second, okay?"

"This house, it's in the country, isn't it?" Kemble said, knowing what Laura had got out of Kohlman. "A farmhouse."

"Could be," said Fawcett, still sniffing.

"You don't know where it is. But Marc does, doesn't he?"

Again Fawcett's tears were stopped by surprise. Again his eyes gleamed with low calculation. "Hey, wait a minute, man, you're right! Marc knows where the house is – Rosa said so herself. Why didn't I think of that?"

"You did think of it," Kemble said coldly, getting to his feet. "But you didn't say it. You don't have the guts to lie for your friends, Fawcett, and you daren't tell the truth for the law. Well, you've lost this time, all ways."

Fawcett's jaw dropped at this parting shot. The cigarette, unlit, was still in his hand.

Kemble, at the door, tossed him matches. "Let's have those lists – the members and the weapons. Work hard at that and I'll do what I can for you."

Back in the ops room, standing together by the screens, Kemble and Laura saw the owner of the Babylone taken from his cell. As he was led away handcuffed, Bensaïd's unshaven face was resigned.

"Where's he going?" Kemble asked Daladier.

"Somewhere the press do not see," replied the Commissaire darkly. "And now, monsieur, you may have your reward. It is time to telephone your paper."

"Can I use your office?"

"Of course, you are my guest. But please, do not make embarrassment for the French police. It is necessary not to tell the origin of some information."

"Understood," said Kemble with a nod. "You can trust me."

At the mention of trust a small, short sniffing sound came from Laura Jenkinson's nose. Smiling, she followed Daladier down to the room where the press were assembled.

Kemble, left alone, rang *The Times*. First he asked to speak to the editor, in order to explain the dimensions of the story, since some very fast re-setting would have to be done to the news pages. Aussie Holroyd was shrill with annoyance at the lateness of the call. His accent, as always in stress, went straight back down under, especially when Kemble began to talk new terms.

"This is mainline stuff, Frank, not a contract feature, so I think we can move the pennies up a bit. And since you won't take me on the payroll, I shall have to charge you by the column-inch, same rate as the US dailies. Do you mind?"

Holroyd minded. Yelping as though he'd been kicked, he said that whatever the hell this story was, he would get it from *The Times* man in Paris. And anyway, what was it?

"Harvey's been kidnapped."

Waiting to be hooked up to a copy-taker, Kemble felt a deep glow of pleasure, better than drink really, or any other physical sensation. And that was when he noticed a small commotion down in the ops room. People were gathering at a run round

490

the street-plan of Paris, where the tracking of the Babylone's waiter, Lucien Seznec, was still being shown.

Lucien Seznec could hardly believe he had escaped. His drive from the café had been terrifying, even by his own reckless standards. His small yellow Renault, built to racing perform-ance, had been furiously chased by a pair of police saloons. Both of them had crashed in the Latin Quarter. Close behind him, in hot pursuit through the maze of narrow streets, each police car in turn had made a violent, spectacular error. Other cars, cruising the outer boulevards in wait, had moved in too slowly to take up the chase. For about three minutes the *flics* had milled about in disarray, and that had been enough; he'd got out and away, over the river and up to the Porte des Lilas. Nothing came after him. To be quite sure of that, he had driven for an hour around the north-eastern suburbs before circling back towards Austerliz Station. He had parked near the Bois de Vincennes, and now he was walking along with the railway tracks to his left. The station loomed a short way ahead. The big khaki trains rumbled by him, picking up speed as they clattered out of town across the points, their electrical antennae hissing, sparking, flashing in the network of overhead cables. To his right the setting sun had put a golden shine on the Seine, and between the river and the railway, along the *quai* where he walked, a heavy stream of traffic poured back into Paris from the country, horns blasting irritably at any impediment, dust and exhaust fumes rising together in a yellowish haze. Lucien watched it all carefully as he reached the long wall of the station proper. He had gone through every trick he knew to check that he wasn't being followed; and he knew a lot of tricks, having spent his whole life in various sorts of petty crime and street combat.

But Joop knew more tricks still, he thought to himself. If this too-easy escape was a set-up by the *flics*, Joop would soon sniff it out.

The tough young waiter had a deep respect for the great Dutch terrorist's prowess. Joop Janssen had outwitted every police force in the western world, and so it was necessary, when meeting him in dangerous circumstances, to show some professional class. With this in mind Lucien approached the station with exaggerated care. Walking round to the front of the grand stone building, whose outer clock was showing 8.30, he kept dawdling and switching direction. Eventually, after more checks, he entered the terminus at 8.45.

He was walking normally now, neither fast nor slow, without looking round. And there was nothing unusual about his appearance. Though still in his waiter's uniform, he had put on a crumpled cotton jacket, beige in colour. He carried a pistol in one of its pockets.

The arrangement, made earlier that day, was that Joop would wait until midnight at Austerlitz Station. Any members of the Iskra who wished to escape should present themselves on the station's concourse and stand there until they were approached. Lucien had hoped to keep this rendezvous with Mitzi. He had planned to smuggle her out of the café and carry her off to a life of international crime in the sun, spiced with perfect, endless sex. Instead he came alone, disappointed and surprised at the way she had dumped him for Kohlman; but still too nervous to be very sad about it.

He placed himself beside a row of phone booths. The concourse of the station was busy, although it was Sunday. Crowds of people drifted about. There were women in saris, with caste-marks on their brows, and many American college girls in sensible footwear. Every time a train prepared for departure a priest-like male voice announced its destination, intoning each stop on its journey in a chant that evoked dreams of distance, escape to the end of the line. This got Lucien down. He began to miss Mitzi sharply. For her there would be no escape now, no run to the sun. By the time she got out she'd be forty, and probably fat. He shut his eyes in horror, unable to forget her little girl's body, her sweet-tasting mouth, her pale little legs parting sweetly, wetly, for his frantic desire. Love with Mitzi had been like no other in his life. Since she had joined the Iskra, four years before, he had lived for her sudden descents from Berlin. Last night she had come to his bed from the kidnap. Trapped in the café, she had let him plan their flight. And then she had left him to flee on his own, surrendering to stay with a man she had never even mentioned. Lucien couldn't understand it.

He scanned the concourse of the station. Joop had still not appeared, but he knew that the Dutchman would be watching, and sure enough at nine o'clock exactly the telephone rang in

492

the booth beside him. Lucien picked it up and heard the voice of his hero, curt with annoyance.

"You're hot, kid. So far I've counted four of them."

"That many? *Merde*, I had wondered."

"Wonder more. This is careless. Where's Mitzi?"

Lucien explained what had happened at the Babylone.

Joop listened in silence. "Well, there you go," he said after a pause. "The krauts stick together. What about Marc? Was he taken too?"

"I didn't stop to see."

"Okay, don't worry, I'll catch it on TV. Now listen, kid, here's what I want you to do. Go away home and take the *flics* with you. Then I can get out of here quietly."

"You're going? Without me?"

"I regret, but yes. Has to be. Make a run if you like, but I don't advise it." Joop's voice adopted a fatherly tone. "Hand yourself in and pretend you know nothing. You won't get a long stretch. Maybe they won't even charge you."

"You want me to do that? Really?"

"Best thing, if you think about it."

"Very well, if you advise it, that's what I'll do," said Lucien, feeling a heavy weight descend on his heart and all his limbs, as though the force of gravity had suddenly increased. All his adult life he had dreamed of escape from this city where he lived with a tray in one hand, trotting miles on the same spot each day. "Goodbye, Joop. Good luck."

"You too, kid. Till one of these days."

Lucien hung up. A few yards away, only four booths along from the one in which he stood, an Arab in worn grey suit and dark glasses, his head wrapped up in a red-checked scarf, continued to talk on the phone for two minutes longer, although his receiver was silent. Eventually he shuffled off into the crowd and stood looking up at the departures board. The Arab remained in that position until Lucien Seznec left the station. Then he bought a one-way ticket to Bordeaux. While he was waiting for the train to come in he sat in the station's main bar and watched the news on television. The news caused a sensation in the bar, drawing a crowd around the set. But it seemed to hold no special interest for the Arab. He kept his dark glasses on.

17

The news of Harvey's kidnap exploded over Europe like a bomb. At least that was how Laura Jenkinson imagined it. As she sat at the back of the crowded press conference, watching men dash from the room, she pictured a series of shock-waves booming outward from Paris in widening circles, like those drawn on maps to show what a bomb can do – fireball, blast, radiation, fall-out.

And she knew how deep the tremors would run. Europe was continually shaken by outbreaks of terrorism, but this was the first to strike at the heart of its economic system. Harvey's abduction would rattle the bank-vaults from Zurich to London. Shares would slip on the news. Rich men would wake in the night, troubled by dreams of dispossession, and doubtless some of the really big cash would flit away unnoticed in the hours of darkness, shifted out of range to New York or Hong Kong, until the dust settled.

This vision of fright among the Eurodollars was interrupted by the runners of the news agencies, who hurried back into the room, still panting as they took up position behind her. At the announcement of the first bare fact, FORMER BRITISH PREMIER KIDNAPPED IN FRANCE, they had sprinted off in search of telephones. Reuters and *Agence France-Presse* had scrambled to be first on the wire, not knowing that Kemble had won the race already and was sitting upstairs at his ease, dictating to *The Times*.

Laura had felt first amused by this rush, then a little uncomfortable. The whole of her working life had been spent within the castle of officialdom, flinging scraps of information to the press-dogs who roamed beyond the moat. Now she herself was down among the scavengers, waiting to pick up some bits for *The Times*. Did she like it? No, she wasn't sure that she did. Here I am, free at last, she thought; and what am I doing? I am sitting with a pad on my knee, waiting to take down the words of one man so that another man can use them in his story. It's either very funny or very annoying.

The conference room was hysterically modern, like the rest of police headquarters. The chairs were moulded out of brilliant red plastic to the shape of the human bottom, of which there were many – about two hundred, male and female – sitting tensely still for the statement of Commissaire Daladier. Extractor fans sucked cigarette smoke into the ceiling. Photographers prowled the edge of the scene, leaping up, stretching, crouching, dropping to one knee as they looked for the telling angle. Flashbulbs popped all the time. Half-way back from the platform, bunched to left and right, were the television cameras. The lenses of some were held steady, others roved like guns in search of a target. The platform itself, cluttered with microphones, was exposed to the fierce white glare of the TV lights, the heat of which was making the poor fat Commissaire sweat. He dabbed at his brow with a handkerchief, folded square, then dabbed his moustache as he told the world in rapid, articulate French how the Iskra had been hunted down.

"All the members of this gang have been identified. A list will be passed to you later. Most of them have been arrested in their countries of residence, but four remain at large in French territory, pursued by the forces of order. It is these four persons, we believe, who are holding Sir Patrick Harvey a prisoner."

Daladier slowed down for the note-takers and spelt out each name with care, repeating it twice. Rosa Berg, Mario Salandra, Stephen Murdoch, Joop Janssen.

Details followed of their careers. Photographs of them were projected on a screen, then prints were distributed round the room, along with typed particulars of their physical characteristics, their dress when last seen. Their car was described to the last small dent in its bodywork: a nearly new Citroen, hired at Nice Airport. Then Daladier moved across to a large map of France, which descended from the ceiling. He took out his pipe and used it as a pointer.

"It is possible these people are in Paris. However, we do not believe so."

That the Dutchman had been seen, and lost, in the city went unmentioned. Daladier had artfully pushed proceedings on to discussion of the hideout.

"The evidence suggests they are using a house in the country, perhaps a farm. This dwelling is probably in some remote location. It could be anywhere within the borders of France, but again we may venture a little precision. It is unlikely to be more than six hours' driving from the town of Tours, which is here. And we may also say that the most probable direction of the gang's escape was southward. So the region in which our search is presently concentrated is the one circumscribed by this line – from here, to here."

The black briar pipe travelled round the edge of a downward-bulging semi-circle, drawn in red felt on the map. The southernmost point of its arc almost touched the Pyrenees.

"As you see, the region is a large one." Daladier turned to speak directly to the television cameras. "I therefore avail myself of the present opportunity to issue an urgent appeal for the public's assistance. Any person who has seen these people, or their vehicle, should contact the nearest police post or unit of gendarmerie."

The appeal to the public went on for a minute, getting down to points such as what to watch out for in isolated farms: suspicious behaviour by unrustic strangers, shutters kept closed in hot weather. Then Daladier moved away from the map. As he prepared to sit down again, he undid the jacket of his dark grey suit, from which his belly seemed to swell, only held from total prolapse by a thin leather belt. He had changed his shirt for the occasion, Laura noticed. And now he had finished his opening statement. He tidied up the papers in front of him and smoothed down the ends of his moustache, then took from his pockets all the kit required to stuff and light his pipe, which made Laura smile. Pipe-smoker's delay, she knew from experience, was the dread of all TV interrogators. An ambassador she'd worked for had been notoriously good at it.

But the Commissaire wasn't alone on the platform. On his left sat a smooth young official from the Ministry of the Interior, with busy little eyes and lips shut tight – the sort who'd go far by saying nothing. And on his right was Nielsen, chief of the

Berlaymont's information services, who had flown in from Brussels to deal with the press. A corpse-thin Dane with a wispy beard, easily given to despair, Nielsen had given up the editorship of a small political weekly in Copenhagen to join the staff of the Commission. He had twice won the Belgian marathon, but was better at long-distance running than press relations. Already his lips were working soundlessly, as if he both wanted and dreaded the questions which would follow Daladier's statement.

But now there was an interval, suggested by Daladier himself, for those who wished to communicate immediately with their papers. He was keen to have the appeal to the public in the early editions, he said, and though there was more to come, the main facts had now been covered.

Another stampede to the telephones followed. During it Laura remained in her seat, examining the photographs that had been handed out. She was interested, especially, in that of Rosa Berg: the dauntless grey eyes and flat-featured face, fringed by hair cut short as a boy's. That Harvey, the great man of state, was now in the power of this woman was something she could not imagine or feel much about. Her mind kept returning to Kohlman, locked in his cell. Poor Erich, the truth was she'd never much liked him. But the thought of him sealed up for years to come, like a person entombed before death, filled her with horror and pity.

She was still thinking about it as the room filled up again. Then the conference resumed.

"How do you know that Harvey's still alive?"

The opening question was fired simultaneously, in English, by the *Mirror* and the *Sun*, both speaking at once. Daladier, replying, switched to English himself, and made it seem an insult – a tiresome concession to a barbaric race.

"We don't know that he is alive. And his chauffeur certainly is dead. But there is no evidence that Sir Patrick himself has been harmed. And it would be contrary to the logic of the affair if, at this stage, they had killed him."

The Iskra's logic had not yet occurred to any of the press. The fact that this same gang had mounted attacks on BMG and Mobital, in Coventry and Rome, was taken to be part of their general revolutionary mayhem. Nobody present had guessed the connection between these incidents and Harvey's abduction. And the very special trickiness of this press conference consisted in the effort to conceal that connection. The idea was to announce the kidnap but not the merger.

So now Laura's interest sharpened. Surely, she thought, the Commission's big secret couldn't hold much longer, if only because of the way Nielsen's beard was twitching.

But she had not allowed for the mental level of the two British papers now holding the floor.

"What logic?" asked the *Mirror*. "You mean he's being kept alive for a purpose?"

Daladier's nod was regally slight. "One must assume so."

"For ransom?" suggested the *Sun*.

"For money, yes, that is possible," replied the Commissaire.

"But surely, with these people, the motive's more likely to be political," said the *Mirror*, inspired. "They've grabbed him as a hostage."

Daladier, in gratitude for this contribution: "A hostage, yes. Maybe so."

Mirror: "But what are they going to trade him for?"

Sun: "Safe conduct, perhaps. They're wanted for murder, all four of them."

Mirror, agreeing, to *Sun*: "And they'll probably want their friends released – the ones who've been arrested."

Sun, to Daladier, aggressively: "Well, what do you think?"

Daladier, shrugging: "We shall know when they tell us."

Sun: "Surely you must have a theory."

But the Commissaire had finished with the two British tabloids. Switching back into French, he addressed the press corps as a whole. "It is not good practice, ladies and gentlemen, for me, as investigating officer, to speculate in public on the motive for this crime. The motive will be known when the criminals reveal it. If a message is received from them, we shall decide, at that time, on the manner of our response. In this, of course, the French police will maintain close liaison with Lady Harvey."

"Where's she?" asked a voice.

Immediately, from the changed tone of his reply, Laura guessed that Daladier had planted the question. "Lady Harvey is in Kraainem," he said. Then he turned to the group of radio reporters, pausing until they had switched on their machines. "Lady Harvey is at her house in Kraainem, just outside Brussels, waiting for news of her husband. And naturally she is in

498

great distress and anxiety." He paused again, then addressed the whole room. "Ladies and gentlemen, I must ask you, in the name of the French police, not to telephone Lady Harvey for the present."

"Why's that?" asked the same voice. A woman at the back, clearly French; not so clearly a journalist.

"Let me repeat, Lady Harvey is distressed." Daladier paused for a third time. "She does not wish to be further distressed by unnecessary phone calls, either from yourselves or from sympathetic friends. If you were to mention that wish in your reports, it would be of some assistance."

The press stirred and muttered. Slowly they understood. Daladier wanted to keep the lines to Kraainem clear and at the same time convey to the kidnappers, through every news bulletin, that this was the way to make contact.

And he would be obeyed, Laura saw. Flattered by the Commissaire's little pretence, the press were exchanging nods and smiles.

Only the man from the *Sun* was still annoyed.

"So you don't know, and you can't guess, why this has happened," he said, frankly presenting the anti-French slant he meant to print. "Has it occurred to you to ask Scotland Yard?"

Daladier's shrug was contemptuous. "This is an international effort," he answered in French: a rebuke as telling as the first switch to English. "It is I who speak to you, because the crime occurred in France. But of course the British police are assisting."

After that the popular press stepped back. *Sun*, *Mirror*, *Bild*, *Il Giorno*, *Paris-Jour* sat down or ran off to the telephones, and the mood of the conference became less charged. The questions came fast but automatic, a routine trawl for usable filler, drifting further from the sensitive point. What weapon had been used? What were the Iskra's links with Baader-Meinhof, with the IRA, with the Red Brigades, the Basque ETA, the PLO? Why had the French police said so much, said so little, acted prematurely, acted too late, devoted so many resources to the case, devoted so few?

These must be crime reporters, Laura thought, most of them youngish and sharply dressed. Some had already left for the telephones. Each identified his paper as he spoke, trying to link the case to something back home. *L'Aurore*, *Le Figaro*, *Daily*

*Mail, Daily Express, Il Messagero, Berliner Morgenpost, Frankfurter
Allgemeine Zeitung* – Daladier dealt with them in turn, matching
their briskness with his own staccato, adding little of substance,
referring them back as often as he could to the written particulars of the four wanted terrorists and the missing car.

Then came the evenings, *France-Soir, Paris-Presse, Corriere
della Sera*, whose urgency was not so intense, though greater
than that of the Americans, *Washington Post, New York Times*,
who had a six-hour advantage. Laura had seen this performance so often she recognised each character in the play. Each
reporter stepped forward in turn with a question put from his
routine angle, which the others relied on him to do. *L'Humanité*
spoke from the left, *Il Tempo* from the right. For the Dutch, left
and right, it was *De Volkrant* and *De Telegraaf. Avanti* and *Combat*
took inside positions, leftward, while the *Guardian*, as always,
stood pat in the middle.

Eventually the daily reporters, as a body, withdrew to the
telephones. Then the magazines took over. Many of these were
women, better dressed, with hard painted faces. What they
wanted was more about Rosa and her background: those she
had loved, those she had killed, any more photographs. *Der
Spiegel, Oggi, Paris-Match, Epoca, Newsweek, L'Espresso*, wherever they came from, they asked their questions in French,
since in all this lavish expense at the Quai des Orfèvres no
money had been spent on interpretation facilities. And Daladier made no effort to charm them. Though he dealt politely
with each in turn, he refused absolutely to help these pushy,
painted ladies find the entertaining angles they sought. His
answers were short and straightforward.

Another group had hardly spoken yet, and these were the
ones that Laura knew best, some of them by name: slower,
greyer men, who wore the distinction, sometimes bogus, sometimes genuine, of the diplomats and statesmen they watched.
Their task was to write on Community affairs for the
heavyweight papers of Europe, *Neue Zürcher Zeitung, Svenska
Dagbladet, Le Monde, Die Welt, La Stampa, El País.*

They had sat making casual, occasional notes during all this
vulgar fuss. But now their moment had come. And so had
Nielsen's. The skinny Dane's beard bobbed in anxious anticipation as Daladier handed him the stage.

To begin with, nothing went wrong. The questions, the

answers were routine stuff. Laura's attention drifted, and the room itself started to empty. Pens were being pocketed, recorders switched off. This wasn't news, it was Eurotalk. The show was over. Even the television lights had faded, making the platform seem dark, when a particularly silvery man from the London *Daily Telegraph*, respected for seniority rather than intelligence, asked what exactly it was that Harvey was doing in Tours.

"It was a private trip," Nielsen answered in English. "Sir Patrick was staying at the house of a friend."

"But his staff were with him."

"Two of them, yes."

"So it was a business trip"

"Partly, yes."

"What sort of business?"

"That has not been made public."

"I know it hasn't. That's why I'm asking," snapped the *Telegraph*, uncharacteristically nettled. "It was a Community matter, I assume. Something industrial, may we say, since that is Sir Patrick's department within the Commission?"

Nielsen shook his head pompously. "I am not at liberty to give the details. There were discussions of an industrial nature, it is true. But they must remain confidential."

There was a moment of silence. Then pens came out again, machines were switched on. Those who had started to leave sat down again, opening their pads. Nielsen, in an effort to change the subject, searched the floor for another question. None came. The *Telegraph*, whose prize he was, was left to take him.

"Just a moment, Mr. Nielsen, let me see if I've got this straight. Sir Patrick was engaged in secret industrial talks, held in a private house in France, when he was abducted by a gang who had just attacked the chairmen of two major European car companies. Are we being asked to believe that this is a coincidence?"

Before he could answer or parry the question, or avoid it, or do anything, Nielsen was caught by the TV lights, which came back on again. Held like a panic-stricken rabbit in their ruthless glare, he kept repeating negatives, shaking his thin, white, fluff-bearded face as questions were shot at him from every side.

"I cannot enlarge on what I have said . . . I'm sorry, but that's all . . . I can give you no further information."

Poor fellow, Laura thought. For two years she'd watched Nielsen struggle in the job, and seeing him now, trapped and speechless in the lights, she thought of a diplomatic saying which arose from the fact that when a joke was made in a meeting using interpreters, the laughter followed at irregular intervals. "The Danes laugh last," it was said among the Eurofolk.

The questions kept coming. Nielsen, still stalling, began to look utterly desperate. The bland French official on the platform refused to help, his face expressing the view that it mattered not at all what Sir Patrick had been doing this weekend in Tours, or whether it was known to the press.

Daladier's behaviour was odd. His face had expressed no surprise or dismay at this turn of events, merely an interest in the outcome. Then, as the questions became more aggressive, he had jumped up and left the platform. He had been gone two minutes. But now here he came again, bringing an extra chair. Behind him, a moment later, a small bald man appeared, his rotund face shining pink in the lights behind a pair of gold-rimmed spectacles. To Laura's surprise, there was little reaction in the room. Most of the journalists present had no idea who this newcomer was. But Nielsen was very glad to see him. Looking ready to faint with relief and exhaustion, as after a long-distance run, the Dane stepped aside and sat down. The small, bald man then spoke.

"My name is Otto Riemeck. I am President of the European Commission."

A stir of interest swept through the room; reporters ran back in; flashbulbs went off like fireworks round the platform. Riemeck took no notice. He spoke as if expounding a nicety of constitutional law to his students, but in English, since that was the language of Nielsen's clash with the *Telegraph*. Turning to toss a glance of pardon at the Dane, he admitted that Sir Patrick had been in Tours for private talks between BMG and Mobital. And then, before anyone could ask him, he told them the rest.

"The Commission has been invited to consider a merger of these two companies, assisted by Community funds. In view of its urgency this project, if it can be agreed in outline, will be presented directly to the European Council, at the session to be held next Wednesday in Rome."

The uproar following this statement was hardly less than that caused by the kidnap. Newswise, the merger of BMG and Mobital was an almost equal sensation. Once again the agency men were sprinting for the door. Chairs were knocked over in the rush, a woman fell down with a scream. Several reporters were on their feet at once, shouting questions. But Riemeck went on with his careful statement, talking straight to the cameras from a text in his hand. Having given a brief description of the BMG-Mobital scheme and its origins, he admitted it was probably the cause of Sir Patrick's kidnap. Apparently the gang's objective was to stop discussion of the merger. But in that they would be frustrated, he said, since this sort of violent intervention could not be allowed to deflect the business of Europe.

"You mean you're going on with it?"

Laura, who was getting down every word, looked up from her pad in surprise. The interruption had come from the *Telegraph*, whose excitement had overcome his manners. This was his moment and his blood was up. Subjected to a flash of annoyance from Riemeck, he put the question again in his normal courtly manner.

"Excuse me, but are you saying, Herr President, that the talks between the Commission and these two companies will continue, even in the present circumstances?"

For the first time Riemeck hesitated. His reply, when it came, was careful. "I do not believe that ideas should be abandoned because they are opposed with force," he said slowly. "This was a personal initiative of Sir Patrick's, not yet discussed within the Commission as a whole. There are a number of problems about it. But every effort will be made to prepare it for discussion in Rome as intended."

Having said this, Riemeck went on to admit that Harvey had been betrayed by a member of his staff, and answered the questions this third sensation brought. He then went back to his written remarks about the united stand of European governments against political terrorism. He finished with hopes for Sir Patrick's safety, sympathy for his family, and an urgent appeal for full cooperation with the French police.

Standard crisis stuff, Laura thought. But she wrote it down

anyway, in case *The Times* wanted standard crisis stuff.

Further questions were still being shouted from various parts of the room, but Riemeck would answer none of them. He put the text in his pocket and walked off. Surprisingly, this exit worked. Without a murmur all the journalists present, hack and serious, took this as the close of proceedings. Within a few minutes the room had cleared.

Laura, back upstairs, reported to Kemble.

"Poor old Nielsen, they told him to keep back the merger, but they never really thought he'd succeed. Daladier actually hoped it would come out. And Riemeck was waiting all the time with that artful little statement."

"You mean it's not true?"

"The stuff about business as usual isn't true." Laura sat down in Daladier's office, which was empty except for the two of them. "The merger is dead as a duck without Harvey. Riemeck knows that very well. And Riemeck doesn't care. He never much liked the plan in the first place, though he hoped to get the credit if it worked."

Kemble studied her pad. "So this is a bluff," he said after a moment. "About the merger going on."

Laura nodded. "Just automatic fighting talk for the press."

"But the Iskra don't know that, do they?"

"Oh, they won't be fooled."

"Are you sure?"

Laura thought of the coldly intelligent eyes of Rosa Berg, staring from the circulated photograph. "Unless Harvey's rescued pretty quick," she said, "and I mean within hours, the whole thing is finished – for this summit, anyway."

Kemble was still staring at her notes. "Hm," he said, "I wonder."

"Wonder what?"

"If you're right."

"Well, that's what I think. Or aren't I supposed to?"

"Not in print, until you're senile." He looked up and smiled, then waggled the pad at her. "So we'll go with the quotes and hold on the comment, okay?"

"Terrific."

"Want to quit?"

"I haven't been hired yet."

"Exactly. Now leave me to finish here, and then we'll get over to the Ritz. I've got another job for you."

"Gee, Mister, thanks."

"Interview with Clabon and Guidotti – can you fix?"

"If you kiss my feet."

"I'll start with your feet. But work before pleasure." Kemble uncupped his hand from the phone, preparing to dictate more paragraphs to *The Times*. "Go watch the Frogs while you wait."

Too weary to retaliate, Laura withdrew to the ops room, in the centre of which stood Commissaire Daladier, surrounded by a bunch of subordinates. The Commissaire looked too busy to interrupt, so she nosed around by herself. A fresh set of women, crisply dressed and newly coiffed, were pushing coloured markers round the map of French territory, but nothing new had happened, so far as she could tell, except that the runaway waiter from the Café Babylone had given up his circular flight through the city. Lucien Seznec had surrendered in Austerlitz Station. Now he was down in the cells, being question with the rest.

Laura took this fact to Kemble before he rang off. But as they left the ops room neither of them paused to wonder why, if the waiter had been caught, there was still a green marker on the map, hedged around with red pursuers.

18

Immediately after the news on French television, Joop Janssen left the bar at Austerlitz Station. The concourse was crowded with police and uniformed gendarmes. They stood at the entrance to each platform and roved in pairs among the crowd. But none of them glanced in his direction. And even if they had, they would not have looked twice, so expert was the Dutchman's disguise.

His alert, roving eyes were hidden behind cheap sunglasses, of the mirror-lensed kind. His head was wrapped in the red-check *keffiah* of a Palestinian Arab. Underneath it his tufted grey hair had been blackened with a washable dye. The exposed portions of his skin had been stained an even olive brown, though nothing could erase from his face the uncertain touch of a plastic surgeon in Prague, the baby-smooth grafts and traces of pale mottled burn-scar, close to the hairline.

He had changed from blue denim to an old grey suit and worn leather shoes, of the kind that derelict Arabs wear in Europe. His own clothes, along with a large sum of cash and all necessities for the journey, had been packed in a small plastic kit-bag, which he carried by the rope drawn tight around its top. The rope was twisted around his left hand, so that in one quick movement he could swing the bag across to his right hand, rip away the bottom and snatch out the Makarov pistol concealed there.

Joop had practised this movement many times in the day, until there was a gap of less than two seconds from upward heave to first shot. But he did not think it would be necessary. His appearance would pass any check in this station. His Arabic was good enough for any French gendarme, and so were his papers. In his pocket was a passport issued by the government of Syria, stamped with a valid entry visa for France and matched by a number of supporting documents. This unemployed Palestinian from Damascus was the last and the best of Joop's false identities. Taken into the house of reliable friends, he had spent the afternoon preparing the role. Now even his walk, as he crossed the station's concourse, had become the slow, hopeless shuffle of a refugee.

Soon he was back in a phone booth under the clock. The voice that answered was Murdoch's.

"Hello, it's Brother Jewp. Nice of you to ring, mate. When shall we see you?"

"Let me speak to the lady."

"Okay, okay. Here she is."

Annoyed by the mention of his name, Joop waited for Rosa. Her voice, when she came on the line, was calmer than it had been that morning, but strangely lifeless.

"Still there then," he said to her.

"Yes," she replied with a touch of acerbity. "Waiting for you."

"No trouble?"

"Not yet."

"How's the patient?"

"Alive."

"Did you catch the news?"

"No," she said, sharpening up. "Why? What's happened?"

"Switch on and keep watching," Joop told her. "The hunt is on. And our friends have been caught, I am sorry to say."

Since it had not been mentioned in the television bulletin, he managed to convey by circumlocution that among those arrested at the café was Erich Kohlman. But the downfall of her secret informant drew no reaction from Rosa. There was a silence.

"We must have been betrayed," she said.

"Perhaps."

"We'd better move out of here then."

"No, don't move," Joop told her. "That's why I'm calling. Our friend from Algeria won't talk. And you won't get far, not in that car. Stay put until I get there."

Rosa considered this advice for several seconds, then drew in

507

her breath with a sharp, decisive hiss. "Yes, you are right," she said. "But hurry. Come tonight."

"Not tonight, no. I'll be there tomorrow."

"Tomorrow? What the hell are you doing, Joop?"

"Making preparations."

"For what?"

"For us."

There was a silence. Then her voice fell back to the dull, flat tone in which she had begun. "I want to finish this. And I want you here," she said. "I'm tired, Joop. Tired."

Joop had never heard her like this in his life. "Watch the road all the time," he said. "And if anyone comes calling, don't answer the door. Have you got that?"

"Yes."

"Keep the place looking as if it's unoccupied, that's the important thing."

"Understood," she said; then chuckled. "Are you taking control of me?"

Joop smiled in relief at this change of manner. "Of course not, my general."

She grunted. "I want you. And that's an order."

Joop's head was bowed in the phone booth, his smile concealed by the Palestinian head-cloth. Coarseness, in Rosa, was a sign of tranquillity. At ease, her mind sank to the trough – belly, loins, sleep. But this call had lasted long enough.

"Listen," he said to her, "I'll have to go now. I'll reach you when I can. If I'm not there tomorrow, say sundown, take off. But don't use that car. And don't try to take him with you, will you?"

Joop rang off before she could answer. He tucked the *keffiah* round his chin, reached for the bag between his feet and twisted the rope round his hand again, composed himself into an attitude of dejection, then shuffled back out into the crowded concourse. Behind his mirror-glasses his eyes were busy, darting this way and that as he counted and assessed the opposition. The station was swarming with *flics* of every sort, but he saw a few ways to run. Numbers were a help, since sten-guns couldn't be fired into a crowd, so to let the congestion build up he stood staring up for several minutes at the swiftly changing departures board – the poor puzzled Muslim, confronted with western science.

At 9.20 he joined the queue to board the slow overnight train to Bordeaux. His ticket was inspected and returned. He was asked for his papers. He showed them. The detective at the barrier studied his passport, then glanced at his face, requesting him politely to take off his spectacles. Joop did so. The policeman nodded, without expression, and handed the passport back, turning his attention from the most wanted man in Paris to the woman who happened to be next in the queue.

Ten minutes later the Iskra's professional was on his way. Having chosen a position in the centre of a central coach, to give himself warning of an end-to-end search, he sat by the door of a smokers' compartment with his blue plastic bag on his knees. When the train pulled out it was almost night.

The green plastic marker, meaning contact under surveillance, moved slowly across the map, out of Paris and then further south, along the line of the railway, intermittently shifted by one of the girls with her croupier's stick. Following each inch of its progress, the eyes of Commissaire Daladier glowed in triumph. He chewed his unlit pipe in excitement, then snatched it from his mouth and spoke to the half-dozen men gathered around him.

"Is he armed?"

"Yes, sir. The detector picked up a trace in his bag – probably a hand-gun."

"How many people have we got on the train?"

"Two, sir."

"Positions?"

"One in the same compartment, and one in the corridor."

"Not enough," snapped Daladier. "Biffaud, are you there?"

"Commissaire."

The bristle-topped Inspector pushed forward. Daladier spun round to face him. "Take charge," he barked, prodding at the smaller man's chest with the stem of his pipe. "Get on the train yourself, take a look around. But don't stay. Run it from the air."

The pipe prodded upwards, to the helicopter pad.

Biffaud ran off, taking three men with him.

Daladier watched the green marker again, as though it might escape if he took his eyes off it. After a minute he lifted his head and looked round the room.

"The English journalist – has he gone?"

"Yes."

"The girl too?"

"Yes."

Satisfied that only official personnel were present, the head of the BRVP returned to his office, opened the grey steel door behind his desk and summoned forth a man from the room beyond. This was the room to which prisoners were brought for questioning, but the man who stepped out of it now was Reinaldo Herrera Valdes, Cultural Attaché of the Embassy of Cuba.

Still dressed in the white shoes and brass-buttoned blazer he had worn that morning, the plump young Cuban was sweating with fright. Emerging from confinement, he dabbed his brow and palms with a big white handkerchief, folded square like a poultice. His eyes rolled nervously about, in expectation of a trap. Released into the Commissaire's office, he kept trotting in different directions, taking a pace or two in his white shoes, pulling up, swivelling, going another way, like a wound-up toy.

Daladier put him in a chair and poured drinks: for the Cuban a small medicinal cognac, for himself a cold beer. He raised his glass in salute.

"Thank you, Señor Valdes. You have been of valuable assistance."

"You have found him?"

"We have. On the Syrian identity, as you advised."

"I wish it to be known," huffed Valdes in halting French, "that neither I nor my government can accept responsibility for this man's actions. His approach to me this morning was made on the basis of a brief encounter in the past, a coincidence which can in no way be used to implicate the people of Cuba . . ."

"Yes, yes, of course. All that has been taken care of, Señor Valdes, between your government and mine – and also those people over there."

Daladier extended his beer-glass in a general north-easterly direction, towards Porte des Lilas and the Soviet Union. Then he sat down himself. "As I have already said, no mention will be made of this Dutchman's political connections. His training, his purpose in Europe – all this, although fully known to us, will be concealed by the government of France on condition that you give us your help in the present situation."

510

There was a moment of silence. Valdes, beginning to relax, sipped his drink.

"All this has been arranged, señor. And at the highest level, as you know. So be at your ease." Daladier sat back and emptied his pockets, for lighting of pipe, phase one. "However, until our operations are concluded, I must ask you to remain in this building."

"I am a prisoner?"

"No, señor, a guest. You will sleep in the cells, because that is where the beds are. But you will be perfectly comfortable." Tamping in shreds of mixed leaf, Daladier looked up and smiled serenely. "There are people who say, you know, that this is the best hotel in Paris – for the price."

19

Others would have said that the best hotel in Paris, at any price, was the one to be found at 15 Place Vendôme. But to find it, you had to look hard, for the Ritz was as self-effacing as the other commercial establishments in the perfect seventeenth-century square: the shy little banks with no money in sight, the lawyers' and stockbrokers' offices marked only by polished brass plaques. Even the shops did little to spoil the square's harmony with their uniform, gilt-lettered names and softly lit windows, their restrained displays of silver and gold, silk scarves, crested linen, foulard ties and diamonds laid on black velvet.

Laura Jenkinson, catching a glimpse of this finery as the taxi swung in from the Rue de Rivoli, felt a small thrill of sensual pleasure. Inordinate wealth had for her the same attraction as unabashed sex – something she never could quite carry off but liked to contemplate.

Kemble was almost asleep. His eyes, now only kept open by hunger, travelled straight to the steps of the hotel. "Oh-oh," he said. "Look. We're in trouble."

The Ritz was besieged by press. Pulled up among the big shiny Citroens and sleek Rolls-Royces were several vulgar little cars, out of which had tumbled a crowd of raucous investigators, some with cameras. They were being held back by a posse of gendarmerie, who had come to the aid of the hotel's doorman. And the press didn't like it. Rights had been infringed, free passage denied. A furious row was in progress, getting close to blows, as Laura and Kemble came up the steps.

But Laura passed through it like royalty. Holding out her diplomatic card, tossing out a few words of French, she parted the gendarmes and drew a salute from the doorman. Kemble, sticking close, followed her into the hotel's foyer, which called to mind a wedding cake – creamy paint and curlicues of ornamental plasterwork, gilt-edged. Underfoot was a richly patterned carpet, across which liveried flunkeys were passing to and fro. Somewhere a fountain was splashing, and from close at hand came the rhythmic swish and rattle of a cocktail being shaken in ice.

Thirst struck Kemble like a blow. "Full marks," he said. "We're in. How do you do it?"

Laura shrugged, without vanity. "I go with the decor."

And that was true. Even bare-legged, in a cotton dress and sandals, she looked a million francs. Place Vendôme was Jenkinsonville. Glad to be in her tow, Kemble waved back to the doors, beyond which the forces of order were still doing battle with the forces of truth. "Who did you tell them I was?"

"I told them that you were my husband, Jack."

"And how did I do?"

"You passed."

"You mean I get the part?"

"You'll be lucky, chum." She smiled, diamond-bright. "This way."

"Which way is this?"

"The way to the restaurant."

She walked boldly on. And her instinct was sure. Just as she had guessed, John Clabon and Carlo Guidotti were dining together: a curly ginger head and a silver-smooth one, bent side by side in the soft recessed light of a small private alcove. Cast aside by events, the chairman of BMG and the chairman of Mobital were nibbling despondently at the liver-paste of force-fed geese, mixed with truffles, spread on squares of crust-free toast and washed down with bubbly white wine from a silver ice-bucket. It really was very bad luck, Kemble thought.

Laura crossed the restaurant without a pause and was standing beside the pink-clothed table, set with a centrepiece of white gardenias, before they noticed her.

"Hello," she said.

Guidotti jumped up in pleasure and surprise, immediately advancing round the table. But Clabon sat and glared, a piece of toast half-way to his mouth. "You," he said.

"Yes, me. And this is Mr. Kemble of *The Times*. May we join you?"

Clabon's glare instantly switched to Kemble. "So here he is at last – the darkie in the woodpile. You've got a bloody nerve coming here, fellow."

"The nerve is the lady's. I'm just tagging along," Kemble said, eyeing him back. "I'm sorry about what happened, and I've known Sir Patrick for longer than you have. I have spent the day trying to help. At the moment my main aim in life is food, but if you want some sympathetic copy on the merger, I shall be glad to oblige. Take it or leave it, Mr. Clabon. But make up your mind, please. Restaurants are closing all over Paris – even this one, I notice."

"Sit."

"Obliged."

"But you pay for yourself."

"Of course."

"And for her."

"And for Miss Jenkinson, naturally, since she is the head of our nerve department." Kemble sat down. "So what's the problem here? The Thunderer will pay for all, if you wish."

"That will not be necessary," rumbled Clabon, unable to keep a smile off his face. "Flaming cheek. Here, have some of this."

He lifted the bottle from the ice and filled two more glasses. They ordered food, selecting from a menu as big as a statute book, and it arrived quickly – for Kemble a fillet steak *au poivre*, flamed in the pan, running red in the middle. To go with the main course Guidotti chose a Burgundy thirty years old. Kemble and Clabon drank most of it as they talked through the day's events in a mood of rapidly diminishing sobriety.

After a while the merger came up again: its origins, the talks, the points outstanding, the muddle about the money. In fact, said Clabon, the kidnap was not even necessary – that was the really crazy thing. The merger was doomed in any case, since Riemeck would not accept the cost of it. This had become very clear in the course of the afternoon, when talks had been resumed in the Ritz, to see what was left. Nothing was left. That was the truth of it. Bloody President Riemeck was totally negative about the whole plan, and now any chances remaining had been cocked up by disclosure to the press. It really was a bloody shame, said Clabon. Enough to make you bloody weep.

Watching the chairman of BMG shake his head slowly from

side to side, like a bull in the ring just prior to the moment of collapse, Laura felt a sudden, strong, rising urge to giggle.

Guidotti had almost come to a stop. Eyelids half-closed, he sat without moving or speaking, like an ancient wrinkled iguana. He had eaten and drunk very little. Occasionally he took a languid puff at one of his yellow cigarettes, of which he had smoked so many that he was now using a short filtered holder, made of amber and gold.

Kemble was trying to get the facts straight, all of them at once, clamped down in one place, so they wouldn't run about overnight. "So," he said, "it's off, right? The merger is off."

Clabon, who had chosen a very large cigar from the Ritz's selection, and was now trying to insert his thumbnail under the paper band, paused in this difficult task. "Off," he agreed. "Kaput. Finito. All over. Right, Carlo?"

Guidotti nodded, without expression.

"And a damn shame, too," mumbled Clabon, returning to work on his cigar. He was determined to get the band off.

But Kemble was dissatisfied. Frowning, slumped back in his chair, he was staring intently at the table cloth. Suddenly he sat up and spoke in a loud, frustrated voice. "But if the goddamn merger is off, then why has Otto Riemeck just told the whole goddamn world that it's *going ahead*?"

Laura quivered.

Clabon smiled knowingly. He wagged his finger, then laid it against the side of his nose. "Orders, Jack."

"What!"

"That's what the French cops told him to say – don't you see? Merger goes on, let's see who jumps. Seems bloody risky to me, for us as well as Patrick. But there, that's the Frogs for you. Just like their traffic laws. Get from A to B, shortest time possible, never mind who gets squashed on the way."

The table had been cleared except for coffee, cheese, fruit, and now liqueurs. Kemble had lit a cigarette. "So how do you know all this?" he asked with his eyes narrowed, still searching for a catch. "Did Riemeck tell you himself?"

"Yes," said Clabon, smoking with the band on, "he told us. When he got back here – not until."

"Okay. So where is he now?"

"Riemeck?"

"That's the fellow."

"Upstairs." Clabon pointed at the ceiling, like an orator denouncing the gods, then turned to his fellow-suffering friend. "Wouldn't eat with us, eh, Carlo? Oh no. Wants to guzzle in private with Lord Arnold Doublett. You know, these Europeople make me sick. They live like kings, wining and feasting, taking suites in fancy hotels. And it's all on our money."

Oh dear, thought Laura, I'm not going to make it. She bit her lip.

Kemble's face was first nonplussed, then outraged, as he realised the facts had slipped his grasp again. "Now just a minute," he said, thumping the table for silence. "Just a minute, if you please. *Who*, for Christ's sake, is Lord Arnold Doublett? What's he *doing* in this?"

Clabon, stopped short in mid-tirade, was too surprised to answer the question.

So Laura did it for him, thinking that speech might aid self-control.

"Lord Doublett," she began with great care, correcting the solecism, "is the Nuffield Professor of . . ."

She could not finish. She bowed her head, took a breath and tried again.

"He's a professor of . . ."

Still she couldn't say it. Crumpling, she gave way to helpless, tearful, silent mirth.

The other three stared at her, astonished. And then the trouble spread. Guidotti's mouth rose at the corners and began to emit little grunts, like a man being punched in the stomach. Then Kemble, though still bewildered, began to cackle too. Clabon's laugh shook the whole room.

Immediately a hush fell upon the restaurant of the Ritz. Diners turned to look, waiters paused in their tasks. But fortunately no photographers were present to record the deep personal distress that the kidnap had caused to the friends and staff of Sir Patrick Harvey.

Upstairs, in the largest of the hotel's suites, Professor Lord Doublett stood by himself at an open window, looking down at the solitary floodlit pillar which rose in the centre of the square outside. As a scholar of the ancient world, he had recognised immediately that it was a copy of Trajan's Column in Rome. The

516

statue on top, in toga and laurel wreath, was Napoleon dressed as Caesar. He had not always stood so pretty, though. In 1871 the Parisian rebels, enraged by this monarchist-imperialist totem, had dragged the thing down and smashed it in two. But then up it went again, as most things in France, and now there it stood in the warm starry night, with pigeons on top and cars parked around it, an item of urban decoration whose origin was surely no better remembered than the campaigns of Emperor Nerva Trajan Augustus of Rome – against the tribes of the Dacia, wasn't it? Yes, yes, the Dacians. 101 to 108 A.D.

Ah well, thought Doublett, ah well. *Sic transit gloria*, and a jolly good thing too. Poor world if powerful men weren't turned into pigeon roosts.

And what about Patrick Harvey, he wondered, turning back into the room. Would anyone put up a statue to him? Poor old Patrick, he would rather like one, no doubt of that. But he wouldn't get spotlit on a pillar, and probably not even put on a plinth in Parliament Square. Perhaps his old school would stump up for something.

Doublett found it hard to believe that his friend was alive. So many of his contemporaries had already been carried off in less violent ways, struck down on the golf course, falling into their soup at high table, that survival of kidnap seemed impossible. He thought Harvey must be dead, yet was still too confused to feel proper sorrow. Shocked he felt, certainly, and above all inadequate. What could he do? How could he help? He couldn't help at all. Snatched away to this smart hotel in Paris, still dressed for Sunday in Oxford, Doublett was conscious of his own absurdity and feebleness. It saddened him.

Another shaming problem was that in spite of the *canapés* gobbled up earlier with cocktails, he was so ravening, belly-aching hungry that he couldn't think properly of anything else. Two hours had passed since he normally dined in college. Otto Riemeck had ordered supper here, for two, to be brought up. It hadn't arrived yet.

To ease the pain, Doublett walked about the room, which had been designed for comfort by the masters of comfort: thick carpet, fine tapestries on the walls, deep English sofas and a very French balcony, adorned with the famous sun emblem of Louis XIV. Through a half-open door he could see a huge canopied bed, and laid out on it, trivial by comparison, the blue-striped pyjamas in which the President of the European Commission would, having eaten – if eat he did – eventually sleep.

There was a marble bathroom; and next door to this room, going the other way, a small conference room or maybe a dining room, for those who liked to eat. Riemeck was in there now with his staff. And they weren't eating. Clabon and Guidotti were eating, downstairs, in the restaurant. But Riemeck was talking business. He was sitting at the table next door – a table surely meant, *prima facie*, for eating – with a bevy of Commission officials. They were going through the briefs for the summit. Associate membership for Turkey, emergency aid for Northern Ireland, European Monetary System, Lomé Sugar Protocol – Doublett had read the labels on the files, and the files were thick. This could take time, he thought gloomily. But since Otto Riemeck wished to sup *à deux*, for reasons not yet made clear, there was nothing to do but wait.

And this subordinate problem was soon put right. Ten minutes later food arrived on a trolley. Riemeck dismissed all his staff and sat down at last to supper for two, laid out on a small round table at the side of the room, beneath the largest tapestry, which depicted Heracles cleansing the Augean Stables.

The mood of this meal was uneasy. Since the late afternoon they had called each other "Otto" and "Arnold", but despite their common academic background – perhaps because of it – a wariness existed between them. Intellectual rivalry threatened. To Doublett is seemed not quite decent that a professor of law should hold such high public office. Riemeck's attitude to the presence at these proceedings of a master of classical history had so far gone unstated. But now he had a bone to pick. And he came quickly to it, without preamble.

"So, let us talk about four billion Ecus, Arnold. That is a very big amount. With some of the other Commissioners I could understand it. But Sir Patrick was always careful about money."

Immediately Doublett bristled, almost as much to his own surprise as Riemeck's. "Why? Are you going ahead with his plan?"

"They asked me that at the press conference."

"And you answered?"

"I gave no direct answer."

"Surely the search must come first. Find him, get him out alive. All that matters now."

"Naturally, that is the first priority."

"Cars can wait."

"If necessary, yes."

"Yet you wish to talk about the money." Doublett, eating fast, shook his head. "Sorry, Otto, goes against the grain. Money another day, if I may suggest." The Englishman's mood was not improved by acute disappointment in the supper. Ordered without his aid, it consisted of omelettes and croquette potatoes, with a large green salad on the side, two portions of camembert cheese and two apples. To drink, there was a bottle of mineral water.

They ate in silence.

Then Doublett said, relenting a little: "Man's an old friend. Upsetting business."

"We are all his friends, Arnold."

"Quite so, quite so. However, for me, at this juncture, not easy to talk about money or cars. No offence meant." Doublett, having got these conciliatory remarks off his chest, and the whole meal into his stomach, went on in a more analytic tone. "Besides, some danger here surely. Purpose of kidnap is to stop merger. *Ergo*, if merger continues, kidnap has failed. Further action by gang required."

Riemeck nodded stiffly. "That is the calculation of the French police. They wish to provoke some response from the kidnappers."

"This is healthy? For the hostage?"

"It may help to find him. If he cannot be found, he cannot be saved."

Doublett's head bobbed up and down, up and down, several times. "Yes, yes, understood. So French want merger to go on."

Riemeck laid down his fork and spread his hands, palms upwards, on the table. "The police, Arnold, wish me to *say* it will go on. The company chairmen wish to go on in fact. My staff are praying on their knees that I will forget the whole matter. Now, if you please, what do *you* say? I wish to hear your opinion."

The mood was still chucklesome, and progress a little unsteady, as Kemble, Laura, Clabon and Guidotti came up from the restaurant to see what was cooking on the Ritz's top floor.

The businessmen walked ahead discussing low-drag co-efficients for their plastic-bodied, no-petrol miracle. Behind them Laura and Kemble were arm in arm. And Kemble was happy to be tugged along. His unauthorised presence at these proceedings appeared to have been forgotten. Well aware of his luck, wondering if it would last, not so tiddly as he seemed, he tried to hear what the businessmen were saying as they strolled in front down the carpeted corridor.

Without a knock, Clabon and Guidotti wandered straight into Riemeck's suite. Following, Kemble and Laura came into a miniature conference room, which was full of Commission officials. The mood was harassed. Some of the Brussels men were sitting in silence round the oval-shaped table, either reading through or staring in dumb dismay at deep stacks of paper awaiting their President's attention. All work had come to halt while Dr. Riemeck had supper next door, shut up alone with Lord Doublett.

Laura, having found this out, gave Kemble a whispered guide to those present.

The pretty girl half-asleep in the corner, her curly blond head laid sideways on her arm, was Harvey's Scots typist, Lucy Maclean. Also in the room was Harvey's Director-General, the senior official of the industry department, a Luxembourgeois of stately appearance and little initiative. Nielsen, the bearded information officer from Denmark, had the appearance of a man still hoping to wake from a bad dream. Together with the head of Commission Security – an Irishman, also present – he had turned the Ritz into a fortress. Every entrance was blocked by gendarmes and police, and the hubbub that this was causing could be heard from the square below. The press were still baying at the hotel's doors.

"Attention! Listen to me, please."

The voice cutting through the subdued, anxious chatter was Riemeck's. Having stepped through the double doors which opened from the sitting room, the President stood at the end of the table and rapped its surface for silence.

At his side stood Lord Doublett, blinking in the too-bright light of the glass chandelier. The professor from Oxford was dressed in an old tweed jacket and rumpled yellow corduroy trousers, so short they exposed his patterned socks. Still tucked into his waistband was a napkin belonging to the Ritz.

Laura began to quiver with laughter again. Kemble stepped on her foot to shut her up as Riemeck addressed the whole assembly, speaking English.

"Thank you for waiting. It is late, so I will be brief. The following are my decisions. There is no time to discuss them. I ask you to put them into action with your best ability."

A hush of mingled dread and expectation had settled on the room. Everyone, it seemed, had guessed what was coming. And Riemeck's voice was flat as he made the announcement.

"The merger will go on. A plan will be presented to the European Council in Rome, as Sir Patrick intended."

Clabon took his hands from his pockets and clapped them silently, high above his head, for all to see. Guidotti's face was immobile, but his eyes shone with pleasure. Riemeck looked sternly from one to the other.

"I must warn you," he added, speaking only to them, "that there are many difficulties. To be honest, I do not know if this project will succeed. However, we shall go on with it, and we shall do so with full commitment. For this I will give you two reasons. It seems to me that Europe is challenged by the problems of the car industry, and in particular by the problems of your two companies. So – there is nothing new in that. We talk always of problems and challenges. But now we have been challenged by these kidnappers. That is a new thing, at least for the European Commission. And we must resist it. We cannot, as a matter of honour, allow this Iskra to succeed. We cannot, as a matter of policy, allow these companies to fail. For these two reasons we go on. Am I clear?"

Kemble was impressed. Laura had described Otto Riemeck as small and pompous, pushed into politics by mistake, a man of ambiguities and procedures.

"So," he went on, "there is much to be arranged. Sit down, please."

There were two gilt chairs by the window. Kemble motioned Laura to one and sat on the other, quickly lowering his profile as the general head-level sank. Nielsen was staring at him now with a panicked expression, having guessed, or been told, who he was. Kemble tried a reassuring smile. Laura made a placatory signal. The Dane, unconvinced, turned to Riemeck and opened his mouth to speak. But the President, now seated at the head of the table with Doublett, had resumed.

"First, let us settle the procedures," he said to Clabon and Guidotti. "I myself shall not be able to join your discussions, due to pressure of other commitments. In the interim Professor Doublett has agreed to take Sir Patrick's place. Is this acceptable to you?"

Kemble almost laughed aloud at the businessmen's reaction. First astonishment, then annoyance, then amusement passed across their faces; and finally base cunning, as they realised the possible advantage to themselves in this extraordinary appointment. They agreed to it.

Riemeck, with a quick nod of thanks, turned next to Laura. "Miss Jenkinson, you will keep the record, please, and make all the usual arrangements – meals, accommodation, travel."

Laura, taken quite by surprise, took a moment to find her voice. "But I have left the Commission, Herr President."

"I am asking you to return," said Riemeck with a cold stare. "Until this matter is concluded, at least. I take it you will not refuse."

A further short pause, then her shoulders dropped; her breath came out in a sigh. "No, of course not. I'll do it."

"Nielsen, you have one task, and that is to keep the press out of this. We have told them the talks will continue. That is all we shall tell them. No further details, please, until the summit is over."

Nielsen nodded at Riemeck. And Kemble nodded at Nielsen, to say that he would honour this embargo. The Dane hesitated. His mouth was slightly parted, ready for speech. But Riemeck had moved on already.

"And we cannot remain in this hotel. Tomorrow we must find a more discreet place."

A new venue for the talks was discussed. Once this was arranged, the meeting relaxed a little. Two men at the table lit cigarettes. The President, preparing to move from procedure to substance, was passed a bundle of documents. To Kemble, watching him, it seemed that Otto Riemeck was enjoying the exercise of power. This German doctor of law was in the position of a lifelong birdwatcher who has suddenly discovered that he, too, can fly. At first he could hardly believe it, but after some nervous experimentation he had spread his wings and taken to the air. Now he was sailing about the sky.

"Very well, let us now consider what items remain for decision. As you know, the record of proceedings in Tours was destroyed." Without any change of expression, he picked up a stapled typescript. "However, here is a new record, prepared last night by Erich Kohlman. This was done at the request of the French police. Miss Jenkinson, will you look through it, please?"

The document was passed to Laura, who placed it on her knees and immediately started to read, bent over on the small gilt chair.

"However," Riemeck went on, "I think it is already known what the main points are, from our previous discussions today. I have made a list of them."

Taking out a small sheet of paper, handwritten, he started to read from it, looking up after each item to gauge the businessmen's reaction.

Kemble stayed still as a fly on the wall, amazed that Nielsen still hadn't exposed him. But the Dane was staring resolutely into space, his face drawn tight with the effort to pretend unawareness. He'd left it so late now, action would get him into worse trouble than ignorance.

Riemeck went on down his list – a scheme for workers' directors, joint production of the Mobital Sparta, selection of a new joint chairman – until Carlo Guidotti interrupted politely to say that there really wasn't much point in going on with this project unless and until the matter of money had been cleared up.

"Yes, yes, that's right, the money," echoed Clabon, immediately turning belligerent. Now plainly drunk, as the brandy inside him caught up with the Burgundy, he bunched his fist and stuck out his chin. "Well, Dr. Riemeck? The money – is that on your list? You say one billion, Sir Patrick said four. Some reduction of this small discrepancy would be helpful to me and my partner here."

Riemeck met the sarcasm with an untroubled smile. "I have discussed the question of finance with Professor Doublett," he said in an even voice, "and I now agree that the earlier figure was too low to be useful. We shall aim for a sum of four billion."

The shock on the faces of the men from Brussels was like that

523

of people bereaved. They stared at Riemeck in appalled, breathless silence. Kemble, too, was holding his breath. A light breeze was playing through the room from the flapping of his ears.

And then, damn it, Laura got the giggles again. Bent over on the gilt chair beside him, she started to quiver and quake. Tears of laughter dripped onto Kohlman's record of the talks in Tours. The typescript shook in her hands.

No, not laughter. She was crying.

First Kemble noticed; then, very quickly, they all noticed. Several of them jumped up and came to her aid, fussing round her with clucks of concern.

To explain, Laura held out the typescript. "Look," she cried, "it's perfect – every word! He wrote down everything, just the way it was. Oh dear, excuse me . . ."

She broke down completely.

Kemble, standing up, put his arm round her shoulders. "I'll take her home," he said. "I know where she's staying."

"Who is this man?" asked Riemeck from the opposite end of the room.

The President was answered, or rather deflected, by Clabon, who said in a loud, bustling voice: "Leave this to me, Otto. Back in a moment."

Kemble made quickly for the door with the sobbing, sniffing girl. The chairman of BMG came with him, and also the chairman of Mobital. Out in the corridor, Guidotti took over the care of Laura. Clabon pulled Kemble aside.

"Right," he said, "here's what you do. One favour deserves another. Leave out the Sparta, will you? Just say a joint car at 1500, because a lot of my men are going to get the chop, and I'd rather they heard it from me than *The Times*."

"Okay," said Kemble. "Agreed. What about the four billion?"

"Print it, chum, print, before they change their minds. But one more favour, if you please."

"What's that?"

"Skip the workers."

"Two directors in five, you mean?"

"I do mean," said Clabon. "Once that's out, we're lost. The monkeys will take over the zoo."

"Progressive fellow, aren't you?" Kemble said with a laugh. "Okay, second item suppressed – just for you."

"Scout's honour?"

"Mother's grave."

"Good lad. *Orryvoir* now. Take her away. Sleep well."

Clabon said good night with a lecherous wink. Guidotti handed Laura over with a sad, knowing smile of regret. Then they turned back together, chuckling softly, through the door into Riemeck's suite.

20

Escaping from the Ritz in a taxi, through a gauntlet of flashbulbs and shouting reporters, Kemble kept his arm round Laura's shoulders. She, to hide, pressed her face against his chest, and then kept it there, as they sped away westward down the Rue de Rivoli, between the lantern-lit gallery and the high-walled terrace of the Tuileries.

"God, I'm such a *fool*," she moaned into his shirt. "How did that happen?"

"I thought you were laughing."

"I nearly was. I just went the other way. Give me a handkerchief, will you?" She sat up and dried her face, then drew back from him. "And for heaven's sake stop being so ridiculously *gallant*."

Kemble took his arm from her shoulder. "Me? Gallant? Don't kid yourself. I'm just hoping to take advantage."

She laughed then, weakly. "Oh yes?"

"You bet. Lady cries, take her home. See what she does next."

"Tried it before, have you?"

"Uh-huh," Kemble said, watching the Place de la Concorde pass by, the Champs Elysées like a pathway of light. "Reckon to score about fifty in a hundred."

"You're disgusting."

"That's the plan."

She tossed the handkerchief back, then flopped into the soft woolly seat. "Really, I should have laughed," she said a moment later. "I mean, just think. He plots to wreck the merger, then helps to patch it up again, leaving us a nice neat record of progress to date. Now what could be funnier than that?"

"I can think of a few things."

The taxi had turned along the embankment. Laura sighed, staring out at the river. "You're right, it's not funny. It's pathetic."

"Was it love?"

"For Mitzi? Oh no, I don't think so. It was love for a dream."

"Strongest kind," said Kemble, still thinking of the other kind, though sleep was coming up fast on the rails.

"It's the strongest kind in Germany," Laura said. "Oh dear, what dreamers they are. No one makes myths like the Germans. Race, War, all that stuff in the thirties. Back in the twenties it was Peace and Beauty. God knows what's next, but right now it's Work. The hard-working burghers of Germany, carrying everyone else on their backs."

"Isn't it true?"

"Yes, but the point is they get so romantic about it. An operatic cycle, that's what the Germans are."

"Bravo," murmured Kemble, his own head sinking back.

Laura, already recovered, talked on as the taxi hummed over the cobbles. He lost the drift of it, but heard her say after an interval: "Divided Germany, that's the great issue, though nobody even dares to talk about it. Erich was just ahead of his time. And there's your next myth, of course. One Germany. Oh deary me, just wait till that gets going. Ah, here we are. Have you got any money? Jack? *Jack!*"

"Uh?"

"Wake up. We've arrived."

Not much was done in the Ritz after Laura's departure. Guidotti went to bed. John Clabon paid a visit to the Crazy Horse Saloon, where he fell asleep watching topless girls. The men from Brussels dispersed.

Left alone again, Professors Doublett and Riemeck decided to take a walk, since the night was so beautiful. They slipped out through a side-door and strolled together round Place Vendôme in the moonlight, walking in circles round Napoleon's triumphal column while the press, unaware of them, stood bunched in wait on the hotel's steps.

Pleased by this subterfuge, they talked lightly at first. Then Doublett became aware that Riemeck had something to say: a late-night unburdening, probably, on the topic that no one had

527

dared to mention. And so it turned out.

"That boy, Erich Kohlman – he came from Lübeck, you know."

Doublett nodded in instant comprehension. "Border town, you mean – close to the East. Yes indeed. Could explain."

"In Lübeck you can see the other side," Riemeck said in a quiet voice, seeming to talk to himself. "There is only the river between. Sometimes, in the morning, there are people found dead on the western bank. They try to swim across in the night, but the current is too strong. For this boy, Kohlman, that is an ordinary fact of his home. He has grown up with it."

"Must have marked him," Doublett said gravely. "Painful thing."

They paced across the moonlit flagstones surrounding the floodlit column, whose bronze reliefs spiralled into the starlit sky, telling stories of great forgotten battles of Europe – battles, it struck Doublett now, which the French had won largely because, among other things, the Germans were not yet an organised nation.

Then Riemeck stopped, staring down at his small, neat feet. He spoke like that, his hands in his pockets, his bald head lowered, until he had finished.

"It is strange. I know nothing about this boy's life. And yet I know, exactly, why he is in prison – what emotions, what ideas have put him there. Erich Kohlman will tell us that Germany's prosperity, our famous economic miracle, is nothing but a trick – a propaganda victory of American imperialism. We have no reason to be proud of it. There is more justice in the East, he will say, a greater sense of moral purpose. And that is the way we should look, to our countrymen in the East. In fact – he will say this to me, in accusation – our actual constitution, the basic law of Federal Germany, requires us to seek reunification with the east. But how can we do that if we are a puppet of America, attached by so many strings to the West? No, says Kohlman, this is wrong. This must change. The answer, for Germany, must be neutrality. We should make peace with the communists and unite our country. And this will be good for Europe – for the world. Because in Germany, when we are united, the best will be realised of both systems. A state will be organised without waste or hardship, and the dream will come true of brotherhood on earth."

528

On this fantastic phrase the President of the European Commission stopped short and looked up at his companion, no trace of apology or amusement on his face. One might have said the dream was his own. He stared at Doublett in silence, his ruddy features bleached in the moonlight.

"That will be Erich Kohlman's speech, Arnold. Pretty well exactly, I assure you, those are the words he will use when his trial arrives, this boy who has been a spy in our middle. And he is not alone. There are many young Germans who think the same. I have heard them talk. I know what they think. Come, let us walk some more."

Starting forward again, Riemeck took off his spectacles, wiped them with a handkerchief, then looped them round his ears. Turning to Doublett, he smiled.

"You are shocked a little. That I can see."

Doublett, a deep-dyed political conservative, was indeed shaken, almost panicked, by the drift of this conversation. "That you should sympathise with Kohlman? No," he said, "of course not. Perfectly natural."

But Riemeck was quick to correct this impression. "I sympathise with him – yes, perhaps. However, I do not agree. For me a neutral, united Germany comes into the class of impossible dreams. The systems, East and West, contradict. They cannot be mixed."

"And Germans not, by nature, neutral people? Would you say?"

Riemeck nodded. "The Russians, at least, will never believe so – not for many generations. The only Germany they will permit is one they control. Partition is the price we must pay."

He strolled on in silence a while, then spoke in a less solemn tone.

"We old Germans of the war are very cautious people. We do not like to disturb things. And this is why Patrick Harvey annoyed me, do you realise? Scared me, perhaps I should say. That great, so-easy English confidence of his, by which he ignored the procedures in this matter, one billion, four billion, pah, what is that, let us get to business, slap-dash, double-quick – to a German such as myself, who has seen too much breaking of rules, this is shocking. It is dangerous."

Doublett chuckled: a low belly-rumble. "Seem to have picked up the habit yourself, though."

Riemeck only smiled, with some ruefulness. "Yes, it is too late for caution. We have to go for all or nothing."

"Which will it be, do you think? Between ourselves."

Riemeck shrugged. "There are some odds in favour. You must understand, Arnold, that there is a psychology of summits. Often it is the last-minute, crazy idea which works. When heads of government meet, they want something new for the history book. They do not want something safe, produced by a committee of officials. A plan costing one billion Ecus, coming formally from the Commission, would have been rejected in a moment. But a plan for four billion, prepared by a former Prime Minister, who was kidnapped in the task – that is different."

"Especially if he is dead," added Doublett.

"I did not say that."

"You speak of him in the past tense. You have done so all evening."

"I have? Is that so?" Riemeck stopped in mid-square. After a moment he shook his head. "No, I don't believe he is dead."

"You don't? That's good," said Doublett. "Can't help thinking it myself, though."

"Tomorrow we shall know perhaps," Riemeck said coolly. "Tonight we can do no more. So, I shall go to bed. Thank you for taking this job, Arnold."

"You didn't give me a chance to say no."

"That is true, I did not. I treated you as Patrick treated me."

They said goodnight and parted. Riemeck returned to the hotel.

Professor Doublett, deciding to walk a little more, felt better for the job he'd been given. Duty did not call often in his life, and therefore when she called, she was welcome. His head was full of plans for the morrow, and another had just popped into it. He left the square and turned right along the Rue St. Honoré, then right again, towards the church of La Madeleine. Skirting the church to the right, he entered a long narrow street where honky-tonk women stood in doorways. A few, the most desperate, made business propositions. He refused them with muttered apologies, shuffling on until he found what he wanted: a cheap late-night brasserie, still where he remembered it. Furtive as a spy, mumbling low to the waiter, he ordered entrecôte steak and *pommes frites*.

"Of course," said Laura, when she was sitting up in bed, "the great thing about Otto Riemeck is that he won't join the national opera. He never would, you know, even in the war. He is positively anti-operatic, is our Uncle Otto – a non-singing, non-dreaming, unheroic German. He thinks small. But at least he does think, and he listens as well. His students loved him, you know. There was never much trouble at Württemberg."

"Laura."

"Yes, Jack?"

"Why don't we just settle down to the fact that the Germans are a superior race? They're better organised. They're better behaved. And in case you didn't know, I must also inform you they are better at football."

"Yes, Jack."

"So now we can talk about something else."

"Yes, Jack. What else shall we talk about?"

"Oh, I expect you'll think of something. Meantime let's try not talking at all."

Kemble was sitting on the edge of the bed, still dressed, with a generous whisky in his hand; no water, no ice. He swung his feet up on the bed and lay beside her, cupping both hands round the glass.

They were back in the sumptuous, all-white flat. The bed-room, too, was white, with a long-haired carpet that made him think of Hollywood. On the wall were some erotic paintings. Sometimes the present scene seemed to be heading in that direction, sometimes not. But Kemble did not greatly care how it ended. His desire for sleep was almost equal.

Laura's desires were unclear. She was leaning against a heap of fluffy white pillows with a hot *tisane* in her hands, made from a tiny bag of herbs attached by a cord to the handle of her mug. She still gave off the fragrance of a pine-scented bath. She was wearing a night-gown of broderie anglaise, white with blue ribbons, which showed off the tan of her thin neck and arms. Her black hair fell loose to her shoulders – the sort which recovers from anything with a few quick strokes of a brush. And the frown had gone from her brow. Having laughed, having cried, her whole face had softened, which was the essential improvement. Once she relaxed, she really wasn't bad, thought Kemble. In fact, with a little encouragement . . . No, forget it. Too tiring. Too late in the day. And for you,

531

brother, too late in life. Stick to Scottish Comfort.

"So," he said, "enjoyed your day, did you?"

"In parts."

"You're a public menace," said Kemble, "that's what you are. Holy cow, what a dance you led us – me, the French, the Germans. You can't even go to the races without causing trouble. Do you realise, you actually managed to get in the same bloody betting queue as the KGB stooge who's running the Dutchman?"

"I did?"

"You did. He's a Cuban – small-fry attaché at their embassy in Paris. Regular punter at Longchamp."

"That must have been confusing."

"It certainly warmed things up in the flichouse," Kemble said, smiling at the memory. "But what really muddled them up was your behaviour in Tours – yes, now there's a subject. Forget Uncle Otto. Let's talk about Uncle Harvey. Tell me now, honestly, why *did* you quit on him like that?"

Laura shut her eyes and shook her head, reluctant to think about it. "Oh dear, I really was terribly rude to him."

"So what tipped you over?"

"God knows. The way he gave me a bit more responsibility, I suppose. Normally I just do the menus and plane tickets, but this time he brought me into the work. And on the way down he took me out to lunch. For once he treats me like an intelligent person, more or less on a level with himself. But as soon as I try to tell him what I think, he slaps me back down again, like a servant who's forgotten her place. So, I don't know, I just went on shooting my mouth off. It became a sort of deathwish, I suppose – a compulsion to see how much he'd take. Does that sound crazy?"

Kemble laughed. "I bet it puzzled Harvey."

"I am *not* a domestic servant."

"No, Laura, that you are not."

"And I'm not going back to the Berlaymont, whatever happens. After Rome I quit."

"Quite right. Good girl."

"Can you really get me onto *The Times*?"

"You know, I believe I can." Kemble lit a cigarette and blew smoke upwards, towards the naughty paintings. "When I said it, maybe not."

532

"Bastard."

"But now I can really twist Holroyd's arm."

"You've twisted it already. How much is he paying you?"

"Dunno. Lost count," Kemble said with a sharky grin. "I'll have to ask for you as a tip."

They chuckled, lying side by side on the bed; then fell silent. Their minds drifted off on separate tracks, or maybe the same one. The silence went on for several minutes, seeming to deepen. The night-sounds of Paris were far off. The room was their own: enclosed, warm, luxurious. The pictures winked and nudged from the wall. Kemble emptied his glass and put out his cigarette. When his head came back to the pillows, Laura had turned towards him, so her lips were close beside his face. He could feel her breath on his cheek, speeded up, in little pants.

"So here we are," she said huskily, mock-seductive, trying to make a joke of it.

"Yes," he said, inwardly sighing, inwardly chuckling at the utter predictability of everything – her hesitations, his own bad behaviour. "Here we are."

"Well?"

"Well what?"

"Aren't you going to take advantage?"

"Dunno. What do you say?"

She sat up with a jerk. "Me? What do *I* say? Don't ask *me*. I'm just waiting to be scored by Mr. Hot Shot, fifty out of a hundred." She slumped back on the pillows, face upward to the ceiling. "My word, you *are* a disappointment."

"Oh yeah?"

"Yeah."

"Try this then."

He turned, rose up on one elbow, descended to her face and kissed her. She half-resisted, then fully yielded, murmuring appreciatively as she pulled him down. Then she stopped, froze still, pushed him back and said: "No. Wait. This is silly."

Kemble sat up. "What's the problem?"

"We ought to think about it."

"No, we are not going to think about it. We're just going to do it. Now take off that thing and switch out the lights. I'm prettier in the dark."

She dived for the switch as his trousers came off. But she herself would not undress. For a time they lay side by side in the blackness, then gently he took off her night-gown. She let him, but made no other movement. She was shaking.

"Take it easy," said Kemble. He caressed her cheek, then patted it. "Just lie there. I'm going to call Commissaire Groucho."

He rolled away, switched on the light on his own side and picked up the telephone. Soon he was through to the Quai des Orfèvres, the ops room, one of the girls on the special exchange. Then Daladier came on, sounding strangely cheerful. "So," he said, "where is my English *biographe*?"

"In bed."

"In bed? What is this? You have gone turvy-topsy in the *priorités*?"

"My priorities are fine, thanks." Kemble sat up in suspicion. "What's going on?"

But the Commissaire's attention had been distracted. Voices could be heard in the background. "Wait," he said, no longer bantering. And a few seconds later: "Give the girl your number. I will call in the morning."

With that he was gone. Passed back to the girl on the switchboard, Kemble gave her the number to call, then rang off and sat back frowning in thought, propped against the bedhead of padded white silk. He lit another cigarette. Laura, curled up below the duvet, watched him.

"Well?"

"Something's happened."

"Harvey?"

Kemble shook his head. "No, can't be that. Daladier wants me in at the kill."

"Are you sure?"

"I'm sure. This copper is vain, Laura. He wants his deeds in print."

"So he'll let you know, then, won't he? If anything happens."

"Yes, I suppose so."

"Switch off the light, Jack. And put out that horrible cigarette. You're right, you do look better in the dark."

But her boldness was gone in a moment. As he slid down beside her, she started to tremble.

"Please," she said. "Don't rush me."

But Kemble was in no rush. It took him some time to forget

534

the French police. And when he did get back to wanting her, patience was easy, since he did at that moment feel a wave of affectionate tenderness towards her, this funny flighty creature from England he had chased for four days, now fluttering like a bird in his hands. He took his hands off and lay still. Eventually she settled and shifted towards him, entwining her long, lean limbs with his own. Her skin was warm to the touch and smooth like a child's, except for the angular bones beneath. Her breath was on his face and his ear, and when she took him in her arms he felt his heart turn right over, to his own great surprise, and some alarm. He had thought it was dead.

In the half-empty ops room Daladier was still at his task. Pondering the big map of France, beside which a single tired girl still stood, he momentarily thought of himself as a doctor examining the body of a patient. Once the problem had been found, he could operate. But meanwhile all he could do was wait, watching carefully to see what happened as pressure was applied to three different sensitive points of this brightly lit, supine anatomy.

Here in Paris the Algerian, Marc Bensaïd, was now undergoing the toughest degree of continuous interrogation allowed by the law of the French Republic.

And somewhere down there, towards Spain, was Rosa Berg herself, who would soon know, perhaps already did, that the merger of BMG and Mobital was going ahead. That would hurt, Daladier thought. That would bring a scream.

Meanwhile here, where the green plastic marker was, just outside Orléans, moving south through the night to Bordeaux, was the point of most delicate pressure. Too much, or too little, would be fatal.

But Biffaud was on the train now, taking a look.

After Orléans the train picked up speed, roaring through tunnels, rumbling over bridges, faster and faster, until it was dashing at a steady, even pace through the moonlit countryside south of the Loire.

In the cheap compartments the lights were dimmed. A single bulb glowed in the ceiling of each, less bright than the moon. Most people were asleep, sprawled about on the hard, green, upright seats. Territories had been staked out for the night.

Disturbance was unwelcome, but there was still some settling in to be done by the people who had got on at Orléans. They chose their places and disposed their luggage to general irritation, amid sighs and grunts, half-watched by tired eyes.

Joop Janssen had taken off his dark glasses, but his head was still wrapped in the Arab check cloth, his face turned away from the rest of the passengers. His bag was laid across his knees, with the base of it placed a few inches from his hand. His body was relaxed. His eyes were shut. But he wasn't ready to sleep until he saw who came to occupy the empty seat opposite.

The door was drawn back. Looking in from the corridor, a middle-aged man in steel-rimmed spectacles and black leather jacket, with hair cut short as a toothbrush, asked if the seat was free. People shrugged and grunted. No one knew. Pretending to sleep, Joop watched the newcomer by opening his eyelids the merest, invisible fraction. The man sat down, without luggage. He looked around and settled in. Then the previous occupant, also male, short-haired, middle-aged, came back and said the seat was his. Crewcut apologised, without surprise, and went off down the corridor, the way he had come.

For a few minutes longer Joop watched the second man, who had been in the seat since Paris. Then he closed his eyes and relaxed. Instantly sleep overwhelmed him with the force of a drug. His jaw dropped open, his head fell sideways, and he started to dream of a railway in Russia, the track stretching off without a stop, without a curve, through a limitless forest of pines.

"Thank you," she said.

"My pleasure."

"Can I talk now?"

"If you must."

There was quite a long silence in the dark, during which Kemble sensed several things pass through her head and then out again, unspoken. What she eventually said was: "Come to London. Let's live together."

"Well now, that might be nice."

"We'll work on *The Times* and give smart little dinners in Fulham."

"But I did that . . . twenty years ago." Kemble laughed at the thought, then clicked his tongue. "Shit. Twenty years."

"Relive your youth. With me."

"Yeah, yeah. Wouldn't mind doing that," he said, caressing her. "Just leave it for now, will you? Let's go to sleep."

"I mean, we could . . ."

"Laura."

"Right, Jack. Whatever you say, Jack. Sleep."

She rolled away. They lay back to back in the dark, not touching, but conscious of each other's breathing. Kemble, still alarmed by his feelings, was glad to be left in silence. Her present high spirits were hard for him to share. Old joys revived were not the same as new ones discovered, and if they went wrong, would hurt more. It was he, not she, would suffer at the parting of the ways. He could see the whole path from here to there, and was scared to go on. This road was mined.

"You're not asleep," she said, rolling back suddenly. "You're brooding. I can tell."

This time she stayed on his side of the bed and kept her limbs entwined with his own, hot-skinned and damp in the crevices. Kemble, thus wrapped, sank towards slumber. The situation seemed too good to be true, but he was too tired to look for the traps. He hadn't the strength to shake her off, nor the wish.

One thing undone still bothered him. Half-conscious, eyes closed, he mumbled into her ear: "I should have called Groucho back."

"Want to now?"

"No, too late. Is there an alarm here?"

"Yes," she said, "I've got one."

"Set it early. Say seven."

She set the clock, then came back to him, curling up. "The job comes first, eh?"

"Always," he murmured. "You too. Job first. Safest thing. Don't forget."

A few minutes later, just before midnight, he added with the sudden, strange lucidity of a man in delirium: "Infidelity to wives I can handle. It was being unfaithful to my job brought me down."

Laura stirred, too drowsy to answer.

"And this thing has rescued me," Kemble went on with perfect clarity. "So I feel rather guilty. In fact I've suggested a way I might help, which is so bloody dangerous I must have been mad."

But Laura, now close to sleep, failed to take this in. "Poor man," she murmured. "Think they'll find him?"

"They'll find him. The question is, will he be alive?"

"Oh dear, I hope so. Goodnight, Jack."

"Goodnight."

"Don't leave me."

"We'll see."

Monday

1

With the first light of day came a scuttling and scratching of small clawed feet on the tiles overhead. Then tentative flutterings began, and soft guttural sounds: a first nervous clearing of forty slender throats. At sunrise, suddenly, they started to coo. The new day seemed to alarm them. Afraid to venture further from their loft, they huddled together on the roof, but eventually some of the braver spirits took off, setting out for the trees at the bottom of the garden. They were not long gone. Within a few minutes they came flapping back. And the news from the trees was not good, it seemed. The coos of the flock went up a note; the fluttering of feathers increased. Soon there was general commotion.

Margaret Harvey found menace even in the early routine of the pigeons who lived on top of her house in Kraainem, Belgium. Normally she liked nothing better than to listen to the chatter of these soft, silly creatures at a time when they thought the world their own. Normally, in order to wake with the light, she kept the curtains of the bedroom open. This morning, hoping to sleep, she had drawn them. But it was no good. The early sunlight struck easily, fiercely through the flower-patterned chintz. The sun was too bright and the birds were too shrill. Even nature, it seemed, her friend in old age, had turned against her.

She closed her eyes and tried to be calm. This was silly, she thought, this was just drugs. And her own fault, too. She hadn't managed the night very well.

Get some rest, the police had said, we will wake you if anything happens – that must have been about midnight. To stop them fussing, she had come to her room, but had not slept.

541

Wanting to be prepared, she had sat for two hours in the chair beside her bed, attempting to read a book. Then Mary had come, the British Ambassador's wife, who had been so kind. Sleep, said Mary, was the important thing, since the next day, Monday – this day – might be crucial, and she should be refreshed for it. Pills had been Mary's answer.

Margaret Harvey had yielded and taken two: a thing she'd resisted all her life. And the tablets had given her three hours' sleep. The trouble was they hadn't fully worn off. Now she was awake again, not tired and calm as she might have been, but fuddled and tense, with a headache.

Pills had been a mistake, she thought. But well meant. Mary Brent-Ewing, though not a close friend, had been understanding and only slightly bossy. Perhaps it was Mary's light snores that had woken her, for Mary, asleep next door in the spare room, had kindly left the doors open.

Mary had been very kind. And others were being kind downstairs, moving softly about in the drawing room and kitchen. There was nothing so disturbing, Margaret Harvey thought, as large men trying to be quiet. In the night they had been doing technical things to the telephone. Now they just seemed to be moving about. The house was full, as for a party. There were Belgian police down there, British people from the embassy, and Berlaymont officials of several nationalities whose names she should know but could never remember – all trying to be kind. There were more policemen in the garden, quietly standing on her flowers and placed behind trees with machine-guns. They had put an armed cordon round the house. Others were holding back the press at the bottom of the drive. To judge from the stir, there was quite a crowd down there, and a jam of cars already. Perhaps that had upset the pigeons.

She got up and closed the door of the bedroom as softly as she could, hoping not to be heard. If they knew she was awake, they would draw her back into the drama. Cups of tea would be brought up, bits of news, declarations of sympathy, fresh instructions. But obviously nothing important had happened. For really good news, or really bad, they would have woken her. So it would be back to guessing and planning the next move, of which she had taken as much as she could. How could she face a house full of foreign policemen, let alone take in their complicated orders, when she was fuddled with drugs? Let them wait, she thought. And Mary, too. Let them keep their kindness to themselves, and their plans. Please, just leave me alone, that's all I want.

No, that was not all she wanted. Abashed at the selfish thought, annoyed at her own irrationality, she went into the bathroom and dashed her face with cold water. She dried herself roughly, brushed her hair, then crept back to the bed, feeling a little more capable. She was still wearing the housecoat in which she had slept, to be decently dressed if anything happened. And now could be the time. If it happened at all, they said, it would probably happen this morning. The clock at her side said 7.30.

She tried to think about what she had to do. It had been rehearsed several times before she came up to bed, and had seemed to her then a frightful, unfair responsibility. To dwell on it now would scatter her wits entirely. She was just a piece of equipment, rather less reliable than the things attached to the telephone downstairs – that was the way to think of it.

As to the bigger issues, any thought by herself was not really possible, or of the slightest use. Kidnapped? Who by? How? Why? She had been told, but it made little difference. Politics, to her, was all the same: a world full of violent, obsessive, hysterical people. She had tried to make him give it up. Once, when he was down with shingles, she had almost succeeded. But he had gone back to it, time and again, as a sailor goes back to the sea. And now it had swallowed him up, just as the sea swallows sailors. Well, he had known what he was doing. The risks were part of the lure; his skill at survival was a matter of pride to him. He, the politician, would understand.

No, that was wrong, he would not understand. Physical risks were not the sort he took. He'd always had a special fastidious horror of violence, even on the games field – an utter dud, poor thing, at manly sports and military pursuits. Words, not guns, were what he understood. He expected the world to be rational and moderate, like himself, and was always pained when it turned out not to be. So this would have taken him quite by surprise. Confronted by an actual fanatic with an actual gun, he wouldn't know what to do at all.

As in Wales, and many times since, Margaret Harvey's mind wandered off in a desperate effort to visualise her husband's circumstances. But all she could see was his physical effects in the bedroom around her – suits, shoes, shirts, brushes, pills, lotions, books. In these things only his presence was real; her emotions could fix on nothing else, so she gazed at one item after another, beginning to see them as relics. Horrified, she caught herself wondering which things to keep, which to throw away . . .

Then it happened.

The buzzer plugged in beside her bed buzzed once, long and loud, to wake her. There was a silence of about two seconds, then it continued to buzz in three short consecutive spasms, several times repeated – the pre-arranged signal to warn her that a call had come through from the kidnappers.

She jumped off the bed and stood frozen beside it, heart leaping, her mind in the wildest confusion. One moment she had been trying to imagine his plight, the next she had started to think of him as dead; now, on a buzz, she was told to be ready to speak to his captors. For Margaret Harvey, aged 68, dulled by drugs, worn out by anxiety, this was too abrupt a switch of attention. As the buzzer went on buzzing it drove every detailed instruction from her head.

After that nothing happened as rehearsed.

The system set up for receipt of this call was of the utmost mechanical complexity. The Belgians had set up a special exchange in the house. Their equipment, which filled the drawing-room and extended to a long blue van on the drive, was designed, in the first place, to keep the line clear. Family, friends, relations, well-wishers, newspapers, cranks, informants, tipsters – each incoming call had been taken by a Belgian female operator, of whom there were four on the switchboard. Their job was to answer the number, posing as the Harveys' Flemish housemaid. But as soon as it was clear that the speaker was not a kidnapper, the call was taken off the line and diverted to a team of police and officials, who sat ready to handle each enquiry. Official calls, relating to the search, came to the van, on a different number. A continuously open line had been established from the van to police headquarters in Paris, and also, more important, to the French communications monitoring centre at Les Invalides. Once the kidnappers came on the line, the call could be traced to source, but this would take time – exactly how much time no one could say. The trace could take from two to eight minutes. So the task, in Kraainem, was to keep the Iskra talking. First the Belgian operator would dawdle, pretending to be the Harveys' maid, then an intermediary would come on the line. Several people stood ready for this purpose. And among them now, unknown to Lady Harvey, was her son, John Harvey, the father of David, who had been in the house a few minutes only, having stepped straight off a military jet from Kenya. He, it was hoped, would do as a spokesman for the family. But in case Lady Harvey was required, the buzzer to her room was left connected. As soon as she heard the triple signal, she was supposed to come down and take over the call. Simultaneously, through a headphone placed to her free ear, Commissaire Daladier, talking from Paris, would advise her how to keep the Iskra on the line.

If the task had been to invent a torture specifically for Margaret Harvey, this would have been a good one: to keep up a conversation for at least four minutes, eight minutes if possible, with a different foreigner speaking in each ear and her husband's life in the balance. She had hardly ever talked on the telephone for eight consecutive minutes in her life. For her it was a useful but hostile instrument, to be kept in its place, like the television. Just as TV was for listening to particular programmes, the phone was for passing or receiving particular information, and then goodbye. Her brusqueness on the line was famous: a joke to her friends, a complaint of enemies, and the source of some injured feelings in the diplomatic *salons* of Brussels.

This Margaret Harvey herself had tried to explain at the previous evening's rehearsal. The plan wouldn't work, she'd said. It was too complicated. She, at least, wouldn't be able to carry it out.

Nobody really believed this until it was noticed that, although the alarm had buzzed in her bedroom, Lady Harvey had not come down.

Several people dashed up the stairs at once. When they burst through the door, they found her standing quite still.

"Quiet!" she said to them imperiously, raising her hand. And then, to their total consternation, she picked up the phone by her bed, which was not, at that moment, connected to anything.

They tried to tell her she was on the wrong extension, she

should be downstairs. But too many people spoke at once. She didn't understand. So one of them started to tug her towards the door. She resisted crossly. Then Lady Brent-Ewing, wife of the British Ambassador to Belgium, dashed in from the spare room and showed why some of the junior staff at the embassy had given her the name Bloody Mary. Barking like a sergeant-major, all kindness for the moment abandoned, she got the elder woman on the move. The whole group, moving in a cluster, had started down for the kitchen, when, from below, came voices raised, and a single desperate shout, immediately followed by the burly figure of John Harvey, who abandoned his position at the switchboard and dashed upstairs to his mother.

"John!" she cried, seemingly not very pleased at this unexpected appearance. "What are you doing here?"

He made no reply, but dashed straight past her into the bedroom, where he picked up the phone she herself had just dropped, listened momentarily, then cupped his hand over the mouthpiece and held it out.

"Quick," he said, "take it here. You're connected now."

"You take it."

"I already have, mother. It's you they want, and they won't wait. Now, quick, come on, speak. Say anything, before they ring off."

And so came the terrible, ludicrous climax of Margaret Harvey's long career as a politician's wife. She took the receiver. As she did so, it rattled against her cheek. Her eyes, comprehending, filled with fear.

"Hello. This is Margaret Harvey speaking. Who are you?"

Outside in the van, in the operations room at the Quai des Orfèvres and the secret monitoring centre near Les Invalides, Paris, tape-recorders listened and turned.

"This is the Iskra," said a woman's voice; stern, rather gruff, almost hoarse, speaking English with a heavy French accent. "We have your husband. We shall kill him unless our demands are accepted."

"Please, let me speak to him." Lady Harvey's response was instinctive. Then, prompted by a mutter in the background, she added: "What demands?"

The woman refused to answer the question. The line was silent.

"What do you want?" asked Lady Harvey, going on quickly. "Please tell me your demands. Hello? Do you hear me?"

Still there was no reply from the woman. Then, to everyone's surprise, a man's voice came on. "Hello. Is that you, Margaret?"

A catch of breath at Lady Harvey's end. "Patrick?"

"Yes, this is me. Hello there."

"Patrick! Thank God! Are you . . ."

"Yes, all right. A bit warm, that's all." He was stopped, then went on: "Please, don't speak. There isn't time. They want me to read off the headline in this morning's *Figaro* – to prove I'm alive, you know. So I will now do that. Are you ready?"

In Brussels, in Paris, every listener heard the rustle of a newspaper, and those who were professionals appreciatively noted the skill with which Sir Patrick was stalling, seeming to be brisk while not actually getting along very fast with the business. By mentioning heat he had dropped a clue to his location, and now he added another, by quite superfluously giving the paper's edition number and time of going to press. Then he started on the headline. *"Disparition de Patrick Harvey. Attentat mystérieux en Touraine . . ."* His voice tailed off in a manner which implied there was more to come. And that was possible, given the usual length of French headlines. But he had been interrupted, by someone who had realised this business had lasted long enough. The paper was snatched from his hand, it seemed, and immediately they heard him say in a fast, low voice: "Tell Otto to go right ahead, Margaret. No deals –"

Sir Patrick was stopped by a sharp, indecipherable sound. It could have been a blow or a report, the crack of a whip, the slam of a door, something snapping or dropping – perhaps the phone itself.

Immediately the woman came back on the line, more harsh than before. "Believe me, he will be executed," she said. Then her voice went up to a shout. "At eight hours tomorrow, you hear? You have one day, that is all."

At which point Margaret Harvey at last remembered her lines. "Please tell me clearly and slowly what it is that you want," she said in a high commanding voice. "I will take it down in writing, so there is no mistake. I have a pencil and paper here. And then I will pass your demands to the people concerned . . . Will that be all right?"

The woman made no reply.

"Do you hear me?"

Still there was silence.

"Hello? Are you there?"

But Rosa Berg had gone. The line was dead.

The next voice heard was that of Commissaire Daladier, speaking from Paris. With grave, deliberate politeness the French policeman thanked Lady Harvey and her son for their help. From the moment of link-up to disconnection, he said, the call had lasted one minute and forty seconds. It had been traced to the area exchange in Bordeaux, but no further.

Afterwards a hush fell upon the house in Kraainem, Belgium. Nobody dared to speak. Margaret Harvey had sunk to a sitting position on the bed, erect, staring forward, still holding the phone. Her son took it from her, hung up, then sat beside her in silence. Even Mary Brent-Ewing said nothing. Showing some diplomatic tact, the Ambassador's wife withdrew from the room and took everyone with her except John Harvey.

Left alone together, mother and son did not speak for a while.

John Harvey was a merchant banker in his forties, with receding hair and bulky figure: a more ponderous man than Sir Patrick, in both body and mind. Though tanned from watching hippos, still dressed for safari, he was not an adventurer of any sort. He seemed to make a point of worthy dullness. His face, even in middle age, had the wary, withdrawn expression of a boy who has learned to grow up with a famous father and a rather less attentive mother than modern psychologists recommend. He had survived his parents; and now he was bringing up his own son, David, in the sort of warm, dull home from which dynastic brilliance repeats. It was probably his biggest achievement.

However his mother was aware of him now, and glad of his presence. Reaching out suddenly, she took his hand and held it in her own. "Was that our fault, John?"

"No," said John Harvey easily, being something of an expert in the assertion that all was for the best and no one to blame for anything. "The woman was too clever. She gave us ten seconds to put you on the line, so she knew exactly how long she'd got."

"Of course, she'll kill him. She sounded quite mad, don't you think?"

"It is much too early to assume that," said John Harvey

548

sternly, correcting his mother in the firm, judicious voice that filled his bank to the brim with deposits. "Let's wait and hear what she wants."

"She didn't say, did she?"

"She'll tell someone."

But Margaret Harvey had a deep premonition, unreachable by logic, that she would never talk to her husband again. "Oh the poor, stupid *fool!*" she burst out in anguish a moment later. "Do you realise that for once, just once in his life, the only thing he had to do was talk to *me*, about anything at all, for just a few minutes?"

"Yes, he needs practice at that," said John Harvey, switching to a strenuously jocular manner. "I'll have to have a word with him when he gets back."

This effort to lighten the mood fell flat. Lady Harvey stood up and walked round the windows, yanking open each curtain in turn. When the room was full of light, she stood looking down into the garden and said to her son without turning her head: "Please, go downstairs, will you, and bring me up a strong black coffee? You'll find some rolls in the larder."

Such rebuffs were a very familiar thing to John Harvey, who was used to the fact that his mother, so quick to fling bricks at her husband, would not accept a word against the great man from any other person; and that included her son. As to the great man himself, well, he would surely survive, thought the portly merchant banker, descending to the kitchen. And that thought stopped him on the stairs. It struck John Harvey there and then, on the stairs of the house in Kraainem, that he could not believe and never had been able to believe that his famous, brilliant father would die.

2

Still pulling fresh clothes from the case she had packed for Tours, Laura had put on a smart grey suit with a nice suggestion of executive stripe. The jacket had sharp mannish shoulders, but underneath it she was wearing a frilly white blouse, the opposite of businesslike, with a cameo pinned at the throat.

She likes to keep the customers guessing, thought Kemble, still lying on the bed in an off-white linen kimono he had found in the all-white bathroom. Ten hours in the home of these rich French anti-chromatics had left him with a wierd sense of visual deprivation. He had a strong desire to go out and stare at a London bus.

Instead he watched Laura apply a deep red lipstick. And then her gloss was complete. Quickly, neatly, she put away her bits of cosmetic equipment and stood for his inspection, turning circles on the fluffy white carpet.

"Will I do?"

"You will do," he said with a smile. "In fact, for a pair of tired old tycoons, I would say you were probably too much."

She was like a very expensive chocolate, he thought to himself. What made you want to eat her was the hard, sharp shell as much as the soft, sweet centre. At first he had thought she was too hard to bite through; and then last night, to his slight consternation, his teeth had sunk into teenage marshmallow. But this morning she was, after all, just right. Sharp and sweet, hard and soft. Seeing her now, packaged to go, he wanted to undo the wrapper and take another mouthful. But none of this would do to say aloud, not to this girl. So instead he just thought about it, watching her legs as she left the room.

Spread around him on the bed were that morning's news-

550

papers, the British, the French, and others in languages that only Laura could read. She had gone down to the square and bought the whole European press before he woke up. The kidnap of Harvey and the cause of it, the car merger, were screamed across every front page in massive double headlines, some the tallest and heaviest type that Kemble had seen in his working life. After she had gone to the kitchen he went back to scanning his own stuff in *The Times*, swearing at each editorial cut. But there weren't too many. Paid by the inch, he was rich. He was also famous: the author of the news in one paper, a subordinate subject of it in all the rest. He had come to Europe to score. He had scored. And it felt good. He slapped the layers of print in pleasure, then lay back and lit himself a cigarette.

In two different parts of the apartment Laura had a radio and television on, both of them rattling out news. Not understanding French at such speed, Kemble wandered into the *salon* and watched the TV for pictorial clues to the latest development. The set was of the miniature sort, with a screen only six inches square, black and white naturally. One by one the characters left in the play flitted over it. Mug shots came up of Rosa Berg and her Dutchman, Joop Janssen; then the other two kidnappers still on the loose, Stephen Murdoch and Mario Salandra. There was an extract of Daladier and Riemeck, facing the press last night. Next came a glimpse of the car chiefs, Clabon and Guidotti, conferring at the Motor Show in Paris last year. Then the young French female announcer, shuffling paper, receiving fresh reports by telephone, found a pause long enough to introduce the star of the crisis.

Harvey's face was first seen in still, then clips came up showing various points of his career: Harvey as a young man with Churchill in the war, on the hustings as a rising politician, entering Number Ten himself as Prime Minister. His triumphs in office flicked by in quick succession, and then he was a Knight of the Garter, looking deeply uncomfortable in a floppy velvet ostrich-plumed hat as he walked in procession at St. George's Chapel, Windsor. The last clip showed him addressing the European Youth Conference at Strasbourg. It was hard to tell on so small a screen, but to Kemble it looked as if some of the youths were asleep.

The RTF lady reappeared at her desk, still in charge of the world; made a few remarks too quick for mortal ear, then withdrew for what appeared to be a live outside shot of the Harvey's house in Kraainem, Belgium. This was followed by another, of the present scene at the Ritz Hotel, Paris.

"Hey, look at this," called Kemble to Laura. "How are your tycoons going to get out? Not to mention the poor old prof."

The hotel's front entrance was blocked by a crowd of two or three hundred people, mostly newsmen and photographers.

Laura came over to the set. "The *flics* will just seal up the square until they've got away." She glanced at him, deadpan, then sashayed away. "No fooling about with freedom of the press in France, you know. This is a civilised country."

Kemble put out his cigarette and followed her into the colour-free kitchen. "I'll take two eggs," he said, "sunny side up."

Turning with a white-toothed smile, she propelled a steaming mug across the white counter. "Coffee, instant, one cup. No sugar, no milk."

"Ha!" he said, shook his head and sighed. "The voice of Eve down the ages."

"Wrong, brother, wrong. Eve does fry-ups. Always has."

"But now she is taking industrial action."

"*C'est ça.*" Still smiling, Laura picked up her own mug. "I'm really not sure, you know whether I can take all this cock in the morning. Now shut up and sit down here. Find Choisy le Roi."

She had spread a map of Paris on the counter. Kemble pored over it, perched on a stool. "Choisy le Roi," he said, "Choisy le Roi," casting his eye around the outer suburbs. "Is that where they're meeting?"

"Yes," she said, leaning over him in a waft of scent. "Twelve, Rue Darthé, Choisy le Roi. I've never heard of it. Must be miles out."

"Why so far?"

She shrugged and turned away. "Apparently the Commission owns a house there. Riemeck's man rang to say a car would pick me up. Bring my own pad."

"So it's business as usual."

"The world goes on."

"The merger goes on, and Eve will keep the record. *Vive le merger.*" Kemble lost interest in the map, unable not to notice, even through the sweet reek of lilies of the valley, that the kitchen was filling with a warm and bready aroma. "Are you sure you're not cooking?"

Laura put her hand in a padded glove and moved to the oven, bending to open it. "You're not going to make a *Hausfrau* out of me, you know, just by waving your magic wand. However, in the circumstances, I thought . . . you deserved . . . some of these."

Grimacing from the heat, she straightened up and banged down a baking pan, in which lay curled four steaming *croissants*, perhaps cooked a little too much for their good. She had bought them when she went to get the papers, she explained as she got together plates, knives, butter and jam. "Come on, let's eat them outside."

Mugs in hand, plates balanced on knees, they sat side by side on one of the balconies, just wide enough for two, which hung above the Avenue du President Wilson. Below them Paris was already roaring, jostling, hooting to work. High up, where they sat, small birds were screeching and swooping about the steep leaded rooftops. Everything seemed to be in exuberant motion, but further off, over the river, the Eiffel Tower stood in a still summer sky, without a cloud, without a breeze.

Kemble felt on top of the world. He was alive with expectation. Or rather, to be exact, a number of different, half-formed expectations were stirring inside him; not only hopes, desires, but some trepidation as well. Close at hand all was delightful, as in the view. But further off hung the promise of a storm.

A break in the actual weather was forecast; and people were waiting for it in a mood of snappy tension. The papers were full of freaky behaviour by animals and men, put down to the long spell of heat. They'd probably have made it the headline, Kemble thought, if the Iskra hadn't provided a better one. And who could tell where it would end? Next thing the birds would start to fly backwards and middle-aged journalists would fall in love.

His happiness was not at all spoiled by a sense of danger in the distance. Yes, he thought cheerfully, anything could happen today. As they say on those stupid cards, it could be the first day of the rest of my life. Or, God help me, it could be the last. If Daladier accepts my suggestion . . .

"I suppose you think it's just sex."

Laura, interrupting with this remark, put her hand out to his.

553

Her face was perfectly solemn, raised to the sun as though in worship.

"Well," she went on, "it was nice, of course. But really I'm just happy to share things with someone. To talk, you know, and have a few laughs. I seem to have missed . . . oh damn, there's the car."

A buzz had sounded in the flat, coming up from the concierge's office. Laura picked up the house-phone and said she was coming. Kemble went with her to the door.

"Don't shirk it, Jack, will you? Just call your wife and tell her. Then you'll feel better."

"Will I?"

"Eventually, yes."

"Eventually I won't feel anything."

"All right, be a coward, leave it. But don't run away while I'm gone."

"I won't run away." He opened the door and stood back. "*Au revoir*, Eurogirl. Have a nice day at the office."

She put on a bright expression, but immediately the smile fell off again. She rushed up against him and kissed him long on the cheek, her lips moving slowly across the surface of his face while her hand, looped around him, caressed his back. Finally she walked away to the lift. Waiting for it, she turned back and pointed a finger at him.

"And leave the place tidy. Wash up. Make the bed."

"Yes, sir. Right, sir."

Kemble stood to attention, saluting, as her head descended in the slow, creaking lift. Then she dropped from his mind. He turned back into the flat, closed the door, and immediately started to think about his next despatch to *The Times*.

To bring himself up to date, he needed another conversation with Daladier. Something had happened in the night, he was sure of it, but now the Commissaire had turned evasive. Twice already, since waking, Kemble had telephoned the Quai des Orfèvres. Each time he had been put off. Now, at 8.45, he tried again. He was told that the Commissaire would call him back.

"How soon?"

"When he is ready, monsieur."

Disgruntled, uneasy, Kemble brewed another coffee. Then, cross-legged on the bed, he checked the new points picked up in the Ritz.

554

Grouped in one list on his pad were the things he could tell. *Merger goes on, cost four billion, joint car at 1500, Commission to choose top man.* Underneath were the two facts he'd promised to hold. *BMG Pilot to be scrapped, workers to choose two directors in five.*

For a long moment Kemble stared at these two latter points, assessing the impact of each in turn. Important, were they? Yes, they were pretty hot stuff. But he would hold them as promised. Clabon was a pretty nice guy, after all. And Clabon had a far bigger secret to protect. Indeed the chance might arise to put a little pressure on John Clabon, nice guy as he was, by telling him he couldn't have all three secrets. If he wanted to keep the first two, he should open up about the battery car.

Thinking over these tactical options, Kemble relaxed into drowsiness. There was no rush to call *The Times*. The presses of the workers' cooperative wouldn't roll for another twelve hours. In London it was only eight o'clock.

In Bethesda, Maryland, it was three in the morning.

And that was no time to tell a good woman you weren't coming back. He took his hand off the phone and lay back, to see how bad he could feel. He thought about the meals she had cooked for him, the clothes she had washed; those cool tissues she used to dab his face with in the huge summer heat. The way she cried in bad movies, cried when he drank. Cried all the time.

He closed his eyes.

When he opened them, half an hour had passed. The clock beside the bed said 9.45 and the telephone was ringing between his legs. Expecting Daladier, he picked it up. "Yes? Hello?"

"Who are you?" said a man's voice. English, not friendly.

"Kemble's the name. Jack Kemble."

"Oho, the Yankee from *The Times*. I thought it was you. Is Comrade Laura there?"

"No, she's out. Who is this speaking?"

"My name's Murdoch."

Kemble sat up in the bed, very carefully, holding his breath, in that odd way he had of not wishing to upset a lucky break by any precipitate movement. "Hello, Murdoch," he said with equal care, in the voice he would have used if called by a long-lost friend. "Can I help?"

Murdoch spoke away from the phone, consulting someone

else at his end. Then he came back. "Yes, you'll do, scribbler. Get out your pad and listen to me. Here are the terms for Harvey's life."

3

Choisy le Roi, though swallowed by the outward spread of Paris, had been swallowed whole, and could still be recognised as the small provincial town it once had been. At the heart of the drab modern suburb that bore its name, old Choisy stood almost intact. The church and the *hôtel de ville* were still in position, either side of a handsome square, and out at one end of the principal street was a large nineteenth-century mansion, set in a park. On the site of this house had once stood a château where the kings of France came to hunt. Now the big house belonged to the Brussels Commission, who were turning it into the Institute of European Law.

And 12 Rue Darthé had been bought as well, as a residence for the Institute's Director. This was an altogether more modest place, though still in the old part of Choisy. Rue Darthé was one of several similar residential streets built around the turn of the century. The houses, each standing in just enough ground to be detached, were tall and thin, with steep slate roofs and ornate manorial touches of the sort which please the provincial bourgeoisie. No. 12 was slightly bigger than the rest, with a high wall around it and a garden, all gravelled, just big enough to take the three cars now parked in it. Outside the gate stood two gendarmes, sub-machine guns slung by straps across their shoulders, and another car was parked beside the pavement, containing four plain-clothes police. But nobody took any notice. The only thing happening in the street was a children's game. Two boys were playing frisbee, tossing the plastic disc lazily backwards and forwards while a dog barked frantically between, trying to catch it.

Despite the heat of the morning, the air inside the house was cool, almost chill. Nothing had been done to the place since it was bought, so it had the cheerless feel of a home abandoned. There were stains on the walls and cobwebs in the corners. The furniture, filmed with dust, was of the sort previous occupants leave behind. In the central room stood a plain deal table, on which were now spread heaps of official paper and several glass ashtrays, already filling up. Around the table, quite out of keeping with its rustic look, was a set of high-backed chairs, made of dark stained wood and heavily upholstered in red. And on these chairs, more out of keeping still, were all the people now taken up with the merger of BMG and Mobital.

Jack Kemble, ushered into this strange setting a few minutes after 10.30, was struck by the thought that it must have been in just such a house that the talks to end the war in Vietnam had begun. The image passed quickly, but left him feeling cold. His light-hearted mood of the morning had evaporated. And Laura, too, seemed on edge, unable or unwilling to look him in the eye while it was discussed how the Iskra had come to know her home number. Beside her were Clabon and Guidotti. At the head of the table, in the umpire's position, was Professor Doublett. But the car talk had not yet begun. This was a council of war, and the dominant presence was that of Otto Riemeck, although he was sitting slightly back from the table, without any papers, not meaning to stay. Standing by the door was Commissaire Daladier, the latest to arrive. And it was Daladier who had the room's attention at the moment.

First he told what had happened at Kraainem: the gang's call to Lady Harvey, the threat to Sir Patrick. And then he went on to exonerate Laura. It was not a matter of surprise, he was saying, that the kidnappers knew where to find her. They had probably been tracking her for months, in Paris as well as in Brussels. They would have known where she stayed in the city, and in any case must have overheard her make arrangements by telephone, from the château La Maréchale.

Daladier paused, his hands out in front of his belly, held vertical, parallel, a little apart, as he chopped the case for Laura into neat French logical slices and served it up to the table. Kemble wondered why he was making such a meal of it. No one was interested. No one suspected her. Then he saw the reason, and was touched by the Frenchman's pains. Laura herself was upset. Indeed she was terrified by this new complication. Of course there was no cause for her to worry, but she was in one of those all-over, all-purpose moods of anxiety that women do sometimes fall into. She thinks the others think she is guilty. She thinks I am going to run away and leave her. If I told her now that she takes my breath away, sitting there in her frilly white shirt and grey suit, she would say I was just a smooth talker. If I told her I'm sorry for my wife, she would scream.

"They are not fools, this Iskra," Daladier went on, speaking English. "They will not announce their demands to Lady Harvey, because that would take too much talking. In two minutes, three minutes we can trace the call – they know that. So Miss Jenkinson gets the tinkle."

Laura lifted her head with a wan, relieved expression. Slowly, uncertainly, she smiled in reply to Kemble's wink. Then Lucy Maclean, the non-speaking blonde from Scotland, came into the room and walked round the table laying down a typewritten sheet in front of each person present, top copies for Riemeck and Daladier, flimsy carbons for the rest.

KIDNAPPERS' DEMANDS

As stated by telephone to J. Kemble, 9.45, Monday 22 July

1. *All surviving members of the Iskra, now held in jail, to be released and flown to political asylum in a socialist country – this to be clearly seen on French television.*
2. *The present negotiations for the merger of BMG and Mobital, with the mass redundancies envisaged, to be suspended – this to be clearly stated on French television by both chief executives and the President of the European Commission.*
3. *A public undertaking to be given, by the governments of Britain and Italy, guaranteeing full employment and production in both companies.*
4. *A public commitment to be given, by the chairmen and boards of directors, that both these companies will be opened to full democratic control by the workforce, and their future, together or separate, decided within this framework.*

There was a minute of silence while everyone studied the Iskra's terms for Harvey's life. To Kemble the wait seemed long, and the hush of suspense was intensified by the small sounds that broke it – the barking of the dog in the street, the shouts of the boys playing frisbee, the rumble of planes out at Orly. Conscious of the luck, still holding, that had brought him to this secret conclave, he made careful visual notes on each person present. As he did so he had the warm, flooding sense of being in just the right place at the right time, with no competitors present. Here, at Choisy, was the news.

Daladier was showing most strain. Although he had shaved and found a clean shirt, the Commissaire was still in the same dark suit, now rumpled and speckled with ash. His movements had grown a little twitchy. He kept wiping his thick moustache downwards – as if it could possibly go up – and chewed on his pipe instead of lighting it. His face had the feverish, obsessed concentration of a general locked into a battle which could go either way. Bags had inflated under his eyes, but the rest of him appeared to have shrunk very slightly in volume, like a barrage balloon losing air.

Clabon was a study in reds. His rumpled reddish hair, red face and red eyes testified to excess of red wine and a night among the red lights of Paris. One of the marks left by the punches of his workers was still red, where his lip had almost split. But he was in fighting form nonetheless; missing nothing, giving nothing away. The bull of BMG, if provoked, would see red.

Guidotti, tired or fresh, looked the same. Silver-locked, sleepy-eyed, his face was as wrinkled as his clothes were not. This morning he was a marvel of elegance, cool in a pale grey suit with a small pink rose in one lapel. The flower, especially, caught Kemble's eye: a magnificent gesture of insouciance.

Doublett was a mess, dark and shaggy, hot and bothered in a buff linen jacket of the sort worn by British professors in tropical climes. On the other hand he had settled in. Having been recruited to the crisis, he belonged to its cast as much as the others. And now that the crisis had engaged his intellect, it seemed that he might be a force. Having read through the Iskra's demands more quickly than anyone else, he stared off into a corner, in a manner which made it almost possible to hear the great multitude of alternative consequences rushing for inspection through his head.

Riemeck, as professors go, was unusually sleek. His tie was of boldly patterned silk and his blue mohair suit, which shone when he moved, was almost spivvy. But the moment that he spoke, all suggestion of flashiness vanished. His manner, though commanding instant attention, was modest, calm and quiet; entirely without self-regard.

"Please tell us again, Mr. Kemble, in what way exactly these terms were delivered."

Kemble repeated his story in detail. The wording of the terms, he said, was Stephen Murdoch's own. The leader of BMG's rebel workers had spoken on the phone without a pause, obviously reading off each demand from a ready-prepared English text.

"Yes," growled Clabon. "I recognise the style."

It was Murdoch who'd delivered the Iskra's terms, Kemble went on. But after that the woman herself had come on the line – Rosa Berg.

"Her English isn't so hot. But she made herself understood. She said these demands were so far private – a message direct from her to you. But at two this afternoon she'll release them to the press. And tomorrow, if there's still no action, Harvey will be shot."

There was a silence, broken by Riemeck. "That was all?"

"No, not quite. When she releases the terms this afternoon, she's going to add a statement to the workers of both companies. She'll urge them to stop work and occupy their factories, until they get control."

Clabon, hearing this, put his hands to his head, as though struck by a migraine. "Holy smoke," he said, "that's all mine need. Strike and occupy – the poor buggers just might be daft enough to try it."

Guidotti's face, too, was long as he stared at the surface of the table. "In Italy also this could cause an explosion. The Iskra – the spark. They have named themselves well."

But Riemeck refused to join the tragic chorus. He wanted only facts. "And the threat, Mr. Kemble? Please tell us again what this woman said."

"She said she would stick to the time she'd given Lady Harvey. You have until eight tomorrow morning, Tuesday, to act on all four demands. And she wants you to do it in a way she can see on TV. If she isn't satisfied, Harvey will be shot."

"She made no mention of negotiations?"

"Yes, she did. She ruled them out. No further discussion, she said. Either you do what she asks or Harvey dies."

Riemeck nodded, seeming grateful for clarity, however grim. "Was there anything else?"

"I asked her how she was going to announce her terms to the press."

"And what was her reply?" interjected Daladier, keenly interested in this.

"She said she has friends who can do it. You haven't caught us all, she said. Her words."

A moment of confused reaction followed, several people speaking at once, until they were pulled up by Riemeck in that surprising voice of authority which was not yet one day old. "Come, let us not waste time on inessentials," he said with some sharpness, and peered down carefully at his watch. "We have twenty-one hours, exactly, to save Sir Patrick's life. So, let us talk about this now." Lifting his head, he twisted in his seat to look at Daladier, who was standing behind him. "First, if you please, we must hear a report from you, Monsieur le Commissaire. What can you tell us about the progress of the search?"

Kemble waited for the answer eagerly, convinced there had been some fresh break since his own departure from the Quai des Orfèvres. But nothing had happened after all, it emerged. Daladier confessed to a night of frustration. Since the arrests at the Babylone, he told the meeting, there had been a total impasse. And one severe disappointment.

"We were hoping for some information from Bensaïd, the Algerian we took at the café. But he did not talk."

No comment was made on this.

"So," Daladier summed up, "our search continues, and it is now concentrated in the environs of Bordeaux. But I cannot promise you any success. Not in twenty-one hours, or even more. I regret, but that is the truth."

He ended before they expected, then started to dig old tobacco from the bowl of his pipe with a penknife, leaning over the table to an ashtray.

"There is nothing more you can tell us?" asked Riemeck.

"Nothing more, Herr President. We have a chance of perhaps fifty-fifty. It is all."

"So what do you wish us to do?"

Daladier shrugged, still absorbed with scratching out bits of old leaf. "For us, the police, some delay would be helpful – some dialogue, if possible. This woman says she will not negotiate. But perhaps, if you make her some offer, she will hesitate, no?'' Abruptly, then, he stopped scooping and looked up, his eyes travelling round the table. ''For us, the police, that would be the best thing. Hesitation is what we desire in this woman.''

''Arnold, what do you say?''

Riemeck, after one quick nod at the Frenchman's suggestion, had turned to his fellow-professor. By this time Doublett had started to draw what appeared to be the map of an ancient naval battle on the blank side of the Iskra's typed terms. But immediately, when called on to speak, he screwed the paper up in his fist.

''We must do whatever is required to save Patrick's life,'' he replied, with none of his usual double-speak ''That is the first priority.''

No one dissented from this proposition.

''And if the police cannot find him,'' Doublett went on at speed, ''then only we can save him, by giving way to this woman's demands. But that, I think, will not be allowed. Total surrender is not an option open to us, whatever our feelings in the matter.''

Riemeck confirmed the point. It had been long agreed by the governments of Europe, he said, that none of them would ever give way to terrorist blackmail, whatever the cost in human life. The Commission itself could not break ranks. A total, public concession to the Iskra was therefore out of the question.

Doublett went on from there.

''Agreed and understood. Not total, not public. So what we are asked to consider is this. Are there available to us any partial concessions or hints of same, public or private, genuine or dissimulated, of a sort which might, by causing delay, assist the police to effect a rescue of the hostage?''

The Nuffield Professor of Ancient History took a customary pause to let persons of normal intelligence catch up with the logic of Oxford. Then, while most of them were still working hard on the question, he answered it himself.

''No.''

The word was said with a grim, regretful shake of the head.

''I have given the matter some reflection already, and that is my own conclusion. No negotiation is possible. The woman wants it so, and so she has made it. If we examine her demands, we shall find she has left us no room for manoeuvre, no room at all."

Riemeck resumed control of proceedings. "So," he said, "let us now do that, starting with the first – release of prisoners."

Each of the Iskra's demands was then considered in turn. The discussion lasted twenty minutes, from 10.45 to 11.05, and Kemble kept track of the answers. Afraid to take any notes, he recorded the meeting in his head.

1. Release of captured members of the Iskra.

An impossible demand, it was quickly agreed. No release of prisoners was article number one of international anti-terrorist practice. Daladier especially was firm on the point.

2. Present merger talks to be suspended.

Also impossible, a precise public promise having just been given that the talks would go on. As to partial concessions, there was only one thing which might be said. Any loss of jobs arising from the merger would be discussed with the unions. But that, it was agreed, would not be enough to melt the heart of Rosa Berg.

3. Guaranteed support for both companies by the British and Italian governments.

Also impossible. In fact the whole purpose of the merger, as perceived by Brussels, was to avoid this. Intervention by governments was not the right way to save BMG and Mobital. And it certainly wouldn't save Harvey. The discussion, getting gloomier, moved to the last of the Iskra's demands.

4. Workers' control.

On this, agreement came harder in Choisy le Roi. Each person present had a different stance, Kemble noticed, the gaps between them appearing more plainly as each spoke up on the subject. Doublett led off by denouncing the whole idea. Industrial democracy, he said, was a dangerous absurdity in all its forms, and to introduce it here would be a disaster. Even to pretend flexibility on the point would lead to all manner of trouble.

Clabon, though less dogmatic, agreed. Anything said on this now would look like weakness, and would be hard to retract later. There were men in BMG who might exploit it.

Guidotti's opinion began by sounding similar. In Mobital, he said, the balance of power between workers and management was delicate, and should not be tampered with.

"However, on this point, I think it is necessary we give away something."

Kemble saw Laura's head lift in surprise. Concessions from this man she had not expected.

"This woman, Rosa Berg, has been intelligent," Guidotti went on through a cloud of cigarette smoke. "Please notice, she does not demand that there is no merger at all. The merger should be decided by the workers, she says. And to some people that will seem not such a stupid idea. If we refuse even to talk about it, we shall be criticised."

Kemble was watching Riemeck's face, but could catch no hint of the presidential verdict to come. The German sat plump, pink and blank as the elegant Italian concluded his speech.

"On Saturday we were talking in private," Guidotti wound up. "We hoped to settle this matter before the world heard of it. But that has changed. Now it is this woman Berg who is sitting with us here, at this table. She has made other proposals, and all the world is listening. We cannot say nothing, do nothing. That would not be intelligent."

Guidotti stopped there. For the third time Riemeck nodded in thanks. No further views were required. It was time to declare his own. There was a pause while he wiped his spectacles: a nervous mannerism now occurring every few minutes.

"You are right," he said, answering Guidotti, "we cannot do nothing. But Arnold, I regret, is also right. There is nothing we can do."

For a moment the meeting considered this unhelpful paradox. No one spoke. Then Kemble, to his surprise, was addressed by Riemeck.

"You will please use your discretion in reporting these proceedings."

"Yes. Of course."

"And now, perhaps, you can assist us."

With that Riemeck glanced at his watch and stood up. He seemed to be waiting for something. He walked to the window, peered into the garden, came back to the table. Finally, still standing, the President announced his plan. As he did so he stared at Kemble, the unfinished conversation between them promoted to a general address.

"This is now a matter to be conducted in the press, is it not? These wars, I mean to say, between terrorists and authority – they are always won or lost in the media." He paused and raised one finger, like a schoolmaster. "So, perhaps here there is an advantage to us – one thing we can do."

"Meaning what?" asked Clabon impatiently.

Riemeck, unruffled, turned to answer, his blue mohair suit changing colour in the light. "I shall talk to the press before the woman does. I shall tell them myself what she asks, and why we cannot agree to it. And then I shall present our own structure for the merger. In this way the public will hear our view before they hear hers. What do you think of that, Mr. Kemble?"

"I think it's a good idea."

"Yeah, I bet you do," Clabon said sourly. Then, to Riemeck: "Surely you're not going to give this fellow any more scoops?"

"Scoops?"

"Exclusive stories."

"No," replied Riemeck, understanding, "there will not be any scoops. Mr. Kemble will print the same story as the others. Only first he will help us to prepare it. Yes?"

Kemble could only nod in obedience, though dismayed to see his scoop snatched away. By not phoning London straight after the Ritz, he had lost his chance to blow the details of the merger to *The Times*. Nor could he now pump Clabon for details of the battery car. He had, in fact, made the classic error of second-rate war correspondents. Instead of observing the battle from an outside position, he had been drawn into the troops on one side.

Riemeck expected nothing less. "So," he said without thanks, "let us prepare a statement."

Discussion began energetically. The problem was to crack up the virtues of the merger without revealing too much of its detail. Neither Clabon nor Guidotti were ready to come fully into the open; nor was Riemeck. So vague forms of words were drafted to reassure the workers that some form of consultation would be provided, some protection of jobs – the two points Rosa would strike at. The time drifted on to 11.25. Everyone was pleased to be doing something, but as the meeting went on it became ever clearer that there was, in truth, nothing to be done. As Doublett had warned, no response could be found which had any chance of saving Harvey's life.

And this struck Kemble more forcibly at the moment he heard a car arrive, bringing Lady Harvey from Orly. The poor blundering bastards, he thought to himself, looking round the others at the table, they really have boxed themselves in. Thanks to their tactics, the hostage has less than a day to live. And here comes the hostage's wife.

But what upset Margaret Harvey was the smoke.

"Please open a window," she said, sitting down. "This is really disgusting."

And she had a point. The air in the room had been fouled by two cigarettes, one cigar, and the Commissaire's pipe, which smelled like smouldering peat. Daladier quickly passed it to a subordinate, who took it, still smoking, from the room. The others used ashtrays. The shutters were pushed further back, the door left open.

"Forgive me, Commissaire. But after that flight I do not feel strong."

"You look very well, madame."

And indeed she did look surprisingly well, Kemble thought. Her thick white hair was firmly in order and there was no pallor in her pink-cheeked, robust, outdoor face. She wore no make-up. She was marked by lines of sadness, but they had been a long time in the making, and gave an impression of strength. Her eyes were clear. She was dressed for the weather in a plain cotton frock, many years out of date.

It had been Daladier's idea that she should come. Her son had been left in Belgium, to take any further threatening calls, while Lady Harvey herself was brought closer, to be on hand for instant consultation. As in a case of dangerous surgery, things might have to be done requiring permission from the next of kin. The Commissaire explained this tactfully, and brought her up to date on the search. Riemeck handed her the list of the gang's demands. She started to read them, then pushed the sheet away with a shake of her head.

567

"Please," she said, "tell me yourself."

"It is a confused situation," Riemeck began, more ill at ease than at any point so far. "There are several possibilities which we have been examining . . ."

She listened in cold, calm silence until he had finished. "You mean," she said, "there's nothing you can do."

Riemeck met her eye. "Very little."

"Unless he is found, the woman will kill him."

Riemeck nodded bravely. "It is what you must prepare for, Margaret. I am sorry."

She stared at him, so steady and clear of eye that she seemed, momentarily, a much younger woman than she was. She had grasped the situation now, errors and all. The others looked down or away as Riemeck, alone and erect, awaited her wrath. But then her eyes dulled into stoic resignation.

"Oh yes," she said, "I'm prepared. And really it's not very complicated, is it? You've heard what he told me on the phone this morning?"

"Yes. We have heard a tape."

"Tell Otto to go right ahead, he said. No deals. So, Otto, you had better do that. Go ahead, no deals. And I'll support you, if that's what you want." She stopped, then added in a lower voice: "But please don't expect me to cheer."

4

Soon after that the meeting broke up. Only those involved in the merger – the businessmen, Laura, Doublett – remained in hiding at Choisy. The rest dispersed back to Paris. Lady Harvey was taken to the residence of the British Ambassador. Riemeck and his staff went to the office of the Commission, modest premises in Avenue Victor Hugo, where they planned to hold a press conference at noon. Daladier and Kemble, travelling together in the BRVP command car, returned to police head-quarters at the Quai des Orfèvres.

This was Daladier's own suggestion, and Kemble was glad to accept it, still hoping to keep on the inside of the French police operation. That was what counted now. A huge hunt was being set up to find the Iskra's hideout, believed to be somewhere in south-western France. And time was short. If Rosa Berg kept her promise, only twenty hours and twenty-two minutes re-mained before Harvey was killed.

As Margaret Harvey had been quick to see, her husband's predicament was perfectly, brutally simple. Either the French would get him out or they wouldn't. Nothing else that anyone could do, certainly not Otto Riemeck's press conference, would make a scrap of difference. And so here in this car, Kemble thought, at Daladier's side, was the right place to be at the moment. Somehow the Commissaire's coat-tails had to be clung to, from now until the end.

"It's all on you then," he said as they drove away. "Tough shit."

The expression momentarily puzzled the Frenchman. Then he nodded, with the same strange cheerfulness he had shown on the phone the night before. "To this, my friend, we in the French police are accustomed."

"Think you'll find him?"

"I think it is possible."

"Chances? Off the record?"

"Fifty to fifty, as I have said – off the record." Daladier, still evasive, if jolly, stabbed his thumb over his shoulder at the suburb of Choisy, disappearing fast behind. "The old lady, Harvey's wife – she was very fine, no? Very British. This I admire."

"She made good copy. Wait while I remember it." Kemble put down Margaret Harvey verbatim, then held his pad out at arm's length, as if he were judging a picture. "This I admire."

Daladier smiled at him, amused. "You are writing a book?"

The question, Kemble thought, was not quite so casual as it was made to sound. "Yes," he said, answering it lightly, "of course I'm writing a book. Why? Do you want to be in it?"

"I hope I am in it already."

"You're in. But to do a proper job I'll have to stay close."

Daladier nodded, now frankly serious. "The difficulty is that I need a reason. You must assist in some way."

"Well, there is one way," Kemble said, referring to a previous suggestion of his own.

But the conversation ended there, the Commissaire seeming to forget it as other matters pressed for his attention. In the front passenger seat an officer of the BRVP, wearing headphones, was continually taking radio messages, scribbling each one on a memo pad and passing it back to his chief as he started to take the next. Daladier had kept on reading these sheets while he talked. Now he dictated rapid replies, pausing between each one as his words were repeated into the radio. And all this time the car was hurtling into Paris, preceded by another car of the same type which cut a path through the traffic with flashing light and hee-haw siren. Kemble stared at the faces and buildings flashing past, and was thinking of something else entirely when Daladier spoke to him again.

"*D'accord*. I shall keep you with me."

"You will? Well, thanks."

"But you must do exactly what I say, not more and not less, until this matter is concluded. Your mission will be to assist the French police, you understand? You will have no contact with your paper unless I allow it. And you will only tell those facts which I authorise."

"I understand."

"You accept these conditions?"

Just as long as it suits me, thought Kemble, and not a second longer. "Yes," he said, "I accept them."

Daladier stared at him thoughtfully, then seemed to lose interest again, turning away to look out of the window. "Good," he said. "So that is agreed. And now there is something I shall tell you, not for your paper. We have found the Dutchman."

"What! You've caught him?"

"No, of course not. He is under surveillance."

"When did this happen?"

"Yesterday night."

"I thought there was something."

"We picked him up on a train to Bordeaux. And now he is in a hotel there. We are watching where he will go next."

"He'll take you to the hideout," Kemble said. "This is good news."

"Perhaps."

"But why didn't you tell them? Back there, I mean." Kemble thumbed over his shoulder at Choisy. "You didn't want to raise any hopes, I suppose."

"That is one reason."

"And you don't want this break to get out."

Daladier nodded. And then, quite casually, he added a third reason. "I also hoped that they would negotiate. If they are very afraid for Harvey, I was thinking, they will make an offer to Rosa Berg. And this will give us more time."

Kemble was stunned by the ruthlessness of this calculation. And then, remembering the courage of old girl Harvey, he was annoyed. "My God," he said, "you really are . . ."

"Tough shit?"

"Yeah. Right."

"The French police are not sentimental, my friend. Put that in your book."

"Okay, okay. I'll write the book, you do your bloody job."

The Commissaire nodded in agreement, his face expressing no hint of perturbation. "Yes," he said, "that is the arrangement," and went back to work on the radio.

At the Quai des Orfèvres there was pandemonium. The crowd of press had multiplied many times over, swelled by swarms of British, come to cover the fate of their former Prime Minister. Several of them recognised their colleague.

"Good God, it's Kemble! Where have you been, you old lush?"

"Talk, Jack! You owe me one."

"Where's Harvey? Is he dead?"

"Come on, Jack, spread it around! What's going on?"

Kemble, stepping out of the car, pushed through them, himself now the tight-lipped celebrity. "Relax, boys, you're in the wrong place. Statement from Riemeck coming up at midday. Now, come along, let me pass here. Let's have a path for the Thunderer, please. Make way for the people's paper."

"And where the hell are you going?"

"Inside."

"Oh? What for?"

"Assisting the Frog police, old sport. I'm a witness, remember?"

Kemble pushed on up the steps. They turned away from him then, as they spotted Daladier behind. But the Commissaire also had nothing to say. The whole raucous crowd were referred to the Commission's offices, 103 Avenue Victor Hugo. Some of them didn't believe it. Others immediately set off at a run, hunting taxis. A taxi appeared. They fought for it. A woman fell down in the street.

Kemble and Daladier passed through glass doors and into the lobby. When they were alone in the lift, the Commissaire raised his eyes to the ceiling and said with a smile: "So whose job is the most bloody?"

The ops room was just as Kemble had left it, except that the single green marker on the map, indicating contact with a member of the Iskra, had moved from Paris to Bordeaux.

Joop Janssen, still using his Arab identity, was now in a sleazy hotel on the waterfront, a district frequented by merchant seamen and dock workers, drug traders, prostitutes, smugglers. He had gone to the hotel at dawn, directly from Bordeaux railway station, and had been there all morning, shut up in his room. Since getting off the train from Paris he had met no one and made no phone calls. He had not received or delivered any messages. Inspector Jacques Biffaud, deputy chief of the BRVP, had the hotel staked out with a team of twenty people, some watching and listening, more ready to follow. But there was nothing to report. Janssen's purpose at the moment, it seemed, was simply to get more sleep.

Sooner or later, some time this day, the Dutchman was bound to make a move. And then, whatever he did, the BRVP would be ready for him, assisted by local police and gendarmerie, who knew every cranny of the quayside district. Standing by was a crack team of shadows, ready to take up pursuit if Janssen left the city. Bordeaux was one of his haunts, and a good place for him to be at the moment. A Cuban-crewed ship was in port from Angola. An Algerian vessel was due in with peanuts, and another, from Guinea, was unloading baux-ite. Downstream, in the deep-water channel, a Libyan tanker was pumping oil into a refinery. All four ships were under close watch.

Bordeaux itself was surrounded by roadblocks, and standing by on a runway at Mérignac Airport, ready to scramble into trucks and helicopters, was France's squad of anti-terrorist commandos, known as the GIGN. If the rescue of Harvey came to a shoot-out, the GIGN would do the shooting.

Kemble, who was told of these dispositions quite freely, began to add them up. In and around Bordeaux at this moment, he reckoned, there were something over 400 operatives of French law enforcement, all of them waiting for the Dutchman in Room 23, Pension de la Mer, to wake up and get out of bed.

The question was where, when he woke, would he go? Or would someone come to him? One way or another, Joop Janssen must soon make contact with his colleagues of the kidnap. And here was the specially dangerous problem. The only way to find Harvey was to let Janssen join the rest of the gang; on the other hand, if that reunion took place, the odds against Harvey's safety would worsen. At the moment the Iskra were without their professional, and Janssen himself was equipped with no more than a hand-gun. But Rosa, wherever she was hidden, had an arsenal. A description of the ordnance in her box had come from Hal Fawcett, whose recollections had been sharpened overnight by consultation with a pair of weapons experts, one French and one from the US Army. The consequent list was put in Kemble's hands.

Mulloy AP shrapnel mines, 4
Claymores, NATO, 2
Smoke grenades, estimated 6
M26 grenades, 2 boxes (12)

Viking pump gun, ball ammo
Armalite sniper's rifle, .233
2 Kalashnikov assault rifles, AK 47

Skorpion .32 machine-pistol, VZ 61
CZ 50 automatic pistol
Webley 42, single-shot
Assorted other pistols

Flex-X plastic explosive, 6 kilos
Dynamite, est. 15 sticks
Detonators, NATO Mk. III, one box
Assorted firing mechanisms

Iris intruder-detection system
Tobias geophones, 8
Trip-flares, est. 10

Philips 88 Interceptor-transceiver
Hand radios, 3
Gasmasks
Medipacks, US Army, 2

Kemble, having copied down the basic list, went through it from top to bottom, noting points which might be of interest to bloodthirsty readers of *The Times*.

As Fawcett had warned, the Iskra even had mines, but small ones, anti-personnel, of a type which were set off by trip-wires. The claymores exploded horizontally, spraying an area with something like grapeshot. The M26 grenades were American, green eggs of thin metal sheet stuffed with steel fragments and a yolk of TNT. Their casualty radius was 50 feet.

Of the firearms, the most impressive were the Viking and the Armalite. It was the first, the pump gun, which had killed Harvey's chauffeur. On that occasion it had been loaded with a scatter cartridge, but it also fired solid shot, half an inch in diameter. The French police used this gun in tight spots. So did the Mafia. Anyone expecting a close-quarters shoot-out was well advised to carry a Viking in their luggage.

The Armalite was more of a high-precision instrument. Indeed this one here, if Fawcett's description was accurate, was one of the most advanced and expensive rifles in the world, a type known in full as the Armalite-Stoner Hi-Fire. It was small in calibre but extremely high in velocity, with a lightweight plastic stock and all kinds of deadly variations among its ammunition. Its magazine held 20 shots, but it also had the option of being fed by belt, in which case it could be fired like a machine-gun, spraying in long continuous bursts. Fawcett could not remember seeing any belts. But he knew there was a telescopic sight, an infra-red night sight, and another attachment called a single-point scope, for rough and rapid aim at close quarters. This was Joop's own weapon, he said. The Armalite was the Dutchman's pride and joy.

Among the pistols, Rosa Berg's own was the CZ 50, which had killed Guidotti's bodyguard in Rome. It was a neat little automatic, Czech-made. But the one which had everyone frightened was the Webley 42. This was a collector's item, a long-barrelled single-shot gun with built-in silencer, made by the British in World War Two specifically for assassination. It was sometimes called the Webley Permanent Silencer.

And then there were the explosives, enough to make a very big bang. That had the French especially worried, since the hardest of terrorists to rescue a hostage from were those prepared to blow themselves up. If the Iskra's hideout had been wired for detonation, Harvey's chances were slim indeed. And it could be hard to get near. The next items listed were all designed to warn of a human approach, by rays or sonar sensors or flares. The radio receiver could pick up police messages, the masks ruled out a rush with gas. The Iskra's shopper had thought of everything.

And that shopper was surely Joop Janssen. None of the others were trained to use this box of deadly tricks.

So the problem at present had two sharp edges. Without their professional the gang couldn't do much; yet unless Janssen joined them, they couldn't be traced. No wonder old Groucho was losing weight.

In Bordeaux the Dutchman refused to make a move, while here in Paris the Commissaire was sweating out a visit from high quarters. Kemble kept tactfully out of sight while the French Minister of the Interior was brought up to date.

He decided to find a phone. Riemeck's press conference, put back to 12.30, would be starting in a few minutes, at which point he was free to release his own story on the Iskra's demands. Though sworn to discretion on the merger, he thought he might accidentally mention the figure of four billion. *The Times* would surely find a way to hide the source. But the first thing to do was find a quiet telephone, while Daladier was otherwise engaged.

So calculating, Kemble trotted up the steps to the mezzanine offices and into the room where the two girls sat at the switchboard. One of them was now his friend in a mildly flirtatious way. She gave him a line on a nearby extension. But just before picking it up, Kemble caught sight of a man in Daladier's office: fortyish, fat, unshaven, in a blazer and white shoes.

"Who's he?"

The girl took a look round the door. "He is the attaché of Cuba," she said without interest.

"Cuba? Really? What's he doing here?"

She shrugged and went back to her mirror, making up between calls. "He waits there all night. He must stay close to us, the Commissaire says."

Kemble, who had picked up the phone, put it down again, starting forward to question the Cuban. But just at that moment, 12.30 to the second, he was stopped by a terrible shout from the well of the ops room. Guiltily he froze to the spot, then saw that the shout was not directed at him. The Commissaire, brick-faced, was yelling at someone on a telephone.

Two minutes of total confusion followed, but by 12.32 the cause of this outburst was known to all present.

Biffaud had called from Bordeaux to say that the Dutchman was not, after all, in the quayside hotel. The bed in his room was disarranged, in a way that made it look occupied, but Janssen could not have slept in it, or used the room at all for more than a matter of minutes. Given the very tight watch put on the hotel, the Dutchman must have got away across the roof immediately after his arrival, before the police had a chance to put a man up there. In that case he had been gone for six hours.

After the fury and muddle, there was a moment of silent despair in the ops room. Then Daladier took a decision. In view of this setback, more time was needed. The Iskra must somehow be stalled. In which case Riemeck's statement, about to go out, was far too strong. The press conference must be stopped . . .

But it was too late.

Riemeck was already talking, and must have been so for several minutes, because right at that moment, 12.34, the teleprinters set in a row at the side of the room began to rattle with the first news agency reports. By the time Kemble tore off the still unreeling sheets, Riemeck's unyielding response to the gang had been flashed world-wide.

Daladier, understanding, hung his head dumbly. At least the Minister of the Interior had gone.

5

For eight whole minutes, from 12.28 to 12.36, the lizard was perfectly motionless. At 12.36 he made a sudden dash and swallowed the fly. His jaws snapped, his belly heaved once, and then he was still again, stuck to the wall by his splayed prehensile feet. He would probably stay like that for another ten minutes, digesting his lunch and thinking things over. He didn't like to be rushed between meals. Sometimes he was still for so long that he seemed to have forgotten his own existence; but then he moved faster than a fly could fly. Like the best of statesmen, he wasted no energy, this lizard, but applied all he had to one particular thing at a time – the single, simple task of the moment. After careful thought he acted with speed and resolution. He was a natural leader of lizards. He called by two or three times a day, scuttling in through the slats of the shutter and straight up the blotched white wall. Next he would probably visit the cobweb, top left. Or he might cross the ceiling and take a look in the crack above the door. That was what he did last time. This time he hadn't yet made up his mind. He was still thinking. Two minutes' meditation was short for this lizard. He could stay put for ten or even twelve minutes. His record for total immobility was twelve.

Sir Patrick Harvey, keeping time with friendly interest, glanced again at his watch. It was 12.38, less a few seconds. In the present hiatus between life and death he was glad to have made the acquaintance of the great World-Leader Lizard. He was also, he found, very glad of his watch, this old Swiss timepiece with plain white face and Roman numerals, still ticking away on his wrist as it had for the last twenty years. In his political career he had been given many and much more splendid watches, gold, platinum, electronic, wierd. But the strict British rules had prevented him from keeping them, and he was glad to be left with his old Swiss friend . . . His political career! Already that ordered, timed existence of busy days and many appointments seemed far behind him, so far it might have been a trick of the mind. But so long as this watch, its physical relic, still ticked on his wrist, he could believe he had come from that world.

Meanwhile ahead of him, and close now, the way this was going, lay the next world, hard to imagine but easy to believe in from this short distance. Like the presence of the sea beyond a near horizon of hills, its proximity altered the feel of his surroundings. He was conscious of larger possibilities in the view.

There, just ahead, was the place he was going to; behind was the place he had left. Less real than either, and much less interesting, was this place where he was waiting: a house in France guarded by strangers.

And yet it was the present situation – these people, their hideout – that he was supposed to be concentrating on. The two-day course on kidnap survival, laid on by Europol, obligatory for all new Commissioners, had been insistent on the point. To look back was an error, Europol said. The hostage, once snatched, should try not to worry about the effect of his removal on colleagues and family – the unfinished business, the unsaid endearments. He should cease entirely to think of his eminent post, since this would only aggravate his humiliation. Nor, of course, should he look forward. To dwell on the possible violent end to the business was futile and distressing. The thing to keep his mind on was the present. He should study it closely and react to it flexibly, concentrating wholly on the plain human act of survival, minute to minute.

To begin with, Harvey had done this. Bound and gagged in the boot of the car, he had tried to keep track of the kidnappers' journey. Calculating distance and time, counting towns, noting changes in traffic and the roads, he had managed to hold off panic for several hours. But then had come cramp and nausea together, an unstoppable rising of the gorge and the blind screaming urge to get out.

That had been the worst moment so far. Nothing since then had been nearly so bad. He could still feel the bruises and cuts from that terrible struggle not to choke, and also a dull ache across the chest, where his heart, like a mad thing itself, had hammered to get out of his ribs.

And afterwards he had been dazed. The time of arrival at this place was vague to him, though he knew it had been in the dark. He had been carried from the car and laid in this room, on this mattress, where he had slept fitfully till dawn, half-dreaming, half-swooning, uncertain whether he would wake in this world or the next, and not much caring.

Since then, feeling better, he had kept his mind busy with the puzzle of the hideout's location. And now he could make some intelligent guesses. To get here had taken six to eight hours, he thought, at fairly high speeds – a journey of, say, six hundred kilometres. Certainly the main direction was southward. This place was hotter than Tours; the air buzzed with crickets and smelled of the south – dusty earth, dried grass, baked rock. And yet the landscape was not Mediterranean. The one glimpse he'd had of it, when taken out to speak on the telephone, had shown rolling woods, mixed deciduous and conifer, rising gently to outcrops of rock. The rocks, pale and smooth, eroded with rain, hung over the trees in short concave cliffs pocked with holes. And that was the best clue. Having visited it twice in voluntary circumstances, Harvey was very nearly certain that he was in the prehistoric cave district of south-western France. If so, the fact had a certain resonance. Twenty thousand years ago European Man, pushed south by ice, had smeared these caves with his first works of art. Now here were these modern savages, about to spill blood in the name of social progress.

They had certainly chosen a good spot to hide in. The house stood on high ground approached by a steep twisting track. The car had made heavy work of the ascent. Somewhere below was a road on which occasional traffic could be heard. But no human sounds broke the hot, heavy, cricket-singing silence of this place. And no other human habitation was in sight, so far as he could tell, though he'd not been able to check every point of the compass. Around the house itself were the crumbling remains of some small terraced fields, run to hay and wild flowers, across which self-seeding pines had advanced for several years from the edge of the woods. The forest from which this farm had been hacked was taking it back.

That was the outer situation, so far as Harvey had glimpsed

or deduced it. But all he had got to know properly was the limited view from this room. The single window faced west; and although it was open, hinged inwards, escape had been blocked by an outer wooden shutter, which was closed and nailed up. The shutter had been painted a dark shade of red long ago. Some slats of it were missing, which gave back a little of the view. A strip of blue sky was visible through one gap, high up, and some of the ground through another, lower down. Growing outside the window, Harvey could see, was a fig tree, its fruit still hard and green. Beyond that a short stretch of derelict garden led down to the woods, which on this side came within thirty yards of the house. A few vegetables still grew wild, tall artichokes toppling among the weeds. Insects and butterflies hovered in the heat-shimmer. The sun blazed down on the hard rocky ground, so bright it made the eyes ache, so hot it had already burned Stephen Murdoch a raw shade of pink.

Eye pressed to the shutter's lower gap, Harvey watched Murdoch at work.

Standing at the edge of the trees, half in shade, the English kidnapper had paused to take his shirt off. He mopped himself, wincing at his sunburn, then threw the shirt aside and bent to his task again. His pink freckled skin shone with sweat; his red wavy hair was wet with it. He was hacking at the ground with a pick. He and the Italian, taking turns, had been hacking at the same piece of ground since yesterday morning. And now they were down fairly deep. When Murdoch took up the shovel, stepping down into the hole to throw out the freshly loosened earth, he disappeared up to the waist.

Harvey watched his grave dug without emotion. He had got used to it. And now, he thought, the depth and length would almost do. He would moulder away there under those hazel trees, undisturbed for hundreds of years, perhaps even thousands, until someone came on his bones and handed him over to the experts . . . Ah yes, a fine example of Berlaymont Man. But what's he doing here? And what's this hole in the back of his skull?

Murdoch climbed out and sat down in the shade, exhausted after ten minutes' effort. The time was 12.48. Harvey turned back from the shutter to see where the lizard was, but the great reptilian philosopher-hunter-statesman had gone, being easily disturbed by human activity, of which he had a deep and unsleeping suspicion.

In an effort to lure him back, Harvey sat carefully on the mattress, which was set on the floor against the inside wall, to the left of the door. He kept still for several minutes, his eyes roving round the room, of which he knew every crevice and crack.

Although not large, the room was tall, square and bare, with a ceiling of planks laid over two worm-eaten crossbeams. The planks were painted pale green. The walls were a greyish shade of white, yellow where the rain had broken through, and in places the plaster was swollen with damp, about to crumble. The floor was tiled. Dusty rather than dirty, it was strewn with dead spiders and flies. Cobwebs straddled the room's upper angles. Moths were sleeping in the corners, wings folded. The population of live flies, though not yet intolerable, was rising by the hour. Midges jigged through the air, briefly spotlit as they passed through the sunbeams from the shutter. At Harvey's feet was a cockroach he had crushed, its innards splashed messily outwards. But the lizard, his friend, had gone.

Giving up the search, he put up his feet and lay back on the straw-filled mattress, in which there was also some busy insect life.

Originally the mattress had been set below the window, but he had dragged it across the room and placed it behind the door, against the inside wall, to give himself the safest position if rescuers came in shooting or blew their way through the outer wall -- another of the lessons of Europol.

The only other things in the room were two aluminium-framed deckchairs, of the small folding type that people take out of their cars for roadside picnics. There was also a red plastic bucket, which served as a prisoner's lavatory. A copy of *Paris-Match*, two years old, was placed beside it. Harvey had used the magazine's first page. The bucket had a lid and was half-filled with water. The water had been turned milky white by a liquid disinfectant, which went some way to subdue the smell. But not far enough. The changing of the water in the bucket was now the highest priority in Harvey's life.

The second was a wash. His skin was sticky, his face unshaven. In one place his hair was stiff with dried blood. His shirt, also spotted with blood, smelled strongly of sweat. All his clothes were smeared with dust. His jacket and tie, taken off now, rolled into a pillow, were still encrusted with vomit.

It bothered him to be in such a mess. He felt humiliated by it. Following the advice given out on Europol's course, he had done his best to keep in physical trim, but to clean up properly he needed access to the shower which he'd heard elsewhere in the house. He would ask for that next, he thought, when the bucket had been emptied.

Luckily his cell was fairly cool, despite the glare beyond the shutter. The walls of this homestead had been built thick, to keep out the heat in summer, to hoard it in winter. And the height of the ceiling helped. Above it, Harvey thought, there was no upper storey, but a loft. Probably this room had been the byre for the animals. It must have been converted to human use when the farm had been sold to city folk. The floor-tiles, the magazine, the deckchairs – several touches indicated this was now a holiday retreat for an urban family, when not serving as a kidnappers' hideout. But the new owners didn't come often, Harvey thought. They didn't care enough to chop the weeds or stop the plaster falling. The real life of this house was over. It was sad to imagine the peasant who had lived here and his family, his animals, his tussle with the awkward soil, the rough *maquis* always crowding in on the cultivated patch; the money he kept stashed behind a brick in the chimney, saved up for years but still not enough to buy a dress for his wife or pay the doctor's fees if the children coughed . . . That was the real world, unknown to these pale sick fanatics, and the thought of it brought back to Harvey a picture of his wife's cottage in Wales. Much further back he saw the solid Devon farmhouse to which he had gone as a boy for summer holidays. Though a townsman himself, he had come to enjoy the country more in later life. More and more, as his power declined – power over men, power of intellect – he had come to draw a special deep pleasure from turning his unpractised hand to the simple tasks required at Cwm Caerwen, that sturdy Welsh croft where his wife was so happy. When these people shot him, he would lose the dozen, perhaps fifteen years he had expected to spend with her, growing old in that peaceful place. And nothing the Iskra would take from him hurt more than that. Nothing was more resented. In the currency of happiness, given and taken, he owed Margaret more than he should, and now the chance to pay her back had been snatched away by these bloody people. His anger against them was sharpened by guilt. He minded the cruelty done to his wife more than the ruin of the merger – more even than the murder of his chauffeur, though that too was terribly distressing to remember, and added its portion of guilt. Paolo had been a political innocent, drawn into the crossfire by loyalty to him . . .

But this was no way to let the mind run. Remorse was no help in a kidnap. As strongly warned by Europol, past errors and futures lost were both rotten subjects for the victim's contemplation. Present chances, however slim, were what he should think about. And the thing to watch out for especially was any small clue to his captors' characters. What were their motives, their differences, their weaknesses? What would each of them do if a crisis occurred? What might incline them to mercy? What exactly, in the end, would push them to kill? These were the questions the hostage should keep himself busy with . . . Yes, yes, and no doubt keeping busy was half of the point. But the subject for study was a dull one, thought Harvey. He wouldn't have believed, if told, that any set of people could have been both so boring and so frightening, simultaneously, as the Iskra. He glanced at his watch again, then closed his eyes, still stretched on the mattress. At 12.52 on this Monday morning, day three, he knew where each of them was and could keep track by sounds alone.

Murdoch was back to digging, not with the shovel but the pick. The grave seemed to be his favourite task. Indeed it was open to consideration whether BMG's number-one agitator had ever worked on anything so hard in his life as he had on this hole in the ground. The thought brought a smile to Harvey's stubbled face. It was hard to catch anything but hate in Stephen Murdoch, yet hard to take him quite seriously, perhaps because he was English, and so familiar a type – too clever to be content with his place in the world, not clever enough to improve it. But would he kill for it? Oh yes, he might. Sometimes he seemed to be frightened by what he'd got into, but all his frustration might easily go into one little twitch of the finger, and then he would fill his hole up again, probably dance on it.

Mario, the Italian, was different. Courteous, quiet, even kind at times, he appeared to take no pleasure in the business. His manner expressed only sadness. And yet, when you took a closer look, there was something scaring about him, this plump university lecturer from Rome who had guided the rebels of Mobital. Though he seemed to be free of cruelty or hate, he was also free of hesitations. In everything he did there was a sort of sleep-walking certainty, sad but steadfast, unnerving to watch. Mario's eyes were on a future world of his own imagining. Unless this trance were broken, he too might kill, Harvey thought, as priests had once killed for the faith.

At this present moment the Italian was out on sentry duty, watching the track which led up from the road. The car was somewhere down that way too. They had hidden it in what they called "the mine". Perhaps they meant a stone quarry, dug from one of the ubiquitous cliffs.

Mario and Murdoch took turns to be sentry. Each time they swapped places, at two-hour intervals, the one coming in handed over to the one going out a walkie-talkie radio with telescopic aerial. This was how they kept in touch with the house. Their intermittent reports could be heard crackling through a receiver in the room next door. Harvey could not make out the messages but noticed that they often coincided with the passage of a vehicle down in the valley, its motor sound echoing up through the rocks. So the sentry-post commanded the road. And the echo, he thought, made the road sound closer than it was. The track leading up from it must be half a mile long, as well as steep and twisty, so any approach from that quarter was not going to take the gang by surprise.

Most of this was guesswork, put together from his own observations and some overheard talk between the gang. No one had talked to him direct. His food was brought and taken out in silence. The little he knew about the Iskra had come from his own conversations with the company chairmen, back at the château in Tours. Stephen Murdoch had planned a workers' rising at BMG, and Mario, surname forgotten, was the man whose students had tried to kill Guidotti on Friday.

But the leader was the girl, called Rosa. There was no doubt of that. Just as both company chairmen believed, the brain behind their troubles belonged to a Frenchwoman. Rosa gave the orders, Rosa took decisions. It was Rosa, in the room next door at this moment, who guarded the prisoner – a function she seemed unwilling to delegate, Harvey had noticed. All day and for most of the night she sat by the telephone, took reports from the sentry, and kept abreast of events in the world outside by means of a portable radio, set on the table beside her. She had a television too. At her feet was a big black box, kept padlocked, in which Harvey thought there were weapons. If so, they had not been handed out. The other two seemed to be unarmed. But Rosa had a pistol at the ready all the time, either held in her hand or stuck in the waistband of her skirt. And she never left her post. She stayed indoors. She hardly slept, she rarely washed. From time to time she went to the lavatory. Once she had cooked a meal. At this moment she was cooking again, to judge from the appetising smell, and also the more distant sound of the radio, which she'd carried out into the kitchen. Then she came back to the main room and switched on the television.

Harvey looked at his watch.

12.56.

She was waiting for the RTF news, he thought, due on the hour. She never missed a TV bulletin. The next would be in four minutes. She flicked round the rest of the channels, then turned up the volume, so she could hear, and went back to the kitchen.

Harvey, still stretched on the mattress, listened to her clanking around with pots and pans, whistling tunelessly. He was conscious of her all the time. His whole day and much of the night was spent gauging each small shift of mood in the mind of this unknown woman beyond the locked door of his cell. And he had noticed a change. Since the time of arrival her bodily movements had grown much clumsier, her shifts of mind more erratic. Out of the three she was much the most frightening, because the least stable. She might kill or she might not, depending which way the wind blew in her head. In fact it was getting rather worse than that. Rosa was in charge here, and Rosa should not be, because she was going round the bend.

Maybe the other two would club up against her, Harvey was thinking. Maybe, the way this was going, a means should be found to provoke them into doing that.

This was the first constructive idea he'd had for his self-preservation, and it came to him just as the house resounded to the introductory fanfare of French TV news. He jumped off the mattress and kneeled at the door of his cell, ear pressed to a crack in its flimsy wood. Beyond the door Rosa, barefoot on the tiles, hurried back to the set from the kitchen. Harvey just managed to catch the first headline, which concerned himself, then she turned down the volume, and after that he could only judge the news by its rhythm. The headlines went on unusually long, he noticed. They followed one after another in quick succession before the announcer's return to the news in detail. Giving up the effort to listen, he straightened up and turned away from the door. But suddenly the door was unlocked and flung open. He had not heard Rosa approach it, but now she rushed in, grabbed hold of his arm and jammed her gun into his neck.

"Come," she shouted, pushing him out in front of her. "Come, Harvey, see how much your friends care for you!"

Harvey stumbled and almost fell as, walking in tandem, they went down a short corridor, then up three steps and into the principal room of the house. It was a spacious parlour, for sitting and eating in, with low heavy beams and a big stone fireplace. The TV was a small portable set, set on a long oak table beside the telephone. Darting past him, Rosa dragged out a chair, twisted it round and slammed it down close in front of the screen.

"There," she said furiously, speaking in French, as she always did. "Sit yourself. Watch your kind friends."

Coming back to him, she shoved him roughly into the chair, then stood close behind him, thrusting her pistol up hard against the nape of his neck, just under the hairline.

"Don't speak and don't move," she said, breathing heavily. "If you budge a muscle, I'll evacuate your brains. Just watch and listen. Ah, here he is, Harvey. Here is your judge."

The face of Otto Riemeck appeared on the screen. He was seated behind several microphones, about to make a formal statement.

At the same time a glazed door opened to the left. Stephen Murdoch came in from the terrace which overlooked the garden. And immediately behind him came Mario, up from the sentry-post for relief.

Surprised, the two men paused to take in the scene – Harvey, Rosa, the gun, the TV. Then they advanced and stood beside the set, left and right, to watch the news themselves.

6

Harvey sat upright and still in front of the television set. As he tried to take in the broadcast he was sharply aware of the muzzle of Rosa's pistol, always close to, sometimes touching the back of his neck. The mouth of cold steel, the short tube beyond it, the bullet at the bottom of the tube, the explosive, the firing pin, the trigger, her finger on the trigger, the volatile mind which controlled that finger – so fine and taut was this line of connection that Rosa's own reactions to the news could be gauged by shifts of the gun-barrel, which brushed his skin, jerked in surprise, steadied, withdrew as though relenting, then pressed again angrily, causing charges like electricity to shoot out along his nerves, up and down his spine, to his toes, to his scalp, to the pores of his face.

He had seen her temper already. During the phone call to Margaret in Kraainem, when he'd tried to blurt out a message, Rosa had knocked the receiver from his hand and struck him in the face. His cheek was still sore where she'd whipped it with the pistol. When the call was over, she had kicked him and screamed abuse. An hour after that she had been too disturbed, it seemed, to deliver her own ultimatum. The Iskra's demands had been dictated by Murdoch, in English, to some unidentified party. All morning Rosa had waited in restless, charged silence for some official response. Now here it came, by TV. And she liked it so little her pistol was trembling.

After a short lead-in the French news had cut to a filmed press conference, held half an hour before by Otto Riemeck. This was still being transmitted. Riemeck's pink skull shone with perspiration, his spectacles flashed in the lights as he read out a formal statement. He was seated too low at a desk, half hidden behind several microphones. Only Nielsen, the Danish press officer, was at his side. Reporters were crowded in so close that some were crouched in front of the cameras, keeping their heads down so as not to block the picture. Only their hands appeared, holding up microphones to catch the President's words.

Harvey recognised the Commission's office in Paris, which was really too small for such an occasion. But no doubt Riemeck wished to stress that in this matter the Commission spoke for itself. An early remark seemed to emphasise the point.

"Let me make it clear that I cannot answer questions about the search for Sir Patrick Harvey. That is a matter for the French police. I can, however, tell you of the demands conveyed by his kidnappers to me as President of the European Commission."

Having said this, Riemeck took off his watch and placed it beside him on the table. Then he picked up a fresh sheet of text and read out the Iskra's demands – or rather his version of them. Some clever hand had tinkered with the wording, Harvey suspected, so the gang's ultimatum sounded less reasonable than it had when dictated by Murdoch on the telephone. Riemeck presented each point of it in the most unfavourable way, exaggerating and distorting for melodramatic effect. He made Rosa's coming appeal to the workers, to occupy their factories and write their own merger, sound especially foolish.

"At two o'clock today, this woman has informed us, she will make known these plans to the press. So. Very good. I am sure that you are waiting to hear them with interest. And in Mobital, in BMG, the men of the factories will be pleased, I am sure, to learn this woman's plans for their future, since she is so skilled and experienced in industrial matters."

This heavy-footed German sarcasm brought a titter from the crowd of reporters, who jostled for elbow-room to get it on their pads. Harvey, held at gunpoint by the lady being mocked, was not so amused, but admired the tactics. The story would not now be written Rosa's way, he thought, whatever she tried to do next. And for old Otto Riemeck this was a most unusually skilful bit of press handling, even if he should have found a higher chair to sit in.

Another unusual thing was that the President was speaking English, with French-language subtitles popping up from RTF,

589

so that sometimes his face disappeared altogether. Was this for the British public, who wouldn't want to hear about their former Prime Minister in French? Or was it because the gang's own message had been delivered in English? Harvey couldn't guess. But certainly this carefully scripted, bilingual broadcast was aimed as much at the gang as the public. And the gang hadn't missed a word. Murdoch and Mario were bent towards the screen from either side, while Rosa, behind, was rigid with surprise or annoyance. The pistol had gone rock still.

"So," concluded Riemeck, looking up to camera. "Those are the four demands of the kidnappers. They were conveyed to me indirectly, by telephone, this morning."

There was a babel of questions in French, English, German. Riemeck held up his hand for silence, and got it, more quickly than usual.

"Please," he went on, "I have not finished. It will simplify matters if I say straightaway that, after consultation with everyone concerned, I totally reject these terms. We are not prepared to negotiate with the kidnappers in any way."

"Not at all?" The question was English.

"Not at all."

"Is that the order of the French police?"

"It is the policy of the European Commission. We do not parley with terrorists."

"What does Lady Harvey think?"

"She agrees," snapped Riemeck, grim-faced. "And so do both companies. As I said earlier, this is also the wish of Sir Patrick himself, declared on the telephone to his wife. And we shall respect it. I repeat, there will be no deal of any sort with this gang of political criminals."

Rosa's pistol jumped at the insult. Murdoch raised two fingers at the screen. Mario hissed through his teeth.

Take it easy, Otto, please, thought Harvey to himself. Stand firm, by all means. But don't provoke them.

Among the press gathered in Paris there was also an audible stir. Riemeck's line was harder than expected. The President began to strap on his watch again, to denote the conference was over. But now that he'd taken a stand, the questions, as if by some law of press physics, automatically tried to tug him off his feet.

"Where's Lady Harvey?"

"She has left her house in Brussels. Naturally she wishes to be private at such a painful time."

"But you've talked to her?"

"Yes. More than once. She agrees, without qualification, to what I have said."

"How do we know that?"

"Because I am telling you."

"Can't we have a quote from the lady herself?"

"No, I am sorry. You cannot."

"How does she feel about Sir Patrick being betrayed by a member of his staff?"

"That I have not asked her."

"And you, Herr President? How do you feel about it yourself?"

Harvey listened closely, not knowing yet who the traitor had been. But Riemeck's reply was ambiguous. "Naturally, I am distressed," he said. "Next, please. You, at the back."

"What about the merger?"

"Talks are proceeding."

"Where?"

"In a private place."

"Can we have some details?"

"No, you cannot. I hope to give the details to the European Council, in Rome. That will be on Wednesday. Until then they must remain secret."

"Can't you tell us anything?"

"On the merger, yes, there is one extra point that I should like to make."

Riemeck's bald pate again went down out of sight, dipping under the subtitles as he glanced at a text. "Contrary to the ill-informed accusations of these terrorists, careful thought is being given to the workers' interests in these negotiations. There will be no excessive loss of employment in either company. Any redundancies resulting from the merger will, of course, be discussed with the unions. Furthermore the structure of the new joint company will be considered in the light of the need to provide for some measure of consultation between management and employees, on an ongoing basis, consistent with British and Italian law. Due regard will also be paid to previous European proposals in this area."

In this cautious and inelegant statement, delivered at slow

591

dictation speed, Harvey recognised the work of several hands. Well, it wasn't Cicero, he thought. But it would do. A very accomplished piece of triple talk, aimed at kidnappers, workers and shareholders.

And now Riemeck really had finished. Having strapped on his watch, he stood up to go. Questions were still being put to him as he sidled away from his place at the desk. He spoke them down, insisting that he had to go. But then one question stung him to a halt. It had come from a white-haired man in the front, who identified himself as the Paris correspondent of *Avanti*, the Italian socialist paper. As the cameras swung round on him this elderly man repeated his provocative question to Riemeck in loud, clear English.

"Do you accept that you are, in effect, by what you have said, condemning your friend and colleague to death?"

Riemeck was furious. "It is not I who condemn," he retorted in a harsh voice, leaning forward in anger, his pudgy hands clenched into fists on the desk. "It is they, the Iskra, who control his life. I refuse that they transfer this responsibility to me. And you, sir, have no right to speak in that fashion."

But the old Italian journalist was undeterred. He shot a quick supplementary question, which went unheard on the air but must have touched Riemeck on some raw German spot, because immediately, forgetting his script, forgetting tactics, the good Social Democrat from Baden-Württemberg embarked on a general tirade against the violence in politics. First he raged at the man from *Avanti*. Then, making Rosa's gun jump, and Harvey's heart with it, he turned straight to camera and addressed the kidnappers direct.

"To the Iskra I say this. You consider yourselves an intelligent élite, which has been selected to liberate the masses from subjection and ignorance. Your historical task, you say, is to wake up the people to their own true interest, by violence if necessary. You are wrong. The masses are against you. They see their true interest much better than you do, and they have enough good sense not to listen to your simple, arrogant daydreams."

Riemeck paused, overcome by his own indignation. And in the same instant Harvey's breath stopped, his whole scalp crawled as he felt Rosa's pistol jerk up the back of his neck. She raised it to his skull, and then drew it back, so he felt it no more.

Her breath came quicker, and she let out a grunt, which sounded involuntary, pulled up from her body by sheer force of feeling. Mario and Murdoch, catching the movement, turned inwards. Their eyes immediately widened in fright.

"You, therefore, represent nothing," Riemeck went on from the screen. "There is no moral content in what you are doing, no political meaning. It is simply a crime. And that is why we, as representatives of –"

The President got no further. His egg-like countenance was blown to pieces, the whole scene in Paris disintegrated into chips of flying glass, blue flashes and puffs of smoke as Rosa shot out the television screen. She fired two bullets straight into the set. Her third may have been meant for Harvey, but it went through the ceiling, since Murdoch and Mario had both instantaneously leapt on her with terrified yells of protest and now had hold of her gun arm, forcing it upward. Both men were scrabbling for possession of the pistol, but she held it out of their reach, and then broke free of them, screaming furious abuse in French. She held them away from her with the gun aimed. Her face, which had flushed, drained to yellow. Her lips went white. She was panting like a sprinter. But calmer now, silent. The gun was held steady.

Harvey had been knocked to the floor. Now he was down on his back, half under the table. He thought it the best place to be. Above him stood Murdoch and Mario, still holding out their hands for her gun, beginning to protest again after a short, shocked silence. Harvey's ears were singing so hard from the shots he could hardly hear, but the drift was clear enough. They were pleading with her not to shoot again, pointing down to the road where someone might hear. But Rosa made no reply. She seemed to be off somewhere else on her own. She stared at them dully, no flicker of response in her wide-apart grey eyes. There was no fear in them either. Even interest in what was going on appeared to have left her. Gradually her breathing slowed to normal; two spots of colour returned to her cheeks. Mind returning to body, she glanced from one man to the other, as if surprised to see them standing there. Then she poked the pistol at Harvey.

"Take him away. Lock him up."

Mario stayed with her, surveying the wrecked TV, while Murdoch lifted Harvey to his feet and led him from the room, down the steps, then along the back passage to his cell. This gave Harvey his chance.

"Thank you," he said in a low voice.

"For what?" snarled Murdoch.

"You just saved my life."

"Harvey, I don't give a fuck for your life. I want you put down with less noise, that's all. And then I'm going to dig you into the ground."

"She's mad, you know."

"Is she?"

"She'll get you all killed."

"Maybe she will. But you'll go first, brother. Now just get in there, and shut your face."

Murdoch prepared to lock the cell, but Harvey, turning in the doorway, raised his hand. "Could I make a request?"

"What?"

"This bucket – it's getting unpleasant."

Murdoch's pinched features, burnt pink by the sun, were slowly transformed by a malicious smile. "You are asking me to take away your shit, Prime Minister, is that it?"

"In the public interest," said Harvey, attempting a smile in return.

Murdoch entered the room and took a deep sniff. "Yes," he said, "I see what you mean. Another little chore for the workers, eh?"

"I'll empty it myself if you show me where."

"No, Harvey, you stay here. Lie in your own stink. And I hope it chokes you."

With that Murdoch left, but not before Harvey had seen the whites of his eyes. Despite his tough talk, BMG's Trotskyite was clearly scared stiff. Tipping the helmets off a line of British bobbies was no preparation for this.

The trouble was Rosa held the only gun. And while this was so, she would control the other two. Still, there was some agitation. Bending his ear to the door again, Harvey heard voices raised in argument. He caught notes of anger and panic, but couldn't hear what was said, so deafened was he by Rosa's shots. His whole skull was buzzing, as from a heavy blow. Even Murdoch, snapping out insults to his face, had sounded faint.

594

Remarks made next door were inaudible. Soon he gave up the effort to eavesdrop and sat on the mattress, feeling suddenly faint; unable to draw enough breath, as though his chest were strapped. So far his heart had done well. But more of this could be too much. It was hard to tell. He might last for days or he might, at any second, go out like a light . . .

What was that?

It was Murdoch, outside, running back to the grave to get his shirt. He was carrying the manual radio, for sentry duty. And now he was armed, Harvey saw through the gap in the shutter. Murdoch had a rifle – a Russian one, to judge from the look of it. He was trying to wrap it up in his shirt, for concealment. But that wasn't easy. After a moment he gave up the idea and dashed off.

So she'd made it up to them and handed out weapons. Murdoch was going down to watch for intruders . . . and now here came Mario, also on the run, with an axe. What was he doing? Ah, he was chopping off branches from the hazel trees, sticking them into the earth around the grave . . . They were covering up, then, in case the shots had drawn attention to the house. But this wasn't much cause for hope. The shots might well have gone unnoticed, since these woods were constantly busy with *la chasse.* Yesterday, Sunday, there had been spasmodic firing from dawn to dusk, some near, some miles away. Three shots on Monday morning weren't going to cause much alarm.

Rosa was back in the kitchen, clattering about with more urgency, perhaps to get rid of the cooking smell. Shutters, windows, doors were being slammed. Then she was on the transmitter, calling up Murdoch for news from the road. There was no answer. Murdoch hadn't yet arrived at his post perhaps. Rosa switched off. Her ordinary radio, the portable set on low volume, was putting out pop music between news bulletins. She switched that off too. A silence ensued, broken only by the blows of the axe in the hazel wood. Then they, too, ceased. The Italian came back to the house. Another door was closed. Voices muttered softly, and then Harvey was jumping to sit on his mattress as footsteps approached his cell. The door was unlocked. The Italian came in to shut the window. Harvey watched him, trying once again to assess the plump, dark Latin with a monkish bald patch and stubble which was growing so fast it was nearly back to a beard. Dressed in check shirt and jeans – clothes which looked new, though now dirty – Mario was dripping with sweat from his exertions. A soft man, in body at least. But in mind? That was harder to tell, the more so because his eyes were hidden by mauve-tinted spectacles.

"Excuse me, Mario – is that your name?"

"Yes. It is my name."

"May I ask you a favour?"

"No. You must not speak."

Harvey, ignoring this, pointed to the bucket. "Look, if you're going to shut the window, will you take that away? Or change the contents, at least."

"You are an enemy of the people, Harvey. And this is a people's prison. You cannot expect to be comfortable."

"I suggest you do it for your own sakes. If somebody comes sniffing round here, that smell will give you away."

"Be silent please. Or we shall kill you."

"Yes, the lady might – I can see that. But is it what you want?"

"If it is necessary, it will be done. My wishes have nothing to do with it."

So much for the mutiny. Harvey, disappointed, was left alone again. But it turned out he had scored a point about the stench. Half a minute later the Italian came back. He took out the bucket and brought it back clean. On his third entrance he, too, was carrying a weapon – some sort of sten-gun with a carrying strap.

"No talking please, or you will be dead," he said in a low voice, leaning down to wave the barrel across Harvey's face. Then he left.

From this point onward the issue was clarified. There would be no revolt in the gang, it seemed, and no wavering by the Commission. Otto Riemeck would stand his ground and Rosa would carry out her threat. Failing rescue, death would occur at eight tomorrow morning.

Harvey, left alone in his cell, was strangely relieved by this closing of chances. He had already adjusted to the imminence of death, but now he felt better about it. Like a sick man, informed of the worst by his doctor, he could stop wasting energy on false hope. Like a traveller about to put to sea, now that he knew the sailing hour, he could pack his luggage.

It was more the traveller he felt like, light of heart and full of expectation as he got himself ready for departure. Everything was clear and simple.

When a man is due to be hanged, it concentrates his mind . . . no that wasn't quite right. And who was the clergyman that said it? Davies, Hurd, Dodd – anyway a friend of Dr. Johnson's, and a forger. The sermons he wrote just before his execution were much his best.

Harvey had a pen and the memo pad he always carried in his pocket. He had spent most of his life putting thoughts on paper, but now there seemed little point in that. So what should he do? In theory he should pray, for he went to church on Sundays and, when he had time, believed. But a just English God, he thought, would not be much impressed by any last-minute prostrations. A bent knee and stiff upper lip would suffice.

He tried to analyse his emotions, but this was like hauling a bucket up from a deep well and finding it empty. Looking forward to the few hours left, he was not particularly afraid. They wouldn't hurt him, because there was nothing they wanted from him. He would have been frightened at the thought of torture. But a bullet was different. A bullet, at his age, was almost a kindness.

To be kind was not the Iskra's intention, to be sure. On the other hand they did not hate him. They had treated him as well as they dared, and tried to make him comfortable. The meals had even been rather good. This morning, for breakfast, they had given him a long cut of bread with goat cheese and two peaches. The door had opened a few inches and a hand had put the plate on the floor. The hand belonged to the girl.

For Sunday lunch, yesterday, she had brought him a plate of hot stew . . . And what had become of the meal she was cooking just now, before the news? Perhaps they had eaten it, Harvey thought, feeling hungry again himself. Well, if there was any left over, they would bring it. They didn't hate him enough to starve him.

He was, to them, the symbol of an idea; and it was the idea they hated. The idea was what they would kill him for, in the name of another idea. And to Harvey this was a funny way to go, because ideas had never been important to him. Capitalism, conservatism, parliamentarianism, patriotism, Europeanism – although he accepted these "isms", he rarely thought about them, and never spoke by choice in such terms. His life was a network, often confusing to himself, of practical decisions and personal relationships. Ideas were, at best, a game. You needed to know the language of ideas in order to argue with someone like Rosa, but in a well ordered society they didn't really matter. Indeed, when ideas began to matter, that was a sign that society was in a bad way. Ideas were absolute; often destructive, sometimes murderous. Nothing decent or lasting could be built on an absolute philosophy. Terrorists were drugged by their idea to forget the broken bodies, the physical pain, the grief of families. But his own single deepest conviction was that they were wrong, whatever the idea they killed for. Good social change came the other way, boringly, respectably, election by election, conference by conference, compromise by compromise, incompletely, and often through muddle, in an endless series of practical adjustments between imperfect but well-meaning people, attempting to live together. That was his philosophy, such as it was. Now, in his own ears, it sounded merely pompous. He had no wish to write it down. On the other hand he did not doubt it. He awaited death from Rosa in the firm belief that she, not he, was the enemy of the people.

But the next thing she brought him was lunch. It was the same sort of hot stew as yesterday, only this time she brought it in herself: a tepid but generous helping of beans, pork morsels and sausage.

"Eat up," she said. "Here – take a glass."

She poured him out some yellowish wine from a plastic-capped bottle. And that, if she cared, was a mistake. The label on the bottle showed the wine came from a cooperative in Bergerac, east of Bordeaux. That was no proof, of course, but to Harvey it seemed the sort of cheap wine rarely sold outside its area of origin. If so, these rocky wooded hills were where he thought.

Rosa drank nothing herself, and at first said nothing. Holding the bottle by its neck, she stood watching him in silence, without expression in her face. Then she turned away to the window, now closed. Ducking down, she put her eye to the glass and squinted through the shutter's lower gap. She was checking the grave.

"Mario, I can still see it. More branches please," she called through the cell's open door.

Mario was listening to the radio in the main room. He made no reply, and then he called back to her: "Rosa, listen to this."

Harvey then heard a name mentioned, one he had heard several times before. It sounded like Yope. Mario said it, and Rosa reacted to it. "What's happened?" she cried, immediately dashing from the cell.

"He's in Bordeaux!"

"Quick, let me hear! Turn it up!"

Mario did as she asked. Immediately the house was filled by the sound of a French radio broadcast, turned up loud, and since she had left the door open, Harvey could hear every word.

It was a police message – an urgent appeal to the public for assistance in a manhunt. The name of the man being hunted was J-o-o-p, pronounced Yope. The French spelled it out. His surname was Janssen, nationality Dutch, present false identity Arab. But he used several others. Details were given; names, documents; and then a full physical description, from which Harvey instantly recognised the killer of Paolo, his chauffeur. This man was a dangerous professional killer, the broadcast went on, and anyone seeing him should telephone . . . A number was given in Bordeaux. Joop Janssen had last been seen in the city at seven o'clock that morning. He could be there still, or on his way inland. The following rural departments should be on full alert . . . A list was given, which confirmed Harvey's theory of his own location. The police message ended. Music resumed. Then the radio was switched off. Harvey listened carefully to the ensuing silence.

Rosa was the first to break it.

"He will come," she said.

The Italian was not so sure. "Rosa, how can he? Every road will be watched."

"Joop will come. He will not leave us here."

"If he comes, he will bring the *flics* with him."

"No, he will not. You will see," said Rosa, unshaken. "Joop will get here, as he promised. He'll be here by this evening."

Mario, still doubtful, was silent a moment. Then he said: "Rosa, you have too much faith in this man. You know what I think of him."

"Yes. I know. But spare me your advice." Rosa's voice

thickened. It had a way of going guttural in anger or tension. "Joop will arrive," she said again. "Until he does, we shall follow his instructions. So go out and hide that grave properly. I can still see it."

Harvey, still seated on his mattress, listened to this with interest. His meal, half-finished, was put to one side, since he wanted to catch each nuance of the tiff. But it ended there. The Italian went out with the axe again. Rosa remained in the parlour. She called up Murdoch on the radio transmitter and got an all-clear report from the road. Then she came back to the cell. She had another glass in her hand. She filled it from the bottle, drank half on the spot, then wandered over to the window to assess Mario's work. The axe chopped on, the branches fell. Rosa stood silently watching. Harvey, having finished his meal, decided to speak to her. This would be the first time he'd tried, and the language would have to be French, since her English wasn't good. This was no problem for Harvey; his French had been fluent since boyhood. The problem was what to say. He wanted to test her. But how to begin, after two days' silence?

"That hole is for me, I suppose."

She answered with her back to him, still at the window. "That's right, Harvey, yes. For you. Unless your friends change their mind, of course, and agree to our terms."

"They won't do that."

"We shall see."

"They won't."

"In that case you will be shot. At eight o'clock tomorrow, as I told your wife. Not sooner, not later. We shall wait that long." Rosa's voice was flat, almost nonchalant. She went on staring through the window. Then she added, still speaking over her shoulder: "Are you afraid to die, Harvey?"

"Are you afraid to kill me?"

The question made her turn at last. "If I must, I will. But I shall take no pleasure in it."

"You'd rather leave the job to your Dutchman, I suppose. Joop, is it? Well, I'm not surprised. We've all seen what he can do."

"You are thinking of what happened to your driver."

"Yes, I am thinking of my driver. His name, in case you wondered, was Paolo Santini."

600

"I know what his name was. And I regret his death."

"So you should," said Harvey. "You will burn in hell for it."

The remark was made without calculation, as much to himself as to her. But Rosa stiffened in surprise. Her eyes dilated, then she averted them. For several seconds she made no reply, her head turned away to one side. Eventually she turned back and smiled, more at herself than at him.

"Don't talk to me about hell, Harvey. Your sins are greater than mine."

"You believe so?"

"No one is innocent, but you are more guilty than most. That is why you are here."

"And Paolo?" Harvey said, indignation rising. "What was his offence?"

Rosa considered the question. When she answered, she was serious. "To kill without cause, that is the sin – to waste people's lives without a reason. Such violence as we have committed, with reluctance, had been a logical necessity, forced upon us by the present condition of the working-class struggle."

Harvey's anger rose to a head, then dissolved into wordless disgust. Yes, he thought, the logic of the working-class struggle was just the sort of high-sounding claptrap which killed simple peasant boys like Paolo Santini, had killed them before and would kill them again, world without end. And he couldn't be bothered to argue with it. Losing interest in his effort to test the girl's will, he fell deliberately silent. He wanted her to go. To argue the political toss, to probe for her weaknesses, to talk to her further about anything at all seemed at that moment an insult to poor dead Paolo, the fall of whose body, flung over the road by the force of the Dutchman's shotgun, still haunted Harvey's memory. It was indeed a matter of strange satisfaction to him, almost amounting to a wish, that he would share the same executioner as his chauffeur.

And Rosa herself seemed glad to escape any further conversation. She picked up his plate and stalked from the cell. Then, at the door, she turned back.

"Do you want a wash?"

No doubt, in her own mind, this gesture proved a point: the personal kindness of the Marxist assassin. But Harvey didn't care about that. A wash was what he wanted. He accepted the

601

offer and followed her out to a small tiled room in the back of the house, with shower and basin, where she left him alone for ten minutes. There was a towel and soap. When he came out, she lent him a comb. Harvey used it. Still demonstrating how kind she could be, Rosa then took out a first-aid kit and applied an ointment to the cuts on his head. The medical pack was of the military sort, Harvey noticed, and it came from the black wooden box, which was indeed full of weapons. He made no comment on it. He let her take him back to his cell.

Solitude came as a treat, and soon the cricket-singing silence lost its menace, seeming more like the long afternoons enjoyed on French holidays. Even the axework had stopped. There was no talk or movement from any of the gang. Harvey stretched out again on his mattress with a feeling which was close to contentment. He had washed, he had eaten. The bucket had been emptied. And now he had something to read.

That morning's edition of *Le Figaro*, used in the phone call to Margaret, had been left lying in the room where he had washed. He had quietly removed the outside pages and folded them into his pocket. Now he took them out and read them. The headline was enormous, with many subsidiary headlines below it. There were photographs, columns of factual report, boxed-in articles on related topics, bits of hurried comment and background, a summary of his own career. And now he learned the full names of his captors, along with some detail of their lives – Rosa Berg, Joop Janssen, Mario Salandra, Stephen Murdoch.

But the item his eye turned to first, and then came back to at the end, was the arrest of Erich Kohlman.

This, to Harvey, was a cause of sharp sadness. It was also a great surprise. From the moment of ambush he had guessed that he must have been betrayed by a member of his staff, but had thought the culprit must be Laura. Trussed up and choking in the car, brooding for hours in captivity, he had worked up a mood of bitter animosity towards her. And even now that mood would not clear. Confronted with the truth about his German *chef de cabinet*, he found it easier to forgive than the insolent, disloyal walk-out of that aggressive English girl. Poor Erich, so polite and correct, so *useful*, right to the end – what on earth had made him do it? How could he have fallen for the simple slogans of these Marxist louts?

Le Figaro could only guess. And Harvey could hardly do better. At least with Erich the motive would be sincere, he thought, and it would be serious. However mistaken, it would make a kind of sense. But the reason would not be wholly political. There must have been something else, some emotional ferment stirring all the time behind that bland, pale, unreadable face.

Harvey's sadness was increased by guilt. Like a father astonished by an errant son, he asked himself where he'd gone wrong. Moments came to memory when he could have tried harder to communicate at some level deeper than office routine. Now it was terribly too late.

But remorse, of all emotions, was the most futile, in general as well as in kidnaps. Realising that he had let his mood sink from high to low, in a very short time and to no useful purpose, Harvey folded the newspaper up again and put it away in his pocket. He had a politician's ability to put past errors behind him, and now he applied it. Taking firm hold of a door in his mind, he closed it for ever on the sad young face of Erich Kohlman.

From the room next door came Rosa's voice, talking fast and low. For some time now she had been on the telephone – several separate calls. Glancing at his watch, Harvey guessed that she was planting her story with the press, direct or through sympathetic friends. The time was exactly two o'clock.

2.03.

2.12.

2.30.

Time passed; shadows shifted. The telephoning stopped. A long silence fell, in the house as well as outside. Perhaps they were all asleep, thought Harvey, absorbed once again by the midges which jigged above his head in the sunbeams: that never-ending swirl of tiny particles, inanimate, animate, hard to tell apart, like the dance of atoms under a microscope. He began to feel drowsy himself. His eyes were on the midges, but his mind was on the gang, who had shown themselves to him more clearly in the last two hours. He saw them now as individuals, in thrall to a single idea. Their resolve depended on that abstract spell, the force of its hold upon them. And this was most interestingly true of Rosa. Under that rigid idealogue was an ordinary human girl. Her kindness had not been entirely feigned, Harvey thought. Other emotions were under there, too. Fear of hell, longing for her Dutchman, loneliness, anxiety, doubt – they kept breaking through, betrayed by a twitch of hand or lip, a turn of the head, a flick of the eye. There had been moments when she seemed like a person attempting to wake from a hypnotic trance. Perhaps that was wishful imagining. But what if the spell of her idea were broken? Without its iron logic she might be less dangerous; or she might very well be more so. The only thing that could be foreseen with absolute, dull, depressing certainty was that an argument with this woman would not end in friendly accord.

But damn it, he would try to shake her.

Yes, he thought, changing his mind, he would after all talk it out with her if the chance arose; not to save his life, but to go with his head high. The crude, cruel logic that had ended the life of Paolo Santini and smashed the career of Erich Kohlman should not be allowed to pass without dispute.

Thinking to himself in these high terms, which on a normal day he would have laughed at, Harvey drifted off into sleep.

How long he was gone he could not tell. It could have been a few minutes later, or it could have been an hour, when he woke to find Rosa's hand pressed across his mouth. Her eyes were staring into his from a distance of inches. She was crouched on the floor beside his mattress. She had a long-barrelled pistol in her hand – the one she had used to threaten him in the car.

She pressed it against his right ear, and then, leaning closer, put her lips to his other ear.

"Don't move," she breathed, speaking in a whisper so small he could barely hear. "If you budge or make a sound, you will die. And so will he."

7

Harvey supposed his end had come, but was utterly bewildered by the manner of it. Why like this? Why now? What was happening? Please, stop, wait, explain to me before you do it, he wanted to say, but Rosa had him pinned to the mattress, her hand pressed hard across his mouth. She gripped him like that in a tight, surprisingly intimate embrace with the muzzle of her long-barrelled, silent-shooting pistol pressed against his head. Her own head was raised to listen. Harvey kept still, as instructed. Then they both heard a footstep, coming from the house's other side. Rosa's grip tightened. "Gendarme," she said, still in a whisper. "If he finds us, he's dead. So don't make a move, Harvey, will you?" Harvey shook his head. "Will you do what I say?" Harvey nodded. Rosa stared into his eyes a moment longer, then removed her hand from his mouth. But the pistol stayed rammed against his skull. When he sat up, it followed him, glued to his ear. They waited like that, crouched together on the mattress. The gendarme's footsteps· came closer, then stopped. After a moment of silence he called out and rapped the front door. Rosa jumped at the noise, which reverberated through the shuttered, bolted house. Then her eyes were fixed on the window, widening in alarm as she realised that if the gendarme came round and looked through the gap in the shutter, he would see her. Quickly, on tiptoe, she led Harvey into the opposite corner of the room, where they stood together, pressed flat against the wall. She was only just in time. The gendarme arrived at the window seconds later. His movements could be followed from his shadow, which darkened the room. He bent and peered through the gap in the slats.

All he could see was the empty mattress and the plastic bucket. These two things seemed to interest him. He tapped on the shutter, then bent to look again. The shadow of his flat-topped *képi* appeared on the floor, a dark square in the bars of downcast sunlight. Harvey kept still and held his breath, braced for another killing. Mario must be out in the trees, he thought, aiming at the gendarme's back. A warning from Murdoch, posted down by the road, would have given the other two enough time to set up an ambush for this poor country copper, who must have been sent to investigate Rosa's shots. He probably thought he was after poachers, but if he turned round and looked hard, he would find a freshly dug grave. Move on, man, go home

Wishing this to himself, Harvey was suddenly aware that Rosa, the gun barrel quivering as her nerve weakened, was wishing the very same thing. And a few seconds later their joint wish was answered. The shadow disappeared from the floor. The gendarme passed on. He walked slowly once round the house, testing each door and shutter in turn, and then rode away down the track on a motorised cycle, the putter of its engine soon lost in the silence.

Rosa steadied and relaxed. Releasing her hold, she moved into the centre of the room, where she turned and faced Harvey with a cool knowing smile, as conscious of their moment of collusion as he had been.

"Thank you," she said to him. "As you see, we want no more violence than necessary."

Harvey, still standing stiffly in the corner, made no reply. Now that the danger of a bullet had passed, he was in some danger of buckling at the knees.

Rosa stared at him, seeming to guess this. And then she said: "Would you like me to make some tea? That's what the English do, isn't it?"

He nodded at her. Yes, he would like tea. His mouth was dry.

When she had gone he sat on the mattress and drew up his knees, resting his head on them, until it had cleared. Again he had felt that dizziness and constriction of the chest, impeding his breath, which had struck him first in the talks at Tours. But now he was less worried about it. His first instinct was to cheat these people by survival, but the idea had entered his mind that he might just as easily cheat them with a natural death. That would be rather amusing, he thought. Altogether a very neat exit. But not one that he could arrange for himself.

As he had suspected, Mario had been on guard in the woods. Now the Italian returned to the house. Rosa moved in and out of the kitchen. There was a muttered exchange with Murdoch on the radio; some laughter; and then she came back to her prisoner with tea. Two mugs.

This time she planted herself in one of the small aluminium-framed deckchairs. Both hands cupped around her mug, she drank her tea and watched him, not speaking. Harvey watched her back. If she wanted a discussion, he would take her on. Was that what she wanted? It was hard to tell. But something kept drawing her back to him. For two whole days she had left him alone, but now here she was again, clearly with unfinished business on her mind.

Her eyes gave no clue to her thoughts, fixed upon him with their blankest, controlled expression. Pale grey, almost colourless, set far apart, they had a sort of wide-open clarity. And yet there was nothing to be seen in them, and they in turn seemed to see nothing; or rather they saw what her brain allowed, and this gave a strange effect of blindness. The rest of her appearance suggested crude strength. A big girl, thick-limbed, heavy-breasted, she made Harvey think of an athlete from the Soviet Union. Her skin was pale, her hair cut short. She wore a grey shirt, stained with sweat below the armpits, and a big loose skirt, its printed pattern faded from frequent washing. Her regular pistol, the small one, was now in a holster belted round her waist. She kept the flap of the holster unbuttoned, Harvey noticed, and between sips of tea reached down to touch the butt of the gun, repeatedly checking its position. Her legs were unshaven. They had perhaps never been shaved. Her muscular calves were hairy as a man's. She had kicked off her sandals and was sitting with her bare feet splayed on the floor.

There was something aggressive in this posture, which made him expect a verbal attack. So her first remark took him by surprise. Chucking up her chin to the window where the gendarme had stood, she patted the handle of her pistol. "As you see, I don't like to use it."

"You weren't so benign this morning."

"That, I admit, was exaggerated." She nodded. Then, to his further surprise, her face was suddenly lit by an ordinary, good-humoured smile. "But tell me now, Harvey, haven't you ever wished to shoot a television set?"

Harvey, despite himself, laughed.

"I was annoyed by your friend's stupid insults," Rosa went on, her smile disappearing as fast as it came. "He should take more care how he talks, this Riemeck – for your sake. Don't you agree?"

Harvey very nearly nodded in agreement, impelled by the small bruised twitch of a feeling that Otto Riemeck's televised statement had indeed been on the tough side, given the circumstances. He had the twitch suppressed before it reached his face. But Rosa, with the quick percipience of the nearly mad, had seen enough.

"A hard man, Riemeck," she taunted, her smile returning.

"A strong one."

"But tactless. A German fault, don't you think?"

"He says what he means," retorted Harvey. "A German virtue."

Losing interest in this quibble, Rosa glanced at her watch. "Never mind, I have given him time to save your life. He has sixteen hours."

"He won't, you know."

"He will try."

"You really believe that, don't you?"

She nodded, blind-eyed again. "I know it. This refusal to talk is a bluff. He will keep it up for a time, of course – perhaps until this evening. And then he will make some response to our demands. The workers will force him to."

"The workers?" said Harvey in surprise.

Rosa stared at him, surprised at his surprise. "Tonight the workers of BMG and Mobital will seize their factories, in support of the Iskra's programme. There will be some dissidents, of course. But the activists will lead, and the rest will follow. The workers will take control. It is what we have worked for."

Harvey went through a short moment of incredulity. Aware by this time of her intelligence, he thought she must be pretending. Then he saw that it wasn't so. She believed her own prediction. This expectation of a workers' rising was the fixed idea holding her up. He intended to knock it away, but to do so too soon, too hard, would be dangerous. His best hope was to talk her down slowly, attempting some sort of relationship which would last when reality crashed in.

"So what are your demands?" he asked her eventually. "May I see them?"

Immediately she jumped up and left the room. Half a minute later she came back with two sheets of paper, on which were the Iskra's conditions for their hostage's release, drafted in English and French. She held them out.

Harvey read through the four paragraphs with deliberate slowness, to give himself time to think. And then he decided that on one point at least, the first, he could risk an immediate attack. To demand the release of her friends from jail was hopeless, he told her. "They will not be let out. You know that."

"I know," she said, surprising him with instant agreement. "But I had to try. It was all I could do for them."

"So this, by itself, does not get me shot."

Rosa admitted it. The life-or-death conditions were the other three.

"All right," said Harvey, making a first attempt at friendly domination. "So let's take a look at them. And please, if I speak my mind frankly, don't fly into a rage. We can hardly expect to agree, after all."

Rosa accepted this suggestion. Sitting side by side on the mattress, they went down the list.

Suspension of the merger
State intervention
Workers' control

Gradually, methodically, Harvey attempted to lower her expectation on each point in turn. It was just possible, he said, that the companies might agree to a suspension of the talks. But in due course the merger was bound to go on, either with him or without him, and the moving force would be the Commission, because there was no realistic alternative. Neither company would be rescued by its own national government.

His confidence grew as he heard himself deploy these arguments, speaking as he would have done to the heads of government in Rome. But then, glancing sideways, he was stopped.

Rosa Berg had yawned – and not from weariness. She was bored.

He concluded curtly: "In any case, the loss of jobs won't be as bad as you allege. There will be some natural wastage . . ."

"Wastage!" The word woke her up. She scrambled off the mattress, stood, walked away, then swivelled on him. "These are human beings you are talking of, Harvey, not old machinery to be thrown on a scrapheap. Oh, you disgust me! I ought to shoot you now."

But her pistol remained untouched in its holster.

"Calm yourself," Harvey said, trying to regain his dominance. "You forget that even more will lose their jobs if there is no merger. Both firms will probably collapse."

"I don't give that for your opinions." She leaned down and snapped her fingers in his face. "They count for nothing any more, don't you realise that? Nothing!"

Harvey realised it. For the last two decades his opinions had swayed the destiny of nations; now they were those of a man to be shot. He could repeat them to himself if he liked, but no one else was listening or cared, not even this girl.

"Very well, let's leave it there," he said quietly.

But Rosa was on the offensive. "No, we will not leave it there," she said, standing over him. "Don't you understand, Harvey, that this is what it's all about? The men in these factories are human beings – like you, like me. They spend their lives in this work of making cars, and yet they are at the mercy of those few other human beings who happen to have a store of money and are looking for a way to increase it – a return on capital, as it's called. We, the Iskra, say that the workers are entitled to better arrangements. And that, it seems to me, is a very elementary moral proposition. I find it hard to understand why anyone, let alone a man like yourself, disagrees with it." She paused and stepped back a pace, declaiming at him from the centre of the room. "You accept democracy, don't you – in politics, in cities – even in companies? The holders of shares have votes. So why not the men who do the work? Answer me that, Harvey. Go on, answer that!"

This went on just long enough for Harvey to pull himself together. Seeing that he wouldn't get rid of her, he took up the sheet of four demands again. "So it's this point which matters to you – the last one. Workers' control."

Rosa returned to the mattress and took the sheet from him, to remind herself what she had written. "Yes," she said, handing it back, "workers' control. That's what you will die for, Harvey. And it's a better cause than any in your miserable, misguided life."

Harvey ignored the proferred paper. "In that case allow me to tell you that we have already made some provision for this. In the merger as we had it before you interrupted, and as it will no doubt proceed in any case, there are measures to give the workers a voice."

"Oh?" she said after a moment of disconcerted silence. "What measures?"

This had been touched on in Riemeck's press conference, Harvey reminded her, repeating from memory the President's roundabout words on participation. If more was not said, that was because it was a delicate subject. An unguarded statement on workers' rights at this stage could arouse false hopes or antagonisms.

Rosa stared at him balefully. But now her curiosity was stronger than her anger. "Okay, Harvey, tell me. What were you going to do for the workers?"

So he told her. Two directors in five elected by employees, another two to represent the shareholders. Chairman to hold casting vote.

Rosa listened until he had finished, then reacted with contempt – a little forced. She was clearly surprised by this development. "That is nothing," she snapped. "That will change nothing. You do not fool us with that."

"What's wrong with it?" Harvey said, retaliating. "What reason will you give when you tell the workers that they must not accept these places on the board? Go on, please tell me. It's your turn to answer."

But Rosa refused the challenge. "You damned capitalists," she said in her own time, "you are very clever people – much more so than Marx himself realised. Your favourite trick is to steal just enough from the revolutionary programme to ensure your own survival. And that's what you're doing here, Harvey. Don't imagine that we can't see it."

At that Harvey's anger rose again, beyond thoughts of self-preservation. "It's called reform in my world, and it stops good people like my chauffeur getting shot – unless, of course, they

611

have the misfortune to run into maniacs like you, who can only express their hatred of the world by killing in the name of impossible perfection." He pulled himself up, noting that his loss of control made her eyes glow with triumph. "And anyway, where's the trick? Two directors in five, from none, is an improvement. It will change things."

Rosa sniffed and turned away. "Paint on the corpse," she said dismissively.

Harvey prepared to withdraw from the argument, which was ending just as he'd known it would, in a pointless exchange of abuse. But then, to his great surprise, she struck at a sensitive point.

"Harvey, listen. You have told me yourself, this merger of yours will be ruled at the top by three men, yes? Guidotti, Clabon and a neutral chairman. All the power will be in their hands. The national boards of each company will have no real power at all, will they? And yet it is on these superfluous boards of directors that you will so kindly allow the workers two places. That is not reform. It is trickery."

This required an answer, but Harvey could not immediately think of one. He sat in exhausted silence.

Rosa could have stopped there, to some good tactical effect. But now she was chasing her own train of thought. She seemed to have forgotten his presence.

"In any case, you don't change the nature of a capitalist enterprise by putting two workers on its board of management. You only change the nature of those two workers, who are taught to act like the bosses. As soon as a serious conflict of interest arises – a conflict of class – this little reform of yours will make no difference at all. Because real power goes with ownership, Harvey. Only when the people own the means of production will things be different. That is a fact of economic life."

Harvey noted the shift in her terminology. "The workers" had become "the people". From defending the rights of employees in two specific companies she had started to talk of society at large, and this lapse into Marxist jargon was welcome to him, since he was now standing on slippery ground. Even within his own party, the conservatives of Britain, there were men who had started to argue in strangely similar terms to Rosa Berg. Co-ownership will make the workers behave, because then they will see the world as we do. There will be no conflict of interest.

"So you wish to turn the workers into capitalists, Rosa. Is that what this is about?"

"No, it is *not*," she said, stung as by no other question so far. Eyes blazing in outrage, she advanced towards him, then halted and rubbed her face with both hands – a sudden frantic washing motion, as though she wished to remake her features. It was a very odd gesture. She had done it before, but now it was happening more often. Harvey wondered what it signified.

She looked at him more calmly. "Wait," she said. "I will get Mario. He will explain to you."

She left and shut the door behind her.

Harvey continued to think about the way she rubbed her face. Was she bothered by her own unlovely appearance? No, it was nothing so simple. She seemed to do it most when stuck for an answer, so perhaps it was her brain she was trying to push into shape – her whole self. The plain human girl was troubled by imperfect service to a beautiful, perfect idea.

Although almost certain of this diagnosis, Harvey could not translate it into self-preserving tactics. He had no plan of action, simply the vague yet growing fear that Rosa, in disintegration, would be a very dangerous person.

And just at that moment, as though in confirmation of his own dark foreboding, there came a faint rumble on the air, which it took him a second to recognise as thunder.

8

The thunder rumbled off in the hot, heavy silence. It did not come back. Nor did Rosa. She was gone for some time.

Puzzled by her absence, Harvey glanced at his watch. 4.30. He had thought it was later. The afternoon seemed long, made more long by heated discussion. The room smelled of bodies, hers and his. Swept by a longing for release, fresh air, he crossed to the window, pulled it open and bent to the gap in the shutter, peering out at the overgrown garden, the hay hovered over by butterflies. But this glimpse of freedom tormented him. He returned to the mattress and waited, oppressed by a feeling of confinement and solitude. Even the wise old lizard kept his distance. He wasn't having anything to do with workers' control.

Eventually they came back together, Rosa and Mario, and the talk went on, in French as before. But for Harvey the brief glimpse of sunshine and butterflies had been too much. He could not recover his interest in the argument, especially since it now grew quickly more abstract. Mario Salandra, who soon showed himself to be the Iskra's Think Tank, came to Rosa's aid with articulate zeal. While she stood at the open window, occasionally throwing in remarks of her own, the exact point of theoretic difference which had caused this absurd little war was explained by the fluid-talking academic gunman from Rome.

Industrial democracy, if perverted by Harvey and his like, would mean a few places on the board for the workers, a few shares, a slice of the profits. This limited access to wealth could indeed turn some workers towards a more capitalist style of behaviour, as Harvey had said. Alienated from their less prosperous fellows, they would fight to hang on to their small advantage.

"The people's solidarity would be broken. And this we shall fight against always."

Harvey nodded patiently, refraining from comment. "All right, now let's hear your version."

And so came the creed of the Iskra.

Industrial democracy, correctly interpreted, meant a network of worker-cooperatives in which there would be no property at all. What would happen was this, said Mario. A group of men would work together, in a factory, on a farm, and their labour would give them a say in its direction. Each man would have a vote, and together they would settle their pay, choose the management, decide the big questions of production and investment. But there would be no capital shares. The workers, indeed, would not own their cooperative. The people would own it.

At this point Harvey must have shown some confusion, because Mario took out a sheet of paper and drew him a diagram: a sort of molecular structure consisting of several small circles of various sizes, all linked to a larger one in the centre.

Harvey stared at the strange shape in wonder as Mario explained that this was what Lenin had envisaged at his death. The small circles were self-administering cooperatives, each with some independence. The big central circle was their general assembly – the congress of soviets. Taken all together, the big and the small, these circles formed a pool of resources, which was the people's. Excess profit, in any particular cooperative, would be returned to the centre for general use . . .

Harvey's patience ran out. "All right," he said, "I understand, and it makes a pretty picture – I'd call it the birth of the totalitarian state. But would you tell me what this has to do with the present predicament of BMG and Mobital?"

Mario was happy to answer the question, but in his own time. He approached it through another thicket of theory.

The concept of Marxist revolution, he said, had set into one fixed scenario – that of the instant and unified proletarian uprising, led by the party. The Iskra's conception was different. Revolution, they believed, might come just as easily in pockets, which would gradually multiply and spread, until the gaps were closed and change was complete. If a few model cooperatives could be established and seen to succeed, the movement would gather momentum. Already there were some examples in Europe. But they were still small and scattered. The cooperatives that survived in the West had failed, so far, to combine and pool their resources in defence of the single great idea for which they all stood. What was urgently required to catch this tide of history, the Iskra had realised, was some much bigger demonstration of workers' democracy in action. And so their eyes had turned towards BMG and Mobital, each employing many thousands of people, each clearly coming to the edge of collapse.

"So the Iskra, in its wisdom, decided to give them a push."

Startled by this interruption, Mario sat back and blinked. "No push will be needed," he said. "These companies will fall without our aid. Our task has been to instruct the workers how to turn this development to their own advantage."

"How then? How will they do that?" Harvey asked crossly. "Please tell me how these workers will benefit from losing their jobs."

They would not lose them, Mario retorted. At the moment of collapse each company would be taken over by its employees and forced to continue production as a democratically organised cooperative. These seizures, as planned and prepared by the Iskra, had been scheduled for later in the year. But now the moment had arrived, brought forward by Harvey's own effort at a merger. This evening, or early in the morning – the exact timing was a matter for the activists – the workers would rise and take control.

Glancing at Rosa, who was silent at the window, Harvey left this delusion intact. "And what will they do for money?" he asked. "Making cars costs money, you know, a lot of it. We're not talking here about cooperative basket-weaving."

Precisely, said Mario, unshaken. It was their size that gave these two companies their great revolutionary potential. And because of their size, finance would be forthcoming from the state. Neither in Britain nor Italy would a government of any colour dare to let two such important firms collapse. The workers' initiative at self-employment would be supported; the shareholders would be bought out; protection would be provided for BMG and Mobital against the imported cars of foreign capitalist firms. And at this stage a merger would make more sense. BMG and Mobital, once worker-controlled, would look to each other for assistance. The first of Lenin's links would be formed.

Harvey, though tempted, did not interrupt. He waited with dull resignation for Mario to finish.

That was the Iskra's objective, the democratisation of BMG and Mobital. Admittedly it would only be an interim stage, the Italian concluded, but two great bastions of workers' control would have been raised, and as the experiment was seen to succeed, it would grow; it would be copied. Thus at last, by stages, without a shot fired, revolution would come to Europe.

Harvey listened to this last in amazement. Shots had already been fired, he thought. And at least one more was to come. Could this buffoon have forgotten it?

"But suppose the experiment fails," he said, speaking with deliberate mildness. "What then?"

Mario replied offhand, as though asked to comment on a deeply improbable hypothesis. Even if they failed, he said, BMG and Mobital would start an irreversible process. Their destruction as worker-cooperatives, and the consequent mass destitution in Coventry and Milan, would dramatise the issues at stake. Their fall would arouse the masses to a proper awareness of the nature of capitalism. And that anger wouldn't go away. Nothing would be the same again . . .

"I see," said Harvey, breaking in with less mildness, "so that's what we're in here – a play. Well, I agree with you, that's what it feels like."

Each of them started to object. But Harvey had heard enough.

"Now let me tell you what I think. If either company takes your advice, it will not survive. For a time it might, on public charity. But that won't last. The money, the political support will go. And so will the popular sympathy. Even as revolutionary theatre your plan won't work, because this isn't a play we are in, but the real industrial world. I believe the workers in BMG and Mobital understand that. But if they don't they will very soon learn, because once they have grabbed their own factories, they'll be left with the very same problem their managers face now, which is how to make cars that people want to buy. The democracy of the market – that's the one you leave out. Good cars sell, bad cars don't. It's a matter of money and technical skill and good organisation. Fine social theories have nothing to do with it."

Mario was going to reply, but Rosa did it for him, jumping forward from the window.

"That's where you make your big mistake, Harvey. It is not just money and machines, but people's lives we are talking of here. You don't understand that, because you have not spent your life in a factory. You don't know what it feels like, as a human being, to be valued as nothing more important than an item of productive equipment."

"Do you?"

"No, I do not. But I try to imagine it every day. And it is not I, but you who are sitting here with a pleased expression on your face telling us how . . . in the name of good organisation . . . money . . ."

She couldn't finish. She let out a furious exclamation of disgust, and then swept her hand violently sideways, flinging her tea-mug across the room, so it smashed into fragments on the opposite wall.

But Harvey would finish it if it killed him. He got off the mattress, for self-protection, and spoke again quietly, addressing them both. "Before you people interrupted those talks, I was trying to persuade John Clabon and Carlo Guidotti to accept their workers as partners. If I had been allowed to succeed, that would have been the biggest step forward yet for industrial democracy in Europe."

Rosa shook her head wordlessly, staring at the wall against which her mug had broken. Mario answered for her. "She is right," he said. "Yours is a meaningless formula. Two directors in five changes nothing."

"If it was meaningless, they would have accepted it. As it was, they resisted hard."

"Men of that sort – Guidotti, Clabon – will fight change of any kind."

"But in this case they would have lost," insisted Harvey. "Because I had something they wanted – and that was money. I could have bought your workers some power, you see. And I would have. But instead of that, here I am locked up and arguing with you, about to be killed for a point of dogma. And a very fine point it is, I must say. Workers' directors versus workers' control – I doubt if the wars of religion could match it. Nevertheless I can see I shan't persuade you, so now I suggest we close this discussion. Please leave me alone."

But the last word was Rosa's. Still shaking her head, but calm now, she turned to face him with her old closed expression.

"No, Harvey, you will die for more than that. You have spent your life preserving a world which is rotten and wasteful. That world must go; and you will be destroyed as a symbol of it."

A symbol of an imperfect world, Harvey thought, still trembling with anger after they had gone. Yes, that will do. Let's settle for that.

After this second wrangle with his captors he felt deeply tired. Yet sleep would not come. In its place came disturbance of mind. For a long time he lay on his mattress in the hot little room, going over the contest just past.

Had he won? The question was futile. He had said his say, they had said theirs. Pride was satisfied. Pride was what it was about, he thought. Pride and talk, round and round – the never-ending circles and conflicts of human existence, the dance of the doers and the dreamers. There were those, like himself, who were happy to live in the world as it was, in the present with all its imperfections. On the other hand there were and ever would be those who, like this Rosa Berg, could not bear to live with things as they were, but must dream of a perfect future or past. Forward-gazing, backward-gazing, prophets and reactionaries, in one thing these dreamers were alike – they hated the present. But why was that? Was it themselves, and so life itself, that they hated? Who could tell. Confused, unhappy people . . . and always the same mistake. Like the Millenarian Christians, these Marxists ranted of heaven on earth, they smashed and they killed for it – a particular heresy of Europe, not finished yet. Sad because noble, in a way, yet futile beyond understanding.

Watching the atomic jig of midges in the sunbeam, Harvey momentarily saw both himself and his captors as just another agitated swirl in the life of the world. Then he veered away from such thoughts, for which he had no aptitude, and turned his face back to the present, in which he had always lived. He wondered how the French police were getting on.

By this time their search must be frantic, the more so because of Rosa's deadline. But here they would not now come, since the house had been checked and passed empty by a single inattentive country gendarme. Poor man, he would probably suffer for it.

A first puff of wind stirred the trees outside, but did not last. It whispered away through the woods, leaving stillness as before. From the distance came another roll of thunder. Provoked by it, Harvey's imagination fanned further outwards, envisaging the world-wide uproar his plight must have caused. He had seen the French headlines. The British would be bigger. But he had lived too long with fame to be deceived. Hundreds of men would have put down their papers that morning and said to their wives "I met him once," then gone to work without a further thought. The sense of shock would spread wide but shallow, and in forty-eight hours it would be gone. There would be one more headline when they found him dead. Then the ripples would subside; the pond would be still. A few people would remember him for longer, with different blends of curiosity and regret, diminishing into indifference. Only from Margaret's life had he cut so large a fragment it would not grow whole again.

Still trying not to think of his wife, for the sake of his own morale, he started to count off the others who would care, and found them very few. There had been two other girls, long ago; two or three men whose friendship was real when he was young; his son, who had turned away; and now his grandson, David. It was not a long list for sixty years. True, it had been a crowded life. Colleagues, constituents, secretaries, drivers, messengers – of people that he could remember by name, with some degree of affection, there was a very great number. But what would they say of him? That he had been polite, perhaps; had passed something more than the time of day. Some would say, just as the press had in generous moments, that he was a master of personal relationships. But only he could be the judge of that. And lying on the mattress, waiting for death, Harvey turned the verdict against himself. No, he thought, I never was a master of personal relationships. I merely mastered people. And with one especially I should have tried harder.

To keep his wife out of his thoughts, even if it was recommended by the course on kidnap, seemed suddenly indecent. If these were his final hours, then Margaret should be with him in spirit, and he with her. He wanted no one else. So he let her in at last. And soon she drove out all else. Random images from their long life together flicked through his head. The way she threw the stick for that stupid dog at Chequers, snored at night, brushed her hair, banged the saucepan when annoyed . . . laughed aloud at that preposterous gift from the Saudis, holding it up round her neck . . . turned gruff when affectionate . . . hacked all day long in the heat at Cwm Caerwen, bent over with a sickle, determined to clear the dead bracken by nightfall.

The pictures turned, like pages in an album. For a while this worked to Harvey's comfort. But soon, as warned, it cast him down further. Margaret's present distress was too easily imagined. And in with the memories came regret. Unable to shake off his mood of self-judgement, he was conscious of things he might have done, might have said, to make her happier. But hadn't, and now would not be able to. Time, he thought, there never was enough of it. Work, there was always too much. Lack of time, excess of work were the enemies. . . No, not true, too easy. They were excuses – to ward off that holiday he didn't really want, that evening at home which would have bored him. When the work ran out, he thought, I went and found more of it, because I enjoyed it. Because in my work I felt happy and complete, more confident than ever I was in personal relationships. Poor Margaret.

Harvey's eyes filled with tears, and he wished he had a cigarette – two sensations he hadn't felt in years. But this brought a comforting shift of mind. He thought of John Clabon, filling up the room at La Maréchale with horrid cigar smoke.

Could they really save the merger? Would they try?

Yes, he thought, they'd try. They had said in public that they would, so they would. That was good. That was something.

But what on earth had Otto said when he heard four billion? Perhaps the companies would settle for less. Yes, they would manage on three. And the new chairman shouldn't be a problem. Several men could do it, but really the best . . .

His old friend the lizard was back on the ceiling, staring at him upside-down with cautious concern. But Harvey didn't notice. He had gone back to work. First the problems outstanding rose to mind, and then his own answers. And then his best guesses at the answers Guidotti and Clabon would find for themselves. Imagining them at it, placing himself like a ghost at their side, he willed them on up to the summit in Rome.

9

Flying south from Paris, the plane had hit weather so bad they were forced to put down in Geneva. For an hour they had dawdled at the airport. Switzerland in the rain, they had agreed, was the most depressing country in the world. Colourless lakes and dripping pines, a tent of soggy cloud from peak to peak. Even the mountains got you down.

Then the storm had rolled away westward, and soon after that they were in the air again, bouncing through turbulent draughts into Italy. But their spirits took longer to lift. All three passengers were very tired men. John Clabon fell asleep with his mouth open. Carlo Guidotti, smoking incessantly, stared down at his factories in Turin as if he might find them in flames. Lord Doublett continued to work, reading through the points agreed so far, the small list of matters outstanding. He consumed the written word as he did food – the two great appetites necessary for a professor of Oxford. He was, besides, excited at his new responsibility. Duty outlasted fatigue.

Now, at 5.30, Mobital's jet was back in bright sunshine, cruising smoothly down the west Italian coast. Long yellow beaches passed below, packed with plebs on vacation. Motorboats carved their white wakes on the sea. The island of Elba was coming up ahead, the brown hills of Tuscany were spread to the left.

Apparently the plane could fly by itself. The pilot, to Doublett's alarm, came back with a flask of coffee and three plastic cups. Still, this refreshment was welcome. Clabon woke up and Guidotti smoked on. Doublett made notes in the margin, relieved when the pilot returned to his task. No one yet spoke.

The three of them were on their own now, and glad to be so,

preferring to conclude the business in private, without Commission officials. The talks in Choisy had been adjourned early, since each executive was due to meet his board of directors in Rome. Laura Jenkinson had stayed behind in Paris to prepare formal papers. She would follow to Italy that evening. Nobody knew where Riemeck was, but he had promised to be in Rome by tomorrow, the eve of the summit.

All would be settled in Rome, one way or the other. And the plane would soon be there, thought Doublett, glancing out of its small oval windows at Tuscany: the vineyards and olive groves, the old brown towns on their hilltops. The sight delighted him. This was the land he loved best in the world. Watching it pass, wishing he were down on it, he wondered how much time in the last two days he had spent looking out of windows. Across the aisle Clabon and Guidotti were gazing at Elba. These busy indoor men, they hurtle from meeting to meeting, looking out at real things through glass, thought Doublett, a half-remembered hymn drifting into his mind.

> A man that looks on glass
>   On it may stay his eye
> Or something something through it pass
>   And then the heaven espy.

Perhaps, it struck him with sadness, Patrick Harvey was looking out of some barred window, trying to espy a bit of . . . But this would do no good. Rome was coming up. He reached out and touched Guidotti's arm.

"Still work to do, Carlo. Not much time."

As ever, Guidotti was courteous. Clabon grumbled, but pulled himself upright and turned in to listen.

"This clause on worker participation," Doublett said, passing them the relevant sheet of typescript. "Where did it come from? I refer to section two, para three. Workers' places on the board."

The eyes of both executives turned wary. They took the sheet from Doublett and studied it, then looked at him across the plane's aisle. Both opened their mouths. Neither spoke. They glanced at each other. Then Clabon answered for both.

"The wording is Kohlman's." He almost stopped at that, then added reluctantly: "Patrick was keen on it too."

"How keen?"

"Pretty keen."

"Did he do the detail himself?"

"No, not really. We didn't get round to it."

"As I thought." Doublett took back the sheet. "This clause, as drafted, is pure Brussels jargon. What are we committed to? That I find obscure. What indeed is European policy, as trumpeted by Otto on the box? Also obscure. *In re* workers' rights, the line you are being asked to toe does not yet, in practice, exist."

Neither businessman reacting, Doublett went on.

"I propose a more pragmatic approach. Proper line to follow is your own inclinations, given state of play in each company. What do you say?"

Neither said anything. So on Doublett went again, all this occurring at a voice-level slightly over normal, because of the noise of the plane.

"For what it is worth, my own view is that the workers should work and the management should manage. Pay high and don't consult – that's the trick." Pausing, he glanced down and tapped the sheet, at which he was peering through half-moon pince-nez. "But this, I notice, goes even further than consultation. Each of you is to have a supervisory board, two directors in five elected by the workers. At best that will be a bureaucratic muddle. At worst it will let in the Reds. I suggest, very strongly, that you reconsider it."

There was a pause, both businessmen staring. Then Guidotti said: "Lord Doublett, you amaze me."

"Why so?"

"You are so logical." The Italian smiled and shook his head. "So right," he added, glancing back at Clabon.

Clabon nodded glumly. "Of course, it's all bloody nonsense. I don't like it any more than Carlo does. But we did agree this with Patrick, Arnold. We can't very well go back on it now."

"Nothing was finally agreed in Tours," protested Doublett. "You were interrupted, and there's no proper record – just Kohlman's summary. Patrick wouldn't hold you to that."

There was another pause, pregnant with temptation, despite the roar of the jet. Then Guidotti nodded in agreement with Clabon.

"Dr. Riemeck has already told the world that we will offer new powers to the working force. And that is a promise we cannot escape. If we do nothing, there will be trouble – and is not Patrick then nearer to death?"

Rosa Berg's call for a workers' rising, conveyed to the press through collaborators in Paris, had made both executives nervous. Even so Doublett felt cross, sitting opposite these two rich, powerful men. It was he, the underpaid academic, who had been put in charge here. Also it was he, not they, who was Harvey's friend. He was convinced of the point he was making, and he had already judged the risk in it. Patrick's life would not be saved or lost, he believed, by a phrase in the merger's fine print.

"Back to consultation then," he said in a gruff voice.

They were puzzled. "What exactly do you mean?" Clabon asked.

"We will keep the machinery but take away its gears." Doublett settled the sheet on his knee and took down a pencil which was tucked behind his ear. "These two-in-five boards are described as 'supervisory'. Let us change that to 'advisory'. Agreed?"

Neither businessman answered. To save them embarrassment, Doublett pencilled in the change without a pause, then shuffled the sheet out of sight in the deep pile of paper beside him.

"Consult, consult – that's a waste of time, but not an active danger. You'll manage with that. Now, let us talk about research."

The switch of topic was so sweeping it took both businessmen by surprise. In their eyes was still pleasure, relief, and some guilt at what had been done the moment before. Now these emotions gave way to hostility. Research, their faces said, was not a thing they wished to discuss at this time and place, with this man. Their mouths said nothing.

Doublett was not put off. "Awfully expensive department these days – too big for either alone. Costs less spread between two. Best reason of all for merger. Suggest we discuss it."

Neither man answered this telegram.

"Any projects to propose?" Doublett glanced from one to the other, then rephrased the question. "Any projects already in hand," he said carefully, "that either wishes to share?"

Still there was silence – or rather the monotonous, unceasing scream of jet engines at speed.

"I understand your hesitations," said Doublett, breaking into grammar under stress. "But you cannot afford to be so shy, gentlemen. Carlo has a new light alloy, brewed up by his lab in Turin. And John, you have a non-fuel engine."

Clabon was the first to react. "Tell me what you know," he said grimly.

Doublett obliged by repeating from memory, with absolute exactitude, the performance characteristics of BMG's prototype battery car.

Clabon's face reddened in anger. "Who in the hell told you that?"

"Patrick, when he came to Oxford. You'd taken him for a spin in Wales. He gave me an account of it."

"Did he now?" said Clabon, getting redder, getting louder. "Breach of confidence, that is. And a bloody annoying one, I must say – even if he has got a gun to his head."

"Calm," said Doublett, "calm. He has told me many secrets in the past. I keep them."

"You better keep this one, Professor."

Guidotti nodded in support. "For us it is important, this secret."

"It belongs to you both?" enquired Doublett in surprise.

There was a pause. Again they glanced at each other. Again Clabon answered for both. "Yes," he said. "We have agreed to cooperate."

"Then there's no problem. Praise be, praise be." Doublett's manner relaxed. Pencil still poised, he realigned his eyeballs with his pince-nez, inspecting a new sheet of typescript in his hands. "But this should appear in our formal submission."

"No," barked Clabon. "Leave it out."

"All statesmen impressed by research, you know. Makes them feel modern."

"Please do as John says, Lord Doublett. The battery car must be omitted, or these discussions are concluded."

Doublett's eyes popped up from his half-moon lenses. Such hard talk from Guidotti had not been heard yet.

And instantly Guidotti apologised for it with a slight negating motion of his hand. "We cannot allow this to be known by Fiat. VW, Renault – all of them are working on similar projects."

Doublett's head ducked once, in semi-submission; not the multiple nodding he reserved for full agreement. "General statement on joint research, then, for summit consumption. But I propose confidential annex, Riemeck's eyes only, undertaking to pool information on non-fuel forms of propulsion. How's that?"

"You propose?"

"Very strongly. If forced, I insist."

"All right," said Clabon eventually. "Start drafting, Professor. But I want to hear every word. This cat stays in the bag."

Doublett, suppressing his annoyance, did as he was bid. As he wrote it he read out the new form of words, and at the same time his capacious brain, in which there was room for other activity, computed the altercation just past. Guidotti, he had noted, was keener to keep Clabon's secret than Clabon was. And this was no great surprise. Just as he, Doublett, had foretold in Oxford, it was BMG's electrical motor which was holding the Italians to the deal.

The plane flew on. Work continued.

And twenty minutes later they had covered the ground. Talk ceased; paper was put away into briefcases. Clabon closed his eyes again. Guidotti retreated into private thought. Doublett turned back to the window, watching Rome approach through the warm haze of evening.

His interest in the landscape beneath was now more than casual, and suddenly he saw what he was looking for. The plane, coming in from the sea, had made a first circle of the airport. Waiting for clearance to land, they flew across the ancient port of Ostia, surviving in fragments under the pines. Just outside the fence that ran around the well-tended ruins was a scar of newly excavated earth, in the middle of which stood a pale lump of masonry.

"There it is!'

"There is what?" growled Clabon.

"Demeter's warehouse. Just discovered," Doublett said excitedly, sitting back as the plane banked away. "Chap in charge is a chum. Cambridge man, but first-rate intelligence. Good nose, too. Sniffed it out all by himself. Hunch, you know, hunch is what counts on a dig."

Both businessmen gaped across the aisle. In their eyes now was something close to panic. And Doublett, smiling back at them, understood the cause. Throughout this plane journey and the talks preceding, the unspoken thought in all three minds was that he, Arnold Doublett, might be chosen by Riemeck to be the new chairman of BMG-Mobital. Patrick Harvey had had the same idea perhaps. And Doublett, while uncertain whether to accept, was keen to be asked. The chances that he would be were high and still rising, he thought. It therefore behoved these two wealthy braggarts to get used to classical scholarship as well as a no-nonsense line with the workers. They might have to live with it.

Otto Riemeck, however, was not yet engaged with the third-man problem. He had stayed in Paris for a different purpose, for which he now left the Commission's offices in Avenue Victor Hugo. After a visit to the Ministry of the Interior, where he was brought up to date on police operations, he proceeded to the seat of all power in France, which lay a short distance down the Faubourg St. Honoré. At 6 p.m. exactly his car turned into the gates of the Elysée Palace.

His arrival was expected. The chain which blocked the entrance was raised; the Republican Guards saluted as he passed. His chauffeur, instructed where to park, drove across the forecourt and left him at the steps to the palace's entrance, up which he was taken by an usher in long-coated, black-and-silver livery. At the top of the steps he was taken over by a grander flunkey still, silver-haired, silver-chained, who led him in superior silence across the stone vestibule and up some wide stairs, until he was standing alone in a gilded *salon de réception*.

Riemeck refused to be impressed. Pomp of state was a thing he distrusted. Resolutely ordinary, small of stature, still wearing his shiny blue mohair suit, he waited below the huge tapestries and crystal chandeliers until he was taken in hand by a brisk aide-de-camp, who led him through tall double doors to the men he had come to meet.

The room they were waiting in was even more magnificent, but the President of France and the Chancellor of Germany were ordinary men like himself. Sitting in their shirtsleeves, each with a drink in his hand, they were discussing their business beside an open window. When he came in they jumped up and greeted him warmly, shook his hand, made him a drink of his own, sat him down. Each of them knew him quite well. Each man, like Riemeck himself, was from the political Centre-Left.

Yet Riemeck was not deceived. These men had power. He did not. In Europe, as currently organised, real power lay in this palace beside the Seine and that other flat modern edifice beside the Rhine in Bonn, not in the Berlaymont Building, Brussels. He knew it. They knew it too. That was why they were sitting here, comparing notes before a summit. When the nations of Europe were gathered, these two consulted beforehand, and on one thing they were always agreed. They would not allow their two great states to be pushed about by the men from Brussels, whose task it was to propose and advise, not rule.

However, on the present occasion, Otto Riemeck brought to this room a certain moral clout. He knew this. The other two knew it as well. It emerged straightaway in the conversation about Patrick Harvey, a man whom they spoke of as one of their number. Both were upset by what had occurred. Both had issued genuine statements of shock. The President of France was worried by the conduct of his own police, who seemed to be bungling the search. The Chancellor of Germany was embarrassed that Harvey had been betrayed by a German, a young diplomatic official passed clean and clear for political trust. Each man had to take some blame for the present situation, and neither of them, Riemeck had calculated, would feel quite able to spurn the commercial project which had caused it.

"Well," he said, coming to the point without preamble, "you know what I want."

They nodded, not happily. They knew.

Riemeck took out the papers that Laura Jenkinson had prepared for him and handed them one copy each, got up into elegant dossiers – suitably elegant for statesmen; suitably thin. "Here is the plan as it stands," he said. "Just an outline."

There was a silence, broken only by the murmur of traffic in the Faubourg, the birds in the Elysée's garden. Riemeck waited, not saying more. Abashed by his stare, each man began to read. The first to raise his head was the Chancellor.

"Surely you don't want an answer now, Otto?"

Simultaneously, as on a signal between them, the President of France closed his dossier and laid it aside, also unwilling to do his prep on the spot. They would give their answer in Rome, they said, not before.

Riemeck expected no more. He tried for no more. This was not the place or the time to throw around the little weight he had. After an interview of less than ten minutes he stood up to take his leave, his glass of Scotch whisky untouched.

By 6.20 he was back in his car, nosing out again into the Faubourg St. Honoré. The guards saluted; police whistles blew; the traffic was stopped for his benefit. Riemeck barely noticed. He was tired. He considered a courtesy call on the British Embassy, which lay just along the street, then thought better of it and let his car pass the embassy's arched entrance, the Union Jack hanging limp in the heat. He did not have the energy to comfort Margaret Harvey, who was hard work at the best of times. Nor did he have the time. He told his driver to take him to the airport, where the Commission's plane was waiting. The driver assumed that this was the start of the journey to Rome.

"No," Riemeck said to him, "not Rome."

Where then?

The question was asked by the tilt of the chauffeur's capped head. Riemeck left it unanswered.

In 1815 the Duke of Wellington, arriving in Paris from Waterloo, bought a house from Napoleon's sister. It had been the British Embassy since.

Margaret Harvey hated it.

Patrick's career had brought her here many times, more than she could remember. And always the place annoyed her. Its elegance was so absurdly unsuited, she always thought, to the humdrum business of modern diplomacy. As a house it was also uncomfortable. Typically, the chair she was sitting on now, though it might have won a place in any exhibition of French antique furniture, was hard to relax in. She was supposed to be taking it easy, she was supposed to be having a nice cup of tea. But how could you do these nice simple things in a huge gilded room overlooked by the victor of Waterloo, who stared from his portrait on the wall with a cold but vaguely lecherous expression? H.M. Embassy, Paris, was not the sort of place you took things easy in. It made you ask for lemon in your tea when you wanted milk.

On the pink veined mantelpiece a clock began to whirr. A horrid little cherub struck a gong six times.

Margaret Harvey sipped her lemon brew in solitude, looking

631

out at the trees of the garden. She had dismissed the kind young official detached to keep her company, worn out by his studious chit-chat. She preferred her own anxiety to that.

Sir Godfrey Smethurst, the bachelor Ambassador in Paris, had been called away to a meeting with the French Interior Minister. He had gone off at 5.20. He should be back soon with some news. But this pause had lasted long enough. She had the feeling that something had happened.

At 6.10 this suspicion was confirmed. Sir Godfrey came back with a flustered announcement.

"Well, there's news, Margaret. I'm not sure whether to call it good or bad."

"News? What news?"

"They think they may have found him."

"Found him? Where? Why didn't you say?"

"It's not certain. Now, listen while I . . ."

"Is he alive?"

"So far as they know – yes, he is." The Ambassador glanced at his watch in agitation, checking it with the cherub on the mantel. "But they want you and me on the spot now, in case something happens."

"Where is he then? What's happened?"

"Please, sit down, Margaret. We're not due to leave for a few more minutes."

Having jumped to her feet, Margaret Harvey sat again, taut on the edge of her chair. Patting her back with nervous white hands, Sir Godfrey Smethurst explained.

The French police, he said, were on the track of the Dutchman. They had followed him to Bordeaux. In Bordeaux they'd lost him, by purest incompetence. But now they had traced him to Périgueux, in the Dordogne, by intercepting a phone call which Janssen had made to the Cubans. By the time the French had men on the spot, the Dutchman had vanished. However, he must still be in the town, of that the police were certain. They had the place ringed by hundreds of men. Hundreds more were searching the streets, house to house. "So they want you and me to go down there," Sir Godfrey finished, his pale hands fluttering again over Lady Harvey's lap. "A helicopter's coming to get us. Can you manage that?"

Margaret Harvey nodded, without reply. Either Patrick was dead or he was alive. Either he would return to her or he would not. There was nothing else to it, and nothing to be said. She sat where she was until told to do different. Sir Godfrey went out to make preparations. The nice young official went to find her suitcase. Left alone again in the gilded room, she noticed how beautiful the trees were, lit from the right by a blaze of western sun. She walked to the window and opened it. From the bottom of the garden came a steady hum of traffic: all those millions of people going on with their lives, as if nothing had happened. In the distance already she could hear the clatter of a helicopter. Then a smaller sound, close behind, made her turn. In the doorway which led to the Ambassador's study, smart in a grey striped suit and white blouse, stood a girl whose existence she had forgotten.

"Laura!"

"Hello. Am I intruding?"

"Not a bit. Come in. What are you doing here?"

"They're taking me off to Rome. So I thought I'd pop in and see . . . how you were."

"How nice of you! Please, let's sit down. Help me shut this."

They closed the window, to keep out the helicopter, and moved back to where the tea tray was set.

"I'm so sorry . . . about all of this," Laura said with an effort, as though she were apologising. She paused, took a breath; then made a greater effort. "This morning, at that meeting . . . I thought how brave you were."

"No, not brave. Just bewildered. It's easy to keep a calm face if you haven't the first idea what's going on."

Again Laura took a little breath. Then she raised her brown eyes, wide and grave. "At Tours, you know, we had a frightful row. I walked right out on him."

"Yes, so I heard. Well, I've done it myself once or twice."

They laughed together nervously. Touched by Laura's effort to communicate, wondering why they had never got on better, Margaret Harvey said: "So you really are leaving the job?"

"Yes."

"You won't change your mind?"

"No, I can't do it any more."

"What next then?"

"I'd like to do something original. Perhaps I should go and help the starving."

"Laura, dear. Is that really you?"

"Actually, no. I'm going to be a journalist and live in sin in London."

They laughed again, heartily. But talk was now almost impossible. Margaret Harvey turned with a frown to the windows, now rattling in the helicopter's draught. "Just listen to that thing. Well," she added, rising as the Ambassador appeared, "they're carrying me off to battle." She held out her hand. "Goodbye, Laura dear. And good luck – whatever you do."

No further words were heard. They shook hands; and then, to the slight surprise of each, kissed cheeks.

The French army helicopter landed on the embassy's lawn, blasting the leaves off the trees. Lady Harvey was taken away. Laura, remaining at the window, watched the passengers assemble in the garden. Among them was a pair of British soldiers from the Special Air Service, in pale khaki berets and camouflage uniform. Each of them carried an olive-green cylinder as big as himself. As they hoisted their kit aboard, their faces were set in the far-away expression of athletes about to run.

A few minutes later the helicopter rose. As it turned to the south, Lady Harvey's white hair was visible at one of its windows. Good luck to you too, Laura thought, still touched by the farewell she'd had. She supposed it to be a special message between women.

10

As soon as they were out of the helicopter and into a plane, taking off southwards, Sir Godfrey Smethurst spread a map on his knee and showed Lady Harvey where the Iskra had taken her husband – or rather the town where the Dutchman, Joop Janssen, was hidden. More than that wasn't yet certain.

Périgueux stood a short distance inland from Bordeaux. As could be seen from the map, the town was in a district of low wooded hills and many rivers, all of which ran down into flat alluvial land around the great port. The best vineyards lay around here and here, the Ambassador digressed, his slender finger darting round the plain. And up here, in the hills where they were going, was the land of truffles and *foie gras*.

Sir Godfrey knew his wines and his food. He also knew his history. Périgueux, he said, was the capital of Périgord, a very old province of France. In medieval times it had been a frontier between the French and the English, much fought over. Since revolutionary times, however, this royal domain had become a department, named after its principal river, the Dordogne. "Not so nice. I prefer to call it Périgord."

And so he continued to do. Throughout the flight, Margaret Harvey noticed, the British Ambassador referred to the sphere of operations as Périgord, not the Dordogne, to the general confusion of the French. At one point he even spoke of "our troops in Aquitaine".

Sir Godfrey was a very tiresome man. She wearied of him, yet at the same time was glad of his company. The exasperation he aroused in her deflected her feelings into manageable channels.

The plane, although military, was comfortable; much like a normal commercial aircraft. Inside it, besides the two British soldiers, was a posse of high French officialdom, descending from Paris to take control. There were men from the Ministry of the Interior and the Ministry of Defence, and also several men in uniform, generals and colonels of the army, high officers of the police and gendarmerie. Taken as a whole, they did not inspire Margaret Harvey with confidence. The main thing that this plane was bringing to the crisis, she thought, was a very large cargo of male self-importance.

"Of course this is also the cave district, you realise," said Sir Godfrey, back at her side again; still poring over the map. "The prehistoric paintings, you know, all that. *Grottes* and *gouffres*."

Suddenly, then, she knew where she was going. She took the map from him in excitement. "Yes, of course, we've been here – Patrick and I. We came to do the caves. Here, Les Eyzies – that's where we stayed. A rather nice hotel by a railway."

This late realisation, though it altered nothing, immediately made Margaret Harvey feel better. For the first time her husband's predicament began to take physical, imaginable shape in her mind. So he'd been taken to the cave district. Well, that wasn't so bad perhaps. She remembered it as a benign bit of country, thickly wooded; and the caves had been very interesting. She had been strangely moved by those ancient smears on the rock, the mammoths and antelopes, bison and reindeer, depicted in spare lines of dull red and black. They had called it the Reindeer Age. Twenty thousand years ago, was it? Thirty? Forty? She could not remember. But the beautiful slowness of it all was what had appealed to her most. For a million years, was it, man had learned no more than how to make tools out of stone. And then things had speeded up. Everything was going too fast now, too fast. She could not keep up.

Her reverie was broken by the voice of the pilot, who announced that a big electric storm was coming from the east, but he hoped to beat it. He would land at Bordeaux in twenty minutes.

But a few minutes later, at 7.15, he changed the destination. He was making for the airfield at Bergerac, he said, which had now become the base of operations.

Sir Godfrey, listening, moved his pale finger across the map and tapped the flat country where the wine grew, between Bordeaux and the hills.

There was then some talk of the weather. The military men didn't seem to have a view, but Margaret Harvey felt that a storm was bad news. Oh dear, he hasn't got a mac, she thought to herself, picturing her husband crouched beneath a rock-shelter, still in his suit, while the rain poured down in the forest and the animals roved about.

The picture was too depressing. Needing to think of something else, feeling that some sort of effort was required of her, she tried to keep track of events in the plane. From the general chatter she gathered that trouble was descending on the heads of the French police, who had first concealed and then bungled their pursuit of the Dutchman. She heard the name of Commissaire Daladier mentioned with anger. But instinctively she was on the Commissaire's side. He had been so kind and polite, so calm in the midst of trouble; a big man surrounded by lesser ones. She had faith in him. Daladier was running the search and she was content to leave it to him. He would do a better job than this planeload of popinjays.

The radio in the control van was chattering with agitated messages, some sent from Paris, some from the air; getting louder.

"So this plane's bringing trouble," said Kemble.

But Daladier only shrugged. "The trouble will come later. If I save him, they will give me a medal. If he dies, I shall have no job. *C'est tout*."

"High stakes."

"Too high for them." The Commissaire chucked up his chin in a northerly direction, though the sky was still empty. "These men who are coming, they will not stop my work, or do it themselves, because they will fear to take the risk. This is the lot of policemen. You say that in England?"

Kemble nodded. "We used to. Nowadays songs don't get written for the cops."

"In France, never." Daladier stopped in the middle of the tarmac, sniffing the air. He turned to the east, where the sky had darkened. "But for you, my friend, also, this plane brings some problems. My bosses will not be pleased to find you here. And the British will not dance with joy perhaps."

"That, I agree with you, is horribly possible."

Daladier nodded in decision. "So, okay, we will make

ourselves little. *Allez, au chopper*. Let us go before they find us."

Au chopper, pronounced "Oh chop air", was Kemble's least favourite French expression. Though glad to be moving up to the front, he prepared for a spell of Vietnamese jitters.

Scattering last-minute instructions, the Commissaire hurried on ahead with his odd shambling gait. They were on the airfield at Bergerac, walking clear now of a warlike assemblage of men and equipment which was bunched at one end of the runway. Parked in close to the terminal building was the mobile command post they had just left, a dark blue windowless caravan bristling with antennae, packed full of radio equipment and manned by men of the BRVP. Around it and drawn up further away was a mass of other vehicles, among which were many police cars, marked and unmarked, high-speed pursuit cars, other cars of no detectable purpose, long buses for carrying police in greater numbers and mesh-windowed black marias for prisoners. Further off still was a line of khaki troop-trucks, parked in convoy; and beyond that again were ambulances, fire-engines, slit-windowed riot vans, vans with loudhailers and vans with searchlights fixed on their roofs. There was even an armoured car, complete with turret and field gun.

Spread out on the grass beside the runway were three or four hundred men. A leisurely crowd, they lay smoking and chatting in the bright evening sun. A trolley with soft drinks and coffee circulated slowly among them. Some of them were queueing for a lavatory housed in a trailer. Some were asleep. A few were stripped to the waist. Scattered around them was their equipment, among which could be seen gas masks, helmets, flak jackets, and every variety of weapon.

Easy to identify within this general mass was France's own anti-terrorist assault force, the famous GIGN – *Groupe d'Intervention, Gendarmerie Nationale*. They stood apart, dressed in black, with the air of men whose moment has come. They took nothing off. They did not sleep or even sit. Urination seemed to be unnecessary to them. They checked their equipment repeatedly. Two of them, probably officers, were talking to a major of the British SAS, easily recognised by his buff beret.

Already the GIGN's forward squad had moved up to Périgueux. This back-up unit in Bergerac, split into two groups, stood ready to follow or move to another location. And ready to lift them out, parked at their side on the grass, was a pair of big troop-carrying helicopters, painted the same all-over black as the combat dress of the men.

To Kemble's delight, there were no press present. A pair of local reporters had turned up to ask what the fuss was, but had been held back at the gate with talk of a military exercise. Daladier was not giving anything away. Knowing that the gang would be listening from their hideout, he had put a strict control on all television and radio stations, local and national. Not a word could be said about the progress of the search without police clearance. And the same went for newspapers. From now until the business was terminated, the Iskra must only be given such news as the chief of the BRVP desired them to know.

Kemble had therefore been given the scoop of all scoops. And he was gratefully conscious of it. Never ceasing to think of the story he would write, he filled up his pad with the technical detail.

He was now able to say that the long-barrelled submachine-gun everywhere in evidence was called the MK-49. Aside from pistols, this was the main weapon used by the French police and gendarmerie. The CRS carried the fat-barrelled Webley and Scott anti-riot gun, which could fire cartridges of tear gas. The Army were equipped with the NATO 7.62 mm self-loading rifle, presumably on the theory that, should France wish to rejoin the West's defences in a hurry, they would at least have the right ammunition.

But when it came to hardware, first prize went again to the GIGN. The all-black squad carried pistols on their belts like everyone else, Kemble noticed, but pistols of idiosyncratic variety. Enormous Colt Magnum revolvers and long-barrelled Lugers from the Second War could be seen on their belts. Their torsos were festooned with oval grenades, some of the usual kind, and some of the kind made to stun. Two of them had Viking shotguns and four carried snipers' rifles. For sniping the GIGN used a variant of the NATO SLR, which could blow a man away at a thousand yards, and was certainly the equal of Joop Janssen's Armalite. For close-quarters stuff they had the celebrated Mini Ruger 14. A quick-assembly, quick-aiming carbine, the Ruger shot very small bullets but shot them so fast that the opposition, even if winged, tended not to get up. Most of the GIGN were carrying Rugers. But most unusual of all was their submachine-gun, a funny little thing called an Ingram, with a short thin barrel and no stock to speak of at all. The Ingram was made of grey plastic, but its close resemblance to a toy did nothing, in Kemble's eyes, to diminish the impression of deadliness. In a close fight, he was told, you blasted with the Viking and aimed with the Ruger. With the Ingram you simply sprayed. You were bound to hit something.

He had seen the list of the Iskra's ordnance, and that had been frightening. But now, as he stopped to survey it from the airfield's far edge, Kemble thought the Republic's response more than adequate. All items considered, from mobile toilets to field guns, the forces of order were thoroughly equipped.

Turning, he saw that Daladier was in conversation with the pilots of two light aircraft, which stood a little further up the runway. And a few minutes later both planes took off, wheeling westwards towards Bordeaux. Kemble was told they were escaping the weather. He didn't believe it. The storm would not be here for an hour. The party from Paris would arrive before that, but without a plane small enough to put down in Périgueux, they would be forced to stay at base-camp in Bergerac.

Groucho was thinking well.

From a chopper in flight the storm looked closer. Kemble, strapped down in his seat, peered out at a range of hills to the east, overhung by black cloud. Forks of lightning jumped from cloud to earth. Yet here, where the River Dordogne wound through the plain to the coast, broad and brown, the weather was fine. The rows of vines glowed green in the sun.

Soon they were out of the flat country and flying over thickly wooded hills, the mat of trees broken here and there by short cliffs of rock. Smaller rivers passed below, and patches of farmland, fields of maize and tobacco, plantations of poplar. The roofs of the houses were built on two angles, with a pretty change of tile at the break. The roads were almost empty.

Then Périgueux came into view.

It wasn't a big town, but big for the district, and certainly big enough to hide Joop Janssen. The helicopter circled it once at Daladier's request.

Kemble peered down with interest. There was an old quarter of narrow streets, and a new quarter spread along the usual boulevards. At the edge were the usual blocks of flats, a few factories. The only peculiar thing to be seen was the cathedral, a sprawling affair of low flattish domes and many pointed bell-towers, built of white stone in the Byzantine style. It would have looked better in Istanbul.

Daladier's eyes were on the main roads leading out, of which there were four. On each was a barrier manned by police. If Janssen showed up, they would let him through and follow him.

The problem was the gaps between. Périgueux had a large, rambling periphery. In theory every way out was being watched, but Kemble, looking down, wondered how it was possible to draw so tight a cordon. Hundreds of men must be involved. And what about when night fell? In darkness, surely, the Dutchman could escape. If he was still here, he was waiting for that.

Perhaps they would find him before then. The town was being combed to its corners in a systematic search fanning outwards from the phone booth where the call had been made to the Cuban in Paris. With typical foresight Joop Janssen had made that call from a café buried deep in the town's old quarter. Immediately after it he had vanished inside the maze of narrow streets spreading up from the bizarre white cathedral. Was he still there? That was uncertain. By this time Joop Janssen could have gone anywhere inside this town of fifty thousand people.

Kemble took up the problem with Daladier when the helicopter landed.

"Think he's still here?"

"It appears so."

"And the others – with Harvey? Here too?"

The Commissaire's negative was convinced. "No, but they are close. The Dutchman is in the town, the others in the country – perhaps a few kilometres away." His hand waved round at the town's environs. "The problem is to observe them join together, and we have to do that without any shooting. Any more shooting, and Harvey is dead."

This remark fell into the silence left by the helicopter's motor, which had sighed to a stop. Daladier, still peering round at the lie of the land, seemed overcome by fatigue. He shook his head grimly.

"It is a dangerous conjuncture we are in here, my friend. For myself, as an officer of the police, I cannot remember a problem more difficult. Please say that in your book."

"Cheer up. There's still time," Kemble said. "At least we're getting closer."

But the mention of time was poor comfort. Prompted by it, both of them lifted their watches. The flight from Bergerac had taken twelve minutes. Now it was 7.32. Assuming no error in Rosa Berg's watch or brain, twelve hours and twenty-eight minutes remained.

The Commissaire made no comment on it. Lifting his hand to his face, he wiped his moustache energetically, shut his eyes tight for a second, then opened them wide, to force himself into wakefulness. The grimace suggested a man who shrinks from a sight, then faces it.

"They'll make a mistake," Kemble said.

"Let us hope. Here is Biffaud." Daladier, catching sight of his deputy, advanced towards him; then turned back to Kemble. "Please, monsieur, leave us alone. I will call you if there is news."

This was the first encounter with Biffaud since he had lost track of the Dutchman in Bordeaux. The BRVP's number two was about to descend in the batting order, Kemble thought. Biffaud expected so too. The bristle-topped, sharp-shooting *flic* marched towards his chief with the erect but desperate bearing of a soldier about to be stripped of his medals. But that did not occur. Daladier said a few words to him, then put his arm around the wee fellow's shoulders. Together they walked off towards the command van.

Kemble stayed out on the tarmac and looked around.

The chopper had put them down on an airstrip just west of the town. This was forward base for the search. There were no mobile loos or pop trolleys, no sunbathing infantry, no armoured cars. In Périgueux were only four necessary squads; three waiting to go, one already in action. Kemble identified them quickly in turn.

Grouped around their black helicopter were the black-clad assault group of the GIGN, all set to shoot their way in to Harvey.

Gathered near the airstrip's exit were the *Brigade de Surveillance*, ready to follow Joop Janssen if he tried to make a dash. And Janssen would have to be clever to evade them, even to spot them. Among the pursuit teams were men and women of various ages, in various styles of dress. Some wore jeans and some looked rich. One man was even got up as a priest. They had every sort of vehicle, from motorcycles to sports cars. They had their own helicopter. They even had a spotter plane. And no doubt they had been joined by some local police, who knew the by-ways of the district.

Closer by was a group whose expertise consisted in talking trapped kidnappers into surrender, without a shot fired. Among them were two psychiatrists, and also several women, in case Rosa Berg would listen to her own sex better. Kemble doubted it. But this talk-down squad had had some success in the past, he was told. Only if their methods failed would "those black baboons" of the GIGN be let loose.

There was rivalry in the air at Périgueux. And thunder. Walking back to the command van, Kemble was startled by a long, deep rumble from the east.

The van was smaller than the one in use at Bergerac, but similarly bristling with radio antennae. Gathered around it was the fourth and largest group on the airstrip – those engaged in the search. And here there was already action. Men came and went at the double, cars arrived and left with an urgent screech of tyres. Biffaud had been in charge; now Daladier was stepping up the pace. Both men were shut in the van while subordinates dashed around outside it.

Kemble positioned himself at the heart of the fuss and waited for something to happen. The thunder rolled again, long and low. Nothing else happened. But he knew that something would. Once again he felt the warm and solid certainty, so rarely permitted to a newsman, that he was in the right place, at exactly the right time to be there.

He had no cigarettes but didn't care; nothing to drink, didn't want it. Twice in the day he had thought of Laura, but only to realise how much he'd forgotten her. Waking this morning he'd had a new girl on the brain, in the heart. Now she had dropped out of both. A week ago he'd had a wife. Now she was on the far side of the moon. He was alone and he wanted one thing. He wanted to be on the spot when it happened, alone if possible, ahead of the field. And for that he would take any risk. He would get as close as they let him, go as far, or further, play cop, be a hero, break the rules, shoot a gun, scared of nothing –

except those bastards over there. That's right, keep them out. Me first.

From his central position on the airstrip he watched a bunch of press at the gate, held back by a pair of gendarmes.

And then he noticed something peculiar.

Parked a little way off from where he stood was an armoured police van with meshed glass and small barred windows, of the sort which had carried off the prisoners from the Babylone. There had been one in Bergerac, too. But outside the sealed doors of this one, in Périgueux, stood a pair of armed guards.

Could there be someone inside?

Kemble had started to wonder about this, and was thinking of walking across to investigate, when he was called into the command van. He trotted up the aluminium steps and was met by a cool waft of conditioned air. The interior was like the cockpit of an aircraft, packed tight from floor to roof with flickering, crackling equipment. A pair of BRVP sat at the controls. Biffaud was talking on the radio. Daladier filled most of the available space. Beckoning Kemble to look across his shoulder, he showed him a street-map of Périgueux, pinned under transparent plastic. Chalked in red around the town's perimeter were the outposts of watching police. Spreading in a solid red stain from the centre was the area so far searched. Cordon and search were drawing close at several points, so Joop Janssen, unless he'd been missed, must now be squeezed between the police lines in one of the town's outer suburbs.

"Biffaud is going in to take command. I propose you go with him."

"Suits me," said Kemble, assuming that the Commissaire wished him to get a closer look at the difficulties, in case of eventual failure. Or perhaps this was a pure favour, to put him in closer to the action. A third explanation, that it was to get him out of the way, did not occur to Kemble until he was leaving the airstrip in Biffaud's car. Passing out through the gate, he looked back to see that Daladier was strolling across towards the sealed prison van.

So, it was true. There was someone inside.

Who?

The question was deflected by the hee-haw of a siren, a blue flashing light approaching at speed from the town. Hello, here's something, thought Kemble. But it was only an ambulance, demanding right of way past the roadblock ahead. The gendarmerie waved it through. Biffaud pulled aside to let it pass.

"So who's in the van?" Kemble asked him, pointing back.

As usual, when convenient, the Inspector failed to understand English. Kemble put the question in adequate French. Still he received no answer. Biffaud's lips remained in their usual position, clamped in a tight bloodless slit, as he drove up the hill into Périgueux.

Oriental temple apart, it was a good-looking town. The old streets had ducts in the middle, to carry the rain down their steep cobbled slopes to the river. Strung across one was a banner saying 18e FESTIVAL DU FOLKLORE. There were frilly *patisseries* and several luxurious *salons de thé*. The cafés were putting up defences against the storm, pulling in chairs from the pavement. Some of the shops were open still. Displayed in their brightly lit windows were the goodies of the region, walnuts and truffles, many truffles, a delicacy advertised in one place as *Le Diamant Noir de la Gourmandise*.

Kemble's attention wandered as Biffaud made a tour of his men, driving in ever-wider circles. In the back of the car was a man from the local police, who acted as guide. In the newer parts the streets, getting wider and straighter, were shaded by plane trees. Wrapped around the trunks of the trees were posters of pop stars. Another banner appeared, suspended above the traffic to say that, for those who could wait, coming up was a SUPER NUIT DES JEUNES AVEC JIMMY MULLOT. Biffaud drove under it and on down a wider street still, called Avenue John F. Kennedy. Kemble's eyelids began to droop.

The flap, when it came, caught him napping.

First there was a radio message. Kemble, half-asleep, missed what was said, but it sent Biffaud into top gear, siren wailing, tyres squealing as he u-turned in JFK Avenue and sped away into less crowded streets. The *flic* at the back kept shouting the way, Kemble kept asking what was happening, Biffaud kept on not replying. He was driving flat-out towards the eastern edge of the town, where the main road led out past the airstrip and away along the river to Limoges.

Within two minutes of the radio message they had reached the source of the alarm: a small detached house in the suburbs, brand new, made of scrambled-egg stucco on a base of pointed brick. Outside it already was another police car. An elderly woman in an apron was standing in the garden. She was talking in a loud, excited voice to one of the patrolmen. The other was trying to break into the house.

The truth emerged slowly, getting worse as it went.

The man who lived there was an invalid, and he must have taken a turn for the worse, said the aproned lady, who lived next door, because an ambulance had just come to get him.

Up to a point she was right.

When entry was forced, it was found that the sick man who lived here was still here, and he had indeed taken a turn for the worse. Also still here was the ambulance driver, who had lost his white coat and peaked cap. Both men had been killed with a knife.

The funny thing was, said the lady outside, that the ambulance had been driven off again, without any patient inside it. But she had lost her audience. Biffaud was sprinting for his radio, Kemble was close behind.

11

The ambulance was one of those marginally modified Citroën estates in which it is hard to imagine a patient being fitted, unless he is flat on his back already, and not too bulky at that. The rear end tapered down to a pair of little doors, just big enough to take in a stretcher. The windows were curtained. The bodywork was white. There were crosses on the sides, and one on the roof. The bonnet was the usual shark's nose, and under it was a very powerful engine. If speed of conveyance was the critical factor, then this, of all ambulances in the world, was the sort to get carried off in.

For speed of escape it also served well. In the twenty-eight minutes that had passed since it left the town, waved casually through the eastern roadblock, the ambulance of Périgueux's municipal hospital had covered a great deal of ground. First it had dashed down the road to Limoges, far enough to encourage pursuit in that direction. It had then ducked southward on by-roads, until it came out on the main road to Brive. For several miles it went that way, confusing pursuit still further. But then it had changed direction entirely. Having travelled continuously south-eastwards, it had struck off south-westwards, doubling back through the Fôret Barade. From that point it had gone almost unobserved. Once inside the forest it had kept to the smallest roads it could find, and then, seen by no one, it had left the mapped roads altogether and gone lurching down a rough track. Now it was not even on the track, but doing a mad high-speed slalom through the trees, flattening the undergrowth which lay in its path. It careered down a short muddy slope, then sailed clean over a limestone cliff, up into the air. In the air it performed a graceful arc, like a diver, then dropped sixty feet and crashed on its pointed nose in the narrow ravine below the cliff. After impact it toppled slowly over on its back. The wheels spun a while, then were still. The water of a stream gurgled through its broken windows. The bracken and brambles, torn apart by its fall, closed over its underside. The trees overhanging the gorge almost screened it from sunlight. For all its white paint and crosses, this ambulance would not be found from the air. It would be hard to find on the ground.

And that was the driver's intention.

Picking himself off the soft patch into which he had jumped, Joop Janssen peered over the cliff, then up at the cover provided by the trees. Satisfied, he started to move fast on foot. First he tore off the white coat and cap, bundled them up, stuffed them under a bush. Then, in his usual denim jacket and jeans, still clutching his rope-handled plastic bag, he ran back until he reached the road he had left.

There he lay down in the bracken and waited, well concealed. In the sky could be heard a small plane, circling somewhere to the north; also a helicopter, further off. Neither came close. The storm, too, seemed to have changed its mind. The thunder had veered to the south. He was pleased to hear it. Panting and sweating from his run, he beat off the flies that settled on his face. The air was heavy and still. Little creatures stirred around him in the woods, disturbed by this sudden activity. They seemed to be waiting like himself.

The road was of the smallest sort to be found in rural France. The ferns on the verge tumbled over its pale gravelled surface, on which were no markings. The trees of the forest pressed close on each side. Its emptiness had been an advantage so long as he was still in the ambulance. Now the lack of traffic was a problem. Several minutes passed before he heard a motor.

First to come along was a woman, driving a small brown Renault estate. In the back were two children. He let them go.

Next was a woodsman, puttering along in a pick-up with logs. Too slow. He let it pass.

Third came a red BMW, travelling fast, one man at the wheel. Joop stepped into the centre of the road and flagged it down. The man braked sharply and wound down his window to protest at this high-handed, grey-headed hitcher in denim. It was the last thing he did. Before he knew what was happening a pistol came through the window and was pressed to his chest, so hard that its shot was muffled. He toppled back into the passenger seat, stone dead.

Joop took over the wheel. Within a few seconds he was up through the gears and cruising at speed. The BMW was a car he knew well but had never much liked, for reasons of racial prejudice. Still, it was fast. It would do. With luck it would take him all the way.

He drove on until he found another track, up which he turned, until out of sight. He dragged out the corpse and hid it in the undergrowth, then cleaned up the blood. The man's papers showed him to be an estate agent from Brive, name of Bernard Gallimard. He had a tweed cap and macintosh on the back seat, ready for a turn in the weather. Joop put them on. The disguise wouldn't pass a police check, but might be enough to fool the public. More useful still, Bernard Gallimard had maps. His glove compartment was packed with them. Joop found the one that he needed and spread it on the pink-stained passenger seat. In sixty seconds of intense concentration he had picked out and memorised the route he would follow. He turned the car round and drove back to the road.

The switch of vehicles had taken too long, he thought, glancing down at the neat German instrument panel. He had ditched the ambulance at 8.25. Now the time was 8.43. Eighteen minutes had passed in which he had covered little extra ground from Périgueux.

This made him worried.

He had no definite reason to think the alarm had been raised, and yet there was one small thing. From 8.15 the hospital in Périgueux had started to call for their overdue vehicle. And then they had stopped. For the last two minutes he was in the ambulance its radio had gone silent.

That was enough to make him suspicious. And if the alarm had been raised, he knew what would happen next. The *flics* would work out how far he could have travelled, add a few kilometres for safety, then draw a circle of that exact radius on the map and block every road that passed through it.

So speed was still the main factor. If he could cover more ground than they reckoned, he would be out of the circle before it was drawn.

The chance of that was reduced. However, for the *flics*, drawing circles on the map was easier than putting down a cordon on the ground. If he stuck to the smallest by-ways he could find, heading fast in a new direction, he had a good chance of passing through the circle.

Small roads at speed were the best hope, and yet he should not go too fast, he thought, lifting his foot from the floor. A red BMW screeching around on two wheels would draw some attention in these parts, especially since its owner was probably known.

Slow through the villages, fast through the woods became Joop's tactic after this thought. But he wasn't much held up. There were more woods than villages, mile after mile of them, rolling up and down. There were wild woods of ivy-covered oak and many plantations of hazel, shorn off to sprout from the stump. It was a country of trees and of nuts – chestnuts, walnuts, hazel nuts. The walnut trees stood out in fields, the cattle grouped under them for shelter. Also the truffle-oak grew here, scrounged under by pigs for the trufflle-eating classes. This was good country to eat in, and it was good country to hide in, chosen by him for that purpose. Twice he had come to reconnoitre before Rosa took the house. Soon he would be in the district he knew.

Heading due south now, into the storm, he rushed on down through the hilly wooded land in the red German car. At each bend he braced himself, preparing to meet a roadblock. They would wait round a corner, to take him by surprise. He knew it and held himself ready. All the way, until arrival, there would be danger ahead.

And there would be danger behind.

If he'd been spotted they would follow him, not stop him. The surveillance brigade would take over, catch up, sit tight on his tail. And he knew just how good they would be. Everything that turned up behind was a danger, all the time from now until arrival.

Nothing turned up until Rouffignac.

Rouffignac, for Joop, was a nightmare. The town was holding a fête. He was in it before he could avoid it. There was nothing to do but drive through it. A brass band marched by in scarlet uniform; girls threw rose petals over his car. Little boys rushed up in medieval armour, pulled faces at him through the window, then rushed off to hit each other over the head with silver wooden swords, English invaders versus gallant French. There had been a parade, but now it was over. The floats had been drawn up by tractors around the war memorial. Tables were set out with food and wine, seats had been made from stacked bales of straw. Paper lanterns were strung between the trees. There were dodgems, fairy-lights, fireworks going off, cheers, kisses, laughter, glasses raised to the stranger in the smart red car, shouted invitations to come and join the fun.

Joop smoked a cigarette and stared ahead, left hand raised to his face as he passed through the turmoil, yard by slow yard. He could see the town's gendarme talking to the priest. Neither turned to look. At last he was through.

Leaving Rouffignac, he was soaked with sweat. The car picked up speed but the air hardly cooled him. It rushed in like warm human breath. The windscreen was spattered with insects. Outside the town he passed a field of sunflowers. The giant yellow blooms hung their heads, exhausted by heat and drought. The light was still falling on them, yellow from the west, but ahead now the sky was almost black. Late-evening brightness and stormy darkness hung over the landscape together, a few miles apart. Between them flew a helicopter, disappearing rightwards. The woods closed in again.

And in the woods was a girl, hitching southward from Rouffignac in shorts which showed off her legs. When she heard the BMW coming she turned and stood to thumb a lift, flicking back her curly fair hair from her face, smiling with all her teeth. For a road-walker she was very beautiful. Her backpack was new.

Joop passed her by at a hundred. Keeping his eyes on the mirror, he saw her stick out her tongue, slap her thighs in annoyance. Perhaps she was real.

And then, still watching the mirror, he saw that an English car had come into view behind, a BMG Jaguar saloon, which also refused to stop for the girl. Fast as he was going, the Jag caught him up and sat on his tail, following him round the bends in the woods. Inside were two men, one smoking a cigar. They were talking together and laughing. The driver watched only for a chance to overtake. As soon as the road straightened out, he did so and disappeared ahead, still talking to his passenger. The car's number-plates were English.

And probably real, Joop thought. Many English lived in this district. The Iskra's own hideaway belonged to an English family, whose holiday home it was. Rosa had taken out a lease in the name of Marc Bensaïd's wife, who had signed the paper with her eyes shut.

But Marc knew where the place was. And Marc had been pumped by the *flics* for twenty-four hours.

Despite his faith in the thick-skinned Algerian, this fact worried Joop more than any other. The house must be approached with caution, he thought, in case it was already ambushed. But first he had to get there. Some distance remained.

The Jaguar did not reappear; nor any other vehicle, in front or behind. Suspicion subsiding, he drove on alone.

The road remained empty until he got to Fleurac, where there had been a wedding. Coming out of the village, he got stuck behind the honeymoon car. Smeared with messages in toothpaste, stuck with balls of cotton wool, it was being unsteadily driven by the groom, whose new wife kept trying to kiss him.

Even for the famous *Brigade de Surveillance*, this seemed a little too theatrical. Impatient but not suspicious, Joop followed the car down a narrow defile, into country that he had reconnoitred. Descending steeply to the River Vézère, the road passed through cliffs of overhanging rock. Advertisements appeared for prehistoric sites: big placards of bison and reindeer. At the mouths of the caves were supplementary signs to say that, when it came to settling up, the guide should not be forgotten. In this district caves were big business.

But Joop wanted only to get on and out. The road twisted down, too narrow to pass on. The newly-weds lurched ahead. A girl on a motorcycle closed up behind, wasp-waisted in a tee-shirt, hair flying from her helmet. Joop watched her in the mirror, came to a straight patch, pulled out to overtake the honeymoon car . . . and at the same moment saw the Jaguar in front, stopped for petrol.

There was nowhere to go but forward.

Leaving them all behind in one sprint, he took the BMW fast down the hill. At the bottom, he knew, was the village of Manaurie, from which there were four ways to go. If he moved fast, he could still get away.

But that was not how it happened. All routes out of Manaurie lay beyond a railway level-crossing. And the boom was down for a train.

After one short moment of shattered dismay, Joop Janssen was seized by a ferocious urge to escape, like that of an animal trapped. Several courses of action flashed through his head, from ramming the boom to making a dash on foot across the rails. He dismissed them all and controlled himself. There was nothing to do but stop and sit tight. Scalp prickling, he set his Makarov pistol ready to hand, on the shelf below the dash, and bent across the map on the passenger seat. Moving his eyes but not his head, he saw the bridal pair close up behind. They went on canoodling. The Jaguar followed, the men in it still in conversation. The girl on the motorbike, arriving last, passed to the front of the queue and stopped by the boom, just ahead of the BMW. She took off her helmet and shook out her hair, glancing anxiously up at the sky as she waited. The late-evening brightness had gone. The cloud-mass was almost overhead. Thunder crashed close. The girl winced in fright, then put on her helmet and looked up the track. She was riding a Yamaha.

Un train peut en cacher un autre, said the usual sign. Yes, and one *flic* can hide another, Joop thought, lifting his head to glance round the village. But it was deserted. All the people of Manaurie were shut in their homes, like a western town before the gunfight.

The train came past, on its way to Les Eyzies. A small two-coach diesel like a bus, red and white, it rolled off leftwards with a two-note blare of its horn. The echo bounced up around the cliffs, then was swallowed by another clap of thunder.

The boom was raised.

The girl's Yamaha stalled.

Joop got away first. Accelerating over the tracks, he took the smallest road from Manaurie, straight ahead and up into more wooded hills. After three more kilometres he pulled off into the trees, got out of the car and waited, well hidden, to see which one of the three would follow him – the girl, or the couple, or the Jaguar. One would, he knew it.

But to his great astonishment and growing relief, nothing came after him at all. The minutes passed by, the thunder crashed around, but nothing else came down the road. Only the storm arrived: a sudden rush of wind through the trees, then rain like an army advancing. Lightning and thunderclaps almost coincided; the rain fell harder. Soon he was crouched in a downpour. Water hit the leaves with such violence the trees sagged beneath its weight. It bounced off the road with the force of a pressure hose. The gravel surface vanished in a grey mist of spray. But still the road was empty. Nothing came down it, on foot or on wheel. Only rain, now running like a river.

Joop didn't care about the weather. If anything, it was a bonus. The wonderful thing was that empty road. He stepped out of hiding and rejoiced as the sky cracked and split above his head in great explosions of sound and electrical light. So the trap in Manaurie had all been imagined by his own over-trained, anxious mind. In that case he'd made it. He was free and away, outside any circle that Daladier would ever think of drawing. Only one risk remained, at the bridge just ahead. And that he knew how to inspect in advance. From there it was a short run to the house.

While watching for pursuers, Joop had been hidden in the trees. Now he was standing in the open, still wearing the brown gabardine of the murdered estate agent. Rain had flattened his hair and was running down inside the collar of the coat. Oblivious of the weather, he paused for one more inspection of the road, up and down, and then walked back to the red BMW, which was parked out of sight on a muddy lane between two concave rock-faces. He got back into the car and sat smoking a reflective cigarette while the rain drummed down on the roof. According to the BMW's digital clock it was 9.06. He watched each passing second flash up with ostentatious German precision. He was in no particular hurry. He wanted to get to the house before dark, to take a look around. But there was still time for that. He would finish this cigarette before he moved on.

His thoughts were untouched by the three men he'd killed. He was glad to be free, that was all, and proud of his skill at evasion. Twice in one day he had fooled the best police in France. That was something, he thought. In fact his whole journey from Austerlitz Station, Paris, to this obscure neck of the woods in Dordogne was the best run he'd made in his life.

But there had been some bad moments. The first scare had come on the train, after Orléans, when Biffaud took a seat opposite. The first fear of trap had come there, on the train: that old convulsive surge of stomach, heart and brain. But he had subdued it and slept. So long as he travelled, they would follow. In the night he had worked out a plan of escape from Bordeaux.

And that had gone well. The docks there were full of old friends, a pair of whom had taken him out of the city and left him with a car. Travelling on alone, he had taken his time, looping northward to avoid major roads.

That, too, had gone well. There had been no problems. Outside Bordeaux the *flics* had got in a comical tangle with the wine-growers, who were setting up roadblocks of their own in protest at something or other. But for him this stage of the journey had been easy.

Too easy. Wanting a meal and some supplies, he had gone into Périgueux to call the Cuban. That had been a bad mistake. It was frightening, even now, to think how nearly he'd been caught on the phone. Reinaldo Valdes, talking in circles, had tried to get the address of the hideout. That was the first thing to put him on his guard. It should have been enough to make him hang up. But he'd wanted instructions, an escape route. And finally Valdes got around to it. Harvey should be released, he said, and the others brought to an address in Bordeaux. When it came to instructions, Valdes had been precise and particular, a strangely urgent note in his voice. And then he had started to flannel again.

Sitting now in the car in the rain, Joop could not remember exactly what it was in the voice of the Cuban that had made him slam down the phone and run from the café in Périgueux. But he had escaped by a whisker. Within a few minutes the whole quarter filled with *flics*, and soon after that the town was besieged. He'd had to abandon his car. Several hours of evasion had followed, close calls without number, and always the fear of encirclement.

If I ever see Reinaldo Valdes again, he thought, I will kill him.

Smoking at his ease in the hidden BMW, Joop reviewed his journey with a mixture of pride and bitterness. Three times over, twice in fact and once in fancy, he had gone through fear of trap and joy of escape. Indeed this long day in France, he thought, could stand as a miniature of his whole career. Escape from traps was what his life had been.

The windows of the car had steamed up. He wound down the one at his side and threw out the stub of his cigarette, then wiped the others with a cloth. Outside the rain fell with unabated force. The lightning was so frequent it hardly ceased. Once it had struck very close. The dripping woods were lit by great overhead flashes, every tree, every leaf outlined sharp in the sudden white glares. Thunder banged and rolled around the hills.

Bracing himself for further action, Joop started up the car and returned to the road, looked carefully up and down it – still nothing – and then drove slowly along the route he had plotted, down to the River Vézère. Some of the roads were so drenched in rain that they were like tributary rivers themselves, pouring into the valley. But all were empty of traffic or people. Even the animals had gone to ground. The whole countryside was deserted, strangely lifeless, though tossed and pounded by the storm. As his tyres hissed and splashed through the wet, Joop Janssen was conscious of solitude. And the feeling was pleasant to him. He was alone and he was free, pursued by many, outwitted by none; a fox of the forest no hounds could catch.

And so it had been all his life.

Yes, he thought, this is the last escape of all. Or perhaps the last trap. I shall have to watch my step.

12

As he drove slowly down through thunder and rain towards the River Vézère, Joop Janssen pondered the facts of his life. Brooding rather than thinking, a creature of instinct not intellect, he felt his past pulling him in different directions. Aware of the choices still open to him, at least until he crossed this last river, he allowed the impulses coming from memory free play in his head.

Within a few minutes he would have to do one of three things. He wasn't sure which it would be. He had been thinking about this all the way from Périgueux, between more pressing emergencies. And now the moment of decision was close.

The period his mind drifted back to was his last stint of duty in the Middle East, when his life as a Soviet agent had been bewilderingly complicated by quarrels within the Palestinian camp. The bloody Muslim bandits had started shooting each other, shooting for power, shooting for money. They even started hiring German anarchists. Depraved little girls from Dusseldorf and Frankfurt had popped up behind every sand dune while the Arabs fought like alley-cats and everyone talked in a high moral tone of world revolution.

And this he had not been able to cope with. Killing he could manage; confusion he could not. Whose side was he supposed to be on? Whose side were the Russians on? Which of these squabbling Arab factions carried the seal of Soviet approval? Nobody knew. He received no instructions. Higher authority retreated into cloud, and he felt aggrieved. His masters had deserted him.

In 1977 the Syrians seemed to have Soviet blessing, so he

transferred allegiance to them. But then the whole problem was ended by the swoop of an Israeli Phantom, a white ball of fire rushing over the sand. He thought he was dead.

To wake up in Moscow had been like arrival in heaven: the martyr's reward. Even through the agony of multiple burns he had felt pride and pleasure as the pink smiling face of General Viktor Shuvalov, his original master in Cuba, had leaned down to murmur approval.

And they had looked after him well. The Russians had mended his body. They had trained him to fighting fitness and sent him back to the West.

But for what?

His final briefing had been a disappointment. Uncle Viktor, whose favour could be gauged by the splendour of his lunches, had taken him to an inferior restaurant overlooking the steps in Odessa. The meal had lasted half an hour, broken off without spirits or coffee. His task, he'd been told, was to make contact with progressive groups in Europe and offer such assistance as he saw fit. His link would be Reinaldo Valdes in Paris.

As a farewell this was curt, Joop thought at the time, and thought now again with more bitterness. Furthermore its vagueness had led directly to the present predicament, in which the chief mystery was Reinaldo Valdes.

What was going on there in Paris?

It was possible that Valdes was innocent. The possibility, at least, should be considered that the Cuban didn't know his phone had been tapped. In that case his orders were probably genuine, and the main one ought to be obeyed. The right thing to do was to go to the hideout and set Harvey free. Valdes' escape route would have to be ignored, since known to the French, but Harvey's release could still be achieved. Of the options available, this one had the highest chance of pleasing the Russians. It therefore ought to be considered.

On the other hand, from the business with the telephone – the delays, the way the conversation had gone – it seemed much more likely that Reinaldo Valdes was a traitor. In which case his orders had come from the French, and should be ignored. But was that all? Was Valdes alone in his treachery? Suppose that not only Reinaldo Valdes but General Viktor Shuvalov, along with the whole damn *apparat*, from Havana to Moscow, had turned in their hands with the French. In that case they weren't only working for Harvey's release. They were also suggesting escape to a prearranged dèathtrap.

Joop faced this second theory with deepest aversion. As he did so he felt his whole life take a sickening lurch. Treachery by Uncle Viktor turned day into night. And yet it was possible. Certain small undeniable features of that phone call – Valdes' manner of speaking, his precision, his unusual confidence – made it seem probable, even, that this was the truth. The certainty grew in Joop's mind as he drove to the river. The Russians were in this, too. The Russians were working with the French to trap him and kill him.

To this his immediate, angry reaction was to go in and help Rosa finish the job she had started, even if that meant death for Harvey. After all, the girl had foreseen exactly this. Your Russian masters will let you down, she had said. Before this is over you will have to choose between them and me.

So, he could do that. Yes, he might do that. Rosa had worked this out better than he had. And Rosa was Rosa; the only girl he'd kept for more than a week, the only girl who'd ever kept him. They had been together, it struck him now, almost as long as he'd been with the Russians. And Rosa's loyalty had never once wavered. She had always offered shelter, whatever the risk. Twice she had helped him out of Paris, when trapped and on the run. Rosa had guessed who his real masters were, and yet she had trusted him and fed him and kept her bed warm for him, nobody else. So yes, he would return that loyalty. He would go in there, do what she wanted, and take her out with him.

This second possibility hung in Joop's mind a moment, carried to the fore on a wave of affection. But immediately behind it came a third.

Perhaps he wouldn't go to the hideout at all. He'd finished with the Russians; and he didn't need Rosa. She wasn't worth the risk of going back to. He would leave her to finish off this crazy private war of hers, in which the risks remaining were big. That house was far from safe. Marc might have talked, or the *flics* might have traced it some other way. And once it was traced, the house was a death-trap; there'd be no escape. So perhaps he wouldn't go there. Perhaps, after all, he would just keep moving in this fast German car, which would take him a long way further before he had to swap it for another. The car was hot, but he would find another. His identities were all used up, but he would find others. He would keep on moving fast through the night, southward out of France, on over the mountains and down into Spain, to Algeria, to Libya, and on further eastwards to friends in desert places – or perhaps somewhere else entirely, some new land where he could rest and start his life again; a man alone.

This plan had hovered in his mind since Paris. Now it rose to the front and stayed there.

Yes, he thought, I'll keep on going. Goodbye Europe, goodbye Rosa. I'm sorry, but you know what I am, and you know why. I live for myself. Joop Janssen hunts alone.

This decision had not quite set, firm and final, as Joop approached the River Vézère. He was still trying it out in his mind, and had to keep some concentration for driving. The rain was so hard he could barely see. The fast German wipers were overrun by downpouring water. But there was no other traffic. He passed through no villages even, but kept to lonely roads in the woods, proceeding slowly until he reached a point from which he could see the river unobserved. There he stopped and left the car out of sight. Advancing the last few yards on foot, crouched again under dripping trees, he inspected the lie of the land.

It was now growing dark, but flashes of lightning lit the scene in every detail. He could see as much as he needed to.

Directly below him was the railway, and beside it the Vézère flowed rightward: a wide river, already swollen by the storm. There were rapids frothing white with the force of the current, a few bars and sandbanks disappearing quickly in the flood. In the main channels the water ran deep and fast, muddy brown, its surface lashed by wind and rain.

On the opposite bank was the village of Campagne. He could see the bulbous stone towers of its château, each topped by a conical spire of slate. One was struck by lightning as he watched: a bolt of white fire from sky to earth, accompanied by a deafening crack.

Joop took no notice. In the wooded slopes behind this castle was the hideout. And his hunch was the house hadn't yet been traced. If it had been, the village of Campagne would have shown more activity.

Next he looked rightwards, to inspect the bridge he must cross. It was screened by the cover he was standing in. He shifted position, pulled aside a branch, and then the bridge came into view. Stopped on it were two cars. A striped boom was laid across the road between temporary trestles. Inspecting each vehicle that passed were plain-clothes police, backed by gendarmes and soldiers, six men in all. And the weather wasn't putting them off. They were checking papers; searching each car. One of the drivers had been made to get out.

Joop watched a moment longer, then returned to his car. There were two other bridges he could use. One was downstream in Le Bugue, nearest town to the hideout; the other was in Les Eyzies, a few miles upriver. But he knew that both would be blocked. Unable to draw a tight circle in time, Daladier had gone for the bridges.

So the way to Rosa was cut.

Digesting this fact, Joop sat in the car and lit another cigarette, amused at his own indecision. All night and all day he'd been travelling southward, half-hoping to arrive, half-wanting to be stopped, locked into automatic motion until something happened to make up his mind. Now Daladier had settled what his own instincts couldn't.

Half a minute later, at 9.15 by the clock on the dash, he turned the BMW round and drove back the way he had come. He went uphill into woodland, then down to the railway and left along the river bank, away from the bridge and on out of sight.

13

For Rosa the storm was a breaking point. It had swept up to the house not just with a wind, but a whirlwind, which came through the trees like the blast of an explosion, snapping off branches, ripping up twigs, leaves, dust from the ground and flinging them about in the air with contrary gusts of terrific force. The telephone cable had fallen. Tiles had been lifted from the roof. The shutters had banged back and forth on their hinges, some so hard they had splintered. The shutter of Harvey's room was nailed up tight, but rushing round the house to get the others closed, she had been knocked over by one of them. It had blown back and struck her on the head. Dazed, she had fallen to the ground, struggled up again, got the thing barred, run on to the next one, then fallen again, bowled over by sheer force of air. She had screamed at Murdoch to help her. But Murdoch had never seen a southern French tornado. He refused to come out of the house. She should come inside too, he screamed back, or she'd be blown away. At that she had lost control. Overcome with rage at this English poltroon who had run from Ash Valley, now scared of wind, she had gone back inside and drawn her pistol on him. Shouting at him in French she had forced Murdoch out, at gunpoint, to help her. Together they had got the shutters closed. Then came the rain. And right behind the rain came thunder and lightning, of which she herself was afraid. They had dashed about inside the house, putting out buckets and saucepans to catch the leaks from the roof. But the deluge soon found the holes where the tiles had been. The rain came into the house. And then the lightning came in too. Flashing along the power line which ran down the hill, it spluttered on into the fuse-box beside the front door, which started to put out smoke and then lit up in a blue flickering aura of huge electrical power with nowhere to go. For Rosa this was too much. She had left the electrics to Murdoch, then run away down the track to take over sentry duty from Mario. Pretending more courage than either of them, she had sent Mario up to the house while she stood watch in the woods. There was more safety in the trees, she thought. Lightning struck trees, but there were a lot of them. If she crouched down small and didn't touch the trunks, the bolts from the sky wouldn't find her.

She had been in this position for fifteen minutes. And now her fear had subsided. The storm was crashing overhead, even closer, but she didn't think it would touch her. She hardly cared if it did. Her fear and her fury had given way to cold, exhausted numbness. Soaked to the skin, she sat in the undergrowth and watched the road below.

Down the road was the village of Campagne, out of sight. But the conical spires of its château were visible, protruding from the trees, and one got struck as she watched. Good, she thought, strike it down, the ugly great feudal pile. Hail, fire and brimstone on the homes of the rich.

So she said to herself, but without much feeling. Fury at Murdoch, fury at the rich had subsided into rain-drenched apathy. She felt only cold, inside as well as out. Numbness spread through her like hemlock.

The road was empty. No traffic came along it.

But there was one person in sight.

At the bottom of the hill, where the track from the house met the road, was an open stretch of marshland, and standing in the middle of this wet grassy patch was a man wearing high rubber boots and an oilskin. Bent over, he waded slowly from place to place. Slung over his shoulder was a canvas bag, into which from time to time he put something picked from the ground. Snails, Rosa realised after a while. This man was out in the weather picking snails. For himself? No, of course not. For market. Tomorrow was market day in Le Bugue. She wondered how much he would get for them. How many francs for a snail? How many snails for a franc? She started to count them as he filled his bag. He wasn't finding many, but enough to make him work in the rain, poor wretch. Did snails come up to the surface in storms? How strange, she thought. You'd think they'd go down, scared of lightning like me.

Normally they came up at night, she remembered. When she'd been here in May, to show Joop the house, they had watched the snail-pickers working by torch-light, three of them traversing the marsh in a row.

And where was Joop now, she started to wonder. By this time he should be here, at the house. Perhaps he'd been caught. Perhaps he'd been shot. The very great number of things that could have gone wrong pressed into Rosa's imagination. All day she had worried about this more and more, and now it was nearly night. Joop wasn't here and she didn't think he'd come. Something had happened to stop him.

Hope of Joop's arrival died within her as she sat below the dribbling canopy of leaves. For the first time she faced the prospect of finishing the job without him, and it filled her with fright and dismay. She had brought things this far by her own force of mind and will, but now she had none of either left; no stomach for the task ahead, no energy for escape, no idea which way to run. Overwhelmed by fatigue and despair, she curled up tighter in the undergrowth, snail-fashion, pulling up her knees and lowering her head between them, wrapping her hands round her neck. Numbness spread to her heart. Soon it must surely stop beating. I'll die of this numbness, she thought, like men who lie down in the snow. I am tired, I am weak. I am cold all through, to the heart. I can't do it, Joop. I can't. Without you I'll never finish it.

For some minutes more she sat hunched in this position. Her shoulders quaked; grunts of misery were forced from her lips. Then she took a deep breath and lifted her face to the rain, transferring her hands to her knees. The job must be done. Only she remained to do it.

As in Rome, she tried to brace her spirit with memories of past successes: the great strike and marches of 1968; the raising of the red flag in Nantes. But this time it was no good. For her these grand moments of the past were now as remote, as meaningless as the splendour of trumpet and drum for a soldier in the trenches. She was haunted by memories of the man she had killed, and dread of the killing to come. Now there was nothing else in sight. It was all blood and mud, whichever way she looked.

The soldier, preparing for bayonet work, is glad to dispense with moral reflection. But in her the habit was too strong to shake. Without inner light she couldn't operate. Darkness of soul led only to paralysis. Of course, as with terror of lightning, she knew very well where it came from. This was the shadow that falls on little girls when God turns away his face. She must drop to her knees and grovel for forgiveness before she would feel the warm light of that countenance. So taught the nuns of the Sacred Heart, Nantes. And so their little charges, grown up to big rational girls, could never quite forget. They could, if they had any brain or guts, kick away the whole stupid grovelling voodoo. But they couldn't change their moral emotions – that feverish swing from light to dark, inner warmth, inner cold, right or wrong.

Rosa knew this very well. She knew it better than those who said it about her, and it filled her with impotent disgust. She was ashamed of this self she could not change, the womanly nun-damaged feebleness that made her unable to do what Joop Janssen could.

Usually this rage was a help; a spur to action. The memory of a childhood spent kneeling was enough, of itself, to make her stand up and spit. But today, as she sat in the rain-soaked woods, the usual anger wouldn't come. She examined her origins with abject resignation. I am what I am, she thought. I have done what I could. I can do no more.

Again her head sank between her knees. Again her shoulders shook, but only with cold. No sound came from her lips. She stared at her feet, smeared with mud in their sandals. The rain, still falling on her neck, had slackened; the thunder had shifted to the west. She had one source of strength left, and to this her mind automatically turned before she went back to the house. She understood her weakness and knew ways to deal with it. Like a person who has learned to live with some physical infirmity, she carried old remedies to hand.

It was just another habit from the convent of course – others said so, she knew it herself – but throughout her life as a Marxist she had drawn courage from the founding fathers. Sometimes she made herself happy imagining their triumphs. More often, when cast down as now, she drew consolation from their moments of darkness. She thought of Marx himself, working away on his tracts in London, short of money, wracked

665

with piles in his bottom, pursuing the great abstractions in his head while his family went hungry around him. She thought of Lenin, hanging grimly on to his vision among the hopeless drunks and dolts of Siberia; stuck on cracking ice-floes in the Finnish Channel as he waited for escape by ship; stuck for years in England and Switzerland; stuck again even in 1917, back in Russia, on the verge of success, but forced to seek refuge in the Razliv Marshes while the revolution sank into bourgeois reaction. When stuck, the man to think of was Lenin. *The ability to see straight without overlooking the zig-zags of reality, that is what Marxism teaches.* So Lenin had said. And Lenin always practised what he preached. Stuck in bed, 1922, he had forced himself to work to the end, peering through the zig-zags to come.

For pure illumination she usually turned to Trotsky, her own patron saint. That sharp, bearded face with its thick pebble pince-nez was the one that came most often to her mind. In Rome she had seen him at work on his diary – *I can see the light above the wall* – but now, in the darkening woods, her effort to conjure him up was half-hearted. That peaceful moment of his Mexican exile seemed inappropriate, the words in his diary too facile.

Nothing she could think of brought light. Head bent in the rain, she saw only her own muddy feet, and always the face of Patrick Harvey – those cool appraising eyes, the small frown between, the wound on his head she had dabbed. She kept thinking of how he had tidied his hair, the way that he tugged his right ear-lobe in thought . . . Harvey was getting too familiar to shoot, that was the truth of it. Three days of physical proximity had made the task harder. And that was her own stupid fault, Rosa thought in disgust. She should have killed the man already, or left him alone. Instead of that, typically, she had tried to make him see the light.

At least when he argued, he annoyed her. There was that to be said for it. If he went on enough, she might manage to shoot him from sheer irritation. But what if he started to agree? Once or twice, it seemed, a glimmer of doubt had appeared in those eyes, a hint of larger feeling in that prim, self-satisfied English face.

Any more of that and I'll start to like him, Rosa thought. So I'd better stop talking to him. If it's me that's got to do it – and neither of the others will – then no more argument with

Harvey. The man is what he stands for, and that must be destroyed. We must finish what we've started. Yes, I will do it. I can shoot this man. I will.

Slowly, though still feeling leaden within, she gathered strength to return to the house. As often, a physical need overtook the twists of her spirit. She wanted food and dry clothes. She had sat where she was for half an hour. It was 9.45, she saw from her watch. She would go up now, dry off and cook a meal.

Suddenly conscious of her slackness as a sentry, she lifted her eyes to the view – or was it a sound that had broken her reverie? She wasn't sure, but the memory-trace of some small noise, furtive and close, seemed to linger in her ears. Nervously she scanned the ground below her. The road was still empty of traffic. The rain was falling softly now; the thunder had rolled away further. It was nearly night. The marsh was in darkness, unprobed by any torch-beam. The snail-picker must have gone. But the gloom beneath the trees was still lit by flickers of lightning, and it was in one of these brief flashes that she first saw the human figure running up the slope towards her – a man, bent low, dashing straight at her through the brushwood. In panic she jumped up and fumbled for her pistol. But she had left it too late. Next instant he was on top of her, tumbling her back into the undergrowth.

"Stay put," he said in French. "Sit still."

Rosa couldn't believe it. She went through a full two seconds of stunned incredulity, and then her mouth opened to let out a yelp of delight.

"Joop!"

14

Having charged up the hill and brought her down, Joop crouched still in the undergrowth. "Shut up," he said, raising his fingers to her mouth.

"How'd you get here?"

"Quiet. Tell you later."

"What's the matter?"

"I've been seen. Who's the fellow in the marsh?"

"I . . . don't know," Rosa stammered. "No one. Just a man. He's been picking snails."

"Well, watch out, he's coming up the track." Joop stood to peer down the slope. "*Zut*, he's seen us. Act normal. Here he is."

"Oh God, I'm sorry. I'd forgotten him."

"Don't worry. Stand up, put your arm round me. Right, that's it. Now let's walk away, nice and casual."

They started to stroll uphill through the trees. Behind them came the putter of a *mobylette* advancing up the track. The little engine slowed with the weight of its passenger, then stalled. The man got off to walk. He fixed them with the beam of a torch. Joop and Rosa half-turned and waved. The snail-picking peasant, a dark shape in beret and oilskin, waved back. "How goes it at La Guillarmie?" he shouted out, calling the house by its local name.

"All right thanks," Rosa called back. "And you? Not too wet?"

"Eh, well – it's my job," the man said. "Quite a wind, wasn't it?"

"Yes," shouted Rosa. "A very big wind."

"Still got your roof on?"

668

"Just," she said, laughing. She turned away from him with another wave, one arm still twined around Joop.

The man's torch stayed on their backs. Then he shone it on his big canvas bag, slung over the handlebars. "Hey! You want some snails?" He picked one out and held it up: a round white shell in the torchbeam.

"No thanks," Rosa called back, half-turning again. "Too fresh."

"Yes, you're right. Oh well, goodnight then."

"Goodnight."

The torch went out. The peasant kicked his *mobylette* back into action and half-rode, half-pedalled away. At a fork in the track, instead of turning right up the hairpins to the house, he travelled straight on and over the back of the hill, towards the village of Péchalifour.

Joop watched him go, then relaxed with a chuckle. "What the hell do you mean, too fresh?"

"Snails," Rosa said with normal cheerfulness, "are no good to eat for a week. They have to be starved or they're too full of shit."

"Oh," said Joop. "Is that a fact?"

"Where have you been all this time? I was starting to think you'd deserted me."

"Nearly did. Changed my mind."

"Pig," Rosa said in disbelief, then took the lean Dutchman in both her strong arms and squeezed him tight, pulling his head down into a kiss. Their bodies collided in a squelch of wet clothing. She mauled him with hungry affection, pressed against the big Russian pistol tucked into his jeans, then stepped back and held him by his elbows. "So," she asked, "how did you get here?"

"Train, car. Several cars. Had to leave a nice one on the other side." Joop gestured back towards the river. "*Flics* on the bridge," he explained.

"What!"

"Don't worry, just a roadblock. They've got them all over."

"They haven't found us?"

"No."

"How'd you get across then?"

"I swam."

"You *swam*? Ah, Joop, you're a marvel." She squeezed him again. "I'm glad to see you."

"It's mutual," Joop said with no more excitement than he ever put into such statements. "So how are things here? No problems?"

"Not yet."

"Harvey?"

"Still with us," Rosa answered in a quiet voice.

"And the other two?"

"Feeble, but trying."

"No trouble? No arguments?"

"No," said Rosa after a pause. "The television's bust. But that's my fault."

"Got annoyed with it, did you?"

"I didn't like the programme."

Joop chuckled with a short sniffing sound: the nearest he ever came to laughter. He disengaged himself from her arms and hitched his bag over his shoulder, twisting its rope round his wrist. "Okay," he said, his left hand placed on the small of her back, "show me round quickly while I can still see something. Then we'll have something to eat."

Hand in hand they climbed up the steep wooded hillside, now trickling with many instant streams. In the little light remaining Joop quickly inspected the terrain around the house, loping at a trot from vantage point to vantage point. Satisfied, he let Rosa take him inside. Stephen Murdoch, he saw straightaway, was entirely out of nerve. Mario Salandra was miserable but firmer. And the two of them had a furtive air of collusion. Clearly there had been some talk in Rosa's absence.

Taking charge straightaway, Joop sent Murdoch to watch the road, then asked to be shown the hostage. He inspected Harvey's cell; then Harvey himself. No words passed between them. The encounter took place by candlelight, since the house was now without power. But Joop saw enough to gauge Harvey's state of mind. In this Englishman's eyes there was no loss of nerve; only defiance, and some hope of rescue – even a sort of serenity. Harvey had kept himself in good mental shape. Physically, too, he was lasting. His face was unshaven, his suit smeared with dust; dishevelment had robbed him of some of his dignity. Yet plenty remained. Harvey was lasting and

Harvey knew it. He had been reading a book by the light of a candle. While under inspection he sat with it lowered on his knees and stared straight back, not speaking or moving.

Joop shut the door on him. Sending Rosa off to the kitchen, he took Mario aside.

"Has she been talking to him?"

"Yes," the Italian said. "There has been some discussion."

"How did it go?"

Mario reported the day's events: the shooting of the television, the arguments that followed.

Joop nodded. For a moment he was silent, then he flicked his head at the door of Harvey's cell. "Go in there and take away his book. The candle, too. Leave him in the dark. At supper bring him out and have another go at him."

Mario disliked this idea. He asked for a reason.

"Just do it," Joop said.

The Italian stood a moment, starting to make a gesture of protest. Then he went off to the cell, like a man condemned himself.

Joop's reason for setting up a confrontation at supper was that he wished to test Rosa's resolve, not Harvey's. An argument under his eye would show the exact state of play between the parties.

Left alone in the parlour, he glanced carefully round it, noting the position of everything. Then he found an empty bedroom and changed into semi-dry clothing. He had swum the river with the bag above water, as much as was possible. He hung his wet denim jacket on a chair, but kept on his jeans to dry out with body heat. He took out his pistol and wiped it clean. Returning to the main room, he checked the weapons in the trunk, then sat at the table with Mario to listen to the radio news at 10.30. The bulletin contained no fresh offer from Riemeck, no information from Britain or Italy. More surprising, to Joop, was that nothing came out about the search. His own escape from Périgueux, if known, went unmentioned. There was no talk of special concentration in the Dordogne department.

This made him vaguely uneasy.

Leaving the sullen Italian alone, he went into the kitchen, where Rosa was cooking by candlelight. She, too, had dried herself and changed. She was wearing a plain woollen dress, working brown. She had several things going on the butane gas stove. As he stood watching she tipped the creamy liquid of a pancake mix into a frying pan, swirling it round to the edges with a cheerful flourish. She was drinking from a bottle of Sauvignon. She held it out.

Joop smiled and shook his head. He took a can of beer from the fridge. Talk of snail-shit and chowy expertise at Breton pancakes were Rosa on best form. But he had seen her in the woods, sitting inert with her head down. Rosa was close to the limit.

Her condition, he recognised, was that known to military doctors as "switch-off": the apathy which overtakes soldiers after several days of battle, caused by continuous loss of adrenalin. Without further rest they can only come to life in short freakish spasms of energy, hardly more normal than their underlying state of exhaustion. Thus Rosa now: exuberant but fragile. Close to the limit.

On impulse Joop walked to the front door and poked his head out. The rain had stopped; the clouds were clearing from a near-full moon. The crickets had started up again.

He turned back into the kitchen. "Come outside. I want a word."

Rosa protested with a flap of hands. "I'm cooking."

"Leave it."

"What, now?"

"Now."

She turned down the burners and joined him outside. They walked across the garden and stood by Harvey's grave, out of earshot from the house. Joop lit a cigarette. Unusually, Rosa asked for one too. A few traffic sounds had started to come up from the valley, oddly loud in the stillness. They spoke together in low voices.

Joop's first question was his main one. "Are you sure you want to go on with this?"

And Rosa expected the question. Her answer was quick and decisive. "No, I don't want to go on. But we must. We can't stop now, or we're nothing, Joop. All that we've done comes to nothing. People are in jail for this. Others are dead. If we don't finish it, all that is wasted." She turned to him. "Why?"

Joop replied cautiously. "I was thinking, on my way here. Perhaps you've done as much as you can."

"So what? We just leave?"

"It crossed my mind."

Rosa's voice sharpened. "You and me, you mean. We just walk off into these trees and ditch the other two, who'll let Harvey go and hand themselves in. Is that it?"

"Something like that."

"Joop, have you been talking to the Russians?"

"No, of course not. But they won't much like this, I can tell you."

"I don't like it. None of us like it." Rosa, as usual, went guttural in anger. She threw down the cigarette and stamped on it. "But we're going to stay together and finish the job. That's settled."

Quickly, to see how she took it, Joop shifted his ground. "All right, so let's do it now, then get out. This place isn't safe, you know. In fact it's damn dangerous."

"I know it's not safe," she said to him, calmer. Then she added with odd loss of logic: "But we can't go travelling with Harvey, can we?"

"Certainly not."

"Right. So we'll stay here and take the risk. Until the morning, anyway. We act at eight tomorrow – not sooner, not later. I gave them that long. I ought to keep my word."

"What – out of honour? They won't show you much, let me tell you, when they come up that hill."

"No, not honour," said Rosa, slowing down. "It's a question of effectiveness. We mustn't forget that we're trying to achieve a political result here. If Riemeck makes a good enough offer, we'll let Harvey go. Or, if the workers take the factories, then maybe you'd be right – we'd have done all we could."

"Rosa, let me ask you, frankly. Do you expect either of those things to happen?"

"An offer from Riemeck, probably not. A rising in the factories, perhaps." Her voice dropped low. "Frankly, I don't know. Steve and Mario promise strong action by their men in both places . . ."

"Those two. They lead from behind."

Rosa ignored the jibe. She smeared her face with her hand, then looked at her watch. "So we wait, Joop, right? Nine hours. That's all."

"That's plenty," Joop said with another sniff of grim semi-laughter. Eventually he nodded in agreement. "Okay, until eight tomorrow. But then we go. You and me."

"We'll all go."

Now it was his voice that hardened. "No," he said, "four in a bunch is too many. The other two can go through Marseille. You and I through Spain. We can meet them again in Algiers."

Rosa nodded wearily. "Very well, if you insist. You seem to have worked it out." She started back to the house, then paused and turned back. "Will you tell the other two? They're not going to like this."

"I'll tell them in the morning. When we see how it finishes." Joop trod out his cigarette. "Now cook us a meal while I get this place organised. I want everything out of the trunk. We'll spread it around before we eat. And nobody sleeps, understood? The three of us will keep watch outside while you stay inside with Harvey. No sleep, no lights. I've got some pills to keep us awake."

Rosa nodded again, too tired to reply. "There is one thing. When we come to it . . ."

The sentence tailed off. But Joop understood. He put his arm round her shoulders. "Yes," he said, "don't worry. I'll kill him."

15

Eye pressed to the gap in the shutter, Patrick Harvey watched them talk at his graveside, this girl and this man who'd decided his life should end. It gave him a peculiar feeling to watch them there, talking and smoking in the fitful moonlight. One moment they were visible, the next they disappeared into shadow, the Dutchman's cigarette still glowing like a firefly. Above the hazel woods great woolly storm-clouds were still drifting over the face of the moon, but beginning to thin and grow ragged. Already clear patches of starlight had appeared to the right, above the spikier outlines of firs, larches, spruce and pine – the wilder mixed woods that covered the slope to the road.

His peculiar feeling arose from the fact that his death seemed too personal, too intimate a matter to be in the hands of these strangers. And from this unsettling position there were only two ways to go. Either his death wasn't intimate, or these people weren't strangers. To start with, he had gone the first way. He had seen his execution as a public matter with public causes, to be carried out by just the sort of incomprehensible, outrageous strangers that political life had so often thrown up in his path. But after three days of close cohabitation, the event had become more personal. And watching them now, he swung fully round to the second way of looking at it. His killers were no longer strangers. He knew these people. He felt his own destiny intimately linked to theirs, a private matter to be worked out beneath the light of the uncaring stars. He wondered intensely what it was they were saying to each other in such low voices. Two days ago he wouldn't have cared. But now he was interested. He wanted to know.

Everything else had fallen far behind him now. His days as

Prime Minister, his post in Brussels, the merger, his staff, his friends, his family, even Margaret herself was remote from the matter in hand, which was simply between himself and the odd set of people in this house. There were four of them, but the two who counted were those two, standing by the grave – Joop Janssen and Rosa Berg. They would decide the issue.

He withdrew his head from the shutter as they walked slowly back to the house. The girl's head was bowed. The Dutchman had his arm round her shoulders. Were they lovers, Harvey wondered. What bound them? What drove them, together, to commit such acts? He continued to listen, but once within earshot they ceased to speak. He was left with no clues.

Towards the girl he no longer felt any grudge. He pitied her. He even half-admired her. Her political hopes were a fantasy, wildly unrelated to the facts of her political time. On the other hand, it had to be admitted, in Rosa's manifesto there was something rather grand. The mighty were going to be put down from their seats, the meek exalted for ever; the poor were going to take over the earth. It was all the most utter baloney, of course. And yet, Harvey thought in his new mood, it was honest. Honest dreams, however deluded, served to show the sad state of reality; they forced a response of some sort, and from such small improvements progress was made. His own task had been to make the improvements. Rosa's was to scoff at their smallness. He was the practical citizen, she was the prophet in the wilderness.

This long view of the matter had come to him in the late afternoon as he lay on his mattress, exhausted by argument, watching the dance of the midges. It had stayed with him through the hours since. The right way to go, he thought, was in humility, taking an all-round view. This girl is God's creature as much as I. We are locked together, knocked apart by the strange counter-stepping gavotte of existence – right and left, man and woman, fact and dream.

At a less mystical level it had occurred to him that what made them jig was time – sometimes known as the generation gap. His own generation, remembering the war, was content with any sort of harmony between the nations, however uninspired. Rosa's, not knowing the war, took the present for granted and wanted to improve it, however much conflict they stirred. Maybe the next lot would be more cautious. Thus the world spins, but never in quite the same circle. History the science of what never happens twice.

Sitting on his mattress in the dark, allowing these random reflections to pass through his head, he realised what strange thoughts they were – unusual for him, at any rate. He was not used to spending much thought on mysteries. Too much thought, indeed, inhibited action; he had always been well aware of it. The problems of the moment were not eased by glimpses of eternity – not until now. Now, here, the opposite was true. Easement of the problem was exactly what contemplation had brought. Was this wisdom, Harvey wondered, or was he going crackers? Either way he felt happy. And that, in the circumstances, was strangest of all. Since early in the evening he had been taken over by a light-headed feeling of contentment. Not even the visit of the Dutchman had caused him the slightest disturbance of spirit.

Joop Janssen – now there was a mystery of creation. Everything about the man, though chilling, was slightly unreal. His face was like a waxwork which had stood too close to a radiator. His hair was grey and tufted; in places it was missing. But the most striking thing was his eyes, simply because there was nothing to be seen in them. They were like empty water, blue and still. No trace of human emotion stirred their surface or their depths: no malice, no compassion, no remorse. If they had an expression at all, it was that of a plumber who has come to do the job.

So here was a true professional of death. Joop Janssen would do a good job, Harvey thought; quick and clean. And this was a sort of relief, both to himself and no doubt to the others – Mario, Murdoch, Rosa – none of whom would manage the deed without hesitation. Any one of them might make a horrible botch of it. So better for all that the plumber had come.

On the other hand the chances of rescue were certainly reduced. Since arrival the Dutchman had been tightening up. And now he had put the Italian to work, Harvey saw, drawn back to the shutter by noises outside. Mario and Joop had lugged the wooden crate from the parlour to the garden. Each equipped with a torch, they were taking things out of it; going off to the woods, coming back for more, going off again. It was hard to see exactly, but they seemed to be laying down lines of some sort.

677

Trip-wires? Flares, perhaps. Or some sort of mine. Defences, in any case, which brought down the chances of survival. The house was being turned into a fortress.

But even this new development failed to disturb him. Harvey no longer calculated chances of survival; he had given up hoping or plotting for rescue. This resignation was not entirely healthy, he realised. And yet it was not morose. It was all of a part with this mood of airy contentment which had come over him and wouldn't go away.

The book must take some of the blame. A tattered English paperback, stained with sun-oil, it had been brought in by Murdoch, who had cracked his first smile as he threw it on the mattress.

"Here you are, Harvey, something to read. Just the sort of infantile trash to appeal to a fascist-imperialist mind like yours."

And Murdoch was right about that. The book had seemed perfectly suited to the moment. *Biggles Fights Back*, it was called, by Captain W. E. Johns. Pilot-Officer Biggles had just taken off in a Bristol Fighter, away to save the world for the English with Flight-Sergeant Ginger in the navigator's seat, when Mario had come in and confiscated this dangerous item of anti-party literature.

Yes, the book was a loss. For a few minutes Harvey had fun making up Chapter Two. Then the gallant Bristol Fighter flew off into the blue, out of sight, out of mind. He lay down and closed his eyes. The moon was obscured again. The cell was so dark that it made no difference if he closed his eyes or opened them. Still happy, despite loss of book and candle, he began to play games with the luminous hands of his watch, timing the pulse of his heart. It was steady. Heart and watch were ticking on nicely.

Soon he would sleep. But first they would bring him a meal, he thought. He could smell it. Rosa was busy in the kitchen again. Listening to her, Harvey felt obscurely grateful that she should bother to feed him. He forgave her. He forgave them all. Even in the Dutchman there was nothing to hate. You couldn't hate a plumbing machine.

At eleven o'clock he heard the whole crew assemble in the parlour. On the hour they listened to the news on the radio, which aroused no comment. Then Rosa brought in her meal, to jocular cries of appreciation, led by herself. She invited them to dine at the Hotel Guillarmie, *"sa cuisine soignée, ses vins réputés!"*

"Son parking ombragé," shouted Mario, taking up the joke.

"Sa terrasse explosive," said Joop with grimmer humour.

There was more laughter; some busy eating; the clatter of cutlery on plates. Then Murdoch proposed a toast.

"To the Iskra," he said with harsh solemnity. "Let's hope the spark lights the flame."

But this brought no audible reaction. Comrade Murdoch, as often before in his life no doubt, was out of tune with the mood of the meeting. By five past the hour he was on his way back to the road.

The others talked on a while, too softly for Harvey to catch what was said. Then, to his surprise, he was summoned to join them. Fetched from the darkness by Mario, he was led to the table, where a plate had been set for him. On it were two rolled pancakes, some small red sausages, a pile of white beans.

"Sit down, eat up." Rosa waved at the plate, then went back to reading a newspaper – or was about to, when she looked up again and threw him a pale, tight smile. "Welcome to the life of the rural guerilla."

Harvey sat down. Now he was among them he did not feel so forgiving. He ate in silence, looking round the low-beamed room.

There were two dripping candles set in saucers on the table, but the main source of light was a hurricane lamp. Its wick was turned up bright. A fire of pine cones was burning in the big stone hearth, but not all the smoke was going up the chimney, so the room had a hazy atmosphere, fire-smoke added to that of cigarettes. Laid out on the floor and against the white walls was a frightening array of weapons. Rifles, pistols, a small machine-gun, grenades and ammunition boxes were the only things Harvey could recognise – and the shotgun which had killed Paolo Santini. At the sight of it his forgiving mood took another jolt.

Set on the sideboard were two radio receivers, one big, one small. The big one, Harvey gathered after a while, was tuned to the French police frequency. The smaller one was tuned to Murdoch, who sent up bored reports from the road. There was nothing, he said. Just a few cars.

At the table's far end sat Rosa, still engrossed in yesterday's newspaper, *Dimanche Sud-Ouest*. At her side was a portable radio of the ordinary type. Music was coming from it, just loud enough to hear. From time to time she turned to other wave-bands, seeking news. Earlier she had seemed exhausted, but now she was alert. Her eyes had a strange bright stare.

Joop Janssen was standing outside on the terrace. He had a rifle now, and on it was a sort of fat telescope, which seemed to work at night. He kept aiming at things in the dark. He was also busy with other bits of warlike equipment, but what he was up to Harvey could not tell.

Terrasse explosive?

The atmosphere inside the room was awkward. There was some obscure tension between these three people.

The only one speaking was Mario, who sat across the table with a bottle of wine. To Harvey's great boredom, and Rosa's own evident restlessness, the Italian began once again to explain the political purposes of the Iskra. Rosa stared on at her newspaper; Mario talked on; and Harvey ate on, pretending attention, though in fact hardly listening. He made no effort to argue, or even reply, feeling too far removed from the world to talk any more about worker-cooperatives. But at length he was goaded into a retort when the Italian came up with a saying of Victor Hugo's – the one about no army being able to withstand an idea whose time has come.

"Come, has it?"

"It is coming."

Harvey smiled benignly as he won a change of tense. "But taking its time."

Mario wouldn't have that. Christianity had taken three centuries to get off the ground, he was saying, a remark at which Harvey was about to laugh, when Rosa interjected casually: "God or Marx, Harvey. There's your choice."

"It's not one I've ever had much difficulty with."

"Oh, really." She yawned and went back to her paper.

Conversation ceased. Thunder rumbled to the west, further off now. Then Joop Janssen stepped inside from the terrace. Backing into the light, he unrolled white cable from a carton drum, then set it down carefully on the floor. He glanced at Mario, then took a smaller reel from his pocket and started to apply strips of brown sticky tape to the glass of the double doors which led to the terrace.

680

From the glance between the two men, Harvey got the impression that this conversation had been set up. Mario was talking to order; and the order had come from Joop. Rosa's lack of interest was genuine.

But Mario had lost his lines. He went on drinking in gloomy silence. So after a pause Harvey worked himself up to taking the initiative in this three-cornered conversation, though presumably it had been devised for his own humiliation. And having seen the shotgun on the wall, he felt like shooting back hard. His forgiving mood had vanished entirely. He was ashamed of it.

16

God or Marx.

The silence which had fallen on the room since Rosa's casual challenge reminded Harvey of that which falls on cabinet meetings when some tactless minister broaches the point which all at the table know to be the heart of the matter, yet none are keen to discuss.

And another minute passed before talk resumed. Moths fluttered and died in the candle flames. Joop went on sticking brown tape to the windows. Rosa stared on at her newspaper, Mario into his glass. What they were thinking their faces didn't show. Perhaps they weren't thinking at all. But Harvey, having made one evasive reply, was thinking up a more aggressive one.

Central to his political attitudes was a statement once made by D. H. Lawrence. "Socialism is a dud," said the coal-miner's son. "It makes a mush of people." However, as an articulation of central belief, this was itself a little too mushy, Harvey thought. And much too English to translate. For this cabinet of international fanatics, which was being conducted in French, something sharper was required.

"Perhaps there's no choice to make," he said after a while.

Rosa looked up from her paper with a start. "What do you mean?"

"I mean perhaps it's all the same thing – God or Marx. People need a faith of some sort, don't they? A holy book, a set of laws. A simple explanation of the world, complete with myths and saints."

Harvey had shot more from impulse than calculation, but he saw straightaway that he had hit a mark. Rosa's eyes, already

682

wide and bright, widened further, lit by outrage, as she took in a breath and answered: "No, it is *not* the same thing. There is a great deal of difference between a rational theory of history, by which the poor can be led to improve their condition, and a primitive grovelling superstition which instructs them to wait for reward in the next world while a few have a good time in this."

"Even so, I think the similarities are interesting. And perhaps they're greater than the difference," Harvey said, encouraged to press the point. "Only earlier today I was thinking how similar you were to the Christian millenarians. Like them, you promise a thousand-year reign for the just, and in troubled times I dare say you'd sweep the board. A lot of simple folk would rise up and follow you. But these are not troubled times, Rosa. At least they're not troubled enough for this kind of talk. The workers you address aren't a desperate rabble, sunk in medieval chaos. No, not at all. And they're not simple-minded either. They're more like the medieval craftsmen in their guilds. They know where their true interest lies, and they club together to protect it. They want to improve their material conditions – that's what matters to them, and that's about all. Although they might like more say in the running of their companies, they're not going to risk much to get it."

"That's where you're wrong, Harvey. You wait and see."

Rosa, as she made this rejoinder, was smiling. She had quickly recovered from agitated anger to confident calm; and then had come a smile of amusement, unnaturally bright. Harvey wondered if she'd taken some drug.

Joop, though still busy with tape, was taking in every word.

Mario had been staring down at the table with the ostentatious patience of a wise man compelled to wait until a fool has finished. Now he raised his head and pushed his tinted glasses up his nose. "So, Harvey, what is your own political faith?"

"Don't tell me," Rosa broke in sarcastically, frowning and putting her hand to her brow, as if for a guessing game. "Democracy – right?"

"Yes, I'll settle for that," said Harvey. "It's an abused term these days, but any sort of system which lets people run their own affairs will do. Democracy, I'd say, is a political expression of human sympathy. It's also a tribute to human intelligence.

The individual's right to be different is recognised, and also his right to a view about the common interest. Yes, that'll do."

"Marx was a democrat."

"Oh no he wasn't, Rosa. Karl Marx believed in the tyranny of the mass, led by a few clever people like himself. And hence, precisely, the horrors of Russia. First the people are led by the party. And then, before anyone notices the difference, the party is speaking for the people. And pretty soon the leader speaks for the party. Anyone who argues with the leader speaks against the people, so is wrong, and gets shot. It's an old trick, and it gets things done. But don't let's call it democracy."

With the air of a man repeating old stuff, Mario came to the defence of early Soviet Russia; forced to protect itself against civil war, cut off by the failure of supporting revolutions in Europe. Still, he admitted, the shift into rigid party rule was an error.

"Lenin saw the error," chipped in Rosa. Trotsky had not seen it, she went on quickly, conceding the point before Harvey could make it. "But we follow Trotsky in two other things. He saw that revolution must be carried right through once it's started. If you stop half-way, the wheel turns back. And the other thing he saw is it has to be global. So long as revolution is confined to individual nations, it's blighted. You get success, but in isolated pockets, too weak to survive. And that will be a danger with BMG and Mobital, as we have admitted to you. Even when controlled by their workers, they will be at risk until the whole system changes."

She's giving plenty away, Harvey thought. What's making her so confident? For the first time he got the impression that something had happened he didn't yet know about. "So full revolutionary success is uncertain," he said. "Yet for this you go to war."

"Yes, we do. A war without frontiers."

"There's a thing called a ballot-box, you know. How come your system's never arrived through the vote?"

"That's not true. In Chile it did."

"Yes, and look what happened in Chile," said Mario, going straight on to the thesis that no ruling class had ever yielded power without a fight. In the end, he said, it always came down to bullets not the ballot. Democracy, as now seen in the West, was a trick.

"In what way a trick?" asked Harvey.

The trick, said Mario, was this. The institutions of western democracy were so distorted by the interests of the propertied class that the power they offered was illusory – a sort of dream, in which the people went through the motions of exercising choice, but were in fact blinded to their own real interest. And the task of groups like the Iskra was to break this spell by which the people were held.

"So you see," the Italian concluded, "the Iskra is only the spark that lights the flame. We do not wait for revolution. We create the condition for it. And that is why we must go ahead with this action, even if the outcome is uncertain."

This, for Harvey, was the spark that lit the flame.

"I've noticed that this is what your sort always say. I've never heard a Trotskyist talk any different. The people can't see what's good for them, but you, the intellectuals, can. Well I have a higher opinion of them. It's you, not they, who are living in a dream. The people can see their own interest very clearly, and if it was thwarted, they'd revolt. They always have, they will again. But right now they're not revolting, are they?"

"You wait," said Rosa. Her smile had come back.

But Harvey refused to be stopped. "This is what I'm here as a symbol of, isn't it? Well, I accept that. It's rather an ordinary age we've got here, you see, and to run it the people vote for ordinary men – like me, like themselves. People are ordinary, Rosa. The world they make is an ordinary place. But you can't bear that, can you? Like your founder, Marx, you just can't accept the world as it is, the people as they are. You want to tidy them up, make them better, happier, more equal. You want them to fit your own fantasies."

Harvey stopped, watching Rosa's reaction. The tussle was between him and her now. Mario was drinking alone, having retreated into silence with the facial expression, simultaneously defeated and superior, of an adult who gives up trying to talk sense to a difficult child. Joop had finished taping the windows and was sitting on the sideboard, fiddling with the larger of the radios, from which came only a soft airy rustle of static. If it was tuned to the police, Harvey thought, the police were keeping awfully quiet. Was that a good sign or a bad one? The question passed through his head and out again. His interest now was in Rosa, who in turn was staring at him with a serious, patient, controlled expression, as though she would like to understand him.

"But what do you believe, Harvey? What's your politics *about*? It sounds to me like your idea of good government is no government at all."

"As little as possible, certainly. The best of governments is the one you don't notice," Harvey said. "You can go about your business without its permission, and most people talk of other things. The government isn't a topic, any more than the sewers. It works unnoticed. It goes unnoticed because it works."

"And what is it working *at*?"

Harvey shrugged. "Food and shelter, law and order. Perhaps a bit more. Smoothing out a few rough edges . . ."

This, to his surprise, threw Rosa into a rage. "Oh, you make me sick!" she exclaimed for the second time that day. Slapping her hand on the newspaper, she swept it away to the floor.

"What is it that offends you?"

"You're so disgustingly complacent, Harvey. That's what offends me."

"Complacent? I'd call it modesty."

"Modesty!"

"We politicians, you see, unlike you intellectuals, know just how little we can do. We know we can't remake the world, or even get rid of its injustice. We just aim to keep it from chaos."

Rosa dismissed this with a contemptuous flick of her head. She stared at him with the look of a person who has just heard something too stupid to reply to. "There's one mistake you've made, though."

"Oh? What's that?"

"These nice, quiet, ordinary people of yours – they're not so content as you think. Those factories will be taken. Tonight."

Harvey smiled at her sarcastically. "And if it goes wrong, you'll kill me."

"Yes, we'll kill you. I'll kill you myself if I have to."

"In the interest of the workers of BMG and Mobital."

Rosa slapped the table again, where the paper had been. "Yes!" she shouted. "Yes! For their dignity as human beings!"

"As seen by you, not them."

"As seen by anyone except a smug pimp like yourself."

"No, Rosa, as seen by you. No one else. There's no way you

can spread this around – except among your friends here, if they can take it."

She rose erect in her seat; then flopped back and turned to the other two. "Oh, take him out."

Neither man moved. Mario had sunk into a trance. Joop was standing close to the table, having grown more interested as the talk went on. Before either of them could intervene, Harvey fired a parting shot.

"I have been elected by the people, Rosa, several times in my life. Which gives me some claim to speak for them. But you only speak for yourself. And a sadly distorted individual you are."

"Take him *out*!"

Mario started to obey, but she stopped him, hand out-stretched; leaning taut down the table.

"In what way am I distorted, Harvey? Tell me that."

"The causes I can only guess. But what I'd guess is, you had a strict religious upbringing –"

Harvey got no further. The remark brought her surging to her feet.

"Get him out of here! *Out*!"

She started to stride round the room then, *enmerding* away, and other things Harvey could not translate. He gazed at her, astonished to have caused such effect. Then it struck him she was looking for her pistol. It struck Mario too. The Italian began to pad after her, pleading for calm. Joop watched the drama with empty eyes. It was all the same to him. If this girl wanted to do the job herself, so be it. The plumber had work else-where.

Then in an instant the whole scene changed, in response to a noise outside. Rosa and Mario froze to their spots; Joop Janssen jumped into action. Barking at the other two to douse the lamp, the Dutchman quickly snuffed out both candles, then scooped up his rifle and ran to the terrace. Within a few seconds the room was in darkness, lit only by the glow of the moon. Harvey sat forgotten at the table. Across it loomed the black shapes of Rosa and Mario, muttering together in alarm.

Advancing from the north was the even, rhythmic thackety-thwack of a helicopter.

Soon the noise drowned all others. The machine flew directly over the house, at normal height, continuing over the back of the hill and into the distance, until it was out of hearing. There

687

was no pause or deviation in its flight, Harvey noted with some disappointment. Even so, Joop Janssen tracked it all the way through the telescopic night-sight on his rifle, following it through the sky like a game-bird. Even after it had gone he stood out on the terrace, still watching and listening. Then another sound broke the silence.

"Brother Jewp, are you there?"

The voice was Murdoch's, coming from the smaller of the radio sets. Joop moved quickly to the sideboard and answered in English. Their medley of accents, Midland and Dutch, would have been a comic turn in other circumstances.

"Yes, Steve? What is it?"

"Car here. Went past, came back a minute later."

"What marque, please?"

"Peugeot."

"Colour?"

"Hard to say. Black or blue. Dark anyway."

"Saloon?"

"Yup."

"No light on his top?"

"No. Can't see one."

"Okay, keep watching. We will listen here." Joop straightened up from the set and switched into French, with a prod of his rifle at Harvey. "Lock him up."

Half a minute later Harvey was back in his cell.

Though tired, he was nowhere near sleep. Alternately crouched at the door and bent to the gap in the shutter, he listened to the gang prepare for the night. Murdoch reported nothing more from the road. After a time Joop pulled him up to a closer position on that side of the house, where the track was. Mario was placed behind the house, looking uphill, across the open meadow. The most dangerous side, Joop said to Rosa, was the west, where the woods came up close. This Harvey recognised as his own view: garden, grave, trees. And Joop proposed to watch it himself. He was also going to keep an eye on the north side, below the terrace, though there the slope dropped into the valley more steeply and was thickly overgrown. A silent approach from the north, Joop told Rosa, would be very difficult. He didn't think they'd try it.

The last thing he told her was that the doors to the terrace and all the shutters of the house, except Harvey's own, were now sealed and live. So everyone should remember that. From now until morning it was back door only, or kingdom come.

Soon the three men were out on watch. Rosa brewed coffee for them and took it round to each. After that she came back to the house. Perhaps she lay down somewhere. Harvey couldn't tell. The lamp and candles were not relit. The silence was total, except for the endless singing of the crickets.

In fact only human sound was absent. Total silence there was not. Both radios still crackled softly, kept open. Occasional traffic could be heard on the road. Rainwater still dripped and trickled, inside the house as well as out. And away beyond that were all the small noises of woodland at night, little cracks and stirrings and rustles, each one of which Harvey began to notice with the hearing of a man gone blind. An owl hooted close. A dog barked far off. Then a fox, much nearer. Earlier Rosa had mentioned that the foxes in these parts were rabid: a fact which struck Harvey as the least surprising thing he had heard all week.

For comfort he stared at the luminous hands of his watch. They ticked on to midnight, the same as ever. But his heart had speeded up, he noticed, and was tripping after every few beats. Keep calm, he told himself. Keep your head up. Not long to go now.

Tuesday

1

It was soon after midnight when Harvey's ear was caught by a new sound. Seated upright on his mattress, still alert to every stirring in the dark, he heard a small, soft scuff in the corridor. At first he thought it was a rat. Then he recognised a human step. It was Rosa. She was moving furtively about beyond the door. Now she was just outside it; standing still; breathing. Again she walked quickly up and down; paused; walked; stood again, walked. The noise was the soles of her sandals on the rough concrete floor of the passage, untiled. She was trying to be quiet but could not keep still. Her pacing to and fro, to and fro, suggested to Harvey the moody agitation of a predator who has smelled meat but dare not collect, having also sniffed danger. She did not come in; she could not go away. Then she made up her mind. She came in.

The way she opened the door was brisk and resolute. But Harvey wasn't fooled. He had heard the hesitation in the corridor. Once inside, she crossed to the window and bent to peer through the gap in the shutter, pretending a mission of inspection. The moonlight fell directly on her face, which looked calm enough. For a full two minutes she remained in that position, not stirring. Then she spoke.

"You shouldn't annoy me, Harvey. It's bad for your chances."

"Drat my chances," Harvey answered from the mattress, speaking snappily but softly, as she had. "I was annoyed myself. Standing against a wall in that room is the gun which killed my chauffeur."

To that she did not reply for some time.

As he waited, Harvey was conscious that his indignation at

693

Paolo's death contained a grain of humbug. His young Italian driver had fallen far from his thoughts. Moreover Paolo's death was partly Paolo's fault, it had to be admitted. Amateur gunplay by chauffeurs was not recommended in Europol's kidnap-evasion drill; indeed it was specifically forbidden. Still, there was no need to make a gift of that to the Iskra. Rosa Berg should be made to answer for Paolo Santini.

And in due course she did.

"I'm sorry about that. We meant to bring him here. But he had a gun, and then Joop . . ."

"Yes. I saw."

"I'm not proud of that, Harvey. I regret it. But to me this man's death makes it more than ever necessary that we carry this through to the end, in the way that we said we would, and for the proper motives. That is why we're still here. And it's why we shall spare you if we can. We don't shirk violence, but to us it's a last resort."

After another long pause she turned in from the window, her face disappearing in shadow.

"I'm not a prophet, Harvey. I can't tell what the future will say of us. I can only analyse the present. And that analysis tells me we should act as we have – as we are doing now. Of course, you yourself think I'm mad. I expect that. But please do me the credit of believing that my reasons are sincere, and serious."

"Yes. I believe they are," Harvey said, relenting a little. "They're just hopelessly wrong, that's all. In my view."

Rosa advanced from the window then and sat down in one of the deckchairs, her feet spread out in the square of light cast by the moon. "Your view, my view," she said with a sigh. "We are like people at the opposite ends of the earth, you and I. Each upside-down to the other."

"That's true," Harvey said in surprise. "At last you've said something I agree with."

His interest quickened. He had thought she had come to kill him; then that she'd come for more argument. Now it seemed she sought a reconciliation. And perhaps . . . But hope was premature. He waited to hear what came next.

The aluminium frame of the flimsy little chair creaked and shifted with her weight as she leaned forward intently, her pale face appearing in the moonbeam. "I want you to know it's not personal. Please bear that in mind, Harvey. In there just now

694

you accused me of personal motives, and I nearly killed you for it. I would have killed you from personal emotion. That would have been wrong."

"So what will be the excuse this morning?" he said to her, without any note of sarcasm. "History, I suppose."

"Not an excuse, no. A cause. It would be an excuse if I wanted to kill you, which I don't." She sat back, retreating into shadow. "We are both the instruments of history, Harvey."

"The difference is," Harvey remonstrated, "that I don't see myself as a servant of it. You Marxists always talk of history as though it were a go to be served. But it's nothing of the kind. It's just the record of individual human actions, some good, some bad. What you will do this morning is a cruel act, and you are responsible for it. You can't go putting the blame on history – not when you're talking to me."

Rosa sat still and silent. Her reply, when it came, was measured.

"In the war, before I was born, the English bombed the cities of the Germans. They even bombed the French. That was a cruel act, but you supported it, because you saw it as historically necessary."

"Yes, it was cruel," Harvey said after several seconds' thought. "But it was done with reluctance, wasn't it, by ordinary people who were forced to defend themselves against an insane idea of history."

Rosa's reply was quiet. "This, too, is done with reluctance. But for a better idea." She sat still a moment, then leaned again into the moonbeam, lowering her voice still further. "Now that we're alone, Harvey, let us be honest. This is a matter of life and death, after all. And we are both intelligent, serious people. Whether we agree or disagree, it should be without pretence. I would like to find the truth of the difference between us." She paused. "You will do this? You are not too tired?"

"No, let's talk. I prefer it."

Seeing her face now, passionately earnest in the moonbeam, Harvey thought they might get closer to the heart of the matter. Or they might not. Would she really stop talking in slogans? From his position on the mattress he waited to hear, leaning back against the wall, his hands cupped around his knees. He kept half an ear on the many small sounds of the night while Rosa began a long statement from her chair, her face once again invisible. He could only see the outline of her head. But her voice, as it came to him through the dark, had none of its previous ranting tone.

"It's true that Marx foresaw a society, some time beyond the revolution, when people would be so changed that they wouldn't need laws or authority. He spoke of this state of affairs as though it would last for ever – the end of history. But I have never believed that literally, Harvey. As you say yourself, there never will be a heaven on earth, and there never was a golden age. There's no final, perfect, static solution to human affairs. Yes. I agree with that. But here, I think, Marx was telling a parable – a symbolic story. And I have one of my own. Would you like to hear it?"

"Ah, a story," Harvey said. "Yes, I should like that."

"You are mocking me."

"No I'm not. Please, go on."

"*Imaginez-vous une île déserte*," she began: a story-starting sentence which had more ring to it in French than English. "And imagine that you and I, surviving a shipwreck, discover ourselves upon this desert island. We have never met before. We are strangers. And yet we would help each other, wouldn't we? We would fight together against the wild beasts. We would share what food we could find. We would build ourselves a shelter and share it. The idea of property would seem absurd to us, and power, one over the other, would seem unimportant. You agree?"

"I agree."

"And this cooperation, it would come naturally to us, wouldn't it? It would be an expression of ordinary human sympathy, to use your own phrase."

"All right," said Harvey, catching the drift. "Now try imagining a hundred people shipwrecked on the same island. I think you may hit a few problems."

But Rosa was ready for these new arrivals. "Yes, of course, cooperation would soon break down among so many. There'd be quarrels and fights. Groups would form and claim territory, one against the other. Individuals would rise to power over others. And some would amass possessions, a better shelter or a bigger store of food, which they'd guard, and preserve for their children. After a while the island would look as the world does now, Harvey – yes, I agree. And by the time the islanders grew old, they would say it had always been so. 'You can't change the island', they would say to their children. 'It's always been like this, from the start. It's sad, but that's how things are and always will be.' These old islanders are a very depressing bunch of people. They talk just like you, Harvey. But they aren't being honest, now, are they? Or maybe their memory is faulty. Because it can't be denied that things were better at the start, before groups formed and individuals took power, before some people got greedy and started to hoard more stuff than they needed. At the start it wasn't like that. Everyone helped each other, each doing what they could."

"From each according to his ability, to each according to his need?"

"Exactly. Good marks, Harvey. I see you're following my story well."

"But Europe is not a desert island, Rosa. There are more than a hundred of us. Some people's ability is for power. And need is a hard thing to measure, as I'm sure you know. Take cars. Who needs them? Who doesn't? I'm glad I never worked in a government which had to settle that one."

"Don't interrupt. This is a parable, Harvey. And it's not finished yet."

Harvey's smile was hidden by the darkness. "Go on then. Finish it."

When Rosa leaned into the light, he saw that she too was smiling. "Now," she said, raising a finger, "suppose that these people are rescued. After many years on the island they are found and taken off in a ship. But on the way – hup! Their ship is wrecked again." Describing this unlikely catch, her finger jumped backwards and up: a uniquely French gesture. "So once again these people find themselves on a desert island, the same hundred as before. Only this time, of course, they have the wisdom of experience. Now, Harvey, tell me. Would they make the same mistakes again?"

Harvey laughed aloud. "Yes, Rosa, they would. That is exactly what I think they'd do."

"They might," she said, "they might. Okay. But perhaps they might not. It's conceivable, you must admit, that on this second island the survivors would arrange things better. Remembering the quarrels which broke out on island number one, and how hellish miserable life became there, this time they organise themselves in such a way that the spirit of early cooperation is preserved. They make rules for themselves, forbidding too much power or property to any one group or individual. Naturally this is opposed by the ones who did well on the first island. But they are voted down. 'Down with the greedy ones', say the rest. 'No more of that.' This time there will be no exploitation, it's agreed. The divisions between man and man will be stopped before they can start again . . . No, Harvey, don't interrupt. This is the way the story goes. These twice-wrecked people aren't such fools as you think. Pretty soon they've got a system worked out to protect the common interest, while everyone can still see it clearly and no one is arguing to preserve his own advantage. And this new system is a success. It works. It lasts. After some years it even becomes a natural habit. The people who live on the island are changed by it. The young ones who grow up within it are formed by it . . . No, all right. We mustn't exaggerate. The story's not quite such a happy one as that. The habit these people have lost, Harvey, is that of being able to satisfy their competitive instincts just when they feel like it. They haven't become perfect people, of course. They have the same faults as before – greed, aggression, the wish to do better than the next man and dominate him. But these instincts aren't admired any longer. They're not encouraged by the system. So people have got in the habit of restraining them. They still break out of course, but less so as time goes on, because the habit of equality has also become very strong – as strong, say, as respect for property in our own society. In general people obey the system and support it in their hearts, because they can see the good it brings them. And now it is hard to find anyone who wants to go back to the ways of the bad old island." Rosa brushed her hands and sat back.

"Is that the end?"

"Yes, that's the end."

"Of history?"

"No, just the story."

"Well, it's a nice one," Harvey said. "To me it sounds a little optimistic. But then I'm a very old islander."

Rosa had dropped the light tone of narrator. "To me it seems possible, this story. And we should try to make it come true."

"The system forbids a lot of things, though, doesn't it? You

698

don't think it might come to feel oppressive, the life on this island of yours? A bit dull perhaps?"

"That is a risk, I admit. But I'll take it."

"You'd like to live there yourself?"

"Yes, Harvey, I would. And when I compare it with the world I do live in, I am filled with disgust. Ours is the ugliest civilisation in history."

"Come, Rosa. That's just not true."

"Not the most openly barbaric, perhaps. But ugly all the same. Cruel, wasteful, immoral. And all the more disgusting because we are intelligent, experienced people. We have less excuse than earlier societies. In fact we modern Europeans, I would say, are in the position of third or fourth-time islanders. We have the whole of history to learn from, and yet we are content with a system in which all other human rights are suppressed in favour of the right to own – to trade."

"Now that's not true either. You know it's not."

"It's truer than it ought to be. Property and commerce are the great gods of Europe. Everything else is subordinate. We waste the earth's resources making things we don't need, because in our system the only way we have of deciding what to make is to leave those with money to make what they like – whatever will bring them most profit. And the people are tricked into buying these things. Their desires are created by advertisements, until they seem like needs. The rich manufacture for personal profit, the poor work to satisfy imaginary needs. Everyone is caught in a tangle of money."

Harvey sat in silence, discouraged by this speech, which came so hard on the heels of the desert-island story it took him by surprise.

"And this was a thing that Marx understood," she went on. "He was the first to see it clearly. You say that he was material-ist, Harvey. Marx spoke too much in terms of money, you say. But that was only how he described the present state of history. What he said was that man was *distorted* by money – divided and trapped into groups who can only exploit and injure each other. And this was against human nature. He looked to a day when man would be complete. That was his word for it – complete. He said that we should proceed to a state where man's natural dignity was restored, and his instincts of co-operation set free."

"Should proceed? Or would?"

"Should and would. This was the goal of history – the ideal to which it moved. And to anyone who'd seen this clearly, there was a duty to join that movement, and assist it."

At that she paused to draw breath, and did literally draw it: a sharp inhalation, then exhalation, as though she had got something off her chest. It was funny. While orating she had seemed to be talking to herself. Now, to him, she was more philosophical.

"God or Marx, we said back in there. But the question should have been God or Man. Because that's the real difference, isn't it, Harvey? Christians like you take a poor view of man's capacities. Your ideas are based on the worst assumptions about human nature. But Marx believed in man's essential goodness. He saw and explained the possibilities for realising it." Again she paused and took a breath. "Well, Harvey, that is what I believe too. I believe it, millions of others do. So are you going to sit there and tell me that this is just religious neurosis?"

"No."

"Thank you."

Having leaned tensely forward on the question, she sat back. After a moment she went on.

"They are quite different faiths, you see. And I have always been aware of that. It was the difference which drew me from one to the other."

"All the same, you serve Marx as you might have served God – in an extreme fashion."

"Yes," she said quietly. "Perhaps."

"That's not your fault, of course. We can't help our natures."

"No. We can't."

"But we ought to be aware of them before we go killing people," Harvey said, dropping his voice to match hers. "That's all I'm saying, Rosa. Take a close look at yourself before you do this."

She was silent. Then her voice sharpened up again. "You leave my personality to me, Harvey. Let's hear your beliefs."

On an ordinary day Harvey would not have replied. Religious discussion with strangers was wildly against his normal form. But this was his last night on earth. There was nothing left to do but pursue this terminal tussle of words with his executioner, and he was glad of the chance. No hope remained except that of changing her mind. So he answered her, finding it easier to do because of the dark that enveloped them both.

"Spiritually I don't get very high. I'm afraid I never have. Even so, I look for a creed which contains more than man – especially man explained in economics."

"But it's more than economics," Rosa protested. "You yourself called it a faith." She paused to pick her words, then added: "The way I'd put it myself is, Marx is the hope of the poor."

Harvey's resolve to communicate flagged. "Would you find it totally preposterous," he said to her after a moment, "if I were to suggest there might be one or two mysteries which apply to rich and poor alike? Which, indeed, stretch beyond man?"

"No, Harvey, that will do for your beliefs. It's time for sleep."

"Yes. I agree."

But still she did not go. Head turned away to the window, as though to catch a longer perspective, she said in a rather sad voice: "For me Marx has always been more than an intellectual concept. For me, Harvey, this was my home. That was how I felt from the day I first found it. A home for me, a hope for the poor – these are my loyalties." She turned back towards him. "So, you see, we both have a faith. God or Marx – different ideas, but same human impulse, as you said yourself. Perhaps you were right." Then her voice turned teasing. "Would you go so far as to say I was doing God's work?"

Harvey was embarrassed. "Only in the sense that we all do. You are part of his creation. So am I. There's the mystery."

Rosa chuckled at the thought. "God's work, eh? Well, that's new." She got to her feet and walked to the window. "No one's accused me of that in a long time."

"Well, I could be wrong," Harvey said curtly. "But I'll soon know the answer, won't I? Seven hours from now, if you mean what you say."

The remark acted on her like an insult. She stiffened. "One day we'll both know," she snapped back, then spun on her heels and strode out.

"Goodnight, Rosa. Sleep on it, won't you?"

To which no reply. She shut the door and locked it behind her. Harvey heard her walk across the main room and out of the house, using the back door beside the kitchen. Well remembered, he thought to himself. Watch out for the terrace, Rosa, won't you? Or you'll know the answers before I do.

701

2

She went round the house and sat under the hazel trees with Joop, close to the grave. A cigarette glowed between them.

Harvey watched through the shutter, then reeled from sudden dizziness. His head sang and swam as he sank on the mattress. As usual his heart took him by surprise. Moved less by external events than some obscure private flap of his own, it skipped and bounced in his chest. He settled it with respiratory exercises; a deliberate effort to relax. But then it speeded up again, excited by a first snatch of speech from the French police.

The radios in the next room were on all the time, and Harvey had learned to distinguish between them. The one he heard now was the big set, waiting to pick up police talk. So far it had been silent. But all of a sudden, at 1.23, it put out a loud burst of urgent chatter – just as quickly cut off. One second there were several excited male voices, the next there were none, as though a door had been opened and shut on a crowded room. Harvey could not make out what was said. Joop ran in, but was too late to hear.

Rosa brewed more coffee. One by one they came in to drink and chat, then went back on watch. The Dutchman especially was busy. He checked each approach in turn. He briefed the others on paths of escape. He prowled near and far with his sniper's rifle and telescopic night-sight, deep into the woods and back again, up the hill behind and back again. He concentrated on the north and west sides, where Harvey could sometimes observe his patrols, but as soon as the Dutchman was out of sight his movements were hard to distinguish from those of animal life. From the hazel plantation and especially the overgrown forest, further down the hill, came the same continual stirrings and rustlings, soft hoots, yelps and barks, a flap of wings, a snap of twigs, the steady drip of water on fallen leaves. The crickets were quietening down. Traffic on the road was rare.

Harvey stood listening at the shutter, at the door. He lay down again but could not sleep.

He tried to think of his wife, but this had become more difficult. Even his memories of her brought no proper emotional response, in the way that a favourite old record of music can sometimes fail in its effect. At one black point she seemed hardly more than a visitor in his life, who had turned up early but left before the end. He knew the impression to be falsely callous, not caused by lack of affection. This was the isolation that comes before death: the retreat into self before retreat from the world. He had seen it in others. Even so, it saddened him not to think of her better. He stopped trying.

Rosa shifted restlessly about in the parlour. She knocked something over in the dark – perhaps the wine bottle. It fell with a splintering crash and in the silence that followed Harvey heard a series of rhythmic grunts, like the act of love, or a person doing press-ups. Then a violent sneeze; then another. It took him a while to recognise Rosa Berg in emotional distress. The sound brought him no vengeful pleasure. He listened with a mixture of pity and embarrassment. Though cast as its victim, he felt he had broken in on some private tragedy.

At 1.33 a single-engined plane flew overhead, north to south, quite low, along the same path as the helicopter. It did not return.

But Rosa did. A few minutes later she came back to join him in the cell. This time there was no hesitation in the corridor. Her movements were more decided. She seemed to be resigned to something. Harvey wondered what.

This time she sat beside him on the mattress, but apart, at its opposite end, leaning back against the wall, as he was. Maybe she wished to see him better. Exactly between them now, on mattress and wall, hung the last patch of moonlight, cast down from the gap in the shutter's upper slats.

For several minutes more she said nothing, and then, without any preamble, she took up the argument from its last point, as though there had been no interruption.

"So you think this is all God's work, do you? Explain yourself, Harvey. Let me hear this mystery of yours."

Harvey paused to get his thoughts in order; no longer embarrassed by the subject, merely unprepared. But before he could answer she asked another question, more sarcastic.

"Would you say he is here, watching over us?"

"I'd say he was between us." Harvey pointed to the patch of moonlight. "There – the light between. From a source above."

"What? You mean he's not on your side?"

Rosa's jocular manner rang false. Perhaps to her too, Harvey thought, this was the heart of the matter – or had come to seem so.

"No," he said carefully, "I wouldn't claim that. You and I are just left and right, Rosa, right or wrong according to our own point of view. Our quarrel's beneath him."

"You mean he's neutral?" The question was serious. She had given up the effort to sneer, yet her voice was amused as she added: "This isn't Christianity, Harvey. This is Yin and Yang. Your god's Chinese."

"Oh dear, I hope not."

"I think if you ever get out of this, you better go and see your father-confessor."

To Harvey this brought a picture of his local vicar, whose conception of the truth was certainly broad enough to embrace Yin and Yang. He almost laughed and stopped there. But this wasn't England and this was no joke. This was a late-night, last-minute hunt for common ground with a murderous French female Marxist.

"No, I don't think God's neutral," he said to her. "He's simply light, and we are different shades of darkness. But if you don't mind, I'd rather leave him out of this, at least by name."

"Yes. Let's try to keep rational."

"I'm not sure that reason will get us all the way – this is a mystery we're chasing. However, let's call it the creative force. Don't ask me how it works, but in its operation there's always some tension, isn't there? This afternoon it struck me that if people didn't quarrel, as you and I are now, nothing much would change for the better. There's no moral life without moral tussles. But there are always two ways that such tussles can go, Rosa. They can either end in harmony or conflict, can't they? From the first comes creation, from the second destruction. So the first way is better than the second, I'd say. It's not a neutral matter."

"Thesis, antithesis, synthesis," Rosa mused. "That's what it's called in my camp."

"So it is, yes. Well, there you are."

"But synthesis can sometimes be a cheat," she went on quickly. "It can't be achieved by evasion of the issue, or it's worthless and dishonest. You don't get progress from that."

"I agree," Harvey said, "there is compromise and compromise. Sometimes it's just an easy way out. But that's not always true, is it? Sometimes it's a very hard bargain between honest people, each convinced that the other is wrong – an agreement to settle for the little ground shared. And that's not evasion. It's humility."

"Humility! I hate it!"

"Really? I'd say it was a good thing."

"You say, you say." Rosa's mocking tone returned, then she scrambled up and strode to the window, where she stood stiff and still. "What you're saying is I'm doing God's work until I shoot you."

"That, I agree, would be an intervention of the Devil."

"And who are you to say such a thing? Just shut up, Harvey, will you? Shut up! I've heard enough of what you say." She swivelled and advanced a few paces, leaning forward, throttle-voiced, furiously slicing up the moonbeam with her hands. "All this stuff about heavenly light – just clever talk to save your skin. Don't think I can't see that." She turned away; turned immediately back again. "And what do you mean, preaching synthesis to me? You haven't given up much ground, have you? No, none at all. Well, unless your friends do it for you, I shan't give any either. There won't be any cheap compromise here, let me tell you."

"Rosa, listen. Don't be stupid." Harvey himself was now up off the mattress; one step forward. "It's not my skin, it's your soul –"

"Hah!"

"Don't do it, for your own sake. There may be good in what you say. So, fine, keep saying it, keep trying to change things. But don't carry on with this foolish threat, or you're damned. The rest of your life will be . . . ."

Harvey was stopped by her pistol. She had whipped it out

and pressed it to his cheek, stepping forward quickly to his side in the dark. Her face was so close he could feel her breath.

"That's enough," she said, cold as her Dutchman. "Not another word or I'll do it."

"All right, no more. I've said what I have to."

"Sit down."

Harvey sat.

"And stay there," she added, dropping the gun to her side. "Don't move, and don't talk. I've heard enough of your voice for the rest of my life. *Merde! Merde*, you do annoy me, Harvey. Just shut up and sit there, or I'll shut you up for ever."

Harvey did as she told him, more wearied than frightened by the gun-talk. So, he thought, that was the end of that. The dialogue with this girl was over. On the edge of common ground she had backed off and run. A pity, but hardly surprising. Thesis, antithesis were all that existed here; synthesis there never would be between himself and Rosa Berg. How silly to have thought any different.

"Do you want some coffee?"

Her question, uttered gruffly from the window, took him so by surprise that Harvey said yes, he'd like coffee, although it was not the best thing for cardiac arrhythmia. Rosa went out to get it. She came back with two mugs on a tray, a packet of cigarettes; and set on the tray, a lighted candle. She sat on the mattress again, kicked off her sandals and crossed her bare legs below her skirt.

"Do you want one?"

Harvey accepted a cigarette. Even worse than coffee, pulse-wise, and more revolting than he'd remembered. He put it out after a puff or two, then picked up his mug and sipped from it.

Rosa, her face theatrically lit by the candle, was smoking with her left hand. Cradled in her other palm was the pistol, resting on the folds of her brown woollen dress. She stared at it; and then, to Harvey's consternation, she picked the thing up by the barrel and held it out towards him.

"Would you like to see a product of the people?"

"I don't want it."

"Take it. Look."

"No, Rosa, that's yours. Don't . . ."

"Take it, Harvey! *Take it*!" Eyes glaring in wild annoyance, she thrust the gun into his hands. "That's right. Now, take a look at the writing on the side."

Harvey turned the pistol over in his hands and bent to examine two lines of fine lettering etched into its black metal side.

VZOR 1950 CESKA ZBROJOVKA
NAR. PODNIK STRAKONICE

Rosa leaned across to him. "Know what that means?"

"No."

"I'll tell you. The top line says Model 1950, Czech Gun Company. 1950's the year they brought it out. And this, the bottom line, means it was made in the factory at Strakonice. *Narodni Padnik* – People's Factory." She sat back and looked at him, smiling. "Well? Don't you think that's appropriate?"

Harvey had no answer. He stared at her dumbly, wondering what would come next. To his vast relief she held out her hand, with an upward flick of the fingers. He gave the gun back.

But Rosa had more games to play. She stubbed out her cigarette on the floor and transferred the weapon to her right hand. "Did you think you could shoot me?"

"I wasn't tempted."

"Well, you wouldn't have succeeded. The catch is on. See? Down for safe, up for off."

With that she pushed up a lever on the side, then held the gun towards him again, barrel pointed. "Now it will shoot," she said, smiling still. Then she turned it over at an angle. "You see that red dot? When that dot shows, the safety catch is off. But I can never remember, so I have an English rhyme to help me. 'Red is dead', I have to say. Does that amuse you?"

"No, not really."

"Red is dead. Corpse made by the people of Strakonice." She re-applied the catch and bounced the pistol on her palm, as though testing its weight; then held it up in the air for inspection. "Funny things, aren't they? Like toys. I've had it for years, but I never thought I'd use it. I was rather shocked when it worked."

"In Rome?"

She nodded, smile gone. "In Rome. He fell down the steps, just like that. So easy."

She put the gun away then, buttoning it into the holster on her belt. On the belt's other side, Harvey had noticed, were some loops with spare magazines slotted into them. Once rid of the pistol, Rosa stared at the candle morosely, her flippant mood replaced by a look of profoundest exhaustion.

"I shot him through his ear," she said. "And down he went. I don't suppose he had time to feel it, do you?"

"No, I don't suppose so."

"I'll do the same for you, Harvey. All you have to do is turn your head away and hold it still. Will you do that?"

"If I have to, yes," Harvey said. "But I thought your friend Joop would do it. He's the killer here, surely."

"Yes, he'll do it. I'll leave it to him."

"Joop Janssen will do it, but you will decide."

"Yes, that's right, Harvey. I'll decide. And now I think it's time you stopped talking again."

Harvey was happy to stop. It was time to be alone. And Rosa, it seemed, had nothing more to say. Together they squatted on the mattress and stared at the candle flame, which had now attracted a squadron of kamikaze moths, swirling and diving to death with mad abandon. Harvey began to find this upsetting, but soon the slaughter was ended by a curt command from outside. Joop Janssen told Rosa to put the candle out. She immediately did so, leaning forward to blow with the guilty haste of a girl caught playing in the dormitory. The Dutchman wandered off.

Harvey was ready for sleep now. But still Rosa did not go. They sat side by side on the mattress in darkness, each invisible to the other until their eyes recovered. In Harvey's vision the brightness of the candle left an afterglow, gradually fading.

He lost track of time, but after some minutes Rosa spoke to him again in a voice now vague and rambling with fatigue. She asked him if he had ever been to Moscow. When he said that he had, she wanted to know if he'd seen Lenin's tomb.

"Yes," he told her, "once."

"What's it like?"

"It's like a pyramid. Outside, as you know. And even more in. A tomb of the Pharaoh."

"And Lenin himself?"

"Strangely ordinary. Not like a Pharaoh. Small, neat, dry

little fellow, fast asleep inside his glass case. A sleeping bank manager."

Rosa absorbed this in the dark. From the space where she sat came a tomb-like silence. Then she said: "Lenin was a very great man, Harvey. Wouldn't you agree with that?"

"Oh yes, I would. And I felt so at the time. It's an awesome shrine. And the awe rubs off. But I'll tell you another thing, Rosa."

"What's that?"

"I felt a long way from Europe."

"So now you're going to tell me I'm hooked on an Asian cult."

"In Moscow, certainly, that's how it feels. The warrior of Tartary, enshrined with full pomp. A touch of plain oriental power."

"A universal hope. That's what Lenin is."

"Yes, he became so, for a few years. But not any more, I would say. As time passes he's been seen as more Russian – not for export."

She stirred and sighed. "You don't give up, Harvey, do you?"

"The question was yours, Rosa. And that's my answer. Let's not argue any more."

"No, I agree. No more argument."

Still she did not go.

Earlier Harvey had been troubled by the strangeness of this girl who had come from nowhere to finish him off. Now the moment was unnervingly intimate. He could hear her breath and smell her body, too little washed during two days of heat. He could now just see her, slumped against the wall in the last faint rays of the moon.

We are like exhausted lovers, he thought, going over a broken relationship. We know we can't mend it but we're too tired to end it. Without enough energy even to separate, we share a bed in the dark.

Often in political life he had seen a quarrel mended, abandoned at least, through plain fatigue – especially in Brussels. The synthesis of limited stamina, it could very well be said, was what modern Europe was built on.

But he had one more idea to utter.

"You know, Rosa, listening to you, it strikes me you're in the wrong place. Your true cause is not with the workers of Europe, but the poor of Africa and Asia – the wretched of the earth, as you call them. Those are the people you ought to go and fight for."

To this she made no reply.

"But I'm not sure you ought to take Lenin in your luggage," Harvey added.

Still she did not react.

Peering at her form in the darkness, Harvey saw that her head had fallen forward on her chest. And then he caught the deep, even note of her breathing.

Rosa Berg was asleep.

3

Soon it was the blackest hour of night. The moon went out. No sounds of animal life stirred the sleeping, dripping woods. Even the crickets stopped scratching their legs. To Harvey it seemed that all nature held its breath.

Nor was there any sound of man or machine. Traffic had ceased on the road in the valley. No vehicles or aircraft approached, no people. No movement came from the house or its garden, no voice from the radios in the next room. The Iskra's three sentries had either dropped off, he thought, or they were watching in disciplined silence.

He himself tried to drop off but could not. Curled up at one end of the mattress, while Rosa snored at the other, he kept track of time by the luminous hands of his watch. 2.15 came and went, 2.30, 2.45. He marked the hours by the quarter. 3.15 was the last he remembered. Some time after that he must have slept.

But before sleep came a black trough of the spirit, shot with feverish images. Stirred by Rosa's games with her pistol, his imagination leapt uncontrolled to the moment of execution. He flinched from the missile that would smash through his brain, succumbing to an onset of pure naked fear. Verbal upward address not being his habit, he tried to hold his mind still in a moment of concentrated supplication. He offered his spirit to source. But the light of creation had gone with the moon. Now he saw only the black of oblivion, heard only the snore of the girl at his side. He asked forgiveness for his own dim vision, and found himself asking for her as well. If she shoots me, forgive her. If she doesn't, reward her. Show her your light . . . But this thought disintegrated even as he thought it. Uncertain

711

whom he was addressing, uncertain of anything mortal or divine in the utter annihilating blackness, he curled up tight on the mattress and waited for release into dreams.

And sleep must eventually have come, for how long he wasn't sure, when he and Rosa, both, were woken by Joop Janssen crashing through the door of the room.

The Dutchman came hurtling in with his rifle and took up a firing position at the shutter's lower gap. Jumping up from the mattress in joint alarm, Harvey and Rosa saw the hazel woods lit by a blazing white light. One of the flares had gone off, triggered by a touch on its trip-wire. And immediately another ignited with a sharp explosive pop. The ground below the trees was lit as it never was by day. The Dutchman scanned it tensely, ready to shoot. But no human shape could be seen; no animal even. Nothing stirred in the hot white glare below the leaves.

A fox perhaps, Rosa suggested. A fox, yes perhaps, Joop agreed. But he was uneasy. It took a good tug to set off those things, he said. A fox would have been less clumsy. A fox would have picked up the scent of the flare-setter.

The other two, first Mario, then Murdoch, called up in fright on the radio. Joop, speaking into his handset, told them to hold their positions. Keep watching, he said, report any movement.

Then he told Rosa to get the Webley.

And Rosa, still bleary from sleep, did what the Dutchman said. She went out to the main room, using his torch, and then came back in with the long-barrelled pistol she had used to threaten Harvey in the car – the one she had said was silenced. The Dutchman took it and stuffed it in his belt with a quick, cold glance in Harvey's direction. Turning back to watch the woods, he asked Rosa whether she wanted to stay here longer.

Rosa said she would stay. Joop could go if he wanted, but she would stay and see the thing through. The other two could make up their own minds.

Joop grunted. He went off to scour the woods as the light from his fireworks sputtered and faded. A few minutes later he came back to the gap in the shutter, speaking through it from the outside. Yes, he agreed, perhaps a fox. No sign of anything else. Then he gave some last instructions to Rosa.

"Stay with him. You have your gun?"

"Yes," she said.

"Here, take the Webley. Any time you're ready."

"Not yet, Joop."

"Okay, you're the boss. But stay awake. And keep quiet. No lights, please."

The Dutchman went off. Rosa came back to the mattress. Again she and Harvey sat alone in the dark, each invisible to the other. But now the vibrations between them were different. Each was wide awake, each jolted by the incident just past. Harvey's self-doubt had vanished with the short spell of sleep, the violent awakening; and so had all wish to think of higher things. It was too late now to argue ideals or chat about the meaning of existence, he thought, sensing that Rosa felt the same. For her now there was only the wait for more news, the final decision to be made. And his own mind, resolved if fearful, was now held fast by two equal priorities.

If he went, he must go with dignity; jacket on, shirt buttoned, head high, face composed. This was a matter of physical control. He had lived tidily. So he should die.

On the other hand he shouldn't go meek and resigned. From now until the end no chance of survival should be overlooked. Four hours remained. Help might come. And even if it didn't, there was always the chance that Rosa would relent.

So his interest in her now was different; more precise, more pragmatic, more selfish. He was back to the lessons of Europol. The longer he could keep her in play, he thought, the harder he would be to shoot. So from now on the talk should be calm and uncontentious. It was Rosa the girl that might let him off, not Rosa the Red.

He was still wondering how to pursue this, when Rosa herself spoke up. And what she said was a surprise.

"Have you heard of Mondragon?"

"No, I don't think so. It sounds like a sleeping pill."

"Harvey, you really are a disgrace. Where have you been all this long political life of yours?" She laughed to herself in the darkness. "Mondragon's in Spain," she went on. "It's a town where the workers own the means of production. They own the factories, the schools, the hospitals. They even own the banks."

"Oh yes," Harvey said, remembering. "The Basque thing. Started by a priest, wasn't it? After the civil war?"

"Started by a priest and after a war. Yes, I'm afraid so."

"And you have friends there?"

She avoided the question. "Naturally we're interested in Mondragon. But they rather disapprove of us. To them the Iskra is too Marxist. To us they're getting close to big business."

Harvey wondered where this was leading, but she said no more, so he left the topic unpursued. He had finished with workers' cooperatives. "There is one thing I'd like to know, Rosa."

"Yes?"

"How did you persuade Erich Kohlman?"

To this she did not immediately reply, and he feared he had touched a raw spot. But eventually an answer came back from the darkness at his side, with no resentful vibrations attached.

"If you want to believe, you are half-way there. That's what the Christians say, isn't it? Erich Kohlman wanted to believe. He was more than half way when we found him."

"And when did you find him?"

"Soon after he came to work for you."

"Will you tell me about it? I want to hear how this happened."

"Very well, if you wish." Rosa settled herself on the mattress, apparently glad of a neutral subject: something to keep awake on, something to keep her mind off the crisis approaching. "Throughout his career," she began, "Erich Kohlman has had a secret friend in the German Left. She's a girl called Mitzi Hoff. And Mitzi is a friend of ours. Her father was an original member of the Iskra."

"Hoff – you mean the man who jumped from a window?"

"He was pushed, Harvey."

"Really? I didn't know that."

"No, you wouldn't. In any case Mitzi herself joined the Iskra. And one day she told me about Erich Kohlman. We already had our plans for BMG and Mobital, and you already seemed a threat to those plans. Erich Kohlman worked for you. This seemed to me a piece of very good luck. So I fixed to meet him in Berlin."

"Go on."

"We had to be careful. But Mitzi arranged it very well. She borrowed an island on one of those lakes they have there. The Tegeler See, it was called."

"A desert island?"

Rosa's voice was altered by a smile. "A secret one, certainly.

714

There was just the one chalet on it, hidden by pine trees. Erich met us in Spandau late at night and we went out in a private motorboat, also borrowed from Mitzi's friends. They owned the whole island, so we spent a weekend on it, no one to disturb us. Late summer it was, very beautiful. Calm water, calm discussion. Bach in the intervals."

"You don't mean Erich brought his cello?"

"No, there was a gramophone. It worked on a battery. The hut had no electricity or gas, so we cooked on a barbecue. I ate a lot. I always do in Germany. I explained to Erich about the Iskra, but I didn't have to do much persuasion. He and Mitzi talked privately most of the time. To me it was touching, you know, the relationship between those two. I can see them now at the water's edge, listening to Bach. They were both fond of music. And water, too. They had met on a lake, and after that they went on doing so – in Hamburg, in Berlin, even in Brussels, so I'm told. Water and Bach. It was like a ritual. Tranquillity was very important to them."

"Were they lovers?"

"At first I assumed so. But no, they weren't. Only friends. Sometimes they held hands, that was all. Sometimes they would sit in silence, but at others they would talk and talk, as though they'd just discovered their voices. To watch those two talk – it was like a first embrace between teenagers. I felt shy in their presence."

"How did it start?"

"On a holiday, when they were younger. Mitzi's mother got to know Erich's parents." Rosa paused and made a motion in the dark – wiping her face perhaps. "Have you met Erich's parents, Harvey?"

"I did once. In Hamburg. I don't know them well."

"Nazis, yes?"

"Oh no, I wouldn't say that. Conservative, certainly. Old-fashioned, strict. It struck me he was rather young to be their son."

"To him they are Nazis. Too similar, anyway."

Rosa stopped there, as if no more explanation were needed. And at a shallow level none was, Harvey thought with sadness, recalling his visit to Hamburg a year ago. He had gone to give a talk at the Ubersee Club and accepted an invitation to stay with Erich's parents. The house they had used to put him up in was owned by the family shipping firm, a solid prewar mansion overlooking the Elbe, clad in ivy to the dormers, full of enormous furniture. And the Kohlmans had gone with the decor: a heavily handsome couple of the utmost bourgeois solidity and confidence. Like their friends who came to dinner, like the luncheon guests at the club, business was their subject and they were never bored by it. The talk at table had resembled a board meeting. And then, to provide an excusing dash of culture, Erich had been asked to play his cello, which he did, while the guests smoked cigars and their eyes slowly closed.

This picture, returning to Harvey with terrible clarity, contained all he wanted to know. He asked no more questions.

Rosa sat in silence beside him, and now he could just see her outline, head and shoulders framed against the wall behind. He glanced at his watch. 4.05. At that moment Harvey was wondering how to go on, but before he could think of more to say another panic swept through the gang. Stephen Murdoch failed to answer on the radio. Joop dashed round to the east, to see what had happened, while Mario stood guard outside Harvey's shutter and Rosa was posted at the back door. Five minutes of tension followed. Then Murdoch was found asleep.

Joop must have been so angry that he hit him, because next time that Murdoch appeared he had a red weal across his cheek. Murdoch's face was sore, and so were Murdoch's feelings; as Harvey discovered. After this scare more coffee was made and Murdoch was sent to fetch the mugs from the cell. As he stooped to pick up the tray, he muttered resentfully through his teeth: "I don't like this, Harvey. Nor does Mario. We're going to stop it if we get the chance. So keep on your toes. May be a fight."

Harvey had no time to answer.

And after this Rosa kept away from him. She was gone for more than half an hour. Left alone in the cell, he could only prepare things to say to her, prepare plans of action if mutiny broke out. His hopes were running high now, but his fears rose with them in odd combination. The better his chances, the more scared he got. Twice he was seized by cold fright as the light grew from dull grey to milky white, not yet warmed by the sun. The birds began to chirrup, but that did not lift him. It seemed rather tactless of the birds to treat this as an ordinary morning, to be sung and flown about in just like any other. Harvey had

716

never had much enthusiasm for birds. But then he received an early visit from the statesman-lizard, who called in to know what was happening, and stayed to mull it over, glued fast to the wall with dismay. He might have stayed longer, but Rosa's return sent him scuttling.

She had lost composure in the interval. Her face was so pale it looked ill, almost yellow, its flat features carved with strain. Normally smooth, it had picked up new lines overnight. Her movements were jumpy. She could not sit still, and had lost the desire to talk. Each time Harvey tried, she waved a hand irritably for silence.

At five o'clock she went out for news on the radio, but came back with none. When she smoked a cigarette, it shook in her hand. Slumped in the aluminium deckchair, she watched the light of sunrise grow beyond the shutter, until each gap between the slats was tinged gold.

"The light above the wall," she muttered to herself, rather bitterly, it seemed to Harvey. But she held up her hand to stop him asking what it meant. For a few minutes more she was silent, and then she said, going straight back to the point broken off an hour before: "Erich's ideals were very high – more German, perhaps, than Marxist. But he was practical when it came to detail."

"Yes, he was. I remember."

"He was worried by the problem of size. A motor company had to be big, he said, to compete. But this made it difficult to run by the vote."

"I agree with him," Harvey said, perplexed by this new line of talk. "The decisions are so complicated that no cars will get made at all. The poor fellows on the machines will be too busy reading balance sheets."

"Well, I accept the point," Rosa said curtly, nodding as though in decision. "In Mondragon they have put a limit on the size of industrial unit. Five hundred people is the maximum allowed. Communication fails, they say, at any higher number. And the Iskra are conscious of this problem. We realise that democratic organisation is easier in small production units."

As she made this peculiarly formal statement Rosa sat upright in the chair, not looking at Harvey once, but staring straight ahead at the light in the shutter, the patch of sky above. The statement sounded thought out. It was also, from the tone of her voice, unfinished. But half-way through it she had stopped, as if it were a difficult thing to go on with. Her face turned quickly towards him, frowning.

"Would you like some breakfast?"

The question came out in a bark, and then she was up and gone through the door, before he could give her an answer.

Harvey was glad of a moment to collect himself, so strong was the hope now surging up inside him. He was struggling to keep it off his face, but knew it would show when he spoke. And close behind hope were coming joy and relief, either one of which would send him to pieces completely.

How lovely the sun was, he thought, how sweet the birds sounded. And here was his old reptilian friend, head nervously poked from a crack in the plaster to hear the latest news.

Lizard, keep still. *I think she's changed her mind*.

Lizard was unconvinced. His head disappeared as he heard her step.

Rosa no longer bothered to lock the cell's door or even close it. Returning from the kitchen, she brought a tray of coffee, two peaches, stale bread, some oozy butter and an unopened package of cheese.

To Harvey it seemed a fine breakfast, and the peaches especially a wonder of creation, their juicy orange flesh squirting into his mouth as his teeth bit through the furry skin. He continued to eat, head lowered, while Rosa sat pensive in the chair, about to go on with her statement. She took only coffee for herself.

"When the whole system has changed," she said suddenly, "it may be possible to split BMG and Mobital into smaller units. But until then they have to compete. So size is important, to keep costs down."

"You're beginning to sound like me, Rosa. Are we going to agree, after all?"

"No. Wait."

"Sorry, go on."

"Because of these companies' size, I accept that only the simplest and biggest decisions can be put to the workforce as a whole – election of senior management, distribution of profit, settlement of wage rates, major investment plans. Nothing much more will be possible. And this will be even more true when the companies are joined into one."

718

"I agree," said Harvey, keeping his mouth stuffed with bread.

She turned to face him, stern and cold. "The difference between us is this, Harvey. The structure proposed by you is an empty formula. Very typical of the false democracy Mario spoke about. You offer the workers an illusion of power – just enough to dupe them and keep them quiet."

"It's meant to be more."

"But it's not. As I showed you this afternoon, your new board structure is a fraud."

"It may be the best I can do, Rosa."

"In that case you will change nothing." She turned away from him, losing interest.

"Still, I take your point," Harvey said quickly, swallowing his bread. "Why? Are you going to suggest an improvement?"

After a pause of several seconds, in which she appeared to weigh up this whole conversational initiative, wondering whether to drop it or not, Rosa nodded. "I could show you one, for a start." Then she rose abruptly from the chair. "Wait here."

She left the room. She was gone for several minutes, doing something on the table in the parlour. When she came back, she had a sheet of paper in her hand. She held it out to Harvey, then sat at his side on the mattress while he once again stared at the future arranged into molecules.

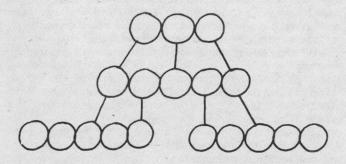

They studied the pattern together. Rosa explained what it meant. She then made some other points about the merger, more practical by far than any she had mentioned before. She was doing this, she said, to show him that she was a reasonable person. She wanted fuller change, yes, but was ready to admit that some reform was better than none. And some reforms were better than others, she added, tapping the paper with a schoolmarmish finger.

She stood up and walked to the window. Again she hesitated, seeming embarrassed. She glanced back; half-opened her mouth; then finished what she had to say with her face turned away to the shutter.

"I can see from your face, Harvey, you think I've decided to let you go. No, I have not. I am waiting until I hear more news, from the factories or your friend Riemeck. My decision will depend on that."

She paused, pointing back at the sheet still held in Harvey's hands.

"If I were offered something like that, I might let you go. But I won't be, will I? We both know that. Well, they'd better offer something. I cannot retreat from what I've said unless I have . . . something. They must give me *something*," she repeated forcefully, turning her back on him again. "If they don't, I shall ask Joop to kill you. And if he's reluctant, I'll do it myself. I have no desire to, but I have the will. Don't doubt my will, Harvey. It's stronger than you think." Her shoulders sagged as she let out her breath, the way that she always did after a difficult statement. Her voice, going on, had a note of finality. "And now I am going to say goodbye to you. They have been interesting, but now these discussions must end, because they are making this harder – certainly for me, and perhaps for you too. We shall talk no more unless there is news to change the situation."

She turned and faced him with a small, wan smile.

"So you see, the thing is out of our hands. We are after all the instruments of history. And the last thing I'll say is what I said before. Remember, please, it's not personal."

Harvey had risen to his feet, intending one last protest. But the words died to nothing on his lips. His mind was empty air, without force of resistance.

She crossed towards the door with her long heavy stride, then stopped to look him in the eye.

"Goodbye."

"Goodbye, Rosa."

For a second he thought she was going to shake his hand, but no, she carried straight on to the door. This time she closed and locked it. Her footsteps retreated through the house. Silence fell, except for the birds and the crickets. The lizard stayed deep in his crack. Left alone in the sunlit room, Harvey sank down and stared at his half-eaten breakfast, the crust of bread and one peach remaining, the butter beginning to melt. The cheese was called Caprice of the Gods.

4

Still it might have ended peacefully. But now in the opposite camp there occurred a most deadly confusion.

It had begun the evening before, at the time when Dr. Otto Riemeck left his audience with the President of France and Chancellor of Germany.

And the pity of it was that Riemeck was blessed at that moment by a perfectly accurate foresight of how the crisis would develop. As he drove away from the Elysée Palace he was worried by his unyielding stand against the Iskra. Was there not something he could do which might help to save Patrick Harvey's life? Specifically, was there not some sort of offer he could make to Rosa Berg which would save her face and yet not seem a blatant concession to any of her four demands? So far he had thought of nothing. But to this problem Riemeck brought the whole of his weary attention in the short time it took him to travel from the centre of Paris to Le Bourget, where his plane was waiting. And by the time he reached the airport he had come up with an answer. Before taking off he wrote this idea on a piece of paper, put it in an envelope and gave it to the chauffeur, who was told to take it back to Laura Jenkinson at the Commission's office in Avenue Victor Hugo.

The message was more than a vague suggestion. Laura, had she read it, would have recognised immediately that this was a Presidential order for instant transmission to the businessmen in Rome. But Laura did not read it. The message never reached her, because she was not where she should have been. She had gone to the British Embassy on an errand of sympathy to Lady Harvey. And soon after that Laura left for Italy, along with all other Commission officials who might have grasped the note's

722

importance. For many hours it sat unopened on an empty desk. In due course it was transmitted to Rome, but orally, para-phrased over the telephone by a young man with scant idea what was happening to another who had even less. Neither had much grasp of English either, the language in which the note was written. And after transmission it was destroyed.

By the time this confusion started to matter, Otto Riemeck, although still in Europe, was a very long way from the battle. For most of the night he was airborne. By dawn he was close to the Arctic Circle. His jet put down at an airstrip cut from a wilderness of trees in the topmost corner of Sweden. He switched to a military jeep and was taken for miles along a track through the forest until he reached a lake of unearthly beauty, set still as glass between precipitous fir-clad slopes. Above the tree-line the slopes rose to mountains whose icy peaks glittered pinkish white in the opalescent light of a premature northern morning. Beside the lake was a house made of logs. A thin wisp of smoke drifted up from its chimney into the chill, windless air. And on the lake was a man in a boat, out fishing already, despite the early hour. He looked up in surprise as the jeep's raucous engine broke the silence, then hauled in his rod and started to row towards the shore.

Even at a distance the fisherman's displeasure was clear. And Riemeck himself was irritated at the very long journey forced upon him by the fisherman's taste for primeval seclusion. The house by the lake had no telephone, no wireless. Riemeck was hoping it had food and warmth, soap and razor. But even if welcomed, he could not stay long – an hour at the most. It made him uneasy to be so far out of touch. As he stood at the water's edge, stiff-limbed from his journey, listening to the soft splash of oar-blades approaching, this uneasiness rose to a definite sharp sensation of alarm. The time by his watch was 5.30. It had taken too long to get here, he thought. It was time to be going already. Exasperated by the slowness of the boat, puzzled that none of the family came out of the house, he had a sudden urge to jump back into the jeep and be off, since definitely and drastically in the wrong place.

What caused this fear he could not say, but afterwards, remembering the time, he wondered if it might have been a subliminal shock-wave, carrying all the way from Milan.

If so, it had taken two minutes to arrive. By 5.30 everyone living in Milan was on the telephone to everyone else. A few seconds after 5.28 the city had been shaken end to end by a mighty explosion. It had come from the Como Road, people said who lived near. It had come from the Mobital factory, said those who lived closer. And they were right. The detonation had shattered every pane in the handsome glass block of the company's head office, and fatally weakened its steel supports. Slowly the whole building started to lean. For one awful moment it hung, Pisa-like, the scream of a woman trapped inside still audible. Then it fell across the road in a heap. Eight people were killed, four staff and four guards. Several others were hurt, but not Carlo Guidotti, who was thought to be in Rome at the time.

He was not, as it happened. Guidotti had been in Rome for most of the night, talking round his board and the unions. But now, as his office was blown to the ground, he was at his apartment in Milan. When brought the news he was found awake and dressed, which gave some people the impression that Mobital's chief executive knew in advance what was going to happen in his company that morning.

And it was not over yet. The explosion was just the beginning. Simultaneously, as at a signal, all the plants in the neighbouring compound were brought to stop by rebel workers, who jumped up and called on their fellows of the night-shift to seize and occupy the factory. Others, less disciplined, began to attack the machines as if the machines were made of flesh and blood. Trolleys of components were overturned, the contents used as weapons. The machines resisted well, so next the rebels ran across to the staff block. They pushed the guards aside, broke in, forced the locks of the filing cabinets and started to make fires of paper on the managers' desks. Then they found the personnel records and began to shout names from the windows – who had been followed, who watched, who was marked down as an agitator, who picked for promotion, who due for dismissal, who was known to vote Christian Democrat, who suspected of collusion with the Red Brigades.

This was good revolutionary theatre, as Mario Salandra would have said. And it quickly drew an audience. Soon a big crowd of workers had gathered in the yard below the window. As the names were called out some men shouted angrily, some were spurred to fresh acts of destruction. Some simply stood by and watched, either in silent disapproval or noisy amusement. The ones who laughed and catcalled were young. Those who disapproved were generally older. At the back were others, older still, whose faces expressed only weariness.

Here in Milan, and in a parallel disturbance at the main plant in Naples, the workers of Mobital quickly divided into three different groups of roughly equal number. There were those known as autonomists, who called for instant and total workers' power. There were the communists, hanging back until they heard orders from the party. And there were the loyalists, who were against this upheaval but certainly not going to risk their necks to stop it. In Milan this last third of the crowd became swelled by indecisive communists, youthful catcallers, and those who lost their nerve as the forces of the state appeared. Down the Como Road came wailing ambulances, flashing fire-engines and police cars screeching to a halt by the dozen, most of them Mobital Sparta saloons. And behind the police in a fast-moving convoy of khaki jeeps came a large squad of *carabinieri*, so large and so swiftly on the spot that some said it must have been waiting close at hand.

The *carabinieri* acted with skill. At first they did nothing, but waited until their ostentatious and numerous arrival could work its sobering effect on the mob. The troops remained in their jeeps, casually displaying submachine-guns, while their officers hopped out to survey the scene in a deliberately nonchalant way. The day was brightening fast. Milan's early ground-mist was clearing. But as the sun rose, excitement fell. Inside the staff block the noise of ransacking died away. The officers sauntered in front of the jeeps conferring in their handsome uniforms, showing the individual courage which comes so easily to Italians. Then orders were suddenly given. The *carabinieri* leapt from their jeeps and ran to take up positions around the staff block, putting a line of armed khaki between the workers inside and those in the yard. The senior officer took up a megaphone and ordered the men to leave the building.

There was a moment of immobility.

One of the ground-floor offices was on fire. Smoke belched from its window, the crackle of flames could be heard inside. Later it was much discussed, and never settled, whether the *carabinieri* had started this blaze, or whether it came from the

725

papers which undoubtedly the rioters had set on fire.

For a few minutes nothing occurred. Then at that precise point, with nicely judged timing, Ambassador Carlo Guidotti arrived on the scene. With him in his car was Giuseppe Vico, the Communist leader. It was later alleged but never proved, that they had been waiting together at Guidotti's flat. Certainly they acted with skilful cohesion. On arrival at the plant they drove straight into the yard where the trouble was, stepped out of their car and took the megaphone in turn.

Vico spoke first. Denouncing the anarchist, adventurist tendencies which had led to this violence, he called on the communists to take no part in it. They should remain at work, he said, and await his considered advice. There was nothing in the present situation, or in the merger proposed with BMG, to justify action outside the law.

His speech was met with cries of *"Traditore!"* But these were only stray shouts from the burning staff block. There was more smoke now, pouring from several windows, and the noise of men crowding down a staircase. Vico continued to call for calm, repeating himself. The *carabinieri* stood waiting at the doors.

Guidotti then took the megaphone and made a direct appeal to the workers as a whole. The merger was for their good, he said. There would be changes, but Mobital would emerge stronger. The unions had already been consulted on the terms of the deal to be done, and they had approved it. His speech came in long flowing sentences, to which the men listened as if to opera, the words less important than the music.

There were now figures looming through the smoke in the doorways. There seemed to be shoving as well as shouting. A man appeared at a first floor window, made to jump, thought better of it, disappeared. Then Guidotti ceased to speak in operatic generalities. Shouting urgently for attention, he told the men in the building not to be fools. If they came out now, they would be taken for questioning, but only those responsible for blowing up the headquarters block would be prosecuted. The company would take no further punitive action. Those who returned to work would keep their jobs, whatever part they had played in the general disturbance.

Guidotti repeated this assurance once more, very clearly and loudly, in words of few syllables, then lowered the megaphone and waited. In the brief pause that followed a few of the loyalists found nerve to applaud him. There was a single shout of "*Bravo!*"

And it was indeed pure art; the touch of a modern industrial *maestro*. Drawn by the offer of clemency, driven by the fire behind, the rebels came out and surrendered one by one. The *carabinieri* moved in to take them, without undue force. There was no scuffle of resistance as the trucks drawn up outside the gate were quickly filled with prisoners. One or two men gave a clenched-fist salute before they disappeared.

And that was all. The fire was taking hold now, but nobody moved to put it out. The *carabinieri* drove off. The yard soon emptied. Guidotti stayed long enough to shake hands with Vico in front of the television cameras, then drove straight off to the airport.

The cameras panned away to the shattered glass head-quarters, collapsed across the road, then lifted their lenses to the smoke-smeared sunrise. As they did so a first low rumble of restarted machinery came from inside the works.

At Ash Valley the style was different. There was no blood, and certainly no sun. But the mood in BMG was in many ways more dangerous. Resentment was still running high from the picket incident, for which some blame still attached to John Clabon. Every factory in the group had been shut down since Thursday, and was shut down still. Yesterday, Monday, the men crushed to death by the truck from Holland had been buried with full proletarian honour. A mass funeral march had wound through the streets of Coventry, arousing emotion still further.

And now to righteous anger were added suspicion and fear. The news of the merger with Mobital had not aroused much enthusiasm. Some were opposed to it. Most were holding back judgement until they heard more, uncertain whether to believe the reports in the press. Suspicion and fear were the dominant emotions. Confusion was universal.

And one truth was hardly denied in canteen or pub, when-ever the men of BMG were gathered. No good thing had ever come to them from mainland Europe. The cold wind of free competition, blowing mainly from Germany and France, had carried many men to the dole and shrivelled the confidence of those who survived. John Clabon, it was true, had a knack of reviving that confidence, for which he was respected, if not much liked. He had his following. His plans would be listened to. But clear in the minds of many thousand men was another plan, preached for many years in their midst by the activists of the Left. Stephen Murdoch, though his politics were not much liked, had been widely admired for his platform eloquence and the keen negotiating intelligence which had won hard cash from the bosses. Now Murdoch was discredited, and some blame attached to his Trotskyist followers. But that did not alter the force of Murdoch's plan, which still had its following in many less political heads. Let's take over the plant for ourselves, many said, demand production on our own terms and screw more cash from the government. We're big enough. We can do it. They won't dare refuse. And let's have quotas against the Krauts and Frogs, not to mention the bleeding Nips. Sod Europe. Buy British, that's the answer. No, said others, that's crazy, stick with the gaffer, let him take us in with Mobital. The Eyeties make effing good cars. Okay, so they'll scrap the Pilot for the Sparta. But it's the best hope we've got, mate, I tell you . . .

So ran innumerable anxious arguments in the great tide of men advancing from all over Coventry in response to a broadcast summons on TV and radio. The time was now 6.10 in Europe. Here it was 5.10, an hour behind. The light was grey. A drizzle was falling. Some of the men came by car, some on motorbikes, many on cycles. Some walked, alone or in groups. Not everybody talked. Some trudged along with their heads down, saying nothing, too bored or sleepy, perhaps too worried to communicate. Some stopped to buy newspapers or gulp washy coffee and thick sausage rolls in the cheap cafés close to the works. There was nothing in sight to please the eye or raise the spirit. The drab brick streets were littered with cans and plastic bottles. Here in industrial Coventry at dawn was the raw stuff discussed at the château of La Maréchale and inside the Ritz Hotel, Paris. It was not so much a hard life as dull. One did it for the money. Why else. Rosa Berg wished to bring it more dignity, involvement; but that too was hard to see in Coventry at daybreak. There were cars to be made, there was money to be drawn. That was all.

This morning, though, there was more. At the gates of Ash Valley itself stood Murdoch's men, still saying sorry for Murdoch as they passed out their leaflets. Sorry about what's

728

happened, they said, but don't let that put you off, brother. Now's the moment.

The leaflet called for general occupation of the works and set out a list of demands. Some of the men passing by refused to take it. Some took it only to screw it up and fling it on the asphalt. But most of them took it and read it.

Also waiting at the gates were many reporters and several TV crews, sampling the views of the workers as they passed. And this gave pleasure to the men of BMG: to those who shook their heads, refusing comment, as much as to those who said their piece to camera. The feeling that he might be important comes sweet to a mass-production worker.

Already inside the factory were maintenance men and some of the night-shift: those who had bothered to turn up the evening before. They were supposed to have the plant rolling already, but it was still silent. The assembly lines, ready to go, would move into action or they would not, depending on the outcome of the present mass meeting. And for it the whole workforce of BMG, night and day, was presently assembled, gathered in crowds around the speakers scattered through the factory. One of John Clabon's innovations had been to wire up all thirty plants of the British Motor Group to a single linked public-address system. It had been used once or twice before, but not for a drama such as this. Excitement spread through the waiting men – plain excitement of congregated numbers, more jocular than defiant; like a football crowd before the match. The English are generally cheerful in the mass.

Had somebody worked that out beforehand? None of the men stopped to wonder, though the Trotskyists started to worry.

They worried even more when the press were let into the works. This was a very unusual step. Who had authorised it? Nobody knew. Few cared. The Trots protested, but the others roared them down. It pleased the men of BMG to have their decision recorded on TV. The influence this might exert was a point too subtle to be heard in the hubbub.

At 5.30 speeches began.

All parties were given a turn at the microphone, even the Trotskyists. And here the skill of an organising hand became more apparent, though no one was sure, then or later, whose hand it was.

729

Until the last moment the BMG Committee of Workers' Control, which included more groups than the Trotskyists, was told it could not speak at all, on the grounds that the action it proposed, occupation of the factory, was unlawful. The committee protested that not all their members supported occupation. This argument went on hotly behind the scenes right up to the start of proceedings. And then, at the very last moment, the committee were told they could speak after all. They could speak first, and for five minutes only, and their spokesman must come from the Industrial Workers' Alliance, since that was their largest constituent group.

So the first voice to come from the public-address system was that of an unprepared orator quickly thrown in by the IWA, the hardest-line Trotskyist group, already discredited by Stephen Murdoch. He was greeted by jeers and boos. He spent the first two minutes of his five disclaiming all connection with the Iskra, which left him only three to explain why this act of terrorism in France was an irrelevance, brothers, and did not affect the main issue. The main issue was that the merger was a capitalist plot. It was in fact a European takeover, which would mean the end of BMG. The present production models would be scrapped. The group would be left knocking up Italian cars under licence, thousands of jobs would be lost. That was why it was necessary now, this morning, to occupy the factories and keep production halted until . . .

Until what, nobody heard. The IWA's time was up. Their spokesman was removed from the microphone, his voice rising into a last inarticulate shout, which drew guffaws of derision.

After that it was over. The Trotskyists knew it, if nobody else. They started to drift away. Some of them walked from Ash Valley that moment and were never seen on the premises again. Others stayed to carry on the fight, heads hung in bitter disappointment.

History, in which these men believed, should have made them a bow at that moment. For the Marxist there is no place on earth so hopeless as England, where ideas of social revolution are met not with hatred but laughter.

The last three statements to issue from the speakers came from the Hilton Hotel in Rome. Two were recorded on tape. The last was broadcast live from a telephone.

First came a senior spokesman for the fourteen trade-union

leaders flown out to Italy for consultation. They were recommending the merger, he said, by a vote of ten to four. They had talked to John Clabon all night, and though they had failed to get a guarantee against redundancies, they were convinced that the link-up with Mobital was in the best interests of their members. Even the four dissenting unions favoured a merger in principle, if not yet satisfied with the terms.

"We are therefore recommending, by unanimous vote, that normal working be resumed. No further action should be taken at this time. That is all. Thank you."

A good-humoured groan went through the crowd at the mention of return to work.

Second last came a recorded announcement by Michael Oppenheim, Director of Finance and Planning, who declared unanimous support for the merger in the groups's board of management.

This was greeted in indifferent silence.

Last of all came John Clabon, speaking live by telephone from Rome. His remarks were short and blunt. His normal cigar-roasted voice, distorted by the long-distance line, amplified by the speakers in the roof, slammed through the cavernous tin works like a steam-hammer.

"Good morning. Sorry to have hauled you in so early, but this thing has to be settled on the spot. And it had to be cooked up in private. That's the way these deals are done, or not at all. I can guess what your worries are, but take it from me, I'm here in Rome trying to save your jobs. Some will have to go in any case – I'll tell you that now. But if I don't succeed, then all your jobs are at risk. We need this merger. We can't live without it. I've been in this business a very long time, and I know what I'm doing. I shall get the best deal I can, for us all, and it has to be done tomorrow. There's no time for argument or hesitation. I ask for your full support. And if you've got any sense, you'll trust me."

In plants spread from Scotland to Bristol a hundred thousand workers listened to this without a murmur. At Ash Valley, Coventry, the silence was solemn as a church. Clabon made no mention of the plan to occupy, as though it were simply too stupid to discuss. His last remarks referred to the kidnap of Sir Patrick Harvey.

"I can guess what most of you think about that. I expect your

731

feelings are similar to mine. But let's put this to the test. Will those of you who think we should give in to this French-woman's demands now please raise your hands."

The television cameras panned across the sea of workers' heads.

"All right," said Clabon. "Now will those of you willing to let me negotiate this merger, on the best terms I can and without further reference, please do the same. Hands up."

No count was necessary. A short pause followed while each plant reported in.

"Thank you," said Clabon. "That's a very clear majority. Now I'm going to work, and you do the same. Let's get some cars made."

And that was all.

The night shift went home, the day shift remained. The noise of restarted machinery, ready to go but not yet moving, grew from a hum to a rumble. In the glass-walled control room alongside the automated body shop of the BMG Pilot 1500, Assembly Building 14, the red lights went off one by one as the computer men pressed the buttons on their console. The first things to move were the robots, making a car that was already doomed.

Soon after seven o'clock, Italian time, John Clabon and Carlo Guidotti were sitting at breakfast together on the balcony of Clabon's suite at the Hilton Hotel in Rome. Below them the domes of the city's many churches showed above a thin morning haze: St. Peter and his pups. Across the river a bell tolled for mass. Doublett had not been asked to join them. Both by now had a certain respect for Doublett, but were more at their ease without him. Doublett, besides, had no more to do. The merger was ready as it could be. Boards, unions, even employees had been won over to the project. Only the twelve heads of government remained to persuade, the leaders of Europe's Community already assembling here for their summit.

Meanwhile there was the matter of Harvey's life, of which fifty minutes remained, if Rosa Berg meant what she said. Both Guidotti and Clabon assumed that she did. They did not discuss it. Both were too tired to waste any speech on speculation. They sipped black coffee and picked at the Hilton's limp toast, seated either side of a white iron table in the early sunshine. Each went to the bathroom in turn to clean up. They were waiting to be called to a studio in the hotel's basement, where the cameras of French television were waiting. Daladier of the French police had telephoned to ask for a last joint statement, in which it should be pointed out to the Iskra that further bloodshed was useless, since the merger had now been accepted by the workers of both national companies. But the tone should be moderate, the Commissaire advised. Some concession should be made to the woman's pride if possible. Any small thing could tip the balance.

Guidotti and Clabon had done their tired best. Each now had in his pocket a carefully drafted, handwritten text. Clabon would deliver it in English, Guidotti in French. But neither believed it would make any difference. And both thought the job should have been done by Riemeck, who was still delayed in the air. They knew by this time that he had gone to Sweden, and they knew why. The reason was a good one. They approved. Even so, they felt, Riemeck had not organised his time with much skill. At this hour, of all hours, he should have contrived to be here. They muttered about it resentfully as they sat on the high sunlit balcony, waiting to be called downstairs to the studio. Then Clabon was struck by an afterthought.

"Did I tell you he left a message in Paris?"

"No," said Guidotti. "What was that?"

"I was phoned last night by one of his young men. Otto, it seems, has got the idea that once it's through the summit we ought to put the merger to a ballot, yea or nay. He wants a referendum, one man one vote, total workforce both companies. What do you think of that?"

Guidotti rolled his eyes and shook his head. "God forbid it."

"That's what I said. Well, we shall have to talk him out of it. Maybe Arnold will – ah, here we go."

Laura Jenkinson had appeared in the suite off which the balcony opened. With her was Nielsen, the wispy Dane. They said the studio was ready. Both businessmen rose and went inside, automatically straightening their clothes for camera. Behind them across the city, with different voices, deep, shrill, old, new, the bells began to strike 7.30.

Half an hour was left to save Harvey.

5

Since first light of day the town of Le Bugue, in south-western France, had been coming slowly to life.

First there was only the river. Its brown waters, swollen with rain, flowed fast and silent through the town, hidden by a thick early mist. Swifts swooped and dived below the arches of the bridge with small bat-like squeaks. Along the bank silver-leafed poplars quivered in a breeze so slight it could hardly be felt. Then two boys with rods came to fish in the river very early. Their voices carried in the misty stillness.

The mist began to lift after sunrise, but no one was yet on the move. The Tricolour hung limp from its pole above the *Mairie*. The streets were washed clean by the rain. Around the war memorial – *Le Bugue à ses glorieux morts* – the flowers were still wet and battered from the storm. The night had not been a quiet one. First there had been the storm, and then in the early hours of darkness a great amount of traffic had passed through the town. Cars, vans, police buses, motorcycles, trucks one after another – a regular military convoy had come through from Bergerac and Périgueux. All of it had gone up the road to the village of Campagne. None had come back. Later there had been some fast driving in the night, to and fro, but that was not unusual. Now things were quiet. Only the voices of the two boys fishing could be heard.

But as soon as the sun lifted over the poplars, the town filled up like a stage under lights. The priest emerged to say early mass. A gang of men started to fix up the stalls in the market place. Shutters were opened and awnings extended. People shook hands and lit their first cigarette, discussed the storm, discussed the heavy traffic in the night. On the road to Campagne, someone said, where it crossed the river at the eastern bridge, the *flics* had now put up a total roadblock. Nothing was being let through either way.

Then somebody mentioned that his phone was out of order. Two other people said the same. Soon everybody found that their phone was out of order. Not one telephone was working in Le Bugue.

This was discussed in Oscar's Bar, which quickly filled with old men in berets flinging back small potent drinks to start the day. Storm damage, that was the general explanation. But no one was perfectly happy with it. Someone went looking for the gendarme, to see what he said. The gendarme was out. His wife said he'd been out all night, but where or why she refused to add.

From that point the morning acquired an air of mystery, of very great pleasure to all. Something was up, it was realised; and very likely something to do with the kidnap of the Englishman, Harvey. Yesterday there had been roadblocks all over, and the gendarme had been checking houses in the district. He had asked Marie-Louise at the Post Office whether there was anyone staying at La Guillarmie.

The sense of drama increased, but business continued as usual. In the Place du Marché, among the trimmed acacias, the stalls were erected and occupied. In a short time the square went from empty to crowded. From the villages and hamlets around Le Bugue came a throng of smallholders bringing their produce to market, just as they did every Tuesday. No, that was not quite true. There were gaps in the market this morning. The stalls booked by people living on the far side of the River Vézère, in an easterly direction, stayed empty. Nobody, not even customers, came from Campagne or Péchalifour. The road was sealed tight by the police on the bridge.

But everything else was normal. By 7.15 the square was full of people. The sellers had arrived, and now came the first of the buyers, taking their pick. Small vans were parked in every gap between the trees. A little out of order in the absence of the gendarme, hooting traffic jammed the streets. Empty boxes and discarded packaging spread across the pavement. And spread on the stalls in a colourful, sunlit display were the good things of the district. There were piles of golden peaches and crimson nectarines, green apples, yellow pears, punnets of strawberries, huge red tomatoes and shiny purple aubergines, crisp lettuce, spiky onions, long carrots, bagged potatoes. The cheeses were sliced in cross-section, their centres oozing white. From the river came perch, carp, crayfish and bream. There were trout in a tank. There were chickens and rabbits running live in wooden cages. Skinned hares hung with their eyes wide in death.

At the edge of the square the products grew more frivolous. Hippies were selling leather belts and silver jewellery. There was basketwork and pottery, even a painter. On the steps leading up to the *Mairie* were women selling flowers.

And to this position, as was her custom, came the gendarme's wife at 7.30. She placed herself on a leather cushion with a flat open basket at her side, full of the big white shells so skilfully collected by her husband.

Immediately somebody chaffed her about her price, which had risen since the week before.

"Yes," she said, smiling mysteriously, "they cost more to-day. You will see, these snails are historic."

Le Bugue's chief of gendarmes, an ex-army sergeant in his fifties, was a veteran of Indochina. He had known Daladier as a serving soldier, and had asked to speak to the Commissaire in person when he telephoned. The call had come through to the command van in Périgueux soon after dark had fallen, and with it black despair. The Dutchman had escaped, all hope was lost, when Daladier heard the voice of this long-forgotten comrade in arms, who greeted him formally, with solemn respect, and then announced his news in three short words.

"*Ils sont trouvés.*"

Daladier said he'd get a medal for it.

Kemble had met the old fellow in the night and sketched a word-profile for the readers of *The Times*, who would learn of his existence in a boxed side-feature complete with photograph.

The gendarme got no sleep for his pains. All night he was kept close at hand to advise on local terrain. He had helped to lead the snipers into position. And at daybreak he led the command party over the back of the hill for a downward view of the house from the rear. Kemble was taken along.

Everything was done with the utmost caution. From the command post, tucked out of sight behind the cone-roofed château of Campagne, they were taken along the road in an old covered lorry smelling strongly of dung. Two officials from Paris, Daladier, Biffaud, the gendarme, a general in camouflage uniform, another in black who led the GIGN, two other parties not identified and Kemble himself all stood inside the vehicle in silence, holding on to the ribs of its canopy, as they passed the point at which the lorry could be seen by the Iskra's lower sentry. The one watching the road was Stephen Murdoch, according to the snipers. After another mile or so of level tarmac they had climbed a steep hill, the truck grinding and lurching upward, until they arrived at Péchalifour. This village lay behind the house and out of its sight. Even so, no chances were taken. All the people of the village were confined to their homes. All the dogs and geese had been shut up. All police or troops were kept tightly under cover.

In Péchalifour there was no outward sign of the huge siege mounted overnight. But Kemble now began to get some idea of its shape.

Under cover of darkness three separate cordons had been placed around the hideout. The outer one consisted of regular troops, whose task was to keep the area cleared of unwary civilians. The second cordon, further in, was sterner stuff; mixed police and military, heavily armed, standing by at all points through which the kidnappers might try to make an outward dash. The inmost one was purely men in black of the GIGN, France's crack hit squad.

The GIGN were split into three assault groups, two as close as they could get to the house on the ground, the third standing by in a helicopter some miles away. Also in position were a number of snipers, who already had the Iskra's three male sentries in their telescopic sights, though the Dutchman was awkward to watch. He kept moving about.

Some of this Kemble knew already. The rest he picked up in a barn at Péchalifour, where a conference with maps was held on arrival. Then followed a cautious advance on the house. In single file, with himself in the rear, the command party followed the gendarme out of the barn and through a field of maize, heads bent below the tall crop, which rustled like old brown paper as they passed through it. They stopped behind some empty cob-racks, then scampered across an open patch into trees. Behind them a cockerel started to crow in the village, then stopped with a screech, as if strangled.

The woods were dripping wet from the storm. The trees were mixed deciduous and conifer, many long fallen and rotten, others blown over in the night. Vines trailed between them. Most were choked in ivy. On the barks of others grew exotic fungus and lichen like disease. They were very untended woods, and very quiet. The Frog police had locked up the birds, Kemble thought to himself, close to laughter as he brought up the rear of the column. He was creeping along the mossy path behind one of the men from Paris, whose suit was getting satisfactorily mucky. It was still very early. But the sun was up now, striking prettily into the clearings on patches of gorse, ferns and lavender.

The Iskra had chosen their hideout well. It was devilish difficult to approach unobserved, and the Dutchman's defences had made the problem harder. It was known that he had a receiver in the house, so no use of radio was possible. As well as mines and flares, laid with trip-wires, he had sonar sensors and an anti-intrusion device which worked by ray. He had scattered these sophisticated gadgets in the woods and disposed his sentries with such professional skill that the GIGN could not get close enough to rush. Once in the night they had set off a flare, which gave everyone the jumps. Daladier had pulled them back again. All night Kemble had been witness to a heated tussle between the GIGN and BRVP. The boys in black kept wanting to charge; Daladier kept on pulling them back. The prime objective, he kept reminding them, was not to kill the gang but rescue the hostage. That was not so easy. The girl, Rosa Berg, stayed inside the house with Harvey. There had never come a moment in the night at which it was possible to knock out all four of the Iskra at once, before any one of them could get back inside to the prisoner. Twice, when Rosa came out, it had nearly happened. But Daladier refused to give the order. He was waiting for a better chance in daylight.

Now daylight had come, and time was short. A decision would have to be taken after this reconnaissance.

Eventually the gendarme raised his hand. The column stopped and spread sideways in silence. They had reached the observation point. Puffed and perspiring from the climb,

Kemble hauled himself up beside the Commissaire's fat form, which was now spread prone on a rock.

The rock was at the crest of the hill which lay between the house and Péchalifour. It was called Le Roc du Sang, because of a massacre during the Hundred Years War. Who had been massacred, English or French, Kemble had not yet learned. But such marginal copy could wait. He was now looking down the hill's far slope with eager interest.

Below the rock were a few last trees, thinning to seedlings, then the ground lay open all the way to the house in an overgrown meadow of hay and wild flowers, about three hundred yards in length. Below the house and on either side of it was more woodland. Kemble could not see him, but was told that Mario Salandra, the Italian, was watching the meadow from a derelict water-cistern slightly above and behind the house, outside the back door. Only the cistern itself was visible, a square tank of half-crumbled concrete, overgrown with brambles.

The house had once been a farm, called La Guillarmie. Now it belonged to an English magazine, who ran it as a staff recreation centre, but had most unwarily let it to the Iskra to cover some libel expenses. It was built of timbered brick with a double-angled roof, half orange pantile, half a darker shade. Up its walls grew thick creeper, already turning pink. Its maroon wooden shutters were closed. Close beside it to the right was a barn, against which a vine grew, bright green leaves on a half-collapsed trellis.

The Dutchman was inside the hazel plantation to the left. No moving thing was in sight except butterflies, already bobbing like scraps of coloured paper over meadow and garden. Then a magpie flew across the field from right to left. No mate followed. Kemble ignored the ill omen. He was thinking how lovely the view was, backed in the distance by more wooded hills. The uplands were bathed in early sunshine, but down in the valley, where the road was, a blanket of mist still lingered, which gave the scene an over-the-clouds look, birth of the world, half-way to paradise.

Hysterical copy tumbled into his head. His joy at simply being here, in at the kill with no competition, kept threatening to break into open laughter. He had the story now and nothing could stop it. His gratitude to Commissaire Daladier was deep, and edged with half-fearful, half-hopeful curiosity. What was the man going to do?

Nobody yet knew that. The Commissaire had kept his intentions to himself all night, except to rule out the use of the talk-down squad. To that squad's bitter objection he had held them back at operational headquarters in Campagne, confined to the grounds of the château whose conical tips were now peeping up through the mist in the valley. He had flatly refused their suggestions of an open approach to the house with searchlights and megaphones. No, he said, that wouldn't work with Rosa Berg. Salandra and Murdoch it might intimidate. But Rosa would be talked up, not down. And there was no way to talk to Janssen.

So Daladier had ruled out the soft approach and the hard. If he had another plan, he had not divulged it; and now he was not saying anything. For a long time he scanned every inch of the scene through binoculars, his huge bulk spread on the Roc du Sang. Then he lowered them and wiped his moustache. His cheeks were dark with bristle. Sweat dripped from his chin.

After more silence he muttered a few words to the military men on his left; then turned to Kemble, who was lying on his right.

"So, my friend, let us hear a little sideways thought from you. What shall we do here?"

Kemble replied as addressed, in a voice just over a whisper. "There is that idea we discussed in Paris."

"There is."

"I still think it's best," Kemble said. "At least I haven't thought of a better one."

"So you wish to be a hero."

"No, I want the story. And this lady is rational, whatever else. She'll see it's the best she can do."

"She is rational, but not always calm. That is the danger."

"Right. So we have to be cool," Kemble said. "Straight in there, straight talk. Take her by surprise before she blows up."

Daladier nodded, seeming too tired to speak. "Surprise, yes. With that I agree." Again he raised the binoculars and scanned the scene slowly from side to side. He lowered them; paused; thought some more. Then he handed them rightward with a swift decisive motion. "Very well. Take a look. It is time that we say hello to these people."

"You mean . . . we're going in?"

"We are."

Delight and terror struck Kemble together. His heart jumped into his throat. "So you'll come too," he said, raising the glasses. "Well, I'm glad of that."

"Of course. I am responsible."

"What shall I look at?"

"Examine the ground to the right, between the house and the barn. That is where we shall arrive," Daladier said, pointing. "There will be one other in the car. And Biffaud will cover us there – from the trees behind."

The binoculars bumped and jiggled against Kemble's eyes. He could not hold them still.

"In a moment I will show you the other positions," Daladier murmured, dropping his voice still lower. "But now I must explain to the general. He will not be delighted."

This occurred at 6.15.

At 7.15 a car came looking for Lady Harvey in Les Eyzies, the other nearby town along the river, overlooked by its statue of primitive man, who peered from his niche below the cliffs with a look of pained bewilderment. Since all the hotels were full, the official party from Paris had been put up in a local research centre, proclaimed by the sign above its gates as *L'Institut pour L'Étude de l'Évolution d'Êtres Organisés*. But Lady Harvey had been found a room at the Hotel Crô-Magnon, where she had stayed once before. The management had put her to bed with her clothes on in their private quarters.

At 6.45 they were told by telephone to prepare her for instant departure. But Lady Harvey was not in her room. By the time a police car came to collect her, the town was being frantically searched by the hotel's staff. At 7.15 they found her, alone in the church by the railway station. She was not on her knees or lighting candles, but sitting stiffly upright in a protestant attitude, thinking of no one knew what. As they led her to the car she seemed bewildered.

The car sped away down the street, then stopped to pick up the British Ambassador, Sir Godfrey Smethurst, from the Institute for the Study of the Evolution of Organised Beings. He was the last person left there. The rest had been called away earlier to join the reconnaissance.

741

Sir Godfrey had therefore had no information to give Lady Harvey. He was unable to tell her what had happened.

At this she woke into open annoyance.

"Really," she snapped, "you might just as well have stayed in Paris."

Sir Godfrey stammered some reply, but Margaret Harvey did not listen. She sat in silence, staring rigidly ahead as the car travelled quickly along the winding bank of the River Vézère. A few minutes after 7.30 it reached the village of Campagne and turned straight into the grounds of the château, where the French police had set up headquarters. Spread over the drive and the lawns was the great assembly of vehicles and equipment that had come from Bergerac and Périgueux. The number of men was now reduced, but gathered around the command van were the dozen or so most senior, engaged in last-minute conference with Commissaire Daladier.

Jack Kemble, standing apart, watched Lady Harvey step out of the car and join the brass hats. Her white hair was more awry, her face set more stoic still, but otherwise she looked much the same as when he had seen her first in Brussels, before there was anything to worry about. The poor old girl had lived so long in the shadow of crisis, he thought, that one more hardly made a difference. She listened without much expression as Daladier told her the plan. Kemble saw her nod in consent. Then, to his surprise, she walked across to him.

"Mr. Kemble, are you sure you want to do this?"

"No," he said, smiling when she did. "But I'm going to – for reasons you'd better not ask me."

"You want to be there, you mean, to see what happens. Yes, that's natural. You are a newspaper man."

"No, it's not natural," Kemble said. "It's disgusting. But there is this idea, you see, that if the woman, Rosa Berg, is given the chance to make a public statement, she might back down."

"Yes, I've been told."

"She's off the phone. Can't do it any other way."

"So they're taking you in. Do you think it will work?"

"No, I don't think so. But it might distract her, just for a moment. She certainly won't be expecting it."

Lady Harvey nodded, her eyes turning absent. She frowned and glanced around, as though trying to remember where she was. "Well, come back in one piece. And bring him back with you, if you can. I shall wait here. That's what they've told me to do."

She wandered away. The Ambassador took her arm and led her off into the château. The door closed behind them with a boom of heavy oak.

The time was 7.45.

With fifteen minutes to go, Kemble stood waiting on the drive. He had started to feel rather ill in the stomach. To steady himself he kept noting detail. On the lawn now, among the hardware, was a cardiac unit from Bordeaux. And parked beside the command van was another big windowless trailer with aerials on the roof. It belonged to RTF, the French broadcasting service. From inside came continuous radio chatter and the flicker of many small monitor screens. No word had gone out on any channel to alert the gang to the fact they had been discovered. On that there would be silence to the end. But about to begin any moment was a special simultaneous all-channel broadcast, advanced from the normal news time of eight o'clock. Rosa was going to hear live statements from union leaders in Coventry and Milan, reporting the failure of both factory revolts. That would be followed by a joint appeal from Clabon and Guidotti in Rome. Riemeck had taped a statement before leaving Paris. Last would come the President of France, promising fair trial if Harvey was released.

Kemble's faith in this massive assault of the airwaves was nil. Come on, he thought, let's get in there, before she gets excited. Before I throw up.

His nerve was not improved by the sight of Inspector Jacques Biffaud doing practice jumps from the back of a small blue van. The van, an old Renault model belonging to the postal service, was being driven in circles on the drive. Three times the crewcut Inspector tumbled out through its back door, rolled on the gravel and came up at a crouch, pistol drawn. Kemble stood watching, unimpressed. But then he himself was called over and shown what to do. Seated in the back of the van, he had to reach out while it was moving and shut the door after Biffaud had tumbled. They practised it once. After that Kemble was introduced to various weapons secreted in the vehicle.

"No good to me," he said. "If there's any of that, I'm going to run."

This was done by 7.50.

Then Daladier came over and tried the driver's seat.

At the same time another vehicle entered the grounds of the château and pulled up. It was the prison van Kemble had seen at the airstrip in Périgueux. He had forgotten all about it. The doors were opened. The prisoner stepped out, handcuffed to a guard.

Astonished, Kemble turned to Daladier, who was still in the driver's seat of the van. "Is he coming too?"

The Commissaire nodded, also watching the prisoner. "He will sit beside me, and you in the back. That is how we shall go."

"But what's he going to do?"

"Endeavour to persuade Rosa Berg. He will try first, and then you. I myself will make the introductions."

Daladier hauled himself out of the Post Office van, which rose on its springs, relieved of his weight. As the prisoner was led towards it, he muttered a further aside to Kemble.

"I told him the Dutchman had murdered Jews, you see. And that was enough. So, let us go. Take your place."

Biffaud was already in the back of the van. But Kemble stood rooted to the spot a moment longer, unable to speak for surprise as Erich Kohlman stood on the gravel, his wrists held out for the cuffs to be removed. He was perfectly clean and smart, still wearing the suit he had worn at arrest, though his tie had been removed. The Commissaire said a few words to him. Kohlman nodded, then walked to his place in the passenger seat.

6

Sir Patrick Harvey, still alone in his cell, was aware of the passage of time. It ticked through his being. But he no longer bothered to look at his watch. He had worked up a state of intense concentration in which he was noting each detail of his last few minutes on earth – the insects and the sunlight, the crickets and the birds, the traffic in the valley, the voices on the radio. Though dry in the mouth and reluctant to go, he was no longer fearful or depressed. The whole of his consciousness had bunched itself into a tight crouch of anticipation. It was not the sensation of a bullet he dwelt on; nor was he wondering what might come after. He was merely suspended on the edge of existence, waiting and watching to see what happened next.

And in this state of extreme alertness he suddenly became aware of something.

The traffic had stopped on the road.

Many minutes had passed since any sound at all had come from the valley. He wondered if the others had noticed. Surely, he thought, the Dutchman must soon start to wonder about it.

But perhaps it was Joop who had now come into the house. One of the men had. Rosa was talking to someone as she listened to the radio.

And then, on the radio, Harvey caught the voice of John Clabon.

"This merger is not being done for the personal profit of Mr. Guidotti or myself. Nor is it merely to please our shareholders. It is done in the interest of all employees, in both companies. The men in our factories have shown that they understand this. We therefore ask that this verdict be accepted by those who are holding Sir Patrick Harvey. We appeal to them to release him."

Clabon's voice, as he read out these careful remarks, was halting and awkward. And Harvey, listening, found room in his death-prepared mind for amusement. Poor old John, he was no good at all with a diplomatic text. He sounded exactly like the local non-worshipping magnate whom the vicar occasionally persuades to read a lesson in church.

Now other voices were speaking in French. Harvey recognised Riemeck, then the President of France, who was stopped in midflow. The radio had been switched off.

Rosa said something to the man who was with her. But if it was Joop, he made no reply. The same silence fell as before. Only the crickets and the birds dared to speak. The rest of the world stood still. Then came two other simultaneous sounds, one close and one far away. Footsteps approached the door of the cell, and approaching down the valley was the motor of a single small vehicle. Though magnified by the echo of the hills, it did not seem to Harvey the drumbeat of rescue. Calmly he stood up and buttoned his jacket; smoothed his hair; straightened his tie.

The lock turned. The door opened.

Yes, it was the plumber, empty-eyed as before, dressed in blue working denim. Slung over his shoulder by a strap was his rifle. In his hand was the pistol called a Webley, the one that made no noise.

Having opened the door, the Dutchman stood aside and motioned Harvey through it. Harvey walked out to the parlour, where Rosa stood gazing through the doors to the terrace. She did not turn her head.

Stephen Murdoch, posted down by the road, had also noticed the strange lack of traffic. But he was dull from lack of sleep, and much more worried by events in the house. He was wondering whether to go back up there, join forces with Mario and call a halt – call for a last discussion, at least. So far exhaustion and fear had held him pinned to the spot, irresolute. Scared by the act to be done, equally scared of the Dutchman, he was tempted to run down the hill and away.

But now into these greater fears rose anxiety at the peculiar desertion of the road. He was about to report it on his radio handset when he saw the van approaching from Campagne. As it drew closer he saw it was a postal delivery van, which immediately made him more nervous still. The English who owned La Guillarmie had directed all mail to London in their absence, but Rosa had been worried from the start that the postman might come to the house.

Still Murdoch did not act. Twice yesterday this van had passed by.

This time it slowed. Then it turned up the track.

He jumped to his feet in alarm.

Even now there were two other houses the van could be going to, up the track's leftward fork. But Murdoch, aware that his warning would come too late, immediately scrambled into terrified action. Leaving his rifle on the ground, he half-rose from hiding to see which way the van would turn at the fork, and at the same time raised the handset to his mouth.

"*Attention!*" is what Stephen Murdoch would have said – one of the few French words that he knew. But before the first syllable came out he was struck a mighty blow from behind which sent him tumbling head over heels down the slope beneath the trees. The shot came from a silenced weapon, fired at a distance of thirty yards. It did not kill him. But before Murdoch's mouth could utter a squeak of pain or terror he was smothered by black-clad commandos. They leapt from the bracken all round him, then one stood to wave the van up the hill. The driver of the van waved back in acknowledgement. He turned right at the fork and changed into bottom gear, then started to climb the muddy hairpins to the house.

Daladier, driving, growled and swore as the van's wheels spun in the mud, but he kept it going up, round one bend, then another. The engine note rose with the effort. The vehicle lurched and bounced across the ruts, its upward angle steepening with the gradient.

Erich Kohlman neither moved nor spóke. He sat like a dummy in the passenger seat.

Kemble hung on to a strut at the back, to stop himself sliding across the van's floor.

Biffaud, holding something on his own side, was now on his feet in a crouch, ready to jump. He was dressed in woolly black, like the GIGN. Held in his right hand was a rifle like theirs, a Ruger 14. Strapped about his person were several magazines and his pistol, a Colt .45.

Daladier shouted.

Biffaud jumped.

He went out backwards, feet first. The door of the van, lightly held by a tape, burst open as his rubber-soled boots kicked it back. He landed on the track already running, slipped, scrambled up again and dashed up left into the trees.

Kemble, hanging on with one hand, leaning out with the other, reached for the door and pulled it shut.

The van went on up.

For a few seconds after Harvey reached the parlour, coming from his cell with the Dutchman behind, nothing happened. Rosa stood at the glazed doors leading to the terrace, now criss-crossed with brown sticky tape. She was staring through a gap in the strips at the view across the valley, the trees close by hung with trailing tree-moss, the sunlit hills in the distance.

Half-way across the room the Dutchman paused. He seemed to be waiting for a final instruction. Rosa gave none. She neither moved nor spoke, though Harvey could see she was trembling. Her whole body shook from head to foot. But she said nothing. So the Dutchman proceeded. Coming up alongside, he laid a hand on Harvey's elbow and guided him out towards the back door.

Then two things happened at once.

The vehicle had turned up the track from the road. Harvey, who had never ceased listening, had noticed this already. And now Joop Janssen noticed it too. Immediately he jumped to the smaller of the radio sets on the sideboard, snatched up the microphone and called up Murdoch. There was no answer. Rosa, eyes widening, turned inward, and at that same instant Mario Salandra burst in from outside. He came through the back door beside the kitchen. In his hands was a Russian Kalashnikov, a weapon that even Harvey recognised. He held it levelled at the other two. The short barrel shook in his hands. Yellow-faced with fright below his three-day beard, the Italian began to shout in French.

"This must stop, Rosa. We are not assassins. Release him, or I warn you . . ."

That was as far as Mario got. His voice trailed away as he realised the crisis had been overtaken by another.

Joop, ignoring him, dashed from the main room to the

kitchen. On the way he put down the Webley pistol. Leaving it behind on the table, he unslung his rifle, scooped up a belt of ammunition and stuffed some grenades in his pockets. As he moved he was shouting instructions to the other two. They, like Harvey, stood rooted to the spot.

The vehicle drew rapidly closer. They heard it mount the track, turn by turn, engine toiling with the effort. Joop now was out of sight in the kitchen, dismantling his booby-trap on the shutters. Something fell to the floor. The shutters were thrown open with a screech of old hinges. The window he had gone to commanded the ground on that side of the house, where the track came up from the road. Harvey knew this, although he had only seen the area once, at the time of his first arrival.

At more shouted orders from the Dutchman, Rosa and Mario jumped into action, snatching up bits of equipment from the arsenal spread around the room. They seemed to go mostly for boxes of grenades and spare magazines of ammunition. Rosa left her pistol in her belt and picked up another weapon, bigger, with a strap hanging down from it. But Harvey neither caught the orders nor saw what they did. And they took no notice of him. He was left standing alone, ignored in a frantic rush of movement, surrounded by the metallic clatter and clack of firearms being readied for action.

As he waited he was conscious of his heart, as usual less calm than its owner. The silly thing stopped, did a flip, and then stumbled on with a hop, skip and jump.

After the last of the hairpins the track was less muddy, less steep. As the van climbed on to the top Daladier drove slower, but spoke at speed. His final orders were in English, delivered in a rapid flat monotone to both of his passengers. The moment that he himself stepped out, he said, Kemble and Kohlman should do the same. They should move promptly but slowly, revealing themselves when he did. Biffaud would be in the trees to the left. If there was talk, it should be calm. And the main thing was to avoid sudden motion – unless there was firing. In that case down flat and lie still.

Kemble needed no second telling. His last thought was I must be mad, plain mad, what in the hell am I doing here, I don't even like the old bastard, never did, I must be mad.

It was Harvey he was thinking of, the remote man of power

whom he, the man of words, had chased all his youth and now in middle-age was risking his neck for. In the midst of panic came a dash of old resentment. Even when riding to his rescue, Kemble felt that Harvey was calling the shots. What a pity I couldn't write movies in the sunshine, he started to think, but there was no time for regrets. For one brief second he was gripped by self-preserving panic and annoyance at his lot; the next all thought and feeling stopped. The van reached the top of the track, wheeled left and pulled up.

From now, any instant, the bullets could fly.

Daladier had picked his spot to the inch. He stopped on the first level patch that he came to, pointing the van at the house's back door, which lay about fifteen yards ahead. Immediately to the right was a dip in the level of the garden, close enough to be reached in one leap. To the left, not so close, were the trees in which Biffaud was hidden.

Kemble, pressed tight to one side in the back of the van, peered forward at the house over Erich Kohlman's shoulder.

The back door was open. No one came out, but resting on the sill of the nearest window was the barrel of a rifle. A head was just visible behind it.

"That is the Dutchman," Daladier said softly. "Don't move."

Several seconds of immobility followed. To Kemble they seemed the longest of his life.

Then Daladier slowly drew a pistol from under the dashboard, at the same time opening the door on his side.

"Okay, now we descend," he said. "Move slowly. Stand still while I talk to them."

The Commissaire waited till Kohlman was out, Kemble noticed, and then laid his pistol carefully on the driver's seat.

They stepped from the van, all three.

Daladier and Kohlman stood semi-shielded by their doors, into which armour plate had been hurriedly fixed. Kemble got out of the back, protected by the body of the vehicle.

"Stay still," a voice shouted in French from the house. It came from the head behind the rifle. "Lift up your hands."

They did so, all three.

"Step clear," the Dutchman shouted. The rifle barrel wagged right and left in command.

Daladier stepped left, towards the trees. Kohlman and Kemble edged right, towards the dip in the garden.

"Stop there," yelled Joop Janssen. "Keep your hands raised." His voice was heard talking to someone in the house, then it came loud again through the open window, though his head never shifted from the rifle. "What do you want?"

Daladier answered in French, speaking slowly and loudly, like a politician making a speech to a very simple section of the public. The house was surrounded, he told them; no escape was possible. Therefore better to hand Harvey over. Here to urge sense was their friend, Erich Kohlman. And here, to take a statement if they wished, was the press – a man they would recognise to be an English journalist.

There was further consultation in the house. It was interrupted by Daladier, who now raised his voice to a shout.

"Rosa Berg, do you hear me?"

A second head appeared in the shadowy gloom behind the Dutchman's. Rosa was standing, half-bent for cover, in the centre of the room. In her hand was a gun like Mitzi's.

"I hear," she called.

Daladier repeated his message.

She thought about it, then shouted back: "Throw away your guns. Let me see you do it."

"We're not armed," said Daladier, lowering his hands to open his jacket, then raising them wide again. "We have come to end this in peace. We have Murdoch already. He's unhurt."

The Commissaire then spoke more quickly. Kemble missed exactly what he said. The suggestion seemed to be – it was more of an order now – that Harvey should be sent out first. The rest of them should then come forward with their hands up. If they did so, they wouldn't be harmed.

In the pause that followed, when no reply came from the house, Daladier muttered at Kohlman in French. He told him to go ahead and speak. But Kohlman either could not or would not. From where the German stood came a small gasping sound, of the kind made by a man in pain. Daladier and Kemble glanced at him together. His hands were trembling in the air. His head went down, and then jerked up again, his feather-soft hair flopping forward then back. Erich Kohlman was breaking down.

Daladier's head flicked to Kemble, standing just behind. "Now you," he said in English, with a sharper note of urgency. "Go ahead, speak. Keep them talking."

Kemble tried. His voice came out in a croak. He cleared his throat and tried again.

"Rosa Berg, can you hear me?"

"I hear."

"You understand English?"

"Enough."

"Okay, use your head," Kemble shouted. "If you kill him, you won't achieve a thing. There are men on your side in those factories. But once you kill Harvey, you'll lose them. If you care about results, let him go. Then give me a statement. That's what I'm here for. That's news. We'll print it." He paused, then ended with a stronger shout. "Come on now, think. It's the best you can do."

Even as he spoke Kemble started to feel it was not going to work. Violence was already stirring in the air, like a breeze before the storm. From the woods behind he heard little sounds of movement as the French assault squads crept closer. They were still held back from the garden's perimeter by the Dutchman's snares, but the way up the track was now clear.

And then, while still saying his piece to Rosa, Kemble noticed black shapes advancing at a crouch down the meadow behind. That was a surprise. It meant the Italian must be in the house, not watching from his post in the overgrown cistern, from which there had been no movement since the van's arrival.

They were inside the house, then. All three of them.

This was new. This was unexpected. No plan had been made for it. The GIGN had a chance to move in, unobserved; and in they were coming without delay.

Kohlman must have realised the same thing. Daladier had noticed it too. From the Commissaire's direction came a hiss of breath indrawn and a click of the tongue.

Kemble knew these to be signals of dismay in the imperturbable Frenchman. But God save us all, he thought, it will take more than that to stop the boys in black.

Harvey had followed these developments by ear. He was still standing where the gang had left him, inside the main room of the house. Mario was with him, but not as a guard, or in any sort of threatening posture. Since the vehicle drove up the Italian had fallen into a trance. He stood by the door to the kitchen, rifle lowered.

Harvey himself was close to elation. He had gone without hope so long that now the first touch of it carried him away. It's going to be all right, he thought. It's all over now.

He even found a moment for amused contempt at Kemble, the sneaky press hack playing hero. What a preposterous sham the man was, he thought. And what an extraordinary idea of the French police to bring him here. Compared to the prospect of an interview with Kemble, the grave had a certain attraction.

This relief of Harvey's was premature. It was ended by Rosa running in wild-eyed from the kitchen. She had a sort of small machine-gun, but as she came towards him she looped it over her shoulder by a strap and took her Czech automatic from the holster at her waist. She paused to cock the pistol, pulling back some movable part with a grimace of effort. It snapped into place. Then she grabbed him by the arm and hauled him to the kitchen for display. There, still holding him tight with her left hand, she placed her pistol hard against his head. Joop was crouched below at the sill, training his rifle on the three men outside, whom Harvey was able to see now. They were standing round a small blue van in bright sunshine. There was Kemble, and there was the French policeman: a bulky fellow with a bushy black moustache. Erich Kohlman looked ready to drop. His stance was unsteady, his face pale as death. Poor boy, Harvey thought, and kept on thinking even when he felt Rosa's pistol pressed to his temple. Poor boy, let him go. Let him start his life again.

Then the Dutchman, never shifting his position, called Mario into the kitchen. They crouched at the window in hurried consultation.

"Ready?" Rosa said.

"Yes," said Joop, "ready. Tell them now."

Kemble was watching the black-clad commandos, now half-way down the meadow, when Rosa called out her answer.

"Daladier, are you listening?"

"Yes, I hear you."

"We're coming out now, and we're bringing Harvey with us. One move from you and he's dead. We're taking that vehicle. We want safe conduct to an airport. Give us a plane out of France and we'll let him go the other end. Do you agree?"

Daladier's tongue clicked again. Rosa's voice rose to a shout. "Come on, *flic*, answer! Or he's dead, right now."

"I agree," said Daladier. "Come on then."

Immediately Joop's head and rifle vanished from the window, and in the very short moment that followed, while the Dutchman's aim was lifted, Daladier seized his chance. He made a quick signal with his hands to the men in black advancing down the meadow. They sank out of sight in the tall wild grass. They were still about a hundred yards off.

Next instant Joop Janssen hurtled from the house, trailing belts of ammunition. He looked about him as he ran. Holding his Armalite ready to shoot from the hip, sweeping the ground with it, this way and that, he darted from the back door up a short rise behind the house and then dived headlong into the cover of the disused water-cistern. There he took up a new firing position, from which he could see the whole terrain, the meadow behind, the woods and the garden, the flat patch of grass where the van was parked. Janssen could now see the whole zone of battle, but could not himself be seen. He was hidden by brambles and walled in with concrete.

Kemble watched this move with dry-throated fear. The Dutchman had chosen a perfect foxhole, and was fully equipped for a firefight. He was clanking with grenades and spare magazines. Every pocket of his denim bulged with something. A pistol was stuffed in his belt, and wrapped around his shoulders were belts for the Armalite, a hundred rounds in each.

It was possible to see straight off that his rifle was the Armalite from the straight stock and overhead carrying-handle, the high projecting foresight on the muzzle. And just as Hal Fawcett had warned, this one was the Stoner variation, with belt-fed option. Joop Janssen was carrying the most expensive, most deadly firearm in the world.

Kemble's sense of doom increased. He held himself ready to jump rightward and down, into the dip of the garden.

It was a very shallow dip.

Kohlman, meanwhile, had steadied up. He was standing with more resolution than before. What swayed him, from fear to courage, was not in Kemble's power to guess.

Next to come out of the house was Mario Salandra, who advanced towards the van with a Russian Kalashnikov, easily recognised by its short-nosed barrel and gas chamber, the curved magazine. Salandra held it pointed level from the hip. He was coming to inspect the vehicle.

Kemble realised the moment of crisis had arrived, but couldn't guess how it would go. He waited in horrified dumb fascination to see what would happen next, and when things did begin to happen, they happened so quickly that he was not sure what order they happened in.

For a short moment longer nothing happened at all.

The barrel of the Dutchman's Armalite poked from the cover of the cistern, resting on its crumbled concrete wall. His head was concealed by the brambles.

Mario stopped just in front of the vehicle. He seemed to be wondering which way to walk around it.

From the trees to the left, where Biffaud was hidden, came a movement of leaves.

Then Rosa did an incautious thing. She emerged at the back door with Harvey.

She was holding her Czech automatic to his head. The pockets of her brown woollen dress were bulging with grenades, and strapped across her shoulder was another Czech weapon which Kemble recognised as a Skorpion machine-pisol – long slim barrel, straight magazine – a gun of the same type as that used by Mitzi Hoff at the Babylone.

Rosa Berg was well equipped. But she wasn't thinking so well. As she came to the doorway she had Harvey beside, not behind her. They stood close together in shadow, about to come forward.

Did the shot come first, or Kohlman's shout of warning? They were so close together it was hard to tell. Afterwards Kemble gave first place to Kohlman's shout, by the merest fraction of time, because he heard enough of it to think the word used was "*Achtung!*"

And Biffaud's shot just missed, which could only have happened if Rosa, reacting to Kohlman's cry, had moved her head a split-second before. The bullet from Biffaud's carbine slammed into the brickwork behind her, sending out a shower of fragments. But Rosa had moved, and Rosa survived. Already she had pulled Harvey round in front of her and was dragging him back through the door. Biffaud got no second shot.

But his first gave Daladier time to kill Mario. The Italian stood turned in surprise towards the trees for all the time it took the fat but fast-moving Commissaire to shoot him through the chest, using the pistol placed ready on the driver's seat. Only in death did Mario Salandra retaliate. As he toppled over backwards the AK 47 went off in his hands, firing a burst of automatic at the sky, sharp reports like a fire-cracker, three or four rounds. Then he was peacefully flat on his back.

The trouble was Mario should have been dead before that. As soon as the shooting began, both he and Janssen should have been hit by fire from the snipers.

This did not occur.

Why it did not was the subject of later enquiry. The answer was hushed up, but came out anyway, as all scandals do in France.

There was no fire from the snipers because their commander, the general of the GIGN, had decided to move them inward. They were half-way down the meadow, lying flat in the grass with the upper assault group. This made no difference in the case of Mario Salandra. The more drastic consequence was that Joop Janssen, holed up inside the concrete cistern, was now firing free and fast with the Armalite.

Daladier had already lived through the Dutchman's first shot, which came as he dived back into the protection of the van. The bullet hit the driver's door. It went through the armour plate like tinfoil but missed the Commissaire's body by inches. One inch lower, two inches to the left and the chief of the BRVP would have had no buttocks. As it was, he only got hit by the armour plate, which was carried clean away from the door.

Joop Janssen should have held his aim on the Commissaire, if the chief of operations was his principal target. But his second shot went through Kohlman.

Why the Dutchman did this could only be guessed in the acres of newsprint that followed. Had he not heard the loyal shout of warning? Perhaps he thought Kohlman had helped to set the trap. Perhaps he just wanted to put a last bullet through a German.

In that case he did so, to terrible effect. The bullet of an Armalite-Stoner .223, fired from a distance of twenty yards, travelling at four thousand feet per second, leaves nothing for the doctors to mend. It hit Kohlman full in the chest and carried him, disintegrating, high through the air, to land with a thump in the dip of the garden.

Kemble was already there, having jumped for his life with more speed. He was pressed flat behind a low wall of stones, face to earth, when Kohlman flew over his head.

What happened next Kemble heard but did not see, since too scared to raise his head.

First there was a most tremendous bang, much bigger than that of any firearm. It came from a claymore fixed against the wall of the house to cover the approach from the track. Suspended from the sill like a window-box, this item had been nervously eyed by Kemble throughout the attempt at a talkdown. And now it exploded, set off by a cord which Rosa must have tugged from inside the kitchen. A blast of miscellaneous shrapnel hit the van with a multiple whang of metal tearing metal. Such was the force of this impact that the van was rolled over on its side. But once again Daladier survived. And now, with the van rolled over, the Commissaire had better cover to hide from Joop Janssen, who was spraying the whole of the area with long bursts of automatic fire. The bursts were so long, with such short gaps between, that he must have been using the belts. Kemble could feel the bullets whipping through the air above his back. The wind of lead and stuttering crack of the rifle were simultaneous, indistinguishable one from the other, a continuous storm of death sweeping round the points of the compass. Kemble whimpered and swore in terror, grunting four-letter words as he pressed down flat as he could get, trying to melt into mud. The ground was still sodden from the storm, and spreading towards him, though he hadn't yet noticed, was a river of blood from Erich Kohlman.

So intense was the Dutchman's fire that the whole French rescue force was held at bay while it lasted. Daladier hid behind the van, Biffaud hid in the wood. Even the assault groups of the GIGN, advancing up the track and down the meadow, were forced to keep their distance. Two were scythed as they rose from the hay, another mown down in the garden.

Then the Armalite stopped firing. Before it was realised what he was doing the Dutchman had fled from the trap he was in. He flung out a pair of smoke grenades, one up, one down, and then he was out of the cistern and into the trees behind the barn. Dodging Biffaud's fire, flinging out more smoke, he plunged away eastwards and down through the woods.

The noise of battle went with him.

A short lull followed, in which could be heard a desperate cry from Rosa, still trapped in the house.

"Joop!" she screamed, "*J-o-o-o-p!*"

But her Dutchman had gone. Rosa Berg was alone.

No, she still had Harvey – and now the best hope of rescue was a rush, which came from all sides at once. Daring to raise his head at last, Kemble saw the French commandos charge down the meadow, and over the brow of the hill came a helicopter, with more of them dangling from ropes. As it hovered low across the field they jumped and ran on down the hill. More were running up from the track, Daladier and Biffaud were running from the trees. Kemble got up to run himself.

Then everyone fell flat again as Rosa began to lob grenades from the window. She threw four in quick succession. They rolled across the garden with horrid little pauses, the green oval spheres of the US Army, type M26, packed with steel coil and TNT. *Whoomph* they went, *whoomph*, going off with gusts of brown smoke, clods of earth and singing fragments. One of them rolled awfully close to Kemble, who knew the things from Vietnam, but again he was saved by the blessed scrap of low stone wall left behind by the blessed French farmer who had tried to level up his garden into flat strips for cultivation. God bless and preserve the good man for ever.

Rosa's barrage was coming from the kitchen, but the French were unable to retaliate, for fear of killing Harvey. Their own grenades were quite useless. Their bazookas and fat-barrelled gas guns, their shotguns and rifles and dinky submachine-guns, the whole huge armoury brought from the airfield at Bergerac was useless when it came to the point, because of the danger to the hostage. The forces of order could only take cover and wait.

Then Rosa ran out of missiles. She was seen by Daladier to flee from the kitchen, back deeper into the house. And the Commissaire now had a megaphone. He stood up and bellowed through it, pointing the assault groups forward. The rush recommenced.

Kemble was up again, chasing after a squad who had charged straight past him from the exit of the track. And then he was down again, knocked over by something from the under-growth bordering the garden to the right. One of Joop's mines had been tripped off by an unseen foot. Kemble was vaguely aware of the explosive thump, the bushes blowing outward in a wind. He was peppered with twigs, leaves, pebbles and sharper things which hit him in two or three places. The ground came up to meet his face.

I'm dead, he thought, falling. Oh God, I'm dead and I haven't phoned *The Times*.

No, I am not dead. I am alive. I am getting up. I am in marvellous good health.

He stood a moment dizzily, getting used to this new idea. He was almost blown down again by the draught of the helicopter, flying out over his head, and then a great surge of happiness passed through him. His luck had held. He had the story. His life was still his and it had come good.

Before he could go any further he saw the GIGN rush the terrace of the house. Bulky men in black, grotesquely swollen with body armour, they dashed up a short flight of steps, smashed a pane in the glass doors, dropped in a stun grenade and stood back to wait for the bang. They got a bigger bang than they expected. The whole of the terrace went off with a mighty boom, which brought down part of the roof on that side. The commandos who were nearest fell back down the steps. One stayed down. The others charged up again and disappeared inside.

Kemble staggered after them, fumbling for his camera. Something sharp had gone in, he could feel it, but he was on his feet and moving forward.

At the same time he saw Daladier and Biffaud run in from the left, through the door beside the kitchen.

All parties converged in the house's main room, which was scattered with wreckage from the terrace, still swirling with dust and smoke, and then all were flat on the plaster-strewn, glass-strewn floor as Rosa raked the room with automatic fire, shooting from a door at the back. The weapon she was using was the Skorpion, but she was no good with it. She hit no one. Perhaps she meant not to.

Then one of the boys in black had a go at her. He sprayed the doorway with an Ingram. The fire of the little grey plastic gun was so rapid it sounded like an engine. *Brrrrrrrrp*, it went, *brrrrp, brrrrrrp.* But all it hit was the wall and the door-frame, the corridor behind.

Rosa had gone.

Then they heard her voice, from further down the corridor.

"Keep back!" she yelled. "Keep back or I'll kill him!"

She was heard to struggle with the Skorpion, trying to change the magazine, then she gave up and threw the thing down with a clatter.

Now was the time.

Two or three commandos jumped forward, but Daladier got to the doorway before them and barred it with his arm. He held them back and beckoned Biffaud to join him. The Inspector ran forward through the smoke, put down his Ruger and drew out his Colt. The pistol was already cocked. He thumbed off the catch, then eased the hammer forward for a first-pressure shot. The two men stood close, conferring in whispers. Daladier poked his head into the corridor, then turned back and nodded at his deputy.

The nod said "go".

Biffaud raised his pistol and went.

Harvey had been in his cell since Rosa retreated from the kitchen. She had dragged him with her, pushed him back inside and left him alone there. And there he was stuck. Escape was impossible. Rosa left the door open but stood close outside it, waiting to shoot from the corridor if anyone entered the house.

So Harvey did the next best thing. He went immediately into the cell's far left corner, which lay behind the door as it opened. Here he sat down, in the angle formed by the room's inside wall and the back wall of the house. This put him into the last corner which would meet the eye of a person entering, the furthest corner from the window. To protect himself he pulled up his knees and lowered his head, wrapping his hands round the back of his neck.

These were the lessons of Europol. Harvey remembered them. He was stunned by the shock and noise of battle, but not much afraid. He was trying to think. With what little force he had left he was trying to do the right thing.

Outside was the racket of battle, near and far. Explosions and firing still came from the woods into which Joop had run. All round the house were the shouts of men advancing. One was giving orders through a megaphone. Harvey heard the clatter of a helicopter, the thump of a mine. The hazel wood blazed with popping flares.

Then came a short lull.

Rosa waited in the corridor. He heard her cock the machine-gun: a quick metallic slide and snap. This was followed by a tinkle of glass, then a stupendous boom as the terrace went up. The whole house quaked. Plaster fell on Harvey's head.

Amidst the rattle of cascading debris he heard an exclamation of fear or pain from Rosa, half-way between a scream and a grunt. And then she was firing – two long bursts. A click. The gun was empty. She yelled at them to keep back, flung the gun down, and next second rushed backwards into the cell with her pistol drawn. For a moment she stood aiming at the door, then she turned to him, panting like an animal at bay. Her face was drained yellow, her hair white with dust. Desperate sounds were coming from her throat. Her eyes were staring wide.

Harvey raised his own to meet them. In hers he saw fright and despair, but also a wild last fury.

Then she rushed at him.

He tightened every muscle, but she did not shoot. She dived down into the corner beside him. Jostling him aside, she got behind him, deep into the angle of the walls, then grabbed him and pulled him back on top of her. Her left arm was looped around his chest in a tight convulsive grip, her head was exactly behind his own. Harvey could feel her breath on his neck. She pulled him even closer. He felt her lips. Then, as they both heard a movement outside the cell door, up flashed her right hand, jamming her pistol hard against his head. She thrust the muzzle into his ear.

Harvey, clenched tight from top to toe, shut his eyes. But still she didn't shoot. Another second passed; then the door of the cell crashed back and a man dived through it.

By the time Harvey opened his eyes the man was crouched opposite, a few yards away across the cell. His pistol was levelled straight at them, held two-handed with both arms out. The face behind the gun was scarcely visible in the dust still swirling through the room, the smoke let in through the door, but Harvey could see a pair of steel-framed spectacles, a head

761

shaved close in bristly, grizzled crewcut. Here was a professional tough. Here, from all France, was the man picked to do this job.

But Rosa had been too clever for him. He couldn't get a shot at her. His pistol shifted fractionally left and right, searching for some part of her to hit. But it did not fire. Harvey kept still, and Rosa kept still, her head held right behind his. Only her breasts rose and fell, squashed tight against his back.

"Get out," she said to the man with the pistol. "Get out right now, or I'll kill him."

She must have said it loud, her lips against his neck, but to Harvey's stunned ears her voice was faint.

"Tell him, Harvey. Tell him."

"Better go," said Harvey in French, only able to guess at the loudness of his own voice. "Let me talk to her."

The man straightened up, still aiming. Then he glanced to the door, where another head appeared, with a black moustache – the fat man who had stood by the van.

"Out!" yelled Rosa. "Get out!"

Harvey spoke to the fat man. "Are you in charge?"

The man nodded.

"Then please do as she says," Harvey told him. "Is that journalist there?"

The fat man's head disappeared; came back again; nodded. He came a little further into the room, pointed back to the corridor and said something Harvey couldn't catch. But the words did not matter. Obviously Kemble was outside the door.

Harvey had already formed a good opinion of the fat man, who was as calm as himself. The calmness of each reinforced the other. Throughout this hectic encounter unspoken messages of mutual comprehension passed quickly between them, eye to eye. The fat man told Harvey, by eye, that he was responsible and yet momentarily impotent, since unable to judge the girl's temper. And Harvey understood the fat man's problem. Leave this to me, his eyes replied.

Aloud he said, raising his voice and switching into English: "Kemble, listen to me. You will please witness that I am requesting the French police to leave this room. I am grateful for their efforts, but that is what I want them to do. I rely on you to report that fact accurately, whatever the result. Now please go – all of you. I wish to talk to this woman alone."

762

Harvey repeated the instructions in French.

The fat man looked doubtful, but eventually nodded in consent as Harvey stared back at him commandingly. He withdrew from the room and called off the crewcut marksman, who was more reluctant still, and never once relaxed his aim as he backed away pace by pace.

Then the room was empty.

"Shut the door," called Rosa.

"Yes," said Harvey. "Shut it."

The door was shut.

Kemble, now standing in the corridor, was also dizzy from the shock of battle. His ears were singing and his middle was sore. Something had gone in there. But this was where he wanted to be. This, indeed, was closer to the kill than he'd ever dreamed of getting. He held himself upright, propped against the wall, and watched each thing that happened.

Biffaud was crouching with his pistol raised ready, his ear pressed close to a crack in the door. Daladier, meanwhile, had scuttled away down the corridor, and Kemble knew what he had gone to do.

The boys in black wanted to go in to Harvey's rescue the other way, through the room's window. This had been stopped when it was found that every shutter in the house was booby-trapped with plastic explosive and broken-link fuses. Now it was known that this window was clear. Even so, the Commissaire wanted no hasty assault. The men outside were being told to stand ready, but on no account to make the first move.

As he waited, Kemble heard distant firing, for which there could only be one explanation. The Dutchman was still on the run, trying to break through the outer cordons. Incredible.

Then the Commissaire hurried back into the corridor. He had been gone for less than half a minute. On return he brought with him a police technician, carrying radio equipment. Quickly laid on the floor and opened up, it was a sort of heavy black briefcase inside which were many knobs and dials, a neatly packed assortment of microphones and earphones.

But before the technician could go to work a murmur of voices was heard from the cell. Biffaud tried to catch the words, but could not. What was said at that moment between Rosa Berg and Sir Patrick Harvey was never known.

763

She sat slumped in the corner, her pistol lowered to her side. Harvey, released from her grasp, had straightened up. He sat turned towards her, between her splayed legs.

"Well?" he said, putting the sheet of paper back in his pocket. "What do you say?"

She said nothing.

"Come on, Rosa, please. Be calm now. Think."

Still she did not react. In her eyes was a faraway, desolate expression; beyond reach. She was listening to the firefight in the woods, following each stage of the Dutchman's bid for freedom. Then the firing ceased. All sound of battle ceased. Whatever had happened, it was over.

For a short while longer she kept listening, then her head dropped back against the angle of the walls. She shut her eyes. A single large tear fell from each and rolled down her face.

Harvey let the moment pass; and then he tried again, gently urging. "They won't wait much longer, I'm afraid. Listen. Do you hear them? There are men outside that window. Come on now, let's end this in peace. We'll walk out together."

At that her eyes opened, dry again, but dull with defeat. She stared at him without any guessable intention.

For one short moment Harvey thought she was persuaded. But then came the cold, closed look that he had got to know.

"Clever Harvey," she said in a voice more weary than sarcastic. "Clever, clever Harvey, still talking for your skin. No. The answer is no."

She lifted the pistol and peered at the side of it, checking to see that the catch was off. It was. The red dot was showing. Harvey could see so himself. She raised the gun towards him.

"Turn your head away," she said in a whisper of unremitting bleakness. "Look at the window."

The technician, working quickly in the corridor, had thrust an antenna through the door-frame, just above the hinge. To Kemble it resembled one of those transparent plastic ice-sticks used to stir American drinks. Once it was through and resting firm, the man bent to tune the knobs, then snatched off his earphones and handed them up to Daladier with a nod. Biffaud, relieved of the need to listen, straightened up and stood poised to go through the door.

Harvey had still not obeyed.

At this Rosa's calm disintegrated. Her eyes lit with desperate anger and she jabbed his chest with the gun, her free hand flying out leftwards to point at the window.

"Turn away," she said, louder. "Look there – at the light."

When he started to protest she raised the gun and held it, quivering, straight into his face. "Do what I tell you, Harvey. *Do it*. Do it now. Turn away."

Slowly Harvey turned his head away to the light from the shutter, the bright gap of sky where the upper slats were broken. Just as he did so, he saw the pistol move, spun back and lifted his hand to knock it away, crying "No! Don't –"

Daladier's whole frame jerked upright, as though the head-phones had given him an electric shock, and in the same instant his hand hit Biffaud on the shoulder.

The Inspector flung himself through the door.

The men outside smashed in the shutter.

At the same time a single shot cracked through the house. The echo of it bounced round the hills, like answering fire.

Well before the echo had finished Daladier rushed after his deputy, snatching off the earphones as he went.

Kemble stumbled in behind.

Sir Patrick Harvey had fallen over sideways, face down to the corner of a mattress. His hands had gone up to his eyes and his knees were drawn up beneath him, so he looked like a Muslim at prayer. The back of his suit was white with dust.

Rosa Berg was still propped in the corner. She had shot herself through the head.

Her aim had not been quite true. As the room filled with people her body arched upwards convulsively, then slithered to the floor and lay twitching, like that of a dog in a dream.

A medical team was brought in at the run. Some went to work on the girl straightaway. Another walked over to Kemble, who was propped against a wall taking pictures. Others helped Harvey to his feet. They tried to lead him from the room. But strangely, he would not go. He could not watch yet he would not leave. He stayed with Rosa Berg until she died.

7

A nearly full moon hung over the Tiber, magnified to twice normal size, its colour deep yellow in the warm haze of evening. Night had not yet fallen on Rome, but already the city was illuminated. One by one the monuments had stepped out into their floodlights, like gorgeous women arriving for a party. Light made beautiful the multitude of domes, large and small, which Clabon and Guidotti had seen from the Hilton that morning. It fell in a beam on Marcus Aurelius and his bronze horse, brought out of the museum where they were convalescing from pollution, restored to pride of place on the Capitol. Light rose to spectacular effect on the ruins of the Palatine and the Baths of Caracalla, where already the crowd was jostling for an open-air performance of *Aïda*. Light appeared on the Alban hills, where bonfires blazed above the lake. Up there rockets exploded in the dusk with a crackle too far to be heard, and down along the bends of the Tiber itself every bridge was bathed in light. The most splendid of these was the Ponte Sant'Angelo, its parapet lined by the angels of Bernini, their draperies twisting fantastically in the baroque high wind which held them fixed yet moving for ever. At the end of the bridge, also floodlit, was Castel Sant'Angelo, the great round fortress of the popes. Above its topmost battlements the Archangel Michael, cast in bronze, spotlit, was sheathing his sword after ridding the city of pestilence. He and the battlements had been there for centuries, but never had they been so finely lit as they were on this Tuesday evening. Italy had more than her share of modern pestilences, industrial and political, but tonight these ills were forgotten as Rome did honour to the rulers of Europe.

When it came to summits there was a certain competition

between the capitals. And for style the winner was always Rome. The occasion had brought out a mass of flags as usual, but tonight in Rome they looked better than usual, lit up on their poles beneath the Archangel Michael. The colours of the twelve nations repeated themselves in an unbroken circle round the castle's upper terrace, the poles massed tight as pikemen along the edge of the wall. As the sky turned dark above them the flags furled and unfurled slowly, stirred by a wind more gentle than Bernini's, and from time to time the British one was stretched out enough for it to be seen that the Union Jack was upside-down. But nobody cared about that. Tonight in Rome it was not the detail that mattered, or even really the substance. What mattered at summits was style.

Parked in the courtyards of the Castel Sant'Angelo, lined up in the streets outside, was a very great number of dark shiny cars. From the castle's brightly lit rooms came the buzz of many voices. Already under way here was the first of many receptions to be held in the course of the forty-third session of the European Council, as the summit was more properly called on the big white invitation cards sent out by the President of the Italian Republic. These cards were carried as proof of identity by the guests arriving, proof of *bona fides*, proof of importance, and were now being handed in to four huge footmen in tails and white ties who stood at the foot of the castle's staircase. The wide marble stairs were flanked by men of equal stature in parti-coloured medieval dress, each carrying a flaming torch. At the top of the stairs the Italian President, sadly normal by contrast, stood receiving the line of guests, his resplendent wife at his side. Heads of Government and Foreign Ministers were ushered straight into a tapestried room on the right and served with champagne. Others began the long scrimmage for lesser wines and foods in the adjoining apartments.

John Clabon and Carlo Guidotti, arriving together, had their hands pressed with special warmth. Words of support for their project were murmured like a blessing on their heads, and then the chief executives of BMG and Mobital were guided in a different direction, down a passage which led to a small room full of armour. Pikes, halberds and broadswords criss-crossed the walls. Wax musketeers in suits of armour, beautifully chased, glared across the room from each corner, and out of one niche loomed a riderless horse, richly plated and caparisoned for war. More to the point, at the room's far end was a table set with wine, cold turkey, Parma ham, many salads and a bowl of fruit. Behind it stood a solitary waiter in white jacket.

"La Sala della Pace," said Guidotti, pointing with a smile to the name of the room, painted over the door on a scroll.

Clabon, drink in hand, took in the massed instruments of death.

"Arms for display, not fighting," Guidotti added. Taking a glass for himself, he sighed. "Italy was civilised then."

After that they drank together in silence. Neither had energy for small talk. The waiter stood and watched them in suspicion, uncertain whether this private supper was a sideshow or the heart of the whole affair.

Next to arrive was Professor Lord Doublett, who hurried in untidy and sunburned, eager for food and drink. He was followed at once by Dr. Otto Riemeck, at whose appearance the waiter began to liven up. And with the President of the Commission came the Arctic recluse he had found in a fishing-boat on a lake in northern Sweden: a man who was now revealed to be of amazing thinness and tallness, with a face much lined yet expressionless, and hair so blond it was hard to discern where the white of age began. Riemeck began to introduce him formally, but that was unnecessary. The others knew him. In turn they stepped forward to shake the hand of Count Ingmar Nordstrom, former deputy chairman of Saab-Volvo. In turn they told him how pleased they were that he had agreed to be chairman of BMG-Mobital. The pleasure of Clabon and Guidotti was genuine. To them Nordstrom was a good choice, especially in view of the Swedish involvement in BMG's battery engine. Doublett was a little disappointed, but could not deny that Nordstrom was the perfect third man. His congratulations, twice repeated, contained no trace of sulk.

"Thank you," the lofty Swede said to them in return. "If the heads of government agree to my appointment, I will accept the post. If my health permits, I will do it for three years." Count Nordstrom's tone was perfectly pleasant but gave no hint of his feelings. Softly musical in accent, his voice went up and down with the carefully polite inflexions of a recorded announcement.

"There is still some work to do," said Riemeck, addressing them all. "That is why I have arranged this private room. I must

768

report to you on my discussions with the French and Germans, which have been satisfactory. And we must finalise the form of presentation for tomorrow."

"Meanwhile, Otto, meanwhile, a little of this fare would not go amiss. A start could be made, I suggest. Eat as we talk – yes?"

Doublett's presence at these events was coming to seem ever more bizarre as they returned to normal. Riemeck stared at him a moment in slight irritation, then nodded and made a forward motion with his hand, turning round to include them all. "Of course," he said, "go ahead. Eat."

But Riemeck did not himself eat. And a few minutes later he dismissed the waiter, so that they could speak in privacy.

The secret discussion that followed was about BMG's electric car. Clabon said he was prepared to let the secret out if that would help to part the summit from their money. In fact he had brought the prototype to Rome. It was hidden inside a British lorry in the suburbs, locked up and under guard, but to swing this deal he was ready to take any head of government for a demo drive round the Colosseum or half-way to flaming Naples if required.

This bit of sales panache delighted everyone. It even brought a distant, arctic smile to the lips of Count Nordstrom. But Riemeck ruled the stunt out. He himself was very glad to know of the battery car, he said, because it made the merger a good commercial bet. But that didn't mean the summit should know of it. The mood tomorrow should be more in the nature of poor old Britain, poor old Italy, what can be done to help them?

Clabon and Guidotti exchanged nods of approval. This German professor of law, their looks said, has come a very long way in one week. He will soon be as crafty as we are.

Then the waiter was let back in. He returned to work with the aggrieved, wary look of a minor country left out of major talks. And with him came Laura Jenkinson.

Laura had come to the Castel Sant'Angelo prepared to glitter or work. At present she was glittering, as she had all the way up the staircase to the presidential hand. She was in a sheath-style dress of iridescent turquoise silk, half-green, half-blue, trimmed with gold at the edges. A white gardenia was tucked in her hair, which was swept up to show off a pair of gold earpendants. She was an oriental princess. But her face was strained below the painted mask, and the men in the room knew why.

Circulating in Rome all day had been a number of rumours about the state of health of Jack Kemble, the man from *The Times*. Apparently he had been hit in the final battle with the Iskra. After it he had been taken to the hospital at Bordeaux, then moved to the one at Toulouse. No one was sure where he was now, but someone had said it was bad. Kemble, one rumour went, had been hit in the stomach by fragments from a shrapnel mine.

To the men now gathered in La Sala della Pace it was a matter of deepest indifference whether Jack Kemble lived or died. But they knew he had been a friend of Laura's, so they tried to be sympathetic. They asked her how he was. Laura did not know. She had no accurate information. Kemble had been moved from Toulouse to Paris, she said, but she couldn't find out which hospital.

So that was the end of that subject. Laura was given a plate and a glass. There was more eating and drinking, some desultory conversation in the room full of armour. But further business was put off. The occasion had an incomplete air. An expectant hesitation hung over it.

Finally Doublett raised the question in everybody's mind.

"Well, where is he? Are we going to see him?"

"I understand that he is to come here," answered Riemeck. "I will be warned."

"He'll never get in," said Clabon. "There are so many press down there they'll kidnap the poor chap all over again."

"There is a side way into the tomb," said Riemeck. "You will see."

By this Riemeck meant the tomb of Emperor Hadrian, which the Castel Sant'Angelo had originally been, until it became a fort to keep out the Goths. The change of use had occurred in 527.

And Sir Patrick Harvey, Knight of the Garter, former Prime Minister of the United Kingdom, European Commissioner for Industry, was on his way at that moment to the party being given by the President of Italy.

Since rescue he had fallen out of the Commission's hands.

The nations had competed for his care. The French, having saved him, had patched him up medically and soothed his heart with drugs. Then they had flown him across to the Italians, who had met him on a military airfield with precautions of the very thorough kind that occur in a stable when the horse has gone. Finally he had been handed back to the British, who were putting him up at the Villa Wolkonsky, their embassy in Rome.

It was from there that Sir Patrick was coming in a black Rolls Royce with a British pennant fluttering from its mudguard. Four Italian police were escorting on motorcycles fore and aft. Beside him sat his wife Margaret, and also John Harvey, his son, who had flown in from Brussels that afternoon. Opposite, facing them on the car's jump-seats, sat the British Ambassador and his wife.

Not much was said. Those around him during this first day of his release were still carefully tuning their manner to Harvey's own, not sure what his mood would be. Harvey himself was showing very little. For the moment he seemed content to watch Rome pass by. The car circled round the Colosseum at a stately pace, then passed by the Forum, the Capitol and Marcus Aurelius on his horse. Soon they crossed the Tiber under Bernini's angels, who loomed above the Rolls-Royce in windswept postures like that of the silver lady on its radiator. St. Peter's appeared to the left, and then they drove into the Castel Sant'Angelo, wheeling away from the waiting crowd of press towards a private entrance.

Harvey stepped from the car with care. Then he stood a moment, head raised to look at Archangel Michael, the deliverer sheathing his sword.

"Fine city, isn't it?" he said in a quiet voice, speaking to no one in particular. "Yes. I'm glad to be here."

John Harvey came up to him, immediately worried by this mooning. "Are you all right, dad?"

"Yes. All right."

"Take care now. This could be a crush."

"Patrick, why don't you walk ahead?" his wife said to him. "Go on, enjoy yourself. We'll come along behind."

But Harvey disliked this idea.

"No, Margaret. We'll walk together."

"Oh, all right." Margaret Harvey let him take her by the arm, but stood at her husband's side restlessly, chafing as they waited to be led forward. "Come on then. Let's get it over."

When they heard a burst of excited noise in the entrance hall, Laura and the four other men of the merger walked back down the corridor from the room full of armour to see what was happening. They emerged into a fierce blaze of television light. Harvey, his wife just behind him, had taken his place beside the Italian President. The two men were standing at the top of the stairs, hands clasped for the cameras, in front of a huge painting of the Virgin Mary being swept to heaven by massed cherub-power.

Harvey had been found a suit which hung quite well on his shoulders but was baggy lower down. He was noticeably thinner. There were unfamiliar hollows under his cheeks. His face had a gaunt, haunted quality even as he smiled at the lights and at the President, smiled at the hundreds of guests who came crowding out of the salons and lined the balustrade around the well of the staircase. Halfway down, the guards in medieval dress stood shoulder to shoulder across the stairs, blocking them. Two were now carrying pikes. Below them seethed a mass of journalists and cameramen, shouting and shoving for position, while the wispy Dane, protected by the pikemen, shouted out in his reedy voice: "Press conference tomorrow! *Per piacere, domani, conferenza di stampa! Messieurs, demain, à onze heures!*" One camerman knelt, took a shot through the legs of a pikeman, then tried to crawl up the stairs. The pike came down on his back. On the balustrade two ladies began clapping with gloved hands. The other guests took up the applause. Those nearest to Harvey saw him put a hand out to steady himself. His wife stepped forward to take his arm. And then he turned away from the crowd to the closer, calmer circle of colleagues who were waiting to greet him. When he caught sight of Riemeck, his smile changed to one of real relief.

Soon after that the two of them, Riemeck and Harvey, contrived to withdraw together, but not straightaway to the small supper-room packed with armour. Instead they went back to the narrow stairs which had brought Harvey up from the street. They followed it upwards, Harvey pausing twice to rest, and then they were out on the battlements, walking on a high open terrace beneath the yellow moon. Above their heads was the huge bronze archangel, sheathing his sword. Now Harvey ignored him. Once he stopped in his walk and breathed in deeply, his face raised to sky, moon and stars. But for most of the time they paced with heads lowered, round and round, among the potted oleanders, taking no notice of the marvellous view. The street below them had been cleared of unofficial cars, but beyond the river the fierce cries and trumpeting of Roman traffic never stopped.

Riemeck, politely concerned, began to ask questions about the kidnap. But Harvey, politely evasive, did not want to talk about it. He wanted to talk about the merger. His voice, which was normally clear and strong, was husky and strained. He seemed to hoard his words. He would rather not be talking at all, Riemeck guessed. But there was business to be done. Unfinished business, that was what had brought Patrick Harvey from his bed of rest, and that was what would hold him together, so long as it lasted.

Seeing this, Riemeck brought him up to date on the merger. He told him about Count Nordstrom. He described his own approach to the leaders of France and Germany.

This last news stopped Harvey in his tracks. He turned on the terrace in surprise. "You mean you've already asked them?"

"Yes."

"And they've agreed?"

"Yes."

"Otto, you're a master. I'd never have dared try that."

"Nor I," said Riemeck, smiling, "unless you . . . had been a victim. That made it easier. They were embarrassed to say no, you see. And so, they said yes."

"Well done, Otto, well done. And thank you. You really have saved this thing."

Riemeck accepted the compliment. "However," he said, "for reasons of . . . emotion, shall we say, it is you who should present the project tomorrow."

Harvey laughed as he agreed. "Yes, that makes sense. Wring their hearts. Hope money comes out."

"You have the strength?"

"Yes, I'm all right. All I need is some sleep."

"And now?" Riemeck asked. "You can come in for a short discussion? We will take you through the main points agreed.

773

An hour, perhaps thirty minutes – more should not be necessary."

"Fine," said Harvey. "Let's go."

So they went back inside and down to La Sala della Pace, where Laura, Arnold Doublett and the merger's ruling trio were still waiting. When Harvey entered the room, they stood up. And then, absurdly, they each shook hands with him. Clabon and Guidotti did so without words, but Clabon's grip was fierce with emotion. Count Nordstrom muttered a formal word of greeting. Doublett impulsively converted his handshake into a Russian statesman's hug. No one knew what to say. Then Harvey noticed Laura.

"Laura? I didn't expect to see you here."

She smiled at him nervously. No words came up as Harvey shook her hand too.

"Have you rejoined the colours?"

"No," she said, "sorry. Just holding the fort."

"Goodness, look at you. So smart. Really, you look lovely."

The way Harvey said this, perfectly serious and a little bemused, still holding her hand, startled everyone present. Most of all it startled Laura, who shifted uncomfortably in her blue-green dress, trying to get out of the way. But Harvey simply went on smiling at her in the same delighted way, as though he had come across an old friend in the street. "Shall we have a private word?"

They withdrew to a corner of the room and stood beside a wax musketeer, talking softly. At first their conversation was grave. The others, trying not to listen but unable to fill up the silence, heard the name of Erich Kohlman mentioned. They heard Harvey say the word sorry. And then they heard Jack Kemble's name, raised interrogatively by Laura. There was a pause, then more talk, followed by laughter. Sir Patrick and Laura were laughing beside the wax musketeer. They were still laughing when they came back to the table, on which the finished documents were spread for inspection.

Harvey controlled himself and stared at the work to be done, but amusement lingered in his face. "Shall I tell you something?" he said, looking round at them one by one. "After the experience of the last few days I have come to a decision which I have put off for the whole of my life." He paused and smiled specially at Laura. "I am going to switch to the *Daily Telegraph*."

Meanwhile, in a bar across the city, the editor of *The Times* was hearing how he had come to lose so eminent and faithful a reader.

"No, no, Frank, let me tell you. Listen. It was beautiful. First I make out I'm in pretty bad shape, see, so I get to go with him to Bordeaux. Fine. We get to Bordeaux, general repairs. Harvey has his heart fixed. Then they want to take him off to Toulouse, damn it. So I get this Frog medic to put me on a stretcher and say I'm at death's frigging door, right? Only place can cope is Toulouse, superior facilities for gut wounds, so forth. Right, says Harvey, put him in the chopper. Can't leave this poor boy to die. Okay, so we're in the chopper. More questions from gallant hack on stretcher, more answers from big man in seat beside. Then, shit, Toulouse. There's an army plane waiting to take him to Rome."

"So Jack gets better."

"Right. Jack gets better, Jack jumps off stretcher. Seems to be okay after all, blunder by ignorant Frog medic. Please, sir, take me to Rome."

"Well?"

"He wouldn't do it. Took off and left me to come through Paris. And I saved this guy's *life*, Frank, right?"

Holroyd nodded. "Right," he said. "The bastard. Boss always said he was a bastard. Boss was right. Harvey is a bastard. Shall we have some more of this?"

They were in Harry's Bar, at the top of the Via Veneto, where it meets the edge of the Borghese Gardens. Across the road the pines of the park loomed black in the moonlight. Swirling around them, flashy and fast in the warm summer night, was *la dolce vita*, pretty girls with very brown skin and pretty men in pure white suits, sporty cars cruising up and down the street with exuberant blasts of their horns, money and sex on parade.

Jack Kemble's clothing was rumpled, still stained with blood and mud. Frank Holroyd, the famous Australian seducer, was smart in a light grey suit. He had lifted a bottle of champagne from the ice bucket; their second. He tipped it over their glasses. It was dry. Harry, or whoever it was, brought another. They went straight to work on it.

"My God," said Kemble, sitting back, lighting a cigarette, "isn't Europe marvellous? Just look at it. The *variety*, Frank, that's the thing. London, Paris, Rome – different lingos, different worlds, Hebrides to Greece. Fantastic."

Aussie Holroyd, for reasons mysterious, seemed stricken with gloom at this thought. "And no shits to beat the English," he said. "The prize shits of Europe, that's what the English are."

"Yeah," said Kemble happily, "yeah, you're right. But I'm staying. Because that's what you miss over there, you know – the variety." He waved his hand at the Borghese park, which seemed the most likely direction for the New World to be. "America's all the same, Frank. Country looks different, state to state. But it ain't. All the same, end to end, coast to coast. And now I'm going to tell you what it'll cost you, Frank, the whole story A to Z, exclusive plus pics. Are you ready?"

"Go on."

"Twenty grand."

Holroyd laughed aloud at such folly; then ceased to laugh. "Eight," he snapped.

"Fifteen. Expenses on top, and usual percentage on all you syndicate."

"But you never sussed out the battery car, Jack. That's what I wanted."

"If I do, it'll cost you on top. This is worth fifteen without."

"Ten, all in."

"At fifteen I stand, plus extras as stated. Take or leave." Kemble raised his glass above the cloth like a hammer.

"Twelve," said Holroyd, "all in."

"Fifteen, as stated. Nothing less."

"All right, damn you."

"Done at fifteen." Kemble's glass came down on the cloth, overflowing. "And then I hash it into a book, my copyright. If you want to serialise the book, that's on top."

Holroyd nodded, too blitzed to reply. "And now I suppose you want a job as well."

"No, Frank. I want two jobs."

Holroyd sighed, without surprise. "All right, Jack. Tell me. Who is she?"

There had been a time in the afternoon when Laura thought Kemble was dead. Now she knew he was not, and in the swing of her feelings between, as clearly as if they had been drawn on a cardiograph, she could read the strength of his hold on her heart. The answer was rather shocking. When the news was bad she had been upset, yes, but mainly on her own behalf. She had felt briefly sorry for herself, then resolved to continue with her plan regardless. Grief for Jack Kemble had hardly come into it.

Now she had him back, she was glad. He would already be in Rome somewhere, and when this was over she would go to find him. But she knew now that what made her heart rise and fall was this inner, private business of her own – the effort to leave behind a life she disliked and move on to one she liked better. And where did that leave Jack Kemble? The rather awful truth was it left him standing in the street: a bold-talking stranger who had turned up one day along the way and said "Yes, go on, do it". Still, she was glad he wasn't dead. And yes, she would find him as soon as this was over.

Meanwhile, sitting at the table in La Sala della Pace, she tried to hold her mind a little longer on the job she was going to quit.

This was the last pre-summit discussion of the merger. There was nothing of substance left to argue. The main purpose was to bring Harvey up to date on the points agreed, and Laura herself had little to do except guide Sir Patrick through her own set of papers.

But then something very peculiar happened, which knocked Jack Kemble from her mind entirely.

8

The meeting had started well. Twenty minutes had passed and it was still going well. The waiter had gone. The table of green-veined marble, from which supper had been cleared, was now deep in papers. They sat round it on hard, high-backed chairs. The medieval weaponry shone from the walls in the bright light of chandeliers. It was a funny place to talk about cars, Laura thought, but in a way that seemed to help. No one could make much fuss about knock-down engineering in the presence of the wax musketeers of Castel Sant'Angelo.

In any case the car talk went well. Now the car talk was over and the money talk had started. Uncle Otto Riemeck was passing round a schedule of finance, prepared at high speed by the clever young men in his office. This had already received the nod in Paris, Bonn, London and Rome. The other member-nations had just received a copy and were studying it now, overnight. There were bound to be some worries among them; some resentment too. There had never been such a big hand-out before. The objections would come in the morning, Riemeck warned, and since there was no time before, they would come in the meeting of heads of government. The mood of that meeting was therefore essential, and the merger should be hurried on through before the mood had time to turn sour. The matter would be raised as a special agenda item, first thing tomorrow, before any other hard subjects were tackled.

Riemeck had been explaining all this at high speed, anxious to let Harvey go as soon as possible. But Harvey was having some difficulty following it, as Laura was the first to notice. Seated at his side, she was shuffling the papers for him, like a person who turns the sheet music for a pianist. She kept bringing the relevant item to his eyes, then snatched it away and held out another page as Riemeck rushed on. But Harvey kept trying to stop her, holding his hand on the previous item with small grunts of protest. He was confused. He could not keep up. And soon he stopped trying. He sat, head bent to the table in bleary bewilderment as the meeting moved on to other things.

None of the others had noticed yet. They took his silence for consent. Only Laura was aware that Harvey had ceased to read the score she put before him. He appeared much the same as he had at the talks in Tours, but was not, and she had the feeling that he never would be again. In three days he had aged a dozen years. He was an old man.

This came to Laura as a shock, and a sad one, despite her earlier resentments. Here was a great man's fall, and the fact that it should be occurring so quietly, in this silly room full of armour, unnoticed by lesser men preoccupied by lesser matters, seemed to her wrong, and even sadder. There should be a crash, and then a solemn silence, not this prattle on money and motor cars.

And then, to her horror, she noticed something else. Making no attempt now to read what she passed him, Harvey had turned to a page of his own choice. And his eyes were no longer bleary. He was staring in sharp displeasure at the diluted clause on workers' participation.

It was not this which caused Laura's horror, but the fact that earlier in the day, when she herself spotted the change to this clause, she had scribbled a comment in the margin of it.

> *Je participe*
> *Tu participes*
> *Il participe*
> *Nous participons*
> *Vous participez*
> *Ils profitent.*

This celebrated graffito from Paris 1968 had risen to her mind when she found what the two tycoons and Doublett had done, sneaking off in their private plane to Rome. And down it had gone on the page, not meant for any eyes but her own.

But Harvey did not react to the doodle at all. His eye had

travelled straight to the altered clause. And on that it was now resting, with something of its old hawkish gleam.

"Arnold, is this your doing?"

The question stopped the meeting. The others, deep into some other matter, stared at Harvey in incomprehension. But Doublett, quick, clever, guilty Doublett, immediately understood.

"Yes," he said, shifting in his seat, shuffling his own set of papers, "yes, yes, my doing. We made a small change there. Consultation, as you see, not participation. Should turn the wheels smoother."

As Harvey read out the offending clause in a clear accusing voice, neither businessman looked at him. They stared at the surface of the table. And Harvey did not glance at them. When his head came up, his eye was on Doublett.

"Changed it? You have destroyed it," he said quietly.

And now Laura saw him mustering strength for some last premeditated effort. At the same time she found herself wondering if among all those medals and stiff shirtfronts in the party outside there was one good plain working doctor.

"Consultation changes nothing," he went on. "There must be more – a real shift of power. I thought this before, and after the last few days I am sure of it. I have had a strange opportunity to . . ." His voice tailed off. He turned to her. "Where's the text we had before?"

Laura didn't have it. No one could find it. But it was not needed. Not many words had been altered, and all could remember the words that had been there before. They were quickly restored. So the text became what it was before. The boards on which would sit directors elected by the workers, in a ratio of two to five, became once again "supervisory", not "consultative".

On this Harvey insisted, and he got his way, without much resistance. But then came the great surprise. He went further. Having got the original structure restored, he treated this as only the start of the matter, not the end.

"The trouble is, you see, that even this is rather an empty formula. And I'm afraid it will be seen as such."

Nobody knew what he meant. They listened in guarded silence as he told them.

The company boards, he reminded them, were due to vote

away most of their powers to the merger's ruling trio. The workers would be quick to spot that, and would say, with some reason, that they had been sold a pup. To meet this objection, therefore, the boards should retain full powers over matters relating directly to the workers' welfare – pay, conditions, jobs lost, jobs created.

"But Patrick, all matters relate to the workers' welfare. How are you going to draw the line?"

The objection came from Clabon, but with none of his usual explosive vigour. He spoke as if forced to break painful news to a friend.

And Harvey couldn't take it. He waved Clabon's protest aside with an agitated motion of his hand, as though an interruption of any sort might make him forget what he was trying to say.

Oh dear, thought Laura, this is sad. Please, somebody, stop him.

But nobody dared. After a pause to collect himself, Harvey went on, speaking more and more slowly, his brow knotted into a frown of intense concentration.

The boards should be given full powers over workers' welfare, he repeated. And in order that policy between them was harmonised, a joint board should be created above them, drawn from both companies, still with the workers represented two to five.

From outside the room, down the corridor, elsewhere in the castle, came the hum of the Italian President's reception. In the room there was no sound at all. Laura and the four other men sat round the table in astonished silence as Harvey reached into the pocket of his suit and drew out a piece of paper.

He must have had it with him for days. It was wrinkled and smeared with dirt. Carefully he smoothed it on the table in front of him, then called the others round him to look. But Laura, leaning forward at his side, could already see that on it was his new board structure, drawn in a sort of molecular pattern.

Talking on with slow precision, Harvey explained the drawing from bottom to top. As the others leaned over his shoulder, his finger travelled along the two lower bunches of circles. These were the company boards, he said, two in five. W meant a workers' director. And S meant, loosely, a spokesman of the shareholders. C and G were Clabon and Guidotti, in the centre

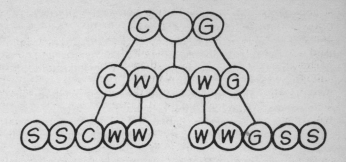

as company chairmen. They went up to the joint board –
Harvey's finger rose to the second row of circles – and with
them went a worker's spokesman from each company, so the
balance was maintained, two in five.

Harvey rested his finger on the second row. The blank circle
was for Nordstrom, he said, who would chair this joint board
whenever it met – quarterly might be sufficient.

His finger hopped up to the top.

And here was the ruling trio, the same as before. They would
run the merged group at a strategic level, meeting as often as
they liked. But on matters affecting the workforce they would
not have power to overrule the joint board, level two.

Harvey's finger hopped down again, then away off the
picture, at which all continued to look for a moment longer,
leaning over his shoulder.

Laura was wondering when and where this pattern had been
drawn. Perhaps the others were too. If so, they didn't mention
it. They returned to their seats.

"I don't pretend it will be easy to operate," Harvey said,
slumped a little deeper into his seat. "But I do believe it's an
improvement, and I think we should try to build it in. There's
time."

There is not time, Laura thought. There is not, there is not.

She could see that Riemeck was thinking the same, but was
scared to cause Harvey offence, because Harvey was needed for
tomorrow. Approval of the merger was far from a foregone
conclusion. Only Harvey, appearing in person, would have the
clout to swing the summit in favour. Riemeck knew it. Nord-

strom knew it. And maybe Harvey knew it too, though Laura could catch no hint of calculation in his remarks. On this matter of molecular boards he seemed to be speaking from the heart. And now, having spoken, he was silent.

The silence lasted no more than seconds, but was long enough for Laura to pick up a glance between the two businessmen. Clabon and Guidotti not only disliked this new idea; they were instantly resolved to stop it. Once again it was Clabon who spoke for them both.

"Patrick, this is mad. We need you. We can guess what you've been through. But please, don't make us commit suicide."

Harvey made no immediate reply. His head had gone down to his chest, and now his concentration seemed to have wandered. His voice was husky as he answered eventually that this was not just a matter of business, it was politics. And something new should be tried.

His eyes were resting on the drawing in his hands.

"It's only a symbol, of course. But that's the point . . . a symbol. We should give them that. And then perhaps the blood won't be wasted."

Seeming suddenly to realise that these words might sound strange to the company, he looked up and smiled in apology.

"Yes, you're right, I am thinking of that – what I've been through, as you say. I've been wondering if . . . perhaps we can use it somehow. Make something of it. But I am very tired."

Down the corridor they could hear the shuffle of departing guests. From the courtyard came an amplified Italian voice, relayed to the street outside through loudspeakers. Cars were being called to the entrance by number.

Then John Clabon did a clever thing. He started to object to the plan for workers' directors as it stood, not as Harvey meant to change it.

"Patrick, you know our trade union movement. They'll jump straight into this gap you've made for them, and that isn't going to be democracy, is it? Sitting with us on these boards will be the same old officials we have to deal with now, put into power by the very few men who take enough interest to vote."

Harvey made no response. He was flipping through the papers in front of him, apparently without any purpose.

The point was dealt with by Nordstrom.

"So," he said, "compulsory voting, yes?"

Speaking in sing-song, cool and clear, the man from Sweden suggested that existing trade-union machinery should be bypassed when it came to selection of workers' directors. They should be chosen by a ballot of all employees, one vote per job. And the ballot should be compulsory.

This was the first contribution Count Nordstrom had made, and it impressed everyone. Compulsory voting. Brilliant. The change was written in.

But Clabon's intervention had dragged the meeting backwards. By the time it was dealt with, Harvey had lost the strength he had gathered. His diagram had disappeared back into his pocket. For a hopeful moment Laura thought he had forgotten it, but then he raised his head and asked in a rather querulous way what they meant to do about his new suggestion.

It took them six minutes to talk him out of it.

He was taken away by a side door, back to his wife and the black Rolls-Royce. Laura went down to see him off. She thought he had forgotten her presence, but at the end he did have one more thing to say. It was strange. There had been a moment in the talk upstairs when she had thought to herself that for this, poor Paolo Santini had died. Perhaps Harvey thought the same thing. Half into the Rolls, he asked if she would go to see Paolo's family, which he would do in person as soon as he could.

"Of course. I'll do it tomorrow."

"Thank you," he murmured, then again shook her hand. "Well, goodbye Laura. Stay in touch, won't you? Come and see us."

"Yes, Laura, do," echoed Margaret Harvey from inside the car. "Now come along, Patrick. Let's get you to bed."

The Rolls moved off with hardly a sound. As it disappeared out of the fortress, the motorcycle escort closed around it like a squadron of noisy fighter-planes.

Laura's last assignment for Europe was over. She walked as far as the bridge, then found a taxi. She was glad to get away.

Waiting at her hotel was a handwritten note. *Come to Harry's Bar*, it said. *Meet your new boss.*

Laura kept the taxi and took it on to Harry's. At Harry's was another note. *Come to Rosati's*, it said. *Will wait for you there.*

Rosati's was in the Via Veneto, so she walked there: a match for any woman on the street in her dress of kingfisher silk. Several young Romans fell into step beside her, offering their services. She told them that she was in search of her husband. The young Romans nodded, undisturbed by this news. Come with us, they said. We shall assist you.

But Mrs. Kemble, despite the many young Romans now coming to her aid, could not find Mr. Kemble at Rosati's. Nor was he in the Café de Paris, next door. At this point she started to think of going home. But the helpful young Romans were not in the mood to quit. When they heard that her husband was American, a man of the press, they thought that he must be in Doney's, which was just across the street from Rosati's. Doney's was where the Americans went, they said. Doney's was the café for Americans.

So Laura crossed the street to Doney's while her troops held back the flow of cars. And in Doney's, they were right, Jack Kemble had been. He had just gone, the barman said, but he had left a message with the girl at the door. A message was found. *Gone to call Times*, it said. *Meet you at Harry's in an hour.*

Laura walked back up the street to Harry's. Turning to address her young Romans on arrival, she said there would be refreshment inside. At that they hesitated for the first time, unwilling to let her buy such a large round, yet unable themselves to pick up the tab for even one drink at Harry's.

Laura saw the problem.

"Don't worry," she said. "This is on my husband."

The advance resumed.

Soon after eleven o'clock two men peered into Harry's, unnoticed in the general hilarity. They seemed about to move on, then one of them pulled the other back and pointed across the room.

"There you are, Frank. There she is. Now you can find her a place, can't you? Put a bit of class in the co-op."

"Nice, Jack, nice. This dolly is in. Introduce me."

Later on, towards midnight, Jack Kemble took off his clothes. This he had to do with great care, partly not to fall off his feet, partly not to touch the dressings round his middle.

"Jack! You *are* hurt."

"Well, like I said, a few things went in."

"It's lucky you're so fat."

"Yeah," he said, not much amused. Fat and luck, that's what I've got. Plenty of each."

Some minutes passed. They lay side by side on the bed. Kemble seemed to have fallen asleep. But then he said: "You know, when I came into Harry's and saw you sitting there, I thought . . ."

He stopped. Surprised by how serious he sounded, Laura sat up to look at his face. "Well? What?"

Kemble's mouth hung open, still hesitating. "I have a lot of luck," he said after a moment. "That's what I thought."

"Ah, Jack. You did?"

"Don't run off now, will you?"

Wednesday

1

The Italian Prime Minister had taken the chair beneath the great Velasquez portrait of Innocent X, the Doria Pope. There had been many summits in Rome since the European Community was founded, but this was the first time the Princess Doria had let them use her palace. And it made a difference. Microphones, interpreters in glass boxes, name-plaques, drinks of fizzy water, all were there just as in Brussels or Luxembourg. So were the heads of state and government, sitting as usual in alphabetical order. But here they were dominated by the old Pope, the cardinals in procession, the Virgin and her infantry, who loomed from the walls of the room as once they had loomed over Europe.

At the start a band of photographers had swarmed around Harvey, shoving, flashing, calling out for his attention. Then the press had been removed and Harvey had taken his seat beside Riemeck, at the opposite side from the Italian chairman.

When the chairman began by saying how pleased they were to see him safe in their midst, Harvey ducked his head in acknowledgement. There was a ripple of applause; soon over. They had clapped him the night before. Heads of government do not clap twice. The meeting moved on to business.

During the short introductory proceedings Harvey sat with his head lowered. He was composed as usual, prepared as usual. There was no last-minute scuffle for papers. And yet there was something in his posture which indicated effort; and afterwards someone remarked that when he raised his head, as he did once or twice, he seemed to be looking at something in the room which wasn't there.

But when the merger came up, all was well. Harvey introduced the Commission's paper in his usual competent manner. Without any drama, he spoke clearly and briefly. He made no reference to the violent events of the last few days. His voice was rather husky, it was noticed, and several times he stopped to take a sip from a glass of water. But otherwise he was as always: thin and grey, well-brushed, essentially just an experienced Englishman who had learnt the language of Europe.

Nor was there any peroration. His last words were: "And so the Commission, apologising for the short notice of this proposal, strongly recommends it to the Council, believing it to be essential for the future of the European motor industry."

The Italian chairman thanked him. And then there was a silence, in which could be heard the jingle of a horsecab outside in the Corso.

Many round the table were unhappy with what was proposed. The merger was hugely expensive; it benefited only two member states; it was based on all sorts of untested assumptions; it had not been properly examined at lower levels. Ordinarily there would have been enough searching questions to force delay.

These men were practised democratic politicians, however, and they knew a political fact when they saw it. That morning Harvey, not his paper, was the political fact. Inside the room he was what his plaque called him, European Commissioner for Industry and Research. Outside he was hero and martyr, commanding all power of press and television. They could not refuse him, that was the fact. There was some talk about the financial details. Then even that petered out.

"Any more questions?"

Silence.

"It is agreed then."

The meeting moved on to the rescheduling of Turkish debt.

At Ostia Antica the archaeological team was doing well. The newly discovered foundations were being cleared of earth. It was certainly a warehouse, probably for corn from Egypt. But what was the meaning of the mosaic pavement which they were now uncovering? It showed a fisherman with his rod and three speckled fish. It might have some Christian significance or it might be just a Roman fisherman with fish.

The problem was that the pavement lay in part under the

road. They had already dug up to the verge. The rest was under tarmac.

The road should be diverted, suggested a stout and shaggy Englishman who had joined the party that morning – a friend of the professor in charge. He was told that roads could not be diverted in Italy. And shortly afterwards, as though to prove the point, two cars approached at speed from opposite directions, forcing each other off the road. The archaeologist ran forward anxiously. Three tiny tiles of the mosaic had been crushed by a tyre.

"Damn cars," said Arnold Doublett.

At midday Jack Kemble phoned his second wife. Six in the morning, American time, seemed as good an hour as any for divorce.

And it went well. Kim Kemble was not upset to hear about Laura Jenkinson. She was pleased. This made it easier, she said, for her to tell Jack about Randolph Miller.

"Who the hell's he?"

"You know," she said shyly. "Randy, at the club."

Kemble could not remember Randy Miller at the club or any other place, but was very pleased to hear that he wished to marry Kim. He was even more pleased when Kim revealed with less shyness that Randy intended to keep her in a style far above that to which she was accustomed, so she wouldn't need any of the fee from *The Times*.

"What, none of it?"

"No, Jack, you keep it. Just don't drink it."

She always had been a good woman, but this was too good to believe. Kemble had difficulty keeping suspicion from his voice as they wished each other luck and swapped lawyers.

Having tidied up his life, he lit a cigarette and went back to work. Within a few minutes he was back at Laura's typewriter, tapping words, taking a puff, tap and puff, tap and puff, as in Hampstead seven mornings earlier.

Then he paused for longer, staring through the window at Rome. He could smell Laura's scent in the room. No, he thought, this can't be true. There's a catch here somewhere. There must be.

In a town to the south Laura Jenkinson parked the hired car by the fountain in the piazza. The Via Cavour was easy to find. It was cobbled and led uphill between white walls punctuated by heavy doors. Signora Santini had a caretaker's flat in a house with a courtyard, lined with oleanders. She was old and bent, dressed in black. Laura could not understand her, because of the thickness of the dialect, and was not sure that she herself could be understood. However, she had practised her speech, so she made it. She said she was a friend of Paolo, and not until she uttered the words did it strike her that they would be taken to mean she had been Paolo's mistress. It didn't seem to matter. The old lady listened; fetched a glass of wine; listened again. Neighbours began to appear, other old women, told by some ancient system of communication that something of interest was happening. Laura finished her story, and they sat in silence. There were no demonstrations of grief. The old lady was quiet and dignified. When Laura rose to go, she once again hobbled to the sideboard, rummaged in a drawer and came back with something in her hand. For a second Laura thought it might be money. But no, it was a photograph of Paolo before his first communion, brushed, scrubbed, solemn, ready for the world.

In France it was the mother of Rosa Berg the press wished to speak to. A crowd of them had waited all morning at the gate of her house in Nantes. But only a priest was let in. Madame Berg would not come out or make a statement. She refused to let the priest speak on her behalf. Nor would she take any part in arrangements for disposal of her daughter's body. Her policy seemed to be that she had no daughter at all, and so there was nothing to make any fuss about. The priest, emerging, said the person to talk to was the dead girl's aunt on her father's side, a Madame Simone Salvador in Le Havre. But Madame Salvador was in prison, the journalists informed him. She was being held on suspicion of harbouring weapons. The priest showed no interest in this news. He got in his car and drove off. From the press, as he went, came a chorus of blasphemies, but not very loud ones.

And into Spain, on this Wednesday morning, came Joop Janssen.

He had run from the battle, run through the three besieging cordons, run from France. He was still running. Behind him, over the last seven days, lay a trail of fourteen corpses. Now he was on his way to Mondragon. Soon after crossing the border he telephoned Rosa's friends in the town. They were a newly married couple living in and operating a worker-run petrol station. They promised to put him in touch with the Basque guerillas. So he continued southward, and began to draw close in the heat of the early afternoon. With the Pyrenees behind him he descended on foot into the lower, fertile hills of the Basque land. He kept to lonely tracks and rocky terrain. Where possible he used the cover of trees. He was coated with a light film of dust. His skin was scratched, his denim clothing torn and spotted with blood. In the places where hair would grow, his face was stubbled with beard. He had no papers left he could use. He had no money. For a weapon he had only his Makarov pistol and two magazines of ammunition. He was dizzy with heat. He was very, very tired.

But his instincts were still at work. Coming down towards Mondragon, he was cautious as a fox. Soon he reached a high observation post and settled there to keep the town in view until nightfall. The workers' flats and workers' factories, workers' banks and workers' schools looked the same as those in any other place. Nor was there anything unusual about the petrol stations, except for the one manned by Rosa's friends. It was on the main road to Bilbao, half a mile below his rocky eyrie, and after a while Joop noticed that it was serving the same cars twice. They went through and then they came back again half an hour later, the same cars in the same order, five minutes apart.

By sundown he was heading back into the hills.

2

To go to Wales directly from Rome was Lady Harvey's idea. The doctors thought it a good one, and Sir Patrick himself approved the plan heartily. He could think of no better restorative than some days with his wife in that cool, green, watery land. He had dreamed in captivity of the small grey cottage couched in ferns; and now, on release, Cwm Caerwen seemed the right place to go – the obvious, the only place.

So they went, without stopping for anything. Thanks to official magic carpets of every description, they were there by the late afternoon. Passing through Builth Wells, Margaret Harvey bought a bottle of rather good whisky, malt, ten years old, the kind that her husband liked. But that was medicine for later in the day. On arrival at the cottage she put him to bed, and he fell asleep straightaway. The police stood guard at the end of the track. Nothing approached except sheep, nibbling grass, and from all around came the soft ceaseless trickle of water – just as imagined in absence.

While her husband slept Margaret Harvey aired out the house, made tea, and then sat down to rest. She must have dozed off. It was early evening when she heard him coming down the steep wooden staircase from the two attic bedrooms. He said he felt better. And he looked better. She brewed another pot of tea, refilling the kettle directly from the stream outside, since the taps were dry. It was always so on arrival. And by long tradition it was Patrick's job, if present, to make the taps flow again. So after tea she sent him up the hill to clear the blockage in the tank. She thought it would do him good.

The ground looked different, Harvey thought to himself, slowly climbing the hill behind the house. Here was the path which the sheep used, found easily enough, for it ran along the edge of the stream. But the bracken was now at its full summer height, which altered the look of things. The thorn bushes had grown too; and the elders. It must be at least two years, he thought, since I came up here with a scythe. Well, never mind. There'll be time for that now.

The rain had stopped soon after he had woken. Now the sun was out; still above the rim of the hill, but going down. Yes, and the midges were out. This was their favourite time of day. He had forgotten to smear his face with the anti-insect ointment which lived on the shelf above the gumboots. Well, never mind. It would take some time to pick up the old routines of Welsh life. But time there was now. Plenty of time.

Pausing in his climb, Harvey stopped on the sheep-nibbled hillside to wonder if he ought to stay on as Commissioner in Brussels, and became so absorbed in the question that he forgot what he was climbing for. Then it came back to him. Margaret had sent him up to clean the filter, because the taps in the cottage were dry.

From here, where the stream began to wander, there had been a short cut to the water-tank. But now the bracken was high and very wet, so he would do better to stick to the side of the stream, he thought, even if it did wander. The stream fed the tank, so the tank must be on the stream. That was logical. But there was no hurry, he thought, pausing to watch the water flow past his feet. He put his boot into it and cleared a pile of sticks and leaves, which had formed a little dam. The rush of the water released was a nice thing to watch. He climbed on.

The sheep ran away at his approach. The ewes had been shorn so recently that they were still nervous of men. Their pelts still bore the mark of the clippers. Without their wool they looked naked, and smaller than their lambs, who lifted them clean off the ground as they nuzzled for milk. Harvey stood to watch. The lambs would soon go to slaughter, he thought. They were nearly fat enough, but they didn't know it, and their mothers didn't either, which was rather sad. Sheep were a sad sight on the whole.

Further on, higher up, he passed the spot where the cottage's refuse was dumped. Cast among the rusty tins, he noticed, was an empty champagne bottle, still in its foil. What celebrating could that have been? He could remember no champagne at Cwm Caerwen.

The tank should be just beyond the next bend, if he had any memory left at all. Yes, there it was, in the same old clearing dotted with anthills, always hard to find because of the mossy slabs of concrete which covered it. A rowan hung over the stream here. Yes, there was the rowan. All as usual.

He stood in the centre of the clearing, then sat down to give some thought to the filter routine. It was really quite easy. You lifted the slab and felt around with your hand in the tank, trying not to stir up too much mud, until you found the filter attached to the mouth of the pipe. You pulled the filter off the pipe, brushed it clear of bits, leaned in and put it back on again. The water then ran down the pipe to the cottage. You got a mucky hand of course, a cold one too, and wasn't it strange the way she kept wiping her face? Kept trying, all the time, to wipe herself away. Did in the end. Poor Rosa. Well, I'd better get on with it. They won't like me being up here.

Still seated on one of the anthills, Harvey took off his coat and rolled up his sleeve. His shirt would not roll up his arm, and any second now, he was sure, they would come up and look for him. He started to hurry, then cringed back. Someone was up here. And they had a gun.

Gripped by the sure sensation that he was being aimed at, Harvey kept still, his eyes on the bushes around. From close at hand came the munching of sheep, the bleat of a lamb. Then the terrors faded, as quick as they had come. Of course there wasn't a gun. That was just a trick of the nerves. Rosa was dead. And Erich had been killed too, which was sad. There was no one up here. That was finished, and there was no need to rush. Margaret had specially said not to hurry. All right then.

He left his jacket on the grass and moved to another position. His shirt-sleeve fell loose to his wrist as he sat on the turf and leaned against a rock. The rock was warm in the sun. The thing to do was sit here and rest a while, try to get things straight.

A short while later he noticed that the sun was hot on his face. And for some reason, even though he had no ointment, the midges stayed clear. How peculiar, he thought. I've put nothing on and yet they keep away.

The sun had just set. The hills were etched sharp against a splendid lemon sky. A pair of buzzards were gliding in circles high above the cottage, their thin cries faint on the windless air, when Margaret Harvey put on her boots and crossed the garden, noting that a deer had broken down the fence and trampled on the only flowerbed. Beyond the garden was a paddock, yellow with ragwort. That would have to be pulled, but she would need gloves to do it. Beyond the paddock the path began, and from that point, if you knew where to look, you could see the clearing by the tank. She was coming out to look, but was not really worried. She had told him not to hurry. And he liked to take his time up there, enjoying the view, thinking his thoughts. He was not the quickest filter-cleaner in the family. He was possibly the slowest. Even so, he had been gone rather long.

Her pace quickened. She reached the spot where the tank came in view and looked up. The clearing was screened by a frothy growth of new green fern. His head could not be seen above it.

"Hello," she called out, "are you there?"

Her voice carried clearly through the stillness. But no answer came.

"Patrick, are you there?"

She called him again by name, several times. But still there was no reply or movement. Her worry turned immediately to fear. She started to hurry up the path. She took the short cut to the tank, but quickly got into difficulty. The fronds of bracken closed around her, showering rainwater as she pushed them aside. Once she stumbled and grazed her hand. For a minute she was lost. Then she was in the clearing. And there he was, slumped back against a rock with his jacket off, his head fallen over to one side.

He stirred at her touch, and then sat up, peering round. His hair fell across his face.

"No," he said, starting back, "please, don't do that."

"Patrick!"

"Oh, hello . . . It's you."

She took his hand. "Patrick, we're here, at Cwm Caerwen. It's over."

"Good," he said, "good." And then he leaned back on the rock again, sighing. "That's very good."

"What happened? Did you fall asleep?"

"I came to do the filter, Margaret." He looked at her sternly. "There's no water in the taps."

"Yes, I know." She twisted round and sat beside him on the grass, still holding his hand. "I know, I know. So what happened? Did you have one of your dizzy spells?"

"No, no, nothing like that. I sat down to rest."

"That's all right then. You must have slept."

"Yes, I suppose so." His head went down, chin on chest. "I do feel rather tired." He sighed again deeply. For a moment he stared at the patch of turf between them. Then he squeezed her hand, looked up and smiled. "Sorry to give you a scare."

After that it was all right. They sat a little longer, admiring the sunset. The buzzards drifted off to the east. A breeze stirred the rowan. Feeling the first chill of night, they got to their feet and started down the hill, arms linked for support. The light was fading fast, and the breeze began to blow cold. But their progress was slow and cautious. There was no room for them abreast on the path, so after a time she went first, pulling him gently forward by the hand. Wherever it was difficult or slippery, she stopped to let him lean on her. He was very weak. Several times she thought he might fall. But she guided him down without mishap to the last of the bends in the stream, from which they could see the cottage. As she waited there, so he could rest, she started to think of other things she must do.

The doctors had warned her what to expect; and at his age, they said, it could be hard to pick up from. Return to health was the best he could hope for. Return to work was out of the question.

Patrick himself had not yet heard this. She was still hardly able to believe it herself. But now, as she stood looking down at the cottage, feeling his weight on her arm, Margaret Harvey took in the truth of what the doctors had said. And immediately images rose to her mind of other homes that public life had swept her through. She thought of the long-windowed drawing-rooms at 10 Downing Street, the starlings swarming in the trees of St. James's Park. She saw the rose garden at Chequers, Patrick sitting in a deckchair, an open red box full of papers at his side, officials in a circle about him. Could it really be over? Yes, it was over. Banquets and speeches, trumpets and palaces, cabinets, journeys and summits, elections, ovations, triumphs and defeats, all were behind them now. However long they both had to live, these things were gone, in the past. To her they were no loss, of course. But what about him? Could he live without them?

Perhaps he would just sink on down out of boredom, she was thinking fearfully, when he gave her elbow a tug.

"Hey, just a minute, we forgot to clear the filter. We still have no water."

She turned to see him smiling in the dusk. Her fears fell away, and she laughed. "Well, we can manage tonight," she said in her old brisk tone. "You can fix it tomorrow."

"Yes," he said. "Plenty of time tomorrow."

The edge of the sky was pale blue now, pierced by an evening star.

Together, in silence, he leaning on her arm, they went on down to the bottom of the track, then crossed the paddock and entered the cottage.

ALSO AVAILABLE FROM CORONET